The
BIBLE
of
CLAY

ALSO BY JULIA NAVARRO

The Brotherhood of the Holy Shroud

The
BIBLE
of
CLAY

JULIA NAVARRO

Translated from the Spanish by
ANDREW HURLEY

BANTAM BOOKS

THE BIBLE OF CLAY
A Bantam Book / April 2008

Published by
Bantam Dell
A Division of Random House, Inc.
New York, New York

This is a work of fiction. Names, characters, places, and incidents either are the product of the author's imagination or are used fictitiously. Any resemblance to actual persons, living or dead, events, or locales is entirely coincidental.

All rights reserved
Translation copyright © 2008 by Random House, Inc.
Originally published as *La biblia de barro*
Copyright © 2006 by Julia Navarro
© 2006 Random House Mondadori, S.A.
Travessera de Gràcia, 47-49, 0802' Barcelona

Book design by Susan Turner

Library of Congress Cataloging-in-Publication Data
Navarro, Julia, 1953-
[Biblia de barro. English]
The bible of clay / Julia Navarro ; translated from the Spanish by Andrew Hurley.
p.   cm
ISBN 978-0-385-33963-6 (hardcover)
I. Hurley, Andrew. II. Title.
PQ6664.A8932B53 13 2007
863'.7—dc22   2007043432

Printed in the United States of America
Published simultaneously in Canada

www.bantamdell.com

10 9 8 7 6 5 4 3 2 1
BVG

For Fermin and Alex, always,
and for my friends, the best you could ever dream of

The
BIBLE
of
CLAY

1

RAIN WAS FALLING ALL OVER ROME WHEN THE TAXI STOPPED at St. Peter's Square. It was ten o'clock in the morning.

The passenger paid the fare, told the driver to keep the change, and tucked a newspaper under his arm. He was lean and well tailored in an obviously expensive suit, his white hair combed carefully back, his resolute demeanor that of a person accustomed to giving orders. He headed straight for the first entry point, where visitors were inspected to make sure they entered the basilica properly dressed—no shorts, no miniskirts, no cleavage.

Inside the cathedral, the man rushed past Michelangelo's "Pietà"—the only work of art among the vast Vatican treasures that had ever moved him—without a glance. He paused for a second, orienting himself, then walked toward the confessionals, where priests from an array of countries listened in their native languages to the faithful who came from around the world to visit the Holy See.

He approached a confessional whose sign indicated that the priest heard confessions in Italian, and he stood, leaning against a column, waiting impatiently for the communicant already inside to finish. As soon as he saw the velvet curtain open and a man step out, he moved purposefully toward the confessional.

The priest coughed quietly, ready for the new communicant to begin confession.

"*Mi benedica, Padre, perché ho peccato.*"

"What is it you wish to confess, my son?"

"Not a past sin, Father, but a sin I am about to commit." He leaned toward the priest and smoothed the lapel of his suit jacket. "I intend to kill a man," he said. "May God forgive me."

With that the man stood, rushed from the confessional, and disappeared among the hordes of tourists crowding the basilica. It took the priest a few moments to recover from his shock.

The stunned cleric stepped out of the confessional and picked up a crumpled newspaper lying on the floor. He glanced at the headlines— ROSTROPOVICH CONCERT IN MILAN; DINOSAUR MOVIE A BLOCKBUSTER HIT; ARCHAEOLOGICAL CONFERENCE IN ROME—and scanned the text below the last, where something had been marked: . . . *with world-renowned professors and archaeologists in attendance: Clonay, Miller, Schmidt, Arzaba, Polonoski, Tannenberg.* The final name was circled in red: *Tannenberg.*

Another man had approached the confessional and was asking insistently, "Father, Father—are you all right?"

"Yes, yes . . . no, I'm sorry, I'm not—excuse me . . ."

The priest folded the newspaper and, his gaze abstracted, walked away, leaving his latest supplicant openmouthed and unshriven.

"I'd like to speak with Signora Barreda, please."

"May I say who's calling?"

"Dottore Cipriani."

"One moment, Dottore."

The old man ran his hand over his hair and was suddenly seized with claustrophobia; the room was too small. He forced himself to take a deep breath while his eyes ran over the objects that had surrounded him for these last forty years. On his desk sat a picture frame with two photographs: one, now sepia-colored with age, of his parents, and the other of his three children. On the mantel was a photo of his grandchildren. Across the room a couch and a pair of wing chairs were softly illuminated by a floor lamp with a cream-colored shade. The room's walls were lined with mahogany bookshelves containing hundreds of books; Persian rugs covered the floor; the entire room smelled of pipe tobacco. . . . This was his office, he was at home: He had to get control of himself.

"Carlo!"

"Mercedes, we've found him!"

"Oh, Carlo . . . My God! What are you saying?"

The woman's voice was filled with dread—and expectation.

"Get on the Internet and look in the Italian newspapers, any of them—the Culture pages. His name's right there!" The intensity in his voice matched hers.

"Are you sure it's *him*? There are thousands of Tannenbergs around the world, Carlo."

"But not thousands in the upper echelons of the archaeological field. The article is about an upcoming conference in Rome."

Mercedes was breathless. And convinced. "Yes, of course, yes. Then he . . . All right, then. We'll do it. At last! Tell me you're not having second thoughts."

He looked at the picture of his parents. "No, never. And you aren't either, I see. Neither will Hans and Bruno, I'm sure." He fingered the buttons on his telephone. "We need to meet. I'll call them now."

"Do you want to come to Barcelona?" Mercedes asked. "I have room for us all."

"It doesn't matter where. I'll call you back—I want to talk to Hans and Bruno now."

"Wait, Carlo—is it really him? We have to be sure. Have him put under surveillance, no matter what it costs. If you want me to, I'll wire a transfer now. We cannot lose him again."

"I'll see to it immediately. We won't lose him, Mercedes. Don't worry. I'll call you back as soon as I can."

"Call me on my cell phone, then. I'm going to the airport. I'm taking the first plane to Rome. I can't just sit here; I need to—"

"Mercedes, don't move until I call you. We can't make any mistakes. He won't escape now—trust me."

He hung up, feeling the same anxiety he'd sensed in Mercedes. He suspected that in two hours she'd be calling him from Fiumicino Airport. She was a woman incapable of sitting and waiting for anything, much less this.

He dialed a number in Bonn and waited, tapping his fingers impatiently on the desk, for someone to answer.

"Hello?"

"Professor Hausser, please."

"Who's calling?"

"Carlo Cipriani."

"Carlo! It's Berta! How are you?" the woman responded delightedly.

"Berta, dear, how nice to hear you! How are you? And your husband and children?"

"We're all fine, thank you—dying to see you. It's been three years, Carlo! Father talks about you as if you were here yesterday."

"Oh, Berta, I'd love to see you all again as well—you know you have an open invitation to stay with me in Rome." Carlo paused and lowered his voice, allowing the urgency he felt to come through. "Listen, is your father in?"

"Yes, I'll put him on now. Are you all right?"

"Yes, my dear, I'm fine. I just wanted to speak to your father a moment."

"Here he is. Take care, Carlo."

"Ciao, bella."

The rich baritone of Hans Hausser came on the line within seconds. "Carlo . . ."

"Hans! He's alive!"

There was a long silence. Then Hans finally spoke.

"Where is he?"

"Here, in Rome. I found him by accident, reading the newspaper. Look, go online right now and read any Italian newspaper, the Culture section. You'll see for yourself."

Carlo's explanation was accompanied by a series of rapid keyboard clicks on the other end of the phone. "I'll hire an agency to keep him under surveillance," Carlo added. "They'll follow him anywhere he goes, even if he leaves Rome. We all have to meet. I just called Mercedes, and I'll call Bruno now."

"I'm coming to Rome."

"I'm not sure it's a good idea for us to be seen together here. Perhaps somewhere else . . ."

"Why not? He's there and we have to do it. We're going to do it. Finally."

"I know, and we will. I'll do it myself if I have to. Or we'll find someone to do it for us. I've thought about this moment my entire life, Hans—how it will happen, how it will feel. My conscience is at peace, but I wonder if it will remain that way."

"That, my friend, we will know when it's over. May God forgive us, or at least understand us—"

A shrill chirp interrupted Hans' words. "Hold on, Hans, my cell phone is ringing." Carlo picked up his cell and looked at the small screen. "It's Bruno. I'll call you back. . . . Bruno!"

"Carlo," said the taut voice.

"I was about to call you."

"Mercedes just did—is it true?"

"It's true."

"Then I'm leaving for Rome right away—I'll book the next plane out of Vienna. Where shall we meet?"

"Bruno, wait—"

"No, I'm not going to wait. I've waited for more than sixty years, and if he's finally turned up, I won't wait a minute longer. I want to be there when it happens, Carlo."

"You will be. . . . All right, come to Rome. We'll all meet here together. I'll call Mercedes and Hans again."

"Mercedes has already left for the airport; I'll leave here in an hour. Tell Hans."

"I will," said Carlo. He opened his desk drawer and took out a bag of fine pipe tobacco. "Come to my house," he said as he hung up the phone and turned to his computer to pull up the number of the president of Security Investigations.

It was midday. He still had time, he thought, to go by the clinic and have his secretary reschedule all his appointments. His oldest son, Antonino, was already tending to most of his patients by now, but some old friends insisted that Carlo and Carlo alone pronounce the official word on the state of their health. He had no complaints about that; it kept him active and forced him to contemplate yet again each day the mysterious machinery of the human body.

He hailed a taxi, and then as he sat back for the short ride to his office he felt a sharp pain in his chest. No, not the warning of a heart attack; it was anguish, pain—and rage at a God whom he didn't believe in yet prayed to and cursed. But Carlo was certain that he wasn't listening. God had never concerned himself with Carlo. Never. God had abandoned Carlo when he'd most needed him, at a time when he naively thought that faith alone could bring salvation. How stupid he had been! But think about God he did nonetheless. Carlo was approaching seventy, and now that he was closer to the end of his life than the beginning, facing the inevitable journey toward eternity, the alarm bells of fear began to ring.

He paid the taxi and this time did not tell the driver to keep the change. The clinic, located in Parioli, a quiet, elegant neighborhood in Rome, consisted of a four-story building in which some twenty specialists and ten general practitioners had their offices. This was his life's work, the fruit of his will and dedication. His father would have been proud of him, and his mother . . . He realized that tears were coming to his eyes. His mother would have hugged him tight, whispering that there was nothing he couldn't do, nothing he couldn't achieve, that a man's will made all things possible—

"*Buon giorno, Dottore.*"

The voice of the clinic's doorman brought him back to earth. Carlo stood tall as he walked through the door and made his way to his office on the first floor, nodding politely to the other doctors and shaking hands with patients who recognized him.

He smiled when he saw his daughter, her slim figure silhouetted against the light at the end of the corridor. Lara was patiently listening to a trembling woman who clutched a teenage girl's hand. Lara touched the girl's hair softly, tenderly, and comforted the woman as she said good-bye. She hadn't noticed Carlo, and he did nothing to call attention to himself as he walked on by; he'd stop by her office later.

He entered the waiting room of his office. Maria, his secretary, looked up from the computer screen.

"Dottore, you are so late today! You have a stack of telephone messages, and Signore Bersini is about to arrive. His results came in: Every test negative, but he insists on seeing you and—"

"I'll see Signore Bersini as soon as he comes in, but cancel all my other appointments. I may not be in the office for a few days; some old friends are coming to Rome and I must see to them."

"Very well, Dottore. What date should I start making appointments for?"

"A week maybe, two at the most. I'll let you know." He looked around the room anxiously. "Is my son in?"

"Yes, and your daughter too."

"Yes, I saw her. Maria, I'm expecting a call—the president of a company called Security Investigations. Put him through even if I'm with Signore Bersini, will you?"

"Yes, of course, Dottore. Did you want to speak to your son?"

"No, that's all right. He's probably in the operating room. I'll call him later."

He found the morning newspapers stacked neatly on his desk. He picked one up and flipped quickly to the last pages. The title of the column read: *Rome: World Capital of Archaeology.* The article detailed a conference on the origins of humanity sponsored by UNESCO. And there, in the list of attendees, was the name of the man the four old friends had been seeking for more than half a century.

How was it possible that he was suddenly here, in Rome? Where had he been? Had the world lost its memory? It was hard for the doctor to understand how this man would be allowed to take part in an international conference under the auspices of an organization such as UNESCO.

He saw his old friend and patient Sandro Bersini and made a superhuman effort to pay attention to Sandro's description of his symptoms. He assured Sandro that he was as healthy as a man half his age—which happened to be true—but for the first time in his life he had no qualms about seeming just the slightest bit unimpressed by his old friend's hypochondria, and he cut the consultation short with the excuse that other patients were waiting.

The ringing of the telephone startled him. A weight lifted from his chest when he heard Luca Marini, the president of Security Investigations, on the other line. The two men consulted briefly, and Marini assured Carlo that he would immediately place six of his best men at the conference site. But within minutes he was back on the line to inform the doctor that this might just be a case of mistaken identity: There was no Alfred Tannenberg at the conference. Just a young woman named Clara Tannenberg.

Carlo's heart plummeted. There had to be some mistake, unless . . . The man they were looking for was older than they were, so he had to have children, grandchildren. Or perhaps Mercedes was right. There were thousands of Tannenbergs around the world.

He felt a stab of disappointment and rage—they'd been outwitted, perhaps by time itself. He had actually believed that the monster had reappeared. But something inside told him not to quit just yet. He instructed Marini not to drop the surveillance of the conference—there *had* to be a connection. And they would go where they had to go to find him, no matter what it cost.

"Papa . . ."

Antonino had entered his office unnoticed, with a look of concern on his face. Carlo made an effort to pull himself together.

"How's everything, son—all right?"

"Yes, fine as always. Something on your mind? You were so absorbed you didn't even see me come in."

"You still haven't learned to knock—just like when you were a boy!"

"Hey, whatever it is, don't take it out on me!"

"What am I taking out on you?"

"Whatever's upset you. It's all over your face. What happened?"

"Nothing happened, Antonino. But I may not be in the office for a few days—not that I'm needed around here anyway."

"What do you mean, you're not needed? God, how dour you are today! Why won't you be coming in to the office, then? Are you going somewhere?"

"No, Mercedes is coming. Hans and Bruno too."

Antonino frowned. He knew how important his father's friends were to him, though their visits often left his father uneasy, unquiet.

"You ought to marry Mercedes, Papa," he joked, trying to lighten his father's dark mood.

"Don't be foolish!"

"Mama died fifteen years ago, and you seem to get along with Mercedes. She's alone too."

"That's enough, Antonino. I've got to go now."

"Have you seen Lara?"

"Not yet. I'll stop by and see her before I leave."

At sixty-five, Mercedes Barreda still retained much of the beauty of her youth. Tall, thin, olive-skinned, and dark-haired, with an elegant bearing and polished gestures, she was an imposing woman who seemed to make men quail. That may have been the reason she'd never married: She'd never found a man worthy of her.

Mercedes owned a prominent Barcelona construction company. She'd made a fortune by never resting and never complaining. Her employees considered her tough, a reputation she earned by never laughing and rarely smiling. But she'd never left them in the lurch: She paid judiciously, made certain they all had health insurance, and respected their personal lives. No one could accuse her of being authoritarian or of having even once raised her voice. She inspired respect, and just a touch of fear.

Dressed in a tailored beige suit and a string of pearls, Mercedes was striding swiftly through the corridors of the Fiumicino Airport in Rome. A voice came over the loudspeaker system announcing the arrival of the flight from Vienna that Bruno was coming in on. They would take a taxi to Carlo's house together. Hans should have already arrived, an hour earlier.

Mercedes and Bruno embraced. It had been more than a year since they'd seen each other, although they spoke often on the phone and e-mailed regularly.

"How are your children?" Mercedes asked.

"Sara just became a grandmother, imagine! My granddaughter had a little boy."

"Which means you're a great-grandfather. Not bad for an old relic like you. What about your son, David?"

"A confirmed bachelor—unmarried, like you."

"And your wife?"

"Unmanageable. She didn't want me to come to Rome. She'd rather I'd forget my past. You know, she's afraid, I think, terribly afraid, though she can't admit it, even to herself."

Mercedes nodded. She couldn't blame Deborah for her fears or for wanting to hold on to her husband. She had great affection for Bruno's wife: She was a good woman, easy to get along with, quiet, always ready to help others. But Deborah didn't feel the same way about Mercedes. She couldn't hide the fear "the Catalonian," as she called Mercedes, inspired in her.

Mercedes, actually, was not Catalonian, but French. Her father was a Spanish anarchist who had fled Barcelona just as the Spanish Civil War broke out. In France, he, like so many other Spaniards, joined the Resistance when the Nazis entered Paris. There in the underground, he met Mercedes' mother, a young Frenchwoman who acted as a courier. They fell in love; their daughter was born at the worst time, in the worst place.

Bruno Müller had just turned seventy. His hair was as white as snow, and his eyes as blue as the sky. He limped, aided by a silver-headed cane. He'd been born in Vienna. He was a musician, an extraordinary pianist, as his father had also been. His was a family that lived for music and earned their livings by it. When he closed his eyes, he could see his mother smiling as he performed four-handed pieces with his older sister. His son, David, too, had dedicated his body and soul to music; his world was the violin, that delicate Guarini that was always almost literally within his reach. Bruno had retired from concert touring three years ago; until then, he had been considered one of the greatest pianists in the world.

Hans Hausser had arrived at Carlo Cipriani's house half an hour earlier. At seventy-two, Professor Hausser was still impressively tall, over six foot three, and his extreme thinness made him look fragile, though he was anything but. Over the last forty years he had been teaching physics at the University of Bonn, theorizing on the mysteries of matter, peering into the secrets of the universe. Like Carlo, he was a widower, and he allowed himself to be cared for by his only daughter, Berta.

The two friends were enjoying a cup of coffee when the housekeeper showed Mercedes and Bruno into the doctor's study. They wasted no time on formalities. They had met to kill a man.

"Well, I'll explain where we are," Carlo began. "This morning I came across the name *Tannenberg* in the newspaper. After speaking with you all, I called Security Investigations. As you all know, I've hired them in the past to try to track down Tannenberg—to no avail, of course, beyond strong indications that he was involved in high-level archaeological transactions from time to time, but at a shadowy remove. At any rate, the president, a patient of mine named Luca Marini, called me a few hours ago to tell me that there is, indeed, a Tannenberg at the archaeological conference being held here in Rome at the Palazzo Brancaccio. But it's not our man—in fact, it's a woman named Clara Tannenberg, an Iraqi. She's thirty-five years old, an archaeologist who studied in Cairo and the United States. Despite her youth, she's directing one of the few excavations still going on in Iraq, no doubt thanks also to the influence of her husband, Ahmed, an Iraqi archaeologist himself connected to the Hussein regime. He studied in France and received his doctorate in the United States, where he lived for several years. They met there and were married. This is her first trip to Europe."

"Does she have anything to do with him?" Mercedes asked.

"With Tannenberg?" Carlo answered. "Like you said, it's quite a common name. But it's possible. The investigators found links to the Middle East in the past. A Tannenberg of Iraqi heritage making her way into archaeology: That's more than just a coincidence. She may be his daughter, for all we know. And if she is, I imagine we can get to him through her. I don't think he's dead."

"No, he's not dead," declared Mercedes. "I know he's not dead. I would feel it in my bones. So Clara may be his daughter?"

"Or granddaughter," added Hans. "He must be close to ninety."

"Carlo," Bruno asked, "what are we going to do?"

"Follow her no matter where it takes us. Security Investigations can send men to Iraq, although it will cost us a small fortune. But let's be clear about one thing—if that madman George Bush invades Iraq, we'll have to find another company."

"Why?" Mercedes' voice was impatient.

"Because pulling off a job in a country at war requires men a bit . . . less scrupulous than those employed by Security Investigations."

"You're right," Hans agreed, crossing his legs uncomfortably in

Carlo's leather office chair. "What happens if we find him, if this Clara Tannenberg actually has some connection to him? We need a professional—someone who doesn't mind killing. If he's still alive . . ."

"And if not, then we'll find his children, his grandchildren, anyone related to him, just as we swore." Mercedes' voice was filled with barely contained rage. She was unwilling to admit the slightest impulse of mercy or compassion.

"I agree." Hans nodded. "What about you, Bruno?"

The most admired concert pianist of the late twentieth century did not hesitate to answer with another decisive yes.

"All right, then. What other company could do the job?" Mercedes asked Carlo.

"Luca has assured me that there are a couple of British companies that hire former members of the SAS and other special-forces groups from armies all over the world. There's also an American company, a security-specialty multinational—although *security* is a euphemism. They hire private soldiers who'll fight for any well-paid cause, no matter what country. He's going to give me two or three names, and we'll decide about that tomorrow."

"Good," Mercedes shot back. "Because if we don't find anyone, I could kill them personally."

They all believed her. They had felt the same hatred, a hatred that had grown hotter and hotter the longer they had lived in the monster's hell.

2

"... I HAVE THE PLEASURE OF INTRODUCING CLARA Tannenberg."

Ralph Barry, the moderator of the Mesopotamian culture panel, left the lectern to a dull round of applause as the small, determined-looking woman, clutching a sheaf of papers to her chest, approached to begin her speech.

Clara Tannenberg was nervous. She knew how much was at stake. Her eyes sought her husband in the audience; he gave her a smile of encouragement. For a moment she lost her concentration in his dark eyes. Ahmed was tall, thin, handsome. Though he was older than her by fifteen years, their passion for archaeology connected them deeply. Gripping the lectern to steady herself, she began.

"Ladies and gentlemen, today is a very special day for me. I have come to Rome to ask for your help, to plead with you to raise your collective voice to avert the catastrophe that hangs over Iraq."

A murmur spread through the hall. The men and women attending this panel—twenty or so of the world's leading authorities on ancient Mesopotamia—were not about to take part in an impromptu political rally led by an unknown within the field, a woman whose reputation had been saved from obscurity only by virtue of her husband's position as director of Iraq's Bureau of Archaeological Excavations. Barry's annoyance showed in his face. His worst fears seemed to be confirmed: He had known the presence at the conference of Clara Tannenberg and her husband, Ahmed Husseini, would be problematic. He had tried to persuade them diplomatically not to come, at the behest of his very powerful employer, Robert Brown, president of the Mundo Antiguo Foundation, which was funding most of the conference. But Brown's influence was limited in Rome, and this Iraqi woman seemed neither to need nor to fear him.

Robert Brown was, in fact, a legend in the world of art. He had provided museums around the globe with unique objects and artifacts. The collection of Mesopotamian tablets exhibited in the foundation's galleries was considered the finest in the world.

He had made the business of art his life. In the late 1950s, barely thirty years old, Brown had been trying to make a name for himself as a dealer in New York when he came under the tutelage of one George Wagner, a man he came to refer to as his mentor. Wagner redirected the course of Brown's professional life by helping him set up a lucrative business: convincing important multinational corporations to donate money to a private foundation to finance research and excavations around the world. That way, the multinationals saved a fortune in taxes and acquired a degree of respectability in the eyes of ever-dubious citizens. Helped by Wagner's influence in Washington, Brown set up the Mundo Antiguo Foundation. On the board sat important bankers and businessmen, ensuring large donations. Brown met twice a year with the board, the first time to hammer out the foundation budget and the second to present the financial report. The next report was scheduled in just two weeks, at the end of September.

Robert Brown had made Ralph Barry his right-hand man, bolstering the foundation's stature with the uncommon distinction Barry held in the world of academia. As for George Wagner, the man who had helped him to the top, Brown professed absolute loyalty. For all these years, he had carried out Wagner's orders without question, he had done things he would never have thought himself capable of doing, he was a puppet in Wagner's hands. But he was happy to be one. Everything he was, everything he had, he owed to George. Wagner rewarded discretion above all, and Brown went to great lengths to maintain his patron's anonymity. Even Barry knew little about Robert's so-called mentor.

Brown had been adamant that Barry was to keep Clara Tannenberg and her husband from taking part in the conference, and if that was not possible, he was to at least keep Clara from speaking. The edict had seemed odd to Ralph, because he knew that his boss was acquainted with the couple through their relationship to Alfred Tannenberg. But in the end, Clara pushed hard and forced his hand, threatening to make a scene unless he allowed her a few minutes at the lectern. So here she was, against everyone's wishes.

Now, as the murmur rose and the crowd stirred restively, Clara's face flushed with anger. She swallowed hard before continuing.

"I assure you, ladies and gentlemen, that I have not come here to talk about politics but rather about archaeology, history, religion, culture—art. Human history began in Mesopotamia, and if there is war, much of that history will disappear. And so, I'm asking that you help us save the artistic and cultural heritage of Mesopotamia. I'm asking you for aid—nonfinancial aid."

No one laughed at her feeble attempt at a joke. Clara realized that things were going from bad to worse, but she was determined to push on, no matter how strongly she felt the audience's intense irritation—even though the surface of her skin seemed to burn.

"More than half a century ago, during an archaeological mission near Haran, my grandfather Alfred Tannenberg found a well-shaft lined with pieces of broken tablets. As you all know, certain artifacts—like writing tablets—were often reused to provide structural material for buildings. Even today we find tablets that farmers and shepherds used to build their houses.

"Most of the tablets that lined this well-shaft were covered in cuneiform text detailing the surface area of fields and the volume of grain from the last harvest. There were hundreds of them. But upon further inspection, two of the tablets seemed not to belong. Judging by the lettering, the incisions in the clay itself, it was clear that one scribe had not entirely mastered his stylus."

Clara's voice became tinged with emotion. She was about to reveal her life's mission, the dream that had led her to archaeology, which she cherished more than anything in the world, including Ahmed.

"For more than sixty years," she went on, "my grandfather has kept those two tablets on which someone, no doubt an apprentice scribe, wrote that a relative of his by blood—a man named Abraham—was going to reveal the creation of our world by an omniscient and omnipotent God, who at one point, angry with men, flooded the earth. You must see what this means. . . .

"We all know what importance the discovery of the Akkadian creation poems, the Enuma Elish, the story of Enki and Ninhursag, and the story of the deluge in Gilgamesh held for archaeology and history, and also of course for religion. Well, according to these tablets, the patriarch Abraham added his own vision of the creation of the world, influenced no doubt by the Babylonian and Akkadian poems on paradise and the creation.

"Archaeology has also proven that the incarnation of early books of the Bible we've come to know were written in the seventh century before Christ, at a time in which the Israelite rulers and priests needed to unite the people of Israel, and for that they needed a common history, a national epic, a 'document' that would serve their political and religious purposes.

"Though sometimes it is hard to separate legend from history because they are so intermingled, it seems clear that the stories represent traditions handed down from generation to generation, tales of the past, ancient stories that those shepherds who emigrated from Ur to Haran carried still later to Canaan. . . ."

Clara paused, waiting for some reaction. Her audience had been listening to her in silence, some people doubtfully, others with some interest.

". . . Haran . . . Abram . . . In the Bible we find a detailed genealogy of the 'first men,' beginning with Adam. That list takes us down to the postdiluvian patriarchs, the sons of Shem, one of whose descendants, Terah, begat Nahor, Haran, and Abram, whose name was later transformed into Abraham, father of nations.

"Despite the detailed story in the Bible in which God orders Abram to leave his house and his lands and go into the land of Canaan, no one has been able to show that there actually was a first migration of Semites from Ur to Haran before they arrived at their destination in Canaan. And the encounter between God and Abraham had to have occurred in Haran, where some biblical scholars maintain that the first patriarch must have lived until his father, Terah, died.

"The Bible tells us that when Terah moved to Haran—and I am now going to quote from Genesis 11—*Terah took Abram his son, and Lot the son of Haran, and Sarai his daughter-in-law, his son Abram's wife; and they went forth with them from Ur of the Chaldees, to go into the land of Canaan; and they came unto Haran, and dwelt there.* We know that at that time families were much like small tribes, who moved from place to place with their flocks and their possessions and who settled down periodically and farmed a piece of land to meet their needs. Therefore, when Terah left Ur to settle in Haran, he did so in the company of many members of his family, more or less closely related. We think—my grandfather, my husband, Ahmed Husseini, and I—that a member of the family of Terah, no doubt an apprentice scribe, may have had a close relationship with Abraham, or Abram as his name was then, and that Abraham explained to this apprentice scribe his ideas of the creation of the world, his conception of that one God, and who knows how many other things. For years we have searched in the region of Haran for other tablets by the same scribe. Our searches have been unsuccessful. My grandfather has devoted his life to investigating an area a hundred kilometers around Haran, and he has found nothing. But the work has not been entirely without its discoveries—in the Baghdad Museum, the Haran Museum, and the Ur Museum, and many others besides, there are hundreds of tablets and objects that my family has unearthed down through the years, but we have not yet discovered those other tablets that bear the stories of Abraham—"

With a brusque, irritated gesture, a man in the audience raised his hand and waved it about. Clara broke off, disconcerted.

"Yes? You wanted to say something?"

"Yes, just to be clear about this—you're saying that Abraham, the patriarch Abraham, the Abraham of the Bible, the father of our civilization, told an anonymous somebody, an apprentice scribe, his ideas of God and the world, and that this anonymous apprentice scribe wrote it down on clay tablets, like some reporter, and that your grandfather, whom none of us has had the pleasure of meeting, has found these tablets and held on to them for more than half a century?"

"Two preliminary tablets, on which the scribe declares his intention to record Abraham's dictations, yes."

"I see! So tell me—why has this discovery never been reported until now? In fact, would you be so kind as to tell us who your grandfather and father are? We already know something about your husband. At this conference, we all know one another, and I'm sorry to tell you that to us you are a complete stranger, whom I, for one, on the basis of your presentation, would categorize as uneducated, infantile, and—to put it mildly—overimaginative. Where are these tablets you're talking about? What scientific tests have they been subjected to in order to guarantee their authenticity and the period to which they belong? Scientists and researchers come to conferences such as this one with solid evidence, not with family stories—family stories from a clutch of amateur archaeologists."

A murmur ran through the auditorium; Clara, flushed with anger and embarrassment, froze. She took a deep breath, struggling to recover her composure. And then she saw Ahmed stand and glare at the man who had interrupted her.

"My dear Professor Guilles . . . I know that you have had thousands of students in your long career at the Sorbonne. I was one of them; in fact, throughout my years of study you always gave me the highest marks. In five years I graduated summa cum laude. Later,

Professor, I had the privilege of accompanying you on excavations in Syria and Iraq. Do you remember the winged lions we found near Nippur in a temple dedicated to Nabu? What a shame that the figures were not intact, but at least we were lucky enough to find a collection of cylinder seals dating from the reign of Ashurbanipal. . . . I know that I have neither your knowledge nor your reputation, but I have been directing the Bureau of Archaeological Excavations in Iraq for several years—though today it is inactive, because we have been the victims of a cruel blockade, and the oil-for-food program yields barely enough money to survive as a nation. Iraqi children are dying because there are no medicines in the hospitals and because their mothers cannot afford to buy them food, so there is very little money left for digging into our own past—or, I should say, the past of all humanity, of all civilization. All our archaeological missions have halted and are waiting for better times.

"As for my wife, Clara Tannenberg, she has been my assistant for years; we have excavated several sites together. Her grandfather is a man who is passionate about the past and who has helped to finance a number of important archaeological excavations—"

"Tomb robbers!" someone in the audience called out.

That voice, and the sound of the nervous laughter in the audience, were like knives through Clara's heart. But Ahmed continued impassively.

"As I was saying, we are reasonably certain that the scribe who made the two preliminary tablets discovered by Clara's grandfather also went on to transcribe the stories that he says Abraham told him. Other research—including tablet fragments—hint strongly at this. We could be talking about one of the most important discoveries in the history of not just archaeology but also religion and biblical study. I think we should allow Dr. Tannenberg to go on. Clara, please."

Clara threw a look of gratitude at her husband, took another deep breath, and shakily prepared to proceed. If another of these old fogies interrupted her, she was going to shout them back down. Lord knows she was more than capable of doing it. If her grandfather had witnessed the scene she was going through now, he would have been appalled—and enraged. He had been against her asking the international community for aid. "They're a bunch of arrogant sons of bitches who think they know something," he had said. Her father would never have allowed her to come to Rome, but her father was dead. And now, with the invasion looming, they had to find a way to move forward quickly.

She scanned the audience briefly and forged ahead. "As I was saying, for several years we concentrated our efforts in Haran, searching for some trace of these other tablets we are certain exist. We found nothing. But on the upper part of the two my grandfather found, the name *Shamas* appears, clearly written by the same inexperienced hand. In some cases, scribes put the name of the supervisor of the transcription on the top of the tablet, as well as their own name. In the case of these two tablets, there was just the one name: Shamas. Who is Shamas? you may ask.

"Since the United States declared Iraq its most dangerous enemy, aerial incursions have occurred more and more frequently. You will recall that just a few months ago American planes flying over Iraq claimed to have been attacked by land-to-air missiles, to which they responded by launching a series of cluster bombs. In the bombarded area, between Basra and ancient Ur, in a village named Safran, the explosion revealed the remains of a structure and a wall, and we calculate the perimeter of the wall to be more than five hundred meters.

"Given the situation in Iraq, it has not been possible to give this structure the attention it deserves, despite the fact that my husband and I, along with a small contingent of workers, have begun to excavate. We believe that this structure may be the storage room for the tablets belonging to a temple or some similar building. We cannot be certain of this, of course, as our work has not progressed far enough to verify any of our findings. We have, however, found many pieces of broken tablets, and much to our surprise, the name *Shamas* appears clearly on one. Is this the same Shamas associated with Abraham?

"We do not know, but it may be. The Bible says that Abram, as his name was then, undertook the journey to Canaan with his father's tribe. Some believe that Abraham remained in Haran until his father died and only then began the journey to Canaan. Was Shamas a member of the tribe of Abraham? Did he accompany him to Canaan? These are some of the questions we hope our excavation may answer. However, the spirit is willing, but the funds are weak, you might say.

"And so, I want to ask you to help us. Our dream is to put together an international archaeological mission. If we were to find those tablets . . . For years I have asked myself at what point Abraham abandoned the polytheism of his contemporaries and began to believe in a single God. These tablets could hold the answer."

Professor Guilles raised his hand again. The old Sorbonne professor, one of the world's most renowned specialists in Mesopotamian culture, seemed determined to stop her in her tracks.

"Dr. Tannenberg, I insist that you show us the tablets you continue to rattle on about. Otherwise, please allow those of us who are here with something real to contribute to proceed with the conference."

It was the last straw. Clara's blue eyes flashed with fury.

"Professor Guilles, can you not bear for anyone but yourself to herald the glory of Mesopotamia, even to make a discovery? Is your ego so fragile?"

Guilles stood up slowly and deliberately and turned to the audience.

"I will return to the conference when we resume serious discussion."

As Guilles strode from the hall, Ralph Barry stepped forward and took the microphone. He cleared his throat and addressed the remaining archaeologists who, with varying degrees of amusement or disgust, had witnessed the scene between the archaeological legend and the unknown woman.

"I truly regret all this," Barry said. "I don't understand why we can't all be a bit less inflexible in our positions and listen to what Dr. Tannenberg has to say. She is an archaeologist like us—why such prejudice? She is presenting a theory; I say let's hear her out and then we can express our opinions. Discarding it *a priori* seems to me not very scientific."

Professor Renh, a middle-aged woman from Oxford University with a face tanned leathery by the sun, held up her hand to speak.

"Ralph, all of us know one another here. Dr. Tannenberg has come to us with a story about some mysterious tablets that she hasn't shown us, even in photos. She has presented no supporting evidence whatsoever. She has made statements about the political situation in Iraq, as has her husband, that I personally am sorry she's made, and she has presented us with a theory about Abraham that frankly seems more the result of an overactive imagination, as Professor Guilles so diplomatically put it, than of scientific fieldwork.

"Let me remind you, we are attending an archaeological conference, not sitting around a campfire. And while our colleagues in other specialties are presenting papers and drawing conclusions in the conference halls next door, we . . . we, I have the impression, are wasting our time. I'm sorry; I agree with Professor Guilles. I'd like to get down to work now."

"But that's what we're doing!" Clara shouted indignantly.

Ahmed stood, and as he straightened his tie he addressed the audience without looking at anyone in particular.

"I would like to remind you all that several of the world's greatest archaeological discoveries have been made by men who paid attention to and followed up on legends. Yet you refuse to even consider what we're saying here today. But you wait—yes, you wait and see what happens the moment Bush attacks Iraq. You are all illustrious professors and archaeologists from the *civilized* nations, which means that you're not going to stick your necks out to defend an archaeological project that entails actually going to defenseless Iraq. I can understand that, but what I can't understand is the reason for this close-minded attitude that prevents you from even listening and trying to find out whether some part of what we're saying is, or might be, true."

Professor Renh raised her hand again.

"Dr. Husseini, I insist that you show us some proof of what you say. Stop judging us, and above all, stop bringing politics into it. We're all adults here, and we're here to discuss archaeology, not politics. Stop portraying yourself as a victim and be an archaeologist. Show some evidence to support your claims."

Clara Tannenberg spoke up without giving Ahmed time to reply.

"We don't have the tablets here. You all know that given the situation in Iraq, we were not allowed to bring them. We have some photos. They are not of the best quality, but you can at least see that the tablets exist. We are asking for your help, help in excavating. We do not have the resources to do it all ourselves. In today's Iraq, archaeology is the absolute last priority—we have enough trouble just surviving."

A heavy silence accompanied Clara's words this time. Then, one by one, the audience got up and left the auditorium.

Ralph Barry approached Ahmed and Clara and gestured sadly at the empty hall.

"I'm sorry. I did the best I could, but I told you when we talked earlier that this didn't seem the best forum for your presentation."

"Yes, indeed, Ralph. You did everything you could to keep us from speaking," Clara snapped.

"Dr. Tannenberg, the international situation affects us all. But in the world of archaeology we must keep a wall between our work and politics. If we didn't, it would be impossible to excavate in certain countries. Ahmed, you know that given the political situation, it just isn't feasible for the Mundo Antiguo Foundation to consider an excavation in Iraq. The president would be removed if he did anything of that sort on his own authority, and the board of directors would never approve it. I advised you to maintain as low a profile here as possible and take private meetings, but you've insisted on having it your way. I only hope that news of our little contretemps this afternoon doesn't blow up further and undermine the credibility of the conference."

"We are not politically correct, I know, Ralph," Clara spat out furiously. "Such talk, of course, corrupts your distinguished proceedings."

"Please! I've been as forthcoming and sincere as I can be." Ralph

Barry paused. "Even so, don't lose hope. I noticed that Professor Picot was listening very attentively. He's an odd chap, but he's also an authority in the field."

The moment he mentioned Picot, Ralph Barry could have bitten his tongue. But it was true—alone among his peers, the eccentric professor had been listening to Clara with great interest. Though, knowing Picot, his interest might not have been strictly academic. . . .

Ahmed and Clara returned to their hotel exhausted, an uncomfortable silence stretching between them. Clara knew her husband was furious. He had defended her, of course, but she was sure he was disgusted with her performance. He had asked her, pleaded with her, tried to reason with her—she shouldn't mention her grandfather or her father; she should give a straightforward presentation limited to the recent discovery of the tablets in the librarylike structure. Given the situation in Iraq, no one there would be checking on what they said in Rome. But she had wanted to credit her grandfather and father, whom she adored and from whom she'd learned everything she knew. Not including her grandfather's discovery would have been robbing him of his due.

They entered their room just as the housekeeper was finishing tidying up. They spoke not a word until she left.

Ahmed picked up a glass, dropped in some ice cubes, and went to the minibar, where he poured himself a whiskey. He didn't offer her a drink, so she poured herself a Campari. Then she sat on the couch, waiting for the storm to break.

"You've made a fool of yourself," Ahmed said, his voice hard. "Talking about your father, your grandfather, and me. Good God, Clara, we're archaeologists; we're not *playing* at being archaeologists. This wasn't some graduation party, where you have to thank Daddy for all the things he's done for you! I told you not to mention your grandfather, I told you and told you, but you had to have your own way, with no regard for the consequences. You brought this on yourself! Ralph Barry asked us to keep a low profile. He made it clear that his boss, Robert Brown, supports our excavation but that he can't help us directly—his board of directors would have his head. He can't tell the board that he's interested in some unknown archaeologist who's the granddaughter of an old friend and married to an Iraqi in what they call Saddam Hussein's 'inner circle.' Ralph said it loud and clear—Robert Brown would be digging his own grave. And now you've made it worse. What on earth were you thinking, Clara?"

"I was thinking of my grandfather! Why can't I talk about him and my father—or about you? I have nothing to be ashamed of. Why shouldn't their contributions be recognized? They were distinguished antiques dealers, and they've spent fortunes helping to excavate in Iraq, Syria, Egypt—"

"Wake up, Clara! Your grandfather and father are just business-men, not great financial backers of cultural preservation! Grow up! Stop climbing on your grandfather's lap!"

"You're right, he was a businessman, but he loves Mesopotamia more than anyone, and he passed that love down to my father and me. He could have been a great archaeologist, but he didn't have the chance to pursue that. But it was he and he alone who discovered those two tablets, and it was he who kept them for more than fifty years, who spent his own money so that others could find more evidence of Shamas. I'd remind you that the museums in Iraq are filled with pieces from excavations financed by my grandfather."

Ahmed gazed at her with an expression of such disdain that Clara was shocked. Her husband was suddenly a stranger.

"Your grandfather has always been a man who shunned the spot-light, Clara, and your father was the same way. They have never made any gratuitous shows of their money or their archaeology. Your actions today would have disappointed them. It's not what they taught you."

Ahmed suddenly fell silent and sank into a chair with a look of weariness.

"The Bible of Clay—that's what my grandfather called it. Genesis as recounted by Abraham," Clara mused in a low voice.

"Yes, the Bible of Clay. A Bible written on clay tablets a thousand years before it was written on papyrus."

"It would be an incredibly important discovery for mankind, one more proof of the existence of Abraham. You don't think we're wrong, do you?"

"I want to find the Bible of Clay too. But today, Clara, you've thrown away the best chance we had to do that. These are the elite of world archaeology. And we do have to apologize for who we are."

"And just who are we, Ahmed?"

"An unknown archaeologist married to the director of the Bureau of Archaeological Excavations in a country with a dictatorial regime whose leader has been condemned to fall because he no longer serves the interests of the powerful. Years ago, when I lived in the United States, being Iraqi wasn't a handicap—quite the contrary. Saddam went to war with Iran because that served Washington's interests. He mur-dered Kurds with weapons that were sold to him by the Americans—

chemical weapons prohibited by the Geneva Convention, the same weapons they're looking for now. It's all a lie, Clara, but we have to tread carefully now. But you don't care about anything that's happening around you; you couldn't care less about Saddam, Bush, and all the people who may die because of the two of them. Your world is your grandfather, and that's it."

"Which side are you on?"

"What?"

"You attack the Saddam regime, you seem to understand the Americans, but other times you hate them. Which side are you on?"

"I'm not on either side, anybody's side. I'm alone."

His answer surprised Clara. They rarely talked so frankly. She was impressed by Ahmed's candor but stung by her husband's sense of alienation.

Ahmed was an Iraqi who'd been over-Westernized. Through the years, as he'd traveled the world, he had lost his sense of heritage. His father had been a diplomat, a man close to the Saddam regime who was rewarded with posts at several important embassies: Paris, Brussels, London, Mexico City, the consulate in Washington. The Husseini family had lived well, very well, and the ambassador's sons had become perfect cosmopolitans: They had studied at the best European boarding schools, the finest American universities, and learned several languages. Ahmed's three sisters had married Westerners; they couldn't have stood going back to Iraq to live. They had grown up free, in democratic countries. And he, Ahmed, had also drunk deep from the well of democracy in every new destination to which his father had been sent. Now Iraq was asphyxiating to him, despite the fact that when he'd returned, he lived with all the privileges accorded the "sons of the regime."

He would have preferred to live in the United States, but he'd met Clara, and her grandfather and father had wanted her near them in Iraq. So he went back.

"So now what do we do?" Clara asked.

"Nothing. There's nothing we can do. I'll call Ralph tomorrow so he can tell us just how big a disaster this is."

"Are we going back to Baghdad?"

"Do you have any better idea? I thought you'd be happy to reunite with your grandfather."

"Don't be sarcastic! But of course—I'm dying to see him. I wouldn't be here at all without him. He taught me to love archaeology."

"He taught you to be obsessed with the Bible of Clay, that's what he taught you."

Then there was silence. Ahmed finished his drink in one gulp, then closed his eyes. Neither of them had any desire to talk anymore.

That night, as she often did, Clara got into bed thinking of Shamas. She imagined him bent over his tablet, intent, as he pressed a thin reed into the wet clay, making his marks. . . .

3

IN THE LATE MORNING, AS HE LEFT THE HOUSE OF TABLETS, Shamas had seen Abram herding the goats, seeking green grass in which to pasture them. He had followed Abram, though he knew that his kinsman preferred to be alone and speak to no one. Indeed, for some time Shamas had found his "uncle," as he called him, much changed. He had become a man who sought solitude, who shunned even members of his own family, saying that he needed to think in peace. But with Shamas, Abram showed patience, so the boy had dared to pursue him . . . and now he would dare to draw him out, for indeed he delighted in asking questions that sometimes provoked his uncle, even if he already knew the answers himself.

"Uncle," cried Shamas, as he ran between the slow-moving goats to reach Abram. "Who made the first goat?" he breathlessly asked.

Abram slowed and crouched to converse with his nephew. "He did."

"And why a goat?"

"For the same reason He made all the creatures that live on the earth."

"And us, then—what are we for? To work?"

"It is God's desire, at least for you, Shamas, that you master your stylus."

Shamas fell silent. He knew he should still be in the house of tablets, completing the work that had been assigned him. His other un-cle, the um-mi-a—the master scribe—would complain to Shamas' fa-ther, and Shamas would once again be scolded.

"But I am bored at the house of tablets," the boy said, seeking an excuse.

"Bored? And what is it that bores you? Do you not find your dub-sar's lessons a welcome opportunity to hone your craft?"

"Ili the scribe is not a happy man. Probably because he has not yet mastered the stylus as well as the um-mi-a Ur-Nisaba would like him to. And Ili does not like children. He has no patience for us and makes us write the same phrases over and over until, in his judgment, they are perfect. Then, at noon, when he demands that we repeat the lesson aloud, he becomes angry if we stammer, even a little, and he shows no mercy in our mathematical assignments."

Abram smiled. Shamas was right: The master was too rigid. But Abram dared not feed the boy's rebellious nature by siding with him. Shamas was the most intelligent boy of the tribe, and his mission was to study so that he might become a scribe, or even a priest. The tribe needed wise men to carry out the calculations necessary to build canals through which water might flow to the arid land, men who could bring order to the granaries, control the distribution of the wheat, make loans, men who could preserve the tribe's knowledge of plants and ani-mals, of mathematics, who were able to read the stars. Men whose pur-pose was greater than simply feeding their broods.

Shamas' father was a great scribe, a master, and the boy, like many other members of his family, had been favored with intelligence. His must not be wasted, for intelligence was a gift that God gave some men so that they might make life easier for others and so that they might combat those who had become infected with evil.

"You should go, before they begin to look for you and your mother begins to worry."

"My mother saw me follow you. She knows nothing will happen if I am with you."

"But she will be cross with you nonetheless, because she knows you are not taking advantage of your education."

"But, Uncle, dub-sar Ili makes us invoke Nidaba, the goddess of grains; he insists that it is she who has given us the power to know the signs."

"You are learning what the dub-sar teaches you, then."

"Yes, I know, but do you think it is Nidaba who gives us the power of knowledge?"

Abram did not reply. He did not want to confuse the boy, although he could not keep silent about how he felt, about the path that had led him to the certainty that the gods his people worshipped were not filled with any spirit but were simply vessels of clay.

His father, Terah, modeled the clay himself and provided temples and palaces with those god idols. Gods made by his own hands! Abram still recalled the pain and grief he had caused when years ago Terah found him in his workshop, surrounded by the shards of dried clay that had once been the figures left to dry before being fired and transformed into gods.

Abram had thrown them to the ground and stamped upon them with his feet, these false idols born of his father's hands before which men stupidly bowed their heads in the conviction that all gifts and all misfortunes descended from them. Abram did not know why he had acted as he had in his father's workshop; he simply could not but follow his instincts.

Then he had sat down to await the consequences of his act. There was nothing in those figures; if they were gods they would have unleashed their fury upon him—they would have struck him dead. But nothing had happened, and the only wrath that descended upon him was that of his father when he saw the fruit of his labors shattered in a thousand pieces.

Terah had reproached him for sacrilege, but Abram had responded disdainfully. He knew that there was nothing in those figures but clay, and he urged his father to reflect upon it.

Then he asked his father's forgiveness for destroying his work, and he cleaned up the remains of the figures. He even kneaded the clay so that his father might make more gods to sell.

Now, many years later, although all the members of their tribe recognized the authority of Terah, the respect given his son was just as great, and the men of the tribe often came to Abram in search of counsel and advice, many to hear his quiet but assured meditations on the one true God. Terah was not offended by this, for he was an old man now and he slept most of the day. At his death, Abram would become the tribe's leader.

And that was precisely why Shamas admired him. That and the fact that Abram was in fact a distant relative of Shamas' mother, a person who spoke to the boy as an equal, as one who could reason as a man, curious to know all, unsatisfied with rote learning. And it was that quality that Abram had to remind him of now.

"What I think, Shamas, is that you must learn what Ili teaches you, for that will enable you to uncover the difference between truth and untruth. The day will come when you alone will separate the wheat from the chaff. But until then, you must not look down upon any knowledge, no matter its source."

"The other day I spoke to Ili about . . . Him," the boy said, turning his eyes upward, "and Ili became very angry. He told me that I must not offend Ishtar, Isin, Inanna. . . ."

"And why did you speak to Ili of Him?"

"Because I never stop thinking about what you tell me. Uncle, I cannot believe there's a spirit inside the figure of Ishtar, which I can see and touch. But *because* I cannot see the one God, I am all the more certain He exists."

Abram was surprised by the boy's reasoning; he believed in what he could not see precisely because he could not see it.

"Does He speak to you?" Shamas asked with a glint of hope in his eyes.

Abram, cautious not to override Ili's teachings, responded reservedly. "I feel that He does."

"And does He speak with words, as you and I speak?"

"No, but I can hear Him as clearly as I hear you." Abram knelt and put his hands on his nephew's shoulders. "But you must refrain from angering your teacher with this."

"I will keep your secret, then."

"I'm not asking you to keep a secret, Shamas—I am asking you to be discreet. Go, now, off to school with you—and no more provoking Ili."

The boy got up from the rock on which he had been sitting and stroked the long neck of a white goat chewing grass with obvious pleasure, indifferent to everything around it.

Shamas bit his lower lip and then, smiling, made a request of Abram.

"Uncle, if you tell me how He created us, and why, I will write it down. I will use the bone stylus that my father gave me. I only use it when the dub-sar gives me something important to write down. It would be good practice for me, Uncle—please."

Abram's eyes gazed long upon Shamas before he replied. The boy was ten years old—was he able to understand the complexity of this God who would be revealed to him? Abram made a decision.

"I will tell you what you ask of me, and you will write it down upon your tablets and guard them jealously. You will show them only when I say you may. Your father shall know what we are doing, and your mother also, but no one else. I will speak with them. But I will do this only under one condition: that you not miss school again. And you are not to dispute with your teacher—you must listen and learn."

The boy nodded happily, then turned and ran off to school. Ili would be angry with him for returning late, but he didn't care. Abram was going to tell him the secrets of God, a God who was not fashioned of clay.

Ili frowned when he saw Shamas run into the house of tablets, sweating and still breathing hard from his exertion.

"I shall speak to your father," the scribe said to him sternly, then went on with the lesson that Shamas had interrupted. He was teaching the boys mathematics and, more than that, leading them to understand the mysteries of numbers, the abbreviations with which the tens were drawn.

Shamas' reed moved over the wet clay tablet, documenting everything Ili explained, so that later he might read it to the satisfaction of his father and mother.

"Father, I'd like some tablets . . . for my own use," Shamas meekly proposed.

Jadin raised his eyes from the tablet he was holding, astounded by his son's request. He had been noting observations of the sky, as he had done for many years. Of his eight children, Shamas was his favorite but also the child who gave him the most concern, for his curiosity was perhaps too great.

"Has Ili given you lessons to do at home, then?"

"No, Father. I am to record Abram's story. Has he not spoken with you about this?"

"He has not—not yet anyway," his father responded with a tinge of curiosity.

"Abram has found our Creator outside the clay figurines we are taught to worship."

Shamas' father sighed. He knew it would be useless to forbid Shamas to listen to Abram's stories; his son was devoted to his uncle. Abram was a man of clean heart—and too intelligent to believe that a piece of clay contained a god. Jadin knew better as well, though he never expressed his disbelief. Abram believed in a God who was the beginning and the end of all things, and Shamas' father much preferred that his son know about that God than be bound by idolatry— preferred that his son be a "heretic" than have his curiosity stifled.

"Have you told Ili what Abram proposes?"

"I've mentioned his ideas, much to Ili's disapproval. But, no, I haven't told him about Abram's project for me."

"All right. You may write everything that Abram tells you."

Shamas ran to embrace his father. "Thank you! I will take good care of the tablets. I will keep them with me always."

"Don't you want to take them to the house of tablets? Are you certain Ili would not understand?" Jadin asked with a smile. "Ili is intelligent, even though he has little patience as a teacher. You must not forget that, Shamas—you must give Ili your respect."

"I respect him, Father. But Abram decides to whom God will be spoken about and in what fashion."

"I see. Then do as Abram has told you, and be mindful of his discretion."

"Thank you, Father. I'll ask Mother to help me look after the tablets, to be sure that no one touches them but me."

And the boy skipped gaily out of the house to find his mother. After he spoke to her, he would take clay from the little deposit where his father went to make his own tablets. The next day he would sit down with Abram. His kinsman always went out with the goats before dawn, because, he had explained, it was the best time of day to think.

The boy was impatient to begin, for he was sure that Abram was about to reveal great secrets to him, secrets he had wondered about as long as he could remember. Some nights he could hardly sleep, wondering where the first man had come from, and the first woman, the first chicken, the first bull, and who had discovered the secret of bread, and how the scribes had awakened the magic of numbers. Yearning for answers, he would turn these questions over and over in his head, until he would fall asleep at last, exhausted and still restless, for even in his dreams he sought knowledge.

Men were sitting expectantly before the door of Terah's house. Abram had asked Terah, as the tribe's leader, to call the men together. It was, however, Abram who wished to speak to the heads of the houses of the tribe.

"We must leave Ur," Terah told them. "This is a decision not made in haste. Come, my son Abram will explain." He extended his hand toward his other son. "Come, Nahor, sit beside me while your brother speaks."

The men's murmurs quieted as Abram, standing before them, looked at each of the men in turn. Then, with a voice touched with emotion, he announced that Terah would lead them to Canaan, because it was a land blessed by God. There they would make their settlements and bear their children, and their children's children. It was, quite simply, God's will. He urged them to begin preparations for a departure, for they would be setting out as soon as everyone was ready.

Terah responded to the men's questions and calmed their disquiets. But the fever of Abram's monotheistic revelation had caught and spread among the tribe; most would do anything Abram asked of them. Nahor was animated and enthusiastic as well, so that the others would take heart. Leaving the land of Ur would not be easy; their fathers had been born there, and their fathers' fathers. Their flocks had pastured there, and they had labored among those flocks and in the fields for generations. Canaan seemed a far distant place to them, but despite their misgivings, the hope of a new life began to take fire in all of them, for Canaan was said to be a land rich in fruits, in pastures for their flocks, in strong rivers where their thirst might be always quenched. And it was the place where God commanded that they live.

Some of the men of Terah's tribe were scribes and thus enjoyed the protections of the palace and the temple. There were also fine artisans among them, and abundant flocks. In Ur, however, most struggled against the desert, digging canals to bring the waters of the Euphrates so that their lands might yield grain with which to knead bread. Theirs was not an easy life. Their goats and sheep provided them with milk and meat, but still they spent much of their lives looking up at the sky, hoping that the gods might bring the gift of rain to water the ground and fill the pools and cisterns.

Now they were to gather all their belongings and their flocks, and set out along the Euphrates toward the north. It would take days to carry out all the preparations and take their leave of other kinspeople and friends. For not everyone would make the journey—the sick and aged, who could hardly walk, would remain under the care of younger members of the family, who someday would be called to the land of Canaan but until then would remain in Ur. Each family was to decide who would undertake the journey and who would remain.

Jadin called his wife, his sons and their wives, his uncles by blood and their children, who came also with their children. All the members of his family sat down with him at dawn in his home, where they took shelter from the chill of the morning.

"We will go with Terah to the land of Canaan. Some of you will stay here, in the care of those we leave behind. You, Hosen, will be the leader of the family in my absence."

Hosen, Jadin's younger brother, nodded in relief. He did not want to leave; he lived in the temple, where it was his task to compose letters and commercial contracts, and he wanted nothing more than to continue exploring the mystery contained in numbers and stars in the land of his father.

"Our father," Jadin went on, "is too old to leave. His legs barely allow him to stand, and there are days when his eyes stare off and he can speak no word. You, Hosen, will see that he lacks nothing. And of our sisters, Hamisal shall remain with you, for she is a widow without children and will be able to care for our father."

Shamas listened in fascination to the words of his father. He felt a tickling in his stomach, caused by eagerness and impatience. If he had his way, he would already have set out in search of that land Abram had spoken of. But suddenly he felt a pang of concern—if they were setting out on a journey, would he then not be able to write the history of the world that Abram had promised to recount to him?

"How long will it take us to arrive at this land of Canaan?" Shamas blurted out mid-thought.

The boy's question disturbed Jadin, for children were taught not to interrupt their elders. The father's stern gaze made Shamas flush with embarrassment, and he lowered his eyes to the ground and muttered an apology.

Jadin, however, spoke to the boy, to calm his unease.

"I know not how long the journey to Canaan will be, nor whether we may have to stop for some time in some other place before we reach it. Who knows what may happen when a tribe undertakes a long journey? Now go, all of you, and make preparations so that you will be ready when Terah calls for our departure."

Shamas saw the silhouette of Abram's lean figure against the horizon and ran toward him. He had been seeking an opportunity to meet with his kinsman for two days now: This was the moment.

Abram smiled when he saw the boy, whose face was red with desert heat and exertion. He plunged his shepherd's crook into the ground, while his eyes sought out a tree under which they might take shelter from the sun.

"Come, rest," he said to Shamas. "We can sit in the shade of that fig tree, beside the well."

"Uncle, if we are leaving, we will not be able to bake the clay to make tablets. My father will not let me carry with us more than is necessary. You will not be able to reveal your story." He lowered his head.

"Shamas, do not worry yourself about this. You shall write the story of Creation later. He will simply decide when and how you shall do it."

The boy could not hide his disappointment. He didn't want to wait—he wanted to write the story now. And despite his intense desire, he had to confess something to Abram.

"Is Ili coming?"

"No."

"I will miss him, Uncle. Sometimes I think he is right to be vexed with me when I do not listen to his explanations, and . . ."

The boy hesitated, unsure whether to continue. Abram gave him no encouragement, asked no questions, but only waited for the boy to decide whether to finish his sentence or not.

"I am the worst scribe in the school, Uncle; my tablets are filled with errors. Today I made a mistake in a calculation. . . . Ili will not abide me. I have promised him that I will do better, that he will have no reason to scold me again, but I want you to know all this, because you may want to draw upon one of the other students to record this history. One who doesn't make so many mistakes with the reed."

Shamas fell silent, waiting for Abram to speak. The boy bit his lip nervously, ashamed he wasn't a better student. Ili often scolded him for wasting his time asking absurd questions. He had complained to Shamas' father, and Jadin had scolded Shamas—he was disappointed in him. Now Shamas feared that Abram, too, would be disappointed and that he might put an end to his dream of writing the history.

"You do not try hard enough in school."

"I know," the boy replied timorously.

"Yet even so, you think that if I tell you the story of Creation you can write it down without error?"

"Yes! . . . Or at least I will try. I have thought about it, Uncle, and I think it would be best if you tell it to me little by little, and then I can write it down slowly, at home, carefully, with my bone stylus. Then each day I can show you what I wrote the night before, and if I succeed, you can continue telling me the story."

Abram looked at him for a long time. It mattered little that the boy's impatience might lead to errors, or that his speculative mind might question Ili, or that his desire for freedom might lead him to pay too little attention to the scribe's explanations. No, the boy had other virtues, the principal one of which was his ability to think. When he asked a question, he expected a logical answer. He was never content with the answers that adults generally gave children.

Shamas' eyes shone with eagerness and excitement, and Abram realized that of all the men, women, and children in his tribe, this boy was the one who might best understand God's plan.

"I will tell you the story of Creation, Shamas. I will begin with the day on which He decided to separate the light from the darkness. But now I want you to go back home. I will call you when the time is right to begin."

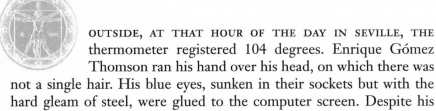

4

OUTSIDE, AT THAT HOUR OF THE DAY IN SEVILLE, THE thermometer registered 104 degrees. Enrique Gómez Thomson ran his hand over his head, on which there was not a single hair. His blue eyes, sunken in their sockets but with the hard gleam of steel, were glued to the computer screen. Despite his eighty-plus years, he was fascinated by the Internet.

The ringing of the telephone startled him. But he was not surprised to hear the voice of George Wagner when he answered. His longtime comrade went straight to the point, as he always did.

"Enrique, Robert Brown just called me. The girl spoke at the conference in Rome."

"And said . . ."

"Everything we wanted to prevent her from saying—she's put it all out in public."

"Have you talked to Frank?" Their old friend and business partner would surely want to hear the bad news as soon as possible.

"We hung up not a minute ago."

"What are we going to do?"

"What we'd planned if something like this happened. Alfred was warned."

"And have you set the plan in motion?"

"Yes."

"Will Robert be able to carry it out?"

"Robert? He's smart, and he takes orders well. He does what I tell him to do and doesn't ask questions."

"When we were kids, you handled the puppets we got at Christmas better than anyone."

"Men are a little more complicated than puppets."

"Not for you. And the time has definitely come to put a stop to this. What about Alfred? Have you heard from him again?"

"No, not so far."

"We ought to talk to him."

"We'll talk, but it's useless. He's clearly going his own way. He wants to play the game by his own rules, and we can't allow that. He's given us no choice—he's put his granddaughter out in front on this and we have to keep her in check. I've got her monitored wherever she goes. They're not going to take what's rightfully ours."

"You're right, George, but I'm not looking forward to a confrontation with Alfred. There has to be some way to make him listen to reason."

"After all these years, my friend, Alfred has decided *not* to listen to reason. It's a complete betrayal of everything we pledged to each other. Treason. There's no way around it."

Enrique ran his hand over his head again as Wagner terminated the call. He looked up as his grandson, Alvaro, dressed in riding clothes, burst into the room. In spite of the troubling phone call, Enrique smiled at the sight of the tall, thin, nice-looking young man.

"Hello, *abuelo*. I stopped by to see if you'd like to have lunch with me." Alvaro ran his arm across his forehead and laughed. "Gosh, am I sweaty."

"So I see. Not too bright, my boy, going riding in this heat. Where's your father?"

"In his office."

"All right. And thank you for the invitation, but I need to work."

"But, *abuelo*, you should retire! Let it go. Come to the club with me for lunch."

"You know I hate those people at the club."

"You hate everyone in Seville. You don't go anywhere anymore, *abuelo*—*abuela* is right, you're an old bore."

"Your grandmother is always right. And I am an old bore, but I can't bear those people."

"That's because of your English upbringing, old man."

"Where's your sister?"

"She's gone to Marbella. She was invited to stay with the Kholls."

"And she couldn't be bothered to say good-bye. You two are worse every day."

"Don't be so old-fashioned! Besides, Elena hates being in the country. You, Papá, and I are the only ones who like the house here—*abuela*, Mamá, and Elena can't abide it. They hate all the bulls and horses." Enrique nodded in rueful agreement as Alvaro returned to his original entreaty. "So, will you come to the club, then, or not?"

"Not. I'll stay here, thanks. As hot as it is, I've no interest in going out anyway. Now leave me be—I have to think."

When the old gentleman was alone again, he smiled to himself. His grandson was a good boy, not nearly so scatterbrained as his sister. The only thing he reproached them for was their all-too-frequent involvement in the social whirl of Seville. He had always made it a point not to socialize too much and focused almost exclusively on his business.

In that respect, his wife Rocío had been a blessing. She was the daughter of a provincial representative to the Spanish parliament in the Franco regime, who had gotten rich after the war through the black market. Over time, his father-in-law had reluctantly brought Enrique into the business, though Enrique had later broken away into import-export, where he'd become a very wealthy man. He would always be grateful to his wife. Without her, he'd never have gotten where he was today. But whatever his success, Enrique Gómez Thomson had always been careful to call as little attention to himself as humanly possible. His was a respectable Sevillan family that had never allowed itself to be the butt of gossip. No scandal had ever touched any of them. Nor would one, if he had his way.

His thoughts turned to Frankie and George. They had been fortunate too, although in truth, no one had ever given them a thing. They'd just been smarter than the others.

Robert Brown slammed his fist down so hard on the desk that he hurt his hand. He'd been on the phone for over an hour. First Ralph had called to tell him about Clara Tannenberg's little speech at the conference in Rome. Just thinking about it gave him a pain in his stomach. Then he'd had to break the news to George Wagner, who'd dressed him down for not having prevented the whole episode in the first place.

Clara was a spoiled child, and pigheaded to boot. She always had been. How was it possible that Alfred had such a granddaughter? His son, Helmut, had been different. The boy had never given Alfred a bad night. A shame he'd died so young. He was an intelligent young man who always carried himself with discretion—Alfred had taught him to be invisible and the boy had learned well. But Clara . . . Clara behaved like a headstrong little princess. Alfred allowed her to do things he'd never allowed Helmut even to think of; he was putty in her hands.

Helmut had married Amira, an Iraqi woman with a cascade of black hair and the profile of a goddess carved in ivory. Alfred had approved heartily of the advantageous marriage. With it, his son had become a member of an old Iraqi family that was not just influential but also wealthy—very wealthy, indeed. They had ties with powerful friends in Baghdad, Cairo, Amman, and the other capitals of the region, which meant that they were respected and their opinions valued across the Middle East. In addition, Ibrahim, Amira's father, was a cultured, educated man of great refinement.

Amira was distinguished by nothing but her beauty, yet Helmut had seemed utterly enchanted by her. Of course, the woman might have been more intelligent than she seemed. With Muslim women, one never knew for sure.

Alfred had lost his son and daughter-in-law in a car accident when Clara was a teenager, and he had spoiled his granddaughter royally ever since. Robert had never liked Clara. It set his teeth on edge when she called him Uncle Robert; he was irritated by her self-assurance, which bordered on insolence, and bored by her incessant chatter regarding her grandfather's archaeological ambitions.

When Alfred sent her to the United States to study and asked Robert to watch over her, he could never have imagined how tiresome that undertaking would be. But he couldn't say no to Alfred, who was, after all, a business partner and special friend of George Wagner. So he arranged her enrollment at the University of California at Berkeley. Fortunately, she'd fallen in love with and married Ahmed Husseini, an intelligent man with whom one could actually deal. Alfred and Robert had hit it off perfectly with Ahmed, who had turned out to be a tremendous asset in Alfred's business. The problem was Clara.

The conversation he'd had with Ralph Barry had given him a splitting headache just when he was about to have lunch with a close adviser to the President of the United States and some friends, all men of business interested in the forthcoming invasion of Iraq. But the conversation with George had been even worse. Wagner had ordered him in no uncertain terms to take charge of the situation, now that the Bible of Clay had been publicly announced and Alfred and his granddaughter were making their move to find it for themselves. Normally, they all would have shared in its profits, but it was now clear that Alfred had abandoned their long-standing partnership. Wagner's edict had been unambiguous: Get the Bible of Clay—if it actually existed, of course.

Robert pressed his intercom for his secretary. "Smith, get Ralph Barry for me again, please."

"Yes, Mr. Brown. And, sir, Senator Miller's assistant just called to confirm that you'll be attending the picnic the senator's wife is having this weekend."

Another stupid woman, Brown thought. Every year she organized the same farce: a picnic at their farm in Vermont, where guests were forced to drink lemonade and eat sandwiches as they sat on cashmere blankets spread on the ground. But Brown knew he'd have to go, because Senator Miller was a Texan with interests in the oil sector. The secretaries of defense and state, the attorney general, the national security adviser, the director of the CIA, and who knew who else would be at the damned picnic. And so would George Wagner. It was an ideal occasion for some high-stakes dealmaking in full view of the oblivious crowd.

A buzzer signaled that Barry was on the line.

"Is there anything that ties Clara Tannenberg to us?" Robert asked him without preamble.

"No, no, of course not. I told you not to worry. The onus of her behavior lay squarely on her and Ahmed. Mundo Antiguo has no connection to that speech whatsoever."

"All right, I suppose that puts us more or less in the clear. You still should have kept her out."

"I told you, Robert—I couldn't. Once Alfred allowed her to attend, nobody could have kept her from signing up for the panel on Mesopotamia, much less from talking. Believe me, I tried to convince her—there was no way. She insisted that she had her grandfather's consent, and she said that ought to be enough for you."

"Alfred must be gaga."

"He might be, who knows? At any rate, his granddaughter, at least, is absolutely obsessed with this Bible of Clay. . . . Do you think it actually exists?"

"It seems likely, from what we know. But we had no intention of making that information public—at least not yet. But that doesn't matter now. We'll make sure we're there, if and when it's found, and we'll secure it for ourselves. We'll just have to cut Alfred out of this one."

"But how?"

"In view of what's happened, we have to change our plans. We were going to assemble our own team, quietly. But she's left us no choice.

One way or another, they're going to put a group of archaeologists to-gether and push ahead with their excavation, so we'll find a way to make sure they have financing. We'll figure something out. And then we'll place our own man in the excavation."

"Jesus, Robert, the situation in Iraq is not exactly propitious for an archaeological excavation. All the Western governments have put out travelers' warnings. It could be suicide to go there now. We ought to wait."

"Am I hearing you right, Ralph? This is the *best* time to go to Iraq, man. We'll be there, and we'll do it our way. Iraq is the new land of op-portunity—only a fool wouldn't see that."

Barry didn't argue further. After a pause, he went back to the events at the conference. "A professor named Yves Picot, who's very well re-garded in the field, is the only one who seemed to show any real inter-est in what Clara was saying. He told me he'd like to talk to Ahmed. If he goes, maybe we can slip a man into his team."

"Let him talk to Ahmed first. Trust Ahmed. He knows what he's supposed to do. But first ask him to send his wife to Baghdad, or to hell—anywhere, but get her out of there before she ruins us all."

Ralph laughed to himself. Robert Brown's misogyny was notorious. He hated women—and was clearly uncomfortable in their presence. He was a confirmed bachelor who'd never been known to have emo-tional relationships of any kind. It was even hard for him to be cordial to his friends' wives. Unlike practically every other businessman in the world, his secretary was a man—Smith, a polyglot, stick-up-his-ass sixty-year-old who'd spent his entire adult life at Robert's side.

"Okay, Robert, I'll see what I can do to get Clara back to Baghdad. I'll get Ahmed to help me. But she is not an easy woman—she's arro-gant, and she's stubborn."

Like her grandfather, thought Brown. *But without his intelligence.*

The president's adviser enjoyed Mediterranean cuisine, so they chose to lunch at a Spanish restaurant near the Capitol.

Robert Brown was the first to arrive. He was punctual to a fault. It infuriated him to wait; he hated people who were late for appoint-ments. He hoped the president's adviser wouldn't be delayed by some last-minute emergency.

One by one the others came in: Dick Garby, John Nelly, and Edward Fox. They all were owners or directors of construction firms, oil interests, equipment companies. The man from the White House was the last to arrive, and he was in a foul mood.

He told them that negotiations with the Europeans over the Security Council's support of military action against Iraq were getting complicated.

"There are fools everywhere. The French, of course, can be counted on to go their own way every time. But the Germans have stabbed us in the back; that red-and-green government is more worried about what the liberal press will say than about keeping its commitments."

"We can always count on the UK," Dick Garby put in.

"Yeah, but it's not enough," Bush's adviser replied. "We have the Italians too, and the Spaniards, Portuguese, Poles, and several other countries, but what are they worth? A hundred soldiers each? Even the Mexicans are waffling now, and the Russians and Chinese are rubbing their hands together, watching us twist in the wind."

"When do we invade?" Robert Brown asked straight out.

"As soon as the boys from the Pentagon tell us they're ready. We'll soften up the country with aerial raids first. I figure five or six months at the outside. This is September, so figure March, sometime in early spring. I'll let you know."

"We need to start getting the Committee for the Reconstruction of Iraq up and running," Edward Fox said.

"Yeah, we've thought about that. I'll call you in three or four days. It's a big pie, but you've got to be in line early to get the best pieces of it. Tell me which parts you want and we'll start working on it."

Almost all of them ordered bacalao al pil-pil, a specialty of the Basque: cod cooked with olive oil, garlic, and a chili pepper for spiciness in a pan rotated over the fire constantly to bring out the delicious juices of the fish. As they ate, the men laid the foundation of their future business dealings in Iraq. There was so much that was going to be destroyed, and so much that would have to be rebuilt. . . .

Lunch was profitable for everyone. They agreed to meet again, over the weekend, at the Millers' picnic. They could continue their talks then—if their wives would let them.

The office of the Mundo Antiguo Foundation was located in a steel-and-glass building not far from the White House. The views were wonderful, but Robert had never really been able to bring himself to like Washington. He preferred New York, where a branch of the foundation conducted its business in a large brownstone in the Village that dated from the eighteenth century. It had been the foundation's first headquarters, and despite the fact that it no longer was of the slightest practical use—though Ralph Barry, too, preferred to work there—none of the directors had ever had the heart to dispose of it. When he was in New York, Robert held his most important meetings there, or sometimes in the private office he maintained on the lower floor of his own home, a splendid duplex overlooking Central Park.

"Smith, I need to talk to Paul Dukais. Right away, please," Robert said as he returned to the office after lunch.

Dukais' hoarse voice came on the line less than a minute later.

"Paul, my friend, I was calling to see if we could have dinner together."

"Sure, Robert, of course. I'd be delighted. When?"

"How about tonight?"

"Tonight? I can't," Dukais said, his voice apologetic. "My wife is dragging me to the opera. It'll have to be tomorrow night."

"There's not much time left, Paul. Fuck the opera—we're about to start a war."

"If I'm going to war, I've got to be sure the domestic front is at peace, my friend, and Doris is always complaining that I never go with her to these social events—which she claims give us what little respectability we have." Dukais laughed. "I promised, Robert—promised Doris and my daughter both. So even if we declare the Third World War, I'm going to the opera tonight. We can have dinner tomorrow."

"No, let's make it breakfast. We need to get moving. Come to my house; it's best to meet there, anyway. Is seven all right?"

"Jesus, Robert, take it easy. I'll be there at eight."

Brown closed himself up in his office. At seven-thirty Smith knocked softly at the door.

"Do you need me, Mr. Brown?"

"No, Smith, thanks. Go home. I'll see you in a day or two."

He worked for a while longer. He'd drawn up a detailed plan for the next few months. The war was about to start, and he wanted to have everything in place.

On his way out of the Palazzo dei Congressi in Rome, Ralph Barry passed a thin, dark-haired man arguing with one of the security guards to let him in. As he waited for the taxi he had called, Barry was struck by the young man's insistence. He wasn't an archaeologist, a journalist, or a historian—he flatly refused to reveal his identity—but he was determined to enter. Just then, Barry's taxi pulled up, and his mind turned to his upcoming meeting.

The sun was gilding the obelisk in the Piazza del Popolo. Barry and Ahmed Husseini had a date for lunch at La Bolognesa. As always, the restaurant was full of tourists, the two of them included.

"Tell me exactly where the remains of the structure are located," Ralph said to Ahmed. "Brown insists that you give me the coordinates. I also want to know what resources you have at your disposal and what you need. We can't publicly intervene; you have no idea the uproar it would cause if an American foundation were to invest a penny right now in an excavation in Iraq. But, of course, we may be able to help in a more . . . discreet fashion. Another thing—your wife, Clara. Can you control her? She's . . . excuse me for saying so, but she's just too out there."

Ahmed was visibly uncomfortable with the reference to his wife. In that respect, he was very much an Iraqi. One did not speak about women, much less about a man's wife.

"Clara is proud of her grandfather."

"That's admirable, but she does a disservice to her grandfather by shining a spotlight on him. Alfred Tannenberg based his success on discretion; you know how careful he's always been about his business. That's why we don't understand your wife's very public announcement, at this premature point, of the Bible of Clay. In a few months, once the United States has had its way with Iraq, we could have organized a full-blown excavation. But now . . . Perhaps you might ask Alfred to speak with Clara, to explain certain things to her."

"It was Alfred's decision to reveal the existence of the Bible of Clay."

Ralph Barry sat back, puzzled.

"I know that this is the first time he's broken with George Wagner and Robert Brown," Ahmed went on. "But you know Alfred—it's hard to change his mind once he has it set on something. Besides, he's very sick. I'm not going to bore you with the list of his medical problems; he's eighty-five years old and the doctors have found a tumor on his liver. We don't know how long he has to live. Fortunately, his mind works perfectly. He's still got a terrible temper and refuses to turn over the reins of the business. As for Clara, she's his granddaughter: She can do no wrong in his eyes. He wants this for her."

Ahmed paused and gazed levelly at Barry. "And, Ralph—forget about the notion that the American presence in Iraq is going to be a walk in the park. It's going to be terrible."

"Don't be pessimistic," Barry replied. "You'll see how things will change. Saddam is a problem for everyone. And nothing will happen to you and your family. Robert Brown will make sure that you can return to the United States safely. Please, talk to Alfred."

"It won't do any good. Why doesn't Wagner, or Brown, talk to him? Alfred is much more likely to listen to his old partners."

"You know that telephone calls into Iraq are being monitored. Robert can't call him there—it could be recorded. As for George Wagner . . . He's God, and I am not a member of his heavenly parliament. I'm just a foundation employee. I *am* expecting a letter Robert wants you to take to Alfred. Someone will bring it from Washington; he'll give it to me, and I'll give it to you. Just as it's always been— communication by personal couriers. We'll pick up Alfred's answer in Amman this time, instead of Cairo."

Ahmed nodded thoughtfully. "Don't worry about Clara; she won't be a problem in Iraq. I'll let you know what resources we'll need for the excavation, but I wonder whether we'll be able to excavate with a blockade in place. The last thing on Saddam's mind is finding cuneiform tablets. We may not be able to find enough people to work, and the ones we do find, we may have to pay every day."

"Just tell me how much you need; I'll see that you take it with you when you go back."

"Money's just one of our problems. We need more archaeologists, equipment, and materials. And the experts are in Europe, in the United States."

"Listen to me—money is *the* problem. Alfred shouldn't finance this mission, at least directly—it will draw too much attention. There are thousands of eyes in Iraq. It would be more practical to find financing abroad—some European university, for example. And as for field experts, Yves Picot is interested in talking to you. He's from Alsace, a very, shall we say, interesting man. He taught at Oxford and—"

"I know who Picot is. He's not my favorite archaeologist, a bit heterodox for my taste. And people say he was asked to leave Oxford because he had a relationship with one of his students. He's a man who doesn't always like to follow the rules."

"You can't be telling me that you're worried about the rules. Picot has a group of former students who love him. And he's rich. His father owns a bank in the Channel Islands; actually, it originally belonged to Picot's mother's family, and everybody in the family works there except him. Because he's independently wealthy, he can come across as an unbearable pain in the neck, even somewhat of a despot. But I've got to admit that he's accomplished. He may not be everybody's Prince Charming, but he's the only archaeologist who's taken any interest in those two tablets that Alfred found—not to mention the only person crazy enough to go off to Iraq right now to an archaeological dig. You decide whether you want to talk to him."

"I'll speak with him, but I don't like him for this project."

"Ahmed, you have no other option. I'm sorry to put it so bluntly."

"You know something?" Ahmed said. "I wonder why Alfred finally chose to make the existence of those tablets public too. And why Brown, if he's so furious about it, has decided to help us."

"Yeah, well, I don't know either, Ahmed, but I've never known either of those two to be wrong."

5

THE FOUR FRIENDS WERE HAVING DINNER AT CARLO Cipriani's house, waiting for the delivery of Security Investigations' latest report. They had received an initial dossier that morning. But the messenger was already an hour late, and Mercedes was growing increasingly uneasy.

"Please, Mercedes, eat something," Carlo pressed. "The food is fantastic—don't let it go to waste."

"I'm not hungry," Mercedes responded flatly.

"Well, make an effort," Carlo insisted.

"I'm sick of waiting. Call him, Carlo—something may have happened."

"Always so impatient," Hans Hausser declared, his voice flat.

"Nonsense. I've controlled my impatience for decades, and I've done it very well, thank you. The people who work with me will tell you I never show my emotions," Mercedes answered.

"They don't know you!" Bruno Müller laughed.

"Besides, Mercedes, the paperwork takes time, for God's sake," said Carlo.

Finally they heard the distant sound of the doorbell and then footsteps coming toward the dining room.

The housekeeper opened the dining-room door and led a man in.

The president of Security Investigations had brought the report himself.

"Carlo, I apologize for the delay. I imagine you were all impatient."

"Yes, as a matter of fact we were," Mercedes answered. "A pleasure to meet you, nevertheless."

Mercedes Barreda held out her hand to Luca Marini, a well-preserved man in his sixties, elegantly dressed, with a tattoo on his wrist covered discreetly by a gold and stainless-steel watch.

The suit is a little tight, Mercedes thought. *Trying to conceal his weight problem. But those Michelins around his waist give it away.*

"Sit down, Luca. Have you had dinner?" Carlo asked solicitously.

"No, not yet. I came straight from the office. And, yes, I'd love something. A glass of wine most of all."

"Wonderful. Let me introduce you to my friends, Professor Hans Hausser and Maestro Bruno Müller. You've met Mercedes."

"Signore Müller, I'm sure people tell you this all the time, but I'm a great admirer of yours," Luca said.

"Thank you," Bruno murmured uncomfortably.

The housekeeper set another place at the table and brought around a large platter of cannelloni. Luca served himself generously, ignoring Mercedes' impatient glare.

She decided she didn't like Luca Marini. She didn't, in fact, like anybody who was slow, and the president of Security Investigations could not have been slower. He seemed to her the most inconsiderate man on earth—smacking his chops on cannelloni while they sat waiting.

Carlo Cipriani, on the other hand, patiently passed the time by chatting about the news of the day—the situation in the Near East, a fight in parliament between Berlusconi and the Left, the weather. Mercedes knew he took pride in his exquisite manners.

When Luca finished his dessert, Carlo suggested they retire to his office, where they might enjoy an *amaro* and discuss the findings.

After they were all seated, drinks in hand, Carlo began. "We're listening."

"Well, the girl didn't go to the conference today."

"What girl?" Mercedes asked, irritated by Marini's macho, paternalistic tone.

"Clara Tannenberg," answered Marini, by now irritated himself.

"Ah, Signora Tannenberg!" Mercedes exclaimed sarcastically.

"Yes. Signora Tannenberg preferred to go shopping today, apparently. Between the Via Condotti and the Via della Croce, she spent over four thousand euros. She seems to be a compulsive shopper, with no lack of funds. She had lunch alone at the Caffè Il Greco—a sandwich, dessert, and a cappuccino. Then she went to the Vatican and was in the museum until closing time. As I was on my way here, I was informed that she'd just gone into the Excelsior. Since I haven't been called again, she's still inside."

"What about her husband?" Professor Hausser inquired.

"Her husband left the hotel late and wandered around Rome until two, at which point he stopped by La Bolognesa for lunch with Ralph Barry, the director of the Mundo Antiguo Foundation and a very influential man in the world of archaeology. Barry is a former professor at Harvard and highly respected in academic circles. Although this conference is under the auspices of UNESCO, the Mundo Antiguo Foundation is its main financial sponsor."

"I wonder why Barry and Husseini had lunch together," Bruno Müller mused aloud.

"Two of my men were able to get a table nearby, and they picked up parts of the conversation. Signore Barry seemed very perturbed by Clara Tannenberg's behavior, but Ahmed defended his wife quite vigorously. They talked about someone named Yves Picot, one of the archaeologists attending the conference, who apparently might be interested in the two tablets that were mentioned in this morning's report. In the dossier, you'll find a report on this Picot and information on some of his adventures. He's quite the ladies' man, and something of a troublemaker. Husseini doesn't seem ready to trust him.

"Husseini mentioned that in addition to financing, he needs archaeologists, people ready to work. And this is the most interesting part: Ralph Barry told Husseini that tomorrow or the day after, he'd be handing over a letter from Robert Brown, the president of the Mundo Antiguo Foundation, to be delivered to a man, someone named Alfred, who is apparently the girl's grandfather, and—"

"It's him!" cried Mercedes gleefully. "We've got him!"

"Calm down, Mercedes, and let Signore Marini finish. We'll talk later."

Carlo Cipriani's tone of voice brooked no reply, and Mercedes, abashed, sat back quietly in her chair. He was right. They could talk when Marini was gone.

"It's all in the report, but my men think that this Alfred and Signore Brown have been communicating with each other for years, through letters sent by intermediaries, and that Alfred's answer will be picked up in Amman.

"Husseini is to have breakfast tomorrow with Picot; afterward, if there have been no changes to their plans, he and his wife will be flying to Amman. They have a reservation on Royal Jordanian Airlines at three. You need to decide whether I should send my men on that plane or leave it at this and close the case now."

"No, follow them, wherever they go," Cipriani ordered, lighting a pipeful of tobacco. "Send a good team—it doesn't matter how many men you have to send, I want to know everything about this Alfred: whether he's Clara Tannenberg's grandfather, as we surmise he is, where he lives, who he lives with, what he does for a living. We need photos—it's important that you get photos and, if possible, video surveillance of him. We want to know everything, Luca."

"It's going to cost you a fortune."

"Don't worry about our fortune," Mercedes interjected. "And try not to lose sight of them."

"Do whatever you have to, Luca, but stay with them." The grave tone of Carlo Cipriani's voice made its intended impression on the president of Security Investigations.

"I may have to hire people on the ground there," Marini told them.

"Whatever you have to do. And now, my friend, if you don't mind, we'd like to read your report in detail. . . ."

"Yes, of course. If you need any further help tonight, don't hesitate to call. I'll be at home."

Carlo walked with Marini to the door, while Mercedes, champing at the bit, tore open the envelope and began to read.

"The suit and expensive wristwatch don't hide what he is," she murmured.

"Mercedes, stop—no need to air your prejudices here," Hans Hausser scolded her.

"Prejudices? He's a nouveau riche in a tailored suit, that's all. A tight-tailored suit, as a matter of fact."

"He's also resourceful," said Carlo as he returned to them. "And he was a good cop. He spent years in Sicily battling the Mafia; a lot of his men were killed, and some of his friends. Finally, his wife gave him an ultimatum—either he left the police or she left him. So he took early retirement and opened this business, which has made him rich."

"You can't make a silk purse out of a sow's ear," Mercedes insisted.

"Mercedes! That's a terrible thing to say!" Hans' tone was reproachful.

"Enough about Luca," Carlo broke in. "He's good at his job, and that's what's important. Let's see what's in the report."

Luca Marini had made four copies, one for each of them. They sat in silence, poring over the details that had been gathered about Clara Tannenberg and her husband, Ahmed Husseini.

Mercedes was the first to break the silence. Her voice was grave and tinged with emotion.

"It's him. We've found him."

"Yes." Carlo nodded. "I think so too. But I wonder why he's decided to surface after all these years."

"It hasn't been voluntary," Bruno Müller said.

"I think it has been," Carlo replied. "Why would his granddaughter take part in this conference and ask for international aid for her excavation? It's put the spotlight on her, and her name is Tannenberg."

"But that need not have been his intention," Hausser countered.

"Why not?" asked Mercedes. "How can we know what his intention was in exposing his granddaughter?"

"According to this report, Ahmed Husseini says that Alfred Tannenberg adores his granddaughter," Müller answered. "So there must have been some powerful reason for letting her come into the open. He's been invisible for over sixty years, I presume in hiding, underground somewhere."

"Yes, there has to be some reason behind these events now," said Carlo, "but what's most intriguing to me is his relationship with this Robert Brown, to all appearances an extremely well-respected American who moves in the highest circles, a personal friend of almost all the big players in the Bush administration, the president of an internationally renowned foundation. I don't know, but something doesn't fit."

"Of course, we don't know if Tannenberg is even in the same line of work anymore. It's been decades," Müller said.

"He's an antiques dealer, according to the report," Hausser pointed out.

"That could mean anything. . . . But how has he managed to stay hidden all these years if he has such friends?" Mercedes wondered aloud.

"We'll have to look deeper into this Robert Brown. Luca can do that for us. But now we have to decide what we're going to do, don't you think?"

They all agreed with Carlo. The time had come to decide what further steps to take. They agreed that Mercedes, Hans, and Bruno would stay in Rome for two or three more days, until some news came from Amman. They would also ask Marini—through his company or another one that he might recommend—to prepare a dossier on Robert Brown.

"Now, let's assume that this Alfred Tannenberg is the man we're looking for. How do we kill him and when?" Mercedes asked.

"I asked Luca about agencies that do specialized work of that kind, and he gave me some names. I've told you that," Carlo replied.

"Well, let's talk to one of them and hire a man," Mercedes insisted. "We have to be prepared when Tannenberg's identity is confirmed. The sooner this is done, the better. The day that monster is dead, I will finally be able to sleep."

"We'll get him, Mercedes; there's not the slightest doubt about that," Bruno Müller declared. "But we have to do it the right way. I don't think you can just knock on the door of these 'agencies,' as Carlo put it, and say you're looking for an assassin. I think, Carlo, that we should take advantage of your friendship with Marini and ask him to explain to us how one goes about hiring a hit man."

They went on talking until dawn. No one wanted to leave a single detail unplanned, unconsidered. They felt in their bones that they were near the end now—at last they would fulfill the oath they'd sworn together so many years ago. None of them thought this vengeance they were planning had come too late; all that mattered was that it had come.

They each took their assignments, and they agreed to set up a bank account from which to pay Luca Marini and the man who would, finally, kill Alfred Tannenberg.

The Via Condotti was practically empty. Carlo Cipriani and Luca Marini were having a cappuccino at Il Greco. It was warm for September, and the tourists hadn't yet taken over the Piazza di Spagna and the Spanish Steps. Nor, at this hour of the morning, had the elegant shops along the street opened their doors. Rome was still yawning and stretching after a late night.

"Carlo, you saved my life many years ago. That tumor . . . I've always been grateful for your help. I'm not going to judge you for anything you do, but tell me the truth—what's behind all this?"

"My friend, there are things one can't talk about. I just want the name and address of one of those agencies that hire men willing to do anything."

"When you say 'anything,' what are you talking about?"

"What we want is someone who can defend himself, because he may be going into the lion's den. Going to the Near East these days is not like going to Disneyland. Depending on what your investigation uncovers, the destination may be Iraq. How much do you think a life is worth in Iraq today?"

"You're lying. I still have my cop's instincts, you know."

"Luca, I want you to put me in contact with one of those agencies, that's all. And I want to be able to count on you not to say anything about this to anyone—consider it privileged information. You told me yourself that if there was a war, you couldn't have your men there; it was you who suggested that we hire specialists."

"There are a couple of companies made up of former members of the SAS. The Brits are very professional; I prefer them to the Yankees. In my opinion, the best of them all is Global Group. Here," he said, handing Carlo a business card, "this is their address and telephone number. Their headquarters is in London. You can ask for Tom Martin, tell him I referred you. We've known each other a long time. He's a good guy—tough as nails, not easy to pull one over on, but good at what he does. I'll tell him you're going to call." Luca took a sip of hot coffee. "He'll charge you a fortune."

"Thanks, Luca."

"Don't thank me—I'm worried. I can't figure out what you and these friends of yours are after. The one who really scares me is the woman, Mercedes. There's not a drop of human kindness in that woman's eyes."

"You're wrong about her. She's a wonderful woman."

"Either way, you're about to get in over your head in this, whatever it is. If you do, I'll help you as much as I can. I still have good contacts with the police. But be careful, all right? And don't trust anybody."

"Not even your friend Tom Martin?"

"Nobody, Carlo, nobody."

"I'll keep that in mind. Now, I need another report—this one on Robert Brown. We want to know everything there is to know about this big wheel."

"Sure, no problem. When do you want it?"

"Yesterday."

"I figured. Let's say three or four days."

"If that's the best you can do."

"That's the minimum, I assure you."

At that same hour, in the dining room of the Hotel Excelsior, Ahmed Husseini and Yves Picot were also sitting down to breakfast.

The two men were about the same age, both also archaeologists, cosmopolitans. Curiously enough, fate had marginalized them both, made them suspect within their own profession, though for very different reasons.

"I was very interested in what you and your wife were saying," Picot began.

"I'm glad to hear that."

"Monsieur Husseini, I don't like to waste time, and I imagine you feel the same, so I'll get straight to the point. Show me, if you have them, the photos of those two extraordinary tablets you and your wife spoke about."

Ahmed took some photos from an oversize old leather passport wallet and handed them to Picot, who examined them closely, without speaking, for a good while. There were two distinct tablets, full of the cuneiform Clara had described, signed at the top by "Shamas."

"Well? What do you think?" asked Ahmed finally, a bit impatiently.

"Interesting, but I'd have to see the tablets themselves in order to make any sort of definitive judgment. What is it you and your wife want?"

"We want an international archaeological expedition to help us excavate the remains of the building that was uncovered by the bombing. We believe it may be a storehouse for tablets next to a temple, or perhaps even a room in the temple itself. We need modern equipment and experienced archaeologists."

"And money."

"Yes, of course. You know it's not possible to dig without money."

"And in exchange?"

"In exchange for what?"

"The material, money, and archaeologists you say you need."

"*La gloire*, Professor Picot, *la gloire*."

"Are you joking?" asked Picot, irritated.

"No, I'm not joking. If we find proof of Genesis as told by Abraham, the discovery of Troy and Knossos will pale in comparison."

"Please. Don't exaggerate."

"You know as well as I do how important a discovery of this magnitude would be. It would change history, with repercussions in religion and even politics."

"And what would you and your wife gain by it? Your determination to do this now is remarkable, given the situation in your country. It's just short of insane to be planning a dig when within a few short months the Americans are going to be dropping bombs all over Iraq. And your, uh, patron, Saddam: Is he willing to allow a foreign archaeological expedition in right now to start excavating, or will he do what he so famously does—detain us all and accuse us of spying?"

"Don't make me repeat what you know better than I—this will be the most important archaeological discovery in the last century, at least. And the war is precisely why Clara and I are so driven to begin now, before it starts. Who knows what will happen, what might be left or who will be in charge afterward. As for Saddam, he will most certainly allow European archaeologists to enter Iraq. It will give him prestige, even leverage. There will be no problem there."

"Until the Americans let loose, at which point he will very quickly lose interest in archaeological missions and likely round up the foreigners. Plus, I doubt the Americans even know where Ur is—it could be bombed out of existence, and the mission with it."

"It's your decision."

"I'll think about it. How can I reach you?"

Husseini gave him his card and discussed a few more details as they finished their meal. They parted with a firm, almost comradely handshake.

Another man, sitting at the next table, absorbed in a newspaper, had managed to record the entire conversation about the war, the dig, and the pictures of two extraordinary tablets in the possession of a man named Alfred Tannenberg.

6

"TANNENBERG! TANNENBERG! I'M TALKING TO YOU! CAN you hear me?"

The young man opened his eyes and looked up blankly at the man who'd been speaking to him.

"What, Professor?"

"You should be working with the rest of the students; I assigned you to dig at the west wall, and here you are asleep."

"I'm resting, resting and waiting for the mail. I want to know what's happening in Berlin."

"Get back to the excavation! We all have to work. And you're no more privileged than the other students."

"You're wrong. I'm here because my family is paying for this expedition and paying your salary. In fact, you're *my* employee."

"How dare you!"

Alfred stood, a foot taller than Professor Cohen. "You, Professor, are an insolent Jew! My father should never have entrusted this mission to you."

"Your *father* has entrusted me nothing! The *university* sent us here!"

"Come now, Professor, tell me who is the largest donor to our hallowed university? You and Professor Wessler have been in Syria for two years thanks to a grant from the university. You should go back. You should be with all the other Jews. Someday, the chancellor of the university will have to answer for his part in sending you here."

The severe features of the middle-aged professor hardened. He began to reply when he was interrupted by the shouts of a boy running toward him.

"Professor Cohen, come! Come! Hurry!"

The professor waited for the boy to get to him.

"What is it, Ali?"

"Professor Wessler sent for you; he's found something important, very important!"

Young Ali was smiling like the sunshine itself—he was always happy. He had been very lucky to be hired by these crazy people who were digging in the earth searching for statuettes and who seemed to take great pleasure in pieces of clay with strange inscriptions.

Professor Wessler and Professor Cohen were the leaders of the group of university students who had come to excavate in Haran. But their dig was coming to its end, and although nothing of great substance had been unearthed Cohen had hoped to return to Germany with something to justify all their efforts.

Professor Cohen followed Ali to the wellhead located a few hundred yards from the archaeological site where they had been excavating over the last few months. He didn't notice Alfred Tannenberg following him, intrigued by the discovery that Professor Wessler had made.

"Jacob, look what it says here!" Wessler said to Cohen, handing him two dusty tablets.

Jacob Cohen took his gold-rimmed spectacles out of a metal eyeglass case he carried in one of his jacket pockets and began to run his index finger under the lines of cuneiform incised into a clay tablet about thirty centimeters square. When he finished reading, he looked at his colleague and they embraced.

"Praise God, Aaron! It's real!"

"It is, my friend, it is. And we found it, thanks to Ali."

The boy smiled proudly. It had been he who told Professor Wessler that there was a well near the excavation site with the same squiggles as those tablets the professor was always so excited about. Wessler was curious but skeptical, knowing that the local people often used pieces of clay tablets in various structures, even their houses.

The well looked like any other, and only expert eyes would have noticed that some of the "bricks" that lined its walls were actually clay tablets.

Professor Wessler began to examine them one by one, deciphering those signs that held such fascination for Ali, who could barely believe that they were letters his ancestors had written.

Suddenly the professor cried out; Ali jumped up, afraid that he had been stung by a scorpion. But Wessler was euphoric, barely able to coherently ask Ali to bring his tools so that he could pry out a couple of the bricks—an operation, as Ali soon saw, that in no way affected the structure of the well wall.

So he had run to the house where Professor Wessler slept at night, grabbed the tools, and brought them back as fast as he could. And then the professor had sent him running for his friend Professor Cohen.

"Now we know that when the patriarch Abraham departed for the Promised Land, he took with him the story of Genesis. God had revealed it to him," declared Aaron Wessler.

"But who is this Shamas?" asked Professor Cohen. "There is no reference in the Bible to any Shamas, and the story of the patriarchs is most detailed."

"You're right, but these tablets are clear: *S-H-A-M-A-S*. There must be more—more tablets on which this Shamas inscribed the Genesis story as told to him by Abraham." Professor Wessler's excitement cooled as he tried to reason out the puzzle.

"They must be here. Abraham spent years in Haran before moving on to Canaan; we must find them!" Professor Cohen exclaimed.

"So Abraham himself revealed Genesis to our ancestors," mused Aaron Wessler to himself.

"More important, my friend, is that if these two tablets are authentic, then there is a Bible, an entire Bible written on clay, inspired by Abraham."

"A bible of clay! My God, if we find those tablets it will be the most important discovery ever made!"

Alfred Tannenberg was fascinated as he listened to the conversation between the two professors, who in their excitement had not even noticed his presence. He wanted to tear the tablets out of the hands of those Jews, and he was about to when another young member of the expedition came running over, waving a telegram.

"War! War! Alfred, we're at war! We are going to take back what those Polish dogs stole from us! Danzig will be part of our homeland again! Alfred—it's what we've hoped for! Hitler will make Germany great again. Here, there's a telegram for you too."

"Thanks, Georg—at last. What a grand day! We must celebrate," the young Tannenberg exclaimed as he began to read his telegram under the worried eyes of the two professors, who had fallen silent and turned pale at the youngster's news.

"My father says we're giving a good thrashing to the Poles," Georg declared.

"And mine says that France and the United Kingdom are about to declare war against us. Georg, we must go back; I want to be there, we must be with Hitler. He will bring back the glory of Germany, and I want to be a part of that."

"You're both mad!" Jacob Cohen burst out. "Germany's as much my home as anyone's. I was born there, as were my parents. What Hitler and his thugs are doing is horrific."

The two young men turned and looked with unrestrained hatred at him.

"How dare you insult us with this filth?" Alfred said, grabbing the old professor by his shirt front.

"Let him go!" Aaron Wessler ordered.

"Shut your mouth, Jewish pig!" said young Georg.

Ali contemplated the scene before him with horror. He did not know what had come over these two young men. They began beating the two professors, hitting them over and over again in a frenzy with their fists, until the two older men finally fell to the ground, covered with blood. Then Georg and Alfred turned to the cowering boy, who had seen everything. They gave each other a complicit, evil look and began kicking Ali, who tried futilely to cover his head and body against the onslaught.

"That's enough! Enough! You're killing him!" Professor Cohen cried from the ground.

At that, Alfred took out a small pistol he carried in his pants pocket and shot Cohen in the head. Then he turned to Wessler and shot him between the eyes. The last bullet was for little Ali, who lay on the ground, writhing.

"Jewish pigs," Alfred spat out as Georg looked on in amusement.

"That's better than they deserved," replied Georg, "but I don't know how we're going to explain this to the rest of the team."

Alfred sat down on the ground, lit a cigarette, then poked his finger at the column of smoke that rose from it and curled in the afternoon breeze.

"We'll say we found them dead."

"That's all?"

"That's all. Anyone might have come along and killed them in order to rob them, *nicht wahr?*"

"Fine . . . as long as we stick to the same story." Georg glanced sidelong at his friend. "You know, you're right. Germany will realize Hitler's dream; these foreigners are sucking our lifeblood and polluting the Fatherland."

Alfred walked toward the well. "I have something to tell you, something important that we will share only with Heinrich and Franz."

"What?" asked Georg, intrigued.

"Look at the well."

"I'm looking at it. So what?"

"Two pieces are missing from the wall, two bricks. Do you see? These tablets, there, lying on the ground next to the professors."

"And what is so wonderful about them?"

"According to those two old Jews, the tablets contain a revelation. It seems that the patriarch Abraham transmitted the story of Genesis to . . . to his people. That means that what we read in the Bible about the creation came down to us from Abraham."

Georg squatted down and picked up the two tablets, though he couldn't read a word of the cuneiform that covered them. He was only in his second year at the university, after all.

Both the young men wanted to be archaeologists—all four of them, rather, because Franz and Heinrich, their best friends, did too. They had gone to the same school, had the same hobbies, had chosen the same career. Even their parents had been friends since childhood. The boys' friendship, as deep as it was indestructible, had been forged by their admission into one of Hitler's Napola schools, based on their unsullied physical and racial characteristics. They were all *echt deutschen*, fully German, without a trace of non-Aryan blood—an honor of the highest distinction in Hitler's Germany. History, biology, geography, mathematics, music, and sports—especially sports—were the major disciplines in the Napolas, which had taken over the buildings that had formerly housed training academies for the imperial German and Prussian high command. In the earlier academies the boys were organized into a paramilitary corps, where they played at taking a bridge, reading a topographical map, clearing a forest occupied by "enemy" troops, and marching all night long.

The Napolas, in addition to that military purpose, were intended to educate and train the elite dreamed of by the Führer. That was why boys from the wealthy classes shared classrooms with boys from the working class who had distinguished themselves in their local schools with superior physique and bloodline.

When Alfred, Georg, Heinrich, and Franz finished their studies at the Napola and passed the examination with flying colors, they had to decide what to do with their future—should they go into the army, the party, government administration, industry, or academia? Truthfully, there was never much of a choice; their fathers demanded they go on to the university and earn their doctorates.

All four of the young men were eager to bring change to impoverished Germany, although none of them personally lacked for anything. Alfred's father was a textile manufacturer. Heinrich's was a lawyer, as was Franz's, while Georg's was a physician.

Adolf Hitler was their hero, and a hero to their fathers and most of their friends. They believed in him and were thrilled by his stirring speeches, convinced that whatever he did would return Germany to its former grandeur.

Alfred and Georg agreed on what they would say about the three dead bodies they had "found," and then they carefully hid the tablets. They would ask Professor Keitel, a loyal follower of Hitler and an expert in cuneiform, to reveal to them their exact content.

Professor Keitel owed a debt to Alfred's father. His family had worked at the textile factory, and he had worked there too, until he was hired at the university as an assistant professor with the help of Herr Tannenberg, who had great influence with the university board. Keitel bore the humiliation of working with Cohen, a Jew whom he despised, because he knew that someday all the Jews would be eliminated from his society.

Their faces filled with mock horror, the boys ran back to the camp, near the site of the main excavation. They played to perfection the part of distraught young men who'd come upon the tragic scene of the triple murder, relating in vague detail how they had discovered the bodies of the two professors and poor, helpless Ali.

Professor Wessler had told Alfred and Georg he was going over to take a look at the area near the old well. After a time, Professor Cohen had remarked to Alfred that he was worried by his colleague's delay and was going to take Ali to look for him. When none of them returned, Alfred had walked to the old well himself, and Georg, who wanted to give him the telegram from home, had followed him. When they got there, they found the professors dead, and Ali too. There was no sign of anyone else, no hint of what had happened. Trying to help their teachers, to rouse them, they became smeared with blood themselves—all this came out in a rush as the boys fought back tears and terror.

With other archaeologists and students, the boys went back to the well to help retrieve the bodies as they struggled to regain their composure. Once there, many of the party were overcome at the sight of the two dead professors and the boy and did nothing to hide their emotions.

It was no secret to any of the professors and other students that Alfred and Georg didn't like Jews, but while they were not overly grieved by the deaths, they were clearly frightened, and they remained disturbed and distressed through the hours that followed.

Professor Keitel, at the urging of the students, became the temporary expedition leader. It was he who went to the local authorities to report the crime and send a messenger to the German consul reporting the news of the unfortunate event. He asked for the consul's aid in contacting the dead men's families as well.

Shortly thereafter, Professor Keitel announced that the expedition would be terminated at once, since Germany was at war and the Fatherland needed its citizens.

By the time they arrived in Berlin, Professor Keitel had deciphered the tablets' secret and confirmed what the professors had said: A scribe named Shamas wrote that the patriarch Abraham was going to tell him the story of the creation of the world. Before the expedition had left Haran, the four friends and Professor Keitel had tried to find the other mysterious tablets Shamas wrote of, but they had been unsuccessful. Undaunted, the friends swore that they would return for them. Still, they did not return to Germany empty-handed. Secreted throughout their luggage were the two telltale tablets and any number of other priceless objects that had been unearthed from the sands of Haran.

7

ROBERT BROWN LIVED ALONE. OR NOT ALONE, EXACTLY, since his butler, Ramón Gonzalez, also lived in the large two-story house outside Washington.

It was a grand house: five bedrooms, six bathrooms, a living room, a parlor, a large sitting–music room, a dining room that seated twenty, a library, and Brown's private office, in addition to the service wing, where Ramón had a private apartment.

Brown was an employer who demanded absolute discretion, but he rewarded loyalty. Ramón had been working for him for over twenty years and was absolutely faithful. He could afford to be, for he enjoyed the relative ease of working for an unmarried man who did not require a great deal of caring for and who paid very, very well.

Ramón had laid breakfast out in the rear room of the house, where pale sunshine was beginning to filter through the large bay window. It was two minutes before eight; Brown would be coming down at any moment. The doorbell rang, and Ramón went to greet Mr. Brown's guest.

"Good morning, Mr. Dukais."

"Hello, Ramón. Cool this morning. I need a cup of good strong coffee, please, and I'm starving. This traffic makes a man hungry."

Ramón's only reply was an understanding smile and a gesture for Paul Dukais to follow him to the breakfast room, where Robert Brown was now waiting. Ramón served breakfast and promptly left the room, closing the door behind him so that the two men could speak freely.

Brown was not a man to beat around the bush, much less with someone like Dukais. After all, Brown held a large block of stock in Dukais' company, Planet Security. They'd met when Dukais was just another corrupt customs officer on the New York docks.

"I need you to send some men to Iraq."

"I already have several thousand ready and waiting. I've been hiring men for months. The minute the war starts, security needs are going to skyrocket. My contact in the State Department called me yesterday; they want my people to cover several locations around the world once our troops are in Baghdad."

"I know how the business works, Paul. Just listen. I'll want you to send several teams, some via Jordan, others via Kuwait, Saudi Arabia, and Turkey. We'll hold some of them along the borders, pending further orders."

"What orders?"

"We'll get to that."

"Okay, but I figure the Iraqis are already sealing their borders, and if *they're* not doing it, the Turks will, or the Kuwaitis or whoever. You want men on the borders and inside Iraq too. Can't you just wait like everybody else?"

"I'm not telling you to send them in tomorrow. I'm asking you to ready several teams until I give the order. Try to find men who can blend in."

"It's dangerous to send men in too early. Our friends in the Defense Department tell me the fireworks will go off in a few months—sometime this spring. Let's not make any mistakes that might put the job in danger."

"I told you—they don't have to get there too early. I'll let you know the exact date they need to be inside. Then they'll get out as fast as they went in. They won't be there for more than three or four days after the bombing starts."

"What are we bringing out?"

"The history of humanity."

Paul Dukais put down the coffee he had been slowly sipping and stared at Robert.

"Your men will be under the command of others, who'll be waiting for them. And that's enough information for now."

Robert Brown's eyes scared Paul Dukais. The two men had been partners for many years, and it had taken a long time for Dukais to get behind his elegant demeanor. He had learned that Brown was not a man to trifle with. This man of perfect manners was capable of anything. He decided to forgo more questions. What did he care what they were going to do in Iraq?

"Now, I want you to take a letter to Rome and deliver it to Ralph Barry," Brown continued. "You'll bring me the answer back in two weeks, from Amman."

"Okay."

"Paul, there can't be any screwups here. This is the most important operation we've undertaken. We have the chance of a lifetime here—you better not fuck it up."

"Have I fucked any up so far?"

"No, you haven't. Which is why you're rich."

And alive, thought Dukais.

"When you've got the plan ready and the men lined up, I want you to lay it all out for me, every detail."

"Not to worry, I will."

"Paul, you may run across some members of the board. I don't have to tell you that this conversation never happened. Nobody can know about my connection with this job. Clear?"

"Clear. I told you—not to worry."

The meeting of the board of directors adjourned. It was noon, time for lunch, but George Wagner used the hour for a quiet nap in the privacy of his office. The noise of the street didn't rise as far as the twentieth floor of the tower in New York from which he ran his empire.

The years had not passed without taking their toll, and he was tired. He rose early because he didn't sleep well at night, and he filled the predawn hours reading and listening to Wagner. He rested best at midday, when he loosened his tie, hung up his jacket, and lay back on the couch. His secretary had strict orders to hold his calls and not to disturb him, no matter what.

He had just fallen asleep when the almost imperceptible buzzing ring of the cell phone he always carried startled him awake.

"Yes."

"George, it's Frankie. Were you asleep?"

"Almost. What's wrong?"

"I spoke to Enrique. We should go to Seville and spend a few days with him or meet someplace on the coast, in Marbella. It's full of old folks like us, and September is still nice and warm in Spain."

"Go to Spain? I don't think that's necessary. We've put out lots of bait—let's not get tangled in our own nets."

"And Alfred?"

"He's turned into an old fool—he's lost control."

"Don't be so sure. Alfred always knows what he's doing."

"Not anymore. And don't forget what happened before. He was determined to stick his nose in where it didn't belong, pull strings that didn't want to be pulled, and now he's doing the same thing all over again."

"George, it was his son—you'd have done the same thing."

"I never had any children, so I wouldn't know."

"But I did—children and grandchildren—and you can't just sit back and take anything that comes. You've got to help them."

"But you *should* just sit back, you *should* accept things for what they are. He can't bring Helmut back to life. The kid thought he was smart. Alfred knew the rules, he knew what might happen. He made a mess then, and now he's making another with that pigheaded granddaughter of his."

"I don't think he'll let himself, or her, become a danger to us. He knows what's at stake, and his granddaughter is an intelligent woman."

"Who's got the old man wrapped around her little finger—he's been making mistakes on her account for some time now. We told him to tell her the truth. He didn't want to listen; he'd rather carry on the charade in front of her. No, Frankie, we can't just sit idly by. We haven't come this far to let a sentimental old man fuck it all up."

"We're old men too."

"And I want to go on that way. I've just finished a board meeting; we have to prepare ourselves for war. We're going to make a lot of money, Frankie."

"Neither one of us cares about money anymore, George."

"But we still like our power. Now, if you don't mind, I need to sleep."

"All right. Listen, I'll be in New York next week."

"Then, old friend, we'll work out a way to see each other here."

"Maybe we could tell Enrique to come to New York."

"Well, I'd rather see him in New York than Seville. I don't want to go there; I don't feel good about it. Let me put some thought into it— we can't risk endangering the operation."

"You've always been a little paranoid, George."

"What I am is prudent, which is how we've come this far. There are many more who haven't, because they made mistakes. I want to see Enrique too, but not at the risk of derailing our plans. I'll be in touch."

Frank kicked back a whiskey as he hung up. George, careful, mistrustful George, had always turned out to be right.

He rang a little silver bell on his desk, and a second later a white-uniformed man came in.

"Did you need me, sir?"

"José, have the gentlemen I was expecting arrived?"

"Not yet, sir. The control tower will let us know as soon as the plane begins its approach."

"Very well. Keep me informed."

"Yes, sir."

"Where's my wife?"

"She is resting, sir. She had a headache."

"And my daughter?"

"Miss Alma left early this morning, with her husband."

"That's right. . . . Bring me another whiskey, please, and something to eat."

"Yes, sir."

The servant left silently. Frank liked José. He was quiet, efficient, and spoke very little. He took better care of Frank than his flighty wife ever had.

Emma was too rich. That had been her main defect, although for him, it was an advantage. Her lack of beauty had also weighed on him, though, he had to admit. She was short and had a tendency to gain weight. And there was no glow to her dull dark skin—too dark; *olive* was a euphemism. She was nothing like Alicia.

Alicia was black. Totally black, and scandalously beautiful. They had been together for fifteen years. He'd met her in the bar of a hotel in Rio while he was waiting for one of his business partners. She had just turned twenty, still almost a girl, with long legs and a neck that never ended. She'd gone straight to the point, offering herself in the most matter-of-fact way. And they'd been inseparable—emotionally—since then.

He had looked good for a seventy-year-old, but he was still just an old man, which was why he paid her magnificently, maintained her in a lavish loft in Ipanema, showered her with jewelry. When he died, Alicia would be able to spend the fortune he was leaving her. She was his, she belonged to him, and she knew what would happen to her if she was unfaithful to him, ever.

He'd call Alicia—she could meet him at the Rio airport.

The fact was, he didn't like to leave his immense estate on the edge of the jungle for too long or too often. He felt safe here, with his men patrolling the five-mile perimeter of his property day and night and the sophisticated system of sensors, security cameras, and alarms that made break-ins impossible. But thinking about Alicia had given him a jolt of energy, and at his age, he had to seize the day. He'd divert to Rio on the way to New York.

8

GIAN MARIA RUSHED INTO THE FOYER OF THE HOTEL
Excelsior, where Clara Tannenberg and Ahmed Husseini
were impatiently waiting for their town car. Neither of
them paid attention to the agitated young man as their black Lincoln
pulled up, and they were well away when he hurried out of the hotel
and shouted in the direction of the vanishing car.

Gian Maria hurried back inside to the front desk.

"They've gone. Could you tell me, were they going to the airport?
Were they leaving Rome?"

The desk clerk looked at the man mistrustfully. Despite the fact
that Gian Maria looked perfectly respectable—thin, pleasant demeanor, very short brown hair, well-modulated voice, though dressed a
bit casually—there was an intensity about him.

"I can't give out that information, sir, I'm sorry."

"It's very important that I speak to them."

"Please understand, sir: We don't know where our guests go when
they leave the hotel."

"But if they called for a car they must have said where they were
going. Please, it's very important."

"I don't know what to say, sir. Let me check with—"

"If you could please just tell me if they were going to the airport . . ."

Something in the man's voice and look led the veteran desk clerk to break the profession's rules.

"All right, yes, they were going to the airport. This morning they changed their departure date for Amman. Their plane is leaving in about an hour. They came down late, the lady was delayed. . . ."

Gian Maria ran outside again, quickly flagged down a taxi, and jumped in.

"The airport, quick!"

The taxi driver, an old Roman, looked in the rearview mirror and proceeded to drive very deliberately to Fiumicino, despite the desperation he must have seen reflected in the face of his fare. But as a priest, Gian Maria couldn't bring himself to chastise the man.

Once at the airport, he scanned a monitor to find the flight departing for Amman. Then he moved as quickly as he could through the crowds toward the gate.

Too late. All the passengers had gone through customs already, and the carabiniere refused to allow him to pass.

"They're friends of mine! I couldn't say good-bye—I'll just be a minute. For God's sake, let me see them!"

The guard was unmoved and ordered him to step back.

Gian Maria wandered through the airport, not knowing what to do or whom to confide in. He knew one thing only: He had to speak to that woman, wherever she was, whatever it cost—even if he had to follow her to the ends of the earth.

As they exited the plane onto the boarding steps, they felt the slap of heat in their face and inhaled air thick with the smell of spices. They were home again, home in the East.

Ahmed, carrying a Louis Vuitton bag, preceded Clara down the steps. Behind her, four men, scattered throughout the queue of passengers, moved forward to keep her in sight, trying to go unnoticed.

Ahmed and Clara had no problem passing through customs. Their diplomatic passports opened every door, and Amman, however much it had sworn loyalty to Washington, had its own foreign policy, which did not include confrontations with Saddam Hussein, even if his policies were not always to Jordan's liking. The East was the East, after all, and the otherwise very Westernized Jordanian royal family were experts in the subtleties of diplomacy.

A car was waiting for the couple just outside the terminal, and it drove them to the Marriott. It was late, so they had dinner in their room. There was still tension between them.

"I'm going to call my grandfather."

"That's not a good idea."

"Why not? We're in Amman."

"And the Americans have eyes and ears everywhere. We'll be crossing the border tomorrow. Can't you wait?"

"Really, I can't. I feel like talking to him."

"God, I'm tired of you doing whatever you feel like. You should be more prudent, Clara."

"I've spent my whole life hearing that I ought to be more discreet, that I ought to be more prudent, and nobody ever told me why."

"Ask your grandfather," Ahmed shot back nastily.

Clara did not respond to that. The truth was, she wasn't sure whether she wanted Ahmed, or anyone, to confirm her intuitions, which had only grown through the years. There were so many loose ends. . . . She'd been born in Baghdad, like her mother, and spent her childhood and adolescence between that city and Cairo. She loved the two cities equally. It had been hard for her to convince her grandfather to let her finish her studies in the U.S. She finally managed, even though she knew it made him terribly uneasy.

She'd loved California. San Francisco was where she'd grown into a woman, but she'd always known she wouldn't stay and live there. She missed the Middle East—its smells, its tastes, its sense of time—and she missed speaking Arabic. She thought in Arabic, felt in Arabic. That was why she'd fallen in love with Ahmed. American boys seemed dull, flat to her, even though they'd taught her all the things that were forbidden to her, as a woman, in the East.

"I don't care," she said finally, reaching for the phone. "I'm going to call him."

She rang the front desk and asked to be put through to Baghdad. It was several minutes before she heard Fatima's voice.

"Fatima! It's me, Clara!"

"My darling girl, how wonderful to hear you! Let me call the master."

"He's not asleep?"

"No, no—he's reading in his study. He'll be so happy to hear you."

Over the phone, distantly, she could hear Fatima calling Ali, her grandfather's manservant, telling him to call the master.

And then he was on the line. "Clara, my dear . . ."

"Grandfather . . ."

"You're in Amman?"

"We just got in. I'm dying to see you, to be home again. To be honest, Rome didn't go very well."

"I know."

"You know?"

"Of course I know, Clara."

"But how?"

"It surprises you that I know things?"

"No, of course not, but . . ."

The old man sighed wearily. "Where's Ahmed?"

"Right here."

"Good. I've prepared a wonderful welcome for you both. Now let me speak to your husband a moment."

Clara held the telephone out to Ahmed, and he took it and spoke for a few seconds with his wife's grandfather. Alfred wanted them back in Baghdad as soon as possible.

First thing the next morning, Clara and Ahmed were in the lobby, waiting for the car that would drive them to Iraq. Neither of them noticed the four men watching them, scattered around the busy lobby.

The night before, the men had sent their report to Security Investigations, straight to Luca Marini. So far, everything looked perfectly normal. Crossing the border presented no problem to Ahmed and Clara, though it did to Marini's men. They'd decided to divide up into pairs and hire drivers to take them across. It hadn't been easy— only Jordanians with family in Iraq, or smugglers, had any interest in going into Iraq.

The drivers had been recommended by the hotel, and Marini's men had managed to persuade them by paying very generously—and sweetening the deal by offering them a bonus if they never lost sight of a green Toyota SUV that had left the hotel ahead of them.

There was not much traffic on the highway to Baghdad, but enough to let them see that it was a conduit for just about anything imaginable.

It was night when they reached Baghdad. One of the cars followed the Toyota to a neighborhood in the city, while the other headed for the Hotel Palestina. They'd been told that was where most Westerners stayed, and they were presenting themselves as businessmen, however suspicious it was under the circumstances that anyone would be going to Baghdad on business.

The green SUV pulled up in front of a pair of wrought-iron gates and waited for them to open. Marini's men didn't stop. They now knew where Clara Tannenberg lived. The next day they'd scope the place out more thoroughly.

The two-story Yellow House, named for its always freshly-painted golden hue, stood proudly in a wealthy residential neighborhood, in the midst of a well-tended garden. Once the residence of a British businessman, it was now guarded by a complement of unseen, heavily armed men in the employ of its current owner.

Fatima was waiting in the entry, sitting in a chair, dozing. The sound of the car door woke her. Clara ran to her and hugged her tight. The woman was a Shiite and had cared for Clara since infancy.

Fatima had been very young when she'd lost her husband and had to go to her mother-in-law's house to live, where she was never welcome, never well treated. But she bore her destiny without a word while she raised her only son.

One day her mother-in-law sent her to the Yellow House, where a foreign gentleman lived with his young wife, an Egyptian woman named Alia. And there Fatima had remained. She served Alfred Tannenberg and his wife, accompanied them to Cairo, where the couple had another home, and above all took charge of the couple's son, Helmut, and then their granddaughter, Clara. At first, the little girl had been frightened of Fatima's black clothing, but she grew used to it and soon found in her the sweetness and affection that her mother lacked.

Now Fatima was an old woman, who had lost her son in the terrible war with Iran. She had nothing now but Clara.

"My girl, you do not look well."

"I'm tired."

"You should stop traveling and start having children—you are growing older, you know."

"You're right, Fatima," Clara replied, laughing.

"*Ay*, my girl, be careful that what happened to me doesn't happen to you! I had just one son, and when I lost him I was left alone."

"You have me."

"Yes, my darling, I have you. If I did not, I don't know what there would be to live for."

"Oh, Fatima, don't start. I just got here! Where's my grandfather?"

"He's resting. He was out all day, and he came in tired and worried."

"Did he say why?"

"No, just that he didn't want any dinner. He shut himself up in his room and ordered that he not be disturbed."

Clara knew that Alfred's orders were to be respected by strangers and family members alike. "I'll see him tomorrow, then," she said.

Ahmed went to his room while the two women talked. He was tired. The next day he would go to his office in the ministry, where he had to present a report on the conference in Rome. What a disaster! But he was privileged. He couldn't forget that, no matter how nauseating it was to find himself in such a position. For years now he had been uncomfortable, first when he discovered that his family belonged to a dictatorial regime's elite. But he hadn't had the courage then to renounce the privileges; he'd preferred to blind himself to the consequences of his status by believing that his loyalty was to his family, not to Saddam. Then he had met Clara and Alfred Tannenberg, and his life had fallen irretrievably into the abyss. He had become more corrupt than he'd ever imagined. And he couldn't blame Alfred. Ahmed had voluntarily entered Alfred's organization, voluntarily become Alfred's heir, knowing exactly what that entailed. If his position vis-à-vis Saddam was solid because of his own family ties, he became untouchable when he joined forces with Alfred.

But it was becoming harder and harder for Ahmed to live with himself and even more so with a woman like Clara, who refused to see what was going on around her, living in ignorance rather than facing the truth about those she loved.

Finally he had come to the realization that he didn't love her anymore—perhaps he never had. When they'd first met, in San Francisco, their Arabic heritage united them. They spoke Arabic to each other, had mutual friends in Baghdad, were both archaeologists, and enjoyed the same feeling of freedom and adventure in the United States, although they both missed their country and their people. Clara had had money—a great deal of money—in her checking account, and he himself had more than enough to live comfortably in a spacious loft from which he could watch the sun rise over San Francisco Bay.

Eventually, they moved in together.

When Ahmed's father visited him in San Francisco, he ordered Ahmed to marry Clara. It was a marriage of many conveniences, and Ahmed's father sensed that things in Iraq were about to change. Among diplomats, information flowed freely, and it was clear that Saddam was no longer favored by the U.S. administration. One had to think about the future, and so Ahmed married the grateful, immensely wealthy, spoiled, and overprotected girl.

Clara came into their bedroom, and Ahmed jumped.

She launched right into him. "How can you not say hello to Fatima, Ahmed? You walked right past her without saying a word."

"I said good evening. I have nothing else to say to her."

"You know what Fatima means to me."

"Yes, I know what she means to you."

"What's wrong with you, Ahmed?"

"I'm just tired."

Ahmed's tone surprised Clara. Lately her husband had been behaving as though he was always upset, irritated with her, and as though she was a burden increasingly hard to bear.

"I know you, and I know something's wrong," she pressed.

Ahmed stared at her. He felt like telling her in no uncertain terms that she didn't know him, that she'd never known him, and that he was sick of her and her grandfather. But it was too late now to escape. "Let's go to bed," he said, turning away. "We both have to work tomorrow. I have to go to the ministry, and I've also got to get started right away on serious preparations for the excavation. Everything I heard in Rome only confirmed there will be a war, even if no one here wants to believe it."

"My grandfather does."

"Yes, your grandfather does. Come on, let's go to bed. We'll unpack tomorrow."

Alfred Tannenberg was in his study the following morning with one of his Egyptian business partners, Mustafa Nasir. They were in the midst of a heated argument when Clara came in.

"Grandfather . . ."

"Ah, you're here, my dear! Come in, come in."

Tannenberg's icy eyes fixed on Nasir, and Nasir broke into a broad smile. "My dear girl, I haven't seen you in ages! You no longer do us the honor of visiting Cairo. My daughters always ask about you."

"Hello, Mustafa." Clara's tone was unfriendly, echoing the manner in which her grandfather had been addressing him.

"Clara, we're working. As soon as we've finished I'll call you."

"All right, Grandfather. I'm going out shopping."

"Take one of the guards."

"Yes, yes, of course. Fatima is going as well."

Clara left the house with Fatima and Yasir, one of Alfred's most trusted men, who acted as a chauffeur-bodyguard. They drove in the green SUV to the center of Baghdad.

The city was a pale shadow of itself. The blockade imposed by the United States had impoverished the Iraqis, who now were forced to live by their wits. The hospitals were still functioning, thanks to the help of a handful of NGOs, but the need for medicines and food was increasingly urgent.

Clara harbored a deep hatred toward Bush for what he was doing. She didn't like Saddam either, but she couldn't forgive the people who were strangling the very life out of her homeland.

She and Fatima, accompanied by Yasir, wandered through the bazaar until Clara found a gift for Fatima—it was her birthday. Neither of the women noticed the presence of the foreigners who seemed to be following them through the narrow, labyrinthine streets of the bazaar. But Yasir detected them pretending to be tourists browsing through the stalls, trailing them at every turn. He didn't say anything to the women, so as not to alarm them.

When they drove back to the Yellow House, he went straight to Alfred Tannenberg before Clara could reach him. Mustafa Nasir had gone.

"There were four men, two and two," the bodyguard explained to his employer. "They were following us; there is no doubt. The way they dressed, their faces—I am certain they were not Iraqi, or Egyptian, or Jordanian. But they didn't speak English. I believe it was Italian."

"What do you think they wanted?"

"To know where Miss Clara was going. I don't think they intended her harm, although . . ."

"One never knows. Be certain she goes nowhere alone, nowhere, and that two men, armed, are always with her. If something happens to my granddaughter, neither you nor they will live to tell it."

There was no need for the warning. Yasir had no doubt that if something happened to Clara he would pay for it with his life; he would be neither the first nor the last man to die at the express orders of Alfred Tannenberg.

"Yes, sir."

"Add more security around the house. Inspect everyone who comes in and goes out. No unknown gardeners replacing sick cousins, no irresistible street vendors. I don't want to see a single unfamiliar face unless I personally authorize it. We're going to turn the tables on these mysterious men who are interested in my granddaughter. I want to know who they are, who sent them, and why."

"It will be hard to grab them all."

"I don't need them all—one will be quite enough."

"Yes, sir, but we will need Miss Clara to leave the house again."

"Yes, Yasir, that is true. My granddaughter will be the bait."

Yasir nodded solemnly.

Tannenberg called in his granddaughter. For an hour he listened to her complaints about what had happened in Rome. He had known that things would not go well. His friends had wanted him to wait until Saddam fell before uncovering the rest of the site the U.S. bomb had exposed. It would be a mission to uncover not just the Bible of Clay but other tablets, perhaps a statue or two, like so many other missions he had financed.

He would not wait this time. He couldn't. He knew that he was living the last days of his life. He had four, six months at the most. He had demanded that the doctor tell him the truth, and the truth was that he was approaching the end. He was eighty-five years old, and his liver was covered with small tumors. Less than two years ago, almost half of it had been removed.

Clara would have Ahmed and enough money to live comfortably the rest of her life, but he wanted to give her a real gift, the gift she'd been asking for since she was a child: the glory of discovering the Bible of Clay. That was why he'd sent her to Rome—so it would be she who publicly announced the existence of the two tablets he had found when he was younger than she was now.

They might laugh about the story of Abraham's tablets, but at least the members of the archaeological community had been notified of their existence, even if most considered them a fantasy. No one could take away his granddaughter's glory now, no one, not even his closest friends.

He had already written the letter that one of his men would take to Amman and deliver to a courier, who in turn would take it to Washington to the home of Robert Brown, so that he, in turn, could deliver it to George Wagner. But before he sent it, Alfred had to tend to these meddlers who were following Clara—he might have to add a postscript. And he'd speak to Ahmed in the evening, when he returned from his office. This morning when he'd brought in the letter from Brown, he'd seemed tense.

Alfred trusted Ahmed because he knew how ambitious the younger man was and how desperate he was to escape Iraq. But Ahmed could escape Iraq only with Alfred's money, the money that Clara would inherit and that Ahmed would enjoy only as long as he was with her.

9

MARINI'S SECURITY INVESTIGATIONS TEAM HAD BEEN IN position since dawn. They had found a good spot from which to watch the comings and goings of the Yellow House: a café on the corner on the other side of the street. The owner was friendly, and although he was constantly asking them why they had come to Baghdad, the place was perfect for surveillance unobserved by the men guarding the house.

At eight, the two men stationed in the café saw Ahmed Husseini leave in the green SUV. He was driving, although beside him, in the passenger seat, was a burly man clearly on the alert; his head seemed to swivel in all directions. Clara didn't leave the house until ten. She was accompanied by the old woman swathed in black from head to foot. The same man accompanied them again today, and the threesome drove off in a Mercedes SUV.

There was a crackle of walkie-talkie chat and the other team, sitting in a rented car two streets away, was alerted. They pulled out behind the Mercedes as it passed, with the first two following in another car not far behind.

The Mercedes headed toward the outskirts of Baghdad and traveled for over a half hour before finally turning down a dirt road bordered by palm trees. The men from Security Investigations were uneasy but pushed on, staying back at a prudent distance as the Mercedes sped up. They weren't willing to lose sight of the woman who was their only link to the old man they'd been sent to find and photograph.

The Mercedes raced down the unpaved road, raising a cloud of dry dirt and dust, and then a second later, from two side roads, a swarm of SUVs appeared, apparently intent on crashing into the first of the pursuing vehicles. Marini's men realized too late that it was a trap, as the SUVs surrounded the first car and forced it to stop. The second car stopped short several yards behind the first and backed up fast to a safer distance, keeping their comrades in sight. None of them carried weapons, and the two men in the trailing car had no way of confronting the armed men who raced to their teammates' car, pulled them out, and threw them to the ground. They watched helplessly as the two were beaten and kicked, then they wheeled their car around to return to the highway for help. They weren't running away, they told themselves, although deep inside they knew they were.

They were well out of sight by the time one of their teammates was forced to his knees and shot in the back of the head, while the other vomited. Five minutes later, both were lying dead in the ditch.

Carlo Cipriani covered his face with his hands. Mercedes was sitting pale and impassive beside him, while Hans Hausser's and Bruno Müller's faces reflected their anguish at Luca Marini's news.

They had been called to the office of the president of Security Investigations. Marini had insisted that they come to him. The entire company was in mourning—the employees' silence was eloquent testament to that.

The plane with the two bodies was due back the next day.

Murdered. They had been murdered after being brutally beaten. Their teammates didn't know what they'd told their assailants or who those assailants were. All they knew was that ten SUVs, five from each direction, had forced them to stop. They saw them beaten; when they came back later with an army patrol they'd met on the highway, they found the lifeless bodies. They demanded an investigation but were instead detained as suspects. No one had seen anything, no one knew anything.

The police had interrogated the survivors efficiently, which translated into bruises and cuts on their faces, chests, and stomachs. After several hours they were turned loose and encouraged to leave Iraq as soon as possible.

The Italian embassy filed a formal protest, and the Italian ambassador asked for an urgent meeting with Iraq's foreign minister. He was told that the minister was on an official visit to Yemen but assured that of course the police would thoroughly investigate the strange event, which seemed to the authorities to be the work of a gang of thieves.

Nothing was found in the dead men's pockets—no documents, no money, not even a pack of cigarettes. Nothing. Their murderers had taken everything.

Luca Marini had relived his worst days as head of the anti-Mafia police unit in Sicily, when he had to call the wives of his men to tell them that organized crime had killed one after another of their husbands. At least in those cases there had been official funerals, with the minister of justice in attendance, medals placed on the caskets, and the widows receiving generous pensions from the government. This time, the funerals would be private, there would be no medals, and they'd have to work hard to keep the press from getting wind of the story.

"I'm sorry, Carlo," Marini said as he finished his devastating summary. "This has gone well beyond anything I could have expected or even imagined. I'm canceling our contract. You've gotten us into something very nasty, without the slightest indication that we might face murderers like these. They killed my men to send a message: Leave whoever it is you're looking for alone."

"We'd like to help the families of these men," said Mercedes. "Tell us how much might be appropriate. I know we can't bring them back to life, but at least we can help those they left behind."

Marini looked at Mercedes in surprise. So she wasn't as callous as she seemed. She had the practical sense that many women have, and she didn't waste time shedding tears.

"That depends on yourselves," he replied. "Francesco Amatore left a wife and a two-year-old daughter. Paolo Silvestre wasn't married, but his parents could certainly use some compensation, since Paolo was helping them put his brothers and sisters through school."

"Do you think a million euros would be enough—half a million for each family?" Mercedes asked.

"That's very generous," replied Luca Marini, "but there's another matter that we have to discuss. The police here want to know why four of my men were in Iraq, who paid to send them, and why. So far I've dodged the questions as best I can, but I've been called in to the inspector-general's office tomorrow. He wants answers from me, because the minister of justice wants answers from him. And although we're old friends and he won't hold my feet to the fire more than he has to, I have to give him those answers. Now, tell me what you want me to tell him and what you want me to hold back."

The four friends looked at one another in silence, aware of how delicate the situation was. It was just too complicated to explain to the police why a retired doctor, a physics professor, a concert pianist, and the owner of a large construction company would hire the services of a detective agency and send four men to Iraq.

"Tell us what the most plausible version would be," Bruno Müller suggested.

"Well, the fact is, you've never even told me why you wanted information on this Clara, Ahmed, or Alfred."

"That's nobody's business," Mercedes said, her voice icy.

"There are two men dead, signora, so the police think it's become their business."

"Luca, would you let us talk in private for a moment?" Carlo Cipriani asked.

"Yes, of course, you can use the conference room. When you come up with something, let me know."

He showed them into a conference room next to his office and then closed the door softly behind them.

Carlo was the first to speak.

"We have two choices: Tell the truth or find a plausible explanation."

"There are no plausible explanations with two dead bodies," said Hans, "much less the bodies of two innocent men. If at least they'd been on the other side . . ."

"If we tell the truth, the jig's up, as they say in the old movies," Bruno said morosely, his voice heavy with defeat and despair.

"I'm not willing to give up now, so let's think of a way to deal with this situation," said Mercedes. "This is not the worst thing that's ever happened to us, it's only another roadblock—tragic and unexpected, but a roadblock just the same."

"My God, you're hard-hearted!" Carlo's exclamation came from the bottom of his heart.

"Hard-hearted or not, here we are," she said, headstrong as ever. "We've seen worse. So instead of wringing our hands and bemoaning our fate, let's think."

"I can't," Hans Hausser said softly. "I can't think of a thing."

Mercedes looked at him with disgust. Then, sitting up straighter, she took charge.

"All right, Carlo, you and I are old friends; I'm passing through Rome and I've told you that in view of the inevitable war, I want my company to be among the ones that bring home a piece of the reconstruction pie. So despite my age, I'm considering the possibility of going to Baghdad myself to see the situation firsthand and determine what the country will need postwar. You've told me I'm a crazy old woman, that that's what investigative agencies are for—they have people who are trained, who can assess the situation in a war zone. You've introduced me to another friend of yours, Luca Marini. At first I was doubtful; I preferred to hire a Spanish agency, but I finally took your advice and hired Security Investigations. We accept the Iraqis' story—Marini's men were killed in a robbery. Nothing strange about that, given the situation in Iraq. Naturally, I'm devastated and I want to help the families with a sizable amount of money."

The three men looked at her with renewed respect. It was incredible—in seconds she had come up with a fully formed scenario. Even if the police didn't believe it, it was more than plausible.

"Do you agree, or does somebody have a better idea?"

They agreed to tell the story Mercedes had invented.

Marini thought the story over when they told him. It wasn't bad, as long as no one in his office leaked the other aspects of the investigation, but his was a tight-knit group that kept its business to itself.

"Of course," mused Marini, "we don't know what my men said before they died. More than likely, they told them they were working for Security Investigations and had been sent to follow Clara and Alfred Tannenberg."

"Probably so," Hans broke in, "but the Iraqi police don't know anything about the real killers, nor, so far as we know, does the ambassador. In fact, the Iraqis have all but closed the case. So I see no reason for it not to be closed here."

"Signore Marini," said Mercedes, very seriously, "we've been sent a message with the murder of these two men. A gruesome message. It's his way of showing us what he's capable of doing if we get any closer to him and his family."

"What exactly are you talking about, Mercedes? What are Alfred—this old man—and his family capable of doing?" Luca couldn't contain his curiosity. He was tired of these four old people's mysteries.

"Luca, it's better that you don't know the specifics. This is the best we can come up with. Help us if you think this story won't fly with the Italian police," Carlo said gravely.

The president of Security Investigations gazed at him for a long moment. Cipriani was his doctor, an old friend who had saved his life when other doctors thought it was useless to operate, that he was a goner. So he'd help him, despite the grating abrasiveness of this woman Mercedes Barreda and how troubled he was by the entire undertaking.

"All right, Carlo. I'll do what I can with Signora Barreda's story. I hope my friends on the police force are feeling flexible. My men's families are devastated, but they think they died because of the chaos in Iraq. Neither Paolo nor Francesco talked to them about the details of their work. Bush will have recruited two Italian families for his war against his Axis of Evil. So they, at least, won't cause any big stink, and if on top of that you're willing to pay them compensation . . . all right. I'll call you and let you know how it goes with my police pals."

"Luca, forgive me, but are you sure no one knows who hired you?"

"Yes, Carlo, I'm sure. You didn't want anybody to know about you except me, and when I give my word I keep it."

"Thank you, my friend," said Carlo, his voice breaking a bit.

And without any further conversation, the four of them left Luca Marini's office and went their separate ways for the rest of the dark day.

They each needed a few hours alone, a few hours to process all that had happened and all that was about to happen.

Alfred Tannenberg was listening impassively to the Colonel. They had met many years ago, and the Colonel had always provided Alfred excellent service. It was expensive—very expensive—but worth it. The Colonel was among Saddam's inner circle; they were both from Tikrit, and the Colonel was assigned to state security. Tannenberg was kept well informed of the goings-on in the presidential palace.

"Come, Alfred, tell me who sent those men," the Colonel was insisting.

"I swear to you I don't know. They were Italians, from a company, Security Investigations, hired to follow Clara. That's all we could get out of them. They didn't know any more than that. If they had, you can be sure they'd have told us."

"I cannot imagine that anyone would want to harm your granddaughter."

"I can't either, but if someone does, it would probably be to get at me."

"And you, my old friend, have many enemies."

"Yes, and friends too. I'm counting on you."

"You know you can, but I need for you to tell me one more thing. If you don't, it will be hard for me to help you protect Clara. You have powerful friends. Have you offended any of them?"

Alfred remained impassive. "You have powerful friends too. No less than George Bush, I believe, who is going to send in his marines and push you into the sea."

The Colonel burst out laughing as he lit an Egyptian cigar; he enjoyed their aromatic flavor.

"I assure you," Alfred said, "that I have no idea who sent those two men. What I'm asking you to do is to redouble the security around the Yellow House, keep your antennae up for information, and help me find out who is behind all this."

"I will help you, my friend, I will help you. But I'm worried. I think the war is coming, even if the palace thinks Bush is only blustering. My gut tells me he's going to try to finish what his father started."

"I think so too."

"I would like to send my wife and daughters somewhere safe. My two sons are in the army, so there is little I can do for them at the moment, but the women . . . I'm worried about what it will cost me."

"I'll see to them."

"You are a good friend."

"As are you."

Alfred Tannenberg closed the door as the Colonel left his office. It was true—he really had no idea who had sent the men to follow Clara, or why. They were Italian, which meant someone had hired them in Rome and they had followed his granddaughter to Iraq. Perhaps he himself was the target. But who was behind it? His old friends, warning him not to break the rules, signaling they wouldn't allow him what was rightfully his, the Bible of Clay?

Yes, he thought, that had to be it—but this time they weren't going to have their way. Clara *would* find the Bible of Clay, and the glory would be hers. He was not going to allow anything or anyone to interfere in that.

He felt faint, but making a supreme effort, he gathered himself and went outside to his waiting car. He mustn't exhibit any sign of weakness to his men. He'd have to postpone the trip to Egypt. The specialist there was waiting for him, to perform some new tests and operate if necessary. But he was not going under the knife again—especially now. He could be eliminated so easily under anesthesia—they could do away with him forever. His old "friends" were capable of that and more. They might still love him—old bonds such as theirs died hard—but no one could be above the rules. He, more than anyone, knew that. Besides, he thought, no matter how hard the doctors tried, it was absurd to pretend that they could extend his life indefinitely. No—he would devote whatever time remained to him to ensuring that Clara could begin her excavation and find at last the treasure he had dreamed of for so many years.

He instructed the driver to take him to the Ministry of Culture. He needed to speak with Ahmed.

Ahmed was on the phone when Tannenberg came into his office; Alfred waited impatiently for him to finish his conversation.

"Good news—Professor Picot," said Ahmed when he hung up. "He won't promise anything, but he says he'll come and have a look. If he likes what he sees, he'll come back with a team and we can begin the excavation. I'm going to call Clara; we have to start organizing."

"When is this Picot coming?"

"Tomorrow. He's flying in from Paris. He wants to be taken directly to Safran. He also wants to see the two tablets. . . . You'll have to show them to him."

"No, I'm not going to meet this Picot. I never see anyone I don't need to."

"I've never known what the rule is for seeing some people and not seeing others."

"The rule needn't concern you. I want you to see to it all; and I want this archaeologist to help. Offer him whatever you have to."

"Alfred, Picot has plenty of money; there's nothing we can offer him. If he thinks the ruins at Safran merit his help, he'll come. If he doesn't, there's nothing we can do to convince him."

"What about Iraqi archaeologists?"

"You know we've never had top-notch archaeologists. Only a few of us are any good at all, and those who could, left the country a long time ago. Two of the best are teaching at American universities, and now they're more American than the Statue of Liberty—they'll never come back. Don't forget that for months those of us employed by the government have been working for half pay. This isn't America, where there are foundations, banks, businesses that finance expeditions. This is Iraq, Alfred, Iraq. You're not going to find any archaeologists available except me and one or two more—and those one or two will help us only grudgingly."

"We'll pay, then, we'll pay well. I'll speak with the minister. You'll need a plane to go to Safran or, better yet, a helicopter."

"We can go to Basra and then to—"

"Let's not waste time, Ahmed. I'll speak with the minister. What time does Picot arrive?"

"I'm not sure—sometime in the afternoon."

"Take him to the Hotel Palestina."

"Can't we invite him to stay with us? The hotel has seen better days."

"Iraq has seen better days. Let's be civilized European-style. In Europe no one would invite a stranger to stay with them, and we don't know Picot. Besides, I don't want anybody wandering around in the Yellow House. We'd wind up running into each other, and so as far as Picot is concerned, I don't exist."

No one contradicted Alfred Tannenberg. Ahmed would do as he said, as he always did.

"Did the Colonel have anything to say about the men who were following Clara?"

"No, he knows less than we do."

"Was it necessary to kill them?"

Alfred frowned at the question. In fact, Ahmed was surprised at himself for asking.

"Yes, it was. Whoever sent them now knows whom they're dealing with."

"They were after you, weren't they?"

"Yes."

"And the Bible of Clay?"

"That has yet to be seen."

"Alfred, I've never asked you—let's face it, nobody dares to talk about it—but was your son murdered?"

"Helmut had an accident in which he and Amira were killed."

"Was he murdered, Alfred?" Ahmed looked hard at the older man, and Alfred stared back, unblinking. He hadn't even winced when Ahmed touched the still-open wound left by the death of Helmut and his wife.

"Helmut and Amira are dead. There's nothing more you need to know."

The two held each other's eyes for a few more seconds, but it was Ahmed who finally looked away. Alfred's steely, icy gaze was too much to bear. The old man seemed to him more grotesque and frightening by the day.

"Are you wavering, Ahmed?"

"No."

"Good. I have been as honest with you as I can. You know the nature of my business. Someday you will take charge of it, no doubt before you expect, probably before I want you to. But don't judge me—don't do it, Ahmed. I do not permit anyone to do that, even you—

and if you should begin to judge me, not even Clara will be able to protect you."

"I know that, Alfred. I know what kind of man you are."

There was no contempt nor judgment of any kind in Ahmed's tone
of voice. Merely the recognition that he knew he was working for the
devil himself.

10

AT FOUR IN THE AFTERNOON, THE HOUR OF SIESTA, NOT A soul was stirring in Santa Cruz, the neighborhood of narrow streets and secluded plazas that more than any other barrio contained the essence of old Seville.

The shutters on the windows of the two-story house occupied by the Gómez family were tightly closed; the September sun had heated the city to an unbearable 104 degrees, and despite the air-conditioning that cooled the interiors, no one in their right mind would have opened their home to the blazing light. It was cooler when the house was in shadowy darkness.

The impatient messenger rang the doorbell for a third time. The irate housekeeper who finally opened the door had clearly been roused from her afternoon lethargy.

"I have an envelope for Don Enrique Gómez Thomson. I was told to deliver it in person."

"Don Enrique is resting. I'll give it to him."

"I'm sorry, I can't do that. I have to be certain that Don Enrique receives it."

"I told you I'd give it to him!"

"And I told you that either I give it to him personally or I take it back where it came from. It's my job, doña; I'm just following orders."

Quick footsteps sounded inside in the wake of their raised voices, and a woman appeared behind the housekeeper in the doorway. "What's wrong, Pepa?"

"Nothing, señora—it's this messenger. He insists that he has to deliver this envelope to Don Enrique personally, and I'm telling him I'll take it."

"Let me have it," the woman told the messenger.

"No, señora. I'm sorry, I can't give it to you. I either deliver it to Señor Gómez or I take it back."

Rocío Alvarez Gómez measured the messenger from top to bottom, seriously considering slamming the door in the young man's face. But she knew she had to be very careful when it came to anything involving her husband. Grudgingly, she sent Pepa upstairs to call Don Enrique.

Enrique Gómez came down at once, and he, too, took the messenger's measure in one look, concluding he was just that, nothing more—a harmless courier.

"*Rocío, Pepa, no se preocupen, no es nada*—I'll deal with this gentleman."

He made sure to emphasize the word *gentleman*, so as to put the sweaty, impertinent young man with a toothpick between his teeth in his place.

"*Oye, jefe*, I didn't mean to interrupt your siesta. I just do what they tell me to do, and they told me to put this envelope in your hands and nobody else's."

"Who is it from?"

"No idea, *jefe*. The company gave it to me and told me to bring it here. If you want any more than that, you'll have to call the company."

Enrique didn't bother to answer. He signed the receipt, took the envelope, and closed the door. When he turned around, he found Rocío at the foot of the stairs, looking at him with concern.

"What is it, Enrique?"

"What's what?"

"It's bad news, isn't it? I knew it as soon as I saw him—there's bad news in that envelope."

"Good lord, woman! The messenger was a pack mule, nothing more; he was told to deliver this envelope directly to me, and that's what he did. Go on upstairs and lie down—with this heat, that's all anyone can do. I'll be right up." He jerked his head toward the stairs, and Rocío turned and left him without another word.

Enrique went into his study, sat down at his desk, and with some misgiving opened the large, bulky envelope. He grimaced at the photos he found: pictures of two dead men at the side of a dirt road, both shot in the head, execution style. There was a brief typewritten report identifying them as operatives of an Italian firm, Security Investigations, and the place as a district of Baghdad. Finally, Enrique withdrew a note from the envelope and was not surprised to see the crabbed old-man handwriting of Alfred Tannenberg.

There were just three words: *Not this time.*

The hotel coffee shop overlooked the beach at Copacabana. The two men looked up from their breakfast as the bellman murmured an apology and proffered a bulky manila envelope to the older of them.

"Excuse me, sir, this was just brought in for you, and the front desk told me you were here."

"Thank you, Tony."

"You're welcome, sir."

Frank dos Santos put the envelope in his briefcase and continued his conversation with his business partner. At noon Alicia would be arriving, and they'd spend the afternoon and evening together. It had been too long since he'd been in Rio, he thought. Living on the edge of the jungle caused a man to lose all sense of time.

A little before twelve he went up to his suite. He looked at himself in the mirror in the entry hallway: He might be an old man of eighty-five, but he still looked all right. It made no difference either way. Alicia would act like he was Robert Redford—that was what he was paying her for.

George Wagner was about to board his private plane when he saw one of his assistants running across the landing strip.

"Mister Wagner! Wait!"

"What's wrong?" George snapped, obviously annoyed.

"Here, sir, a messenger just brought this envelope. It arrived from Amman, and apparently it's urgent. He insisted that you should have it immediately."

Wagner took the envelope wordlessly and continued on up the plane's boarding steps.

He sat down in one of the plush club chairs and tore open the envelope, while his personal flight attendant poured him a whiskey.

He examined the photos with a look of disgust and crumpled Alfred's three-word note in his fist.

His face filled with rage, he got up and strode back to the exit, gesturing toward the attendant.

"Tell the captain we're not leaving yet. I have to go back to the office."

"Yes, sir."

As he crossed the asphalt toward the private-aircraft terminal, he took out his cell phone and made a call.

Goddamned Dorothy Miller! Robert Brown's back hurt from sitting on a blanket in the garden of the Millers' mansion. And to top it off, he still hadn't seen Wagner, who hadn't shown up at the picnic.

Now the senator's boring wife was yammering on about his making a "generous donation" to aid the future orphans in Iraq.

"You know, Mr. Brown, that the war will have grave consequences. Unfortunately, children suffer most from these conflicts, so I and a group of other Washington wives have organized a committee to aid the orphans."

"And you can count on my personal contribution, Mrs. Miller. When you have a chance, tell me where to send the money, whatever amount you think appropriate."

"Oh, how generous! But I couldn't presume to tell you how much to contribute, Mr. Brown. I'll leave that to you."

"Ten thousand dollars, perhaps?"

"That would be wonderful! Ten thousand dollars will help us so much!"

Mercifully, Ralph Barry stepped in and interrupted. He was carrying a bulky manila envelope, which he handed to Robert.

"It's just arrived from Amman. The messenger said it was urgent."

Brown struggled up from the grass, made his excuses to the senator's wife, and went to find a quiet corner in the house. Barry came with him, smiling and relaxed. The former university professor reveled as he always did in rubbing elbows with the cream of Washington society.

They made themselves comfortable in a small den and Brown opened the envelope. His expression morphed from boredom to shock as he examined the contents.

"That bastard!" he exclaimed. "That son of a bitch!"

Brown angrily rammed everything back into the envelope.

"Find Paul Dukais for me."

"What's wrong?"

"We've got problems. Problems with Alfred."

The helicopter flew over Tell Muqayyar, the site of ancient Ur, and Safran came into sight. The cloud of yellow dust and sand that billowed around the copter as it landed did justice to the village name, the Arabic word for *saffron*.

Modern Safran consisted of little more than three dozen ancient-looking adobe houses that seemed frozen in time, save for the television antennae or satellite dishes sprouting from rooftops. The dig site was less than a kilometer away, surrounded by a wire fence laced with DO NOT ENTER red tape and dotted with signs that read NO TRESPASSING and STATE PROPERTY in both Arabic and English.

The people of Safran cared little about how their ancestors had lived; it was hard enough for them to live in the present. They found it strange that a group of soldiers had set up camp alongside the nearby crater where the bomb had struck. The remains of an ancient village lay there, they were told, perhaps even a palace. There might be some treasure down there, many of them thought, but the presence of the soldiers persuaded them to keep their curiosity in check.

The Colonel had been able to send only four soldiers to the out-of-the-way village between Ur and Basra, but it was enough to keep the nearby villagers out. Now those villagers were looking with equal amounts of curiosity and apprehension at the helicopter that had landed in their midst.

Yves Picot was watching Clara Tannenberg out of the corner of his eye. Her steel-blue eyes, framed by olive skin and long, dark chestnut hair, made her extraordinarily exotic to him. But hers was not a beauty that one appreciated at first glance; one had to take her in little by little to see the harmony of her features and her questioning, intelligent gaze.

He had thought her to be a capricious, high-strung young woman at first, but he might have judged too soon. Life had treated her well, no doubt about that; all one had to do was look at how she dressed in her increasingly impoverished homeland. But the conversation they'd had the previous night over dinner together in the hotel led him to suspect that Clara was more than just spoiled and willful. She was beginning to seem a capable archaeologist, though it remained to be seen whether that judgment would prove true.

Her husband, Ahmed Husseini, on the other hand, was unquestionably a solid archaeologist. He was not a man who spoke much, but what he did say was reasonable, judicious, and indicative of a deep knowledge of Mesopotamia, its history, and its current predicament.

The military helicopter had landed near the tent in which the Colonel's four soldiers sheltered. Picot, Clara, and Ahmed jumped down to the ground, covering their faces as best they could. Within seconds their mouths and noses were filled with fine yellow sand.

The place seemed virtually deserted, save for the few straggling villagers curious to see who had come.

The village leader recognized Ahmed and came over to greet him, nodding to Clara and Picot. He and two of the soldiers accompanied the three visitors as they toured the site.

Picot and Ahmed slid down the side of the bomb crater. Even from the top, one could see the remains of a structure. Around the hole, a bare-bones excavation had been started, establishing a perimeter of some two hundred meters.

Picot listened attentively to Ahmed's explanations, interrupting him now and then with questions that the Iraqi answered fully and knowledgeably.

The explosion had revealed a square room lined with shelves, on which the pieces of shattered tablets were heaped. Ahmed explained that the few tablets found intact had already been sent back to Baghdad.

Clara couldn't bear waiting up on the surface while the two men poked about below. Impatient, she asked the soldiers to help her slide down.

The three of them spent hours in the hole, looking, scraping, measuring, rescuing shards of tablets so tiny their cuneiform script was barely recognizable. When they came up again, they were covered by a fine layer of yellow sand and dust.

Ahmed and Picot were talking animatedly. The two men seemed to be getting along despite themselves, having clearly bonded as peers.

Ahmed gestured back to Safran. "We could set up a camp beside the village and hire some men from here to help with the basic work. But we need experts, experienced people who won't destroy the structure as they dig it out. And as you've seen for yourself, we might find more structures, even ancient Safran itself. I could get army tents, though they're not very comfortable, and maybe a few more soldiers to guard the site."

"I don't like soldiers," Picot said flatly.

"In this part of the world, they're necessary," Ahmed replied.

"Ahmed, spy satellites are trained on Iraq day and night. They're going to see a military encampment, which means that when the bombing starts, this place will be wiped out. I think we ought to do things another way. No military tents, no soldiers. At least no more than these four, which will be enough to keep any of the villagers from getting too clever for their own good. If I come to excavate, it will be with civilian teams and civilian equipment."

"Then you're coming?" Clara asked anxiously.

"I'm not sure yet. I want to see those two tablets you told me about in Rome, plus the others that you say were found here with the signature mark of this Shamas. Until I examine them, I won't be able to form an opinion. In principle, this looks interesting. I think, as your husband does, that this is an ancient temple–palace and that we may find many artifacts, not only tablets. But I can't be certain of that. I have to be able to confirm that what I see warrants bringing twenty or thirty people here, with the equipment and supplies for an excavation of this size and the financial cost that would entail, under circumstances that are far from ideal. One of these days, Uncle Sam's F-18s are going to start flying over and dropping more bombs, and people that *I* bring here could all be killed. The Americans are going to practically wipe this country off the map, and there's no reason to think we'd be spared, if we're still here when it starts. So coming here now is certainly running a significant, and perhaps unnecessary, risk. *After* the war is another question. . . ."

"But we can't leave this until then. It might be destroyed." Clara's voice was desperate.

"*Oui, madame*, you are no doubt right. The F-18s will leave nothing, except more yellow dust. The question is whether I want to risk my money, not to mention my life, on an adventure like this. I am no Indiana Jones, and I have to think carefully about how long it would take me to put a team together and bring it here, how long it would take us to achieve some results . . .

"The war will begin in six to eight months at the most," he continued. "Read the newspapers. So, in six months can we find something? In my opinion, no. You know that an excavation of this magnitude takes years."

"So you've made your decision. You've come just out of curiosity," Clara stated more than asked.

"You're right: I have come out of curiosity. But as for the decision, I have not yet made it. I was just playing devil's advocate."

"We wanted you to have some idea of this place," Ahmed broke in. "But you've yet to see the tablets themselves, in Baghdad."

The leader of the village invited them to come to his house, where it was cooler, for a cup of tea and something to eat. They gratefully accepted his invitation and made him a gift of the bags of food they had brought with them. Ahmed and Clara were surprised to hear Picot speak Arabic.

"You speak Arabic well. Where did you learn?" Ahmed asked.

"I began to study it the day I decided to become an archaeologist. I knew many of the countries I would be digging in would be in the Middle East, and I've never liked having to depend on intermediaries—interpreters and overseers and the like. I don't speak it perfectly by any means, but I can make myself understood, and I understand almost everything that's said to me."

"Do you read and write it as well?" asked Clara.

"Yes, both—at least a little."

The village leader was a shrewd man, and he was delighted to be able to entertain these people who, if they decided to excavate, would bring prosperity to his people. He had met Clara and Ahmed when they began the excavations and had been disappointed when they had to call them off for lack of equipment and trained assistants—the men of the village lacked the knowledge and experience to help them without destroying, or half-destroying, what they found. He murmured softly to Ahmed, who turned back to Picot.

"Our host has offered to let us stay in his house tonight if we'd like. Or we can stay in the tents we brought with us. Tomorrow we can visit the surrounding area, so you can get the lay of the land; we could also go to Ur. Or of course we can return to Baghdad right now. You decide."

Picot was happy to spend the night in Safran so he could see more of the surrounding area the next day. Staying the night would add a whole new dimension to Iraq for him. The route from Baghdad by helicopter, the immense solitude of the yellow desert that opened before them, discomfort as an ingredient in the adventure—it occurred to him that if he was never going to come back here, or even if he did with twenty or more people, this was his opportunity to enjoy the silence of the landscape around him.

They pitched two tents near the soldiers guarding the ruins. They had planned that Picot would sleep with the soldiers who had accompanied them in the helicopter, while Ahmed and Clara slept in the other tent. But the head of the village insisted that Ahmed and Clara sleep in his house, which was fine with Picot, who could then have a whole tent to himself.

They drank tea and ate pistachios with some of the village men who had come to the chief's house and who offered to work on the excavations if they proceeded. They were eager to talk about the wages they would earn per day, and Ahmed, seconded by Picot, began a long session of haggling.

By ten that night the village was utterly silent. The locals rose with the sun, so they went to bed early. Clara and Ahmed walked Picot to his tent. They, too, would be starting out at daybreak.

Later, in silence, the couple wandered over toward the remains of the building that so fascinated them. They sat on the sand, leaning back against the ruined adobe walls of the ancient edifice. Ahmed lit a cigarette for Clara and another for himself.

The canopy of stars made the night lovely. Clara half-dozed, trying to imagine what this place had been like two thousand years earlier. In the silence, she heard the voices of hundreds of women, children, men— villagers, scribes, kings; they were all there, passing before her closed eyes. They were as real as the night.

Shamas. What had Shamas been like? She envisioned Abraham, the father of nations, as a seminomadic shepherd who wandered along the edge of the desert, living in a tent, tending his flocks of sheep and goats, sleeping sometimes in the open on starry nights such as this one.

The Bible described him as a clever, hard man, a shepherd of men as well as of his flocks. He must have had a long gray beard and thick, tangled hair. He would have been tall—yes, she imagined him tall— with an imposing demeanor that inspired respect wherever he went.

Clara sat and felt the coolness of the mud walls against her back, pondering why Shamas would accompany the tribe of Abraham all the way to Haran and then come back here. . . .

11

ILI EMBRACED SHAMAS. THE BOY WOULD BE LEAVING WITH HIS tribe on a long journey to the land of Canaan, and while Ili felt sorrow, he was also relieved. Shamas was impossible to discipline. He was intelligent, yes, but incapable of concentrating on anything that didn't capture his imagination. Ili would never see him again, he was certain of that, though this was not the first time that the tribe of Terah had gone off to the north in search of pastures, carrying merchandise for trading.

He had heard some of the men say that this time they might go as far as the bank of the Tigris, to Asur and from there to Haran.

"I will remember everything you have taught me," Shamas promised.

Ili didn't believe him. He knew that much of what he had tried to teach Shamas had been lost in the clouds; during many of the boy's lessons, he wasn't even listening. Still, Ili patted Shamas on the back and gave him several styluses, some of reed and some of bone. It was a gift for a student he would never forget, for the many bittersweet mornings and afternoons they had spent together.

The sun was rising, and the tribe of Terah was ready to begin the long journey. At a sign from Abram, more than fifty men, women, and children set out on the march, with their belongings and their animals.

Shamas looked for Abram, who was leading the procession with Jadin, Terah, and other elders of the tribe. The boy could not get them to pay him any mind, for they were squabbling among themselves. They had not yet come to an agreement over the route they would take, so Terah, weary, ended the dispute by declaring that they would journey along the bank of the Euphrates, which would lead them near Babylonia. They would pass through Mari and go from there to Haran before they continued on to Canaan.

The boy realized that he should wait a few days before asking Abram to begin the story of Creation. First they would have to become accustomed to the routine of the march, for although almost all of them had made such a journey before, during the first days of a migration problems always arose, whether it be friction between neighbors or adjusting to sleeping on the ground, with only the sky above them.

One evening, while the women were bringing water from the Euphrates and the men were counting the flocks, Shamas saw Abram go off along a path near the river, and he followed him.

Abram walked for some time, and then he sat down on a long, flat rock beside the river. From time to time he would absentmindedly pick up one or two little pebbles on the riverside and toss them into the water.

Shamas realized that Abram was meditating, so he did not make his presence known. He would wait until Abram returned to the camp to speak with him.

But suddenly he heard Abram call out to him.

"Come, Shamas, sit down here with me," the older man told the boy, gesturing to a nearby rock.

"You knew I was here?"

"Yes, you followed me from the camp, but I knew you would not speak to me until I had finished thinking."

"Were you talking to Him?"

"No, today He has not spoken to me. I have tried, but I have not felt His presence."

"Perhaps because I was here," the boy replied apologetically.

"Perhaps. But perhaps He had nothing to say to me."

Shamas felt better when Abram said that; it seemed natural that God would not talk unless it was important.

"I brought styluses with me. Ili gave them to me, a gift for my departure."

"So you two finally made your peace?"

"I tried to be a better student, but I know I did not meet Ili's expectations. I want to learn—I do, but . . ."

"Would you rather be with the tribe?"

"Forever?"

"Yes, forever."

"Can I learn everything Ili knows and still go from one place to another?"

"There are other places where you can have lessons. Now that you have left Ili behind, you must think about other things."

"Yes, that is why I followed you. I wanted to ask you to start telling me why and how He made the world."

"I will."

"When?"

"We can start tomorrow."

"Why not now?"

"Because it is growing dark and your mother will begin to worry about you. She does not know where you are, does she?"

"No, you're right. But tomorrow when?"

"I will call you. Come, we must not stay away too long."

But Abram and Shamas did not start writing the story of Creation the next day, or the next, or the next. The long marches, the care of the goats and sheep, incidents between their tribe and villagers in the places they set up camp kept Abram from finding the calm moments he needed to explain to Shamas why and how He created the world. But the boy refused to stop asking Abram about that God more powerful than Enlil, Ninurta, and even Marduk, and so during the long march to Haran, Shamas heard Abram say many times that there was no god but God and that the others were but figures made of clay.

"Then Marduk didn't fight against Tiamat?"

"Tiamat, the goddess of chaos," Abram answered with a smile. "Do you think there is a god in charge of chaos, another in charge of water, another of grain, another of sheep, another of goats?"

"That is what Ili taught us. Marduk fought against Tiamat and split her into two pieces. With one of them he made the sky and with the other he made the earth. And from her eyes sprang the Tigris and the Euphrates, and with the blood of the goddess's husband, the god Kingu, Marduk made man. Marduk told Ea: 'I am going to knead up blood and make bones. I am going to create a savage, whose name shall be Man. I am going to create human beings, men, who shall see to the worship of the gods, so that they may be well pleased.' "

"It sounds as though you did learn something Ili tried to teach you."

"Yes, but tell me the truth—does Marduk exist?"

Abram looked upon Shamas and quietly said, "No, he does not exist."

"The only god that exists is your God."

"God alone exists."

"Then everyone is wrong but you?"

"Men try to explain what happens and they look up at the sky, thinking there is a god for each thing. If they looked within their hearts, they would find the answer."

"You know, I try to look into my heart, as you tell me to, but I do not find anything."

"Yes you do—you have found the path by which you will reach God, because you ask about Him and want to find Him."

Shamas timidly met Abram's eyes. "Is it true that you destroyed the workshop where Terah made figures of the gods?"

"I did not destroy it, I just wanted to prove that they were clay, that inside that clay there was nothing. My father made the gods. Is Terah a god, then?"

The boy laughed out loud. No, of course Terah wasn't a god; how silly. Abram's gray-headed old father with his prickly beard looked nothing like a god. He yelled at the boys angrily when they awakened him under the hot afternoon sun, and he milked the goats at dawn. Gods didn't milk goats, Shamas told himself.

As they marched north, the weather changed. The sky turned gray and then rained infinite torrents of water onto Terah's camp. Huddled in their tents, the men talked while the women prepared the day's last meal, and the children tested their elders by pretending to dart outside the tents, into the storm. An old man announced that they were now very near the pasturelands of Haran, and Terah nodded, saying that they would rest awhile when they arrived there, for certain distant family members of the tribe lived there, and he himself had been born in that place.

Shamas was ecstatic. He was eager to settle down again. He didn't like all this moving from place to place. He even missed the house of tablets where Ili had given him his lessons. Except for his conversations with Abram, no one in the tribe seemed particularly interested in talking about anything except the health of the goats and sheep and events along the way.

That night, under the mantle of the rain, while Terah was explaining that the tribe would stay for a time in Haran, Shamas asked his father whether there would be another house of tablets there, where he might continue his studies.

Jadin was surprised at his son's question.

"I thought you disliked school—as if it were a punishment to you."

"No, Father. I would much rather study than walk."

"That is the way we live, though, Shamas. You must not scorn what we are."

"No, Father, I am not scorning it. I like to sleep where I can look up at the stars and play until sunrise. I have given all of our sheep and goats names, and I have learned to milk them. But I miss my lessons."

Shamas' father sat quietly, pensive. He knew that his son was intelligent and that this journey to the north had clearly changed him—suddenly he longed to learn again. Jadin would speak with Terah and Abram, and together they would decide the boy's destiny.

The tribe made its settlement outside the walls of Haran. With the aid of his sons Abram and Nahor, Terah would once again model gods from clay. But they would shape bricks and make storage jars and other vessels as well, so that they would have a way of earning their livelihood. They would also have their flocks of sheep and goats and several good asses to carry their burdens as they traded.

Jadin asked Terah to find a way for Shamas to start his lessons again, and one afternoon, just at sunset, Abram sought out the boy. He found him playing with some of the other children, though on the boy's face there was a cloud of sadness.

"Shamas!" Abram called out to the boy.

The boy ran over.

"Now that we have arrived, I thought that I might begin telling you the history of the world. We can mold the clay to make the tablets, and with the styluses that Ili gave you, you can document the story of why God made us. Do you know, Shamas, that of all the things your eyes can see around you, the only thing that will remain through time is that which is written down?"

"Has He told you that?"

"I feel it within me. Our children's children will be able to hear and believe the stories of the gods because other men have written them and left them forever on dried clay. Therefore, Shamas, you and I will tell the story."

"You and I?"

"Yes. I will tell it and you will write it. That is what you asked me to do before we left Ur, is it not?"

"Yes! And we will do it," the boy answered eagerly, looking forward to his new responsibility. "When can we start?"

"Have some tablets ready tomorrow at sunset. We will meet in the palm grove near our tent, and I will begin telling you the story of the world."

As Shamas ran toward his tent, a worry came upon him. It had been many months since he had used the stylus on the clay. Had he forgotten how? So he asked his mother and father to let him mold some tablets to practice on. He didn't want to disappoint Abram, but most of all he didn't want to disappoint himself.

When the first tablet was ready, he wrote his name on the top, as Ili had taught him. *Shamas.* Then he began to write his first words in many months:

> *I shall write the story of the world. Abram shall tell it to me.*
> *And in that way, men may know why He created them.*

Shamas looked at the tablet; he was unhappy with the result. He had lost the ease with the stylus that he had once had, and the symbols were uncertain; they had lost firmness; some of the indentations were twisted in the clay. He decided to keep practicing until his writing was perfect.

> *Marduk is but a clay figure. The clay gods are only clay. The*
> *God of Abram cannot be seen, and that is why He is God. He*
> *cannot be shaped in clay, nor can He be broken.*

The boy squinted critically at the tablet again. His father looked over his shoulder.

"What are you writing, Shamas?"

"I am just practicing, Father."

"Don't worry so much," said Jadin affectionately, overlooking the marks made by his son's unpracticed hand. "Be patient. You will improve."

There is but one God who reigns over the heaven and the earth, and He shares His power with no others, Shamas went on writing, and he continued practicing until the sun sank beneath the horizon and its light became night, so that the boy could do nothing more, and he slept.

In the morning, before the sun was fully risen, Shamas asked his father to make some new tablets so that he could practice again. He wanted Abram to be proud when he read what he had written.

Jadin helped the boy mold several tablets before going out to tend the sheep and goats. He had decided to go to the city that day, to speak to the priests and ask their help in completing the education of his son. Terah had promised to come with him, for Terah was a man well known within the city's walls.

To speak with God, we must seek within our hearts. Abram
says that He speaks not with words but instead makes men to
feel what He desires them to do. I seek within myself, but I
am not yet worthy of hearing Him. I believe that among us,
God has chosen only Abram.

And so Shamas went on writing the whole day, until the sun began
its decline. He then got up and went quickly to the palm grove, where
Abram was already waiting for him.

Shamas showed Abram the tablets, and Abram made no sign of
either satisfaction or reproach.

"You have done your best, and that is enough, Shamas."

"I will try to do better."

"I know."

The boy sat on the ground, his back against a palm tree and the
tablet resting against his legs. Abram began to talk, and his words
seemed to emerge out of the growing shadows of the sky.

In the beginning God created the heaven and the earth. And
the earth was without form, and void; and darkness was
upon the face of the deep. And the Spirit of God moved upon
the face of the waters. And God said, Let there be light: And
there was light. And God saw the light, that it was good:
And God divided the light from the darkness. And God
called the light Day, and the darkness He called Night. And
the evening and the morning were the first day. . . .

Abram sat silently as Shamas wrote everything he dictated to him:
God's creation of the heavens and earth, the creation of the animals,
and the temptation of Adam and Eve in the Garden of Eden. The boy
had not lifted his eyes from the tablet, and Abram had seen the effort
he was making to set every mark, every sign in its horizontal line, the
stylus moving right to left, the lines accumulating neatly down the
tablet.

Shamas held the tablets out to Abram. Some characters were hard
to read, but in general the boy had done an excellent job.

"Most of it is fine, Shamas. Now put these tablets away in a safe
place, where your brothers and sisters will not break them and they will
not be in your mother's way. Ask your father—he will tell you where to
put them. So, what do you think about what I have told you today?"

"I think . . ." Shamas hesitated.

"Go ahead; what are you afraid of?"

"I do not wish to make you angry, Abram, but the creation of the world by God is almost exactly like the creation of the world by the very gods of clay we worshipped."

"Yes, but there are differences."

"In what way?"

"For example, in the Enuma Elish that Ili taught you to recite, Marduk creates man by killing the goddess Tiamat and her husband, the god Kingu. But Marduk has also been created. The gods don't create anything; they make man out of what already exists—but who was the First Creator, who created from nothing? God creates because He wishes to, He decides to, and He creates out of nothingness, because He does not need matter from which to continue His creation."

"But what you and Ili have told me are similar."

"Similar, yes. There are those who have had an intuition of the creative principle and have imagined stories of gods to explain it."

"Why have they not learned to hear Him?"

"Because it is not easy to hear Him. We are too concerned with ourselves. God punished us, punished all men—the first men and those who followed and those who will come after us. He condemned us to earn our bread by the sweat of our brow, and to suffer pain and disease, and to wander the face of the earth. And that is why man has little time to seek out God."

"But why did He punish us? And why all of us? I have done nothing wrong, at least nothing very bad."

"You are right, but Adam and Eve—as I've told you, the first two people God created in His own image—sinned, and so mankind was punished."

"That does not seem fair."

"Who are you to judge God, Shamas?"

"But why should I be punished for something I did not do?"

"I will explain more tomorrow. Bring the tablets and the styluses."

The night was falling, so Shamas and Abram walked back to their camp, where the tribe was preparing to rest after the day's labors. Jadin motioned to Abram; he wanted to speak with him alone.

"My son is not happy."

"No?"

"He misses Ur, even Ili. He wants to learn. I went to the temple with Terah; they will allow him to go there to study, but I fear he will dispense your teachings to others and that that will make difficulties for us. Can you tell him not to say that there is but one God? If such talk reaches the ears of the king, we will suffer the consequences."

"Jadin, do you really think the king would punish us?"

"Yes, Abram, I've no doubt of it. And so we must be prudent."

It had been decided that the tribe would settle in Haran for some time before continuing on toward the land of Canaan, so the men began to raise houses of mud and straw in which to live until it was time to depart again. Jadin offered Shamas a small hole dug in the ground to accommodate his tablets.

Each day, Shamas burned with impatience, awaiting the moment he might sit with Abram in the palm grove again.

By now he knew why God had punished mankind. Adam's foolish act had been unpardonable, the boy thought. God had created a paradise for Adam and Eve in which to live, a place with every kind of tree that was good to eat, and in the middle of the garden He had set the Tree of the Knowledge, the only tree that Adam and Eve were forbidden to approach, for if one ate of its fruit, one would die.

"I cannot understand why they ate it," Shamas stubbornly insisted.

"Because God made us free to choose our actions. Tell me, Shamas, do you remember when Ili would forbid you to jump out of the windows at school because you might hurt yourself?"

"Yes."

"Yet how many of you boys did it anyway?"

"Well, I did."

"You did, indeed! You and several of the others, and one of them, I believe, broke his arm. You knew that might happen, did you not?"

"Yes."

"Yet you still did it."

"But breaking your arm is not the same as dying!" Shamas insisted.

"No, it's not the same. But Adam and Eve believed that eating of that tree would make them be as gods, and they could not resist that temptation. When you boys jumped out the windows at school, you were not thinking about the harm it could do you—neither did Adam and Eve."

"Yesterday I also realized that the creation of Eve is like the story of Enki and Ninhursag."

"In what way?" Abram asked, pleased, as always, by Shamas' quickness and natural acuity.

"Enki lives in paradise too," Shamas answered, reciting, *"where the raven utters no cry, the ittidu-bird makes not the call of the ittidu-bird, the lion kills not, the wolf steals not. . . .* Well, you know it better than I do. In that paradise there is no pain either, and Ninhursag, with no pain in her body, brings forth other goddesses into the world. Ninhursag created eight plants and Enki ate the fruits of those plants, for which

Ninhursag grew angry and condemned him to death. Then later, when she saw him suffering, she created other gods and goddesses, one by one, to cure his illnesses and pains. Remember the poem? Ninhursag says to Enki, *My brother, where do you hurt?/ My tooth hurts. / I have given birth to the goddess Ninsutu for you.* Then she creates Ninti, the goddess of the rib, to cure that part of his body. Enki becomes ill because he eats plants he should not eat and he is punished for it; Adam and Eve eat from the Tree of the Knowledge, and from that moment on they are condemned to death. And so are we."

"You will be a wise man, Shamas. I only hope that you use your knowledge to grow closer to Him and that reason does not blind you to the true path."

"How can reason keep me from finding God?"

"Because we humans are a reflection of God. And that can lead you into the temptation of believing that you understand everything, of imagining that you know everything."

12

A THIN, DARK-HAIRED PRIEST NERVOUSLY WANDERED ABOUT St. Peter's Basilica, frantically searching for a quiet, out-of-the-way place to pray privately. The basilica seemed strange to him, a monument to the arrogance of men rather than a house of God. He had passed Michelangelo's "Pietà" twice, and only in the pure lines of the marble had he seemed to see a flicker of spirituality.

For several days now, God would not come to him, no matter how desperately he prayed for his guidance. The priest went out into St. Peter's Square, alone with his unquiet conscience.

He had failed in his search for Clara Tannenberg. By the time his painfully slow taxi reached the Fiumicino Airport, she had already boarded a plane for Amman.

He'd been tempted to buy a ticket for the next flight to Jordan, but once there, how would he have been able to find her?

He was going mad—mad with inactivity. He restlessly roamed from one place to another. His father had called him again that morning and again had been told by his son's superiors that the young priest had simply gone out. Gian Maria couldn't bear to talk to anyone, much less his father.

"Gian Maria . . ."

The young man whirled around, startled by the deep voice of Padre Francesco.

"Padre . . ."

"I've been watching you wander aimlessly like a lost soul."

For over thirty years, Padre Francesco had been hearing confessions in the Vatican, unburdening of their earthly miseries all the men and women who came to the Holy See. Upon becoming a confessor in the basilica months ago, Gian Maria had grown comfortable under the wing of the old priest. And Padre Francesco's look of concern reflected that bond.

"I'd been told you were ill. But seeing you now, I realize this is a sickness of the soul, not the body. What's troubling you, my son?"

"Padre Francesco, I . . . I can't tell you."

"Why? I might be able to help."

"I can't break the bond of confession."

The older priest fell silent. Then, taking him by the arm and dodging the tourists, he led Gian Maria out of the cathedral.

"Let me buy you a cup of coffee."

Gian Maria tried to resist, but Padre Francesco wouldn't hear of it. "I would never ask you to disregard the sanctity of confession, my son," he said firmly as they walked along. "But I might be able to ease this terrible suffering I see in your face another way."

They entered a quiet café outside the Vatican, where Padre Francesco skillfully attempted to assume some of Gian Maria's burden without breaking his vow of secrecy. After an hour of vague hints and general responses, Gian Maria finally asked a direct question.

"Padre Francesco, if you knew that someone was going to do something terrible, would you try to prevent it?"

"Yes, my boy, of course. Priests shrieve man's sins, but we also have the obligation to prevent them."

"But doing that could take me far from here, and even then, I don't know whether I could help. . . ."

"You should try."

"But I don't know where to begin." Gian Maria lowered his head, hopeless.

"You're intelligent, Gian Maria. Once you've made your decision, the right path will reveal itself."

"Do you think the superior will let me leave? I may be gone indefinitely."

"I'll speak with Padre Pio. He's an old friend; we studied together in the seminary. I'll ask him to grant you a leave of absence."

"Thank you, Padre." Gian Maria smiled, as if a weight had been lifted from him. "Talking to you, everything seems easier."

"It may seem easier now, but I sense that what's tormenting you will not be easy to overcome. But at least you can try."

Half an hour later, Padre Francesco had returned to his confessional in the Vatican, while Gian Maria was still pacing the floor, marshaling his thoughts.

The archaeologists' conference was over, and there was precious little information he'd been able to gather about the woman. Most seemed to know nothing about her—those who did said she was a nobody, riding the coattails of her husband, Ahmed Husseini.

Gian Maria knew in his heart how he could find her. This Ahmed, he'd been told, was head of Iraq's Bureau of Archaeological Excavations. Therefore, to find the woman, he must go to Baghdad. The trip would be like a medieval penitence, he thought, but he had to go: It was his sacred duty.

He felt a terrible apprehension yet was filled with happiness and purpose at the same time.

He leaned against one of the enormous columns that encircled St. Peter's Square. His decision had been made; he mustn't lose heart, and he must not turn back.

Gian Maria walked to a travel agency near the Vatican, and there, timidly, asked for a ticket to Baghdad.

But there were no direct tickets to Baghdad. It would be a war zone soon enough. What did he want to go to Iraq for, anyway? the woman behind the ticket counter wanted to know. Gian Maria couldn't reveal to this stranger the intimacies of his priestly duties, so, reluctantly, he lied: He was to lend a hand to some friends at an NGO. At that, the travel agent's suspicions were tempered, and she promised him she'd see what she could do.

Two hours later, he left the travel agency with a plane ticket for Amman, Jordan. He'd sleep there overnight, then go overland to Baghdad, and once there . . . He only prayed that God would help him.

He entered the order's house as quietly and surreptitiously as he could, to avoid any unwanted conversation. He'd wait for Padre Francesco to speak with his superior.

Gian Maria locked himself in his room, and when he was called to dinner, he feigned tiredness and opted to go to bed. Before he retired, in the quiet of his room he composed a vague letter to his family, telling them that he was taking a short vacation because he needed to rest and think. He'd call them later to let them know he was all right. He couldn't say good-bye to his family in person. His sister, surely, would be worried at first, then angry. She'd try her hardest to wring the details of his trip out of him, but he couldn't confide them, even to her.

Gian Maria hadn't drawn the curtains, and he was awakened by the first light of dawn. When he opened his eyes he remembered the course he had set for himself, and he began to silently weep. The day before it had all seemed so easy. But in the light of the new day, he found himself assailed by doubt. He looked at the sky outside his window, and for the first time in his life he asked himself where God was.

Night was falling as Ahmed led Picot into his Baghdad office.

"Are you tired, Yves?" Ahmed asked as he flicked on the light.

"I am. The dinner was magnificent, but it's made me sleepy. Can you make some coffee?"

"Absolutely, let's have a cup—then you can examine the tablets for as long as you like."

Yves refrained from sitting in what appeared to be a *very* comfortable chair, for fear of falling asleep. He heard Ahmed fiddling with the coffeemaker. After traveling this far, would he finally see the tablets?

Ahmed approached with two steaming cups in his hand and handed one to Picot.

"Come with me," he said to the Frenchman.

Picot followed him farther into the warren of offices, past another locked door. He took a sip of coffee, which did nothing to lift his torpor after the heaviness of the meal. But as Ahmed turned on the light, Yves' drowsiness vanished. He opened his eyes wide, focusing on two ancient stone tablets unceremoniously resting on a large gray cloth. Leaning in closer, he saw the name *Shamas* clearly inscribed at the top of each one.

Clara steered clear of her husband's office the next morning, loath to interfere with Ahmed and Picot's work. So she spent the early hours wandering through the narrow, winding streets of the bazaar with Fatima, protected by four armed men who never let them out of their sight.

When it was getting close to noon, Clara made her way to the Ministry of Culture, while Fatima, loaded down with bags, returned to the Yellow House.

Ahmed and Picot were just about to leave when Clara arrived.

"Don't tell me you were leaving without me!" she burst out.

"No, we were going to call from the restaurant," Ahmed explained.

Clara couldn't muster the nerve to ask Professor Picot what he'd decided, nor did their casual conversation as they drove to the restaurant and ordered provide any hint. She waited, hiding her impatience, while the waiter brought the food.

"This is the best hummus in the East," Ahmed declared to Picot.

"Yes, it's delicious." Picot nodded, as the two men chatted away about the regional cuisine.

Finally Clara couldn't contain herself. "What did you think of the tablets, Professor?" she asked, striving to maintain a casual tone.

Direct as her question was, Picot had been expecting it. He wiped his mouth with a napkin and smiled. "Extraordinary. It might not be totally mad to posit a relationship between the Abram of the Bible and that scribe named Shamas. It would be a discovery of immense importance to both science and religion. It's most certainly worth going after."

"Then . . . you'll come?" Clara asked shyly.

"Let's say that I see strong arguments for doing so. I've told your husband that I'll give him a decision within the week. I'm leaving tomorrow, but I'll call you from Paris as soon as I've considered everything. This afternoon we'll photograph the tablets. I want to study them more carefully." Picot paused, his expression shadowed briefly with concern. "I'm sorry to leave without meeting your grandfather."

"He's in bed, resting," Clara said quickly. "He's not well and certainly in no condition to see anyone. I'm sorry too, because he'd have liked to meet you."

"I'd be interested in hearing how he found the tablets—under what circumstances he came across them."

"We've told you," Clara replied carefully.

"Yes, but it's not the same. Forgive me for pressing you on this, but if he improves, I would be so happy to speak to him."

"We'll tell him," Ahmed said. "Him and his doctors, who are the ones to decide, really."

Yves Picot sensed they were making excuses for Clara's grandfather, which made him all the more curious. For the moment, he let it rest with their explanations. But if he decided to come and dig, he'd insist.

Ahmed carefully wrapped the tablets and placed them in a metal box well padded for transport for their return to the Yellow House. Alfred couldn't bear to be separated from them for long; they were, for him, a sort of talisman. He'd even had a safe installed in his bedroom to secure them, where any servant—save Fatima—would enter at the risk of a beating and a swift dismissal.

"Why didn't Picot want to have dinner with us tonight?" Clara asked anxiously.

"He's tired, I suppose. He's leaving first thing tomorrow."

"Do you think he'll be back?"

"I don't know—if I were in his position, I wouldn't."

Clara looked as though she'd been punched in the gut.

"Ahmed! How can you say that?"

"It's the truth. Do you really think it's worth his time to come to a besieged country to try to unearth some clay tablets that may or may not exist?"

"This is not just about 'clay tablets,' Ahmed; it's about discovering Genesis according to Abram. That's like somebody telling Schliemann that it wasn't worth his trouble to look for Troy, or telling Evans to give up on finding Knossos. What's wrong with you lately?"

"Don't you see what's happening to this country, Clara? Other people go hungry so that you can live a privileged life. You don't see the anguish of mothers helplessly watching their children waste away for lack of medicine, so your grandfather can hoard all the medicine he needs. In the Yellow House, the real world doesn't exist."

"What on earth has gotten into you, Ahmed? What have I done to deserve this? You started shunning me in Rome, and since we've come back you've made it clear that you're more and more disgusted and uncomfortable with me every day. Why?"

They stared at each other, weighing the perhaps unbridgeable distance that had opened between them without their knowing when it happened or quite why.

"We'll talk about this later. I don't think this is the time," Ahmed said to her finally.

"I agree," Clara said, turning away from him. "Let's go home."

Four armed men escorted them back through the city.

When they arrived at the Yellow House, Clara immediately ran to the kitchen, looking for Fatima, while Ahmed closed himself up in his office. He listened to Beethoven's *Eroica*, poured himself a whiskey on the rocks, and sat down in an armchair with his eyes closed, trying to pull himself together. He could see but two alternatives: either leave the Yellow House forever and go into exile, or go on dying inside, little by little. If he stayed, he would have to reconcile with Clara, but she was not one to tolerate half measures, especially with regard to her emotions. But could he go on living with her as though nothing were wrong with him, with them?

He opened his eyes to encounter Alfred Tannenberg's merciless gaze.

He kept his voice steady. "Hello, Alfred. What's on your mind?"

"What's happening?" the old man said, his eyes never leaving Ahmed's.

"What do you mean?"

"Where are the tablets, Ahmed?"

"Oh! Of course! Sorry—I should have brought the box to you the moment we arrived. I came straight to my office; I have a headache and I'm tired."

"Problems in the ministry?"

"It's the country that has problems, Alfred. What happens in the Ministry of Culture at this point is irrelevant. There's nothing to do, no matter how well we keep up the pantomime of our normal lives."

"Are you going to start criticizing Saddam now?"

"I could, although someone would surely denounce me and I'd wind up in jail."

"It wouldn't benefit us for Saddam to be killed at this point, Ahmed. The status quo is best for our business."

"Not even you, Alfred, will be able to change the course of history. The United States is going to attack Iraq, and they will take over the country. You of all people should be able to empathize with their rationale—it'll be good for *their* business."

"They won't do it. Bush is a bully, a blusterer. All threats. His father could have gotten rid of Saddam during the Gulf War, but he didn't."

"Maybe he didn't want to, maybe he couldn't. But the past is irrelevant—this time, they will attack. And they'll run right over us. We'll fight, first against them, then among ourselves—Sunnis against Shiites, Shiites against Kurds, Kurds against any other faction, it makes no difference. The die is cast, Alfred."

"What absolute nonsense!" Tannenberg shouted. "Suddenly you have the gift of prophecy, and we're all doomed!"

"You know I'm right—better than I do, I imagine. If you didn't, you wouldn't be pushing so hard for this excavation in Safran. You wouldn't have gone public. I've always admired your intelligence and your cool head. You know exactly what's going to happen."

"Quiet! Not another word!"

"No, it's best that we talk, that we say aloud what we hardly dare think, because that's the only way we're going to be able to avoid making any more mistakes. We need to be honest with each other."

"How dare you speak to me this way! In my own home! You're nothing, Ahmed—nothing more than I've allowed you to be."

"Yes, of course. I'm what you've allowed me to be, what you've wanted me to be—never what I've wanted to be. But now we're all in the same boat. I assure you I'm not looking forward to the next few months. But since there's no longer any help for it, I'll try my best to keep our little vessel from capsizing."

"Say what you have to say. They may be the last words you ever speak in this house."

"I want to know what you've been planning. You always have an escape route, Alfred. But even if Picot decides to come and dig, the most we'll have is six months, and in that short time there's no way we can uncover anything."

"I'm protecting Clara by securing her future. It's clear to me now that *you* aren't the man to protect her. The Bible of Clay is Clara's inheritance, her birthright. When she finds it, she'll never have to worry about anything for the rest of her life. She'll receive international recognition—she'll be established forever as the archaeologist she's always wanted to be."

"Clara doesn't need anybody to protect her. Your granddaughter is stronger than you've ever been willing to recognize. She doesn't need anybody or anything—just the freedom to get out of this mess."

"You're delusional." Alfred's voice was quiet now, cooled from heated to glacial.

"I'm more sane than I've ever been," Ahmed replied in the same even tone. "Iraq will be gone soon, which is why you're preparing to return to Cairo. You aren't going to be here when the bombs fall, when the Americans hunt down Saddam's closest friends and allies."

"I'm dying," the old man said matter-of-factly. "A tumor is destroying my liver. I have nothing to gain—or lose. I shall die in Cairo—within six months, I should think, maybe less. But not until the Bible of Clay is found. Even if this whole country is torn apart, I'll pay as many men as it takes to work around the clock in Safran."

"What if it doesn't exist—the Bible of Clay?"

"It's there. I know it."

"The tablets could be shattered in a million pieces. Then what will you do?"

Tannenberg said nothing at first, but he made no effort to hide his contempt for Ahmed.

"I'll tell you what I'm going to do now—I'm going to take charge of Clara's affairs. I can no longer trust you."

At this, the old man turned on his heel and left the room. Ahmed ran his hand over his forehead. He was sweating and exhausted.

He poured himself another whiskey and knocked it back. Then he poured another, but this one he decided to drink slowly, as he gathered his thoughts.

13

ENRIQUE GÓMEZ THOMSON WAS WALKING UNDER THE stately, shady trees of the Parque de María Luisa. The photographs of the murder—the execution—of those two poor souls had tied a knot in his stomach.

Frankie had insisted that they see each other. They'd met precious few times since they'd gone their separate ways almost sixty years ago. At first, George had opposed the meeting with all the energy he could muster, but Frankie had finally convinced him that they'd be much less visible in Seville than anywhere else. Besides, they would meet only for as long as necessary—a few hours at the most.

The three friends had decided to converge in the dark, cool bar of the Hotel Alfonso XIII. Emma, Frankie's wife, had been determined to stay at Seville's premier hotel.

Rocío, on the other hand, was uneasy. For several days she'd been hounding Enrique with questions that he dodged or simply ignored. Fortunately, that afternoon she'd gone to her sister's house—her niece was having a fitting for her wedding dress and Rocío wanted to be there.

As soon as he heard Rocío leave the house, he left too. He walked through the narrow, winding streets and the half-hidden plazas of the Barrio de Santa Cruz and headed to the park, where he ambled aimlessly, killing time until his appointment with his friends of years long past. He needed some fresh air.

George was sitting at a table in the far corner of the bar. Enrique joined him. Both men's eyes were misty with emotion at meeting face-to-face after so many years. But they did not embrace; they knew they couldn't call attention to themselves.

"You look good," George told him.

"You too."

"We're old men, now—although you're not as old as I am."

"A year younger, George, just a year."

"So where's Frankie?"

"I imagine he'll be along any minute; they're staying here at the hotel."

"Yes, that's what he told me—Emma insisted."

"It's all right. They had to stay somewhere, after all. Tell me what you've been thinking."

"Alfred is dying, he knows that it's just a matter of months. So he's thrown everything aside, with no regard for the consequences."

"That's what I think too. But what does he want?"

"He wants his granddaughter to find the Bible of Clay and to have for herself everything that that will mean."

"What about this Picot he's trying to hire?"

"You can't undertake an excavation of that magnitude without professionals, without real archaeologists. Alfred can hire half of Baghdad to carry the dirt, but he needs competent archaeologists to oversee the operation, and Iraq doesn't have any."

Just then Frank dos Santos entered the bar, peering into the dimness for his friends. He made his way over to them without a gesture and simply sat down and signaled the waiter, who came over to take his order.

"I'm glad to see you two," he said as soon as they were alone. "I don't think we've changed so much—just got an extra few decades on us!" He laughed out loud.

"Well, we can console ourselves with the thought that we're as healthy as we were sixty years ago. Though now I'm afraid we're on our final lap," said George, and then got back to the business at hand. "What do you think Alfred is up to?"

"Oh, Alfred! He's doing what any desperate man would do," Frank replied casually. "Your friends in the Pentagon are about to incinerate Saddam. Who knows whether Iraq will even exist anymore within a few months, so he's got no option: either find the Bible of Clay now or let it slip out of his hands forever."

"We could try to find it after the war," George mused.

"You know how wars start, but you never know how they'll end." Enrique's implication was clear, and his two friends could only nod in agreement.

"When will they start the bombing?" Enrique asked.

"March, at the latest," replied George.

"So we have about six months at most," Frankie said. "Six months to find the Bible of Clay."

"If the Americans hadn't bombed between Tell Muqayyar and Basra two months ago, the structure would never have even been found—fate wanted it to be now," Enrique said without much conviction. "So, what do we do?"

"If he finds the tablets intact, it will go down in history as one of the great archaeological discoveries of all time. Not to mention the value of the tablets on the antiquities market. And that doesn't take into account everything the Vatican will do to get its hands on them, considering that they'd be proof of the patriarch Abraham's divine inspiration," George said, almost to himself. "Genesis told by Abraham: an extraordinary discovery."

"If Alfred does find them," Frank said pensively, "he'll keep them for himself or his granddaughter, you can be sure, so . . ."

"So he'll do anything he can to take advantage of the little time he has," George finished the thought. "But why put his granddaughter out in front on this?"

Enrique had the answer: "He had her stake her claim, so nobody will take the tablets away from her. Now every archaeologist in the world knows that a local group headed up by Ahmed Husseini and his unpredictable wife have found the remains of a temple in Iraq and that it may hold tablets dictated by Abraham himself. Whatever happens, nobody will be able to claim the discovery as his own. Which explains that little number in Rome."

"He's risking a lot," Frank observed.

"Yes, but he's dying, so he has few alternatives," Enrique insisted. "So, George, do your people know who hired the Italians?"

George shook his head. "We know they were men from a company called Security Investigations, hired to follow Clara. But my men haven't found anything in the Security Investigations files—not a single shred. The contract must have been made directly with one of the higher-ups, someone who didn't have to give any explanations, just orders. The owner of Security Investigations is a former cop who made his name going after the Mafia; he was decorated several times and has friends everywhere in the police force. So the slightest error and the only thing we'll have is the Italian police on our tail."

"But we need to know who hired those men and why. We have one whole flank exposed," insisted Frank.

"You're right. We have to take extra security measures and avoid making any mistakes. There's a leak somewhere, or else Alfred has earned himself an enemy among his own associates," George reasoned.

"A black hole somewhere that we just can't see." Enrique felt the knot in the pit of his stomach twist tighter.

"Yes." George nodded. "There is a black hole, and we have to plug it. There's something new here, something we can't control. But Alfred we can handle. Our people over there reported that Ahmed Husseini seems to be breaking from our old friend. A few days ago he was heard shouting at him. Clara's husband has always struck me as a brave and intelligent man. Might we enlist him?"

"Judging by the last report on the activities at the Yellow House, I fear his conscience is beginning to bother him," Frank said. "There's nothing more dangerous than somebody who decides to go straight at the last minute. They'll do anything to try to make up for their past transgressions."

"Then we won't count on him; we'll simply use him," George said decisively. "And now, my friends, this will, I think, be the last time we ever see one another. Let's make the most of it and agree on every step that we're going to take from here on out. There's a very great deal at stake—"

"What's at stake," Frank interrupted him, "is being able to die quietly in our own homes when the time comes."

Enrique Gómez felt another stab of pain in his gut.

The three men went on talking well into the evening, reviewing bulky manila folders George handed around.

It was after ten-thirty when they finally broke off. They had drunk several whiskeys and shared several small plates of tapas. Enrique had received two impatient calls from Rocío, who asked him where he was and whether he'd be home for dinner. Frank called Emma to tell her to go ahead and take a taxi, he'd meet her at the *tablao*, where they had reserved a table for the flamenco show.

I'm glad I don't have to answer to anyone, thought George. It had not been easy to preserve his solitude, especially in the face of never-ending arguments from well-meaning friends who had constantly urged him to find a wife. But he had stood firm and won the game at last. He lived with a staff of servants who cared for him in silence, never interfering with or trying to change his routines. That was all he needed.

He was the first to depart. He walked to the Mercedes-Benz he had rented in Marbella. Given his advanced age, the rental company had been hesitant to let him drive it off the lot, but there was nothing that money couldn't arrange. Besides, he couldn't resist: German technology was still the best.

Frank headed upstairs to his room, while Enrique Gómez stepped out into the warmth of the night, having decided to walk home to his house in Barrio de Santa Cruz. He couldn't breathe. Not even the meeting with his old friends had helped ease his anxiety. On the contrary, he had smashed right up against his past, as though he'd walked into a plate-glass window. His friends were the mirror of reality, a reality he had successfully hidden from his entire family—except Rocío. That was why he knew he'd never be able to deceive his wife. She knew him; she knew who he had been.

14

"ALFRED, NO! I WILL NOT ALLOW YOU TO ENLIST IN THE army. Continue with your studies; you can be just as useful as a civilian."

"Father, Germany needs me," the young man insisted.

"But not as a soldier on the front lines. You will do your part once you complete your education."

"Georg is going to sign up this week; Franz and Heinrich too."

Herr Tannenberg held his head in his hands. "Come, son! You don't think their parents are going to allow that, do you?" His stern gaze fixed on his son. "We've all agreed: The four of you must complete your doctoral studies."

"Germany needs men who are ready to die for the Fatherland."

"Any idiot can die, but Germany cannot afford to lose the best of the nation's youth. Who do you think will run the country once we've won the war?"

Herr Tannenberg knew that his headstrong son remained unconvinced. He would obey, of course, but never surrender.

"Very well, Father, I will do as you wish, but I hope you will reconsider your decision."

"I will think about it, Alfred. Now go talk to your mother. She is making arrangements for a party, a refined evening of music here at home, and she wants you to attend. The Hermanns will be coming with their daughter, Greta. We want you to become acquainted. She will make you the perfect wife. You are both pure, strong, intelligent Aryans and will be able to give Germany fine, strong children."

"I thought you wanted me to concentrate on my studies."

"You're also old enough to find a wife. We'd like that wife to be Greta."

"I have no interest in marrying."

"I understand that at your age you may not wish to marry yet, but in time you'll change your mind. You must begin to think about the future."

"Did you choose my mother or did your father choose her for you?"

"That question is impertinent."

"I just want to know whether it is a tradition in our family for the fathers to decide who their sons will marry." Alfred calmed down and lowered his voice. "But don't worry; I like Greta as well as any other girl. She's pretty enough at least, even though she's perfectly stupid."

"How can you say that? One day she will be the mother of your children."

"I didn't say I wanted to marry an intelligent woman. I do prefer Greta, really. She does possess one excellent quality: She almost never talks."

Herr Tannenberg had had enough. He would hear no more slander against the daughter of his friend Fritz Hermann.

Hermann was a high-ranking officer in the SS, a man who had spent many days with Himmler himself at Wewelsburg Castle, near the historic city of Paderborn, in Westphalia. There, twelve elite officers of the SS, who comprised the chapter of Himmler's "Germanic Order of the Round Table," gathered once a year to perform their secret rituals, the details of which were unknown to Herr Tannenberg. Each member of the group had a chair with a silver plaque on which was engraved his name. Herr Tannenberg was well aware that Fritz had his own chair.

Thanks to his friendship with Fritz Hermann, Herr Tannenberg's small textile factory was doing extremely well, unblemished by the economic crisis that was now crippling Germany. Fritz had recommended to his superiors that they order military uniforms for some units from his friend Tannenberg's factory, and Tannenberg was now also manufacturing ties and shirts for the SS.

But Tannenberg wanted to seal his relationship with Fritz Hermann. How better than a marriage between his son Alfred and Fritz's oldest daughter?

Alfred was right, of course. And although tolerable, Greta was not the most attractive of young women: blond, with blue eyes, though they bulged a bit, and lily-white skin. But she tended toward the *zaftig*, as one could see in her pillowy white hands. Her mother, Frau Hermann, subjected her to strict weight-control measures, and her father required her to perform physical exercise daily, in the vain hope that she might become slim and graceful.

There were no longer any Jewish professors at the university. By now most had fled the country, leaving behind all their belongings. Those who had stayed believed that, in time, reason would prevail—after all, they'd done nothing and were loyal Germans like everyone else. *They* were now housed in concentration camps. Thus, it mattered to no one that neither good Professor Cohen nor good Professor Wessler had ever returned from Haran. Although they were two of the world's leading experts in the Sumerian language, even before their unfortunate deaths they had not been allowed in the classroom. They found work in the expedition to Haran only because the chancellor of the university, who was suspected by many of having Jewish blood himself, had aided their departure from Germany two years earlier. And so they had remained in Haran, staying on even when the other members of the team had returned when the time allotted for excavation was over. Unfortunately, Syria was even less kind to them than Germany would have been.

Alfred had invited his three friends to the evening of music arranged by his mother, hoping they would make the obligation a bit less tiresome. He enjoyed music, but not these concerts at home, when his mother sat at the piano and her friends took up other instruments and "surprised" their guests with pieces they had been rehearsing for weeks on end. He did admit to himself, though, that Greta was a virtuoso on the cello.

He admired his mother. Tall, thin, with chestnut hair and hazel eyes, Helena Tannenberg was a woman of natural grace and elegance who inspired murmurs of admiration wherever she went. There was no woman in the world more beautiful than she.

Seeing her beside Greta reminded him of the story of the ugly duckling and the swan.

"So your father wants you married off to Greta. Lucky man!" joked Georg, pinching Alfred.

"We'll see who your father chooses for you."

"He knows it's no use. I shall never marry, never," Georg declared defiantly.

"You'll have to; we all have to—the Führer wants us producing children of pure Aryan blood," Heinrich said, laughing.

"*Ja*, well, you can have as many children as you want, and one more for me," insisted Georg.

"Come, Georg, surely one of these lovely young things catches your eye! They're not all bad," chided Franz.

"Have you not yet detected my absolute lack of interest in the female sex?"

The others diverted the conversation toward other, less delicate subjects. No one wanted to hear Georg again explain the inferiority of women to men.

Alfred's father joined the young friends; with him was Fritz Hermann.

Colonel Hermann asked after the boys' studies and encouraged them to start thinking seriously about their contribution to Germany's war effort.

"Study, but don't forget that the Reich needs young men like you on the front lines."

"Could we get into the SS?"

Alfred's question took his father aback; his friends, too, were a bit startled.

"You, in the SS? That would be wonderful! Our Reichführer would be so proud to have dedicated young men such as yourselves. I will see to it that you are accepted at once. Tomorrow afternoon I'll expect you in my office—you know where the headquarters of the ESHA are, on Prinz Albrechtstrasse. Already this fine evening has turned out to be even better than I expected!" Fritz Hermann exclaimed delightedly.

Just then, Herr Tannenberg and Colonel Hermann were called away to another group, and Georg quickly rounded on Alfred.

"What the hell are you doing? I don't want to join the SS or the Gestapo or any other of the Reich's glorious organizations. What I want to do is continue our excavations in Syria. I want to be an archaeologist, not a soldier, and I thought the rest of you felt the same."

"Come on, Georg! We're going to have to join the army sooner or later—we can't hold out forever. My father is losing patience with me; he doesn't want me in the army, so fine—I'll join the SS, where my future father-in-law will find me a comfortable desk far away from the front lines. The rest of you should do the same, or you'll wind up in a much less desirable position," Alfred told them.

"You know, my friend," Heinrich spoke up, slightly inebriated, "you're right. I'll go with you to Hermann's office tomorrow. I could use a nice comfortable spot in the SS. I'm tired of depending on my father's largesse, anyway."

"So the SS it is," Franz said, by way of joining the other two.

"What better way to go!" Alfred said, clapping him on the back.

"Absolutely. I'm with you." Franz nodded again.

"What idiots you three are! Where has all this come from?" Georg's voice betrayed desperation.

"From being at war and our duty to the Fatherland. My father is right—any fool can die. We should go where we can do the most good, far from any real danger. Not to mention, we might be able to do some good for ourselves on the side. I think I'll ask Hermann to send me to one of the camps, perhaps Dachau. Seems like a fine place to spend the war."

Colonel Hermann's aide asked them to wait in a room next to the office and told them that as soon as the colonel finished with Herr Himmler, he'd see them.

The four friends looked at one another with smiles and raised eyebrows, then settled in to wait patiently. A half hour later, Colonel Hermann himself came out to greet them.

"Come in, come in! I'm so delighted to see you all. I have spoken to the Reichsführer, and as soon as you've completed the formalities and been sworn in to the SS, I'll take you to meet him."

Fritz Hermann listened as the young men explained their ambitions for service, and he agreed fully: When it was time, Alfred and Heinrich would be sent to the political office of one of the work camps where enemy prisoners and undesirables were held; Franz would be deployed to the front with the Waffen; and Georg would enter an intelligence unit.

"Perfect! Perfect! In the SS you will be able to develop your native intelligence and character to its fullest potential."

That afternoon, the four friends left Hermann's office as members of Hitler's elite SS. Fritz Hermann had most certainly been efficient, and in just slightly over two hours he had found each one a place at headquarters; that way they could finish their studies at the university while they were serving the Homeland.

"To Germany!" said Alfred, raising his stein aloft.

"To us," Georg toasted.

It was a long night; the four didn't return home until the sun had begun to creep above the housetops. They were beginning a new chapter in their lives, but they had each sworn that nothing would destroy their friendship, no matter where the future took them.

Two years later, after their education and service in Berlin were completed, Fritz Hermann sent them on to their respective destinations. Franz was sent to one of the SS's special commando units, while Georg was taken into the Reich Main Security Office—the RSHA, as it was commonly known. The intelligence service was under the direction of feared SS Obergruppenführer Reinhard Heydrich, the "Blond Beast." Alfred would be in Austria, as liaison officer with Reich Security Headquarters, where Heinrich would accompany him as supervisor of the SS Headquarters for Administration and Economy, a unit in charge of supervising the work camps.

In Austria, the major work camp was Mauthausen, one of Himmler's favorites.

15

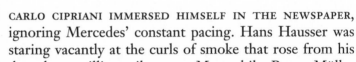CARLO CIPRIANI IMMERSED HIMSELF IN THE NEWSPAPER, ignoring Mercedes' constant pacing. Hans Hausser was staring vacantly at the curls of smoke that rose from his old pipe, his thoughts a million miles away. Meanwhile, Bruno Müller sat stolidly, avoiding eye contact with everyone in the room.

Luca Marini had asked to see them at one; it was now one-thirty and the secretary refused to give them any information, even whether Luca was in his office.

It was almost two when the former police officer entered the reception area and, his face grave, asked them into his office.

"I've just had a meeting with the director-general of state security. I wish I hadn't," Luca said, closing the door behind him.

"What happened?" Carlo asked.

"The government isn't buying Mercedes' account of my men's trip to Iraq. They need something more, something to help them keep drumming into Italy that Saddam is a monster. That way, the government paves the way for public support if it decides to send troops to Iraq. This case is good for the government. It's even being talked about on TV."

"I'm sorry, my friend," was the only thing that Carlo could manage to say. "We've got you into a terrible mess."

"If only we could tell the truth," Luca insisted. "If only you people would tell me what all this is about."

"Luca, please," Carlo pleaded. "You know that's not going to happen."

"All right, then, here's where we stand. I told state security your version of events, and they looked at me like I was crazy. They pressured me, of course, but I stuck to it. They may call you, Mercedes, possibly just to satisfy their curiosity about a person of your age and position sending private investigators to Iraq."

"We haven't committed any crime," Mercedes said irritably.

"No, you haven't. Nor have I. But two of my men are dead and nobody knows why—except the four of you, of course. Since any investigations into your background, Mercedes, will no doubt reveal that you are a person of unquestionable integrity, you're probably safe. But I want to make crystal clear to you that the director of state security is very, shall we say, concerned. Personally, I've never seen a politician actually concerned about anything—I just think he sees a way to make a little political profit off this. But in order to do that he needs a story. And he's going to keep pushing until he gets one."

"That's something that we are simply not able to give," Hans said flatly.

"I think the best thing to do is go back home," Bruno suggested.

"Yes, that would be best," Luca agreed, "because I have not the slightest doubt that we're all being followed. So please don't all leave the building together—leave one by one, and take your time about it. And try to act naturally. As you said, you haven't done anything illegal."

They were all silent for a few seconds, each of them lost in their own thoughts. Then Hans spoke up again.

"Since that's the way things stand, it's best we face them head on. You, Signore Marini, will continue to tell the truth, precisely as you have been doing thus far."

"No, I haven't told the whole truth," Luca protested.

"Yes, you have, as far as you are able. You can't tell what you don't know," the professor reminded him. "As for us, we should talk a bit before we go our separate ways. I think, Bruno, your anxiety is telling you that we should all go back home. Of course we have to go back, but not just now, not running as though we were fugitives. We are all respectable old men—and women, in your case, Mercedes. We are simply a bunch of old friends. So, Carlo, I will very gladly accept your invitation to lunch, if you're so kind as to invite me, and I think we should all go. If the police want to talk to us, we'll tell them the truth, that we're a group of friends who've met in Rome and that Mercedes, who is the dashing and devil-may-care member of our group, has decided that Iraq is a very good place to do business because, when the war is over, everything the Americans destroyed will have to be rebuilt. There's nothing wrong, or even suspicious, in the fact that she, the owner of a very large construction company, might want a piece of that pie. So far as I know, she hasn't led any demonstrations or carried any signs denouncing the war—or have you, my dear?"

"No, not yet at least, although I really thought I might go to the demonstrations in Barcelona." She smiled.

"Well, now you can't," Hans told her bluntly. "Perhaps another time."

"You take my breath away, Professor," Luca said. "Apparently you didn't hear me: The director-general of state security for Italy is determined to get to the bottom of what happened to these two dead men, because his higher-ups want to get to the bottom of it."

"If there's nothing there, there's nothing the police or anyone else can do," Hausser insisted.

"But there *is* something there—there are two dead bodies," Marini replied angrily.

"Enough!" Carlo broke in. "I agree with Hans; we can't act like criminals. We haven't killed anybody. If need be, I'll speak with some friends in the government, patients of mine. But we need not flee the country or leave this office one by one in secret. I refuse to feel guilty."

Defeat and resignation colored Luca's face. "You all seem very secure about this. . . . All right, so much the better. As far as I'm concerned, the case is closed—unless my old colleagues call me again or we all see each other on television. If something comes up, I'll call you."

Once outside, Carlo indeed suggested that they all go to his house for a late lunch, where they could talk comfortably among themselves.

But they ate practically in silence, making intermittent small talk. When they retired to the living room for coffee, Carlo asked his housekeeper that they not be interrupted and closed the doors.

"We have to make a decision," he said when he'd turned back to his friends.

"It's made," Mercedes reminded him. "We'll hire one of those companies, and send a professional to find Tannenberg and do what has to be done. That's all we have to talk about."

"Are we all still agreed about that?" Carlo asked.

The affirmative reply from his three friends was immediate.

"I have the phone number of a company, Global Group. The

owner, a man named Tom Martin, is a friend of Luca's. Luca said we could use his name when we called."

"Carlo, I don't know whether it's a good idea to keep getting Luca involved."

"You may be right, Mercedes, but we don't know anyone else in this business, so I say we call this Martin. I hope Luca will forgive us."

They agreed that Hans would set up the deal. He would make an appointment with Tom Martin in London personally and test the waters. What they intended to ask Martin to do was simple: send a man to Iraq. They already knew where Clara Tannenberg lived, so sooner or later their man would find Alfred. Then he would choose the right moment and kill him. For a professional, that shouldn't be so hard.

Bruno insisted that he wanted to get back to Vienna as soon as possible. He was no longer comfortable in Rome and in fact thought it was past time that they all went their separate ways again. They needed to work out the logistics of staying in touch from their separate locations.

"In case our home phones are tapped, we shouldn't use them," Hans suggested. "We can buy disposable cell phones and use them once only. They're untraceable."

"Let's not get paranoid, please," Mercedes said.

"No, Hans is right," Carlo said. "We need to be careful. I don't think disposable phones are a bad idea. We'll figure out a way to get the numbers to each other, maybe by e-mail," he continued.

"But if they intercept our phone calls, they can do the same thing with our e-mails. The Internet is the least secure place in the world to keep a secret."

"Oh, Bruno, don't be such a pessimist!" Mercedes scolded him. "Each of us will open a fake Hotmail account and send the others the telephone numbers, and we'll stay in contact that way. But we have to be careful, because Hotmail isn't secure; anybody can access our accounts, so we need to be a little cryptic when we send messages."

They devoted part of the evening to deciding the names they would use on the Internet, and Hans came up with a cryptogram in which the letters represented numbers, the numbers of the cell phones they would constantly be buying and discarding once they were used.

It was late when the four friends took their leave of one another, embracing warmly and a bit sadly. The next day, Bruno and Hans would be leaving Rome. Mercedes would linger a couple of days longer so as not to give the impression, if the police were watching them, that the whole group was fleeing.

"So—what's Picot decided to do?" Robert Brown asked impatiently as Ralph Barry hung up the phone.

"My contact says Picot returned from Iraq very impressed, though he does say it would be crazy to go over now to excavate: There's no time. He curses Bush and Saddam both, says they're two of a kind."

"You haven't answered my question, Ralph. I want to know whether he's going to go or not."

"He hasn't decided, but apparently he hasn't discarded the idea completely. In the meantime, he's gone to Madrid."

"Could we get Dukais' Planet Security men into the expedition, if it happens?" Robert asked. George had made it clear to him that they needed their own man on the scene.

"Do you really think Dukais' gorillas can pass themselves off as archaeology students?"

"Of course they can! I need men on that excavation. So Dukais is just going to have to find people with the right look."

"And with a knowledge of history, geography, geology, et cetera—I can't see it, Robert, I just can't see it. Those thugs couldn't even tell you where Mesopotamia is, let alone the difference between it and the newest brew at Starbucks."

"Well, they're going to have to take a quick course in the Middle East, then. We'll give them a bonus if they can manage to pass themselves off as students, or even professors."

"Jesus, Robert! In academia, everybody knows everybody else, at least by reputation. They'll be found out in a second."

Brown opened the door of the office and poked his head out, startling his elegantly suited and very discreet private secretary.

"Is there something I can do, Mr. Brown?" asked Smith.

"Dukais hasn't come in yet?"

"No, sir. I'd have let you know."

"What time did you tell him?"

"At four, sir, as you said."

"It's four-ten."

"Yes, sir. He must have been delayed in traffic."

"Dukais is an idiot."

"Yes, sir."

At just that moment, the imposing figure of Paul Dukais appeared in the doorway.

"It's about time!" thundered Brown.

"Sorry, Robert. The shuttle was running late, and Washington traffic is hell at rush hour."

"You might have left early."

"A little anal lately, aren't we," the president of Planet Security replied coolly.

In Brown's office, after glasses of whiskey had been passed around, Ralph tried to reduce the tension between the two men.

"Paul, Robert wants men on the archaeological mission that Yves Picot may be preparing to organize. I'll send you Picot's dossier, but for now you should know he's French, rich, an ex-Oxford professor, a womanizer, and a bit of an Indiana Jones. But he knows what he's doing, and he knows everybody in the field."

"So what kind of men are we talking about?"

"For a start, they have to be university graduates, men who can talk naturally about academia. They can't be Americans, and can't be tied to us. You have to find them in Europe, some Arab country maybe, but not here."

"Plus they must have impeccable archaeological credentials and be willing to kill whomever we target, right?" Dukais asked ironically.

"Exactly." The tone of Robert's answer left no doubt of his irritation.

"Which reminds me, Robert—I've prepped the teams of men you wanted stationed at the various borders surrounding Iraq. When you give the order, they'll be deployed."

"They'll have to wait a while longer. Let's fix this problem first."

"I don't know how to fix it, Robert. I don't know any university-graduates-cum-mercenaries, or vice versa. I'll look around the Balkans; there may be somebody there."

"Good idea. They've been killing people there since they were kids. There must be university graduates looking for cash who've been on one side or the other."

Ralph Barry listened to their conversation with a mixture of admiration and revulsion. His conscience had been bought off years ago, and it had gone for a mint. He was no longer astounded by the things he heard, although Robert himself always surprised him. He was a Janus, and there were very few people who had seen both faces. Most people would have said he was a well-educated, refined man of excellent taste and manners, a man of his word, incapable even of running a red light. But Ralph knew another Robert Brown, a man who was cruel, unscrupulous, foul-mouthed, with a greed for money and power that had no bounds. Ralph had a feeling that the powerful George Wagner might be the only man before whom Brown trembled. He'd never asked much about that connection; he knew that he'd get no answer, and what Robert valued most was discreet, even hermetic loyalty.

Paul would call them as soon as he'd found any men who might fit the bill—*if* he found them.

Once again, Picot was meticulously studying the slides he'd made of the tablets. Fabian Tudela was watching him out of the corner of his eye. He knew that Yves was coming to a decision and that it almost certainly wouldn't be the right one. But that was the way his friend was. They'd known each other since Yves' teaching days at Oxford, when Fabian was working on his doctorate, the subject of which was cuneiform inscriptions. Both men were quasi-misfits at that venerable institution; they'd hit it off immediately.

And they both were in love with Mesopotamia, a place known today, thanks to the wonders of British colonialism, as Iraq.

Fabian's fascination with Mesopotamia began during his first visit to Paris, at the age of ten. He and his father had seen so many wonderful things in the Louvre, but when they entered a gallery lined with ancient artifacts, Fabian felt a sudden surge of interest within him. He'd never forget the impression the Code of Hammurabi had made, his father's explanation that on that stone pillar were engraved laws as ancient as human civilization, based on the *lex talionis*, the law of retribution. His father explained that Law 196 of the Code said: *If a man put out the eye of another man, his eye shall be put out.* That day, Fabian decided he wanted to be an archaeologist, to go and discover lost kingdoms in Mesopotamia.

"So is it yes or no?"

"It's madness," Picot replied.

"Of course, but it's also now or never. We can only imagine what'll be left after the war."

"If Bush is to be believed, Iraq will become an Arcadia, so we'd be able to excavate as easily as going on vacation."

"But you and I both know that this war is going to turn Iraq into another Lebanon. You know the Middle East—the Iraqis hate Saddam, but they also hate the Americans. In fact, everywhere in the Middle East they hate all Westerners, and they're partly right to do so. We've colonized them, we've given them nothing in return, we've propped up corrupt regimes, we've sold them things they haven't needed, we've been unable to create a middle class or a real intelligentsia, and the people are poorer and more frustrated every day. The religious fanatics are having a field day—they teach for free in the madrassas, they've created hospitals to treat people who can't pay for doctors or medications. . . . The Middle East is about to explode."

"Yes, but that doesn't apply to all of Iraq. Saddam has been a force for secularism, at least to a degree. Seriously, Fabian, will you never stop being such a child of the Left?"

"I'm a bit too old for you to call me a child, Yves. And as for being Leftist—I doubt I'll ever stop seeing the world as it is, even from the comfiest couch in my living room."

"So what would you do if you were on my couch?"

"Exactly what you'd do, even if it was wrong: I'd go. And when it's over, it's over."

"We could be incinerated if they start bombing."

"Yes, Yves—the answer to that, though, is to get out five minutes before that happens."

"And who would fund us?"

"We'd have to do it ourselves. I don't think my university, or any other, would give us a penny for a dig in Iraq. In Spain, most of us are against the war, and an excavation in Iraq right now will certainly seem like madness. Just as you say, it would be like throwing money out the window."

"Which means I'll have to finance it."

"And I'll put together the team. Several students at the Complutense would give anything to be able to go on a dig, even in Iraq."

"You've always told me that there are no great Mesopotamian specialists in Spain."

"There aren't—you and I will be the specialists. What we need are lots of students who'd love to be able to say they've done some real fieldwork."

"I'm not so sure we'll be able to find enough people to join us on this glorious adventure, Fabian. Do you think you can get a sabbatical for a year?"

"I'm not rich like you are; I depend on my check at the end of the month. But I'll talk to the dean to see what I can manage. When would we go?"

"Tomorrow. Today. Yesterday."

"Could I have a real date?"

"Next week is better than the week after. There's no time."

Fabian looked at his old friend. "Well, we should probably get started, then."

Laughing, the two friends gave each other a very American high five, then went out to celebrate with tapas in the Barrio de las Letras.

When in Spain, Picot always stayed at Fabian's place, in a room in the attic. From the little balcony he could see all the rooftops of Madrid. Picot considered it *his* room, in a way, since whenever he could, he ran away to this open, happy city where nobody asked where you'd come from or where you were going.

The morning after he and Fabian had reached their decision, Picot sat down at the desk in his friend's office and tried to call Iraq. It took a while to get in touch with Ahmed Husseini.

"Ahmed?"

"Yes?"

"It's Picot."

"Ah, Picot!" There was a pregnant silence as the Iraqi waited for the verdict.

"I've decided to go, and there's no time to waste. I'll tell you what I need—let me know if there's anything you can't get."

For the next half hour the two men discussed their requirements for the expedition. Though Ahmed was candid—almost brutally realistic—about what could and couldn't be found in Iraq, he did offer to finance part of the expedition.

"You want to put your money in it?" asked Yves, pleasantly surprised.

"It's not that I want to invest, it's that we want to cover most of the expenses. We'll finance the mission as far as we are able; you furnish the people and the equipment—that's the deal."

"And where are you going to get the money, if it's not indiscreet to ask?"

"The government will make an effort, because of what this mission means to Iraq at this juncture."

"Come on, Ahmed—I don't believe that."

"Believe it—it's the truth."

"I can't see Saddam investing a single dollar looking for ancient tablets, no matter how important they are. I want to know who's paying; otherwise, I'm not going."

Ahmed hesitated. "Part will come from the ministry . . . and part from Clara and her family. She has her own personal fortune, inherited from her parents. She's an only child."

"Which means I have to negotiate the Bible of Clay with your wife."

"It should be clear from the outset, Picot, that if we find the Bible, it belongs to Clara—she announced its existence to the world; her grandfather extracted the first two tablets and is investing the money needed for the excavation, no matter the cost. You'll be able to say that you were on the joint archaeological expedition with her."

"Great, now you're imposing conditions on me? Ahmed, without me, there is no archaeological expedition."

"Or without us either."

"I can wait for Saddam to fall and then—"

"Then it'll no doubt be destroyed."

"Why didn't you tell me about these conditions when I was in Iraq?"

"Honestly, I didn't think you'd agree to come."

"All right—shall we draw up a contract, a document that clearly states the part each of us will play in this?"

"That's a good idea. I'll prepare something, and then we'll talk about any changes you think should be made. Can I send it to you tomorrow?"

"No. E-mail it to me in the next hour. We either reach an agreement now or it's over."

By one o'clock, the two men had come to terms.

The document made clear that an archaeological mission was being undertaken, with the aid of Professor Yves Picot, in order to excavate an ancient temple–palace in which Clara Tannenberg believed might be found the remains of tablets resembling those found during another archaeological expedition in Haran years earlier, whereupon a scribe who signed himself "Shamas" had written that Abraham was going to relate to him the history of the world.

Ahmed made it clear that his wife was not going to allow anyone to strip her of the glory that was rightfully hers.

After lunch, Picot strode to Fabian's office and informed him of the details of the contract. Fabian had talked to some of his best students and several other professors about what he and Picot were planning and had invited them to a meeting that afternoon. Of the twenty or so who came, eight students signed up and two or three professors said they'd talk to the dean about a leave so they could go. They promised to meet with Fabian the next day to finalize details.

After the meeting, Picot and Fabian each picked up a telephone and began cold-calling colleagues around Europe. Most of them told the two men they were crazy. Some said they would think about it; all of them asked for more time.

Picot decided that he'd go to London the next day and then on to Oxford to meet personally with some friends, and then he'd return via

Paris and Berlin. Fabian volunteered to go to Rome and Athens, where he knew some professors.

It was Tuesday. They would reconvene in Madrid on Sunday and see what sort of team they'd been able to put together. The objective was to be in Iraq, on the ground digging, by October 1 at the latest.

Ralph Barry came into Robert Brown's office, smiling. "I've got good news."

"Tell me," Brown responded, unimpressed.

"Picot's *in*, Robert! The temptation was just too great for a guy like him. I've been talking to a colleague in Berlin. Picot is there recruiting professors and students for his Iraq expedition. He's also been in London and Paris, setting off quite a commotion in the archaeological community. Everybody thinks he's crazy, but some people have an unhealthy curiosity to go to Iraq.

"I don't think he's going to be able to find any superstars, but he'll convince some students and professors. So far, he's put together the most ragtag bunch you can imagine. They don't have a plan, they haven't done any preliminary surveys of the site, no real analysis of the resources they'll be needing. Apparently Picot's being helped tremendously in all this by Fabian Tudela, a professor of archaeology at the Universidad Complutense in Madrid. He's an expert on Mesopotamia; he got his doctorate at Oxford and has worked on several digs around the Middle East. He's competent, for sure, and he's Picot's best friend. But I doubt they'll be able to do anything. In archaeology, six months is nothing."

"No, it's not, but they could get lucky. I hope they do."

"At any rate, they're moving fast. Shall I tell Dukais? He may be able to slip some of his boys in, if he's found anyone."

"Yeah, fill him in on where Picot is and who he's meeting with. Maybe he's come up with some likely candidates."

"It won't be easy. . . ."

"Just talk to him."

When he was alone, Robert Brown dialed a number and waited tensely for an answer. He calmed down when he heard Wagner's voice.

"I'm sorry to bother you, but I wanted you to know that Yves Picot is organizing a group to go to Iraq."

"Ah, Picot! I didn't think he'd be able to resist. Have you done everything as I said?"

"I'm doing it."

"There can't be any foul-ups."

"I know. There won't be."

Brown hesitated a moment or two before he worked up the courage for his next question. "Do you know yet who sent the Italians?"

George's silence was worse than a reproach. The president of·the Mundo Antiguo Foundation began to sweat.

"See that things go as we've planned."

And with those words, George Wagner hung up.

Paul Dukais was taking notes on what Ralph Barry was telling him on the phone.

"So he's in Berlin," the president of Planet Security stated more than asked.

"That's right, and he's also been in Paris. He'll be going on to London again before he returns to Madrid. It's September—maybe you can enroll your men in one of these universities so they can volunteer."

"You just told me that they're looking for fourth-year students—why would they take somebody who's just enrolled in some introductory course? I don't understand this insistence on joining the expedition. We can find another cover for them."

"Orders from the boss."

"Robert is impossible."

"Robert is nervous. These tablets are worth millions. Actually, their value would be incalculable if we can prove their provenance—a revolutionary discovery. Genesis according to Abraham."

"Okay, Ralph. Let's not go overboard. I've got to get to work. I'll call you if I've got something."

Mercedes was wandering aimlessly through the streets around the Piazza di Spagna. She'd bought a few things in the luxurious boutiques on the Via Condotti, the Via della Croce, the Via Fratina—a couple of handbags, silk scarves, a tailored skirt and jacket, a blouse, a pair of shoes. She was bored. She'd never particularly enjoyed shopping, although she labored over her elegant appearance. Buying classic clothes was an easy way to maintain it.

She was eager to get back to Spain, to Barcelona, to her business, and to start visiting her construction projects again, climbing up the scaffolding—to the terrified looks of the workmen who thought she was crazy.

Constant activity allowed her to live, kept her mind focused. She'd spent her whole life running away, avoiding being alone, although she had no one but herself to blame. She'd never married, never had children; she had no brothers or sisters or nieces or nephews, no living relatives at all. Her grandmother, her father's mother, had died years ago. The old lady had been an anarchist, tough as nails, who'd known far too many of Franco's prisons. She had also been the only person who'd helped Mercedes keep her feet on the ground, helped her feel that she was "just people," just another hardworking woman. "Fascists are who they are," she would say, "so we shouldn't be surprised by anything they do." That was the way she calmed her granddaughter's nightmares—by trying to convince her that everything happened just as it did because it flowed from the behavior of men who bore the stigma of evil.

She'd lived long enough to help Mercedes face life by doing just that—facing it head on.

Mercedes usually had lunch in her own office, just as she dined alone at home, in front of the TV.

Here she had to find someplace to sit down and rest and eat something. Then she'd walk back to the hotel and pack. She was departing the next day, on the first plane out. Carlo had said he'd stop by the hotel to have dinner with her at a nearby restaurant and say good-bye.

Carlo called her room from the lobby. When Mercedes came down, they embraced each other warmly, overcome with the torrent of emotions that had been building over the past weeks.

"Have you talked to Hans and Bruno?" she asked.

"Yes, they called when they got in. They're fine. Hans is so lucky to have Berta—she's a wonderful woman."

"Your children are wonderful too."

"Yes, they are, but I have three, and Hans has only one. He's lucky—Berta pampers him like a baby."

"Is Bruno all right? He worries me; he seems overwhelmed by the situation, scared even."

"*I'm* scared, Mercedes. And I imagine you are too. Our reasons for doing what we're doing don't mean we're above the law."

"That's the tragedy of being human—nothing we do is without its price. It was God's curse when he expelled us from the Garden."

"I didn't know you had suddenly become so religious!" Carlo laughed. "When Bruno called, I heard Deborah protesting in the background. He told me that she's very worried, that she even asked him to never see us again. They had a fight, and Bruno said he'd rather leave her, that nothing and no one would ever break his ties to us."

"Poor Deborah! I understand what she's going through."

"She never liked you."

"Almost nobody does."

"That's because you work at making it that way. You know that, don't you?"

"Is this my doctor or my friend talking?"

"Your friend, who also happens to be a doctor."

"You can heal bodies, but sometimes there's nothing that can be done for the soul."

"I know, but you should at least make an effort to see other people's points of view."

"I do. How do you think I've been able to live all these years? But since my grandmother died, all I have are you three—you're the only thing that keeps me alive. You and . . ."

"Revenge. And hatred. They've brought us this far." Carlo changed course. "Your grandmother was an extraordinary woman."

"She wasn't content to simply be a survivor like me; she had to stand up to everything and everybody. When she got out of prison she refused to change, refused to bend to the Fascists' will; she continued to organize clandestine meetings, cross the French border to sneak anti-Franco propaganda back into Spain, meet with old exiles there. I'll tell you a story: In the fifties and sixties, in every movie theater in Spain they would run a newsreel before the film, about what Franco and his ministers were doing. We lived in Mataró, near Barcelona, and there was an outdoor movie theater in the summer where we kids would play, eat sunflower seeds, that sort of thing. The minute Franco's face appeared, my grandmother would hawk up a ball of mucus, spit it out on the ground, and mutter, 'They think they've beaten us, but they're wrong—as long as we can think, we are free.' And she'd point to her head and say, 'They aren't the bosses up here.' I would look at her in horror, because I thought we might be arrested at any moment. But nothing ever happened."

"I remember she always dressed in black," said Carlo, "with that bun up here on top of her head, and her face covered with wrinkles. She was dignified. Despite the spitting," he added, smiling.

"She knew exactly what we were talking about, what we'd decided to do—she knew about our oath. And she never reproached me for it. On the contrary, she said whatever we had to do, we should do it with our heads and not be led by hate."

"I'm not sure we've done that."

"But we're trying, Carlo, we're trying. I think we're almost at the end now. I think we're very close to Tannenberg."

"I still wonder why he's revealed himself after so many years. I just can't figure it out, Mercedes."

"Monsters have feelings too. That woman may be his daughter, his granddaughter, his niece, who knows. From Marini's report, I think he sent her to Rome to recruit people to help them find those tablets she was talking about at the conference. They must be very important to him—so important that he's risked exposing himself."

"You really think monsters have feelings?"

"Look around, Carlo. Think of all the dictators surrounded by their loving families, grandkids on their knees, pets in their laps. Saddam, for instance—it didn't bother him to gas Kurdish villages, murder women, children, and old people, or dispose of anyone who opposed his regime. Yet people say he's spoiled his sons, given them everything. He pets those two monsters as though they were the eighth and ninth wonders of the world. Ceausescu, Stalin, Mussolini, Franco: All of them absolutely doted on their families."

"You're comparing apples and oranges, Mercedes." Carlo laughed. "You're putting them all in the same bag! You're an anarchist yourself!"

"My grandmother was an anarchist, and my grandfather too. My father was an anarchist. I come by it honestly!"

They sat in silence after that, avoiding going any deeper into wounds that were still bleeding.

"Has Hans called this Tom Martin yet?" Mercedes asked, to change the subject.

"No, but he'll let me know as soon as he's made an appointment. I assume he'll wait two or three days: he just got home, and Berta would be upset—terrified, I imagine—if he left again so soon."

"And what about your friend Luca?"

"You don't like him much, I know, but he's a good man and he's helped us—he's still helping us. He called me just before I came over here. No news; for now, the Italian authorities seem to have backed off. Which is good. But he thinks somebody's been snooping around in his files looking for information. There was nothing to find, because he never opened a case file—he did everything directly himself, kept no paperwork, gave orders to his men with a minimum of background, and never told them who the client was. He thinks somebody's also searched his office. He swept it for listening devices, but it came up clean. Even so, he called me from a pay phone. We're supposed to meet tomorrow. He'll come to the clinic."

"Is it Tannenberg?"

"That's the point—it could be him or it could be the police. For that matter, it could be somebody else."

"It could only be Tannenberg or the police—there's nobody else who would be interested in what happened."

"I suppose you're right."

They went on talking into the night. It would be a long time before they saw each other again.

16

"PAUL, I'VE FOUND A COUPLE OF MEN WHO FIT THE BILL. With a little more time, I can find a few more." Tom Martin's voice was steady and confident. He and Paul Dukais got along. They were in the same business: They provided security to some people, and they killed others. Their businesses were growing; globalization was a good thing. And of course, Iraq promised to be a windfall. They had each already signed several multimillion-dollar contracts and expected to be signing more.

"The only thing I don't have is time," Dukais said. "They've begun the countdown for the war."

"Don't complain—wars are big business. Besides, I've got a proposition for you, something we might do together. How many men do you have?" Martin asked.

"Right now over ten thousand under contract."

"Christ! I don't have nearly that many—but I don't want amateurs or fuckups either; I want men with experience."

"They're not hard to find. I'm starting to hire Asians."

"What difference does it make where they're from? What's important is that they're ready for combat. I've got quite a few former Yugoslavians: Serbs, Croatians, Bosnians—tough guys, maybe a little too eager to pull the trigger. These two I've found for you are real pieces of work; you'll have to keep a tight rein on them. They're young, but they're fucking crazy. They've killed more people than they can remember."

"How old are they?"

"Twenty-four and twenty-seven. Bosnian and Croatian. They finished school before the war in the Balkans heated up. Two survivors who lost most of their families. The Croatian's a good shot. He likes money. He's studying computer science now at the university; the perfect nerd. The Bosnian is a teacher."

"But neither one of them has studied history or archaeology?"

"No, I can't seem to find mercenaries with a penchant for history. But these two are young and they speak English. You know the Europeans salve their conscience by giving scholarships to poor kids from the Balkans, so if you move fast you can point them to something in any university you want to—Berlin, Paris—and once they're in you can find somebody to introduce them into Picot's circle."

"Easier said than done."

"Come on, Paul, think about it—it's easy to get people new identities. There are still idealists out there who are ready to put their lives on the line for anybody with a sad story to tell. And these two have a tearjerker. Give me Picot's contact and I'll see they meet him. Picot's paying the students he's taking to Iraq, so these two can say they need money for their studies."

"But why should Picot hire a computer guy and a teacher? He needs archaeologists and historians."

"Well, my friend, this is what I've got. Take it or leave it."

"I'll send one of my men to have a look at them and explain what we want. He'll be there tomorrow. Send me the bill."

"I will. When are you coming to London?"

"Within the week. I have a meeting with some clients we can share. I'll send you an e-mail."

Tom Martin hung up the phone. His Global Group was unquestionably Europe's best security firm; Paul Dukais' Planet Security was the best in the U.S. Together, the two companies controlled more than sixty-five percent of the business around the world. And some missions had to be taken on as joint enterprises; that was what he wanted to talk to Paul about.

He'd ask him to dinner and they'd have a few drinks once they closed the deal he was sure they'd reach, as they had so many times in the past.

17

DINNER PASSED IN NEAR SILENCE. ALFRED TANNENBERG
and Ahmed avoided speaking to each other, so any effort to
play at normality fell to Clara. Finally she'd had enough.

"What's going on between you two? I want all of us to talk. I can't
bear this tension."

Ahmed broke the silence that followed her outburst.

"Your grandfather and I have had a difference of opinion."

"Ah! And that means you've decided not to speak to each other, eh?
Well, we have an archaeological mission to organize and run. I need
help from both of you, and we won't be able to do this if it's like a
funeral home around here. What's this difference of opinion that's so
important?"

Alfred would never back down before his granddaughter, much less
Ahmed.

"Clara, I won't have this conversation. You just see to organizing
the expedition. The Bible of Clay belongs to you; all the rest is irrelevant. And by the way, I'm going to Cairo for a few days. Before I go, I'll
leave you money. Take it with you to the excavation. It's yours to manage as you need. And I want Fatima to go with you."

"Fatima? But how am I supposed to take Fatima on an archaeological mission? What's she supposed to do there?"

"Take care of you."

No one dared contradict Alfred Tannenberg, not even Clara.

"All right, Grandfather. But, please. Can't you and Ahmed put whatever it is behind you, for my sake?"

"Don't meddle where you don't belong, Clara. Just let it be."

When Tannenberg left the room, Clara glared at Ahmed.

"Listen, I don't know what's going on between you and my grandfather, but I do know that for weeks you've been nasty, angry with the world, especially with me. Why?"

Ahmed sighed resignedly. "I'm tired, Clara, sick to death of the way we're living."

"And how exactly are we living?"

"Locked up here, in your grandfather's 'Yellow House,' at his beck and call, his every wish our command. I feel like a prisoner. Don't you?"

"I'm part of the Yellow House; I can't escape from myself."

"I just wish we could have stayed in San Francisco. We were happy there."

"I'm happy here, Ahmed. I'm Iraqi."

"No, you're not Iraqi—you were just born here."

"Now you're telling me what I am? Yes—I was born here, and I went to school here and I've been happy here, and I want to go on being happy here. Everything I want is here."

"Well, I'm not sure where to find what I want, but I know it's not here, in this house or in this country. Iraq has no future."

"Then what do you suggest, Ahmed?"

"I want to go away, Clara. Away."

"Then go—I won't do anything to stop you. I love you too much to want you to stay around if you're unhappy. Is there anything I can do?"

Ahmed was surprised, even hurt, by Clara's reaction. His wife loved him, but she didn't need him.

"Clara, I'll stay for the excavation. You're going to need my help finding the Bible of Clay, especially if your grandfather goes to Cairo. But when Picot and his people leave, I'm going with them. I won't be able to go back to the United States right now, but I'll ask for refuge in France or the UK. And then someday, when Iraqis aren't such pariahs, I'll go home to San Francisco."

"Ahmed, I appreciate your wanting to help me, but I don't see us living for the next few months as though nothing had happened, knowing that you'll be leaving."

"Are you saying you want to separate now?"

"Yes. I'm sorry, I'm very sorry, Ahmed. But I don't think either one of us should give up who we are, or pretend. We'd wind up hating each other."

"If you don't want me to stay and help you find the Bible of Clay, I'll try to find a way to leave Iraq."

"My grandfather will help you."

"I don't think so. At any rate, think about it. I really don't mind waiting a few months. I know I can be useful to you, and I'd like to help."

"Let me think about it 'til tomorrow. Where are you going to sleep?"

"Here in the Yellow House, on the couch in my office."

"All right. We'll have to work out the details of a divorce at some point, but we can do that tomorrow, or another day."

"Thank you, Clara."

"I do love you, Ahmed."

"I love you too, Clara."

"No, Ahmed, you don't love me. You stopped loving me a long time ago. Good night."

The couple sat silently at breakfast with Alfred. The grim meal was interrupted by an urgent call for Ahmed, who went into the library to take it.

It was Picot, and the archaeologist got straight to business. "I've compiled a provisional list of people who'll be taking part in the expedition," he told Ahmed. "I've just e-mailed it to you so you can start the paperwork on the visas as soon as possible. I've also decided to send two people ahead to set up the equipment. I'd like a certain amount of infrastructure ready so we can begin working as soon as possible."

"Absolutely; you can count on me. What are you sending?"

"Tents, nonperishable foodstuffs, archaeological equipment . . ."

"That's great. Look, Picot, I can take care of the first phase . . . but I won't be taking part in the dig."

"What? We're investing a lot of resources in this project; you can't imagine what it's taken me to convince these people to even go to your country, and now you're telling me you won't be there?"

"My presence is irrelevant—you'll have everything you need. Clara is a very competent archaeologist, I assure you. She doesn't need my help in leading the excavation, and you don't either."

"I don't like last-minute changes."

"I hate them, but that's life, my friend. Anyway, I'll get to work on those visas. You want to speak to Clara?"

"No, not right now. Later."

"All right. We'll be in touch." He hung up, then found Clara watching him from the doorway. She'd heard at least the last part of the conversation.

"Picot doesn't trust me."

"Picot doesn't know you. If you're Iraqi, you're supposed to wear a veil, be incapable of taking a step without your husband. That's the image the West has of the Middle East. He'll change his mind."

"He's worried that you won't be there."

"Yes. But that shouldn't worry you. You don't need me for anything. You know the plan, and you know Safran better than anyone. I think you should make Karim your assistant. He's a competent historian, and he'd love to work on an archaeological expedition. And he's the Colonel's nephew."

"How will you explain your absence?"

"We have to talk about that, Clara; we have to decide when and how we tell people, what we do afterward. We'll do what's best for you, for me, for everyone."

Clara nodded. She sincerely hoped that they could manage the break-up without reproaches and without making scenes. But at the same time, she wondered when they would release all the pent-up emotions they had, and what would trigger that release.

"What did Picot want you to do?"

"He's sending some material and equipment on ahead, and he doesn't want any problems with customs. Let's go to work. There's no time to lose. I have to call the Colonel. Do you have the projected schedule we worked up?"

"My grandfather has it—he wanted to review it."

"Well, go get it, and when you're ready, we'll go to the ministry and get started. We have to get some people to Safran. One of us should probably go on ahead."

Alfred Tannenberg was still in the dining room, and he didn't conceal his anger when Clara returned.

"Since when have you been so rude as to leave me sitting here by myself at the table? What exactly is going on?"

"It was Picot."

"And the world has to stop when Picot calls?"

"I'm sorry, Grandfather, but you know it's important. There are a thousand things to do. We're so close to achieving your dream—"

"It's not a dream, Clara. The Bible of Clay is a reality; it's out there—you just have to find it."

"I will."

"Good, and when you do, you take the tablets and bring them back here as soon as you can."

"Nothing will happen to them, I promise you."

"Give me your word that you won't let anyone—anyone!—take them away from you."

"I give you my word."

"All right. Now go to work."

"I need the plans, the schedule that Ahmed and I drew up."

"It's on the desk in my office. And as for Ahmed, the sooner he goes, the better."

Clara looked at him in astonishment. How could her grandfather possibly know what was happening between Ahmed and her?

"Grandfather . . ."

"Let him go, Clara; neither one of us needs him. He'll be sorry, though—without us, he's nothing."

"How do you know that Ahmed is leaving?"

"How stupid would I be if I didn't know what was happening in my own house?"

"I love him—I won't have you harm him. If you do, I'll never forgive you."

"Clara, don't tell me what I can or cannot do."

"But I am telling you, Grandfather. If you do anything to Ahmed, I'll leave."

Clara's tone of voice left no room for doubt.

Clara's face was tense as she climbed into her husband's SUV.

"What's happened?" Ahmed asked.

"He knows we're getting a divorce."

"And how did he threaten me?" Ahmed asked, a note of pure hatred in his voice.

Clara felt her heart wrenched apart by the two men she loved most in the world.

"Ahmed, don't talk that way about him. He's always been good to you."

"I know him, Clara, which is why I'm afraid of him."

"Why would you say that? He's bent over backward to help you; there's nothing you've wanted that he hasn't given you."

Ahmed had never revealed the dark side of Tannenberg's businesses to Clara—businesses that he himself had taken part in, and profited from. He wasn't going to start now.

"Your grandfather has been generous, there's no doubt about that, but I've worked beside him faithfully, never questioning what he did. What did you tell him about us?"

"Nothing, but I didn't deny that we're getting a divorce. He wants you to leave as soon as possible."

"I agree with him there. I'm going to move out of the Yellow House. Go to my sister's."

Suddenly, Clara felt a sharp pain in her chest. It was one thing to talk in the abstract about a separation, quite another to see it come to pass. She was on the verge of telling him that she didn't want him to leave, that she wanted to call it all off. But she gritted her teeth, held on to her dignity, and remained silent.

By the time they entered the ministry, they had moved on to discussing which one of them would go to Safran.

"I'll go," Clara said. "Later on you won't be there, and I'd prefer to know from the start how everything is organized, choose the laborers . . ."

She didn't add that throwing herself into the preparations for the dig would also keep at bay the pain and overwhelming sadness she was beginning to feel.

"You may be right," her husband said. "I'll stay here and help from Baghdad. And I can also start getting organized to leave."

"How will you leave?"

"I don't know."

"They'll accuse you of treason. Saddam might even send somebody to try to kill you."

"That's a chance I'll have to take."

They spent the rest of the morning on the telephone, doing paperwork and making arrangements for visas and permits. At noon, Ahmed went to lunch with the Colonel, and Clara returned to the Yellow House.

Tannenberg finished reading the last page as his interlocutor looked on expectantly. Then he carefully straightened the papers and put them in a folder that he slid into the top drawer of his desk. He turned his steely eyes on Yasir.

"I'm going to Cairo. I want you to organize a meeting with Robert Brown. Use a telephone that can't be monitored."

"Impossible. The American satellites record everything in Iraq."

"Enough, Yasir—I want to talk to Robert. If it's not possible, then do the impossible. Either find a way for us to talk or I'll place calls to them directly, to their offices. We must discuss the plan they sent me. They've made some absurd decisions, and if we carry out the operation as they've designed it, it will be a disaster. I will be in command, as always. I won't have them sending someone else to take over the lead. The photographs I've sent them should make that perfectly clear."

"No one wants to remove you from anything," the Egyptian responded. "They know you are not well, and they are sending in reinforcements."

"Don't start underestimating me now, Yasir—you don't want to make the same mistake they have."

"You should consider, too, sir, that they may be angry about Clara going to Rome and revealing your involvement with the Bible of Clay."

"That was none of their business. Tell them that I intend to speak directly to them, whether they like it or not. What I want is to know exactly what's going to happen and when. We have to organize this very, very carefully. I want one of Paul Dukais' men to report to me for instructions. Paul's people will do as I tell them, when I tell them, where I tell them. Otherwise I promise you that no one will do anything, unless they want a private war as well as a public one."

"What's wrong with you, Alfred? I think you're going mad."

The old man got up, walked over to his longtime lieutenant, and slapped him.

"Get out, and do as you're told."

Yasir's black eyes flashed with hatred. They had known each other for a lifetime, but he would never forgive Alfred for this affront. He left the office without looking back, still feeling the sting of the old man's hand on his cheek.

Alfred found Clara sitting alone at the table in the garden, in the shade of the palm trees, listening to the water dribble down the fountain. She stood and gave her grandfather a light kiss on the cheek.

"Sit down, Clara. I'm glad we're alone; we have to talk."

Fatima finished setting out several serving dishes of salad and rice to accompany the meat, then retired to the kitchen.

"What are you planning to do?" Tannenberg asked.

"Do about what?"

"Ahmed is leaving. What are you going to do?"

"I'm staying in Iraq. This is my country; my life is here. The Yellow House is my house. I have no desire to become an exile."

"If Saddam falls, it will be hard. We will have to leave the country. We can't stay here when the Americans come."

"Will they come?"

"I've just received a report confirming that the decision has been made. I'd hoped this wouldn't happen; I thought that Bush was just an uncouth bully, but apparently the preparations for war are under way. We should start getting ready. I'm leaving for Cairo; I have to organize some things and speak to some friends there."

"You're a businessman. It's true, you've been close to Saddam, but no more so than many others. They can't take reprisals against every Iraqi who's managed to prosper under this regime."

"If they come, they'll do as they please. A victor can do whatever he wants."

"So why are we starting this excavation?"

"Because we either find the Bible of Clay now or lose it forever. It's our last chance. I never imagined that Shamas had returned to Ur."

"To Safran, actually."

"Practically the same thing—they're right next to each other. The patriarchs were nomads; they wandered around the desert with their flocks and settled temporarily in one spot or another. It wouldn't be the first time they'd come to Haran or gone back to Ur. But I always thought that the Bible of Clay would be in Haran or Palestine, since Abraham was on his way to Canaan."

Clara, for once, was unable to focus on ancient history. "When are you leaving for Cairo?"

"Early tomorrow morning."

"I'm going to Safran ahead of Ahmed."

"What will he do?" Alfred's tone was neutral.

"He needs some excuse for leaving Iraq. Can you help him?"

"No. I won't help him. We have some business to finish up. When we do, he can go anywhere he likes. But he has to meet his responsibilities first—he can't leave until he's done what he signed up to do. I need his help to close a deal."

"I thought you wanted him to leave as soon as possible."

"I've changed my mind."

"Then you'll have to talk to him. We've agreed that he's moving out of the Yellow House and going to his sister's."

"I don't care where he lives, as long as he stays in Iraq until the Americans arrive."

"He won't want to do that."

"But he will."

"Don't threaten him, Grandfather!"

"I'm not threatening him. We are men of business. He can't just run off now. Not now. Your husband has earned a lot of money, thanks to me. But he needs to fulfill his end of the bargain."

"And you won't help him if he doesn't want to stay?"

"No, I won't, not even for you, Clara. I won't allow Ahmed to ruin a lifetime's work."

"I want to know what it is that only he can do."

"I've never discussed my business dealings with you, and I'm not going to start now. When you see Ahmed, tell him I want to talk to him."

"He's coming by tonight for some things."

"Tell him not to leave without seeing me."

"He doesn't trust us."

George Wagner was using the flat tone of voice that signaled an oncoming storm to those who knew him. And Enrique Gómez Thomson knew him very well. Even though they were talking by phone, thousands of miles apart, he could still picture the rictus of tension at the corners of his friend's mouth and the tic in his right eyelid.

"He thinks we set up that debacle with the Italians," Enrique replied. "The photographs made that clear enough."

"Yes, and what's worse is that we don't know who actually did. Yasir says Alfred insists on talking to all of us by telephone and that there won't be any operation unless he heads it. He wants Dukais to send one of his men to go over how the operation will be run, and he's threatening to pull the plug unless we do things his way."

"He knows the lay of the land, George—he's right about that. It would be crazy to put the whole operation in Dukais' hands. Without Alfred, it can't be done."

"Maybe. But he's not going to threaten us or impose his own conditions."

"We don't want the Bible of Clay going to some museum, and he wants it for his granddaughter—okay, there's a difference of opinion there. But we can't let everything else fall apart just because of Alfred's stubbornness about who's going to be the boss. We're at a stalemate with him: If he's willing to go ahead with us, we should do it. We can't run the risk of setting off a war between us. We've come this far because we've always performed like an orchestra, everybody playing his part."

"Until Alfred decided to change the score."

"Let's not exaggerate, George—we've got to understand that this whole Bible of Clay thing is for his granddaughter."

"That stupid bitch."

"She's not stupid; she's his granddaughter. You don't understand because you don't have a family."

"We're family—us, just us. Or have you forgotten that, Enrique?"

Enrique didn't say anything for a moment as he thought of Rocío, his son José, his grandchildren. "George, some of us do have families of our own, and we have an obligation to them."

"You'd sacrifice us for that family of yours?"

"Don't ask me that question—there's no way to answer it. I love my family, and as for you three . . . You're my arms, my eyes, my legs—I can't even describe what the four of us are. So let's not act like children asking who loves you more, Daddy or Mommy. Alfred loves his granddaughter, and that's made him vulnerable. He wants to give her the Bible of Clay, but it's not his to give. It belongs to us as much as it does him. There's no sense making a federal case of this right now; let's trust him, as we always have, to carry out the overall operation. If we declare war on him, he'll fight, and we'll destroy ourselves in the process."

"He can't hurt us."

"Oh, yes, he can, George, and you know it."

"So what do you want to do?"

"I say we organize two operations. First, the one we've been planning, with Alfred at the helm. The other, to snatch the Bible of Clay. We do that one on the sly."

"That's what I've been saying from the beginning. Paul has found two men to infiltrate Picot's team."

"Great—that's what we need, somebody who won't let Alfred's granddaughter out of his sight. Someone who can secure the Bible, if they find it. Nobody has to be hurt."

"Do you think this girl will let somebody just grab the Bible? You think Alfred hasn't organized things to make sure we can't get it?"

"Oh, I'm sure he'll have foreseen that possibility—he knows us. But we know him too. So we'll both be playing a little cat-and-mouse game. But if the men Paul sends are any good, they'll be able to get their hands on the Bible and leave before anyone realizes it's gone."

"You know any smart gorillas?"

"There have to be one or two, George. Anyway, let's make force the last option—not the first."

"You know how things are on the ground, we won't be there to evaluate the situation. It'll be the gorillas who decide. They could hurt the girl."

"We'll give them clear instructions not to do that their first day on the job, okay?"

"I'll check with Frank, and if he's on board, we'll do it. He may agree with you; he has a family too."

"And tell Dukais to send somebody sharp to talk to Alfred. It's going to be delicate."

"I know."

"So let's do this right. I don't want anything to happen to Alfred, you understand, George? I don't want anything to happen to him. We'll get the Bible of Clay—he knows it doesn't belong to him, and he'll understand even if he tries to stop us. We'll do what's necessary—but only what's necessary."

18

YASIR WAS SURPRISED THAT A MAN AS VULGAR AS DUKAIS could be so important.

Busily chewing gum, Dukais had taken off his shoes and put his feet up on his desk, oblivious to the fact that his socks were stuck to his skin by rank sweat.

Yasir took a seat in the chair in front of the desk and tried to ignore the man's crudeness. He was tired and already stressed by two days in Washington. Anti-Arab xenophobia was running rampant, and he'd hardly left his hotel.

Yasir was a businessman; his religion was money. But when he visited the United States, a certain nationalism awakened in him. He couldn't bear the Americans' air of superiority, their disdain for those they deemed "underdeveloped."

His country was poor or, more accurately, had been unrelentingly impoverished by a series of corrupt regimes propped up by world powers who considered the globe little more than a chessboard for their opposing interests. Egypt had been under Soviet influence, and now it was under America's. And as his son Abu said, "Where has that gotten us? They sell us what we don't need for a fortune and we're permanently in debt."

He didn't understand why his son, who had had everything, was so entranced with the fanatics who thought the solution to every problem lay in Islam. Before Yasir had boarded the plane for Washington, they'd had an argument about the beard Abu recently grew. For many young Egyptians, it had become a symbol of rebellion. But no matter how much Yasir debated his son's radicalism, he recognized that Abu was right on several counts.

"Alfred will lead the operation," Dukais now acknowledged. "That'll be best. He knows Iraq and we don't. When you go back to Cairo, one of my men will escort you. Mike Fernandez, a former Green Beret colonel. He's Hispanic, dark-skinned, so he won't stand out too much. He also speaks a little Arabic. He'll be in charge of the men, so he needs to meet Alfred, to be briefed on how Alfred wants things done. He knows how to kill and he knows how to think. He left the army because I pay better, a lot better."

Dukais laughed as he opened a silver box and took out a cigar. He offered one to Yasir, who shook his head quietly.

"The only places I can smoke are my offices, here and in New York. It's against the law in restaurants, and it makes my wife hysterical. One of these days I'm going to move in here permanently."

Yasir knew that any time wasted on small talk was more time he'd be forced to spend in this rank office. "Alfred is very ill," he said. "I don't know how long he has to live."

"Is your brother-in-law still his doctor?"

"My brother-in-law is the chief resident of the hospital in Cairo where they're treating his tumor. They operated and took out part of his liver, but the last sonograms and CT scans have shown small nodules. His liver is covered with tumors. He's definitely dying."

"Will he last six months?"

"My brother-in-law says he might, but he's not sure. Alfred doesn't complain, and he's going on with his life as normally as possible. He knows that he's going to die and . . ."

"And?"

"And except for his granddaughter, nothing matters to him."

"Which means he's a desperate man. And that's bad—if you're afraid of nothing, you're capable of anything," Dukais muttered.

"It's not enough for Alfred to leave his granddaughter a pile of money. He wants her to find this Bible of Clay you've all been looking for. He says that will be his legacy to her."

Paul Dukais might be oblivious to the most elementary social graces, but he was extremely intelligent. That's why he'd gotten to the top. And that was why he had no trouble understanding why Alfred was acting the way he was acting.

"Clara doesn't know the first thing about him," Dukais said, "but when he dies she'll have to face reality, and the only way Alfred can keep her from being stigmatized is to make her an archaeologist with an international reputation. Which is why they need this Picot—to give her the patina of respectability that Alfred can't. If they find this thing during an internationally sponsored archaeological expedition, it will be a horse of an entirely different color." Paul took a drag from his cigar. "I've always been surprised that she doesn't know anything, Yasir."

"Clara is very intelligent, but she refuses to face anything that would taint her relationship with her grandfather—she sees no evil, hears no evil. But I wouldn't underestimate her."

"I have a file on her—what she likes, what she doesn't like, her time in San Francisco, her grades in school—but none of that lets you know a person."

Yasir was pleasantly surprised by Dukais' reflection. It struck him that the president of Planet Security wasn't as simpleminded as he appeared to be.

"Give me a few hours to talk to some friends and prepare a report for you to take to Alfred. I'll tell Mike Fernandez to call you this afternoon, so you two can meet and start getting to know each other. It'd be good, too, if you could prepare him some for what he's going to find over there."

"He's never been there?"

"Sure, in the Gulf War. But that wasn't a war, it was a cakewalk. A chance to try out a few new toys the Pentagon bought itself with taxpayer money. He's been in Egypt too, but just on vacation, seeing the pyramids, you know."

When Yasir left, Dukais called Robert Brown, but he wasn't in his office. His secretary said he could be reached on his cell phone; he was having lunch with a group of university presidents to discuss a series of cultural activities for the following year.

Dukais decided he'd call him later.

Fabian was nervous. He was leaving early for Iraq to scout the site, and although he'd been eager to get on the ground there, he'd been working eighteen-hour days, trying to organize all the forward operations and obtain visas for the various stops he had to make on the way.

They'd managed to put together a team of twenty people. It wasn't enough, but it was all the venturesome souls they'd been able to persuade to risk their necks for an excavation on the eve of war. He himself acknowledged that it was madness, but it was a madness that relieved the monotony of his academic routine.

The advance arrangements, such as they were, seemed almost in place, save for a few loose ends. He'd received a call from Magda, one of his graduate students, who'd be going with them for just a couple of months, until Christmas. She wanted Fabian to talk to another student, the friend of a friend of hers, who might be willing to go. He was Bosnian, she said, a teacher, and he'd come to Madrid to study. He didn't have a dime, so when he'd heard that some crazy people were going off to Iraq and that the job paid pretty well, he'd asked if they needed an extra hand or two—he was willing to do whatever they needed.

But what could a young teacher who'd drifted into Madrid to study Spanish do for the expedition? Fabian had made no promises; he'd have to talk to Picot. Plus, Picot had told him there was already a Croatian on the expedition's team, who'd been recommended by a professor friend in Germany; apparently, the young man had studied computer science. "A survivor of the war who hates violence," Picot had been told, but one who had no compunctions about going to a country at war in order to earn some extra money—Berlin was a very expensive place to live.

Having a computer specialist on the team was a good idea. He could categorize their finds and perform other necessary data-processing work. So Picot had brought the Croatian aboard. Now, bringing in a Bosnian might be too much. The Bosnians and Croatians had been killling each other until just months ago, and the last thing they needed on the expedition was that kind of tension. Anyway, he asked himself, what good would a teacher be?

Picot entered Fabian's apartment, whistling. Clearly, his spirits were high.

"Hello! Anybody home?"

"I'm in my office!" Fabian called out.

"What a great day," Picot said. "Everything's really coming together."

"That's good," Fabian replied, "because I'm up to my neck in customs paperwork. You'd think we were bringing in tanks instead of tents. And the visas are driving me crazy."

"Not to worry. Everything will be all right, you'll see. Listen to this—I'm about to close a deal with *Scientific Archaeology* to publish the findings of the expedition in all their editions—English, French, Greek, Spanish, all of them. We'll have the support of the most prestigious journal in the field. I hope by the end of the year we'll have something to report. Either way, we'll write articles as we go along and send them in. I know it's a lot of work, but it'll be worth it."

"That's great! How'd you do it?"

"The London editor called me. He was at the conference in Rome and heard Clara Tannenberg speak. He's intrigued by the idea that Abraham dictated a version of Genesis to a scribe, and he figured if I was going to lead the expedition it ought to be on the up and up. He wants the exclusive; he'll publish whatever we send him."

"I'm not sure I like working with the press breathing down our necks."

"Me either, but given the circumstances, I think it will work to our advantage. I'm not totally sure what we're getting into."

"Now you tell me!"

"There's something strange about this dig, Fabian, beyond the obvious risks. I don't know what it is, but something's off."

"What do you mean?"

"I've yet to meet this mysterious grandfather of Clara Tannenberg's. And they've never told me how he found those first two mysterious tablets, what expedition he was on, even what year it was. They're an odd couple."

"Who? Clara and her husband?"

"Yes. He strikes me as a solid man who knows what he's doing. But there's a lot he's not saying."

"And you haven't liked her from the first day."

There was nothing Picot could say to that.

"Well," said Fabian, "I'm dying to meet her. I suspect she's much more interesting than you paint her."

"You won't have to wait long—when you get there, you'll be working with her. Her husband has informed me he won't be on the expedition itself. What I don't know is why."

"Intriguing—why would he jump ship at this late date?"

"I just don't know."

Fabian shrugged. Not knowing Ahmed, there was nothing he could add. "Oh! I forgot. Magda, the graduate student who's been helping us recruit, called. There's a Bosnian kid who's been recommended, a teacher who's come to the Complutense to take a course in Spanish for foreigners. Apparently he's short of money and would be willing to go with us, to do whatever needs doing. He speaks English."

"What about the Spanish class?"

"I have no idea. I'm just telling you because we could still use a couple of people, although I don't know whether this guy is good for anything we need."

"Let me think about it. We can't take people who aren't useful for something concrete. The Croatian is different; we need a computer geek."

"I also thought that maybe a Bosnian and a Croatian . . . It could be a problem. But I told Magda we'd consider him."

"Okay. Listen, of those we have so far, is any of them a decent photographer?"

"For what?"

"For the journal! They're not sending us anybody; we'll have to do our own photography."

"I thought you said they were all hot about this project."

"They are, but we're going to do all the work. They aren't going to send a team, or even a lone reporter, assuming they had one, to a war zone. *Scientific Archaeology* isn't *Time* magazine."

"As though we didn't have enough work to do!"

"No whining, my friend. So—when are you leaving?"

"In three days—if I don't have any more fights with customs officials. But there's still some paperwork to finish, so there's no guarantee."

"Who have you decided to take with you?"

"Marta Gómez."

"Oh? Marta, huh?" Yves nudged his friend.

"There's nothing between Marta and me."

"But you wouldn't mind it if there was, would you?"

"Marta's a friend, that's it. We've known each other since university, and believe it or not, there's never been any 'thing' between us."

"Well, she's far and away the most interesting woman of all your friends. She strikes me as really intelligent and capable."

"She is, and she's got a gift for dealing with people—whether it's the president of the university or a ditchdigger."

"But we're talking about Iraq."

"Marta's been to Iraq, and on expeditions to Syria and Jordan too. She knows the country—a few years ago she was a guest archaeologist attached to an expedition financed by some Iraqi bank. She stayed on for a couple of months and knows the area of what used to be Haran, where you said this mysterious grandfather found the tablets. And she speaks Arabic. She'll be able to talk to the customs people, the head of the village, the workers. . . ."

"You speak a little Arabic yourself."

"A very little. Marta and you speak it. I misspeak it."

"Well, she seems like a great choice to me. I don't know her as an archaeologist, but if you say she's good . . ."

"I don't think there's anyone anywhere better for the job."

"Fabian, in a job like ours it's important to choose your team and work as comfortably as possible. Things are not going to be easy over there, and Marta is fine with me."

"You can tell her that in person. She's coming over now."

"Wonderful. We've got a thousand things to finish."

19

FRANZ ZIERIS, THE COMMANDER OF MAUTHAUSEN, WAS reserved in his greeting of the two young men sent from Berlin, especially Alfred Tannenberg. Tannenberg had been sent from headquarters; he was a protégé of Fritz Hermann, whose daughter, Greta, he had just married. No one had to tell Zieris that Tannenberg's career was going to be meteoric. Both Alfred and Heinrich represented a category of the SS reserved for university graduates. Zieris had been a carpenter before the war.

Tannenberg, however, over time turned out to be a more competent officer than Commander Zieris had expected. While effectively achieving the Reichführer's work objectives for the prisoners by driving them until they were human ruins, he also exhibited an unprecedented creativity in his methods of ultimately disposing of the non-Aryan pigs.

Life in that village in the heart of the Danube valley—dotted with farms among the abundant fir and spruce trees—was as pleasant as the two friends could have hoped for. The serene landscape, however, stood in macabre contrast to the machine of death that was the Mauthausen work camp and the others that had been built to accommodate the growing volume of prisoners being brought in week after week. There were now over two dozen work camps scattered throughout the area.

The organization of Mauthausen was similar to that of other camps. There was a political bureau, a department of custody, the "health service," the administrative offices for record-keeping, and the headquarters of the military detachment.

Zieris accompanied Alfred and Heinrich during their first tour of the camp, then turned them over to one of his subordinates, Commander Schmidt, for a fuller explanation of their operations.

Schmidt was succinct as he took them through the procedures. "All prisoners wear a triangle that indicates the crime for which they are interned. Green for common criminals; black for antisocial elements such as gypsies, beggars, thieves, and so on; pink for homosexuals; red for political criminals; yellow for the Jewish pigs; and brown for the conscientious objectors."

"Have there been attempts to escape?" Heinrich asked.

"Would you like to see one?" Commander Schmidt asked in reply.

"I don't understand. . . ."

"Come, both of you, I will show you an escape. Down here, at the quarry; come."

Heinrich and Alfred looked at each other in puzzlement, but they followed the commander. After descending the one hundred eighty-six steps—known as the "stairway of death"—that led down into the quarry, Schmidt called over one of the prisoners charged with overseeing the others. He wore a green triangle; the commander told the two new officers that he was imprisoned for murder. Tall, muscular, and lacking one eye, the prisoner-guard inspired true fear in the other prisoners, who had experienced his brutality on many occasions.

"Choose one of these wretches," Commander Schmidt told him.

The murderer did not hesitate a second; he strode off toward a little white-haired man whose hands were tattered and bloody. He was so thin that it was difficult to believe he had the strength to move. He was wearing a red triangle.

"A damned Communist," the guard said as he pushed him toward the commander and the two new SS officers.

Commander Schmidt spoke not a word; he snatched off the prisoner's cap and sailed it off toward the barbed-wire fence that enclosed the quarry.

"Go get it," he ordered the prisoner.

The old man began to tremble, unsure whether to obey the order, although he knew he had no choice.

"Go and fetch your cap!" the commander shouted.

The little man began to walk, slowly, toward the fence, until once again the commander's imperious voice rang out, ordering him to run.

At that, the wretched creature began to shuffle wearily, his steps a bit quicker. When he came near the barbed-wire fence, where his cap had landed, he did not even have time to stoop down and pick it up. A burst of submachine-gun fire from one of the watchtowers cut him down.

"Sometimes the cap falls right on the barbed wire, and when the prisoner tries to pick it up, the high voltage kills him. One less mouth to feed."

"Impressive," said Heinrich.

"Too easy," said Alfred, clucking slightly.

"Too easy?" asked Commander Schmidt, puzzled. "Well . . . we also have other methods."

"Show us," asked Heinrich.

It appeared to be a large room lined with showers, but the smell that impregnated the walls indicated that it was not water that emerged from the pipes.

"We use Zyklon B, which is a most effective organic compound—a poison that acts very quickly," Commander Schmidt informed them.

"And you bathe the prisoners in that?" Heinrich asked with a loud laugh.

"Correct. We bring them here, and by the time they realize what's happening, they're dead. Here we eliminate the newly arrived. When the high command sends more prisoners than we can handle, we eliminate them immediately—they are sent into the showers, and they never come out again.

"The other prisoners have no idea what happens here; if they did, they might be tempted to riot when we bring them in. After they've stayed in the camp awhile and are no longer fit to work, we send them to Hartheim. Of course, we also have other showers—very efficient ones."

"Other showers?" Heinrich didn't immediately understand.

"Yes, we are experimenting with a new system for eliminating the undesirables. When they are done working the quarry, we send them to that pool at the end of the field. They take off their clothes and for half an hour are made to stand in the freezing water while the showers are turned on. Most of them simply fall dead; the doctor says it is due to circulatory problems."

The tour continued that afternoon. Schmidt accompanied them to Hartheim Castle. The place was lovely, and the service in the castle was most pleasant and efficient.

The commander led them down into the old dungeons and subterranean passageways, through heavy iron doors set at intervals through-out the castle's underground. Within the dungeons was another gas chamber, for prisoners who had worked in Mauthausen for several months.

"When they become very ill, we tell them that we are transferring them here, to this castle, which we explain to them is a sanatorium. They climb very obligingly up into the trucks. When they arrive, we order them to strip, we photograph them, and we bring them down here into this cellar. After they have been gassed, they are taken to the crematorium. Before that, though, we have an excellent group of dentists, both here and down below, in Mauthausen, who remove their gold teeth.

"Hartheim is also the destination of other creatures who debase our society. We have done away with more than fifteen thousand mentally ill persons from all over Austria."

"Impressive," Alfred declared.

"We simply carry out the Führer's orders."

20

ROBERT BROWN DROVE THROUGH THE GATES AND UP THE winding entrance toward a neoclassical mansion hidden among a forest of oaks and beeches. A fine rain was falling. When he got out of the car, a butler was waiting for him with an open umbrella.

He was not the first to arrive. The murmur of conversation, punctuated from time to time by laughter and the tinkle of glasses, reached him as he walked up the steps to the house.

George Wagner was at the door, greeting the guests.

Tall, thin, with blue eyes as cold as ice and white hair that must once have been the color of gold straw, he was an imposing figure. No one could doubt that the man held a great deal of power in his hands, despite his years. *How old is he?* Brown wondered, not for the first time, though he calculated he must be well into his eighties.

Inside, past and present cabinet members, almost the entire upper-ranking staff of the White House, senators, congressmen and congresswomen, judges, and prosecutors were rubbing elbows with bankers and presidents of multinationals, oilmen, and stockbrokers. The crowd ebbed and flowed through the house's beautifully decorated rooms, exquisite spaces housing scores of paintings by great masters.

Brown's favorite was a Pink Period Picasso, a tragic-looking harlequin that hung above the mantel in the drawing room, which also held a Manet and a Gauguin. In a sitting room nearby hung a Caravaggio and three paintings from the quattrocento.

Indeed, the mansion was a small museum. There were paintings by the greatest artists of Impressionism as well as canvases by El Greco, Raphael, and Giotto. In cases and on stands and tables stood small marble figures, tablets from the Babylonian Empire, two striking Egyptian bas-reliefs from the New Kingdom, an Assyrian winged lion ... Wherever one's eyes turned, there was a work of art, a figure from antiquity that showcased the sophistication of the house's owner.

Paul Dukais, carrying a glass of champagne, joined Robert.

"So, I see the gang's all here!"

"Hello, Paul."

"Quite a party! I don't know if I've ever seen so many powerful people in one place. All that's missing is the president."

"I hadn't noticed."

"Can we talk, do you think?"

"Of course; in fact, this is the best place to talk. Nobody'll notice us—everybody is talking, doing business. As long as you've got a glass in your hand . . ."

They flagged down a waiter, and Robert asked for a whiskey and soda; then they went off into a corner, just two old friends catching up.

"Alfred is going to be a problem," Dukais said.

"So what's new?"

"I did what you asked me to. One of my best men, an ex-Green Beret colonel, Mike Fernandez, is going to Cairo with Yasir to meet with Alfred. I trust Mike; he's got a good head on his shoulders."

Robert grimaced. "I'm not sure Alfred will be so willing to work with a Hispanic, being who he is."

"He'll have to get along. And I'm sure he'll like Mike."

"This Mike—he's Dominican, Puerto Rican, Mexican . . . ?"

"He's a third-generation Chicano. He was born here, and his parents were too. It was his grandparents who crossed the Rio Grande. You've got nothing to fear."

"I just don't like Hispanics, Paul."

"Robert—let's not waste time with this shit. Tell me how far Mike can go with Alfred."

"What do you mean?"

"If Alfred decides not to cooperate or if he's not being straight with us, what do we do?"

"For the time being, I just want them to get to know each other and get the operation started. We'll see how things go—your man will let us know—and I especially want to know what Yasir says."

"What about the granddaughter?"

"If she finds the Bible of Clay, you and your men will take it away from her, but be sure the tablets aren't damaged. They're not worth anything if they're smashed to hell. The mission is to get them and bring them back here in one piece."

"And what if she doesn't cooperate?"

"Paul, if Clara doesn't cooperate, then it'll go badly for her. Your men are to follow orders—she can give up the tablets the easy way or the hard way."

"Closing the deal?" Both men jumped when they realized George Wagner was standing beside them. On his face was a smile that looked more like a sneer.

"Just tidying up the last few details of the operation. Paul wants to know how far we're willing to go in dealing with Alfred and his grand-daughter," Robert managed.

"It's not easy to find a balance," George said, looking off into space.

"Yeah," Paul said. "Which is why I want clear instructions on the rules of engagement. I don't want this to come back and bite me on the ass, or to get sucked into a 'misunderstanding,' if you know what I mean. I'm glad you're here to lay out exactly what the limits are."

The old man looked him up and down, his eyes glittering with contempt.

"There are no limits in war, my friend. Winning is all that matters."

Frank dos Santos and George Wagner shook hands without much show of emotion. The party was at its peak, with a string quartet as background for the guests' conversation.

"The only one missing is Enrique," said George.

"And Alfred. Let's not be so hard on him."

"He betrayed us."

"He doesn't see it that way."

"How does he see it?" George asked with an air of suspicion. "Have you talked to him?"

"He called me in Rio three days ago."

"He called you! Why not put an ad in the newspaper!"

"I'm sure he used a secure line. I was in the hotel, and I must say I was surprised."

"What did he have to say?"

"He wants us to know that he has no intention of betraying us or starting a war between us. He repeated his offer: He'll lead the operation we've set in motion, he'll ensure its success, and he'll give up his share in exchange for the Bible of Clay. It's a generous offer."

"You call that generous? Do you have any idea what those tablets are worth if he finds them? Do you realize their leverage, *power*, for the person who owns them? Come on, Frankie, don't let yourself be taken in. You and Enrique tend to let him off too easily, time and again. He's betrayed us; it's that simple."

"Not exactly. He tried to convince us to turn over our part of the Bible of Clay if he found it, in exchange for all the profits of the other deal."

"And we told him no, so he decided to go off on his own, and pulled that stunt in Rome."

"Yes, he made a mistake. But now he's furious because he thinks we hired the Italians to follow his granddaughter."

"But it wasn't us!"

"That's what I told him, George. But until we find out who it was and what they wanted, I won't rest."

"So what do you want us to do? Kidnap the president of the Italian security company and force him to tell us who hired him?" George looked around to make sure no one was eavesdropping. "Does it not occur to you that Clara is married to one of Saddam's government officials? Honestly, Frankie, somebody may think that Ahmed Husseini is a spy. Saddam doesn't let anybody out of Iraq, but Husseini comes and goes as he pleases. There must be a lot of people interested in knowing why. Who knows if it was the Italian secret service itself, or NATO—I mean, who knows? It could be anybody."

"But they didn't follow Husseini, they followed Clara."

"Frankie, it doesn't matter. Alfred can't keep those tablets; they don't belong to him! None of us can make decisions or take actions on the basis of our own convenience or interest, ever. All four of us agreed on that long ago."

Frank was momentarily lost in memory. "You're right, of course," he finally said. "How far are you willing to go?"

"There's no forgiveness for betrayal."

"So you're going to have him killed?"

"I won't allow him to steal something that belongs to all of us."

Clara gave a last look around her room. Ahmed was waiting to drive her to the air base, from which a helicopter would take her to Tell Muqayyar. From there, she would be driven to Safran in an SUV.

She'd rejected Ahmed's offer to go with her, and she had also refused to let Fatima accompany her, at least for now. She had enough company with the four armed gentlemen her grandfather was sending to escort her.

Ahmed was no longer living in the Yellow House. For several days now, he'd been living at his sister's.

Clara knew that her husband had had a long conversation with her grandfather before the old man left for Cairo. Neither of them would tell her what they had discussed, but Ahmed did mention that he might put off leaving Iraq until war actually broke out, although he wasn't promising.

"Call me as soon as you get there. I want to know you're all right," Ahmed said.

"I'll be fine, don't worry. It'll only be a few days."

"Yes, but British bombs seem to have a special attraction for that area."

"Nothing will happen, Ahmed."

She got in the helicopter and put on the earphones to muffle the noise of the rotors. By noon they'd be in Safran, and she was looking forward to enjoying the solitude of the excavation site again.

Ahmed watched the helicopter lift off and grow smaller and smaller in the sky, and he, too, experienced a sense of liberation. For a few days, at least, the guilt he felt around Clara would lift. He had made a conscious effort to keep his emotions under control and not to express the slightest reproach. She had made it easy for him, very easy, and had given him no opening to change his mind.

But now he had to make a difficult decision: He could either allow himself to be blackmailed by Alfred and take part in the last operation, or he could try to escape from Iraq.

He could feel the Colonel breathing down his neck—on Alfred's orders, no doubt—so leaving Iraq would be complicated, to say the least. If he stayed, Alfred had assured him that he'd pay him generously and, in addition, help him leave the country.

Only Clara's grandfather could guarantee his escape, but could Ahmed trust him? Wasn't it possible that the old man would have him killed at the last moment? There was no way to know—with Alfred, you couldn't be sure of anything.

He had talked about it with his sister, the only one of his relatives who lived in Baghdad. She, too, dreamed of leaving. She'd come back just over a year ago when her husband, an Italian diplomat, was posted to Baghdad, and she was hopeful that when the drums of war began to beat they'd be evacuated.

For the time being, they'd taken Ahmed into their home, a large apartment in a residential area where many Western diplomats lived. Ahmed was sleeping in his younger nephew's room; the youngster had moved in with his older brother.

His sister urged him to ask for political asylum, but he knew what a difficult situation it would put his brother-in-law in if he showed up at the Italian embassy asking to leave. It might even trigger a diplomatic incident. Besides, Saddam was capable of preventing them from leaving, regardless of how much diplomatic cover Ahmed had or how strongly the Italians protested.

No, that wasn't the solution. He had to leave by his own means, without compromising anyone else, much less his family.

By the time the helicopter set down at the military base near Tell Muqayyar, Clara's temples were throbbing and her head felt like it was about to explode.

Like much of Iraq's war materiel, the helicopter that had flown her here was junk. The Colonel had told her it was the only one he could spare.

Once she'd boarded the SUV, escorted by two soldiers, she began to feel better. Her grandfather's four men followed in another vehicle.

The ride to Safran was hot and filled with dust, which swirled up in clouds whenever they met another vehicle, invading her nose and mouth and making even her saliva gritty.

The leader of the village greeted her at the door of his house and invited her in for tea. They exchanged the usual formalities and then, when the appropriate period of courtesies had passed, Clara reviewed how she saw the project unfolding and what she would need.

The man listened attentively, with a smile, and then assured her that everything had already been prepared for her visit; Ahmed had telephoned with detailed instructions. They had started erecting a number of houses made of clay, a material not lacking in the area. Once the impurities were sifted out, water was added to form a paste and dry straw, sand, gravel, or ash was worked in for strength. The construction technique was simple: Walls were raised in courses, almost like bricklaying, and when one course was dry, the next one was added on. A thatch of straw and palm leaves formed the roof.

A half-dozen had already been completed, and at the rate they were going, another six would be erected before the week was out.

Inside, the houses were very simple and not terribly large. Ahmed had ensured, however, that they would be provided with rudimentary showers and toilets.

Proud of the work he had done in such a short time, the village leader also assured Clara that he himself had chosen the men they needed for the expedition. Clara thanked him and then, treading carefully so as not to offend, said she would like to meet with all the men in the village, since the workers needed to have certain qualifications. A long and complex negotiation followed, which the leader gave in to only when Clara decided to drop the Colonel's name. The next day, he said, she could meet with them all. There were also women available, he told her, to do the laundry and clean the foreigners' tents while they were out excavating.

It was almost nightfall by the time they finished their discussions. Clara had accepted the headman's invitation to stay in his house, with his wife and daughters, until the rest of the expedition arrived. But first, she said, she wanted to walk around the ruins for a while, to think about the work ahead of her. The old man nodded. He knew that Clara would do as she pleased, and besides, she was no responsibility of his—she had brought her own escort from Baghdad.

She asked her bodyguards to keep their distance. She wanted to be alone, without having to feel their constant presence, alert to her every footstep. But they refused. Alfred's orders had been clear: They were not to let her out of their sight, and they were to kill anyone who tried to harm her, although first, if possible, they were to extract the identity of the perpetrator and who had hired him. Anyone attempting to harm Clara would pay for it with his life.

The most Clara could win from her escort was a promise that they would keep a prudent distance—but she would never be out of their sight.

She walked all around the perimeter of the site, which had now been cleared, her fingertips gently brushing the stones that formed the structure for the mysterious building. She observed the ruins from every angle, flicking dirt off a stone here and there, picking up shards of tablets that she carefully slipped into a canvas shoulder bag. Then she sat on the ground and leaned back against a rock and let her imagination wander through the desert, in search of Shamas.

21

"ABRAM, CAN WE GO ON WITH THE STORY OF NOAH?"

"In truth, it is not the story of Noah but rather the story of God's anger with the impudence of men. Everything God saw on the earth was evil, and so He decided to exterminate its most beloved creature: man.

"But God, who is always merciful, was moved by Noah's goodness, and He decided to save him—"

"—And that is why He ordered Noah to build an ark of gopher wood, with pitch inside and out. I know, I've written this before," Shamas said, rereading one of the tablets stacked beside him. "And the ark was built three hundred cubits long, fifty cubits wide, and thirty cubits high. The door to the ark lay on one side, and God ordered Noah to build it three stories tall."

"I see that you have written all that I have told you."

"Yes, Abram, of course. Although I do not like this story as much as the story of the creation of the world."

"No, my son? Why not?"

"I have been thinking about Adam and Eve and how they hid from God because they were ashamed of their nakedness before Him. And about how God cursed the serpent for having tempted Eve to disobedience. It seems unfair."

"Shamas, you cannot choose which stories to like and which stories to question. You asked me to tell you the history of the world. As part of that story, it is important that you know that God decided to punish mankind and so He flooded the earth. If you do not wish to go on—"

"But of course I do!" The boy bit his lip, fearing he had angered Abram. "Forgive me. Please go on."

"Where was I?"

Shamas read aloud the last few lines he had incised in the tablet:

> *Come thou and all thy house into the ark; for thee have I seen righteous before me in this generation. Of every clean beast thou shalt take to thee by sevens, the male and his female; and of beasts that are not clean by two, the male and his female.*

"Ah, yes. Now write as I shall tell you," Abram commanded him:

> *Of fowls also of the air by sevens, the male and the female; to keep seed alive upon the face of all the earth. For yet seven days and I will cause it to rain upon the earth forty days and forty nights; and every living substance that I have made will I destroy from off the face of the earth. And Noah did according unto all that the Lord commanded him.*

> *And Noah was six hundred years old when the flood of waters was upon the earth. And Noah went in, and his sons, and his wife, and his sons' wives with him, into the ark, because of the waters of the flood. Of clean beasts and of beasts that are not clean, and of fowls, and of every thing that creepeth upon the earth, there went in two and two unto Noah into the ark, the male and the female, as God had commanded Noah. And it came to pass after seven days that the waters of the flood were upon the earth.*

> *In the six hundredth year of Noah's life, in the second month, the seventeenth day of the month, the same day were all the fountains of the great deep broken up, and the windows of heaven were opened.*

> *And the rain was upon the earth forty days and forty nights. . . . And the Lord shut Noah in.*

In the boy's hand, the reed passed rapidly across the tablet. Shamas' imagination was stirred by the image of the windows of the heavens opening and the rain pouring out. He thought of a clay water jug breaking, releasing its contents. He continued to write, never lifting his eyes from the clay as Abram went on. . . .

Shamas took advantage of Abram's respite to rest. The task he had undertaken was not easy. His inscriptions demanded his full concentration; his results filled him with self-doubt. And he wanted to go back to Ur. He felt that he was a stranger here in Haran, even with his father, mother, brothers, and sisters. But happiness had long abandoned their home. Now he hardly saw Jadin, and his mother was always ill-humored. They all missed the coolness of the house his father had built at the gates of Ur and longed for the security of a permanent settlement.

"What are you thinking of, Shamas?" Abram asked.

"Ur."

"And what are you thinking?"

"That I would like to be with my grandmother, and to go to school with Ili again."

"Do you not like Haran? You're learning just as much here."

"Yes, but it's not the same."

"What's not the same?"

"The sun, the nights, the way people talk, the flavor of the figs—nothing."

"Oh, you are homesick!"

"Homesick? What illness is that?"

"Nothing you will die from, my son." Abram smiled. "It is the memory of what you have lost, or left behind. It is a yearning."

"I don't want to leave the tribe, but I do not like living here."

"We will not be here for very long."

"Terah is an old man, and I know that when he is no longer with us you will lead us to Canaan, but I am not sure I want to go to Canaan. My mother would also like to go back."

Shamas then fell silent, afraid he had opened his heart too wide and expressed his sadness too freely. He feared that Abram would tell his father and that his father would grow concerned, knowing his son was unhappy.

Abram seemed to read his thoughts. "Don't worry, Shamas, I won't tell your father, but we must try to make you happy again."

The boy smiled a bit, relieved, as he picked up the reed in readiness for Abram's next words.

And so he learned that Noah sent first a raven and then a dove out of the ark, to see whether the earth was dry, and that he had to release a second dove, which returned with an olive branch, and then a third, which did not return. And that God took pity upon Noah and said, "I will not again curse the ground any more for man's sake; neither will I again smite any more every thing living as I have done."

God, Abram told Shamas, blessed Noah and his children and told them to be fruitful and multiply and replenish the earth. He also gave men every moving thing upon the earth, and the green herb, but, said Abram, "He forbade man to eat flesh with the life thereof, which is the blood thereof: 'And surely your blood of your lives will I require; at the hand of every beast will I require it, and at the hand of man; at the hand of every man's brother will I require the life of man.' "

"You mean God allowed men to return to Paradise?" asked Shamas.

"Not exactly, although He forgave us and made man once again the most important of His creatures, for He gave us all things that had been created. The difference is that now, nothing will be freely given. Men and animals alike must struggle for survival; we must work to obtain the seed of the earth, and women must suffer to bring forth children. No, God did not allow us to go back to Paradise; He only promised not to wipe us again from the face of the earth. Never again will He open the windows of heaven and pour rain down in a torrent.

"Now let's stop for the day, Shamas—the sun is setting. Tomorrow I will tell you why not all men are alike and why we sometimes fail to understand one another."

The boy's eyes opened wide in surprise. Abram was right—there was so little light he could hardly see, yet he wished they could go on. Of course, his mother would be looking for him, and his father would want to see what he had learned that day in school. So Shamas leapt up, carefully gathered his tablets, and ran toward the mud-walled house in which his family abode.

The next day Abram did not go to meet Shamas. He sought solitude, for within himself he felt the call of God's voice. That night he had awakened covered in sweat, feeling a great weight upon his chest. When he arose from his bed, he left Haran and wandered aimlessly for hours, until at nightfall he sat down to rest in a palm grove carpeted with soft grass. He was awaiting a sign from the Lord.

He closed his eyes and felt a sharp pain at his heart, and he heard very clearly the voice of God:

Abram, get thee out of thy country, and from thy kindred, and from thy father's house, unto a land that I will show thee. And I will make of thee a great nation, and I will bless thee, and make thy name great, and thou shalt be a blessing. And I will bless them that bless thee, and curse him that curseth thee, and in thee shall all families of the earth be blessed.

He opened his eyes expecting to see the Lord, but the shadows of night had crept into the palm grove, and the only illumination came from the reddish moon and the thousands of stars, like tiny points of light gleaming in the firmament.

Abram was filled with dread and uneasiness once again. God had spoken to him, he'd heard Him clearly, he could still feel the force of the message vibrating within him. He knew that he must now begin his march to the land of Canaan, as the Lord bade him. Even before leaving Ur, God had marked out the destination of his wanderings, which Abram had put off because Terah was old and wished to repose in Haran, the land of his fathers.

Days and nights, then weeks, then months had passed, and the tribe had not moved from Haran, where they found good pastures and a prosperous city in which to trade. They had settled here as Terah had wished.

But now the day to follow the commandment that God had given him to journey on to Canaan had come, and Abram's heart was heavy, for he knew that by obeying God, he would displease Terah.

His old father, with his eyes cloudy and his legs unsteady, half-slept most of the day, his mind lost in recollections of things past and fearful predictions of things to come. How was Abram going to tell him that they had to move on? Grief pressed upon his chest, and tears flowed from his eyes unbidden. He loved his father, who had been his guide throughout his life. He had learned everything he knew from Terah, and by watching his dexterous hands creating statues he had seen that hands do not create a God.

Terah believed in the Lord, and he had been able to plant the love of God in the rest of the tribe, though still today its people worshipped the highly adorned figures of clay upon their altars and in their sanctuaries.

Abram walked quickly. He had to go to his father's house, where Sarai would be waiting, still awake though the sun had set hours ago. He knew that Terah would be waiting for him as well. His father called out for him in anguish when he was not near.

By the time he came near Haran, Terah had fallen into a stupor from which no one had been able to rouse him, and the only word he spoke was the name of his son, Abram.

When Abram entered the house, he sent the women out of his father's room and asked his brother Nahor to let him sit alone with the old man. Nahor, exhausted from his long vigil, went outside to breathe the cool air of the night while Abram sat with Terah.

Those who remained inside heard the soft murmuring of Abram's voice, although they also thought they could hear the weary voice of the old man.

Dawn brought the death of Terah. Sarai's slave made her way to the tent of Jadin, who hurried to console the family of the tribe's deceased patriarch. There he found Abram and his brother Nahor and the two men's wives, Sarai and Milcah, and his nephew Lot.

The women were crying and tearing at their hair, while the men were rendered mute with grief and desolation.

Jadin took charge of the situation and sent for his wife, so that with the other women they might cleanse the body of Terah and prepare it for burial in the land of Haran.

Terah had died in the place he loved above all others, for in Haran, though they had wandered with their flocks and herds in search of grain and pasture, almost all of his ancestors had been born.

The tribe waited the designated time before burying Terah's body in the dry, cracked ground of the Mesopotamian summer. Grief marked Abram's face; now it fell upon him to lead the tribe, into a land where there were green pastures and they could live without fear. A land promised his people by God.

"We will go to Canaan," he announced to them. "We must make preparations to depart."

The men discussed the route they should follow. Some preferred to settle in Haran forever, while others proposed returning to Ur, but most pledged to follow Abram wherever the road took them.

Jadin met with his kinsman Abram, who was now the leader of the tribe.

"Abram, we will not be going with you to Canaan."

"I know."

"You know? How can you know, when until yesterday I did not know myself?"

"I could read in the faces of your family that you would not be going with me. Shamas dreams of returning to Ur; your wife yearns for that city, where her family remained; and even you prefer to lead your tribe back to Ur in search of pasture and grain with which to nourish them. I have nothing to reproach you for. I understand your decision, and I am happy for Shamas especially."

"Indeed, the listlessness you read in my son's eyes has brought me to this decision."

"Shamas is called to his writings. He will be a good scribe, a wise, just man. It is not his destiny to remain a shepherd."

"When will you leave with the tribe?"

"Not before one moon has passed. I have many things to do, and I cannot leave until I have completed the story I am telling Shamas. He must pass it down to our people who remain in Ur and all those he meets throughout his life: who we are, where we came from, and the will of God. Only that which is written is fated to endure, and before I leave I want Shamas to write down all that I tell him."

"Very well. I will tell my son to come to you, and I will prepare enough tablets for him so that he can preserve all that you tell him."

22

 "MADAM! MADAM!"

    The cries of one of the men in her escort woke Clara from her lethargy.

"What is it, Ali?"

"It's late, Ms. Tannenberg, and the leader of the village is angry. The women are waiting for you to have dinner."

"All right, I'll be there in just a second."

She got up, brushing the yellow dust off her clothes and skin. She really didn't feel like talking to anybody, much less the chief of the village and his family. Soon the site would be swarming with people, filled with activity, and she had wanted to enjoy the solitude a while longer.

She'd been imagining Shamas the scribe—her mind had given him a face, and she could almost hear the sound of his voice, sense his footsteps in this place.

He must have been an apprentice—that would explain the imprecise marks of his characters—but he also seemed to be gifted somehow, close to the patriarch Abraham, close enough to have been trusted to document his story of creation.

When Clara arrived at the village leader's house, he was waiting for her at the door with a glacial smile that she chose to ignore. She praised the food she was served, though, and ate heartily, then retired to a room with a narrow bed set next to the village leader's eldest daughter's. She fell deeply asleep instantly, as she hadn't since Ahmed left the Yellow House.

Alfred Tannenberg's home in Cairo was located in Heliopolis, the residential area that housed Egypt's diplomats and its government's highest officials. The windows of his study looked out onto a row of trees and several men guarding the perimeter of the property.

Alfred had grown even more distrustful with age. Now he suspected his old friends, the men he once would have given his life for, of betrayal.

Why was he so determined to keep the Bible of Clay? He had offered his associates almost everything he owned for those tablets. It was not a question of money, though; he had enough money to live out the rest of his days very comfortably and to ensure Clara's future. What he most wanted for Clara was something money couldn't buy—respectability—because the world he'd lived in was beginning to crumble. In fact, the reports he had been receiving from George Wagner for over a year now left no room for doubt. Alfred Tannenberg was a monster, and that would be his legacy to his granddaughter, no matter how wealthy he was. No, he could give Clara respectability only with the Bible of Clay. But George refused to agree to that, and although Frankie and Enrique had families, they didn't seem to understand either.

He was alone, alone against them all, and with one other very inconvenient fact against him: the short time he had to live.

He pored over the doctor's report. They wanted to operate on him again, take out the tumor that was destroying his liver. But he had made his decision: He would never again enter the operating room, much less when, according to the report, there was no guarantee of the outcome. He could actually die on the operating table if his heart gave out. And lately, attacks of tachycardia and high blood pressure had been further undermining his health. His only goal now was to live long enough to allow Clara to excavate in Safran before the Americans started bombing.

A servant knocked lightly at the door and announced the arrival of Yasir and another man, Mike Fernandez. Alfred had been expecting them and walked to the door of his office to greet them. Yasir bowed his head with a slight smile. Alfred knew he had made a permanent enemy when he had slapped Yasir during their last encounter, and that the man would betray him at the slightest opportunity—as soon as their business deal had concluded. But he had no intention of apologizing; after such an insult, there wasn't any use. He would keep his eyes open and block the blow before the other man raised his hand.

Alfred evaluated Mike Fernandez as they shook hands. Mike's firm handshake belied the look of fear in his eyes, as if he was in the presence of a truly evil man. Not that Fernandez was any choirboy himself; according to what Alfred heard, he'd worked for a long time under Dukais, on several more-than-questionable missions. But despite Mike's reputation, Alfred knew that he could still tell the difference between good and evil. Could he sense, though, which nature held more sway in Alfred's mind?

They sat around a low table while a servant came in with a tray of ice water and soft drinks and set it down. Once he left, Alfred turned immediately to Fernandez.

"What's your plan?"

"I'd like to take a look at the Kuwaiti–Iraqi border and points along the Jordanian and Turkish borders. I need to know what type of infrastructure we have in place at potential staging areas and especially what there is in the way of escape routes. I think we can get a good cover from a company that exports cotton, giant bales of cotton, from Egypt to Europe."

"What else?" the old man asked, his voice flat and cold.

"Whatever you want to tell me. You're directing the operation. I'll be on the ground; that's why I want to see what I'll have to be moving through."

"I'll tell you the entry and exit points my men will be using. We've been moving in and out of Iraq for years under the radar of every government in the Middle East. We know the terrain like the palm of our hand. You'll be in charge of the men, but on the ground my men will be in command, and they'll be the ones crossing the borders."

"That's not what we agreed on."

"What we agreed on was getting in and out in as little time as possible without being detected. I can tell from a mile away that you're not Iraqi, and I suspect that will be true of the others Paul is sending. If you're caught, the entire operation will be blown. My people blend in—you'd be as obvious as George Bush. We'll position your men in strategic locations to link up with mine. As for that cotton-export company, I'm very familiar with it: It's mine. But it's not right for this job. We need our friends in Washington to let us travel on their military transport planes to their bases in Kuwait and Turkey—they make stopovers in Europe. Once they're there, we'll see to the rest. Each of us must move on our own home ground."

"And you decide what the home ground of each of us is?"

"You know something? When you travel through the desert, the Bedouins always surprise you. You're convinced you're all alone out there, and all of a sudden you look up and they're there. How did they get there, how long have they been following you? That's something you'll never know. They're part of the sand. . . . You can be spotted from a mile away, but you wouldn't see them if you were five yards from them."

"Are your men Bedouins?"

"My men were born here, in these sands, and they are invisible. This is my territory, and I will not agree to any changes in the way we operate. Or have they gone mad in Washington?"

"No, they haven't gone mad, they just want some control of the operation. I'll speak with Dukais."

"There's the telephone."

Mike Fernandez didn't even get up. He had forced the situation to test the parameters and because he didn't want to be just another extra in the old man's movie. But Dukais' orders had been clear: Do exactly what Alfred said.

"I'll call him later," said Fernandez, surprised, despite all he had heard, at the old man's toughness.

For the next hour, Tannenberg gave him a lesson in military strategy and tactics and outlined how the two teams would rendezvous. He unrolled a map and showed him where the support teams were to be positioned and how they were to move relative to the American bases in Kuwait and Turkey. He even showed him an alternative route through Egypt, just in case.

"And where will your men be, Mr. Tannenberg?"

"That's not your business. Telling you would be like putting an announcement on the Internet."

"You don't trust me?"

"I don't trust anybody. I've told you what you need to know."

"Okay, Mr. Tannenberg—I see that working with you is not going to be easy."

"You're mistaken, Mr. Fernandez; it's very easy. I simply expect every man to know what he's supposed to do. You do your part, I'll do mine, and that's it. This isn't a fishing trip where there'll be a lot of bonding, as you Americans call it—so there's no need for you to tell me how your superiors are going to convince the boys in the Pentagon to lend us their planes or for me to share the details of things on my end. But I will tell you how many men you need."

"You're going to tell me?" Fernandez asked sarcastically.

"Yes, I am. Your men will be escorted by some of mine, to ensure that everything goes according to plan."

"And how many men should I bring?"

"No more than twenty, and if possible, they should speak something besides English."

"Like Arabic?"

"Like Arabic."

"I'm not sure we can do that. . . ."

"Try."

"I'll tell Mr. Dukais."

"He already knows what the men for this mission need to be like, which is why he chose you."

As they came down the steps of the plane, they were hit by the dry heat of the desert. Marta Gómez smiled happily. She loved the Middle East. Fabian felt as though he was having trouble breathing, and he quickened his steps toward the Amman air terminal.

They were standing in front of the luggage carousel waiting for their baggage when a tall, dark-skinned man walked up to them.

"Señor Tudela?"

"Yes?"

The man put out his hand and took Fabian's in a firm, decisive grip.

"I'm Ayed Sahadi. Ahmed Husseini sent me," he said in perfect Spanish.

It was no surprise at all to Marta that Sahadi hadn't greeted her, and much to the man's surprise, she put out her hand.

"I'm Professor Gómez. How are you?"

"Welcome, Professor," Sahadi said, bowing slightly as he shook Marta's hand.

"Señora Tannenberg didn't come?" Marta asked.

"No, Señora Tannenberg is waiting for you in Safran. But first we have to get everything out of customs. Give me your luggage receipts and I'll see that your bags and boxes are taken to the vans."

"Are we going directly to Safran?" Fabian asked.

"No. We've reserved a room for you in the Amman Marriott so you can rest tonight. Tomorrow we'll cross the border into Iraq and drive on to Baghdad, and from there a helicopter will take us to Safran. Within two days you will meet Señora Tannenberg," Sahadi answered.

They completed all the paperwork in customs without the slightest problem; Sahadi's presence seemed to ensure that the officials let them through smoothly. They watched as the containers were loaded into three vans that were waiting for them in the airport loading zone, and then they were driven to the hotel. Sahadi told them he'd be back to take them to dinner; in the meantime, they could rest if they wanted. The next day they would be leaving at sunrise, around five.

"So how'd you like that guy?" Fabian asked Marta as they had a drink in the bar.

"Nice. Efficient."

"He seemed to notice only me."

"Sure—you're a man; he's acculturated to deal with you. It'll pass."

"I was surprised you didn't say anything."

"He didn't mean anything by it. It's a product of his upbringing. Not that you Spanish men are any different," she laughed.

"Well, we're being retooled. We've made a huge effort to live up to you girls—after all, you're the new superheroes."

"Yes—everybody knows that Nietzsche was thinking about his sister when he developed his theory of the superman! But seriously, I'm used to that happening when I come to the Middle East for work. Within a few days he'll give in to the evidence and realize that I'm the boss."

"Oh, so now I've been the victim of a coup d'état—thanks for telling me."

They joked for a while as they sipped at their whiskeys and waited for Sahadi. At eight-thirty he appeared as promised.

Not bad, thought Marta, looking with a critical eye as he came toward them through the bar, wearing a well-cut navy-blue suit and an elephant-print Hermès tie.

"The tie is a bit old-fashioned, but it's elegant," Marta said sotto voce to Fabian as she tried to avoid letting the slightest smile reveal her thoughts to this stiff man who had no idea what he was in for with these two foreigners.

He took them to a restaurant in a residential area of Amman where only Westerners lived. Europeans passing through the city shared tables with Jordanian businessmen and politicians.

Fabian and Marta let Sahadi order for them, and they never let on that they spoke Arabic.

"I'm curious, do you work for Señora Tannenberg?" Marta asked straight out.

"No, not exactly. I work for her grandfather. I will be in charge of the workers at the excavation site in Safran. As a foreman," Sahadi answered, not without a wiggle of discomfort.

"Is Señor Tannenberg an archaeologist?" Marta went on with her questions, ignoring completely Sahadi's obvious uneasiness.

"He is a businessman."

"Ah! I understood that he had spent several years in Haran and found the tablets that have caused such a commotion in the archaeological community," Fabian said.

"I'm sorry, but I really don't know about that. I'm only familiar with Señor Tannenberg's current operations." Sahadi was clearly dodging the question.

"And would it be indiscreet of me to ask what those operations are?"

Marta's question took Sahadi by surprise; he hadn't expected an interrogation.

"Señor Tannenberg has several businesses. He is a very respected businessman, and he prizes discretion above all else," he replied with a certain coolness.

"And is his granddaughter a well-known archaeologist in Iraq?" Marta asked.

"I know very little about Señora Tannenberg. I know she is respected in her field and that she is married to a well-known Iraqi archaeologist. But I'm sure that she will be able to answer all these questions when you meet her in Safran."

Fabian and Marta knew it was time to ease up. They had been hard on their host. This was, after all, the Middle East, and in the Middle East no one asked direct questions without running the risk of offending.

"So you will be staying on with us in Safran?" Fabian asked.

"I will be at your disposal during the entire excavation."

At the door of the hotel, Sahadi reminded them that he'd be picking them up the next morning at five. The vans with the equipment had already left for Safran.

"We put it to him, eh?" Fabian remarked as they said good night at the door of the elevator.

"We pushed hard. Not that I care. But I'd love to know how and when this Tannenberg excavated in Haran—I've been on digs in that area, you know. Before we left, I looked up all the archaeological expeditions that have been located in or near Haran, and no Tannenberg took part in any of them."

"Who knows whether this mysterious grandpa has ever been on a dig outside the backyard of his own house. He could have bought those tablets off some grave robber."

"That's exactly what I was thinking. This could be a total wild-goose chase. But I'm like your friend Yves—I find him intriguing."

The trip to Baghdad the next morning was exhausting, and once they arrived, the city showed obvious signs of the siege it was under. Everywhere one saw poverty, as though overnight the prosperous Iraqi middle class had disappeared.

Marta had some motion sickness in the helicopter and, despite the kindhearted ministrations of Fabian, couldn't avoid throwing up. By the time they reached Safran she was pale and wrung out, but she was determined to make an effort as Clara Tannenberg greeted them.

Clara figured Marta must be in her mid-forties, full of that self-assurance some Western women have: women who've made it on their own and don't take well to being told what to do. Or what not to do, for that matter. Nor did Clara fail to note that Marta was an attractive woman—tall, with beautiful long dark hair and well-manicured hands. Clara always looked at a woman's hands. Her grandmother had told her that you could know everything about a woman by her hands, and that observation had never failed her. A woman's hands reflected her soul and her social status. Marta's were thin and bony, recently polished, the nails painted with a light transparent coat that gave them no color, only shine.

After the greetings all around, Clara told the newcomers that the vans had arrived safely, although there had not yet been time to unload them.

"You can sleep in any of the villagers' houses or, if you prefer, in the tents we've set up. We've started building some simple mud houses, no different from the ones that have been around here for millennia. Some of them are ready, but the mattresses and some other fixtures haven't come in from Baghdad yet—they'll be here in a couple of days. They'll provide housing for almost everyone. We won't have any luxuries, but I hope you'll be comfortable."

"Could we have a look around the site?" Fabian asked.

"Of course. I'll have your bags taken to the village leader's home and we'll walk over to the 'palace,' as I call it. It's not far, and it's not too hot today."

"If you don't mind," Marta said, "I'd rather drive. I got airsick in the helicopter and I'm still not feeling too well."

"Is there anything I can do? Would you rather not go?" Clara asked solicitously.

"No, I'd just like some water and a chance to wash my face a bit . . . and not to walk, if that's all right."

Clara spoke to one of her assistants and in a second their luggage was carried away.

Marta took a few minutes to drink some water and recover her strength. Then they boarded a jeep to drive to the site where they would be working for the next few months.

Fabian jumped out of the car before the soldier driving it had come to a complete stop. He began to walk quickly around the site, stopping to examine the area that had been exposed by the bomb.

"I see that you've been clearing the site," he said.

"Yes. We think we're basically standing on the roof of a building and that what you see through that hole is a room where the tablets were kept—that would explain the amount of shards we've found. So, if that's the case, this is a temple-palace," Clara replied.

"I don't believe there's any evidence that there was ever a temple so close to Ur," Fabian said.

"No, there's not, but I remind you, Professor, that's precisely the value of this discovery. If we excavated through the length and breadth of Iraq, we'd likely find several dozen temple-palaces, because they were the administrative centers of wide areas," Clara explained.

Marta, meanwhile, had wandered off from the other two, looking for a place where she could perhaps get a better overview of the site.

"Is she your wife?" Clara asked.

"Marta? No, no. She's a professor of archaeology at the university where I teach, the Complutense, in Madrid. And she has years of experience in fieldwork. In fact, a few years ago she was here, near Haran, where your grandfather found those mysterious tablets."

Clara nodded silently. Her grandfather had flatly forbidden her to reveal any information about him. She was not to say a word more than necessary, even if people insisted on knowing details of when and why he had been in Haran, so she decided to lead the conversation in another direction.

"It's very brave of you to come to Iraq under the present circumstances."

"We hope everything goes well. It's not going to be easy working under these time constraints."

"Yes, but we Iraqis feel that Bush is just testing Saddam's nerve."

"Don't be too sure of that. He's declared war on you, and when all the pieces are in place, he will attack. I don't think he'll put it off more than six or seven months."

"Why is Spain supporting Bush against Iraq?"

"Don't confuse Spain with the administration in power right now. Most Spaniards are against the war."

"So why don't you revolt?"

Fabian laughed out loud.

"It's funny you should ask me why we don't revolt against our government when you Iraqis live under the heel of Saddam. Listen, I don't agree with my government's support of the United States against Iraq, or lots of other things either, but we do have a democratic government. We can throw them out at the ballot boxes."

"Iraqis love Saddam," Clara said.

"No they don't, and the day he falls, he'll fall hard—and only a few of the men in his inner circle will defend him. People suffer dictators, they don't love them—not even the people who've prospered under their regimes. The only thing that will remain of Saddam is the memory of his outrages against his own people.

"I'm against the war because we don't think innocent people should die just to get rid of a single man, especially since he's the last obstacle the Americans need to hurdle in order to get hold of Iraqi oil. The U.S. wants to control the oil reserves because China is breathing down its neck. But I insist: Don't be misled—those of us who are against the war hate Saddam as much as the war's supporters do."

"You didn't ask whether I was a supporter of Saddam," Clara reproached him.

"I don't care one way or the other. What are you going to do? Denounce me to those soldiers so they'll detain me? I imagine that if you live in Iraq and want for nothing, it's because you at least say you support the Saddam regime. We wouldn't be able to excavate here under these circumstances if your grandfather wasn't a powerful man in Iraq, at least that much is clear. But don't be misled there either—you mustn't think we came here ready to bow down before Saddam or sing the praises of his regime."

"No, you came here to excavate."

"If we can avoid political confrontations, we'll excavate. We think we have the chance to find out whether what you speculated about at the conference in Rome exists. We'll work day and night, against the clock, and if we don't achieve our mutual objective, at least we'll have tried. As archaeologists, we couldn't let this opportunity slip past us."

"Are you friends with Yves Picot?"

"Yes, of course, we've been friends for years. He's a bit heterodox, you might say, but he's one of the best, and of course only someone like him would be able to convince us to come and risk our necks in this place," Fabian said, letting his eyes roam over the site, looking for Marta.

"How many archaeologists will be taking part in the mission?"

"Fewer than we need, unfortunately. The team isn't big enough for the job ahead of us. There'll be two experts in magnetometry, a professor of archaeozoology, an expert in Asia Minor and Turkish studies, seven archaeologists who focus on Mesopotamia, and a number of students in their last years of study. About twenty of us in all."

Clara couldn't conceal a look of disappointment. She had hoped Picot would be able to find more specialists for the mission.

"Consider yourself lucky—getting twenty people to come here for a dig within this time frame is a small miracle, and every one of us has done it for Yves," Fabian said, irritated. "Your country is about to be turned into rubble, and it's no place for an archaeological adventure. Even so, Yves convinced us. We've left our jobs, our families in some cases—and don't think it's easy to tell your dean that you're leaving in September, just when the semester is about to start. All of us have made personal sacrifices to be here and have done so knowing how small the chances are that we'll find anything that's really worth the trouble, that can justify the investment of our time and professional reputations."

"You make it sound like you're doing me a favor!" Clara said in exasperation. "If you're here, it's because you think *you* can find something."

Marta had returned to them and had heard the last part of the conversation.

"What's happening?" she asked.

"An exchange of opinions," Fabian replied.

Clara didn't say anything. She lowered her eyes and took a deep breath to calm herself. She couldn't let her temper run away with her, especially before the mission even got started. She missed Ahmed; he had more tact, he knew how to deal with people, how to say what he was thinking without offending others while still standing firm in his opinions.

"Well," said Marta, "I've had a look around. The site looks interesting. How many workers will we have?"

"Nearly a hundred. There are about fifty men here in Safran; the rest will come in from neighboring villages."

"We need more. There's no way to clear all this sand unless we have enough help to do it. Are those the houses that you're building for the team?" she asked, pointing toward a group of half-finished buildings.

"Yes. They're about three hundred yards away. We'll be living practically beside the site, so we won't need cars to get around in," Clara answered.

"We've brought good tents. In my opinion, the workers should finish what they've started, but the priority should be to get to work here right away."

Marta's tone left little room for discussion.

"Right away? Before the rest of the expedition arrives?" Fabian asked in surprise.

"Yes, absolutely. There's no time to lose. Honestly, I don't think we can do what has to be done in so little time—we need to start tomorrow. We'll go back to the village and meet with the men to explain some of the details of the work they'll be doing. We'll try to get the site as clear as possible, so that when Yves and the others get here we can go right to work on the dig itself. Does that sound all right to you two?"

"You're the boss," Fabian replied.

"That sounds fine to me." Clara nodded.

"Good. Let me tell you how I think we should go about this. . . ."

23

HANS HAUSSER STRODE PURPOSEFULLY INTO THE HUGE
lobby of a glass-and-steel colossus in the heart of London.
A directory on the wall led him to Global Group. He
checked to make sure it was, as he remembered, on the seventh floor.
Resolutely, but not without trepidation, he made his way to the bank of
elevators.

A world-renowned professor of quantum physics was about to hire
a killer to assassinate a man and his entire family. He felt no pity in his
heart, but he wasn't sure he knew how to handle the man he was about
to meet.

The offices of Global Group looked like those of any multinational
corporation: light-gray walls, white acoustic ceiling tiles, modern furnishings, abstract paintings by painters with names impossible to remember, pleasant, discreetly elegant secretaries.

Tom Martin did not make him wait. He shook his hand at the door
of his office, a large space with three walls of beautiful bookshelves in
light-toned wood, a long wall of windows through which one had a
magnificent view of old London and the Thames, leather armchairs,
and not a single personal effect—no trophies, no photographs, just a
huge steel-and-glass desk supporting a laptop and a digital phone.

When the two men were seated in facing armchairs, cups of coffee in front of them, Tom Martin sat back to listen, with some curiosity, to the apparently absentminded old man who had insisted on seeing him.

"Tell me, then, Mr. Burton—how can I be of help?"

Hans spoke calmly. "I'll get right to the point. I know that your company sends men into zones of conflict, so to speak. You have a small army that travels and works both in groups and as individuals. I know that you provide security, but if we do away with the euphemisms, we might say that people get killed in your line of work. Your men, for example, kill other men in order to protect the people who hire them or to defend material interests, be they buildings, oil fields, whatever."

Tom Martin listened with a mixture of perplexity and amusement. Where was this old fellow going with all this?

"Mr. Martin, I need to hire one of your men to kill a man. Actually, he'll have to kill more than one person—I don't know exactly how many right now, maybe two, maybe five; I'm not sure."

The president of Global Group couldn't hide his surprise at this man's request. A distinguished-looking old man in tweeds, who'd called for an appointment under the name Burton and was now sitting quietly before him sipping coffee, was looking to hire an assassin. Just that simple.

"Excuse me, Mr. Burton—you did say your name was Burton?"

"You can call me that," Professor Hausser said.

"That is, your name is not really Burton. . . . Well, but you understand, sir—I need to know who my clients are."

"You need to know that they'll pay you, and I will pay you very generously."

"Why do you want to kill someone?"

"That is none of your business. Let us just say that there is a person whose interests have clashed with mine and some of my associates' and that he has had no scruples in using methods against us that every legal system in the world would consider illegitimate. But he is a powerful man and cannot be reached by the authorities or punished by legal means. Therefore, we want to eliminate him."

"And these other people you also want to eliminate?"

"His family members. Any that can be found."

Tom Martin sat in silence at that, a bit taken aback by the calmness with which this man was asking him to commit half a dozen murders. He had made the request, in fact, with the same tone of voice that he'd have asked for a drink in a bar or said hello to the doorman in the morning—in the kindliest, gentlest way, almost offhandedly.

"Could you tell me what exactly this man has done to cause you and your friends to want to kill his entire family?"

"No. Just tell me whether you'll take the job and, if so, how much it will cost."

"Really, Mr. Burton, I'm not running a murder-for-hire agency here—"

"Oh, come now, Mr. Martin. I know who you are, and I know that your people are considered the very best; everyone praises your company's quiet efficiency. I was told I could put the matter to you directly, without beating about the bush, so that's what I'm doing."

"And the person who recommended me told you that this is a company that hires out killers?"

"Mr. Martin, you don't know me, so you don't trust me. I understand that. But what do you call what your men do in the diamond mines when they machine-gun a poor black man for getting too close to the security fence? And what about those protection teams for businessmen who don't hesitate a second to pull the trigger if their boss tells them to?"

"I need to know who you are, a reference . . ."

"I can't provide you with that, I'm sorry. If you're afraid this may be a trap, don't worry. I'm an old man; I probably don't have much time left, and what time I do have I want to dedicate to settling an old score. That's why I've come here."

Tom Martin sat again in silence, looking at this old fellow who carried himself with such aplomb. No, he wasn't a cop, Tom was sure of that. Finally, his curiosity got the better of him and, putting aside his own security rules, he decided to risk it.

"Who is the man you want killed?"

"You accept the job, then?"

"Tell me who he is and where he is."

"How much will it cost?"

"In principle, we have to scout the locations, then decide how and when to approach the subject, and that costs a lot of money."

"A million euros for the man, and another million for his family?"

The president of Global Group's eyes widened. Either the old man was tempting him with the money or he had no idea of the market price for this work.

"You have that much money?"

"I have three hundred thousand euros on me now. If we shake hands on this, I'll give it to you as a down payment. The rest, as the job is done."

"Who do you want to kill, Saddam Hussein?"

"No."

"Who is this man? Do you have recent photos?"

"No, I don't have any photos of him. He'll be an old man, older than me—around ninety. He lives in Iraq."

"In Iraq?" Martin's surprise now bordered on disbelief.

Hans opened his briefcase. "Yes, I believe Iraq. At least, one member of his family has a house there. Here are some photos of his house. I'm not positive whether he himself lives there or not, but the person who does is a member of his family, and she is to die too—but not before she leads you to your objective."

Tom Martin picked up the photos of the Yellow House that had been taken by the men on Marini's team. He examined them carefully. The house was a colonial-looking mansion, well protected, judging by what the cameras had caught.

In some of the photos, an attractive woman in Western dress appeared; she was accompanied by an older woman wearing a burka that covered her from head to toe.

"This is Baghdad?" he asked.

"That's right—Baghdad."

"And this is the woman," Martin stated more than asked.

"Yes. We believe she is a relative. She has the same last name. She can lead your men to him."

"What is the name?"

"Tannenberg."

The president of Global Group pondered that for a moment. This was not the first time he'd heard that name. Not long ago his friend Paul Dukais had asked him if he had any men he could send to infiltrate an archaeological expedition organized by this woman, this Tannenberg, who apparently wanted to keep something that didn't belong to her, or at least not just to her.

From what he was seeing, the Tannenbergs had enemies everywhere, ready to do whatever it took to get rid of them. Did this man want the same thing Dukais did, or was his beef a different one?

"Will you take the job, then?"

"Yes."

"Wonderful. Let's sign a contract."

"Mr. . . . Mr. Burton, you don't sign this sort of contract."

"I am not going to give you a single euro if we don't have a contract."

"We can draw up a general contract—say, to investigate a certain individual in a certain place."

"Yes, but the individual's name can't be in it. I want absolute discretion."

"You are asking for a lot. . . ."

"I am also paying a lot. I know that what I'm paying is much more than you generally charge for this kind of work. So for two million euros, you will do things as I want them done."

"Of course, of course."

"And another thing, Mr. Martin. I know that you're the best, or so you're reputed to be. I am paying you so generously because I don't want failures and I don't want betrayals. If you betray me, my friends and I have much more money than this—enough to find you under any rock where you try to hide, if we should be forced to. There will always be someone ready to do the work, even someone inside here."

"I won't be threatened, Mr. Burton." Martin pronounced the name with a clear hint of irony. "You don't want to do that, or this conversation is over."

"But it's not a threat. I just want things clear from the beginning. At my age, I'll never be able to spend the money I have, and you can't take it with you, can you, Mr. Martin? So I'm investing it in order to see that my last wishes are respected—while I'm still alive, that is."

"Mr. Burton, or whatever your name is, in my business we don't betray our clients. How long would we last if we did that, eh?"

Hans Hausser gave Martin all the information he had. It wasn't much.

Two hours later, Hausser left the offices of Global Group, sensing that at last they were close to the hour of revenge.

He wandered about aimlessly, sure that Martin had had him followed. He walked into the Claridge Hotel and made his way to the restaurant, where he had lunch, though he didn't have much of an appetite. Then he went into the lobby and got into an elevator; anyone following him would think he was staying here, so he pushed the button for the fourth floor. There he got off and went to the stairs, where he walked down to the second floor. Once there, he caught another elevator and went down to the garage level.

A valet asked where his car was parked, but Hausser didn't bother to respond—he simply smiled, as though he didn't understand English. At his age, he knew he looked like some dotty old man. He wandered through the parking lot and then up one of the ramps outside. At the first corner he turned and walked away from the hotel. He hailed a taxi and asked to be taken to the airport. His flight for Hamburg was to leave a few hours later. From there, he would take another flight to Berlin, and from there, to his home in Bonn. He didn't know whether he'd managed to shake Tom Martin's men, but at least he'd made it hard for them.

"It's me."

Carlo Cipriani recognized his friend's voice. He knew Hans would be calling, since he'd received a coded e-mail and had replied with the number of the new cell phone where he could be reached. Then he'd throw the phone in the trash, the calling card into the Tiber.

"Everything's fine so far. Tom Martin's taken the job, and he'll be going to work immediately."

"There were no obstacles?"

"He was surprised, but Mr. Burton was very persuasive." Hans Hausser laughed delightedly.

"When will he have something?"

"In two or three weeks. He has to put a team together, send it out. . . . It takes time."

"I hope we've made the right decision," Carlo mused.

"We're doing what we have to do, and surely we'll make a mistake somewhere along the line, but the important thing is to keep going. We can't afford to stop."

In the background on the other end of the line, an impersonal voice was announcing the departure of the flight to Berlin.

"I'll call you as soon as I know something. Call the others."

"I will," Carlo promised.

Hans hung up the public telephone from which he had made the call at the Hamburg airport. He'd call Berta from Berlin. His daughter was worried by all these comings and goings, and she had started to insist that he tell her what was happening. So far he had lied, telling her that he was traveling to meet some former colleagues, retired like him, but Berta didn't believe a word of it. Of course she could never have imagined her father going to London to hire a hit man. She would have sworn that her father was a man of peace—at the university he had always been among the most vocal protesters against any war or expression of violence, what-ever it might have been. He had been adamant in his defense of human rights around the world, signing petitions, attending conferences, and contributing money to good causes; his students worshipped him, and the university had made him professor emeritus. He still gave a course or two every semester—no one had wanted him to retire completely.

Mercedes Barreda rushed into the bedroom. She'd left her purse on the bed, and now her disposable cell phone was ringing.

She fumbled at the closure, then dumped the purse's contents on the bed, terrified that the phone would stop ringing before she could answer it.

"Calm down," she heard Carlo say, even before she could catch her breath to say hello.

"I had to run," she said.

"It's all right—we've started things rolling."

"Is everything going well?"

"No problems so far. In a couple of weeks we'll know more."

"So long . . ."

"Don't be so impatient. What we want to do isn't easy."

"I know, but sometimes I'm afraid I'll die before we finish this."

"Look, I fear the same thing. I even have nightmares about it—but now we're almost there."

When the conversation ended, Mercedes fell back on the bed. She was bone-tired. She'd been inspecting a couple of projects that her construction company was involved in, and then she'd had a meeting with several of the architects and quality inspectors who worked for her.

Money had never interested her. She'd made a lot of it, it was true, but she'd never had any real use for it, any cause to put it to. She'd made a will: When she died, everything she had would go to several NGOs and an animal-welfare organization, and the shares in her company would be divided equally among the employees who had worked for her for so many years. She hadn't told anyone about this, because she wanted to be able to change her mind, but for the moment those were the terms of her estate.

It struck her, though, that all the money she'd made during her long life was going to do some good, at last, because she'd invested it in murdering Alfred Tannenberg.

Her housekeeper had left a dinner of salad and chicken breast for her in the kitchen. She put it on a tray and went and sat with it in front of the television, as she had done almost every night since her grandmother had died, so many years ago.

Her house was her refuge; she had never invited anyone into it except the only three friends she had in the world: Hans, Carlo, and Bruno.

Bruno was just finishing dinner when the cell phone in his jacket pocket startled him. His wife, Deborah, went on the alert. She knew that for some time, since he'd returned from Rome, her husband had been buying and destroying cell phones and calling cards without explaining why. Not that he needed to. She knew that the past was still present in Bruno's life. Neither children nor grandchildren had managed to erase it. For Bruno Müller, nothing was as important as what he had gone through sixty years ago.

Deborah bit her tongue—she was determined not to speak a word of reproach, especially that night, when Sara and David were having dinner with them. It was rare that the couple's two children came to visit at the same time, since David, a concert violinist, was constantly traveling, playing with the world's premier symphony orchestras.

Bruno excused himself and walked into the privacy of his bedroom, well out of earshot of his family.

"Everything's going well," said Carlo.

"Oh, thank God. That takes such a load off my mind." Bruno sighed. "I was worried."

"You always are. Hans is on his way home again, and within two or three weeks he'll have something for us."

"So they took the job?"

"Yes—he made them an offer that was just too hard to refuse."

"Are we going to meet again, the four of us?"

"Maybe when we have something concrete. For the moment I don't see the need."

"Hmm. Have you talked to . . . her?"

"We just got off the phone. She's all right but impatient. As impatient as the rest of us, I suppose."

"We've waited so long, Carlo. . . ."

"Yes, but we're very close to the end now."

"Or so we hope."

When Bruno hung up, he took the SIM card out of the cell phone and cut it into tiny pieces, then went to the bathroom and flushed them down the toilet, just as he'd been doing each time he spoke to one of his friends since his return from Rome.

Luca Marini was waiting for the receptionist to tell Carlo Cipriani he was here. He'd spent the whole morning in his friend's clinic, suffering through lab tests as part of his annual checkup. Carlo's son Antonino wouldn't be giving him the results for another couple of days—and even then, they'd be evaluated by Carlo himself. But now he and Carlo would be going out for lunch.

Carlo strode into his son's examining room and embraced his old friend.

"I'm told you're in great shape—right, Antonino?"

"Apparently he'll outlive us all." The son smiled. "I can't find a thing to worry about!"

"What about my shortness of breath?" Marini asked in concern.

"Has it never occurred to you that it might just be old age?" Carlo joked. "That's what Antonino tells me when I complain."

When they reached the restaurant and were seated, Carlo asked his friend straight out about what had been worrying him. "Have you had any more news from your old colleagues in the police department?"

"I had dinner with several of them a couple of days ago, at a friend's retirement party. I asked them in passing and they told me they hadn't completely given up on the case, but it was on the back burner. After the first few days, there was less pressure to solve it, so my friend in charge of the investigation decided to let it slide a bit. If he starts to get pressure again, he'll say he's on it."

"That's all?"

"That's a lot, Carlo—it's the most I can ask. He's doing me a favor. If he starts getting pressured, he'll tell me."

"Do you think they may want to talk to Mercedes again?"

"Perhaps. But wanting to know what's happening in Iraq is not a crime. That's what could save you."

"You have friends, Luca—that's what's saving us."

"Of course I have friends—you're one of them. But I have to tell you—I think she's a nightmare."

"She's not, really—she's a wonderful person, with qualities you can't even imagine. The bravest person I've ever known."

"You really like her."

"Tremendously."

"So why have you two never married?"

"She's a very dear friend, that's all."

"Whom you happen to admire above all other women. When you two are together, it's obvious there's something between you."

"Don't try to see what's not there. Honest, Luca. To me, Mercedes is more than family; she's incredibly important to me, but so are Bruno and Hans."

"Your dearest friends—how long have you four known one another?"

"For so long that if I add it all up I'll realize how old I am!"

Carlo delicately changed the subject. He never said more than he had to about his friends, much less about the shared past that united them—united them in a friendship that transcended good and evil.

24

 YOU DIDN'T HAVE TO BE SHERLOCK HOLMES TO SEE THAT
the tall, ruddy-faced dirty-blond was the alpha male of the
group standing around laughing as they waited beside the
luggage carousel for their bags to come out.

They'd arrived on an earlier flight, and Gian Maria was surprised
to hear them talking about archaeology. Apparently, they were heading
to an excavation in Iraq, and the priest thought yet again that there was
no such thing as coincidence—if he'd stumbled onto a group of archaeologists on their way to Iraq, providence had put them in his way.

He heard them mention that they were going to Baghdad but
they'd be staying in Amman overnight before crossing the border the
next day.

Gian Maria swallowed hard and touched the tall man's elbow.
"Excuse me—may I speak to you?"

Yves Picot turned to look at the man, whose face was red as a beet.
"Yes? What is it?"

"I couldn't help overhearing that you were going to Baghdad. . . ."

"Yes, that's right."

"I know this will sound strange, but . . . but is there a chance I
might accompany you?"

"Go with us? Why? Who are you?"

The young priest flushed even redder. He didn't want to lie—he couldn't; it wasn't in him—but he also couldn't tell the whole truth.

It had been hard to convince the higher-ups in his order to allow him to make the journey. He had explained his sudden quest as a spiritual obligation to do something for those who needed help most; he couldn't sit idly by, he said, and watch the Iraq tragedy from a distance—he had to go and do something. At last his superiors gave way to his undeniable passion and relented, though without much enthusiasm. A friend who had a relative within the Rome headquarters of an NGO called Aid to Children had helped Gian Maria with visas and other paperwork that would allow him to work in the Baghdad branch. NGOs normally preferred monetary aid rather than enthusiastic volunteers, who sometimes got in the way more than they actually helped, but his friend's uncle had finally overcome the NGO's reluctance, and now he had made it to Amman, on the way to Baghdad.

"My name is Gian Maria, and I'm going to Iraq to see what I can do."

"What do you mean, see what you can do?"

"Well, I want to help. Some friends of mine are working with an NGO that helps children in the poorest areas of Baghdad and provides medicines to hospitals. The country needs everything, because of the blockade. People are dying because there are no antibiotics—"

"I know what's happening in Iraq. But you just decided to come and see what you can do? Just like that?"

"I told my friends I was coming, but they can't come to Amman to get me, and I . . . Really, I've never done anything like this before, but if I could go along with you to Baghdad . . . I could help you however you might need me."

Yves Picot laughed out loud, touched by the young man's diffidence and painful shyness.

"What hotel are you staying at?" he asked.

"I don't have one."

"And how had you planned on getting to Baghdad?"

"I didn't know. I figured someone here could tell me how to go about it."

"Tomorrow at five a.m. we're leaving the Marriott. If you're there, we'll take you with us. Ask for me—my name is Yves Picot."

With that, Picot turned and strode away, leaving the surprised young priest no chance to thank him.

Gian Maria sighed with relief. He picked up the little black suitcase that contained his few belongings and left the terminal to find a taxi.

He'd ask the taxi driver to take him to the Marriott—with luck, they'd have a room for him and he'd be near the archaeologists.

The taxi left him at the entrance of the hotel. Gian Maria strode optimistically into the lobby, where the air-conditioning made the heat of the city almost bearable. Picot's group was at the front desk registering, and he lingered in the background until they had finished.

Shortly thereafter he settled himself in a comfortable room, which he had no intention of leaving until the next morning. It had been expensive, given his meager funds, but he wanted to run no risks—especially the risk of getting lost in an unknown city. And it would do him good to rest—he had been in constant motion for days.

He called his superior in Rome to tell him that he'd arrived and would be crossing the border into Iraq the next day.

Then, lying in bed reading, he fell asleep. It was just before three when he woke with a start. In two hours Yves Picot and his team would be leaving. Gian Maria spent the remaining time in his room, debating whether to ask Picot if he knew Clara Tannenberg. They shared a profession, and he very well might, or might at least know where to find her. But Gian Maria decided against it. For the time being it was safer to continue to bear the burden of his silence.

Yves Picot was in a bad mood. He'd gotten to bed late, his head hurt, and he was sleepy. The last thing he wanted to do was talk. When the young man from the airport turned up in the lobby, he was on the verge of telling him to find some other way to get to Baghdad, but again, the man's imploring demeanor persuaded him to act with a generosity he was far from feeling.

"Get in that Land Rover and keep quiet," he snapped, and turned back to supervise the porter.

Gian Maria wasted no time in clambering into the SUV Picot had pointed out. A minute later, three young women joined him inside. They couldn't have been over twenty-two or twenty-three.

"You're the guy from the airport!" exclaimed a short, thin blonde with green eyes. "We saw you when we were waiting for our luggage—you kept staring at us."

The other two laughed as Gian Maria blushed deep red.

"I'm Magda," the green-eyed blonde said, "and those two troublemakers are Lola and Marisa."

They threw him quick air-kisses and chattered away nonstop as the SUV and others in the caravan pulled out.

"What is it you do?" Magda suddenly asked him as they drove along.

"Me?" Gian Maria asked disconcertedly.

"Yeah, you. We know what we do!"

"You're archaeologists, right?" he asked shyly.

"Not yet," answered Marisa, a gangly girl with dark-brown hair.

"We're in our last year of studies," Lola clarified. "We'll be graduating this year. But we've come on this dig because it's a great chance to actually do some fieldwork, and they're giving us course credit too. And doing a dig under Yves Picot—plus with Fabian Tudela and Marta Gómez—is awesome."

"You're Italian, right?" Lola asked.

"Yes."

"But you speak Spanish," she probed.

"A little; not much," said Gian Maria uncomfortably.

"So—what is it you do?" Magda pressed.

"I got my degree in ancient Middle Eastern languages," he answered, praying they wouldn't go on with their interrogation.

"Oh, my God—we called those 'the deadly dead languages'! You must be kidding! What on earth for? God, I hated those classes!" Magda exclaimed.

"Like Hebrew, Aramaic . . . ?" Lola asked.

"Yes, and Akkadian, Hittite . . . ," Gian Maria said.

"But how old are you?"

Marisa's question left him disconcerted again.

"Thirty-five," he answered.

"You're kidding! We thought you were our age!" Marisa whistled.

"Twenty-five, tops," Lola explained.

"And you don't, like, need to work?" Magda asked.

"Me?"

"Yes, you." Magda's patience was wearing a little thin. "If you need a job, I could tell Yves; we're shorthanded."

"What could I do with you?"

"We're going to Safran to excavate; that's near Tell Muqayyar, ancient Ur," Magda explained. "And given the situation, there haven't been a lot of people interested in coming."

"It's a very controversial mission," Lola said. "Most people we know see it as a wild-goose chase, and what makes it worse is this war right around the corner."

"Not that they're so wrong either," Marisa chimed in. "In a few months Bush will be bombing Iraq into the Stone Age, and meanwhile we'll have been digging around in the desert as though it were the most normal thing on earth."

"I'm going to help out with an NGO," Gian Maria said. "They're working in the poorest neighborhoods, distributing food and medicine."

"Oh. But, still, if you want to come and give us a hand, you'd be welcome, I'm sure. I'm going to tell Picot. Plus, the pay is great, so if you need a little money . . . ," Magda suggested again.

The young women moved on to other topics, addressing Gian Maria directly only once in a while. He replied as briefly as possible—part reticence, mostly shyness. They crossed the border without any problems and arrived in Baghdad before ten. Yves Picot had an appointment with Ahmed Husseini at the ministry. The expedition members were to be put up at the Hotel Palestina that night, from which Gian Maria would contact the NGO.

When they got out of their Land Rovers at the door of the Hotel Palestina, Picot's humor had not appreciably improved. He needed a cup of strong coffee, so he left an assistant to sort things out with the front desk.

"Professor! Professor!" yelled Magda, running after him. "You know what? Gian Maria has a degree in dead languages—he might be able to help out."

"Who the hell is Gian Maria?" Picot asked testily. He had long since had his fill of this young woman's crazy ideas, even if she'd helped enormously in persuading students to join the expedition.

"That guy you put in the car with us."

"Oh! My, you're very efficient, Magda—you never stop recruiting, do you?" Picot grinned in spite of himself.

"Well, I mean, I understand why you didn't want to bring over that Bosnian teacher, but a specialist in Middle Eastern languages . . . He knows Akkadian," she said seductively.

"All right—ask him where he'll be staying in Baghdad, and if we need him we'll call him," Picot conceded.

"Need him! Of course we need him! Do you know how many tablets we'll have to decipher?" Magda insisted.

"Magda, this is not my first expedition. Just ask him how we can get in touch with him and—Forget it. Send him to me in the coffee shop or restaurant or bar or whatever they have here. I'll talk to him myself."

"Great!"

Magda ran back toward the lobby, hoping that Gian Maria hadn't already disappeared into the city. She didn't know why, but she liked this odd man—maybe because he looked so shy and hangdog.

"Gian Maria!" she called out when she spotted him.

"Yes?" he said, blushing when he realized that everybody had turned to look at them.

"Professor Picot wants to talk to you. He's waiting for you in the bar, or the coffee shop. You'll find him. Don't even think about it—just go! Come on—come with us!"

Gian Maria tried to beg off. "But, Magda, I promised my friends at the NGO. I came here to help; people are going through a really bad time here."

"I'm sure people are just as bad off in Safran. You can help the people there in your time off."

Magda's apparently bottomless depth of energy and her irresistible enthusiasm overwhelmed the priest. She was full of good intentions—but she was like an earthquake that leveled everything around her.

He found Picot in the coffee shop.

"Thank you so much for bringing me to Baghdad," Gian Maria said at once.

"You're welcome. Magda says you're a specialist in ancient Middle Eastern languages."

"Yes."

"Where did you study?"

"In Rome."

"And why?"

"Why?"

"Yes, why."

"Well, because . . . because I liked it."

"Are you interested in archaeology?"

"Of course."

"Do you want to join us? We don't have many experts. Is your Akkadian any good?"

"Yes, it's very good."

"So come with us."

"I can't. I'm here to help out with one of the NGOs."

"You decide. If you change your mind, we'll be in Safran. It's a godforsaken village between Tell Muqayyar and Basra."

"Magda told me."

"It's not easy to get around in Iraq—I'll give you the number of someone to call if you decide to come. He's the head of the Bureau of Archaeological Excavations, Ahmed Husseini, and he'll help you get to us."

Gian Maria said nothing, but his eyes gave away the impact the name Ahmed Husseini had made on him. When he'd finally managed to get into the archaeological conference in Rome looking for information on the Tannenberg attending, he'd been told that the only

Tannenberg listed was a woman, Clara Tannenberg, who was taking part in the conference with her husband, Ahmed Husseini.

"What is it? Do you know Ahmed?" Picot asked, curious.

"No, no," Gian Maria said, flushing yet again. "Listen, Professor Picot. I'm tired, and my mind's a mess. Your offer . . . I just don't know. I've come to help the Iraqis, and . . ."

"As I say, you decide. I'm offering you a job. We pay well. Now, if you'll excuse me, I need to see how things are going."

Picot left Gian Maria sitting there in the coffee shop, his mind racing, going in circles.

Finally, he made his way back to the lobby. He'd just managed to stumble on the needle in a haystack. Picot knew Clara Tannenberg's husband and had told Gian Maria where he worked. If the husband was in Baghdad, it wouldn't be hard to find the wife.

He needed to put his thoughts in order before he went further with any of this.

He couldn't press for an introduction to Ahmed Husseini. He decided to wait a couple of days before trying to contact him. And he had to think carefully about what to say to him and how to say it. His objective was to reach Clara Tannenberg—the question was how to convince her husband to take him to her.

Out in the street, he hailed a taxi and showed the driver an address written on a scrap of paper. The taxi driver smiled and asked him in English where he was from.

"Italy," Gian Maria replied, not knowing whether that was good or bad, since Silvio Berlusconi, the Italian prime minister, supported Bush.

But the news didn't seem to affect the taxi driver one way or the other—he just went on chatting. "We are going through a very bad time—there is much hunger. It was not like this before."

Gian Maria nodded without replying, fearful of giving offense.

When they arrived at their destination, Gian Maria paid the taxi driver and, black suitcase in hand, walked in through a dilapidated door. A sign in English and Arabic announced the headquarters of Aid to Children, the NGO dedicated to providing support to children in conflict-torn countries.

He walked through an anteroom, where women with children clinging to their skirts were waiting to be seen, and approached the young woman behind the desk. She looked him over from head to toe.

"Can I help you?" she asked in English.

"Well, uh, I've come from Rome, and I'd like to see Signore Baretti. I'm Gian Maria—"

"Oh, it's you! We've been waiting for you. I'll tell Luigi," she said, shifting from not-so-fluent English to fluent Italian, and got up and walked to an office partway down a crowded hallway. She emerged a few seconds later, motioning him to come.

"Go on in," she said, extending her hand. "I'm Aliam, by the way."

Luigi Baretti must have been about fifty. He was going bald and carried a few more pounds than seemed healthy but exuded an air of energy and efficiency. Nor was he one to beat about the bush.

"Sit down," Baretti ordered. "And forgive my skipping the niceties. I have no time for them, I'm afraid. Do you know how many of the children in our care have died this week for lack of medicine? I'll tell you—three. You can't imagine how many have died in all of Baghdad. And now here you are, with your big shots behind you, and a spiritual crisis that can only be fixed by a trip to Iraq to 'help out.' I need medicine, food, doctors, nurses, and money, not people who want to salve their consciences by flying in for a while to have a close-up look at the misery before they fly back to their comfortable lives in Rome, or wherever you're from."

"Have you finished?" asked Gian Maria, after a moment of shock-induced silence.

"What?"

"Have you finished insulting me?"

"I didn't insult you!"

"No? Then thank you for your welcome."

Luigi Baretti was taken aback. He hadn't expected a man who blushed like this one to stand up to him.

"I'm not a doctor or a nurse, Signore Baretti; I have no money. So I'm of no use at all, according to you. But I would like to help, nevertheless."

"We're overwhelmed here," the director said, by way of apology. He decided to choose his words more carefully, given that this man seemed to have friends in high places in the NGO. The fact that he was there at all was proof enough of that.

Gian Maria was surprised at himself. He had no idea where he'd gotten the strength of character to speak to Baretti that way.

"Of course you can help," Baretti said, retrenching. "Do you know how to drive? We need somebody to drive the children who need to be taken home or to the hospital or to go to the airport to pick up the packages that come in from Rome and our other offices. We need help, of course."

"I'll try my best. Whatever you need," Gian Maria said.

"Do you have a place to stay?"

"No, I planned to ask whether you knew of someplace that wasn't too expensive."

"The best thing to do is rent a room in the house of an Iraqi family. It won't cost much, and they can always use the money. We'll ask Aliam. When do you want to start?"

"Tomorrow."

"That's fine with me. Get settled in today, and Aliam can fill you in on how we work."

Gian Maria asked himself again why he was taking on commitments he couldn't keep. He'd come to Iraq to find Clara Tannenberg, and instead he was taking this "spiritual" detour. *What am I doing? Why can't I control what I do? Who is guiding, or misguiding, my steps?*

Aliam told him that one of the Iraqi doctors who worked with them had a spare room in his house that he might be willing to rent out. She was going to the hospital to deliver a case of antibiotics and bandages that had come in that morning from Holland, and suggested he come along to meet the doctor.

Gian Maria settled in beside Aliam in an old Renault. She drove very fast, swerving to avoid obstacles and other cars in the chaotic Baghdad traffic. Once there, Aliam strode purposefully through the doors and led Gian Maria down hallways in which cries and moans of pain mixed with the smell of disinfectants.

The doctors' and nurses' faces were lined and weary, and as Gian Maria's tour of the hospital proceeded, the lack of supplies was a constant refrain. Often, they told him, they had to watch their patients die for want of penicillin.

Aliam asked for Dr. Faisal al-Bitar when they came to the pediatric ward. A nurse made a weary gesture toward the door of the operating room. They waited a long while for the doctor to emerge. When he did, his face was creased with anger.

"Another child I couldn't save," he said bitterly to no one in particular.

"Faisal," Aliam called to him.

"Ah, you are here! Have you brought antibiotics?"

"Yes. A case came in this morning."

"That's it?"

"That's it—you know what happens in customs. . . ."

The doctor fixed his tormented black eyes on Gian Maria, waiting for Aliam to introduce them.

"This is Gian Maria. He's just come from Rome—he's here to lend a hand."

"Are you a doctor?"

"No."

"What are you?"

"I've come to help in any way I can—"

"He needs a room," Aliam broke in, "and since you told me you had one, I thought you might rent it to him."

Faisal gave Gian Maria a smile that looked like a mask, a memory of pleasantness more than a sincere emotion, and put out his hand.

"If you wait until I finish here, I'll take you to my home and show you the room. It's not very large, but it should be adequate. I live with my wife and three children—two girls and a boy. My mother lived with us, but she died a few months ago. That's why we have the spare room."

"I'm sure it will be fine," Gian Maria said.

"My wife is a teacher," Faisal explained, "and a fine cook, if you like our food."

"Yes, of course," was Gian Maria's grateful answer.

"If you are going to work with Aid to Children, you must get to know this hospital. Aliam will show you around, will you not, Aliam?"

The young woman led him down more hallways and through offices, stopping to introduce him to the doctors and nurses they met along the way. They all seemed desperate for supplies and medicines.

An hour later, Gian Maria met Faisal at the door of the hospital. The Iraqi's car, another old Renault, gleamed inside and out.

"I live in al-Ganir; there's a church near my home if you want to pray. It's full of Italians."

"A Catholic church?"

"Chaldean Catholic, but it is more or less the same, no?"

"Yes, yes, of course."

"My wife is Catholic."

"Really?"

"Yes. In Iraq there's a large Christian community that has always lived in peace with the Muslims. Now, I don't know how long that will last. . . ."

"Are you Christian too?"

"Officially. But I don't practice."

"What does that mean?"

"I don't go to church or pray. It's been years since I lost my way to God. It happened one of those days when I couldn't save the life of some small innocent and I watched him die in the midst of terrible pain. I can't understand why it has to be that way. Don't speak to me about God's will, or tell me that he sends us trials to test our faith. That child had leukemia. He fought for his life for two years, with a strength of spirit that was an inspiration to me. He was seven years old; he had never wronged anyone. God had no reason to make him pass some test. If God exists, his cruelty is infinite."

Gian Maria could not help making the sign of the cross over himself at Faisal's blasphemy or looking at Faisal with pity, but his pity was no match for the doctor's grief and rage.

"You blame God for what happens to men."

"I blame God for what happens to children—innocent, defenseless creatures. We adults bear the responsibility for the way we are, what we have done, what we do, but a newborn child? A three-year-old? What have these babies done to make them die in pain? And do not speak to me of original sin, because I do not allow people to speak stupidity to me. What sort of God burdens millions of innocents with guilt for a sin they did not commit?"

"Are you an atheist, then?" Gian Maria asked, fearing the response.

"If God exists, he is not in Iraq," Faisal replied.

They drove on in silence until they reached Faisal's apartment block. His flat was on the top floor of the three-story building.

The sounds of a children's scuffle greeted them as the doctor opened the door.

"What's going on here?" Faisal asked two little girls, identical as two drops of water, who were rolling and tumbling over each other in the spacious living room and screaming unintelligibly.

"She took my doll!" one of them said, pointing at the other.

"I did not," said the other. "It's mine—you just can't tell them apart."

"That's it—no more dolls alike for you two," said Faisal firmly as he pulled them up to kiss each one tenderly on the cheek. The girls hugged their father, paying no attention to the stranger.

"These are our twins," said Faisal. "Rania and Leila. They're five, and they're little demons, I assure you."

A brown-skinned woman in a business suit, her hair pulled back into a ponytail, came into the living room with a little boy in her arms.

"Nur, this is Gian Maria. Gian Maria, Nur, my wife. And this is Hadi, the baby of the family. He's a year and a half old."

Nur put the baby down on the floor and, smiling brightly, shook hands with Gian Maria.

"Welcome to our home. Faisal called to say that you would be staying with us, if you like the room."

"I'm sure I'll like it," was Gian Maria's spontaneous reply.

"Is he going to live here?" asked one of the twins.

"Yes, Rania, if he wishes to, yes," replied her mother, smiling at the expression on Gian Maria's face—clearly, he was asking himself how in the world he was supposed to tell the two girls apart.

Faisal and Nur showed Gian Maria the room. It was not very large, but it looked comfortable, and it had a window that opened onto the street. There was a bed with a headboard of light-colored wood, a night table, a round table with two chairs in a corner, and a large armoire for his clothes.

"This is fine, just fine," said Gian Maria, "but you haven't told me how much it will be."

"Would three hundred dollars a month be all right?"

"Yes, sure."

"With meals, of course," Nur said, apparently to excuse the high price.

"Really, that'll be fine, thank you both very much."

"Do you like children? Do you have children?" Nur asked.

"No, I don't have any children, but I love children. I have two nephews and a niece."

"Well, you're still young; you'll have them in time," Nur consoled him. She showed him through the spacious apartment and then left him to settle into his room.

Gian Maria insisted on paying the full rent in advance, although Nur had suggested he try it out first.

He hung his few shirts and pants in the armoire, where he found a stack of towels and sheets, and then went to find Faisal.

The doctor had gone to work in a little office off the living room, separated by a bookcase he had put up for privacy.

Faisal stood up and seemed pleased that Gian Maria would be staying. "I'll give you keys so that you can come and go as you wish, but I ask that you understand this is a house with children, so . . ."

"I understand—I'll try to be as little bother as possible. I know what it's like to live with a family."

"Do you know how to get to the NGO office from here?" Faisal asked.

"I'll have to learn the way, but I'll manage."

"By the way, do you speak Arabic at all?"

"A little—I think I'll be able to get by."

"Good. Anyway, if you need help with anything at all, just let me know."

"Thank you."

Faisal looked down at the papers he had been reading, and Gian Maria took his leave, not wanting to further disturb the family routine.

He decided to go out and familiarize himself with the neighborhood. He needed to think, which he couldn't do shut up in his room.

"I'm going to take a walk—can I bring anything back?" he asked Nur.

"No, thank you. Will you be eating with us tonight?"

"If it's not a bother . . ."

"No, not at all. We eat around eight."

"I'll be here."

He wandered through the neighborhood. He met with several curious stares, but no hostility. The women dressed Western-style, while the teenagers wore jeans and T-shirts emblazoned with names of rock groups.

He stopped at a stand where an old man was selling fruits and vegetables and chose a selection to take back to Nur and Faisal's house. Gian Maria asked where the church was, and the man directed him two blocks down and to the right.

When he entered the sanctuary, he felt a wave of inner peace embrace him. A group of women were praying, and their murmurs filled the silence with an agreeable hum. He sought out a dark corner and knelt down. With his eyes closed, he tried to find the words within himself to speak to God, and he asked him to guide his steps as he always had. In everything that was happening, Gian Maria clearly saw the hand of God at play again: the group of archaeologists at the airport in Amman; his ability to overcome his shyness and speak to Professor Picot; Picot's escort to Baghdad; and especially his mention of Ahmed Husseini, who was in Baghdad as well, which would undoubtedly lead Gian Maria to Clara Tannenberg.

No, none of that could be mere coincidence. It was God who had guided him, protected him, and aided him in carrying out his mission. God was always there—one simply had to be willing to listen, be sensitive to his presence, even in the midst of tragedy. If only he could convince Faisal of that . . . He would pray for the doctor, a good man whom pain and grief had separated from the Lord.

It was after seven when Gian Maria left the church, so he hurried back to the apartment. He didn't want to be late and create a bad impression.

"Hello!" he said to Nur as he walked in. She was trying to get Hadi to eat some thick sickly-green-colored puree, but the boy was kicking and squirming and closing his mouth every time his mother brought the spoon to it.

"Impossible. He simply does not like to eat," Nur complained.

"What is it you're giving him?" Gian Maria asked.

"Peas with an egg mixed in."

"Ugh, no wonder! I hated peas when I was little too."

"Well, there isn't much to eat here—little variety, I mean. We're fortunate, because we at least have money to buy food. Although to tell you the truth, we needed your rent money. I haven't been paid my full salary for months, and Faisal is the same." She eyed the grocery bag. "What do you have there?"

"Some peppers, squash, tomatoes, onions, oranges. There wasn't a lot to buy."

"But there was no reason for you to buy anything!"

"If I'm going to live here, I want to contribute as much as I can."

"Thank you. Food is always welcome."

"I went to the church too."

"You're Catholic?"

"Yes, and a believer. I have seen the hand of God guiding me throughout my life. Even to Iraq."

"You're a fortunate man, then. We haven't been in touch with God for a long time now."

"You lost your faith too?"

"It is hard to keep it. But to answer your question honestly, I think I have a little left. But I don't see the horrors my husband deals with every day in the hospital. When he tells me that another child has died from an infection that could have been cured with antibiotics, his pessimism rubs off on me. I also start asking where God is."

After dinner, Faisal and Gian Maria cleared the table while Nur loaded the dishes into the dishwasher. Then Faisal put the girls to bed and Nur finished putting Hadi down, though the baby continued to whimper from his crib.

Gian Maria bid the couple good night and retired to his room. He needed to be alone; he still had to think about how to approach Ahmed Husseini. Yves Picot could open that door, he supposed, but he wasn't sure that that was the right way to go.

Either way, he was exhausted. The day had been intense—it hadn't been even twenty-four hours since he'd arrived in Baghdad, although it seemed like months. He was asleep before he even had time to pray.

25

ROBERT BROWN AND PAUL DUKAIS WERE ALONE IN BROWN'S office, but Dukais had a suspicion the other man could be heard down the block.

"What do you mean, you could only get one man in?" Brown shouted.

"I told you. Picot wouldn't take the Bosnian, just the Croatian."

"One man to deal with Alfred! You must be nuts!"

"I don't have the slightest intention of sending one man up against Alfred, although that might be the smartest thing to do. One man doesn't attract attention; several is like putting an ad in the newspaper."

"Does the Croatian even know what he's supposed to do?" Brown asked, lowering his voice.

"Oh, yeah. He's been given very precise instructions. For now, he's to follow Clara and report back in detail, find out everything he can about her routine, et cetera, and when it's all clear to take the tablets, put together a plan and call me for the green light."

"And how's he supposed to get out? In a taxi?"

"He'll get out—and maybe even in a taxi. But if you'll listen to me—I think I can get two more men in, as businessmen trying to profit under the blockade. These two are very sharp, and very good."

"Oh, really? And what are two businessmen supposed to be doing in some dog's-ass village out in the middle of nowhere in Iraq?"

"Robert, don't take me for a fool. I've been in this business a long time, and I assure you I can give my men legitimate covers. So I'll spare you the details."

"Don't spare me—I'm going to be asked and I need to know what to say."

"All right, I'll fill you in. But remember that in my view, the Croatian is all we need to do the job—the others will step in only if necessary."

"It'll be necessary, Paul."

When Brown was alone again, he called George Wagner.

Enrique Gómez Thomson hung up after speaking to George in Washington. The operation was under way. They had a man in place, tailing Clara Tannenberg, ready to do whatever was necessary.

He'd told George again not to harm Alfred, although he knew that if the Croation so much as scratched Alfred's granddaughter, it would hurt Alfred more than any other measure they might take. He knew that the man they'd put in close to Clara would have to make decisions on his own as the situation changed and that he wouldn't run any unnecessary risks just to avoid a death or two. His instructions were clear: Get the Bible of Clay and get out of Iraq immediately, using the contact they'd given him. And that's what the Croatian would do—his prior history had made clear the lengths he would go to succeed.

Enrique's thoughts were interrupted by the telephone, which he snatched up.

"Enrique. It's Frankie."

"How are you? I just talked to George."

"Did he tell you we've got a man inside the expedition? A Croatian."

"Yes, I know."

"Listen, Alfred just called me. He's nervous. Those photographs were just the beginning. He's making threats."

"To do what?"

"He didn't go into detail, but he said if he was going to die he'd take people with him. He knows us, Enrique, and he knows that we're going to try to take the Bible of Clay away from him, no matter what promises we've made."

"If he finds it."

"He's sure we've infiltrated the expedition, and God save the Croatian if Alfred finds him out. He also said that if we don't let Clara keep the tablets, he'll make all the details of our business public. In the event of his death within the next few months, he's left instructions regarding his autopsy: If it's determined the cause of death was a homicide, he's made arrangements to issue a posthumous press release exposing our antiquities dealings."

"He's fucking crazy!"

"No, he's just defending himself."

"So what's he offering?"

"The same thing he's always offered: We let Clara keep the Bible of Clay, and he'll complete his end of the operation we've already started."

"But he doesn't trust us to keep that commitment."

"No."

"Frankie, he wants to keep something that doesn't belong to him. George is right."

"Then I think we're on the verge of committing group suicide."

"What?"

"I've got a bad feeling we're not going to be able to avoid disaster this time, Enrique."

"Look, we've been doing this for decades without being exposed. You have to stay rational."

"I am; that's what's so terrifying."

"I'll speak to him again."

"Isn't it a little risky to call him from Spain?"

"I suppose, but if there's no other way, I'll do it. I have to go on a trip, for business—I'll see what I can do from there."

"Call me."

Enrique hung up the telephone and clenched his fists. He swung around at a sound behind him. His son, José, had walked into the room and was observing him in silence, his face clouded with concern.

"What's happening, Papá?"

"Nothing that concerns you."

"Is that any way to talk to me?"

"José, I've told you not to ask me about my affairs—you know that."

"Yes. Since I was young I've known not to ask you questions or stick my nose in your business. Not that I even really know what that business might be. But I know that it's created a wall between you and your family."

"Exactly. That's the way it is because that's the way I want it. And now, please, leave me alone. I have some phone calls to make."

"You said you were leaving. Where are you going?"

"I'll be away a couple of days."

"Yes, but where? Doing what?"

Enrique banged his fist on the desk. He was an old man, but José stepped back at his fury.

"Get your nose out of my business, I told you! And don't treat me like an old man! I'm not dead yet, not by a long shot. Now get the hell out of here!"

José looked at the floor and left the room. It was difficult to recognize his father in the abusive old man he had just encountered.

Enrique sat back down. He opened a desk drawer, took out a bottle of pills, shook out two, and tossed them down—he felt like his head was about to explode. The doctor had warned him more than once that he mustn't let his emotions run away with him—years earlier he had suffered a heart attack, and though there hadn't been another one since, this stress clearly put him at risk.

He cursed Alfred, then cursed himself for interceding with George. Why couldn't Alfred just do what he was supposed to do, like everyone else did? Like everyone else had always done? Why did he have to go his own way this time?

He pressed a button under his desk and a few seconds later heard a soft knock at his door.

"Come in."

A maid dressed in black wearing a white apron and cap stood on the threshold, awaiting Enrique's orders.

"Bring me a glass of water and tell doña Rocío I'd like to see her, please."

"Yes, sir."

Rocío entered her husband's office with the glass of water and was startled by his haggard appearance. She'd seen her husband like this on other occasions, an icy stranger who seemed capable of anything, and it frightened her.

"Enrique—what's the matter? Are you all right?"

"Come in, we have to talk."

Rocío nodded, put the glass down on the desk, and sat in a chair facing her husband. She knew she shouldn't speak before he did. She smoothed her skirt and pulled it down over her knees, as though she might protect herself from the storm she knew could burst forth at any moment.

"In this drawer here," Enrique began, pointing to the top drawer in his desk, "there is a key to a safety-deposit box in the bank. I've never kept compromising papers there, but there are some that pertain to my businesses. The day I die, I want you to go to the bank and destroy them all. José must never see them. And I don't want you to talk to him about the past."

"I would never do that, Enrique."

He looked at his wife fixedly, trying to peer into the hidden depths of her heart.

"I'm not so sure, Rocío, I'm not so sure. You haven't so far, but I was here to keep you from doing it. After I'm gone . . ."

"I have never given you any reason to distrust me."

"No, you're right. But now swear to me that you'll do what I'm asking you. It's for José's sake. Let him go on as he is. Remember that if those papers get out . . . my friends will find out, and sooner or later they'll take action."

"What would they do to us?" Rocío asked fearfully.

"You can't even imagine. We have rules, and we're sworn to keep them."

"Why don't you destroy the papers yourself? Why don't you get rid of what you don't want us to see?"

"Because while I'm still alive, they're relevant. When I die, just do as I say."

"Then I hope I die before you!" Rocío was terrified and read the threat implicit in his request. She listened quietly as he went on to instruct her to also destroy any papers she found in the safe hidden behind a painting in his office.

Later, when he was once again alone, Enrique called Washington.

"You're right, George," he said without preamble. "We can't afford to be weak with Alfred. He's capable of destroying everything."

"Of destroying *us*. It's he who's broken the rules. I love him too, but it's him or us."

"I say it's us."

The helicopters were lined up on the runway of a military base under heavy watch by the Republican Guard. Ahmed Husseini was emphasizing to the base commander the prestige that the successful completion of the archaeological mission in Safran would bring to Iraq. The commander was listening with a bored look on his face. He had precise instructions from the Colonel to transport these foreigners and all their equipment to Safran, and that's what he was going to do; he didn't need any lessons on ancient Mesopotamia to carry out his mission.

Yves Picot and a few graduate students were helping the soldiers load the cases and crates into the helicopters, as were the other members of the expedition, including the women, and that, not surprisingly in this Muslim country, was causing the soldiers to laugh and whisper among themselves.

Picot had been adamant that everyone wear pants and boots and loose-fitting shirts—no shorts or tight T-shirts that might offend the culture. But even so, the soldiers were clearly enjoying the spectacle of these Westerners, who seemed unconcerned about anything except arriving safe and sound in Safran.

When everything was loaded and the members of the team were divided up into the two remaining helicopters, Picot sought out Ahmed.

"I'm sorry you won't be coming with us," he said as he shook Ahmed's hand in farewell.

"I'll be visiting Safran from time to time, as I told you. I won't be able to stay long, but I'll try to get there every two weeks to see how things are going. Meantime, I'll be in Baghdad, where I'll be able to handle anything that might come up."

"I hope we don't have to trouble you."

"No worries if you do. I wish you all the best. Oh, and Yves—trust Clara. She's a very capable archaeologist and has a sixth sense for finding important things."

"I will."

"Good luck."

They shook hands again and Yves climbed into the helicopter. A few minutes later, the convoy disappeared over the horizon. Ahmed sighed. Once again, he'd lost the reins of his own life; once again they were in the hands of Alfred Tannenberg. The old man had left him no choice—either help complete the antiquities operation under way or he would be killed. Simple as that. Worse yet, Alfred had told him that it would be Saddam's secret police who would deal with him. And Ahmed knew Alfred would have no scruples about seeing him "disappear" into one of Saddam's secret prisons, from which no one ever came out alive.

Alfred had told him contemptuously that if the operation was successful and Clara found the tablets, he'd let him go wherever he wanted. He wouldn't help him escape, but he also wouldn't stop him. One thing Ahmed was sure of was that Tannenberg was having him followed day and night. He hadn't seen Alfred's men, or the Colonel's, as the case might be, but he knew they were watching him.

He returned to his office in the ministry. He had a great deal of work to do. What Alfred had asked him to find wasn't easy, although if anyone could access the information, Ahmed could.

Clara felt a surge of emotion when she heard the sound of the helicopters approaching Safran. Picot would be surprised to arrive and find her team already at work excavating.

Fabian and Marta came up behind her to watch the helicopters land. They, too, were proud of what they had already accomplished.

When Picot jumped down out of the aircraft, Fabian was waiting, and the two men embraced.

"Boy, I've missed you," Picot said, shaking his head wearily.

"Same here," said Fabian, laughing.

Marta and Clara moved forward to assist one particularly sick student, who'd just emerged from the helicopter as pale as a sheet. Clara motioned to one of the villagers to bring a big bottle of water and a plastic glass and encouraged her to drink.

"Here, you'll feel better."

"I don't think I can keep anything down," Magda said, separating herself from Lola and Marisa while politely resisting the thought of putting something in her stomach.

"Come on, it'll go away—I got motion sickness too," Marta consoled her.

"I'm never getting in one of those contraptions again as long as I live," she swore. "I'll go back to Baghdad on a camel first."

"Me too," Marta laughed, "but meantime, drink the water. Clara's right—it'll make you feel better."

Fabian had already begun to show Yves around the camp—the mud houses where the labs would be and where the tablets and other objects would be classified, documented, and studied; the place where the computers would be installed; the one-room meeting house where they would all gather to discuss their findings; and the showers, latrines, and weatherproofed tents most of the members of the dig would be living in over the next few months, unless they opted to stay in rooms that some of the villagers were willing to rent.

They entered the mud house where Fabian had organized their headquarters. Magda, who was following them shakily, collapsed into a folding chair with Marta and Clara still hovering over her. Picot, at least, was more than willing to take some water, and he quickly knocked back over half the bottle.

"Good work," Picot said. "I knew it was right to send you on ahead."

"The truth is, we started without you!" Marta said. "For a couple of days we've been clearing the site and testing the workers to see what they're capable of. They range from the very good to the near hopeless, but they're all willing, at least, so I'm sure they'll be fine. They're no strangers to manual labor, that's for sure."

"Another thing—I made Marta the overseer, and I even gave her a whip," Fabian said, laughing. "She's organized us all into a well-oiled machine. An army would be more like it. And the workers are delighted—they won't move a muscle without checking with her first."

"You always need a good slave driver—I mean overseer," Picot said, and nodded. "The bad thing is that there's nothing for me to do now."

Clara looked on, smiling, but beyond the greetings she and Picot had exchanged politely, she didn't quite have the nerve to join in. Over the past few days the close friendship between Fabian and Marta had become eminently clear to her. One could see how well they understood each other, how they almost read each other's minds, and she sensed the same relationship existed between Fabian and Picot.

"So where do we sleep?" asked Magda, who was still feeling woozy.

"There's a room for you in the house next door; Yves and I will be staying there too. It's got four rooms, so we'll fit. Or, if you prefer, look at the list of villagers who are offering to rent rooms," Fabian replied.

"No, that's fine. If you all don't mind, I'm going to lie down for a while," she almost pleaded.

"I'll show you where it is," Clara offered.

When Clara and Magda were gone, Yves turned to Fabian.

"Any problems?"

"No, really, not a one. Everyone here has an almost reverential respect for Clara. Anything we want to do is fine with her; she's accepted all our suggestions—or Marta's orders, rather. She gives her opinion, but if she can't convince us she doesn't waste any time arguing. She's very intelligent, and she's making no show of running things or vying for the upper hand."

"There's a woman, a Shiite named Fatima, who looks after her as though she were her own daughter," Marta put in. "Sometimes she even goes over to the dig with her. And there are also four guards who are on her like fleas on Rover."

"Yeah, I saw that in Baghdad—she's under constant protection, which isn't surprising given the situation in Iraq. And also, I suppose, given the fact that her husband is part of the regime's inner circle," Picot agreed.

"I think it's more than just politics," said Marta. "The other day, her bodyguards lost sight of her. She was with me—we couldn't sleep, so we got up before dawn and went out walking. When they found us, you'd have thought they were about to go crazy—one of them pleaded with Clara that her grandfather would kill them all if anything happened to her, and he said something about 'those Italians.' Clara looked at me and told them to be quiet."

"Which means she's got enemies," Picot mused aloud.

"Let's not let our imaginations run away with us," said Fabian. "We don't know what the bodyguards were referring to."

"But they were scared spitless, I know that," Marta insisted. "Scared something might have happened to her, and even more scared of what might happen to them."

"The mysterious grandfather no one can manage to meet," Yves groaned.

"And whom Clara refuses to talk about," Marta added.

"We've tried to get her to tell us when and why her grandfather was in Haran decades ago, but it's useless; she won't say a word. All she does is dodge the question and change the subject. . . . Anyway, let's show you the rest of the camp," Fabian said.

Yves congratulated them and then silently congratulated himself on managing to convince Fabian to come along on this adventure. He also praised Marta's work. She was a woman with what appeared to be an innate ability to get things organized, and she had worked wonders already.

"I've named the houses where we'll be working and storing the material," Fabian told Yves. "The building we were just in is our head-quarters. Where we'll be taking the tablets is, naturally, the tablet building. The computers will be installed over there," he said, pointing to another mud house. "I'm just calling it communications. We'll number the warehouses—one, two, three . . . and so on."

The head of the village had invited everyone to a welcoming reception, where he had set out lunch for the team and some of his leading men. Yves couldn't bring himself to like Ayed Sahadi, the man who Fabian said had met them at the airport and who'd been chosen to be in charge of the workers. He didn't know why—Ayed seemed friendly enough and quietly efficient, but there was something about him that suggested he was more than a simple functionary. He was tall and muscular, with a slight military air, and it was clear that he was accustomed to giving orders. And he spoke English, which surprised Picot.

"I worked in Baghdad. I learned there," was the extent of his explanation.

Clara seemed to know him from before, and she treated him with a degree of familiarity, but he maintained a somewhat respectful distance toward her. The men obeyed him instantly; even the head of the village seemed to shrink before him.

"Where'd this Ayed come from?" Yves asked Fabian.

"He cleared our way into Iraq without so much as a question. He seems to know the right people. Not a very talkative chap, though. Clara says she was expecting him because he's worked with her and her husband before. I don't know what to tell you—he seems like some kind of military type," Fabian replied.

"Yes, that's what he seems like to me too. I wonder if he's spying for Saddam," Yves speculated.

"Well, we have to figure they're going to keep an eye on us and that there might be spies at the site. That's the way a dictatorship works—plus, we're on the verge of a war, so we shouldn't be surprised if they've planted him with us," Marta said with apparent indifference.

"I still don't like it," Yves said.

"Let's wait and see what he does," Marta suggested.

That afternoon, once all the new equipment had been unpacked and operations were under way, Yves called the entire team together to review the plans for the excavation. They were all professionals; even the students who had come with them had already taken part in other excavations, so Yves didn't have to waste much time on the basics.

The wake-up call every morning would be at four. Between four and a quarter to five, everyone was to shower and have breakfast and then, before five, be at the site. At ten there would be a short break, about fifteen minutes, and then they would work until two. From two to four, lunch and time for a nap if they needed one; at four they'd start working again until the sun went down.

No one complained—neither the team put together by Yves nor the men from the village. The workers would be paid in dollars, ten times what they'd ordinarily earn in a month, so they were willing to work as hard as they had to.

When the meeting was over, a young Croatian man came over to Picot. His height and everything else about him was average, but the oversize glasses he wore made him look like the perfect nerd.

"I'm having trouble with the computer installation," he advised Yves. "The current is too weak, and the hardware pulls too much power."

"Talk to Ayed Sahadi; he'll deal with it," Picot told the young man. The Croatian nodded nonchalantly and left.

"You don't like him." Marta's comment surprised Picot.

"Why do you say that?"

"I can see it a mile away. Fact is, nobody likes Ante Plaskic. I don't know why you brought him."

"He was recommended by a friend of mine at the University of Berlin."

"I guess we all have our prejudices," Marta said. "Ante is Croatian and I can't help thinking about the Balkans."

"My friend said he was a survivor, that his village had been wiped out by the Bosnians in reprisal for a massacre that his compatriots had carried out. I don't know. In that damned war it was the Bosnians who had the worst of it, so maybe you're right—maybe my prejudices *are* coming out."

"Of course, it's easy to oversimplify—these are the good guys and these are the bad guys. Everything black and white, no room for gray. Ante may have been a victim of the war."

"Or he may have been a killer."

"He's awfully young to have been a killer," Marta pointed out, always the devil's advocate.

"I'm not so sure. He must be close to thirty now, right?"

"Twenty-seven. I think."

"Fourteen-year-olds were shooting guns when all that went down."

"So send him home."

"No—as you say, it wouldn't be fair."

"I didn't say that," Marta protested.

"Then we'll give him a chance, and if I still feel uncomfortable, I'll rethink it."

Fabian came over. "What's up?"

"We were talking about Ante," Marta replied.

"Yves doesn't trust him and is beginning to regret bringing him along—am I right?"

Picot burst out laughing. Fabian knew him too well.

"To tell you the truth, there's something about him that bothers me too," Fabian noted.

"Look, he's computer-savvy, and so far that's all we need to know. Let's change the subject before we get carried away," Marta said, closing the conversation.

Ayed Sahadi was, in fact, exactly what he looked like—a soldier, a member of the Iraqi counterespionage service, a protégé of the Colonel.

Alfred Tannenberg had personally asked the Colonel to send Ayed to Safran—Ayed had taken part in some of the jobs the Colonel had helped with.

Commander Sahadi had a reputation as a sadist, with any number of terrible stories circulating about the grisly tortures he meted out. Enemies of Saddam's who fell into Sahadi's hands prayed to die quickly.

His mission in Safran, in addition to protecting Clara's life, was to try to uncover the men Alfred Tannenberg was sure his old friends had planted in the group to seize the Bible of Clay. Sahadi had positioned some of his own men among the workers hired for the excavation— soldiers like him, experts in counterespionage, who would earn themselves a good fistful of dollars if they found a mole.

Clara had seen Ayed from time to time in the Yellow House with the Colonel. Her grandfather had made it clear that Ayed was going to be her shadow and that she was to put him in charge of the workers, just as he'd insisted that Ayed would coordinate with Ahmed, back in Baghdad, and with Tannenberg himself.

And knowing it was futile to oppose her grandfather's wishes, Clara had grudgingly agreed.

Ante Plaskic had stayed behind in his mud house as the rest of the team rose in the early hours of the morning to begin the day's work. In addition to the computer equipment, there was a room with a cot for him to sleep on. It had been a stroke of luck that they'd given him this private space. He could sense the team's latent hostility toward him, but he'd decided to ignore it. He didn't need to make friends: He was there to get his hands on those tablets and kill anyone who tried to stop him. Anyway, it had been a long time since he'd cared whether he was liked or not. The war had desensitized him. He could live happily without the rest of humanity. If he had his way, he'd kill the entire expedition, one by one.

He was surprised to see Ayed Sahadi enter the computer room— he'd thought he was with the rest of the workers at the excavation site.

"Good morning," the Iraqi said.

"Good morning."

"Is there anything you need, or is everything okay now?" Ayed asked him.

"Everything is all right, for the moment—I hope these things work. They should—they're the best."

"Very well. If you have any more problems, come and find me—I can call Baghdad and they'll send whatever you need."

"Thanks. When I finish up in here, I thought I'd go out to the site to have a look around. There's not much data to enter yet."

"Whatever you like."

Sahadi left the communications building, thinking about the Croatian. There was something about him, about his baby face, about the unfashionable thick-rimmed glasses, that felt fake, but he told himself not to act on intuition alone. He suspected, though, that the man had probably killed any number of Muslims during the war. Not that Ayed practiced the laws of his religion; quite the contrary. But even so, his sympathies resided firmly with the Bosnians.

Frenetic activity continued around the crater and ancient ruins throughout the day. Down inside the hole, Ante could just make out a room where, far in the distant past, someone had lined up hundreds of tablets on driedmud shelves. He decided not to stand there looking but to join in the work, and he took a place beside Clara.

"Tell me how I can help," he said.

Clara didn't think twice—she put him to work clearing out more of the debris.

26

IT HAD BEEN HARD FOR TOM MARTIN TO MAKE UP HIS mind. The mysterious Mr. Burton's brazen request was on the far fringe of Global Group's usual activities. A job in Iraq to kill every Tannenberg he could find—Burton had been luminously clear; there was no margin for misunderstanding.

After weighing his options, Tom finally decided to send one man instead of an entire team. One person would arouse fewer suspicions. And if reinforcements were needed, he could send them later. But men in this line of work—hired killers, not to put too fine a point on it—preferred to act alone. Each one had his own methods, his own habits.

He'd also debated whether to mention the job to his friend Paul Dukais, president of Planet Security. But as luck would have it, Dukais had asked him to help infiltrate a man into an archaeological mission led by one Clara Tannenberg—the client wanted to relieve her of some priceless tablets, and was willing to have her killed for them if need be. So in the end, he'd decided not to say anything to Paul. He was sure the Croatian he'd recommended would do his job of securing the tablets, and then his man would have to do his. His man had an advantage too—Tom knew that the Tannenbergs had pissed off a lot of people, people with money to burn.

There was a knock on the door and Lion Doyle was shown into Tom's office.

"Have a seat, Lion. How are you?"

"Good—just got back from vacation."

"Perfect—you'll be well rested for what I've got."

For the next hour the two men pored over the information Tom had been given and more he had developed himself, including the little he knew about the mysterious Mr. Burton, whom he had had photographed before he left the Global Group building.

"I can't find anything on him. He's not a Brit, of course, although his English is perfect. Our friends in Scotland Yard don't have a record of anybody with that face. Ditto for Interpol."

"Then he's just an anonymous citizen who pays his taxes and hasn't done anything to get himself into the databases," Doyle said.

"Yeah, but upright citizens don't come in looking to hire a killer. Plus, he kept saying 'we'—it's not just him, there's a whole group who want this Tannenberg wiped out."

"From what I'm gathering here, the Tannenbergs are not the most popular family on the block. They're in a dangerous line of black-market work, and they've got a lot of enemies. Whoever's hired you must have been screwed, one way or another."

"No doubt, but I have this feeling there's more to it. That maybe it's personal, not business. I just can't figure it out."

Lion, like most in his line of work, seemed unconcerned with motive. "How much, Tom?"

"A million euros. That's what you'll get. A million euros, tax-free."

"I want half up front."

"I don't know whether that'll be possible—the client hasn't anted up yet."

"Well, tell him I want a half a million. It's that simple. You don't know whether I'm going to have to kill one Tannenberg or a dozen—you don't know whether there are others besides this woman Clara and the invisible old man. There may even be children. I don't like killing children."

"All right. I'll make it happen."

"You know how to pay me. If the money's there in three days, I'll go to Iraq."

"You need a cover."

"If it's all the same to you, I'll work it out—if I need you, I'll let you know. I'll be in touch."

Lion Doyle retrieved his gray minivan from the parking garage where he'd left it and drove slowly, randomly, through London, trying to see whether he was being followed. Then he took the M4 motorway toward Wales.

After almost an entire lifetime away, he'd chosen to return to his old stomping grounds. He'd bought an old farm, spruced it up, and married a professor at the University of Cardiff, a wonderful woman who'd made it to forty-five without marrying. She'd spent her life climbing the ladder at the university, and now she'd been given a chair in romance philology.

Marian had light-brown hair and green eyes; she was tall and slightly pudgy. She'd fallen in love with him at first sight. Lion had dark hair, brown eyes, and a weathered complexion—a rugged, cheerful man who inspired confidence and made women feel safe.

He'd told her that he'd been in the army but finally wanted to settle in a real place of his own, so he'd become a security consultant. The business had done well and he'd earned a good bit of money, enough to buy the farm, fix it up, and make a home of it.

It was far too late for them to start a family, but it was enough that they had each other, that they be able to share good times in the years they had left.

If someone had told Marian that her husband had a secret account on the Isle of Man with enough money to allow him a very early and comfortable retirement—enough to let him live it up for the remainder of his years—she wouldn't have believed it. She was convinced that there were no secrets between them. Besides, they were perfectly comfortable as they were.

That was why Marian was content to hire a cleaning woman to come to the farm three times a week and a man to lend a hand once in a while in the garden that Lion, when he was home, liked to tend personally.

Her husband was away a good deal, often for weeks at a time, but that was his work and Marian accepted it without a word of complaint. She knew that sometimes he forgot to call home, and sometimes when she dialed his cell phone she got his voice mail. But he always came back, as sweet as ever, bringing her some little gift—a handbag, some earrings, a scarf, something to show he'd been thinking of her. Marian had not the slightest doubt that Lion would always come home again.

Hans Hausser had a weakness for Paris. The taxi driver unsuccessfully attempted to make small talk as Hans took in the wonderful view of the Seine.

The day before, he had spoken with Tom Martin. Martin had found the perfect man for the job, but he required half a million euros up front. That was no problem for the resourceful "Mr. Burton," and they hung up in agreement. Shortly after, using their established methods, he'd communicated with each of his compatriots, who had chosen to meet again in Paris. Hans' daughter, Berta, was distressed by his sudden leave of absence, but she couldn't do much more than complain.

At the Berlin airport he'd had time to buy a small carry-on as well as a shirt, underwear, and the toiletries he'd be needing. The desk clerk at the Hotel Louvre found nothing strange about the prosperous-looking, silver-haired man who'd made a reservation by phone and checked in an hour ago.

Hausser walked toward the Place de la Ópera and sat down in a café. He ordered a glass of wine and a canapé. He was hungry; he hadn't had time to eat a bite all day.

Half an hour later another gentleman of the same age waved as he entered the café. Hans stood and the two men embraced.

"It's good to see you, Carlo."

"Likewise, my friend. What an adventure, eh! You have no idea the story I've had to invent so my children would leave me in peace. I feel as though I've run away from home—like some teenager!"

"I know what you mean. I called Berta and she was hysterical. I had to put my foot down and tell her I was an adult and was not going to allow myself to be locked in my room like some wayward child. But I know she's very worried, and that upsets me. Not enough to make me lose my appetite, though—what do you say we eat? I'm starving."

"Perfect. I know a bistro near here with wonderful food. Finish your wine and we'll be on our way."

Hans explained to his friend in person what he'd so briefly reported by e-mail: He'd had a short conversation with Tom Martin, who'd asked for half a million euros immediately. He'd already given him three hundred thousand the day they signed the contract, and the total amount was to be two million. If they gave him another half a million now, it would be tantamount to paying half the money in advance.

"We'll pay, Hans—we've no choice, we have to trust him. Luca told me he was the most honest agent in the business, although given the business . . . Still, I think he'll hold up his end. I brought some money with me, as will Bruno and Mercedes. We've all done what we'd planned—taken small sums of money out of the bank from time to time and kept it at home precisely for this moment."

After their late lunch, the two friends parted ways. Carlo had reserved a room in the Hotel d'Horse, not far from Hans.

At eleven a.m., the crowd at Café de la Paix was sparse. A fine mist impregnated the gray Paris morning and slowed traffic to a crawl.

Mercedes was cold. In Barcelona, the weather had been sunny, and her lightweight business suit was no protection against the rain. Bruno Müller, more farsighted, had donned a stylish khaki trench coat.

The four friends were sitting over coffee.

"My plane leaves for London at two," said Hans Hausser. "When I get home, I'll call you all."

"No, we can't wait until tomorrow," Mercedes, always blunt, replied. "I'll die of anxiety. I want to know that everything's gone well—call us as soon as you know something. Please."

"I'll do what I can, Mercedes, but I have to move cautiously: I don't want Martin's men to find out who this mysterious Mr. Burton is."

"Hans is right," Bruno said. "We have to be patient."

"And pray," Carlo added.

"You can pray all you like—I gave that up," shot back Mercedes.

Hans left the café carrying a shopping bag from Galeries Lafayette. In the bottom of it, beneath a carefully folded sweater, were envelopes that his friends had brought for him: half a million euros, to be hand-delivered to the president of Global Group.

After Hans, Mercedes left, insisting that no one need accompany her. She hailed a taxi and asked to be taken directly to the airport. Carlo and Bruno decided to have lunch before they, too, departed the City of Light.

In London, it was raining even harder. Hans congratulated himself on having bought a raincoat at Charles de Gaulle. It occurred to him that with the money he had on him, he'd be able to go anywhere without worrying about luggage.

He was fatigued, though. The stress of the last twenty-four hours was catching up, but with a little luck he'd be home again by early next morning.

He'd called Berta, who'd pleaded with him to be honest with her. He hardly recognized himself when he told her that if she kept sticking her nose in his business they wouldn't be able to continue living under the same roof. His daughter had stifled a sob before hanging up.

A taxi left him three blocks from the offices of Global Group. He walked the rest of the way, his step as light as his tired legs would allow.

The receptionist announced him.

"You surprise me," Martin told him as they shook hands. "It never occurred to me that you'd come in like this, without a word in advance. You could have made a wire transfer."

"This way is better for everyone concerned. I'll just need a receipt for the half million. When will your man be leaving for Iraq?"

"As soon as he gets his money."

Tom wrote out a receipt for half a million euros, signed it, and handed it to the false Mr. Burton.

"When will you be sending me news?" Hausser asked.

"As soon as I have any. Tomorrow my man will have his money; the day after, he'll move out. Nowadays anybody who enters Iraq is photographed and tracked, and not just by Saddam's police. The Americans are watching everyone, as are my former colleagues at MI5. He has to find a cover for his trip, make the travel arrangements, then find this family. Be patient—these things take time."

"All right. Take this number. It's a cell phone. As soon as you know something, call me."

"The Internet is safer."

"I don't think so. Call me."

"Whatever you say. You're a strange man, Mr. Burton."

"I imagine all your clients are."

Paul Dukais reread the report that Ante Plaskic had sent him. Hiring the Croatian had been the right thing to do; he silently thanked Tom Martin for his recommendation.

On several sheets of paper, in clear handwriting and adequate, if stilted, English, Plaskic had set forth the details of the work of the archaeological expedition and the difficulties he faced:

> *I don't trust Ayed Sahadi, and he doesn't trust me. Sahadi is the foreman of the laborers, and he is responsible for the overall functioning of the excavation. He deals with the workers, assigns their shifts, and is in charge of paying them.*
>
> *In my opinion, Sahadi is more than just a foreman; he may be a spy or a police agent. His mission seems clear: protect Clara Tannenberg. He tries hard not to let her out of his*

sight. There are three or four men always in her vicinity, in addition to her personal team of bodyguards. It is difficult to get near her without being a stone's throw from at least one of them.

She, however, likes to escape from her guards, and two or three times there has been quite a commotion because she has disappeared, always at dawn, to go down to the Euphrates to swim; the first time she went with Professor Marta Gómez, the person who has assumed command of our operation. Another day, she organized a secret "escape" for herself and several of the other women on the archaeological team. No one realized what was happening, not even Picot. And once she decided to spend the night beside the ruins, at the site of the excavation. She took a blanket with her and slept on the ground.

It will be impossible for her to elude her minders again, however, because now two of them sleep on the ground at the door of the house she is staying in.

Picot has had a run-in with her, and he threatened to call her grandfather—in fact, he did try to reach him, and now she never stops glaring at him.

Picot has asked for more workers, and Ayed Sahadi has hired another hundred men. The pace of the work will be, I think, impossible to sustain; the team members hardly sleep, perhaps only a few hours every night, and there is tension among them. One or two of the professors who came with Picot have had some angry confrontations with him over excavation methods. Some students are complaining that they are being exploited, and the workers are exhausted at the end of their shifts, their hands covered in scratches and blisters.

But neither Picot nor Clara Tannenberg seems to care about the exhaustion of the workers or the complaints of their own team.

Fabian Tudela, Picot's right-hand man, is an archaeologist who goes around putting out fires, as they say. He seems to be the only person able to bring peace when everything is about to explode. But things will explode, sooner or later; we are working more than fourteen hours a day.

What they claim to have uncovered is a temple, revealed at first some months ago by an American bomb that blasted into one of the upper stories of the building. They say there was a library in the building, which explains the large number of tablets they have discovered. They have now excavated three rooms and recovered more than two thousand tablets, which were lined up in niches carved into the walls.

The students, under the supervision of four professors, are classifying the tablets after they have been cleaned. The tablets apparently contain the temple's accounts, although in the room they are now excavating they have found the remains of tablets detailing the ancient people's knowledge of certain minerals and animals.

So far, all the rooms measure 5.3 meters by 3.6 meters, although they are saying that there are larger rooms in other parts of the temple.

My job is to enter all the finds into the computer after they have been photographed from various angles and, in the case of tablets, their contents noted.

Three students have been assigned to help me.

All the archaeologists come to the computer house, as it is called, to see how the digitalization of their finds is going. Every day I receive ever more detailed instructions from this Professor Gómez, a zealous, meticulous woman whom I personally find unbearable.

Tablets have been found with the names of scribes on the top. This seems to have been the custom among the ancient people here. Apparently some of the tablets bear the name of this "Shamas," with a catalogue of the region's flora. But they've found no trace of tablets with epic poems or historical events, and this makes Tannenberg more and more nervous, Picot more and more grouchy. Picot, in fact, complains that he is wasting his time.

A few days ago, the entire team met to evaluate the findings thus far. Picot was very negative, but Fabian Tudela, Marta Gómez, and the other archaeologists said they were in the presence of one of the unique archaeological sites of the century, as there was no reference anywhere to this palace or temple. They all believe it is especially important because of its proximity to ancient Ur. Apparently the palace itself is not very large, although the library they believe they are uncovering is a good size.

Professor Gómez favors extending the excavation beyond what they believe is the perimeter of the temple, in order to locate the walls of the city or palace and the houses. In this meeting they argued for more than three hours, but in the end, the headstrong professor won the day, because Fabian Tudela and Clara Tannenberg herself supported her. That is why they have hired more workers and are looking for many more.

It is not easy to find workers, since the entire country is in a state of alert, but there is so much poverty, and the Tannenbergs have so much money and influence, that apparently within a few days a contingent of men will be coming in from all parts of Iraq to join the expedition.

The village leader's son-in-law, the contact you gave me to send the reports through, is one of the drivers who travels through the neighboring villages looking for basic foodstuffs, and he seems to be trusted by Ayed Sahadi, insofar as Sahadi trusts anyone—in fact, if it is not foolhardy to trust anyone here.

If the tablets they are looking for are found, it will not be easy to gain control of them, much less smuggle them out. Men can be bought, of course, but I fear that here, there is always someone willing to better one's best offer—and so it would not surprise me to be betrayed.

27

ABRAM WAS WAITING FOR SHAMAS IN THE USUAL PLACE, OUT-side Haran. They had hardly spoken about Terah's death.

The boy approached shyly, hoping to find the words to express his sadness, to console Abram's grief. But he did not have to say anything, because Abram squeezed his shoulder in a sign of recognition and motioned him to sit down.

"I am sorry I will not see you anymore," Abram told him.

"Will you never go back to Ur, or even to Haran?" Shamas asked, his eyebrows knitting in concern.

"No. There will be no going back after the day I set out on this journey. We will never see each other again, Shamas, but I will feel you in my heart, and I hope you will not forget me. Keep the tablets upon which you have recorded our history, and explain to our people what I have explained to you."

Shamas could only nod, overwhelmed as he was by what Abram was asking of him. It was a humbling sign of great confidence, but it was much to ask of a boy like himself. Shyly, he asked Abram if God had spoken to him again.

"Yes, the day the women were preparing Terah for his burial in the very ground out of which God molded the first man. I must do what He asks of me. And you should know, Shamas, that my race shall spread over the entire earth, and I will be called the father of multitudes."

"Then we shall call you Abraham," said the boy, an incredulous smile coming to his face, for he knew that Sarai, Abram's wife, had given him no children.

"Just as you say—I shall be called Abraham by my children's children, and their children, and their children after them, and so on, down through the ages."

The boy was impressed by the firmness with which Abram declared that he would become the father of many tribes. But he believed him, as he had always believed him.

"I will tell everyone to call you Abraham from now on," Shamas said.

"Yes, do that. Now take out your things, for it is time to write. There is much you need to know before we part."

Once again Shamas and Abraham were surprised by the appearance of the moon at sunset, and they prepared for their walk back to Haran. Abraham helped Shamas carry the tablets. At the door of the house they met Jadin, who invited his cousin into the house to break bread with them.

The two men spoke of the journeys they were about to undertake, each in his own direction, both knowing that they would never meet again.

Jadin wanted to put behind him the life of a shepherd and settle forever in Ur, where Shamas would become a scribe in the service of the palace. Ili would be able to finish teaching him the use of the bullae and the calculi, for which Shamas had shown great promise during his years in Haran.

In the last few years, Shamas had become a young man conscious of the fact that learning required dedication. In addition, the scribes in Haran did not have the patience that his teacher in Ur had had, nor did they encourage his curiosity. And there was still much to learn if he was to become a dub-sar and, after many years as a scribe, come to the end of his life as an um-mi-a.

Shamas listened in silence to the conversation between his father and Abraham, the suggestions they made to one another. The winter had passed and spring was upon them, bringing forth green leaves and tiny flowers and making the sky bright blue. It was the time of year when men set out on journeys.

Abraham and Jadin agreed to take their leave of each other by sacrificing a lamb, in the hope that it would please the Lord.

"Father, when are we leaving?" asked the boy the minute Abraham left the house.

"You heard, my son—within the space of a moon we will be on our way. We will not be going alone, though; other members of the tribe will return to Ur with us." He studied his son's face. "Are you sorry not to be accompanying Abraham?"

"No, Father, I want to go back home."

"This is your home."

"To me, home is where I grew up, in Ur. I will always remember Abraham, but he tells me that all men must follow their own path. He must do what God has commanded him to do, and I feel that I must return to the land of our ancestors. There I will explain to our people everything I have learned, and I will preserve the tablets that contain Abraham's story."

"You have chosen your destination and your destiny."

"No, Father, I feel that God has chosen it for me."

"I feel that I must return too, my son. As does your mother. Her heart is heavy with homesickness, and she will smile again only on the day we set eyes upon Ur. She wishes to die where her people died. This is our house, but we feel ourselves strangers here. Yes, we must go."

Shamas nodded happily. Anticipation of the journey gave him butterflies. For him, life was pointless if it became monotonous. They would journey during the day, pitch their camp at nightfall, and the women would bake bread and cook their meals. He could already feel the cool waters of the Euphrates, hear the conversations around the fire.

He thought of Abraham with a pang of sadness. He would miss him. He knew that his kinsman was a special man, chosen by God to become the father of nations. He did not know how that would happen, since Sarai had given him no children, but if God had promised it, so it would be, Shamas told himself.

He had written down the creation of the earth as Abraham knew it. And Shamas had no doubt that it was all true. His relationship with God, though, was difficult. Sometimes he thought he was on the verge of understanding the mystery of life, but just as he was about to grasp it, his mind became hazy and he was unable to think.

Other times, he could not understand God's actions, His anger, the harshness with which He punished mankind. Why was disobedience so intolerable to the Lord? Shamas became upset, even reproachful toward Him at times, but never lost conviction in Abraham's words. Shamas' faith was like a rock sitting upon the ground for the rest of eternity.

His father had urged him to be prudent when they reached Ur. He could not renounce Enlil, father of the gods, or Marduk, or Tiamat, or any of the other deities.

Shamas knew how difficult it was to talk about a God who had no face, whom one could not see but only feel in one's heart. So, yes, he would be careful when he talked about Him, and he would not try to supplant the other gods. He would have to plant the seed of God in the hearts of those who listened to him and hope that it sprouted.

The day came at last for the farewell. Just before dawn, in the coolness of the morning, Abraham and his tribe were preparing to depart from Jadin and his people. The women were loading the asses, and children were running about, their eyes still filled with the dry crust of sleep, interrupting their mothers' work.

Shamas was waiting expectantly for Abraham to speak to him, and he was happy when the old man gestured to him to step aside, where they could speak.

"Come, we still have time to talk while the others finish the preparations for the journey," Abraham said.

"Now that you are leaving, I feel how much I am going to miss you," Shamas told him.

"I will miss you too and will remember you always. But I want you to do something for me—something I asked you to do several days ago: I want you to guard and protect the story of Creation, just as I told it to you. We men must never forget that we are but a speck of dust, our life breathed into us by the Lord. Sometimes we believe that we do not need Him, yet other times we reproach Him because He is not there to help us when we do."

"I have struggled with those feelings often."

"But how can we comprehend the ways of God, Shamas? We were made of clay, like those figures that Terah and I made. We walk, we talk, we feel because He blew life into us, and when He wishes, He can take life away again, just as I destroyed my father's winged bulls. They were gods created by men, and they were no longer gods when my hands destroyed them.

"No, Shamas, we cannot comprehend Him, much less judge His acts. I cannot answer your questions because I do not have the answers. I only know that there is a God who is the Beginning and the End, the Creator of all things, He who made us and condemned us to die because He allowed us to choose."

"May God be with you wherever your journey takes you, Abraham."

"And you also, Shamas, and all your people. God is everywhere."

"Whom will I talk to about God? My father demands prudence and discretion, so as not to upset others."

"Then speak of Him with your father, who carries Him in his heart. With old Joab, with Zebulon, and with all your kin as you set out on your own journey. And with many of those who remained in Ur upon your return."

"And who will guide me?"

"There is a moment in life when we must look inside ourselves for guidance. You have your father; you can trust in his love and wisdom. Do that—he will help you and guide you."

They heard Jadin calling them for the departure. Shamas felt a lump in his throat, and he made an effort not to cry. He thought that if he did, his people would mock him, since he was almost a man.

Abraham and Jadin embraced each other. They exchanged a few last words, then wished each other the best for the future.

As Abraham embraced Shamas, the boy could not keep a tear from running down his cheek, but he immediately dried it with a clenched fist.

"Don't feel ashamed by your sadness over our separation. I, too, have tears in my eyes, though they do not spill over. I will always remember you, Shamas. And I want you to know that just as I shall be the father of many nations, it is thanks to you that men will know the history of the world and be able to tell that story to their children, and their children's children, until the end of time."

Then Abraham gave the signal to set out, and his tribe began to move. At the same time, Jadin raised his hand to indicate to his people that the hour had come for their own journey. Each tribe went its own way, in opposite directions; some turned to look back, raising their hands in a final farewell. Shamas looked back toward Abraham, hoping the old man would look back too, but he was walking with a firm step, and he did not turn Shamas' way.

It was only when Abraham reached the palm grove where they had sat and talked that he paused for a few seconds, looking all around, as though remembering. He felt Shamas' eyes on him at a distance, and he turned, knowing that the boy was awaiting this last farewell. They did not see each other, but both knew that the other was looking.

The sun was at its zenith now, and another day of eternity was waning.

28

DUKAIS HANDED ROBERT BROWN PLASKIC'S REPORT, AS
Ralph Barry looked on.

"Ante has a gift for seeing the big picture," Dukais remarked. "It's the first report I've ever actually enjoyed reading."

"So?" said Brown.

"Well, it looks as though they haven't found anything. I mean your
damned Bible of Clay hasn't turned up, even though they've retrieved
some two thousand tablets and tons of shards, which might be more
worthless than this whiskey."

"Nobody suspects him?"

"Maybe Ayed Sahadi. The Croatian thinks he's more than a
foreman—probably somebody Tannenberg sent in to watch over his
granddaughter."

"I imagine Tannenberg has men everywhere," Barry added.

"We've been lucky to have Yasir inside Alfred's organization,"
Brown said. "He's got at least a dozen men among the workers, plus his
direct contact with the Croatian. If Ayed Sahadi is more than he appears to be, Yasir will find out."

"I guess Tannenberg went so far that Yasir feels he's freed from his
loyalty? No ties to bind them?" Dukais asked.

"Don't be fooled by Alfred; he knows Yasir will betray him sooner or later, and you can be damned sure he's having him watched. Alfred's smarter than Yasir—he's smarter than you," Brown snapped.

After the other two left, Brown had his driver take him to George Wagner's house. He had been told to hand-deliver the Croatian's report and await instructions, if there were any. With George, he never knew. . . . Sometimes he was as cool as a cucumber, but sometimes his steel-blue eyes were as cold as ice. And when that happened, Robert Brown trembled.

Gian Maria couldn't mask his depression. He felt utterly useless. The spiritual obligation that had led him to Iraq was becoming obscured by the complications he seemed unable to keep from creating for himself—he'd lost control of his own life, and he was beginning to re-alize that he didn't even know why he was there anymore.

He hardly slept. Luigi Baretti was making him sweat for the free la-bor he provided in Baghdad; his workday began at six in the morning and never ended before nine at night.

He would get back to Faisal and Nur's house exhausted, with no energy to spend time with the twins or little Hadi, whom he had grown to love. He ate alone; Nur would leave out a dinner tray for him, which he'd devour at the kitchen table. Then he'd drag himself to bed and collapse.

That morning his superior, Padre Pio, had called from Rome. When was he planning to return? Had he accomplished his spiritual mission?

Gian Maria had no answers, only the feeling that he'd leapt into the dark and had no idea where he might resurface.

He felt Clara Tannenberg weighing on his conscience; every day he searched the newspapers for any reference to her, any reference to any Tannenberg. He found nothing.

Time had passed quickly—too quickly. It was now almost Christmas, and he couldn't keep making excuses. His repeated requests to meet with Ahmed Husseini at the Ministry of Culture had been denied. Ahmed was a very busy man, and Gian Maria at last realized that his only way to Husseini was through Yves Picot. He hadn't wanted to use the archaeologist's name—he felt it would only create complications—but he finally had no choice, really: Ahmed Husseini wouldn't meet with him unless someone interceded, and that someone could only be Yves Picot.

"Today I'll be leaving early, Aliam," he announced to the secretary of the Children's Aid group.

"What's up?" the girl asked, curious.

He decided to tell the truth, or at least part of it.

"I want to contact some friends of mine. They're with a group of archaeologists I met when I first came; they brought me in from Amman. They're excavating in Ur and I was just curious how it's going for them. I'm going to try to locate them."

"Wow. Friends in Iraq. There's more to you than I thought. How are you going to find them?"

"They told me I could contact a man named Ahmed Husseini. I think he's the director of the Bureau of Archaeological Excavations in the Ministry of Culture."

"Oh, my! Consorting with the elite, are we?"

"What do you mean?"

"Gian Maria, Ahmed Husseini is one of the chosen few, so to speak. His father was an ambassador and he himself is married to a very wealthy woman, a half-Egyptian, half-German Iraqi. Her family's a little mysterious, but rich as Croesus."

"I don't know this Husseini; I just know that he can help me find my friends. That's all I want to do."

"Just be careful, Gian Maria—that Husseini . . ."

"All I'm going to do is ask him to put me in touch with a bunch of harmless scientists!"

"I know, but be careful all the same—those people are dangerous," Aliam said, lowering her voice. "They lack for nothing and they live by trampling on the rest of us. If the Americans invade Iraq, you'll see— they'll escape without a scratch. If the marines freed us from the horror those people perpetrate, it would actually justify the invasion, in my mind."

"Come on, let's not get down. . . . And if Luigi asks, tell him I'll be back after dinner."

When Gian Maria called the ministry the secretary told him, as on other occasions, that Mr. Husseini was busy. But when the priest mentioned the name *Yves Picot*, her tone changed immediately and she asked him to please wait.

A minute later, Ahmed Husseini was on the phone.

"Hello?"

"Mr. Husseini, I'm sorry to bother you. Professor Picot told me that if I needed to get in touch with him to call you. . . ."

He answered the questions Husseini asked him, and when the Iraqi seemed satisfied with his responses, he asked him to come to his office that very afternoon. If Gian Maria was willing to join the team, now would be the time. His knowledge could be of great service to them.

But Gian Maria had no intention of joining Picot, much less undertaking the trip south to godforsaken Safran. The only thing he wanted to do was what he should have done the first day he arrived in Baghdad: ask Husseini about his wife and explain that it was of vital importance that he speak with her. She was the only person to whom he could justify his presence in Iraq. He'd come to save her, to save her life, but he couldn't divulge that without betraying everything he believed in, without betraying a secret he'd vowed to keep for the rest of his life, no matter how badly it tore him up inside.

Ahmed Husseini didn't turn out to be the fearsome thug Aliam had described. Moreover, Gian Maria noted with surprise that he didn't sport the thick mustache all Iraqi men seemed to favor. He looked like an executive of some multinational corporation more than a government official in Saddam Hussein's regime.

He offered Gian Maria tea and asked what he was doing in Baghdad, what he thought of the country. He recommended several museums. And then he got to the ostensible reason for Gian Maria's call.

"So you want to join Professor Picot."

Gian Maria bit his lip. He had to proceed carefully. He didn't know how this obviously reserved man would react to a stranger asking about his wife.

"You and your wife are archaeologists too, aren't you?"

"Yes, that's right. Have you heard of my wife?" Ahmed asked, his expression cooling as his guest strayed into personal territory.

"Yes, of course."

Ahmed smiled. "I suppose Picot explained that the mission to Safran is due in large part to my wife's personal insistence. Given the situation our country is in now, it's not easy to obtain the resources for an excavation. But she loves archaeology more than anything, and she's one of our foremost experts on Mesopotamian culture, so she managed to convince Professor Picot to help us excavate what appears to be the ruins of a temple or palace—we still don't know which."

The door to Husseini's office opened and Karim, his assistant, came in, smiling broadly.

"Ahmed, everything's ready for the shipment to Safran. I called Ayed Sahadi to tell him that the truck is on its way. I couldn't reach him, but I got lucky—I talked to Clara."

Ahmed Husseini raised his hand to stop Karim from saying any more, while Gian Maria's eyes lit up. He'd finally found Clara Tannenberg.

He'd have to go to Safran. He felt like an idiot for not having considered the possibility that Clara Tannenberg was part of Picot's mission. He flashed back to the official at the archaeological conference in Rome asking him contemptuously whether he was interested in joining the expedition that Clara Tannenberg was trying to organize. And the newspapers, of course, had reported on Clara's talk, in which she had insisted on the existence of certain tablets she called the Bible of Clay. . . . So, if Yves Picot was there, it was in order to try to find those tablets. Why hadn't Gian Maria been able to connect the dots?

Karim left the office without another word, knowing he'd pay later for his transgression.

"Your wife is in Safran . . . of course. . . ."

"Yes, of course," Ahmed Husseini replied, disconcerted.

"Of course; it's only logical," Gian Maria continued, his inner monologue escaping in half sentences.

"So, tell me how I can help you," Ahmed prompted uncomfortably.

The priest recovered his composure. "Well, I wanted to speak with Professor Picot and see whether he still wanted me in Safran for a couple of months. I don't have any more time—I'm in Iraq to help; I work with an NGO, Aid to Children. I can't stay much longer, but if Professor Picot wouldn't mind my going and giving a hand there, even for just a little while . . ."

Ahmed's demeanor clearly reflected his doubts, as though Gian Maria was making up his story as he went along. He'd have him looked into before he'd allow him access to Safran. His tone was curt.

"I'll speak with Professor Picot, and if he agrees, certainly I have no objection to helping you reach Safran. You know that we are in a state of alert, so unfortunately one can't travel wherever one might like, especially without permission. Questions of security, you understand."

"I do understand, but how long will it take to get permission?"

"Don't worry, I'll call you. Give my secretary your telephone number and address."

By the time Gian Maria left the ministry, he was bathed in sweat. There was no turning back now; he had to prepare for whatever happened. Ahmed Husseini would investigate him and find out who he was. Gian Maria had seen his pleasant mask slip. Maybe Aliam was right: Ahmed Husseini was a man of the regime, and he could have Gian Maria detained or thrown out of the country anytime he wanted.

Ahmed Husseini lost no time—as soon as Gian Maria left his office, he called in Karim.

"Have the Colonel investigate that man. He claims to be an acquaintance of Picot. Wants to go to Safran. If Picot agrees, I'll put the papers through, but first I want to know more about him."

Twenty-four hours later, Karim brought in a two-page report detailing the Colonel's findings. On the third line of the first page, Husseini discovered precisely why this Gian Maria was more than he seemed to be. He decided to call Picot.

Yves Picot laughed when Ahmed told him the story of the wandering priest.

"But why are you so shocked that he's a priest?" he asked Husseini. "I certainly wouldn't object to your sending him here—we've got much more work than we can handle, so a specialist in Akkadian and Hebrew would be wonderful. If your investigators have finished vetting him, put him on a helicopter and send him in."

"I'll have to see—I still have some checking to do."

"He's harmless, Ahmed. He's here to help your people."

"Do you think the Vatican is interested in the Bible of Clay?" Ahmed asked.

"The Vatican? Ahmed, don't be paranoid! The Vatican isn't going to send a priest to spy on us." Picot couldn't help laughing again. "You're an intelligent man. Does it really surprise you that there are good people who want to try to help alleviate your people's suffering?"

"But why didn't he just say he was a priest?"

"As I say, he didn't hide it. It's on his passport, and this is Iraq, where everybody spies on everybody else. How many spies have you got among the workers?" Picot asked, still chuckling.

"You should be more careful," Ahmed warned him. The Mukhabarat was surely recording their conversation.

"Well, you decide. Hold on, here's Clara."

"I have no objections to his coming," Clara assured her husband shortly afterward. She looked toward the sky and smiled. "Besides, he's a priest—we could use all the luck we can get."

Ahmed Husseini was waiting for Gian Maria at the door of Faisal's house to drive him to the airport. From there, a helicopter would take the two men to Safran.

After a long and bittersweet talk, Gian Maria bade good-bye to Nur, Faisal, and their children. Of course, Faisal thought it utter foolishness for a bunch of foreigners to go around looking for buried treasure in Iraq while people were dying for lack of food and medicine, but Nur quickly quelched that conversation with an open invitation for Gian Maria to return whenever he liked.

A short time later, Ahmed and Gian Maria were in the helicopter. "I'm glad you're coming too, Ahmed," the priest said.

"I want to see how things are going out there."

The noise of the helicopter blades made further conversation impossible, so the two men sat silently, each lost in his own thoughts.

Ahmed told himself that he hoped he hadn't made a mistake with this priest, despite the fact that after an exhaustive investigation he'd reached the conclusion that he was harmless.

When they landed in Safran a few hours later, Clara couldn't help running to Ahmed the second he jumped out of the helicopter. She had missed him, more than she liked to admit.

Fatima looked on from a short distance, praying that Ahmed might change his mind about divorcing Clara.

But they embraced only briefly—both of them knew there was no going back on the decision they had made.

Yves Picot greeted Ahmed warmly. He liked him; maybe that was why he hadn't made a move on Clara. His initial disdain for her had evaporated as they worked together, and he was more attracted to her than he'd have liked to admit—especially to Fabian, who was always kidding him, telling him his crush was all too obvious. But despite his reputation at the university, there was no room in Picot's personal code of conduct for flirting with a friend's wife, and although Ahmed wasn't a typical friend, Picot liked him enough to respect his marriage.

Picot turned to Gian Maria and gave him an affectionate pat on the back.

"What do you want us to call you—Father? Brother?"

"No, please, just call me Gian Maria."

"Good. I have to tell you, I found you a little strange. But it never crossed my mind that you were a priest. You're so young."

"Not really. I'll be thirty-six in a few days."

"You don't look a day over twenty-five!"

Gian Maria smiled and looked at Clara out of the corner of his eye, waiting to be introduced. But he was immediately confronted by the three students he'd traveled with from Amman.

"Why on earth didn't you tell us you were a priest?" Magda scolded him.

"You didn't ask," he answered lamely.

"Oh yes we did—we asked what you did and you said you had a degree in ancient languages," Marisa reminded him.

"You just didn't want to tell us—what's that about?" Lola insisted.

"Yeah, why not just out with it?" Magda seconded.

Fabian came over with Marta and other members of the team.

"You're certainly the popular one," he said. "I'm Fabian Tudela. Come on, I'll introduce you to the rest of the team and show you where you can sleep."

When Gian Maria was finally introduced to Clara, he blushed, which caused her to burst out laughing.

"They told me you blushed," Clara said. "But do you work?"

"Yes, of course. I came here to help you. . . . I, I mean, to help you find the Bible of Clay."

"We will. I know it's here."

"I hope you're right."

"It will be a wonderful experience for you, as a priest, if we do, won't it?"

"Will there be time?" he asked timidly.

"Time?"

"Yes, I mean . . . you know, the war. Everyone is saying that the United States and its allies are going to attack."

"That's why we're working as fast as we can. But when it comes to the war, I'm very optimistic. I don't think anything will come of it; it'll all turn out to be gunboat diplomacy."

"I fear it won't," Gian Maria replied sadly.

Fabian led him to a small house in a row of identical structures.

"You can sleep here. It's the only place with room for another cot," he explained, showing him into the computer house.

Ante Plaskic greeted him with unconcealed ill temper. He would much have preferred the relative privacy and independence he had enjoyed so far. But he knew that he shouldn't—in fact, couldn't afford to—protest the presence of this new and unwelcome tenant.

Nor did Ayed Sahadi seem very pleased at Gian Maria's arrival. It was probably the first time he and Ante had seen eye to eye on anything, though for very different reasons.

"I'll try to be as little bother as possible," Gian Maria said to Plaskic.

"You do that," replied Plaskic.

Gian Maria didn't know why he inspired such hostility in the Croatian and the foreman, but he decided he wasn't going to worry about it. He would have enough to do trying to protect Clara Tannenberg.

His secret weighed heavily on his conscience. He'd never imagined that one day such a dreadful dilemma might present itself in his confessional. He had heard the horror that can nest, like a viper, in the human heart, and he had wept in the knowledge that he was impotent to comfort those souls twisted by grief, even those determined to exact the most terrible vengeance—souls who had known a hell in life, whose hearts had been dried to ash, drained of every drop of human compassion.

Now he had to win Clara's trust, find out whether she had any family besides Ahmed, and prevent what he knew, deep inside, to be inevitable, unless God intervened. But could he do it?

After carefully studying all the information provided to him by Tom Martin, Lion Doyle had reached one conclusion: Alfred Tannenberg was virtually untouchable—he had twenty-four-hour protection wherever he went, and his home, the Yellow House in Baghdad, was guarded by members of Saddam's armed forces as well as his own hired thugs; his house in Cairo was also under official protection.

Doyle knew that he could get in and out of Iraq or Egypt, but the risk was tremendous—and from what Tom had told him, the old man was already on the alert over trouble with some old colleagues, so he'd redoubled his security. The granddaughter, then, had to be the passport into Tannenberg's house—hopefully, through the front door. And Clara, from all indications, was near Tell Muqayyar with an archaeological expedition composed largely of Europeans. In any event, she was to die too. It was simply a matter of getting all the targets, or as many of them as possible, into the same room at the same time.

He called Tom Martin and told him he needed help getting identification papers and an authentic press card.

"Journalists from all over the world are flocking to Iraq to cover the war. I'm going in as a reporter."

"You're nuts! War correspondents know one another—the same ones go to all the hot spots every time there *is* a hot spot!"

"I'll go as a freelancer. But I need somebody—some magazine, some newspaper—to give me an ID and to be willing to vouch for me should anybody ask. They need to say they're going to buy my photos. I've already bought some secondhand equipment, so aside from the ID, I'm good to go."

"Jesus." Tom Martin wiped his hand over his face. "Give me a couple of hours, Doyle. I'll see what I can do. I think I know somebody."

"The sooner you get it, the sooner I leave."

Less than two hours later, Lion Doyle was entering a two-story house on the outskirts of London. A sign on the door announced the offices of Photomundi.

The head of the agency was waiting for him. He was a short, thin man with small, sharp-looking teeth.

"Did you bring an ID photo?"

"Yes, here."

"Good—just give me one minute," the man said as he went toward the scanner.

"Tell me about the agency," Lion asked.

"We do a little of everything, from wedding pictures to catalogues, even press photos if a client comes in looking for them. If a magazine needs a photographer for a specific shoot, they call me, I send the photographer, photographer takes the pictures, magazine pays me, end of story. I also help out the government. When a friend of a friend comes in looking for accreditation—like you—they call me, they pay me, and I don't ask questions."

"What if the photographer gets into some sort of jam?"

"That's his problem. I've got no one on the payroll. I just hire freelancers I call in as I need them. I'm a subcontractor, and I subcontract. In this case, somebody tells me you're going to Iraq, you want to take pictures to sell to some newspaper or magazine when you get back. So I give you the press pass, which says you're a photographer for Photomundi, and that's the end of my role in the affair. If you come back with photos, I'll call a couple of friends of mine in the media to see whether they're good enough to buy. If they don't want them, you're out the money for the trip, not me. So, to answer your question, if you get into some sort of jam, it's not my problem. Got it?"

"Got it."

Half an hour later, Lion Doyle left Photomundi with a press card identifying him as a freelance photojournalist. Now all he had to do was pack his bag, pick up his ticket, and board the plane to Amman.

The team members were exhausted, but their spirits were soaring. Two days ago, as the group led by Marta finished clearing a new room, they'd found two figures—winged bulls about fifty centimeters tall—and nearly two hundred tablets almost perfectly intact.

Gian Maria was up to his ears copying and translating the tablets. Yves Picot was as merciless as his old boss at Aid to Children.

But Clara was always very pleasant to him, and she came in quite often to help decipher the complicated language of the ancient inhabitants of Safran. Nevertheless, Gian Maria sensed her desperation, which seemed especially acute that afternoon. Every muscle of her face seemed tense and drawn.

"You know something, Gian Maria?" she said. "I know we're making progress; the temple is turning out to be an archaeological treasure. But sometimes I wonder whether Shamas' tablets are actually here."

Gian Maria's response didn't help. "What if Shamas' record of the story doesn't exist, and never did? What if Abraham never told his version of the story of creation?"

"He had to—it's in my grandfather's tablets. Shamas wrote clearly that he was going to inscribe it."

"But Abraham may have changed his mind, something may have happened."

"I know they exist—what I don't know is where they are." Her voice quavered. "I thought we'd find them here. When the bomb exposed the roof of the temple and we found shards of tablets—some with Shamas' name on them—I thought it was a miracle." Clara's eyes filled with tears.

It struck Gian Maria that it really did seem like a miracle that so many years later, the Tannenbergs had now found more tablets inscribed by Shamas. He was a man who believed that everything happened according to the will of God, but in this case, given everything else he knew, he wasn't at all sure what exactly God was trying to say.

"What if they weren't in the temple?" he asked.

"What do you mean, not in the temple? Do you think they could be somewhere else?" Clara's face lit up, and her big blue eyes shone with renewed hope.

"Well, the scribes had clearly defined roles as administrators of the temple: They kept the accounts, oversaw the contracts. . . . We've found a catalogue of the flora of the region, a list of minerals—everything routine. So maybe Shamas didn't leave the tablets containing the story of the creation in the temple. They would have been precious, special. Maybe he kept them in his home, someplace else."

Clara was silent, thinking about what Gian Maria had just said. He might be right. So far they'd only uncovered administrative work. But the fact was that in ancient Mesopotamia, scribes also transferred their peoples' epic poems to tablets, and the story of creation, even Abraham's version, was just that—an epic poem. Perhaps such accounts would not have been kept in temples. She weighed the possibility of expanding the perimeter of the dig. The problem was, there was no time. Her grandfather had called from Cairo, and for the first time she'd heard doubt, just a hint of pessimism in his voice. His contacts in Washington couldn't have been more direct: Iraq was going to be attacked, and this time the Americans wouldn't stop with just air raids—they were going to invade the country.

Not to mention how difficult it would be to persuade Picot to expand the perimeter. He was as desperate to find the Bible of Clay as she was. And he, too, was beginning to lose hope. But he refused to probe beyond the designated area they had already marked out, because that would mean pulling some of the workers off the main dig. No, the excavation of the temple was the first and only priority. Still, she'd talk to him. Gian Maria might be right.

Clara felt Ante Plaskic's eyes on the back of her neck. It wasn't the first time she'd caught him surreptitiously looking at her when she entered the computer house or sat down with Gian Maria and other members of the team to clean the tablets. Perhaps he was just another backup hired by her grandfather to look after her.

And then there was Ayed Sahadi. But in his case, she felt no sense of unease. Her grandfather had flatly told her that Ayed would kill anyone who tried to harm her. And the fact was, she felt protected. She knew how terrified Iraqis were to lift a hand against anyone within the inner circle of Saddam Hussein, and she and her family were as close to the president as anyone could be. She had no reason to worry.

It was Sunday, and Yves, well aware of the team's exhaustion, had suggested that everyone take the afternoon off. But Clara and Gian Maria had decided to keep working, and they were sitting together cleaning tablets in the computer house as the sun approached the horizon. Ante was there too, studying them, fully aware of the discomfort his presence caused the woman.

It would be easy to kill her. He could strangle her—he needed no weapon but his hands. And that was why he was gazing so fixedly at Clara's throat, thinking of the moment he would squeeze it and wring the last breath from her.

He felt no emotion for this woman—for her or anyone else. He was shunned by everyone; the priest was the only person who made any attempt to befriend him. Even Picot seemed to find it hard to praise his work, although he knew he was doing an excellent job.

But in addition to Clara, he would have to kill that overprotective nursemaid of hers, Fatima, the Shiite woman who followed her around like a faithful dog all over the camp. It drove him crazy to watch her kneel and pray toward Mecca three times a day. He'd also kill Ayed Sahadi, because he knew if he didn't, Ayed would kill him. He no longer had any doubts that the foreman was more than he appeared to be. The soldiers in the nearby garrison sometimes stood at attention when they saw him, although Ayed always made a quick gesture for them to stand at ease, and he inspired obvious fear in the workers, a fear that had nothing to do with their labors. At least half a dozen men reported to Ayed on a fairly regular basis, much in the mode of a military hierarchy.

And Ante knew that he, in turn, was being watched by Sahadi, who openly showed his mistrust for the Croatian in any number of ways, as though warning him not to make any false moves. They were both killers, and they recognized each other.

Alfred Tannenberg strode out of the hospital with a firm, brisk step. He'd been admitted seven days ago and his health was undeniably shaky, but he couldn't allow anyone to see that. Humans, like other animals, sensed weakness in others, and when they did, they knew they could attack.

The conversation he'd just had with his doctor had left no doubt: He had until spring at the latest.

The doctor was hesitant about giving him an exact time frame, but Tannenberg had pressured him and determined that if he lived until March, he'd have beaten the odds. He had to use every minute of the time he had left to secure Clara's future.

He would stay on in Cairo for a few days to put his affairs in order and then go back to Iraq. He was going to surprise his granddaughter and join her in Safran for the time being, to stay near her, until they were told they had to leave the area. Leave the country, actually, and they would do so together—if he lived that long. That was why he needed Ahmed. Because Tannenberg knew full well that once he died, Clara would have no one—she'd need someone who loved her to keep her safe. He paid his men to protect her, but as soon as he was gone they would abandon her to her fate unless someone else took charge. He didn't care whether Ahmed and Clara divorced, but they'd have to do it after they both left Iraq.

Alfred had never doubted that Ahmed would agree to the deal: first, because he wouldn't want to hurt Clara in any way and he knew that leaving her in Iraq was sentencing her to death; second, because opposing Alfred's wishes would be signing his own death warrant; third, and perhaps most important, because he was going to receive a very great deal of money for this last job. Yes, Ahmed would do what he was expected to do. And that was why Alfred Tannenberg had ordered him to make arrangements to stay in Safran from February on. Robert Brown, via Mike Fernandez, had sent him reliable information: The attack was to come in March.

A few days later, Alfred was back in Baghdad, on his way to the

Yellow House in a black Mercedes that didn't bother to stop at traffic lights.

Fernandez was waiting for him in the quiet shadows of the vestibule of Tannenberg's home, under heavy guard as always. Security cameras had been installed even in the trees along the street leading to the Yellow House. The old man wasn't going down without a fight.

"How are you, sir?" Mike Fernandez asked as Alfred came in, with a greater measure of respect than during their first meeting. He no longer wasted time with hostility or evasion. In the time they had worked together, he had seen clearly that Alfred Tannenberg was always several steps ahead of himself and Paul Dukais; he seemed to know not just what they were doing, but also what they were thinking.

"So, Colonel, what news do we have?" Tannenberg asked, skipping over any niceties.

"The men are here, sir. I've gone over the maps with them, and I'd like to know if we could spread out and get the lay of the land where we'll be rendezvousing with your men."

"No, not now. You'll have to make do with studying the maps."

"But your people move throughout the area without any problems."

"That's right. But your group will draw attention, which we can't risk now. Once the operation starts, that's another story. Our success depends on our discipline—if you follow my orders to the letter, you'll get out of this alive, and rich as well."

"Mr. Dukais has made the arrangements for our exit—my men and the cargo will go out on military planes straight to air bases in Europe."

"I hope he's taken my advice and arranged for portions of the cargo to be off-loaded in Spain and Portugal. They're allies of the United States, committed to the cause."

"What cause, sir?" the former Green Beret wanted to know.

"Bush's cause, of course, which has become our cause. This is big business, my friend."

"Another part of the cargo will go directly to Washington?"

"Yes, that's right."

"And you, sir—where will you be when the war starts?"

"That is no concern of yours. I'll be safe. Yasir will deliver my orders to you—we'll be in constant contact, even once our friends start bombing."

Mike Fernandez wondered, not for the first time, whether Tannenberg actually felt any loyalty to anything or anyone, and he couldn't resist the temptation to press him a bit.

"I imagine, sir, that you'll be worried knowing that this time it will be more than a few F-18s—we'll be invading Iraq wholesale."

"Why should I be worried?"

"Well, you have family here, and many important friends near Saddam."

"I have no friends, Colonel, just interests," said Alfred. "I couldn't care less who wins or loses the war. I will go on doing business. Money is a chameleon that takes on the colors of the winner."

"But you live here, you have this beautiful home. . . ."

"My home is wherever I am at the moment. And now, if your curiosity is satisfied and you'll excuse me, I have work to do. Saddam is my friend and Bush is my friend; thanks to them I'm going to close a very nice deal and make a lot of money. As will you, and many others."

"People will die, we'll lose friends. . . ."

"I'm not going to lose any friends, and don't start getting sentimental. People die every day—the tempo just picks up in wartime."

29

ALFRED TANNENBERG AND HEINRICH VON MEISSEN
learned a great deal about themselves at Mauthausen.
They discovered, for example, that it gave them pleasure to take other men's lives. Women and children were not exempt
either. Alfred, like Zieris, the supreme commander of Mauthausen,
preferred to shoot prisoners in the back of the head, while Heinrich
liked to toss their caps onto the barbed-wire fences, just as their commander had demonstrated the first day, and watch their terror as the
guards did the killing for him. There were afternoons when he targeted
dozens of desperate men, some of whom shuffled almost gladly to their
deaths, as though they were on the path to liberation.

The two new officers also formed fast friendships with some of the
camp's doctors, who liked to experiment on the prisoners.

"We are making great strides in science at the camp. Our subjects
are revealing previously unknown secrets of the human body," Alfred
proudly told Greta one winter evening after dinner. He explained in
detail the way healthy men, women, and children were inoculated with
various bacteria and viruses, so that the course of their diseases could be
observed. They even put healthy inmates under the knife so that the
doctors might begin to explore more deeply the minutiae of human
anatomy.

Greta nodded submissively at everything her husband told her, questioning nothing. In Mauthausen, as in the other camps that Alfred often visited, there were no human beings—just Jews, gypsies, Communists, homosexuals, and criminals. Germany had no place for rabble such as they. And if their bodies served to advance science, then at least their miserable lives had some meaning.

"Heinrich, I spoke with Georg today," Alfred said one afternoon. "He says Himmler is pleased with the agreements we are reaching with the large factories. We shall provide them labor and they will produce war materiel for the Fatherland. The factories need laborers; all the qualified German men are on the front lines. But there is more—Himmler says that after the war, the SS must be prepared to finance itself. Here, we have more than enough people to enable us to become self-sufficient."

"Come on, Alfred, these wretches are good for nothing but carrying rocks up from the quarry. We should do away with them all, or we will never solve Germany's problems."

"We can put the women to greater use," Alfred suggested.

"The women? We should exterminate them first. It's the only way to prevent them from breeding; their children are sucking Germany's blood dry," Heinrich argued.

"We have our orders, Heinrich, and whether we like it or not, we must follow them. You are to select the prisoners in the best physical condition. Himmler wants able bodies for the factories."

"I've talked to Georg as well."

"I know, Heinrich, I know."

"Then you know that he will be arriving in two or three days with his father."

"Yes, I've been in my office for hours, organizing everything; Zieris wants the commission to see the camps running as efficiently as possible. Georg's father is one of the high command's favorite doctors, and Georg's uncle, who is also a commissioner, is a distinguished professor of physics. The rest are also prominent civilians toward whom the Führer wishes us to offer our finest hospitality—they are especially interested in learning about the experiments of the Mauthausen doctors. Georg said he's got a surprise in store for us. I have a feeling he may be bringing Franz. He didn't say as much, but what better surprise than bringing us all together again?"

"Well, it would be good to get Franz away from the Russian front.

His last letter was devastating; things there are going from bad to worse."

"Things are not going well anywhere; we both know that. But let's not talk about the war."

"Yes, it's just too depressing. Going back to the commission—have you heard exactly what they want us to show them?"

"You'll be pleased to know that it has to do with the women—the creatures who arrive with their bellies full of children, burdening the camp. We can't keep wasting the Fatherland's money feeding this riffraff. So the doctors want to discover how well these pregnant sows can fare in extreme circumstances. One of them believes they may be able to withstand more than we think.

"He wants *them*, not the men, to go down into the quarry and carry up the rocks, on their backs," Alfred continued. "He'll keep track of how many can stand the work, how long they can last . . . and how many cannot—how many tempt the watchtowers' bullets.

"I think he is going to study the fetuses too. I don't know what he is hoping to find, but he says it will continue to expand our knowledge of the human body."

"And what about their children?" Heinrich asked. "Some of them had their bastards in tow when they arrived here."

"Oh, they'll be at the quarry as well, to watch the medical treatment administered to their mothers. It should be very interesting. Come on, let's talk to the doctor now. He's the one who has developed the formula for the injection. We'll see the effect it has firsthand. We have to bathe them first, though. I refuse to subject our physicians to our prisoners' filth."

"How many women will participate?"

"He has chosen fifty—Jewesses, gypsies, and political prisoners. Some of them are already more dead than alive—they'll probably thank us."

The day had dawned silvery gray, with a fine mist and an icy wind that whistled around the corners of the buildings and penetrated every chink in the barracks. The prisoners shook violently with the cold, but the bad weather had no apparent effect on the two SS officers looking impatiently at their watches, waiting for the procession of cars arriving from Berlin.

Standing in rows, utterly defeated, fifty women waited in silence for whatever fate the officers had planned for them. The prisoner-guards—some laughing loudly, others exchanging conspiratorial looks—had informed them that they would never forget this day. Some of them trembled and held tightly to the hands of their children, whom they had been forced to bring to the exercise field.

Some of the women had survived the camp for two years, working for the factories that supplied the German war machine; others had been there for only a few months. But on the faces of all of them could be seen the ravages of hunger and despair.

They had been subjected to all manner of torture and abuse by their guards, who forced them to work from sunup to sundown, day after day, regardless of their weariness or weakness.

Those who collapsed in exhaustion were beaten with the whips and truncheons the guards favored.

But at least they were surviving in the midst of the nightmare that had become their lives—they had seen many of their fellow prisoners die without a soul to come to their aid. Most simply dropped dead after reaching the limit of their strength. There were also those who disappeared—these were the most exhausted of the lot, the ones who could work no more, and one morning the guards would come and simply carry them away. They would never be seen again; nor was there ever even a hint of their fate.

When they left children behind, the rest of the women made a superhuman effort to care for and protect them as though they were their own, until they were old enough to join the adults at another work gang or another camp altogether.

The procession of sleek black cars drove slowly onto the long parade field. The civilians who emerged from them seemed eager, impatient even. Mauthausen was considered one of the most important of the Reich's work camps, a model to be followed.

Georg and Alfred gave each other a great bear hug after the upraised arm and cry of "Heil, Hitler!" As they stepped back to have a better look at each other, they heard Heinrich's joyous exclamation:

"Franz! My God, you've come!"

"Franz!" Alfred immediately embraced his friend.

As the four gave themselves over to their exuberant reunion, they ignored the disapproving looks from Zieris and the other SS officers. They were self-assured, untouchable, the chosen ones of Himmler himself.

By now, Alfred's father manufactured a good portion of the uniforms for the German army. Franz's father, an attorney, had become a consummate diplomat reporting to the Führer himself. It had been he who, years earlier, had managed to persuade a number of countries to take part in the Olympic games in Berlin—a feather in his cap that earned him a great deal of respect among his peers. Heinrich's father was one of the lawyers whose talents had been put to work constructing the legal system of the new Germany. Georg's father was a doctor who treated many members of the SS high command.

The women watched these four young officers who so clearly stood out from the others, and they gripped their children's hands more tightly.

The children were so malnourished that they could hardly stand, but they obeyed their mothers' insistence on keeping up appearances, for they knew what horror could be unleashed against them if they failed to please the terrible men in black.

The four officers came over to examine the prisoners. Their eyes reflected utter contempt and revulsion.

"What a spectacle," Franz said disgustedly.

"Come, my friend, you'll see, this will be fun! Today is going to be a great day!" Heinrich assured him.

"I'm positively brimming with curiosity," said Georg.

"It will be an unforgettable day, I promise you," Alfred seconded Heinrich.

Then Alfred made a sign to the prisoner-guards. "You're going to enjoy this," he went on.

The women trembled at the words of the SS officers, and a greater sense of dread overcame them.

"An unforgettable day," the SS officer repeated softly, as he smiled at them.

30

WHEN HE HEARD HIS NAME, LION DOYLE STIFFENED AND cautiously turned. A woman he recognized emerged from a large group sitting at the other end of the bar. They were all journalists—you could see that from a mile away—no doubt dispatched by their various agencies to report from the fires of hell itself so that the citizens of the world could know the truth. Lion was, of course, no stranger to the horrors of war, but could he fit in as a civilian on a job?

"Hello, Miranda," Lion said coolly, belying the tension he felt in every muscle.

"Don't tell me you're in Amman on vacation."

"Oh, I wish."

"So, you're on your way to . . ."

"Yep. Iraq, just like you."

"The last time we saw each other was in . . ." Miranda rubbed her chin. "Bosnia."

"The first and last, if I recall."

"And you told me you were driving trucks for an NGO, taking food in to the poor Bosnians, right? That was the last I heard from Lion."

"Come on, Miranda, let's let bygones be bygones."

"You don't think I'm upset with you, Lion?"

"Look, I had to leave Sarajevo in a hurry. There just wasn't any time to say good-bye."

Miranda burst out laughing, then came over and stood on tiptoe so she could reach high enough to give him a couple of quick pecks on the cheek. Then she introduced another man, who had been standing in the background, looking on in bemusement.

"This is Daniel, my partner in crime and the best cameraman in the business. And this is Lion. Lion . . . I don't know what."

Lion shook Daniel's hand without bothering to finish Miranda's sentence. The cameraman couldn't have been over thirty and was wearing a ponytail held carefully in place by a rubber band. Lion liked him instinctively: He wasn't in camouflage like some of the reporters, deluding themselves into thinking they were part of the action. Daniel, like Lion, was simply dressed appropriately for fieldwork: jeans, desert boots, a thick pullover, and a parka.

"So who're you going to save this time?" Miranda asked.

"Nobody—this time I'm going to be the competition."

"What! Since when are you a reporter?"

"Didn't I mention it? I freelance as a photographer when I can get the work."

Miranda eyed him suspiciously. She knew practically every war correspondent on earth, no matter what country they were from. They constantly ran into one another in conflict zones, in Lagos, in Sarajevo, in Palestine, in Chechnya. . . . Lion wasn't one of them—*that* she was sure of.

"I've never done press photography before," Lion added. "I shoot for catalogues and . . . well, when things get tough I do weddings. You know, the happy couples stuffing cake in each other's faces."

"And . . ." Miranda was clearly still dubious.

"And when things get even tougher I do other things. Like driving trucks. The agency I work through has contacts with the press, and the owner told me that Iraq sells big now. They're willing to pay for anything passable I send in. So here I am, looking for that big payday."

"And what's the name of this agency?" Daniel wanted to know.

"Photomundi."

"Oh, I know them," Daniel said. "They hire freelancers by the job—they throw you something, but there's no guarantee they'll even buy your stuff. I hope Iraq goes well for you, because if it doesn't, you're screwed—it'll dig you a pretty deep hole."

"Well, to tell you the truth, it's already costing me," Lion said.

"If we can give you a hand . . ." Daniel offered.

"Thanks, I'd appreciate it—I'm no journalist, I know. Any tips would be great. Taking pictures of a war isn't the same as shooting a can of asparagus."

"No, it definitely ain't," said Miranda, her voice still mistrustful.

Daniel invited Lion to join the group of reporters at the other end of the bar. Lion hesitated. He didn't want to get any friendlier with the reporters than he had to, but he didn't want to arouse suspicion either. So he joined them and was introduced to a dozen or so war correspondents from around the world who were getting ready to parachute, figuratively speaking, into Iraq.

They didn't pay him much mind, which suited Lion just fine. They didn't know him, and the fact that Miranda introduced him as a commercial photographer trying his hand at snapping war pictures brought out their sense of superiority. They looked down on him, there was no doubt about it—they were battle-hardened veterans, tossing down their whiskey and trading war stories, without much time for a newcomer.

Early the next day they would be heading out for Baghdad in rental cars. They invited Lion to join them, as long as he paid his share.

The next morning they all drifted down sleepily to the lobby, looking nothing like the merry gang of the night before. The booze and lack of sleep had left their marks.

Daniel was the first to see him, and he waved, while Miranda frowned.

"What's with you and your friend?" Daniel asked her.

"He's not my friend. I just met him outside Sarajevo in the middle of a firefight. You could say, though, that he pretty much saved my life."

"What happened?"

"A Serbian paramilitary unit was attacking a village near Sarajevo. I was there with several guys from other networks. The gunfire had us pinned down in the middle. I'm not sure how it happened, but suddenly I was all by myself out in the middle of the street, hiding between two cars with bullets whizzing past me. And then Lion appeared, practically out of nowhere, don't ask me how. He pushed my head down and got me out.

"The Serbs could have decided to kill us all, but that day they decided it was better publicity to make their case on television screens all over the world, so we were allowed to escape. Lion put me in a truck and spirited me away to Sarajevo. I've got to say I was impressed by the way he managed the situation. He seemed like . . . he seemed like a soldier, not a truck driver. When he dropped me off, we made a date to see each other later. And he disappeared. I never saw him again. Until last night."

"But you didn't forget him."

"No. I didn't forget him."

"And now you have mixed feelings—you don't know what to think, and you especially don't know if you want to get close to him. Am I right?"

"What are you, a psychoanalyst?"

"I know you, Miranda." Daniel laughed.

"Too well. You and I have been in this shit for what? Three years? I spend more time with you than I do with my friends."

"Work is work. Esther complains about the same thing—I'm with you more than her, and then when I get home I'm exhausted."

"You got lucky with Esther."

"Yeah. Anybody else would have thrown me out on my ass years ago." Daniel laughed again.

Lion joined Miranda, Daniel, and two German cameramen in an SUV parked outside the hotel.

Miranda hardly spoke for most of the way. Lion didn't kid himself about her: Despite her fragile appearance, she was a woman hardened by war coverage. And perhaps also by the battles of life. Although she was small—she couldn't have been over five-three or weighed more than a hundred pounds, with very short black hair and honey-colored eyes— Lion sensed she was a force of nature. She had a temper, and she knew how to get her way, even push people around; she seemed fearless. When he'd met her that day near Sarajevo, he had been surprised and impressed by how she kept her cool despite the situation; any other woman, or man for that matter, would have been in hysterics.

The highway to Baghdad was as crowded as it was dusty: The NGOs had decided to haul in their supplies on the ground from Amman rather than airlifting them. The SUV passed two convoys of trucks, and there were dozens of buses headed in both directions. At the Jordanian border, a bus full of Iraqis was trying to convince the border police to let them through. Some of the passengers were lucky; others, when their papers were examined, were detained—and roughly.

The reporters got out of their vehicles to photograph the scene and interview those in authority. They got no answers, only threats, so they decided to keep going. They'd have enough problems when they reached their destination.

The Hotel Palestina had seen better days. Even so, Lion had a hard time getting a room. There was nothing available without a reservation, he was told by a pleasant desk clerk, who seemed overwhelmed by the avalanche of reporters crowding the desk, impatiently waiting for their room keys. Lion decided to try the short way. A hundred-dollar tip bought him a room on the eighth floor. The faucet in the bathroom sink dripped, the blinds couldn't be lowered, and the bedspread needed a trip to the laundry, but at least Lion had a roof over his head.

He knew he'd find the reporters in the bar as soon as they dropped their bags in their rooms. Nobody would start working until the next day, although everybody was already busy hiring guides and interpreters. The Ministry of Information press center provided foreign reporters with interpreters, but some tried to find their own, since they knew that the official interpreters would be briefing the authorities on every move they made.

"You'll need a guide. A local who knows the city," Daniel told him when they ran into each other in the bar.

"Yeah, but I don't have any money for that; I'm going to try to make it on my own. It's cost me plenty just to get here—" Lion said.

"No, you don't understand. The government will *require* you to have a guide. They won't allow a British photographer to wander around on his own."

"I'll try not to attract any unwanted attention. See, my idea is to do a photo-essay on daily life in Baghdad. Don't you think newspapers will be interested in that?"

"It depends on the quality of the photos. You'd have to have something pretty damned good," Daniel warned him.

"I'll do my best. I'll be leaving the hotel early tomorrow—I want to shoot Baghdad waking up, so I'm going to hit the sack early. Besides, I'm beat from the trip in."

"Have dinner with us," Daniel invited him.

"No, thanks. You guys party too hard for me! I just came down for a cup of tea—I'm going straight back up to bed."

Lion was asleep by the time his head hit the pillow. He woke up before dawn and, after a quick shower, picked up his camera bag and headed out into the street. He had to cover his appearances, so he spent the better part of the morning in the bazaar and wandering through the streets of Baghdad. He photographed everything that attracted his attention, trying to capture the pulse of the city. But under blockade, Baghdad didn't have much to offer. Meanwhile, he tried to come up with a good cover for getting to Safran.

When he got back to the hotel sometime after noon, none of the reporters was around. He decided to go over to the Ministry of Information to see what they had to say about traveling to Safran.

Like almost all Iraqi men, Ali Sidqui wore a thick black mustache. He was a stocky man whose height and proud bearing made him look fitter, perhaps, than he was. As the second-in-charge of the press center in the Ministry of Information, he always tried to give his best smile to the reporters who were flocking to Baghdad in greater numbers every day.

"How may I help you?" he asked Lion.

Lion explained that he was a freelance photographer, and he showed him his press card from Photomundi. Ali took down all of Lion's information and asked about his first impressions of Baghdad. After about a half hour of friendly conversation, Lion got to the point.

"I'd like to do a special report. I heard that there's a high-profile archaeological excavation, made up of archaeologists and experts from all over Europe, going on near Tell Muqayyar, in a village called Safran. I'd like to go there and report on the excavation, show the world that ancient Mesopotamia is still yielding its secrets. I thought it'd be interesting to show that in spite of the blockade, there are academics and other professionals still working in Iraq."

Ali himself hadn't heard about any archaeological expedition in Safran, but he was careful not to say so. As he listened, it struck him that the reporter's project might make for good propaganda. He promised to call Lion at the Hotel Palestina if he was able to persuade his superiors to grant permission to shoot there.

Lion returned to the hotel just at nightfall. Miranda was in the lobby with Daniel. They'd just come in too.

"We wondered what happened to you!" Miranda greeted him.

"I've been working all day. What about you guys?"

"We haven't stopped. These people are going through a really hard time—we visited a hospital that made you want to cry. They don't have anything," Daniel lamented.

"Yeah, I've seen the effects of the blockade. But I'm surprised at how friendly the people are, in spite of what they're going through."

"And in spite of what they know is coming—Bush and his friends are going to see to that," Miranda said angrily.

"Well, Saddam is not exactly a saint either," Lion replied.

"No, no, but Bush isn't doing this to rid the Iraqis of Saddam—all he cares about is the oil."

Miranda's tone made it clear that she was spoiling for a fight, but Lion had no interest in this particular controversy. He couldn't have cared less about Bush *or* Saddam. He was in Iraq to do a job, after which he'd return to his farm and Marian. He let Miranda's remark pass, but Daniel couldn't let the conversation go.

"It's the Iraqis who have to throw Saddam out, not us."

"Sure, but they'd have a hard time doing that," Lion said. "Anybody who tries, Saddam throws in prison, and if he's lucky they kill him quickly. You can't ask for miracles; people live under dictators because it's hard to topple them. They either get outside help or they stay the way they are."

"But usually what they get from the outside is worthless. Saddam was an American puppet, like Pinochet or bin Laden. Once they've served their purpose, it's time to get rid of them. Okay, get rid of them—I've got no problem with that. My problem is that in order to do that, they're going to kill thousands of innocent people and destroy the country. When the war is over, Iraq won't exist anymore," Miranda declared furiously.

"Let's not do this. There's no need to argue—we've all had a hard day. How about something to eat? Dinner, you guys?" asked Lion.

Daniel begged off and headed for his room, but Miranda took Lion up on his invitation. They headed toward the hotel restaurant, which was filled with reporters, and sat at a long table with a mix of journalists from across Europe. Fortunately, they all made themselves understood in English. As they all recounted what they had seen in Baghdad that day, each one knew that the others were withholding the juiciest bits for their reports home. Despite the solidarity among them, they never forgot they were competitors.

After dinner, they proceeded to the bar, where there were yet more reporters. *Birds of a feather,* thought Lion as he listened to the conversations that crisscrossed the tables, raised his eyebrows at the extravagant stories, and took in the personalities of the most colorful of the crowd.

"Have you sent anything in yet?" Miranda asked him.

"I will tomorrow morning. I hope something gets picked up. If I can sell some things quickly, I can stay; otherwise I have to go back."

"You give up fast," Miranda said sarcastically.

"I'd call myself a realist, thanks—I can take certain risks, but bankruptcy isn't one of them. By the way, I've wanted to ask you since Bosnia—where are you from?"

"Huh? Why do you ask that?"

"You work for an independent TV producer. You speak perfect English, but there's an accent there somewhere that I can't place. I've heard you speak French flawlessly, but then you get into an argument about Mexican television and, from the heat of it—and the fact that you hardly let the other guy get a word in edgewise—I'd have to say you're from some Spanish-speaking country. So what is it?"

"I'm not from anywhere," Miranda said, smiling slightly and shrugging. "I hate flags and national anthems and all the shit that divides people."

"But you must have been born somewhere."

"Yeah, Lion, I was born somewhere, but I'm not from there or from anywhere. I'm a woman without a country."

"Is that what it says on your passport?" Lion wasn't giving up.

"I have a passport from one of the EU countries so I can travel. You've got to be from somewhere when you want to cross borders."

"I heard something about that."

"Okay. If you must know, my father was born in Poland, but his parents were German. My mother was born in Ireland, but her father was Greek and her mother was Spanish. I was born in France. So where do you think I'm from?"

"What did your parents do?"

"My father was a painter, my mother was a designer. They were from nowhere and they lived everywhere. They hated national borders."

"And taught you to hate them."

"I learned that on my own, thank you. I didn't need anybody to teach me."

At that, Miranda turned away and joined the general conversation.

Lion overheard someone say that the Spanish reporters were organizing a trip to Basra and that the Swedes wanted to go to Tikrit, the birthplace of Saddam.

"What about you, Lion? Are you staying on in Baghdad?" a French journalist asked.

Lion hesitated a few seconds before answering. He decided to tell the truth.

"I want to go to Ur—what's now Safran."

"To do what?" the Frenchman pursued.

"There's an archaeological expedition in the works near there, and I'm hoping that if I can get a good photo-essay out of the excavation I'll be able to sell it."

"Where is this expedition?" asked a German reporter. "It's Picot's, right?"

"Yeah, I think that's right. The truth is, I don't know too much about it, but it sounds interesting."

"I heard they'd found the remains of a palace or temple or something. That there might be tablets containing a version of Genesis. I read something about it in the *Frankfurter*," the German reporter mused. "I think there are a couple of German professors and archaeologists on the expedition. But it hadn't occurred to me that there'd be anything important to get out of it. As a reporter, that is."

"For you guys maybe not. But if I can get a good photo-essay out of it that the agency can sell, I might be able to stay on here for a while," Lion explained.

"It's not a bad idea, I'll tell you—there may be a good story there," said an Italian reporter.

"Yeah, 'til the bombing starts we've got to fill space with something," mused one of the Swedish guys.

"Whoa—it's my story, guys; no poaching! I'm not on an expense account here!" Lion protested, although the more decoys that accompanied him, the better, as far as he was concerned.

For a while longer, Lion played the role of a worried newcomer to the news game, but then he said good night and went up to his room. He had to prepare for the trip to Safran, whether the Ministry of Information gave him the green light or not.

He was awakened early the next morning by the telephone. Ali Sidqui, the ministry official, sounded very cheery.

"I have good news for you, Mr. Doyle. My superiors think it's a splendid idea for you to go to Safran to publicize a story on the archaeological mission. We'll take you there."

"That's very nice of you; I really appreciate it, but I'd rather make my own arrangements."

"No, no, I'm afraid that's not possible. That area is only accessible with government sponsorship. It's a military zone, in fact, and the archaeological mission is under official protection. No one is allowed to enter without permission from Baghdad and an official escort. So you must either go with us or not go."

Lion accepted the terms. Ali Sidqui told him to come by the press center that morning to begin the arrangements.

When Lion arrived at the ministry, Ali introduced him to his superior, who was clearly enthusiastic about the entire idea.

"European intellectuals have not abandoned us after all," the director of the press center said.

Lion nodded. He couldn't care less what Saddam's flunkies had to say about his mission. All he cared about was filling out the required forms and getting his passport photocopied so he could be on his way.

"We will call you in a couple of days. Be ready. And I do not imagine you will be sick in the helicopter?"

"Me? Dunno. Never been in one," Lion lied.

31

TOM MARTIN DEVOURED THE LONG E-MAIL FROM LION, forwarded by the head of Photomundi. Lion was already in Safran, and with the blessing of Saddam!

I got into Safran today. The helicopter that flew me in was an old Soviet junk heap that roared like a freight train.

There are over two hundred people working here. The leader of the mission, Professor Yves Picot, is obsessed with winning the race against time; he knows they don't have much left. I've met the heads of the team, who have very passionately described the importance of the work they're doing. One of the archaeologists, Fabian Tudela, explained that the temple they're digging dates to the time of a king Amraphel who appears in the Bible. I can only hope the photographs and the report are of interest to the general public.

There has been some commotion in the camp since the grandfather of Clara Tannenberg, the other lead archaeologist, announced he will come to the camp to live, apparently for some time. The news arrived before I did, and it was the buzz of the camp. Some people seem quite agitated about it. They're readying a house for him. Furnishings have been brought in from Baghdad so that he can live as comfortably as possible.

As a sidelight, I'll tell you that this Clara is nothing short of mothered by an old woman, a Shiite covered from head to toe in black. She's apparently a servant who also cares for the old gentleman, and Ms. Tannenberg eats only what this woman prepares for her. I was told that the senior Tannenberg will be accompanied by his granddaughter's husband, who is a high-ranking official in the Ministry of Culture, and by a doctor and nurse, for whom housing is also being prepared. A field hospital is to be set up; it was sent in from Cairo. Clearly, the old man is not well.

I mention this because suddenly everything seems to be revolving around his arrival. With its guards and soldiers, the camp looks more like a fortress than a scientific endeavor, but I hope to be able to successfully finish my photo-essay even under these conditions.

Tom Martin smiled. He had no doubt that Lion Doyle would be able to finish what he called his "photo-essay"—the "sanction" against the Tannenberg family.

He'd been lucky, all right. Finding the Tannenbergs in Iraq would have been much more complicated had he not known about them through his friend Paul Dukais. Life was full of wonderful coincidences—how else could you explain the fact that Dukais had asked him for men to neutralize Clara Tannenberg, when ten minutes later the mysterious Mr. Burton had shown up offering him two million euros to kill her and her entire family?

He still debated telling Dukais about the contract he had on the Tannenbergs, but once again, he decided against it. It was best to keep that little professional secret. Dukais might be working against the Tannenbergs, but that was a far cry from having them killed.

He phoned his client to update him.

"Hello?"

"Mr. Burton, a friend of mine has located your friends, although he hasn't been able to meet with them yet. They're all fine—the grandfather, the granddaughter, and her husband. Unfortunately, the grandfather is ill; we're still not sure how seriously, but we're expecting to receive word soon."

"And there are no other members of the family?"

"None that we know of."

"Will your friend be able to get our message to them?"

"Of course."

"Anything else?"

"No, not for the moment, unless you're interested in further details."

"I want to know everything."

"Your friends are in the southern part of the country, in a charming town called Safran. The granddaughter is working . . . how shall I say . . . as the leader of a large team, and the grandfather will be going there to meet with her. But they're well protected, and not just by regular army personnel; they also have private security."

"Is that all?"

"Those are the essential details. As soon as I know more, I'll call you."

"See that you do."

Hans Hausser's stomach was in knots. Tom Martin had just confirmed that Alfred Tannenberg was alive.

He had to call Mercedes, Carlo, and Bruno to tell them that what once had been a distant possibility had become a reality. The vow they had made when they were children would be fulfilled. The sick old man Tom Martin had described could only be the monster that they had spent a lifetime hunting down.

Hans knew Mercedes hadn't slept and had hardly eaten since the day Carlo had called them from Rome to tell them he thought he'd found Tannenberg.

As Mercedes listened, Hans could hear her breathing growing harsh.

"I need to be there," she told Hans.

"That would be crazy and you know it—besides, there's nothing you can do."

"We ought to kill Tannenberg with our own hands, tell him who we are, let him know his past has at last caught up with him."

"My God, Mercedes!"

"There are things one should see to personally."

"Yes, Mercedes, yes. That would be better. But he's in Iraq, in a town in the southern part of the country, guarded by dozens of armed men. It's enough that he will pay."

"You have a daughter and grandchildren; Carlo and Bruno have children and grandchildren too. But I have no one, and at my age the only thing the future holds is getting older alone. I have nothing to lose."

Hans felt a sudden shiver of terror. He had no doubt that Mercedes was actually capable of getting on a plane and trying to kill Tannenberg personally.

"Mercedes, listen. I—we—will never forgive you if Tannenberg survives because *you* fouled this up. If you turned up in Iraq you'd be detained before you got within a mile of him, and the whole thing would fall apart—everything we've worked toward for so many years. The only thing you'd manage to do is put him on the alert, while you'd be thrown in an Iraqi jail, and we . . . we'd be arrested too."

"That's pure speculation on your part. It doesn't have to happen that way."

"Are you so consumed with hatred, so filled with self-importance, that you can't think straight?"

Mercedes fell silent. She had spent her entire life dreaming of the moment when she would plunge a knife into Tannenberg's belly. She had had so many nightmares, so many dreams of walking up to that monster and gouging out his eyes with her own well-manicured nails. In other dreams, she attacked him like a wolf, bit into his jugular and drank his blood. She wanted Tannenberg to feel pain, infinite pain, pain that she herself inflicted—not some stranger. She wanted Tannenberg looking into her eyes as he died, knowing he was finally getting what he deserved.

"Mercedes, are you listening?" Hans' voice came through the receiver, bringing her thoughts back.

"Yes. I'm listening."

"I'm going to call Carlo and Bruno. I'm not willing to wind up in prison because your arrogance and hate have finally driven you mad. If you go ahead with this, I'm done—I'll wash my hands of this, I'll pull out completely."

"What are you saying?"

"I'm saying that I'm not crazy, and that I refuse to take unnecessary risks. Carlo, Bruno, you, and I are four old people, and we have to resign ourselves to letting someone else kill him for us. If you don't see things that way, tell me, so I can get out of this before you ruin us all. Think about what I'm saying. Now I'm going to call the others. Good-bye."

Carlo and Bruno shared Hans' concern when he spoke to them. They should have anticipated Mercedes' reaction to the news that Alfred Tannenberg was indeed alive. They were afraid of her, afraid of what she might do.

The building that housed the offices of Mercedes' company was on the lower slope of Barcelona's Tibidabo district. The receptionist showed Carlo to a chair. Within a minute, Mercedes strode in. She grabbed his arm and led him into her office. When they were alone, she wheeled on him, glaring.

"Hans asked you to come—"

"No." He held her gaze firmly, his expression serious, concerned. "I came on my own. What are you doing, Mercedes? What are you thinking?" Carlo's voice was filled with pain and sympathy.

He took her hands in his. They talked for hours, long after her secretary put her head in to say good night, going over everything they had been through together and all the things they had talked about in the years since then.

Finally Mercedes took a deep breath and looked into her old friend's eyes. "You're right, Carlo, I know it. But everything I am, everything I've done . . ." She stopped and looked away.

"So what are you going to do?"

"Think, Carlo, I'm going to think."

"Which means I haven't convinced you."

"I would never lie to the three of you. I won't tell you that I'm not going to do something while I'm still thinking about it. I'd rather have you hate me than lie to you."

"You'd rather Tannenberg live," Carlo said coldly.

"No!" Mercedes cried. "How can you say that!"

Carlo looked toward the heavens. "There's nothing left to say, Mercedes. We'll call off the operation. Hans will tell Tom Martin to call in his man. It's over."

Mercedes clenched her fists. "You can't do that," she whispered.

"Yes, we can, and we will. You're breaking our vow, everything we pledged to one another, and endangering us all. If you're not with us, it's over. We renounce our revenge from this point forward. We will never forgive you, never. After so many years of looking for him, we find him at last—Tannenberg *and* his granddaughter. We could have killed them; we're that close. It's hard to believe. But all right, go ahead, do whatever you want. We've come so far together, but from this point forward, you're on your own. And that means whatever road you take, you'll take it without us."

A vein throbbed in Carlo's left temple.

Mercedes felt a sharp pain in her chest.

"What are you saying to me, Carlo?"

"That we will never see each other again. That Hans and Bruno and I will have nothing else to do with you for the rest of our lives. And that we will never forgive you."

Carlo was exhausted. He loved Mercedes deeply and could sense her suffering, but if she persisted, they had come to an end.

"I can't accept your ultimatum," replied Mercedes, her face as white as a wax candle.

"Nor can we accept yours."

Carlo rose from his chair. "I'm leaving. If you change your mind, call us, but do it before tonight. Tomorrow Hans will be flying to London to cancel the contract with Martin." He walked out the door.

He called his friends from a public phone at the airport. They agreed to meet in Vienna, at Bruno's home, the next day.

Deborah greeted Carlo and Hans coldly. It was obvious that she and Bruno had been arguing.

"Deborah's so damned pigheaded. She doesn't understand what we're doing," Bruno muttered when they were alone.

"Does she *know* what we're doing?" asked Hans with alarm.

"No—I didn't mean that. But she knows what we've found. And she's lived with me for a long time. . . ." Bruno didn't need to explain any further.

"I'd have told my wife too," Carlo consoled him.

"Me too—don't worry," Hans said.

Deborah returned to the living room with a tray of coffee. She put it down without a word and turned to go. Then she turned back, glaring at them.

"Deborah, leave us alone, please, we need to talk," Bruno asked her.

"I'll leave you alone, but first I want you to listen to me, all of you. I've suffered just like the rest of you. I lived in hell too. I lost my parents, my uncles and aunts, my friends. I'm a survivor, just like the rest of you. It was God's will that I be saved, and I give thanks for that. My whole life I've prayed to be strong enough to keep grief and hatred from rotting my soul. It hasn't been easy—I won't even claim that I've succeeded. But what I do know is that we can't take revenge into our own hands, because that makes us as bad as them. There are courts, there are places to go for justice here in Austria, in Germany, all over Europe. You could denounce him, bring him to trial. What do you make of yourselves if you have a man and his family killed?"

"Nobody says we're going to kill him," Bruno replied very gravely.

"I know you—I know all three of you. You've spent your whole lives waiting for this moment, feeding one another's thirst for revenge because of a pact you made when you were children. Now so much hatred has built up among you that none of you is able to stop. God will not forgive you."

"An eye for an eye, a tooth for a tooth," Hans replied.

"Useless," muttered Deborah, leaving.

The three men remained in silence for a minute. Then Carlo recounted in full detail his impasse with Mercedes. They agreed to make one last attempt to reason with her.

Bruno got up and went into his office. He wanted to talk to Mercedes where Deborah couldn't hear him. He reached her at home.

"Bruno?" she asked. He had never heard her sound so frail.

"Yes, Mercedes, it's me."

"I'm a wreck."

"So are we. Mercedes, I want you to know that I've never suffered as much as I did when I was a child. Carlo and Hans feel the same way. And we know you do too. But now all these years will have come to nothing—you have destroyed our reason for living. Your grandmother would never have acted this way, and you know it."

Silence fell between them again. Bruno felt wrung out. It was hard to find the right tone—he wanted to leave Mercedes room to reconsider, but he also could leave no doubt as to what her actions would mean.

"I'm sorry for what I'm making the three of you go through," Mercedes finally whispered.

"You're literally taking years off our lives, Mercedes. If you go ahead with what you want to do, I'll have nothing left. What would there be? Everything would be over."

Bruno was speaking from the depths of his soul. He was giving words to his anguish, his friends' collective anguish, and Mercedes knew it.

"I'm sorry. Forgive me. I won't go—I don't think I'll go."

"It does me no good to hear you say you *think* you won't go. I need a promise," Bruno demanded.

"I won't do anything. I give you my word. And if I change my mind, I'll tell you."

"You can't leave us hanging like that. . . ."

"No, I know I can't, but I also can't lie to you." Mercedes paused again. The silence stretched between them. "All right, Bruno," she finally whispered. "I won't do anything. I'm not going to do anything."

"Thank you, Mercedes."

"How are Carlo and Hans?"

"They're terrible, like me."

"Tell them that everything is all right—I won't do anything. I promise."

32

"MERCEDES, DON'T CRY; PLEASE, DARLING, DON'T CRY."
The little girl, shivering with cold and hunger,
barely mustering the strength to stand, clutched her
mother's hand as she wept quietly. The guard had shoved her—hard—
for not standing still in rank with the other women and their children.

She'd fallen to the ground, and her face had landed in a cold puddle
of mud. Chantal, her mother, terrified by what the guards might do,
had yanked her up by the arm immediately. In the camps, the first rule
of survival was to remain unnoticed.

Mercedes felt her mother squeeze her hand. The guard who had
pushed her had immediately been distracted by another child squirming in the line, and in those precious seconds Mercedes fought to hold
back her tears, as her mother had implored her to do.

She watched some of the SS officers from the camp merrily hug-
ging the men who had arrived with the procession of black cars. They
were laughing and slapping one another on the back; they all looked
happy, one of them telling another that it was going to be an unforgettable day.

For a few seconds, Mercedes thought about what those men might
do to make today so special, and again she shivered.

One of the kapos—as the common criminals who served as guards were called—a man named Gustav, came over to the row of prisoners and ordered the children to form another row in front of their mothers. The youngest children didn't want to let go of their mothers' hands, until one of the SS officers prodded them with the grip of a whip, and the mothers begged them to stand where the guards told them.

"*Achtung!*" shouted an SS officer. "A scientific delegation has come from Berlin to see you. You are going to aid science—at least now your miserable lives will have some value. All of you will walk down to the quarry; a gift will be waiting for you there, and you are to bring it up at once. Your bastards will remain here. We have another little gift for them."

Alfred laughed at his SS colleague's little joke, and Georg asked how long the test would last.

"That depends entirely on these sows," Alfred replied.

Mercedes sniffled and wiped away her tears as her mother smiled at her, trying to allay her fears even as she was led away to the steps of the quarry. Her mother was eight months pregnant; seven months ago she had been brought to Mauthausen with Mercedes and put into one of the work details. Chantal was amazed that she was still alive. She had inherited her strength from her own parents—good hearty country people with iron constitutions, as were her grandparents and all her other relatives, as far back as anyone knew. Other women in her condition had died, unable to stand up under the torture and the backbreaking labor that the officers forced on them. Some of them had disappeared after they were called into the infirmary, so that the doctors might "inspect" the progress of their pregnancies. But though she was alive, she was thinner than she had been before she got pregnant, and her belly was hardly noticeable.

She had been detained by the Gestapo in Vichy France as she was trying to flee the country with her daughter. The two of them were deported to Austria, locked in a cattle car. There, packed in with hundreds of other prisoners, she told herself that as long as they were alive, she would continue to hope. Her husband was a Spaniard, and like her had been collaborating with the Resistance. He had been killed by the Gestapo on a bright afternoon in Paris as he'd tried to get past a checkpoint. She had been left alone with Mercedes, not knowing she was carrying their second child. She tried to flee to Spain, which had been decimated during the Civil War, to take refuge with her husband's family. She was planning to go to Barcelona and find his mother; she knew she would help them. The Resistance leaders had agreed to transport her and Mercedes, but they'd hardly gotten to the border when she was arrested.

Once in the camp, she was ordered to strip like the rest of the female prisoners and was given the clothing she was to wear from that moment on—a red triangle with the letter F distinguished her blouse from the others. It was the sign of the political prisoners, and the letter indicated her nationality.

At first, she thought her periods had stopped because of her fear, the torture, the lack of food, the exhaustion. When she realized that she was pregnant, she wept inconsolably, blaming herself for bringing a second child into this prison. But, unlike most of the prisoners, despair gave way to hope, for her pregnancy empowered her—she had to stay alive for the child, and for Mercedes. They both were going to need her; she was all they had, although she'd made Mercedes memorize the address of her grandmother in Barcelona in case someday she managed to get out.

"Why don't they send the bastards down too?" Georg asked.

"Not a bad idea, but we have another surprise for them. They are going to shower over there. We'll see how long they can take it," Heinrich replied, chuckling.

"Let's go down and mark the sows' progress," Alfred suggested.

The cheery group of officers and civilian doctors descended the "stairs of death" to watch the women stagger under the weight of boulders harnessed to their backs. Some of the soldiers were shoving them, commanding them to continue, but many of the women could not bear the weight and fell to the ground, crushed by the stones. Of the fifty women sent down, fifteen died quickly, kicked to death or beaten senseless by the guards' cudgels. The others were screamed at and beaten too as they were forced to begin the climb of one hundred eighty-six steps back up to the parade field.

Chantal could hardly breathe; only the image of Mercedes and the desire to one day see her unborn child enabled her to find strength. She was doubled over, dragging her feet, while at the same time trying to control her nausea. And although her face twisted in agony, she exulted inside for each step she climbed. One, two, three . . .

Suddenly she raised her eyes and saw with horror that the guards were shoving the children, forcing them down the stairs.

She could hardly make out Mercedes, but she knew her daughter was frightened, about to cry. She stood up so that the girl could see her, trying to communicate to her the strength that she herself had exhibited. She couldn't imagine why the SS were pushing the children down the stairs toward them but was terrified by whatever they had in mind.

The idea had been Captain Alfred Tannenberg's, and it was unanimously lauded by the other officers. The children were to take night-sticks and beat their mothers, as though they were beasts of burden.

"They are mules," Alfred told the children, laughing, "and you are the mule drivers. You must be strong; if one of them trips and falls, you must hit her hard, even your own mother. If you don't, we will kill them and put the stones on your backs and whip you until you bring them up."

The little ones were terrified, but they hardly dared even cry. Each one took a nightstick and they began, very slowly, hesitantly, to descend the stairs. The women, who were just making their excruciating way up the first steps, looked up at them expectantly, until they realized the cruel game the perverse minds of the SS officers had concocted.

"Any of you who does not hit the mules will be whipped!" shouted Alfred Tannenberg, as his friends and the other guests laughed at the spectacle.

"Come, come! Begin!" the kapos were shouting.

The children looked in anguish at their mothers, not daring to raise the nightsticks.

"Mercedes, hit me! For God's sake, child, don't worry! Just do it!" Chantal implored her daughter.

Suddenly a woman fell, her face falling into the mud and rocks. One of the kapos went over and kicked her, but Alfred told him to stop, looking around for the prisoner's child.

"You! Come here!" he ordered a little girl so thin she looked like a specter.

The little girl, no more than eight years old, nervously took a few steps toward the SS officer, nightstick in hand.

"Is this your mother?" asked Captain Tannenberg.

The little girl nodded, unspeaking.

"Well, beat this mule until she gets up. Go on! Hit her!"

There were two or three seconds of silence. The little girl did not move. She had barely understood what the man was saying to her—she was deaf and unable to read people's lips accurately.

Enraged, Captain Tannenberg grabbed the nightstick and viciously began to beat the woman lying in the mud. The little girl looked on in horror and then, crying, threw herself to the ground beside her mother, as the SS officers burst out laughing.

Suddenly a boy, two or three years older, came over and tried to help the little girl get to her feet. Tannenberg glared at him with fury, his eyes bulging with rage.

"How dare you, you little bastard!"

He kicked the boy to the ground, then pulled his pistol from its scabbard and shot the little girl. The boy tumbled down to the third stair while his mother moaned, on the verge of delirium. The woman tried to crawl over to the motionless body of her daughter, but a series of kicks in the face and head from Tannenberg left her a lifeless mass of bloody flesh. The boy made a move to stand up, but Tannenberg kicked him again and again, until he was at last unconscious. He lay there, motionless, beside the dead bodies of his mother and sister.

"Come on, you mules! Come on! And you children, either hit the mules or you will wind up like this little bastard here. His mother was a rotten Communist, an Italian whore, but we have seen justice done, to the cow and the cow's daughter—daughter? Was that a daughter? Was that a human being?" screamed Tannenberg, wholly inflamed by his own spectacle.

Mercedes was paralyzed by the sight of her friend Carlo lying on the ground, so still. At ten, Carlo was older than she, but he was always so kind to her, always telling her not to be afraid.

The SS men kept shouting at them to beat the mules, and Mercedes began to cry very quietly. She couldn't hit her mother, and she looked around desperately: None of her friends had raised their sticks. She felt a hand on her arm. It was Hans, whose eyes were telling her to start walking.

"Mercedes, please, don't stop; move the stick like this, up and down, but without hitting your mother."

"No, no . . ." moaned the little girl.

A pregnant woman shrieked as she fell in despair to the ground. She was losing her baby right there, on the stairs, and she writhed in agony and anguish. Frau Müller was an Austrian Jew; she taught piano and had been caught hiding in the house of one of her students after someone had denounced her. She had arrived in this hell with her little boy, Bruno, four months ago.

Captain Tannenberg walked over to her and looked down at her coldly. Then he motioned to one of the camp's doctors.

"Doctor, do you think that Jewish fetuses resemble human beings? We should find out, don't you think? This pig won't be good for much else."

Everyone stood silently, expectantly, as the doctor squatted down and sliced Frau Müller open while she howled; then she arched her back and stopped screaming. She was dead. The other doctors, curious, gathered around her.

Little Bruno had cried desperately throughout the horror. Now he tried to back away, but a kapo grabbed him and forced him to witness the carnage.

Some children, unable to bear the Dantean scene, vomited, while the visitors applauded vigorously.

Chantal had climbed fifteen steps when she slipped and fell; a trickle of blood ran out the side of her mouth.

Tannenberg pushed little Mercedes toward her mother.

"Hit her! Do it! She's nothing more than a beast, a mule—hit her! Do as I say!"

Mercedes was frozen with horror. She couldn't make a sound; her eyes were as big as saucers, and she stared at the man who was pushing and shoving her.

"Hit the mule! Hit her!" Captain Tannenberg ordered, more and more enraged and shouting ever more furiously.

Chantal couldn't speak; her life was ebbing away, and she was powerless to protect her daughter or the child she carried. She managed to put out a hand toward Mercedes, who knelt down beside her mother and started to cry.

Captain Tannenberg strode over to Chantal and kicked her in the belly; she fainted, and blood began to flow from between her legs. Then he started to raise his whip to hit her, but he couldn't—small sharp teeth were biting into his wrist with a fury equal to his own. The visitors from Berlin laughed.

Mercedes looked like a doll gone mad. She was no more than skin and bones, but she had found the strength and courage somewhere to confront this monster.

Tannenberg shoved her to the ground, droplets of blood seeping out from the tiny bite marks. He pulled his pistol, looked at Mercedes, and smiled. Then he unloaded the gun into Chantal's stomach as though it were a bull's-eye—one shot in the center and four around it. He then unsheathed his SS regulation knife and slashed through her abdomen as though he were disemboweling an animal, ripping from her womb her unborn child. He threw the fetus in Mercedes' face.

The child's screams were otherworldly in their anguish, but Alfred Tannenberg hadn't finished with her. He picked her up with one hand and threw her down the stairs. The little girl's body landed among the boulders of granite at the bottom, blood running from gashes in her head.

Hans Hausser ran down the stairs to try to help her, not hearing the horrified cry of his mother, who tried to stop him.

One of the kapos grabbed him as he ran by and kept him from reaching Mercedes' motionless body.

"You worthless Jew! You want to finish her off?"

The kapo beat Hans under the indifferent gaze of Tannenberg and his friends, who had turned back to driving the other women up the stairs of death.

Frau Hausser was one of the few to reach the parade ground, but she had no illusions about her safety, or her son's. She looked back, trying to find him, and she wept when she saw one of the kapos beating him with a nightstick.

Marlene Hausser found the strength to cry out, trying desperately to make her son hear her.

"Hans, hang on! I'm right here, my love!"

The sound of a shot from the watchtower drove her to the ground; the first thing she saw when she opened her eyes were the boots of an SS officer.

"This woman has a heart condition; we must operate on her immediately," said the black-uniformed young man standing above her. He had blond hair and the face of an angel.

One of the kapos picked Marlene up off the ground and herded her to the infirmary along with several other women. The doctors from Berlin and their Mauthausen colleagues were scrubbing up for the improvised surgeries.

"Are we going to waste anesthesia on these pigs?" asked one of the assistants.

"Give them enough so they won't move around too much; I don't like to hear patients screaming as I operate," replied one of the doctors.

Marlene Hausser was lifted onto one of the operating tables, and her arms and legs were strapped down. She felt a pinch in her arm and soon after became sleepy; she couldn't help closing her eyes, although she still heard everything around her. She was unable even to scream when the scalpel cut into her chest, opening her from her neck to below her sternum. The pain was unbearable, and she cried impotently, hoping only that she might die.

Drowsily, she managed to say a prayer for her son, Hans. If God really existed, he might allow him to live.

She felt someone squeeze her heart, and then she was gone.

Marlene Hausser's body was dismembered by the monsters so eager to explore the mysteries of humanity.

One after another, the remaining few survivors of the stairs of death were operated on—hearts, brains, livers, kidneys, vital organs were dissected while the doctors taking part spoke learnedly about their subjects' conditions.

The doctors also entertained themselves with some of the bodies of the women who had died on the stairs. They cut the head off the deaf Italian girl, to study at greater length her inner ears.

Meanwhile, the kapos, at the direction of Captain Tannenberg, had ordered the girls and boys to take their clothes off and get into the shower. A foul tank full of mud and filth spraying frigid water over the tormented heads of those who had just been orphaned was the final piece of entertainment Tannenberg had prepared for his visitors from Berlin.

Some children died of hypothermia, while others simply collapsed, their poor hearts stopping. No more than a dozen survived, although some died hours later.

33

CLARA LISTENED FOR THE SOUND OF THE HELICOPTER THAT was bringing in her grandfather and Ahmed.

She was surprised to hear that her husband was accompanying Alfred to Safran. She was also anxious to see for herself how her grandfather was. Although Ahmed had told her not to worry, the newly erected hospital tent and medical equipment that had been flown in several days earlier were not good signs.

She'd spent the day helping Fatima ready the house where she and her grandfather would stay. She knew how demanding he was, and with his deteriorating health, it was vital that he have every modern comfort during his stay.

From the window she saw Fabian walking quickly toward the house. She stepped outside to great him.

"I think we've got something," he said excitedly. "We've found the outlines of several houses less than three hundred yards from the temple, where we started digging last week. They don't look very large, maybe forty or fifty feet on each side, surrounding a main rectangular room. In one of them we found a figure, a seated woman, probably a fertility goddess. And shards of black pottery," Fabian said, out of breath. "But there's more—Marta's team found a collection of bullae and calculi in the temple. There are several cones, perforated, large and small spheres—some perforated—and a couple of seals, along with the figure of a bull and what appears to be a lion, though it's not in perfect condition. But who cares? Do you realize what this means? . . . Yves is going crazy, and Marta . . . !"

"I'm on my way," Clara cried, hardly able to contain herself.

The figure of Fatima was silhouetted in the doorway.

"You're not going anywhere," she ordered. "We haven't finished here, and your grandfather will arrive any minute."

The sound of a helicopter's approach cut off Clara's reply. No matter how badly she wanted to rush to the site, she needed to wait until her grandfather was comfortable.

It was still early afternoon, but even if it was dark when they finished, she was going.

Ayed Sahadi, accompanied by two armed men, strode into the house without knocking, as though it were his own office.

"Madam, the helicopter is landing. Are you coming?" It was more an order than a question.

"I know, Ayed; I heard it. Wait one second—I'll go with you."

She left the house, shadowed by Fatima. They all climbed into a jeep and drove to the landing pad.

Clara was shocked by her grandfather's appearance. He had grown so thin that his clothes seemed to swallow him. He was barely skin and bones. His steel-blue eyes seemed faded, and he moved a bit clumsily, although he made an effort to walk stiffly upright.

He weakly embraced Clara, and for the first time in her life she was confronted with the fact that her grandfather was a mortal, not a god, as she had always unconsciously imagined him to be.

Fatima accompanied Alfred to his room, where she had arranged his personal effects. The doctor asked everyone except Samira, the neatly uniformed nurse, to leave, so that he might examine the old man and evaluate how badly the trip from Cairo to Baghdad to Safran had affected him. Fatima grumbled when she saw that the nurse was staying.

When the doctor came out, he found Clara at the door, waiting for him impatiently.

"May I go in now?"

"It would be best to let him rest for a while."

Fatima asked whether she should take him something to eat, but the doctor only shrugged.

"In my opinion, he should sleep. He's exhausted. But if you wish, ask him if he's hungry, after Samira comes out. She's giving him an injection."

"I don't believe I've met you, Doctor," said Clara a bit doubtfully to the tall, thin young man.

"You don't remember me, but we met in Cairo, in the American Hospital, when your grandfather was first operated on. I am Doctor Aziz's assistant; my name is Salam Najeb."

"Oh, of course, I'm sorry. . . . Please—tell me how he is, really."

"He's very ill. He's strong, and his will to live is extraordinary, but the tumor is growing and he doesn't want to risk another operation, and at his age . . ."

"If he were operated on, would it help?" Clara asked, though she feared the response.

The doctor stood silently, as though searching for the right words to say to her.

"I don't know. I don't know what we might find if we went in. But as he is now . . ."

"How much time does he have left?" Clara's voice was barely a whisper. She was struggling to maintain her composure, not to break down and cry, but more importantly, she didn't want her grandfather to overhear the conversation.

"Allah alone knows that, Madam Tannenberg, but in the opinion of Doctor Aziz—and I agree—no more than three or four months, maybe even fewer."

The nurse came out and smiled shyly at Clara as she awaited orders from the doctor.

"Did you give him the injection?" Salam Najeb asked.

"Yes. He's resting easy now. He said he wanted to speak with Madam Tannenberg."

Clara stepped between the doctor and nurse into her grandfather's room. Fatima followed her.

Alfred Tannenberg was lying in the narrow bed; he looked shrunken, almost like a doll, under the sheet.

"Grandfather," Clara said softly.

"Ah, Clara!" he breathed, smiling wanly. "Sit down—here, beside me. Fatima, leave us, I want to speak to my granddaughter alone. You can bring me something to eat, though."

Fatima left the room, her face glowing with the pleasure of serving the old man. If Alfred Tannenberg was hungry, she knew exactly what would make him happy.

"I'm dying, my darling girl," he said to Clara when they were alone, taking his granddaughter's hands.

Despair washed over Clara's face, and she struggled to keep from breaking down.

"I won't have any crying, do you hear? I've never been able to stand people who cried. You're strong, like me—so save your tears; we have to talk."

"You aren't going to die," Clara managed to stammer.

"Oh, yes, my dear, I am. I can't prevent it. But I *can* prevent another death—yours. You're in danger here, and I'm going to do whatever it takes to stop anyone from harming you."

"Me? Who'd want to hurt me?" Clara asked, bewildered.

"I haven't been able to find out who was behind those Italians who followed you around Baghdad. But I no longer trust George and Frankie, or Enrique."

"But, Grandfather, they're your friends! You always said they were like your brothers, more than brothers—that if something happened to you one day, they would take care of me."

"Yes, and that was true—once. I don't know how long I have to live; Dr. Aziz gives me no more than a few months, so let's not waste time putting off conversations that we need to have. The Bible of Clay will be your ticket to a life far from here. It will be your letter of introduction to another world. We have to find it, because there's not enough money on earth to buy respectability."

"Respectability? What does that mean?"

"You know what it means—you've always known, even if we've never talked about it. My business dealings have earned me a certain reputation, and that's not what I want for you. My businesses will die with me, although you'll have enough money to live very comfortably for the rest of your life.

"I want you to dedicate yourself entirely to archaeology, make a name for yourself—that's what both of us have always wanted, and that's where you'll find your own path.

"I am respected in this region of the world; I buy and sell anything—I find weapons for terrorists, I satisfy the most extravagant wishes of presidents and princes, I see to it that some of their enemies no longer trouble them. And in return, they do me favors—perhaps overlooking, for example, what some might call the plundering of their countries' artistic and archaeological heritage. I won't bore you with the details; they are what they are, and I'm proud of what I've been able to accomplish. Does that disappoint you?"

"No, Grandfather, you could never disappoint me. I realized a long time ago that some of your business dealings were . . . delicate. But I don't judge you; I would never do that. I'm sure you've always done what you thought you should do."

Clara's unconditional loyalty was the only thing that moved the old man. He knew that in his final moments, she would be the only person he could count on. His granddaughter's eyes were without guile, as they had always been, and he knew that she was being honest with him, that she was not hiding anything.

"In my world, respect has a great deal to do with fear—now I'm dying, and it's no secret. This sort of information has its own way of leaking out. So the vultures are certain to be circling overhead—I feel them; I know they're there. And they will descend upon you when I'm gone. I had thought that Ahmed would take over the business and that he would protect you, but your divorce has forced me to change my plans."

"Ahmed knows about your business dealings?"

"Ahmed is instrumental in my business dealings, regardless of how paralyzed he's become by a sudden onset of scruples over the last few months. But he will protect you until you're safely out of Iraq. I've paid him well. And I sent him back to Baghdad for the moment. He can do us more good there."

Clara felt sick. Her grandfather had just destroyed any possibility of a reconciliation with her husband. She wasn't upset with him; he was simply preparing her for what was to come—and part of that preparation was to inform her that Ahmed was being paid to protect her. Not as her husband, but as one of Alfred's guards.

"Who could want me dead?"

"George, Frankie, and Enrique want the Bible of Clay. I'm sure they've infiltrated men into the excavation here, ready to smuggle it out if we find it. It's priceless—or rather, its price is so beyond all measure that they've refused to accept the deal I've offered them."

"Which is what?"

"It has to do with an operation that's under way right now—my last one, since I'll not live to see another."

Clara swallowed hard. "And you think they're capable of sending someone to kill me?"

"They want the Bible, Clara. They'll try not to harm you if they can get their hands on it easily. But if we don't give it to them, they'll do whatever they have to. I'd do the same thing if I were in their place. So I'm trying to stay ahead of them. Until the Bible appears, you're in no danger, but the moment it's found, your problems will start."

"And you're sure that these men are here, in Safran?"

"Absolutely. Ayed Sahadi hasn't uncovered them yet, but he has his eye on several people working around you. They may have infiltrated as workers, suppliers, even people brought in with Picot's team. Killing someone is just a matter of money, and my old friends have more than they need—as I do, my dear, to spend on protecting you."

The conversation was tearing Clara apart inside, but she refused to show it. Nor would she ever allow her grandfather to think that she was ashamed of him. In fact, deep down she truly felt she had nothing to reproach him for. She had always known that hers was a privileged existence within the powder keg of the Middle East, where only a very select few lived as she and her family did. She belonged to the elite of the elite, which was why she always had an escort of armed men ready to lay down their lives to protect her. Her grandfather paid them a king's ransom to do so. Even as a child she had known that he was a powerful and implacable man, and she had enjoyed the reverential way she was treated in school and later at the university. No, she'd never been unaware of her grandfather's power, and if she'd asked no questions it was because she didn't want answers that might cause her pain. She had protected herself by a comfortable, if willful, ignorance.

"What did you offer your friends?"

"I asked them to let you have the Bible of Clay in exchange for one hundred percent of the profits of the operation that we now have under way. I'm offering them a great deal of money, but they refuse to accept it."

"The Bible of Clay is an obsession for them too."

"They are my friends, Clara, and I love them as I love myself, but not more than I love you. We have to find the Bible of Clay before the Americans arrive. The second it's in our hands, you have to leave Iraq. Our alliance with Professor Picot was a stroke of luck—he is a controversial figure, but no one can deny his stature as an archaeologist. So he will be your entrée into a new world—but that is only possible if you have the Bible."

"And what happens if we don't find it?"

"We *will* find it. But either way you will have to leave Iraq—go to Cairo. There you will be able to live quietly, or relatively quietly, although I've always dreamed that you would go to Europe and live . . . well, wherever you want: Paris, London, Berlin."

"You always opposed my going to Europe."

"Yes, and you should only go there with the Bible of Clay. Otherwise your life in the West would become difficult—and I couldn't bear it if anyone harmed you."

"Who could do that?"

"The past, Clara, the past, which sometimes has a way of washing like a tsunami over the present."

"My past is not important."

"No, it's not. But it's not your past I'm talking about. Now, tell me how the work is going."

"It occurred to Gian Maria that Shamas might have kept the Bible of Clay in his house rather than in the temple, so we widened the perimeter of the excavation. Today they discovered the outlines of houses near the temple; we may be able to discern where Shamas himself lived! And in the temple, in addition to the tablets, they've found bullae and calculi and two or three statuettes. So with a little luck, we could find it, Grandfather."

"This priest, Gian Maria—has he created any problems?"

"How did you know he's a priest?" Clara laughed then, realizing how absurd the question was. Her grandfather knew everything that happened in the camp—Ayed kept him up to date. And Alfred had other men, men of his own, who would not let a single detail escape them.

Tannenberg took a sip of water, waiting for Clara's reply. He was tired from his journey, but he was glad he and Clara had talked. They were two of a kind—she hadn't batted an eyelash when he told her that someone was probably going to try to kill her. She hadn't asked any stupid questions or acted the surprised and innocent virgin about the murky world of her family's business.

"Gian Maria is a good person, very capable. He knows the ancient languages of the region—Akkadian, Hebrew, Aramaic. . . . He's a bit skeptical about whether Abraham dictated his version of the Genesis story to a young scribe—after all, there's no mention of it in the Torah—but he works hard, without a word of complaint. And don't worry, Grandfather, he isn't dangerous."

"If there's one thing I know, it's that people aren't always what they seem."

"But Gian Maria is a priest."

"Yes, that's true—we've checked."

Tannenberg closed his eyes, and Clara ran her hand tenderly over his creased forehead and down over his wrinkled cheek.

"I think I'd like to sleep for a while."

"Yes, do. Tonight Picot would like to meet you."

"We'll see. Now go, let me sleep."

Fatima had moved Dr. Najeb into the house next door and had put the nurse into the room next to Tannenberg's, although she doubted there was anything this Samira could do that she couldn't. Fatima knew what Alfred needed even before he did. A gesture, the slightest movement of his hand, the way he held his body were signs that helped her anticipate what her master was going to ask for. But the doctor had been unbending—Samira had to be near the sick man, to care for him and advise the doctor of any contingency. And the doctor's house was within mere feet of Tannenberg's.

"What's wrong, my child?" she asked Clara as her mistress came into the kitchen looking for her.

"He's so sick. . . ."

"He will live," Fatima assured her. "He will live until you find those tablets. He will not leave you."

Clara let herself be embraced by her old servant, protectress, and friend, knowing that she could count on her, no matter what she had to face. And what she had to face now could not be more disturbing: Her grandfather had just told her that someone was going to make an attempt on her life.

"Where are the doctor and nurse?"

"They're putting together the field hospital."

"All right, I'm going out to the excavation. I'll be back for dinner."

Lion Doyle came over with a big grin on his face, his body covered in sand.

"You've heard the news, then, Clara? They've found the foundations of houses—your colleagues are overjoyed!"

"Yes, I know—I just wish I could have been here sooner. How's your photography assignment coming?"

"Better than I'd hoped, thanks. Picot has hired me."

"Hired you? To do what?"

"Apparently some archaeological journal asked him to send back field notes on the excavation, illustrated if possible, and he asked me to cover the photo spread. So my trip won't have been in vain, after all."

Clara, irritated, clenched her teeth. So Picot planned to take all the credit for himself and send off a report to an archaeological journal?

"Which journal is it?"

"I think it's called *Scientific Archaeology*. He told me they publish editions in France, the UK, Germany, Spain, Italy, the United States. . . . Apparently it's a pretty big deal."

"Yes, it is. You might say that what gets published in *Scientific Archaeology* exists, and what doesn't isn't worth the sand it's covered by."

"If you say so—this is all new to me, although I must admit I'm beginning to be infected by all this enthusiasm."

She left Lion Doyle standing there grinning and walked over to where Marta and Fabian were working.

They had dug out another sector of the temple, and they'd found a syllabary. It seemed as though the site, faced with the unflagging determination of this hodgepodge group, had at last begun disclosing its deepest mysteries.

"Where's Picot?" Clara asked.

"Over there," Marta answered, pointing to a group of workers who looked like they were scrabbling in the ground with their bare hands. Picot was standing among them, bent over to examine what they were uncovering. "He's found traces of ancient Safran's city walls."

"Clara, I think we're standing on the second level of the temple, a sort of terrace. Could be a ziggurat, but I'm not sure. There are traces of an interior wall here, and we've started to uncover what look like steps, a staircase leading inside," Fabian told her.

"We're going to need more workers," Marta declared, delighted by the sudden appearance of so much new material.

"I'll tell Ayed, but I don't think it's going to be easy: The whole country is on a state of alert," Clara replied.

Yves Picot was so absorbed in what he was doing that he didn't see Clara walk over.

"I hear it's a great day," she said to him brightly. "Everything seems to be happening at once."

"You can't imagine. The gods have smiled on us!" he practically shouted. "We've found traces of the outer wall, several courses of blocks, and right up next to them the outlines of buildings, probably houses—come here, look!"

Picot led her over the yellow sand, pointing out the remains of perfectly stacked blocks that only an expert's eye could identify as the remains of ancient houses.

"I've brought half the workers over here to clear this zone. I imagine Fabian already told you that they've made wonderful progress on the mound and that the temple looks like a ziggurat."

"Yes, I saw that. . . . I'll work over here."

"That's fine. Do you think we could possibly find more workers? If we want to clear all this with the time we have left, we're going to need more."

"Fabian and Marta told me. I'll see what can be done. By the way, the photographer, Lion what's-his-name, told me you'd put him on the payroll."

"Yes, I asked him to prepare a photo-essay on our excavation."

"I didn't know you'd arranged for anybody to publish our work."

Clara stressed the "our." Picot turned to her, an amused look in his eyes, and then burst out laughing.

"Come on, Clara, be cool! Nobody's going to steal your thunder here. I know people at *Scientific Archaeology* and they asked me to keep them informed. Everybody's been curious about the Bible of Clay since you announced its existence in Rome. If we find it, it will be a landmark in the history of archaeology. We'll not only prove that Abraham existed, but also that he *revealed* the Genesis story. It will be revolutionary. Even if the tablets don't appear, the importance of the things we've found here should merit publication. We're uncovering a ziggurat that no one knew existed, and in better condition than we could have hoped for. Don't worry, this is already a success, and we all share in it. I've had more than my share of *la gloire, madame*—my career, my name is secure. You have no reason to fear that I'll steal the limelight, or the well-deserved credit, from you. But you're quite right that this is *our* work, because none of this would be possible without Fabian Tudela, Marta Gómez, and the others."

Yves then bent back down to his work without another word. Clara hesitated just a moment, and then walked off to a group clearing the sand and other sediment off another section of ground.

The sun was dropping below the horizon by the time Picot called off work for the day. The workers and team members were exhausted and hungry, and they were more than ready to return to their homes in the village or the camp for dinner.

Fatima was waiting for Clara at the door of their house, and she seemed to be in a good mood.

"Your grandfather woke up hungry, and he's waiting for you."

"I have to take a shower. I'll be there as soon as I can."

"He wants to eat dinner alone with you tonight; tomorrow he'll see the archaeologists."

"That's fine, Fatima—whatever he wants."

They were just finishing dinner when Fatima announced that Yves Picot was at the door, asking to meet Monsieur Tannenberg.

Clara was about to tell her it would have to wait until tomorrow, but Alfred interrupted her.

"Tell him to come in."

The two men measured each other in the few seconds it took to shake hands.

Picot took an immediate dislike to Tannenberg. The older man's steel-blue eyes reflected sheer cruelty, devoid of any sign of human sympathy. Tannenberg, for his part, was instantly aware of the Frenchman's strength of will and character.

Tannenberg led the conversation, so it was Picot who did most of the talking, answering the older man's pointed questions about the progress of the excavation and describing the minutiae of their findings to Alfred's satisfaction. But he was waiting for his turn to ask the questions. And at last, his opening came.

"I've been dying to meet you," he told the old man. "I can't seem to persuade Clara to tell me how or when you found those tablets in Haran that brought us all here in the first place."

"It was a long time ago."

"What year did the expedition take place? Who was in charge of it?"

"My friend, it was so long ago that I can't remember—before the war, when expeditions organized by romantics came to the Middle East more out of love of adventure than archaeology. Many of them based excavations more on intuition than research. In Haran I wasn't digging with archaeologists, I was digging with amateurs: people mildly interested in history who could afford to indulge their love of the exotic. We found two tablets on which Shamas, a priest or scribe, refers to Abraham and the creation. Ever since then, I've believed that someday we would find the rest of the tablets that Shamas pledged to make. I called them the 'Bible of Clay.' "

"That's what Clara called them at the conference in Rome when she took on the leading lights of the archaeological community. And what we've been calling it ever since."

"If Iraq were experiencing a moment of peace in its history, half a dozen archaeological teams would have applied for the exclusive rights to excavate the Bible of Clay. With Saddam's blessing. With war about to be unleashed against Iraq . . . I appreciate your commitment. It took tremendous courage."

"Actually, I had nothing better to do," Yves replied with a cynical grin.

"Yes, I know—you're a wealthy man, so you have no need to face the harsh reality of a paycheck at the end of the month. Your mother comes from an old banking family, isn't that right?"

"My mother is British, the only daughter of my grandfather, who did, indeed, own a bank on the Isle of Man—a financial haven, as I'm sure you know."

"I know. But you yourself are French."

"My father is French—Alsatian, actually—so I was brought up shuttling back and forth between Alsace and the Isle of Man. My mother inherited the bank, and my father now runs it."

"And you have no interest whatsoever in the world of finance," Tannenberg stated more than asked.

"That's quite right—the only thing that interests me about money is how to spend it in the most pleasant way possible."

"Someday you'll inherit the bank, though. What will you do with it?"

"My parents are in excellent health, so I hope that day is far off. And luckily I have a sister—much more savvy than I—who's willing to take over the family business when the time comes."

"Aren't you concerned about leaving something solid for your children?"

"I have no children, nor any interest in having any."

"We men need assurance that we've left something after us. A legacy, if you will."

"Some men—I'm not one of them."

Clara was sitting in silence, listening to Yves' conversation with her grandfather, and she noticed that the archaeologist was doing nothing to make the older man like him. It was Samira who brought an end to the volley. She came in, followed closely by Fatima, who was trying in vain to stop her.

"Monsieur Tannenberg, it's time for your injection."

Alfred Tannenberg looked over at the nurse angrily.

"Out."

The old man's tone was icy and brooked no disagreement. Fatima grabbed the nurse's arm and dragged her out, clucking and cackling at her presumption.

Tannenberg drew the conversation out for half an hour longer, underscoring his undiminished power and ignoring the half-suppressed yawns of Clara, who was bone-tired from her work that day. Then he bid good night to Yves Picot, promising to send him a new contingent of workers.

Minutes later, a sharp cry broke the night, followed by a woman's sobs, which grew quieter little by little, until the house was silent once again.

Clara tossed and turned in her bed. She knew that her grandfather had made Samira pay for her temerity. The nurse would learn that Alfred Tannenberg paid his employees generously because he expected them to make no missteps. Nor was he one to forgive such mistakes. Clara imagined that he had struck the nurse—it was not the first time he had punished people who displeased him.

Ayed Sahadi had had Lion Doyle and Ante Plaskic watched. He didn't trust either of them and was sure that neither was what he claimed to be.

Lion Doyle, in turn, kept an eye on Ayed; the man was no mere foreman. As for Plaskic, Lion was sure he was a hit man, maybe even another operative sent in by Tom Martin. Either way, he was not the peaceable computer geek he painted himself to be.

The Welshman had a feeling the group was reaching its breaking point. They still hadn't found the Bible of Clay, and the excavation was moving ahead at punishing speed. No one would be able to keep up the pace for much longer, and there was more tension in the camp every day. The news from overseas didn't help: At any moment, tons of U.S. bombs would start falling on Iraq.

The workers joked that they'd be hunting Americans like rabbits— that they would never let an American soldier set foot on the sacred soil of Iraq—but they knew that their braggadocio was just that: blustering to keep up their spirits. Many of them had lived through the war with Iran, and they knew how quickly, randomly, life could be taken.

Clara seemed not to distrust Lion. His veneer as site photographer made him an important member of the team. She never avoided his company, and during the day she patiently showed him the shards and fragments of clay objects the team unearthed, explaining the importance of each piece while they mutually chose the best angle to showcase the photograph. *Scientific Archaeology* would be the perfect conduit through which she would demonstrate to the world the massive archaeological value of the dig.

Lion had laughed to himself when the head of Photomundi informed him that his pictures of Baghdad had been bought by a news agency. Their first report in *Scientific Archaeology* had been a success as well, in large part due to the photographs that accompanied Picot's text. Assassination or no, Lion had already turned a profit on this job. The only problem was that the publication prompted several TV channels to post their own correspondents to Safran to report on the ragtag international group of archaeologists excavating despite the drumbeat of war that was sounding ever louder. They had captured the public imagination.

So Lion Doyle wasn't the least bit surprised when he saw Miranda show up with Daniel, her cameraman, and another group of reporters who, under the auspices of the Ministry of Information, had landed in Safran.

"So, Mr. World-Famous Photographer!" Miranda greeted him.

"Good to see you too. Things must be slow in Baghdad if you've come all the way out here!"

"Slow is an understatement. Conditions are bad—really, really bad. People are at their wits' end. Your friend Bush keeps insisting that Saddam has weapons of mass destruction, and a couple of days ago,

Colin Powell went to the UN Security Council with satellite photos purporting to show sites housing WMDs."

"The proverbial smoking gun. Which you don't think exists."

"You don't either."

"Me? I have no idea."

"Come on, Lion, don't play innocent!"

"I don't feel like arguing, Miranda. You've only been here a few minutes!"

Daniel intervened to change the subject. "How was Christmas out here?" he asked.

"Christmas? We didn't have any bloody Christmas out here, pal. Nobody takes an hour off, let alone a day—these people work eighteen hours straight, seven days a week. The food tasted slightly better that night, but that was it."

"In Baghdad, we managed to throw together a party; we all brought whatever we could find."

Miranda, filled with curiosity, left the two men talking while she wandered through the camp. She'd heard Yves Picot and Clara Tannenberg mentioned as the co-leaders of the expedition, and she hoped to be able to interview them both.

Picot and Clara very hospitably made themselves available to the troupe of reporters, although they couldn't disguise the fact that they were eager to get back to work—any interruption in their very tight schedule would cost them, and all hands were needed.

Nevertheless, as the day progressed, it didn't escape Clara's notice that Picot was a bit dazzled by Miranda, whom he trailed like a puppy. Clara saw how they laughed and talked, oblivious to everyone around them. It occurred to her that they might have known each other from before, and she felt a pang of jealousy. Miranda, like Marta, was everything Clara wasn't: an independent, self-made, self-assured woman who owed nothing to any man. Miranda was accustomed to being treated as an equal, without conceding an ounce of her femininity. It didn't surprise Clara that she seemed to know Lion Doyle too—they were both, after all, reporters.

At lunchtime, Miranda shared a table with Marta, Fabian, and Gian Maria, along with Daniel and Ayed, who watchfully sat next to Clara herself. Lion soon joined them, despite the condescending look Miranda shot him.

"There are demonstrations all over Europe," Daniel was saying. "The people are against this war."

"What war? We're not at war. Bush won't attack—he's just trying to scare Saddam," Ayed said boldly.

"Oh, he'll attack, to be sure," Miranda said. "It'll happen in March."

"Why in March?" asked Clara.

"Because he wants to have his operation completely mounted before summer. His troops couldn't handle fighting in this kind of heat. So they come in March, April at the latest."

"Let's hope it's later rather than sooner," said Picot.

"How long will you be here?" Miranda wanted to know.

"According to your calculations, about a month," Picot replied.

"What's your exit strategy? The army won't protect you once the bombing starts; Saddam will need every available man, and sooner or later they'll mobilize your workers."

Miranda's hardheaded observation plunged them into silence. Suddenly they were all too aware that the world was moving at a rate very different from theirs, in this village in which they had spent the last several months searching the sand for a secret as old as time, a secret that might only be a chimera.

Marta broke through the gloom.

"As you've seen, we've discovered a temple, apparently part of a ziggurat. We believe that it dates to two thousand years before Christ. What we're sure of is that no one in the modern world was aware of its existence until now. We're also uncovering the outlines of houses from the same period, although unfortunately only traces of them remain. We're studying the hundreds of tablets we've found in two rooms of the ziggurat. We've also uncovered two statuettes in good condition and a number of bullae and calculi. . . . I want to tell you, Miranda, that the progress we've made is extraordinary considering the length of time we've been here. We've done in four months what would have taken years under normal circumstances. Given that we're on the brink of war, I realize that the work of a handful of archaeologists couldn't matter to people. But if the bombs *don't* destroy what we've found and we're able to come back next year, I assure you this will be one of the most important archaeological sites in the Middle East. I think all of us can be proud of what we've done."

"You've had Saddam's permission to work," Miranda responded.

"Yes, of course. You can't dig in any country without the government's permission. He's allowed us to excavate, and thanks to the resources Professor Picot has paid for out of his own pocket, we have the supplies, equipment, and personnel to do it," Fabian interjected.

"I thought that Madam Tannenberg was the co-leader and financial co-sponsor of the expedition. . . ."

Clara decided to seize that opening to make it clear that this was her expedition and that everything that might come of it belonged to her as well as to Picot.

"That's right—this is a project that Professor Picot and I put together. It is an extremely costly and difficult one, but, as Professor Gómez explained, it has already borne extraordinary fruit."

"But you were looking for something else, weren't you? Didn't you announce at that conference in Rome that you'd found tablets promising the story of the creation as told by the patriarch Abraham? And that there were other similar tablets in the same area? Am I mistaken about that?"

This time it was Picot who answered.

"No, you're right. Clara has in her possession two tablets—which I've studied and dated myself—on which a scribe named Shamas says that a man named Abram is going to tell him the story of the creation of the world. Clara maintains the hypothesis that the Abram referred to by Shamas is the patriarch Abraham, and if her theory is confirmed, the discovery of that story would be groundbreaking. No pun intended, of course."

At that, Fabian jumped in. "Bear in mind, though, that science and history have called into doubt the historical existence of the patriarchs. No one has ever been able to produce evidence about their lives, other than what the Old Testament tells us. If we find these tablets, it would show that the Bible accurately recounts history. You can't imagine the importance that that would have for archaeology, science, even religion."

"But you haven't found them yet," parried Miranda.

"No, not yet," Marta replied, "but we have found many tablets bearing the name Shamas, so we still have hopes of finding the Bible of Clay."

"The Bible of Clay?"

"Miranda, what else would we call tablets containing the story of creation?" Marta shot back.

"You're right, and I like the name—the Bible of Clay. And what do *you* think about all this? Aren't you a priest?"

Miranda's question was directed at Gian Maria, who swallowed hard as his face turned bright red.

"Well, that's a first. I've made a man blush!" Miranda laughed.

Gian Maria remained tongue-tied. As everyone looked at him, waiting for him to answer, Fabian interceded.

"Gian Maria is our resident linguist—his knowledge of the ancient languages of the region has been invaluable. He's been working night and day deciphering and translating tablets. Without him, we wouldn't have been able to make such progress. But until we find those tablets and analyze them—not just us, I mean, but also independent third parties—we won't be able to say we've found the Bible of Clay. So we're still in the realm of speculation. But as Marta said before, what we've already uncovered here more than justifies our work."

"And the two tablets that brought you all here were written by a relatively untrained or inexperienced writer?" asked Miranda, staying on the trail. "How do you know?"

"You can tell by the markings. It's clear that this Shamas wasn't yet well trained with his stylus, which as you probably know was a reed that made incisions in the clay. Additionally, the tablets bearing the name Shamas that we've found here don't look anything like the writing on the tablets that Clara has had in her family's possession for decades. The Shamas from here was a very experienced scribe. And he was something of a naturalist as well, because he left a wonderful list of the region's flora," Fabian, again, answered.

"It's possible that the Shamas who wrote the tablets from Haran and the Shamas from here weren't the same person, although Clara contends he was," Marta added.

"And why do you think it's the same person?" Miranda asked, turning to Clara.

"Because while it's true that the markings on the Haran tablets are different from the ones we've found here, the lines do seem to be made by the same hand, although these are firmer, surer," Clara answered with remarkable self-assurance, given the challenge implicit in the question. "My theory is that Shamas wrote the Haran tablets as an adolescent and inscribed the tablets from Safran as an adult."

Clara knew the tablets so well that she carried them as a photographic image in her mind. And the team's analysis seemed to confirm what she already knew: The two sets of tablets had almost certainly been produced by the same hand.

"But I'd like to know what the Church thinks about all this," Miranda insisted, turning again to Gian Maria.

The priest, recovered from the initial discomfort of being the center of attention, tried to satisfy the reporter's curiosity. "I can't speak for the Church; I'm just a priest."

"So tell me what you think about all this."

"Well, the Bible tells us of the existence of the patriarch Abraham. Naturally, I believe that he did exist, that he was a real person. I myself have no need for archaeological proof."

"And do you believe that Abraham revealed the story of the creation to someone?"

"The Bible says nothing about that, and it's pretty explicit about the life of Abraham. So . . . well, I'm skeptical; I'm not positive the Bible of Clay exists. But if those tablets appear, it will be the Church's responsibility to authenticate them."

"But weren't you sent by the Vatican?" Miranda asked.

"Heavens, no! The Vatican has nothing to do with my presence here," Gian Maria answered quickly.

"So what are you doing here?" Miranda insisted.

"Well, it's a long story," he demurred.

"I've got all day," the reporter said, ignoring the priest's obvious uneasiness.

"Can't you just let him alone?" Lion Doyle had remained silent through the exchange so far, but spoke up now.

"Ah, a white knight! You always ride in just when somebody needs you, don't you, Lion, whether it's a damsel caught in a cross fire or a priest under interrogation?"

"Piss off, Miranda!" replied Lion ill-humoredly.

"I have no problem answering," Gian Maria said, his voice barely a whisper. "I was in Baghdad working with an NGO called Aid to Children, but I'd met Professor Picot and couldn't resist coming out here to see the work they were doing. Especially given that my knowledge of the ancient languages would help, so . . . well, I stayed."

"And as a priest, you can just do anything you feel like?" Miranda insisted.

"I have permission to be here," Gian Maria answered, though he turned red again.

For the rest of the afternoon, Miranda and Daniel filmed the archaeologists at work, who by then were tired of repeating the same story to other reporters who'd arrived.

"God, they're exhausting, especially Miranda—although I do like her," said Fabian.

"They're just doing their job," Marta noted.

"You're always so sympathetic to other people—but we've wasted the whole day with them."

Fabian lit a cigarette and stared into the rising smoke. As always, Marta was right. And it wasn't a total waste, especially if their predictions were accurate about the war starting in March, or April at the latest. That was vital information.

He squatted down and began to brush away the sand and dirt from the side of what appeared to be a terrace—a sort of square patio littered with shards of fired clay and ceramics.

There was almost no sunlight remaining when they decided to return to the camp. The laborers were muttering among themselves about their long hours and especially about the news the reporters had brought, that the war was inevitable and about to begin.

Clara had made arrangements for a meal under the stars. Cloths were laid near bonfires on which half a dozen lambs, seasoned with aromatic herbs, were slowly being spitted. A Dutch reporter was enthusiastically filming the scene, while one of her colleagues from the BBC complained about the satellite connection.

Yves Picot spoke with several of the reporters, showing infinite patience, trying to address their complaints.

"You seem very happy."

Picot turned when he heard Clara's voice.

"I have no reason not to be."

"But tonight you seem happier than usual."

"Well, it's been a while since we've had any contact with the outside world, and these people reminded me that there's more to life than just digging in the sand."

"Ah, so you're homesick!"

"That's quite a leap! No, I'm not, exactly, but we've done nothing but work over the past months. I'd almost forgotten that there's a world beyond Safran."

"Are you thinking about leaving?"

"Not because I miss Europe, but honestly, Clara, I *am* worried about our safety. I'm going to call Ahmed tomorrow. I want him to lay out the details of our evacuation plan. He promised to have everything ready to get us out of here when the bombs started falling."

"And if we haven't yet found the Bible of Clay?"

"We'll have to go, no matter what." He studied Clara's everhopeful face. "You can't be suggesting that we stay while the Americans invade? Do you think they'd make an exception for Safran because a group of crazy archaeologists is here excavating? Clara, I'm responsible for these people; most of them are here because of me, some are my own students, some my personal friends. No one's life is worth risking here, even for the Bible of Clay."

"When will you be leaving, then?"

"I just don't know yet. But I want to be prepared. I think the time has come to face this. I want to talk to my people—we'll make the decision as a group. But I don't think we should delude ourselves; you heard what the reporters had to say."

"Things are no worse than they were a few months ago—nothing has changed."

"They say things have."

"Reporters exaggerate, sensationalize—it's what they do."

"You're mistaken. Some of them may, but when they're all in unison . . . Clara, we have Dutch reporters, Greeks, Brits, Frenchmen, Spaniards. . . . They're all saying the same thing."

"All right, I get the idea. You can leave whenever you want; I'm staying on."

Yves Picot looked into Clara's eyes. He couldn't force her to go, but it irritated him that she would continue without him.

"You'll be working in a hail of bombs."

"Your friends may not win."

"My friends? Who are 'my friends'?"

"The people who are going to bomb us."

"Have you had an attack of nationalism all of a sudden? If you're trying to get me to stay by playing on some sort of guilt you think I have, you're wasting your time. I'll say this once: I believe Saddam is a cruel and murderous dictator who ought to be in jail. I wouldn't cross the street to save him; I couldn't care less what happens to him. But I'm terribly sorry that innocent Iraqis are going to pay for his crimes."

"For Saddam's crimes, or because the Americans want to steal our oil?"

"Well, both. Saddam is the excuse, of course, though. But I'm not a political man—I got off that train a long time ago."

"You don't believe in anything."

"When I was twenty, I was a leftist, a militant, passionate about changing the world, but I soon abandoned my party in disgust. No one was what they appeared to be or claimed to be. I realized that politics and imposture go hand in hand, so I got out before I was corrupted. I defend the bourgeois democracy that allows us the illusion of believing that we enjoy freedom—that's all."

"But what about the others? What happens to all of us who weren't born in your first world? What should we do, what should we expect?"

"All I know is that you're the victims of the big interests you so despise, but also victims of your own rulers, and victims of yourselves. I'm French, and I defend the French Revolution; I think that all countries should have a revolution like ours and that it should lead to enlightenment and reason. But in this part of the world, enlightened men and women like you and your grandfather hoard your nation's wealth and power, protect it against all newcomers, and refuse to share it with your compatriots. So don't ask me what you can do. Figure it out for yourself. I don't feel guilty about anything."

"You think your culture is superior to ours."

"You want me to tell you the truth? Yes, then, I do. The rule of Islam prevents you from ushering in the bourgeois revolution. Until you separate religion and politics, you won't progress. I'm disgusted to see Iraqis swathed from head to toe in black, like that woman Fatima, who follows you around everywhere you go. I'm indignant when I see them walk five steps behind their husbands, unable even to talk to a man."

Fabian came over to them with a glass of wine in each hand.

"We're lucky this country isn't strictly observant. It's not France, but at least we can drink."

As he handed them each a glass, he picked up on the tension in the air. "What's going on between you two?" he asked.

"I told Clara that we have to start thinking about leaving."

"From what they told us," Fabian said, gesturing with his head toward the reporters, "we shouldn't wait much longer."

"I'm calling Ahmed tomorrow," Picot said, "so we can coordinate the evacuation. We'll stay as long as it's safe, but not a second longer."

His tone of voice left no room for argument.

From the little window of her room, Clara could see hardly anything. There was no moon.

For a long time, the camp had been silent. Everyone else was asleep, but her conversation with Picot kept running through her mind as she tossed and turned. And she'd also spoken with Dr. Najeb, who was not one for sugaring the pill. Alfred was drifting in and out of consciousness, and the results of his lab tests were troubling. In the doctor's opinion, he needed to be transferred to a real hospital.

Clara had gone in to see her grandfather and was shocked by how much he had aged in one day. His eyes were sunken and his breathing labored. When she told him that they needed to transfer him to Baghdad and from there to Cairo, he shook his head violently. No, he wouldn't leave until they'd found the Bible of Clay. She didn't have the heart to tell him that Picot was ready to close the site.

Clara's watch read three a.m., and the desert night had turned cold. She pulled on a sweatshirt and, without turning on the light, left her room and walked toward Fatima's. The old woman was dead to the world and didn't wake up even when Clara opened the window and crawled over the low sill outside.

The guards in her escort were stationed at the main entrance and just inside the door, but they seemed not to have taken any measures to protect the back of the house.

She waited a few seconds, until her heart stopped thumping, and then, crouching in the shadows, she began to put distance between herself and the camp. She was going out to the ziggurat. She needed to touch the ancient clay bricks, and to feel the night breeze—she needed a balm for her spirit.

The guards were sleeping the sleep of the just, apparently. Ayed Sahadi would have them killed if he learned that someone could have penetrated the perimeter of the camp without being detected.

Once at the site, Clara found a place to sit down and think. She had an odd feeling, a feeling that her life was about to change completely. Where once there had been only security and certainty, she now foresaw solitude and pain, and for the first time she realized that she had never stopped to think—she had just lived, without worrying about anything, without wanting to know or see anything that didn't suit her selfish comfort.

She was no better than Ahmed, who was being paid a small fortune to protect her—except that she was no hypocrite. She may have been willfully blind, but her conscience was clear.

She fell asleep, curled up on the ground, and dreamed of Shamas.

34

 THE SPECIAL MORNING DAWNED BRIGHT AND CLEAR. THE dub-sar Shamas was to be invested with the title ses-gal, great brother.

Ili, who was now chief priest, would conduct the ceremony, which would take place in the small but glorious ziggurat erected by men sent by the king of Ur. There, the people of Safran paid tribute to the provincial government, presided over by the lord of Safran. And there, too, wise men stored writings concerning the wider kingdom's knowledge of the gods and of more worldly things—flowers, plants, and the sky—whose mysteries the priests alone could decipher. The king's motives in building the ziggurat had been clear: He desired to extend his power beyond Ur.

Jadin's eyes had been blinded by time; his teeth were gone and he was shrunken and stooped. But he would nonetheless follow his son's ceremony of ascension with delight. For many years now, Shamas' mother had been Jadin's eyes, and she described to her husband all that happened around him. Today she would raise her head proudly, celebrating the venerable rank to which her unruly son had risen.

The master was already savoring the ceremony dedicated to his most beloved—and difficult—disciple and apprentice. For indeed,

Shamas—however intelligent, however promising—had caused Ili countless headaches. Shamas had never been content with simple answers. He needed to dissect everything he was told, to find its logic. He would not accept what others told him unless the reasoning was clear and evident. Still, no disciple had brought Ili as much satisfaction.

Long ago, Abram had persuaded the young man that there was but one God and that all things had been created by Him, by an act of will. Ili, in turn, explained that indeed, the order of creation had come down from Elohim, but that there were other gods. Shamas would not hear of it.

But time does not pass in vain, and Shamas' contentious spirit had grown quieter; he was now the best of the temple's many scribes. And today he was to assume a new place, a new distinction, ses-gal, and someday he would also be an um-mi-a above all others, for his wisdom and skill were unquestionable. They were the fruit of his unflagging observation and study.

Shamas' wife, a young woman named Lia, had straightened his tunic and smiled as they walked to the temple.

But as the ceremony began, Shamas' mind was distant. He was thinking of Abraham. He imagined him in the land of Canaan, where Abraham had indeed become the father of multitudes, for news of his patronage had spread all the way to Ur. God had promised him that, and He had seen that it came to pass.

God, though, still seemed to Shamas an inscrutable and capricious being. Though Shamas believed in Him with all his heart, he could not understand Him; sometimes when he tried to discover the logic behind the Creation, he thought his head was going to explode. There were moments when he felt he was on the verge of understanding, but that illusion vanished as quickly as it appeared, and his mind lapsed once again into darkness. After long thought, he concluded at last that he was but a mortal man—he had to be content to acknowledge God's will and trust what he felt in the very core of his being to be true.

The sound of Ili clearing his throat brought Shamas back to reality. He had not heard his master's words, had hardly been aware of the scribes and priests praying beside him to the goddess Nidaba.

He was eager to be alone with Ili, so that he might at last present to him the gift he had been preparing for several years. It was the finest of Shamas' labor: a series of tablets written in clear and elegant signs that told a story of the first days, just as Abraham had dictated it to him. The creation of the world, God's anger with men's evil and the flood with which He punished it, the destruction of Babel and the confusion of tongues—three beautiful legends written on the clay, which Shamas hoped would find a home in one of the rooms in which other histories, other epic tales, were safeguarded.

Later, as night was falling, master and disciple finally had the opportunity to enjoy a few moments of solitude together in Shamas' home, when they could speak to each other privately.

There was not a hair on Ili's head, and his slow feet and white eyebrows attested to his advanced age. But his eyes sparkled as he smiled at his protégé. "You will make a fine um-mi-a someday," he told Shamas.

"I am happy to be what I am. It is a privilege to work here beside you, master, where each day I am able to learn new things."

"Though it is never enough for you. We teach you the wealth of knowledge our culture has to offer, yet still you ask questions. You wish to know the reason for the world and our existence in it, and not even God gives you the answers you seek."

Shamas was silent. Ili was right: Every answer his master offered only elicited more questions.

"For many years you have been a man," Ili went on, "and you must content yourself with knowing that there are some questions for which there are no answers, no matter which god one invokes. Although you have learned at least to respect the gods, you've kept me awake many a long night, fearing that your reckless questions may reach the ears of our lord. That no one has betrayed you, not even those who do not understand you, is testament to the respect you command."

"But, Ili, you know as I do that the gods in our temple are merely clay."

"They are, but it is not the clay we pray to. It is the spirit of the god that the clay represents, and that is what you will not accept. It is difficult for most to pray to nothing, to emptiness, to a god who has no face or form and who cannot be seen."

"Abraham said that God created man in His own image."

"So He looks like us? Do you think He resembles you? Or me? Or your father? If He created us in His image, that means that we can make a figure of Him in clay so that we may speak with Him."

"God is not in the clay."

"I have heard you say that God is everywhere. So why can He not be in that clay that men mold in His image?"

They had been carrying on this argument for so many years now that the passage of time had polished away all acrimony in their words. They no longer became irate with one another, they simply conversed as two grown men, as equals.

"I have brought you a gift," Shamas said, smiling at the surprise on his master's face.

"Thank you, Shamas. But the best gift has been teaching you. You have given me reason to better myself every day, knowing that your hard questions awaited me."

The two men laughed. They had come to love and admire each other sincerely and to accept each other as they were.

Shamas led Ili into his small workroom, and there he presented him with several tablets wrapped in fine cloth. Ili unwrapped them carefully, and his eyes lit up in wonder at the signs made by Shamas' fine bone stylus. They were the work of a master and bore little resemblance to the signs once made by an eager boy, which at times had seemed to defy legibility itself.

"It is the story of the creation of the world, just as Abraham told it to me. I wanted you to have it," Shamas said, his eyes glistening.

Ili's eyes, too, brimmed with tears as he held the package of precious tablets.

"You have spoken to me so much of the legends of Abraham."

"And now you have them, in the very words in which he told them to me. I still have the tablets I made in Haran all those years ago, but my hand was not as firm as it has become now, for I was but a child. These, I hope, may meet with your approval."

"Thank you, Shamas, thank you. I will keep them with me always, until the last day of my life."

That night Lia listened as Shamas recounted the ceremony of ascension and his gift to Ili. She was proud her husband had been made a high priest, an important man within the hierarchy of the temple. They retired for the night, happy with each other and the world around them.

But despite the happy day, Shamas' sleep was troubled. Shadows surrounded him and he dreamed of Ili lying broken and bloody on the ground, his fellow scribes dead around him, his tablets shattered and scattered. His head throbbed in agony, and as blackness began to engulf him he came abruptly awake.

As Lia slept, Shamas rose quietly and stole into his workroom. Stooping to one of the lower shelves, he pulled out a cloth parcel and unwrapped his old tablets, those he had brought from Haran. He contemplated them in silence for a long time. Seeing them transported him to his childhood, his adolescence, the years of his life as a shepherd with his father and his tribe. He felt no longing for the past, for he was happy, but he did wish to see Abraham once more and to speak with him of God. Even for his own people, the God of Abraham was not the only god or the all-powerful god—just a god who was stronger than the others.

Shamas folded the tablets back into their cloth wrappings and returned them carefully to their place alongside the others, arranged in perfect stacks. He asked himself what would become of them when he died.

35

"ARE YOU ALL RIGHT?"

Miranda's voice roused Clara from a deep sleep. She had an intense pain in her chest and found it hard to breathe. The reporter was looking down at her with obvious concern, but Clara couldn't manage to respond.

Daniel set his camera next to the low wall of clay bricks and crouched down beside her.

A clutch of soldiers joined the reporters, clearly terrified at the sight of Clara lying shivering in a fetal ball on the yellow sand, her eyes vacant, as though she were somewhere far away.

The commander shouted to his men, and one of them ran off to get a blanket.

Clara felt paralyzed. Her legs and arms didn't obey when she tried to move them, and her voice still eluded her.

She felt Daniel sliding an arm underneath her head, his other hand grasping her arm, as he helped her to stand. Then he gave her a sip of water.

Miranda felt her pulse while the commander looked on, his eyes wide in fright. If something happened to this woman, it would be his head, literally.

"Her pulse is slow, but I think she's all right—she doesn't seem to be hurt," Miranda said.

"We should get her back to the camp so the doctor can examine her," said Daniel.

The soldier ran back with a blanket, and Daniel wrapped it around her. Clara could feel the warmth returning to her body.

"I'm all right," she murmured, finding her voice at last. "I'm sorry, I must have fallen asleep."

"You're half frozen," Daniel said. "What the hell possessed you to lie down out here?"

Clara looked at him and shrugged. She had no answer to that. Or maybe the answer she had would be too complicated, under the circumstances.

A few minutes later, Clara, accompanied by Daniel and Miranda, was sitting in the tent that served as the dining hall for the soldiers guarding the site. A cup of coffee brought the color back to her face.

"What happened?" Miranda wanted to know.

"I went out for a walk around the site. I like to do that—it helps me think. I fell asleep and had a dream. I can't quite remember . . . ," Clara answered.

"You should be more careful. Desert nights are frigid." Daniel's paternal tone made Clara smile.

"Don't worry, I may have caught a little cold, but that's all. But please, don't say anything about this. I . . . well, it's hard to be alone here. My grandfather is so protective—he worries that something might happen to me. And with the political situation, and the place full of soldiers . . ."

"It was just dumb luck that we found you. We were scouting for a location. Wanted to film the ruins at dawn, do something different before we all leave this afternoon. This place is really very beautiful," Miranda said, looking around.

"And if you're all right," Daniel added, "I'm going to get back to that—but you should stay here, Miranda, and see if Clara needs anything else."

Clara intrigued Miranda, and the reporter seized the chance to be alone with her. There was something about this woman . . . Miranda just wasn't sure what.

"You're Iraqi, but you don't look like one," she remarked, to test the waters.

"I'm Iraqi—and nobody here would say I don't look like one."

"But your eyes are blue, and the color of your hair . . ."

"Not all my family comes from here; my background is mixed."

Perhaps that was the source of the affinity with Clara—they had that in common. She turned the conversation to the dig.

"You know, Professor Gómez told me that the patriarch Abraham may not even have existed."

"If we find the tablets, we will prove that Abraham is not a myth. I'm convinced he did exist, that he left Ur to go to Canaan, that he was the first monotheist, and that from that moment on he carried the seeds of his belief wherever he went."

"I'm surprised that when you were in Rome, no high Church official contacted you to authenticate the tablets your grandfather found."

"I didn't expect them to. The Church doesn't question the existence of the patriarchs. If we find the tablets, good, but if we don't, it won't matter to the Vatican—the foundations of their religion were laid long ago."

"But what about that priest, Gian Maria? He seems so out of place. Why is he here?"

"To help us. He's a good person, very hardworking and good at what he does. He's an expert in the ancient languages of this region, and his participation in this expedition has been nothing less than . . . well, miraculous."

Miranda smiled. "What will you do when Picot and his people leave?"

"Stay on and keep digging."

"Bombs may be smart, but not smart enough to make an exception for you."

Clara shrugged her shoulders again. Until war became a reality, which she didn't think possible, she was content to keep going.

The sound of jeeps broke the early-morning quiet. The day's work was beginning. One of the vehicles skidded to a halt in front of the tent where the two women had been talking. Ayed Sahadi leaped out of it and stormed toward Clara.

"Why do you insist on shaming us? Your grandfather has ordered that the men in charge of your security be whipped, and me—I cannot imagine what he has in store for me. Does it amuse you to bring disgrace and worse to others?"

"How dare you speak to me that way!"

Miranda observed the scene in fascination. The man's behavior was well out of bounds for a mere overseer, although he had been introduced to Miranda as such the day before. He carried himself like a soldier, though in Saddam's country, she supposed, many men were. He and Clara looked as though they were about to leap at each other's throats. Finally Ayed broke the tense silence.

"Get in the car," he snapped, turning on his heel. "Your grandfather wants to see you at once."

He stalked out of the tent and sat at the wheel of his jeep, waiting for Clara to follow him.

Clara took her time finishing her coffee.

"Your grandfather has people whipped?"

Miranda's question caught her off guard. Clara had grown up amid regular demonstrations of her grandfather's harsh discipline, and to her it seemed only natural.

"Don't pay any attention to Ayed," she said curtly, as she rose to leave. "He exaggerates when he's angry."

She left the tent, silently cursing Sahadi for providing the reporter an unforgivable window into their world. Clara prayed that his careless remark would have no further consequences, that the press would not choose to pursue a story about the cruelty of Alfred Tannenberg. If they did, then it would be she, not her grandfather, who had Ayed whipped until he begged for mercy.

Miranda sat pensively, watching them drive away. She didn't believe Clara's denial for a moment, and she shuddered, just thinking about what Ayed had said.

Clara was getting out of the jeep as Dr. Najeb came out of the house.

"I want to talk to you," he said, stepping off to the side.

"What's wrong?" she asked in alarm.

"Your grandfather is getting worse; we should airlift him out to Cairo immediately. Here . . . here, he is going to die."

"Is there nothing you can do?"

"Not here. I don't have the proper equipment."

"Then what good is the operating room my grandfather had brought in?"

"It's good for a contingency, but your grandfather's condition is critical—we don't have any more time."

"You just don't want to assume the responsibility for what might happen, do you?"

"No, I don't. This is madness. His liver cancer has metastasized to other organs, and we are on the outskirts of a dusty village in the middle of nowhere—it makes no sense. But it's your decision."

She turned away from him without replying and walked into the house. Fatima was waiting for her in tears at the door of her grandfather's room.

"My child, the master is worse."

"Fatima, I will not have him see you crying—he would not have it."

She pushed her old nurse aside and entered the room, which was in semidarkness; Samira, the nurse, was watching over him.

"Clara?" Alfred Tannenberg's voice was weak.

"Yes, Grandfather, I'm here."

"I should have you whipped too. How dare you put the entire camp in alarm."

"Grandfather, I'm sorry. I didn't mean to frighten you."

"Well, you did. If anything should happen to you . . . They would all die, I swear I would kill them all."

"Calm down, Grandfather. I'm here now. How are you feeling?"

"I'm dying."

"Don't be silly. You aren't going to die, much less now, when we're on the verge of finding the Bible of Clay."

"I know that Picot wants to leave."

"He'll give us time to find the tablets, don't worry. And if he goes, we'll keep digging."

"I sent for Ahmed."

"Is he coming?" Clara asked with equal measures of hope and trepidation.

"He has to come. He's to update me on our current operation, and we have to finalize some details so that you can get out of here."

"I'm not leaving!"

"You'll do as I say! As long as there is breath left in my body, I will not fall victim to anyone's army. We're both leaving for Cairo. Or I'll go to Cairo and you can go with Picot."

"With Picot? Why?"

"Because I say so. Now go, I need to rest and think. Yasir will arrive with Ahmed later today, and I want to be sitting up when he comes."

Clara found Dr. Najeb in the tent-hospital next to the house. He was mechanically putting the operating room in order.

"My grandfather must live."

"We all want to live."

"Do whatever you have to do."

"If we were in Cairo . . ."

"We're here, and here is where you will do your work. We pay you very well to do it—you have to help him hang on."

"I am not Allah."

Clara struggled to keep her desperation out of her voice. "Treat his pain; keep him strong so that he can appear healthy to his visitors," she said evenly. "We'll talk about returning to Cairo later. As long as we're here, my grandfather has to look like the man he once was."

"That is not possible."

"Then do the impossible."

The frigid edge in Clara's voice left no room for argument, and her once-attractive face was overshadowed by her cold, steely gaze. For the first time Salam Najeb saw her resemblance to her grandfather—down to the cruelty in her blue eyes.

Miranda was waiting for Clara a few yards from the field hospital, smoking a cigarette.

"I'd like to meet your grandfather," the reporter said, smiling slightly.

"He isn't seeing anyone," Clara replied coldly.

"Why?"

"Because he's an old man whose health is unstable, and the last thing we're going to do is subject him to a session with the press."

Clara strode back to the house and closed the door without giving Miranda time to follow her. Once in her room, she fell onto her bed and began to weep.

When Fatima found her two hours later, all traces of distress were gone and Clara was preparing to join the others.

"Where are you going, my child?" she asked.

"The reporters are leaving at noon; we have to see them off. And I want to talk to Picot and have things ready for Ahmed and Yasir's arrival."

It struck the old woman that her onetime charge seemed to have become harder, more determined, just in the space of the morning. She saw in Clara's eyes her grandfather's fierce determination, and she realized that someone or something had brought out in her the worst features of Tannenberg's character.

Yves Picot was talking to the reporters; the looks between him and Miranda weren't lost on Clara. *They're attracted to each other,* she thought, *and they aren't hiding it. That's why he wants to leave earlier than he'd planned—he's sick of being here. The minute she leaves, he'll go after her.*

Fabian and Marta were there too, as were Gian Maria and Lion Doyle.

"Why aren't you working?" asked Clara, trying to make her voice seem casual.

Marta raised an eyebrow in displeasure.

"We're saying good-bye to our friends," said Fabian, forestalling her response.

"I hope you've found what we're doing here interesting," Clara said to no one in particular.

Miranda walked over to Clara and put out her hand to say goodbye. Only Marta, who was watching them, seemed to notice their mute duel of wills.

"It's been a pleasure meeting you," Miranda said. "I hope to see you again someday. I suppose you'll be going back to Baghdad at some point; I'll be there until the war's over, if I don't get killed."

"You're going to stay in Baghdad?"

"Yes, a lot of us are going to stay. Holed up in the Hotel Palestina."

"Why?"

"Because somebody has to tell the people what's happening, because the only way to stop the horror is to show it. If we leave, it'll be worse."

"Worse for whom?"

"For everyone. Come down out of your castle. Look around and you'll understand."

"Please. I'm a little tired of superior speeches."

Picot came over to Miranda just then and, laughing, pulled at her—the helicopter was about to lift off.

"Stay with us until we go," he mock-pleaded with her.

"That wouldn't be a bad idea, but I'm afraid my desk at home wouldn't understand."

They kissed each other on the cheek and Picot helped her into the helicopter. Then he waved his hand as the chopper rose and turned away, its rotors raising a fierce cloud of dust. Picot stood there until the helicopter was but a tiny dot on the horizon.

"You and Miranda seem to have hit it off," Clara said resentfully.

"Well, yes, as a matter of fact. She's a terrific woman. I enjoyed meeting her, and I hope to see her again."

"She's going to stay on in Baghdad."

"So she told me—she's as crazy as you are. Both of you are ready to risk your lives for your causes. Kindred spirits, I'd say."

"We have nothing in common," Clara snapped.

"No, just stubbornness, although that may be a trait common to the entire gender."

"You can leave the rest of us out of it, if you please," broke in Marta, laughing. "Yves, have you talked to Baghdad?" she asked.

"Yes. Ahmed is coming in. I think this afternoon. We'll see what he has to say, then make a decision. But in case we have to leave soon, I'm going to ask Lion Doyle to photograph everything we've found; he's already done the *in situ* photos, so that'll round out the documentation. We need to be as detailed as possible. I want more than stills, I want video—I hope Lion can do that. I think it's a good idea, as you've suggested, Clara, to detail everything we've done and everything that's left to do. If you like, we'll do that after we hear what your husband has to say when he comes in this afternoon. Is that all right?"

Clara agreed. She had no alternative.

36

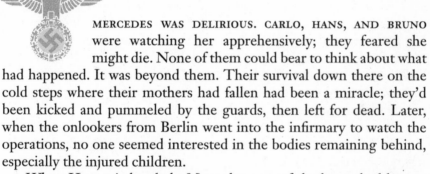 MERCEDES WAS DELIRIOUS. CARLO, HANS, AND BRUNO were watching her apprehensively; they feared she might die. None of them could bear to think about what had happened. It was beyond them. Their survival down there on the cold steps where their mothers had fallen had been a miracle; they'd been kicked and pummeled by the guards, then left for dead. Later, when the onlookers from Berlin went into the infirmary to watch the operations, no one seemed interested in the bodies remaining behind, especially the injured children.

When Hans tried to help Mercedes, one of the kapos had beaten him senseless. Even so, he heard his mother's voice through the torture, strengthening his will to live.

A team of prisoners was ordered to clean up the stairs of death and to take the children to one of the barracks. They were put onto cots, and a Polish prisoner, a former doctor named Lechw, tried to revive them, though he had little more than dirty rags dipped in water at his disposal.

The little girl was in the worst shape. She was unconscious, and Lechw cursed under his breath. There was so very little he could do without medicines. Eventually the orphaned boys would be sent out to work with the men, but the little girl would either be killed on the spot or sent to the infirmary, from which no one ever emerged.

One of the other prisoners, a Russian, removed from inside his mattress a bottle of vodka containing a precious few drops and passed it to the doctor so he could disinfect the wounds. Then Lechw sutured Mercedes' head wounds with the needle and thread that the prisoners used for mending their clothes. The child moaned and writhed in pain, but she remained unconscious.

One of the prisoners was nervous about having a little girl in the barracks.

"If they find her, they'll do something terrible to her, and to us too."

"What do you suggest, that we turn her over to the kapo? That bastard Gustav would strangle her with his bare hands. She wouldn't even make it to the women's barracks, where the poor children came from," Lechw replied.

"You know, you can't tell whether she's a girl or a boy with her head shaved like that," another prisoner observed with a glint of hope in his eyes.

"Are you people mad! If they find her, we'll all pay!" said an older man.

"I, for one, am not going to turn her in; I won't have it on my conscience. You can do what you will," said the Polish doctor.

This little girl reminded him of his own daughter, whose fate he had never learned. Friends of his had assured him that they would protect his wife and daughter, but had they been able to do so? Or was his little darling in a camp like Mauthausen? If she was, he prayed to God that someone might take pity on her as he was caring for this tiny creature lying here unconscious, perhaps never to awaken again.

"Please don't turn her in," he whispered.

The men turned to look at the boy who hours earlier had tried to defend his mother and sister.

"What is your name?" Lechw asked him.

"Carlo," he answered bashfully.

"Well, then, Carlo, you are going to make sure that they don't find her," said Lechw gently. "You and your friends must try very hard not to attract attention. It is difficult—the kapos are not nice men—but it is not impossible," he explained.

"We'll be very careful, sir," Carlo said, as his friends Bruno and Hans nodded.

The boys sat on the floor near the cot where Mercedes was lying, waiting for her to regain consciousness. They, too, were injured, although the most terrible wounds had been inflicted upon their souls.

The entire night, Mercedes remained in a coma, near death. It was a miracle, the doctor said, when she recovered consciousness the next morning.

When Carlo saw Mercedes' eyes flutter open, he squeezed her little hand to let her know he was there for her. He and Hans and Bruno had sat by her cot all night. All three had prayed to God—though they really didn't know whether he was listening—to have mercy on their friend. The doctor told them that God had heard their prayer and had pulled her up out of the darkness.

When the kapos came into the barracks and ordered the men outside into formation, they paid no attention to the wounded children who had taken refuge in a dark corner, trembling with fear and hunger and pain. The prisoners had covered Mercedes with a blanket, so she could hardly be seen. No one went over to the cot to look any closer.

When they were alone, Hans gave Mercedes a little water. She looked up at him gratefully; her head hurt, she was dizzy, but more than anything she was afraid. She could taste blood on her lips—the blood of her dead baby brother that the SS officer had thrown in her face.

"We have to kill him," Carlo whispered, and his three friends looked at him expectantly.

They could all barely move from the beating they'd taken. Their bodies covered by bruises and bloody wounds, they crept closer to Carlo so they could hear better.

"Kill him?" Bruno repeated as quietly as he could.

"The one in charge, with the blond hair. He killed our mothers," Carlo insisted.

"And our little brothers and sisters won't . . . won't be born now," said Mercedes, her eyes brimming with tears.

None of the boys shed a single tear, despite the terrible weight of pain and grief that had settled in their hearts.

"My mother used to say that when you want something very, very much, you get it," said Hans timidly.

"I want to kill him," Carlo repeated, his teeth clenched.

"Me too," said Bruno.

"Me too," said Mercedes.

"Then we shall," Hans said. "But how?"

"However we can," Bruno replied.

"It will be hard to do here," pointed out Hans.

"But when we get out of here . . . We won't be here much longer," insisted Bruno.

"I don't think we will get out of here alive," said Hans glumly.

"My mother said that the Allies are going to win; she was sure of it," Bruno insisted.

"Who are the Allies?" asked Mercedes.

"The ones that are against Hitler," Hans told her.

"We agree, then?" proposed Carlo.

They looked hard at one another for a moment, seeming much older than the children they were, and slowly nodded their heads in a silent oath, aware of the solemnity of the moment. Then they hugged in a sign of solidarity; the embrace of friendship made them all feel better.

They spent the rest of the day imagining the moment when they would kill the SS officer, discussing how they would do it, with what instrument. When the men came back to the barracks that night, they found the children trembling with cold, starving, but with a gleam in their eyes that the men could only explain as burgeoning fever.

Lechw examined them, and an expression of concern came over his face. One of Mercedes' head wounds was infected. He used the rest of the vodka to clean the wounds, but he was pessimistic.

"We need medicines," he said.

"Why upset yourself about it—there is nothing to do," said another Polish prisoner, a mining engineer.

"I am a doctor. I shall do everything in my power to keep these children alive—I shall fight to my last breath!"

"Calm, calm," said another of the Poles. "This one here," he said, jerking his thumb at the Russian, "knows the ones that clean the infirmary—we'll get them to bring us something."

"I need it now," the doctor complained.

"Give us time," his friend said.

It was just before dawn when Lechw felt someone touch his arm. He'd fallen asleep while watching over the children. His Polish friend and the Russian with a talent for finding things were standing by the cot, grinning. They handed him a package, then faded into the shadows, back to their cots.

The doctor unwrapped the little bundle carefully and had to stifle a cry of joy when he saw what it contained: bandages, disinfectant, and analgesics, the most wonderful haul he could ever imagine.

He got up quietly, so as not to wake anyone, and observed the four children's fitful sleep. He unwound the dirty strip of cloth with which he had wrapped Mercedes' head and applied disinfectant once again to the wound. When she felt the cold sting of the Mercurochrome, she woke up and was about to cry out, but he gently placed his hand over her mouth, then smiled and told her not to cry. The brave little girl bit down on the blanket that covered her and, pale as death, lay quietly while the doctor, all concentration, went about treating the wound. Then she gratefully accepted a sip of water and two pills he gave her.

Hans, Bruno, and Carlo were also tended by the doctor, who swabbed the cuts and contusions that covered their bodies. Then they, too, took an analgesic to soothe their pains.

"I heard one of the kapos say that the war is going badly," said a Spanish Communist as he watched the doctor care for the children.

"Do you believe it?" Lechw replied.

"I do. He was telling one of the other kapos; apparently he heard one of the officers from Berlin talking. And I have a friend who cleans the radio room. He says the Germans are nervous; they listen to the BBC all day and night, and some of them are beginning to ask what will happen to them if Germany loses the war."

"Oh, praise God!" Lechw exclaimed.

"God? What does God have to do with this?" spat the Spaniard. "If God existed, he'd never have allowed this monstrosity. I never believed in God, but my mother did, and I imagine she's praying right now that I return someday. But if we get out of here, it won't be God who frees us—it'll be the Allies. Do you actually believe in God after all this?" the Spaniard asked almost sarcastically.

"I do—if I didn't, I wouldn't have been able to live through this. God has helped me survive."

"Then why didn't he give a hand to the mothers of these poor children?" the Spaniard asked, pointing to the four little ones.

Mercedes was listening to the conversation avidly, trying hard to understand what the two men were saying. They were talking about God. When they were in Paris, her mother sometimes took her to church; they went to the Sacré Coeur, near their home. They never stayed inside very long; her mother would go in, kneel briefly, make the sign of the cross, murmur something, and then leave. Her mother told her that they went into the church to ask God to protect her papa. But her papa had disappeared while she and her mother had had to flee, and God had done nothing to stop it.

She thought about what the Spaniard was saying—that God was absent—and she silently agreed. God was not in Mauthausen, she had no doubt of that. She closed her eyes and began to cry, quietly, so that no one would hear. She could still see her mother lying broken and bloody among the rocks on those terrible stairs.

Her friends Carlo, Bruno, and Hans pleaded with the older prisoners to let them stay; they promised to take care of Mercedes; they swore they wouldn't be a bother, that they wouldn't cry, so the kapos wouldn't find them. It soothed her to hear the men agree.

So she would stay there, in those barracks. She was going to pretend to be a boy—she had to act like one and not do anything to attract attention, because if they discovered her there, they would all pay for it. She swore to herself she would never do anything to cause harm to these loving men, or her three wonderful friends.

37

ROBERT BROWN WAS HAPPY WITH THE RESULTS OF HIS meeting with George Wagner. All that was left was for Paul Dukais to pull off his part of the plan and for them to keep Alfred Tannenberg satisfied until the operation was too far along for him to sabotage it.

Brown wasn't deluding himself—he knew that without Tannenberg none of this would have been possible and that the sick old man was still capable of retribution if things didn't go his way.

He took out his cell phone and called Paul. They agreed to meet in Brown's office an hour later. Operation Adam was about to begin, a name Brown had chosen as a nod to the idea of God having made the first man out of clay from ancient Mesopotamia.

Meanwhile, George Wagner was talking to Enrique Gómez, who was at his home in Seville.

"So it'll be on the twentieth?" Enrique asked.

"Yes, March twentieth—I received confirmation hours ago."

"Does Dukais have everything ready to go?"

"Robert says he does. What about you?"

"No problems here. When the package arrives, I'll pick it up, just like always."

"This time it's coming in on a military flight."

"That doesn't necessarily make things any easier, but the contact you gave me on the base already has his advance on the payment, so he's good to go. And he knows what'll happen to him if he decides to make trouble."

"Have you made contact with the buyers?"

"The usual ones, but first I want to see the goods. How are you going to divide it up?"

"Robert Brown has a good man, Ralph Barry, a former Harvard professor who's a specialist in the area. He'll be in Kuwait when the material comes in. Ahmed Husseini has made a provisional list."

"Good idea. You know, George, we ought to start thinking about retiring. We're too old to keep this up."

"Too old? Not me. I'm not going to die in some nursing home, staring out the window with my legs wrapped in a blue blanket. Don't worry, Enrique, everything will be fine; you're going to be living the good life in Seville for a long time to come."

The ringing of Frank dos Santos' cell phone interrupted his conversation with his daughter. Alma frowned; she couldn't believe her father would bring his cell phone the one time they'd been together in weeks.

"Hey, George! . . . Where am I? You wouldn't believe it—I'm horseback riding. Alma decided to take me out. But I'm getting old; my rear end hurts!"

Frank went silent while his friend on the other end talked. George was telling him the same thing he'd told Enrique: The war was going to start on March 20.

"Everything's ready here," Frank finally said. "My clients are looking forward to seeing the merchandise. Will Ahmed be able to fill the list I sent you? If he does, we'll make a killing. . . . Okay, I'll call you; my men are set."

He put away his phone and breathed deeply; he knew his daughter was watching him.

"What's this deal, Papa?"

"Same as always, sweetie."

"Just once you might tell me something."

"Be happy I make a lot of money for you to spend."

"But, Daddy, I'm your only daughter."

"Which is why you've always been my favorite," Frank said, laughing. "Come on, let's get back to the house."

Robert Brown and Ralph Barry were waiting for Paul Dukais. As usual, the president of Planet Security was running late.

When he finally came into the office, grinning broadly, Brown exploded.

"What's so fucking funny?"

"My wife just called to tell me that she's got a migraine, so we're not going to the opera tonight. Is that lucky or what?"

Ralph couldn't help smiling, but he didn't kid himself about Paul Dukais. He knew that under his mask of vulgarity there was an intelligent man with a heart like an iceberg and a careful, deliberate mind, more cultured than he let on, and capable of anything.

"The boys in the Pentagon have set a date for the invasion—March twentieth," Robert Brown said curtly, still irritated at Dukais.

"Good. The sooner our troops go in, the sooner we start making money. And the longer they're there, the more we'll make."

"Ralph is leaving for Kuwait. Talk to your Colonel Fernandez to organize the reception committee."

"He's already in the area. I'll call him, don't worry. But first we need to notify Yasir—he was going to Safran today. Alfred sent for him and Ahmed. The old man is keeping a tight rein on things."

"Okay, get in touch with him. Alfred has to know the date as well."

"I'll use our usual courier," Dukais suggested. "Yasir's nephew in Paris—he's one of Alfred's men. He owes everything he's got to Alfred."

"What about Yasir?" asked Ralph.

"The nephew is close to Yasir, but his loyalty is to Tannenberg," Dukais said with a worldly shrug. "If he has to choose, he'll go with Alfred."

"Just a few weeks . . . ," muttered Ralph.

"Yeah, but everything is ready, not to worry. I trust Mike Fernandez, and if he says that the operation is ready to roll, then it's ready to roll," Dukais declared.

"You should trust Alfred. He's the one who knows how to make things happen, especially over there. He always has been. So don't pin any medals on yourself yet. The only problem with Alfred is that damned granddaughter of his."

38

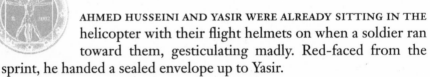 AHMED HUSSEINI AND YASIR WERE ALREADY SITTING IN THE
helicopter with their flight helmets on when a soldier ran
toward them, gesticulating madly. Red-faced from the
sprint, he handed a sealed envelope up to Yasir.

"Your office sent it. Said it was urgent."

Yasir ripped the envelope open and pulled out a short typewritten
note.

> *Sir, you have received an urgent message from your nephew. He says that
> on March 20, he and some friends will come to see you, although he does
> not want you to tell any member of your family. He wants to surprise
> them. You should tell your friends, though. He insists that you should be
> told immediately that he is coming.*

Tucking the note and envelope into one of his jacket pockets, Yasir
motioned to the pilot to take off. Dukais was confirming the date that
the war would start. He had to tell Ahmed and, of course, Alfred.

Night was falling when the helicopter's landing skids touched down
a few hundred yards from Safran. A chilly breeze made the lights in the
houses seem to flicker like fireflies.

Ayed Sahadi was waiting in a jeep to take them to the camp.

"You look down in the mouth, Ayed. What's wrong?" Ahmed asked.

"Living in this village is hell. I've been here too long. Anyway, your wife is waiting for you with Alfred. Picot and his team leaders too. They're jumpy—we've had reporters here telling them the war is inevitable and that given the weather and the state of readiness, Bush will attack any day now."

"I'm afraid they're right," Ahmed replied. "There are demonstrations all over Europe—in the U.S. too. But Bush has already set the machinery in motion; he's not going to call everything off now."

"So they're actually going to attack," Ayed said in disbelief.

"That's what it looks like," Ahmed said laconically. "But for now, my friend, you'll be staying put. The Colonel told me we should keep you here awhile longer."

Ayed drove them into camp. Yasir was to stay in the village leader's house, while Ahmed would be sharing quarters with his wife and her grandfather.

The meeting between Clara and Ahmed was strained. Suddenly they didn't know how to act toward each other.

"You'll have to sleep in my room; we've set up a cot," Clara told him. "I'm sorry, but it would be hard to explain if you didn't sleep here. I prefer to avoid any gossip about us yet."

"That's fine. I'm just sorry to intrude."

"It's okay. We have to make do. How long are you planning to stay?"

"I don't know. Once I talk to your grandfather, I should really go—I have responsibilities that can't wait."

"Of course; that's what he pays you for."

Clara was immediately sorry she'd said that, but there was no taking it back now. And, anyway, she wanted Ahmed to know that he would never again be able to lie to her.

"What are you talking about?"

"About the fact that you work for my grandfather; you're a partner in some of his business dealings and he pays you for that. Among other things. Isn't that right?"

"Yes," he answered, staring her straight in the eye. And then, "Look, so far we've avoided antagonism. We're not enemies, Clara. And I don't want us to be."

"We aren't, because I've chosen not to confront you about this. Let's just leave things the way they are. My grandfather wants to see you and Yasir as soon as possible."

"Give me a minute to clean up. I'll be right there."

Clara went into her grandfather's room. The doctor had just given him an injection, and earlier the nurse had finished administering a blood transfusion, which seemed to have brought the color back to his sunken cheeks.

"I feel much better," Alfred told his granddaughter.

"It's only a temporary improvement," the doctor insisted.

"I'm not expecting a hundred more years. But you'll keep me like this until I tell you not to."

The old man's tone of voice left no room for argument.

"I'll do everything in my power, sir."

"My granddaughter will, of course, see that you are rewarded, generously," he said, looking at Clara.

She went over to her grandfather and kissed his forehead. He smelled like soap. "So, Doctor, do you think my grandfather can come out and sit in the living room and talk for a while?" Clara asked.

"Yes, but not for too long; it could—"

Three light, staccato taps at the door interrupted the doctor.

"Sir, Mr. Yasir and Mr. Ahmed are waiting for you in the living room," Fatima announced.

"Take my arm, Grandfather. Can you?"

"I can do it myself—I don't need your arm. Those jackals think I'm dying. Even if I am, I'm not going to give them the satisfaction of seeing it—not yet."

Clara opened the door and they moved toward the living room. Yasir and Ahmed stood up as they entered.

"Sir . . ." Ahmed, surprised, managed to say.

"Alfred . . ." was all that Yasir said.

Alfred Tannenberg sneered at them, then laughed openly. He knew they'd expected to see him at death's door.

"Did you think you were coming to my funeral? The air in Safran does me good, and being with Clara gives me the strength to live—not that I lack the desire."

Neither of the two men replied, waiting for Tannenberg to sit down. But he decided to walk around the room instead, watching them out of the corner of his eye.

"Grandfather, would you like Fatima to bring something in?"

"No, no, nothing—maybe some water. But I'm sure our guests are hungry; Fatima can bring them something to eat. We have a lot to talk about."

The three men were then left alone.

Yasir gave Tannenberg the note from his nephew. Tannenberg read it and slipped it into his jacket pocket.

"So the war will start on March twentieth. . . . Fine, the sooner the better; my men are ready. Have you done as I've instructed you?" he asked Ahmed.

"Yes, sir. But it was complicated. There were hundreds and hundreds of uncatalogued artifacts in the museums. I had to spend more money than we originally allocated to hire people inside to catalogue the most important pieces in each museum. I gave the lists to Yasir, as you requested."

"I know. Enrique and Frank have already contacted their clients, and there are buyers ready to assume ownership of all the treasures we can bring out. George has also notified his clients, through Robert Brown, so everything's set. What's happening with Dukais' Green Beret?"

Yasir cleared his throat before answering. He knew that question was aimed at him.

"Mike Fernandez is ready too, sir. His men are stationed at the location you chose. There won't be any problems transporting the merchandise, especially in military helicopters. All we have to do now is wait."

"This is the largest art-sale operation we've ever mounted," Tannenberg said. "The truth is, we are doing mankind a favor by saving Iraq's most priceless treasures. If we didn't remove them, they'd be destroyed. Once the war breaks out, mobs will loot everything, and those people can't tell the difference between a Sumerian cylinder seal and a hubcap."

Neither Yasir nor Ahmed replied to Tannenberg's assertion. They were thieves, it was true, but it seemed unnecessary to dwell on that or to characterize what they were doing as something else.

"How many pieces do you calculate we'll be able to extract?" Tannenberg asked Ahmed.

"If everything goes well, more than ten thousand. I've made an exhaustive list of what should be taken from each museum. I have provided the men with detailed floor plans and the locations of the most important pieces. I hope they don't smash up too much."

"How sentimental you are, Ahmed!" Tannenberg laughed.

Ahmed clenched his teeth in anger and humiliation. Alfred Tannenberg's laughter was like a slap in the face.

"As soon as the bombing starts, the teams will enter the museums. They are to gather up the designated pieces in the shortest time possible and get the hell out. Period. Crossing over to Kuwait won't be a problem, as long as the Green Beret does his job," Tannenberg said.

"And what will you do? How long will you stay here?"

Alfred had been expecting Yasir's question.

"That's not your concern, but don't worry, my friend, the war won't touch me. By the time the bombs start falling I'll be in a safe place, I assure you. I'm not ready to die yet."

"What about Clara?" Ahmed asked.

"Clara will leave as well. I still have to decide whether to send her to Cairo or along with Picot's team."

"There's not much time," Ahmed insisted.

"If I think you need to know, I'll tell you when Clara is leaving. But we still have a few more days to find the Bible of Clay."

"But if the Americans attack on the twentieth . . . ," protested Ahmed.

"What do you know? Obey your orders and be happy that you're being paid—and that you'll be getting out with your life."

Tannenberg poured himself a glass of water and drank it slowly. Neither Ahmed nor Yasir had so much as tasted the food that Fatima had brought in.

"All right, let's finish reviewing the operation and the financial details. We're going to make a lot of money, but we've also had to invest a great deal—my men always know that their advance is in the bank waiting for their families in case something happens to them."

Clara dined with Picot and the rest of the team. But Ahmed's presence had put her on edge. It was not going to be easy to share a room with him, even for one night. He seemed like a perfect stranger to her.

"When are we going to see your husband?" Fabian asked.

"Tomorrow, I imagine. Tonight he's meeting with my grandfather; they'll be late."

"Is he going to stay in Iraq, or will he try to leave before the war starts?" Marta wanted to know.

"None of us knows when the war will start. The reporters can't even be sure. They say it's inevitable, but no one knows what will happen, or when," Clara replied.

"That's not an answer," Marta pushed her.

"It's the only answer I can give. At any rate, I want to stay here until . . . well, until I can't stay anymore. Then I'll see. If war does break out, I'll reevaluate my position."

"Come with us."

Picot's invitation took her by surprise, but it occurred to her that his slightly mocking tone left no doubt that her fate mattered little to him.

"Are you offering me political asylum?" she asked in an attempt to be ironic.

"Me? Well, if there's nothing to be done, we can try. Fabian, do you think we can smuggle her out?"

"It's not a joking matter," Marta scolded them. "Clara could very easily find herself in a bind; we have to help her."

They all fell silent until Lion Doyle broke in.

"Clara, I need to ask you a favor. You know that Yves wants me to prepare an exhaustive report on all the items you've discovered here. Do you think your grandfather would allow me to photograph him? It wouldn't take long, and I think it's only fair that a person who's invested so much time and money . . . you know, ought to be recognized for his contribution."

"My grandfather is a businessman; he's financing part of the expedition. I don't think he needs or wants the publicity, but I'll ask him."

"Thanks. Even if he's a modest man, I'd like a photograph of the two of you together, at the least."

"I said I'll ask him—that'll have to do for now."

"I'd like to stay."

Gian Maria's soft voice brought them all back to the issue at hand. Clara looked at him affectionately. She'd come to feel a real warmth toward the young priest, who followed her around like a puppy. Gian Maria actually seemed to suffer when he lost sight of her, when she wandered away. His devotion was moving, though she didn't really understand it.

"Until we talk to Ahmed, it's best not to make any decisions," Yves said.

"Of course, but if Clara stays to work, I'm staying too," Gian Maria declared.

"What are you saying!" Picot almost shouted. "You can't stay here! If the war starts, do you think you can just keep working? There won't be a single man to help you; they'll all be called up. And in any case, you can't excavate if you're being shelled. Or have you not been paying attention?"

Picot had come to like Gian Maria too, and he felt responsible for what might happen to him.

"If Clara stays, I'm staying," the priest stubbornly repeated.

Gian Maria sat in the door of the house he shared with Ante Plaskic and Lion Doyle. He didn't feel like sleeping, and he needed to be alone.

He lit a cigarette and let his gaze wander toward the star-filled sky. He had to put his spirit in order. He'd been here for months now, asking himself who he was, who he'd been, who he had become.

Every day, before the camp awoke to start its labors, he offered a mass—a mass attended by only him and God, because no one else had shown any interest in taking part in it, though he hadn't the heart to ask anyone to. He knew, then, that his faith in God was still firm and unshaken. That, and his devotion to his vows, was the only thing that hadn't changed. He still felt his calling to the priesthood, but sometimes it seemed to him that going back to the calm and order of the monastery where he'd lived since he'd been ordained—a life monastic in every sense of the word—would be an unbearable sacrifice. He was beginning to get used to this new way of life.

It had been a surprise to him when his superior sent him to St. Peter's to be a confessor. At first, he had been overwhelmed by the responsibility, doubting his ability, even his worthiness, to receive confessions. But Padre Pio had convinced him that he was needed in Rome. "The Vatican," he had told him, "needs young men, young priests to keep in touch with the changing realities of the world, and there's no better place for that than St. Peter's itself."

He would have to go back, he knew that, but he would no longer be the same priest who'd arrived in Iraq. He would miss life in the open air, the camaraderie he'd come to know with this motley team—that sense of freedom he'd found. It was strange, under the circumstances, but *freedom* was the only word that seemed to truly describe his experience at this strange excavation, with so many varied people, under the infinite stars of the desert.

And that led him to think about Clara. He had developed a true affection for her. As he strove to protect her, she'd come to be like a sister to him—a difficult, touchy sister, but a sister all the same.

Perhaps the time had come to tell her that he was there to save her life. But no—he couldn't do that without breaking the secrecy, the absolute confidentiality, of the confessional, without betraying God and the man who had made the confession, however misled he was.

Out of the darkness, Clara slowly walked over to Gian Maria's house and sat down beside him. She, too, lit a cigarette and stared off into the night sky. The priest knew that the guards who watched her constantly must not be far away.

"Professor Picot is right. You shouldn't stay."

"That may be true, Clara, but I'm going to anyway; I couldn't sleep at night knowing that you were here alone."

"My grandfather may force me to go to Cairo."

"Cairo?"

"Yes. We have a house there—you're most welcome to come whenever you're in the neighborhood." She laughed.

"So . . . you're leaving?" he asked, not hiding his concern.

"I'm going to resist as long as I can, but my grandfather will force me to leave if war breaks out. You're a religious man, Gian Maria—ask God to help us find those tablets."

"I'll ask, but you should ask too. Don't you pray?"

"No, never."

"Are you Muslim?"

"No, I'm not anything."

"Even if you don't practice, you must have been raised under some religious tradition."

"My mother was Christian, and I was baptized, but I've never set foot in a church, or a mosque either, except out of curiosity."

"Then why this absolute obsession to find the Bible of Clay? It's nothing if not a religious artifact. Is it just out of vanity?"

"There are children who grow up listening to fairy tales or stories of Prince Charming. I grew up listening to my grandfather talk about the Bible of Clay. He's always wanted me to find it. He would tell me stories in which I was the heroine, the archaeologist who finds a great treasure, the most important treasure in the world, the Bible of Clay."

"And you want to make a childhood dream come true."

"You really won't even consider that Abraham would talk to a scribe about the creation?"

"Well, certainly the Bible says nothing about that, and its story of the patriarch is very detailed. . . ."

"You know that archaeology hasn't found some of the cities described in the Bible and that there's no proof of the existence of some of its central figures, yet you believe in everything the Bible says."

"Clara, I'm not saying there's no Bible of Clay. Abraham lived in these lands; he knew the legends of creation, the flood, everything. He could very well have told someone about those legends, or perhaps God revealed the truth to him. . . . I don't know. Honestly, I just don't know what to think about it."

"But you're here, you've been working like the rest of us, and now you want to stay. Why is that, then?"

"If the Bible of Clay exists, I want to find it too. It would be an extraordinary discovery for Christianity."

"For archaeology too, lest you forget. It would be a discovery like Troy or Mycenae, like the discovery of the pharaoh's tombs in the Valley of the Kings. The person who finds the Bible of Clay will go down in history."

"And you want to go down in history?"

"I want to find those tablets of my grandfather's; I want to see him live to hold them. I want to make his lifelong dream come true at last."

"You love him very much."

"Yes, I love my grandfather very much, and . . . I think that I am the only person he's ever loved."

"The men are afraid of him, even Ayed Sahadi."

"I know. My grandfather . . . my grandfather is demanding; he likes to see work done well. As do I."

Gian Maria didn't want to tell her that perhaps Alfred Tannenberg liked to see other people in pain, that he humiliated the humble and sadistically punished anyone who crossed him. Nor did he want to tell her what his personal experience of her grandfather had been.

Gian Maria had been in Alfred Tannenberg's presence on only one occasion, when he went to take Clara a copy of his translation of the most recent tablets they had found.

Tannenberg was sitting in the living room reading, and when Gian Maria knocked, he told him to come in. Alfred interrogated him for fifteen minutes, then seemed to grow bored and sent him to wait outside until Clara came out. Gian Maria left the house knowing that he had seen in Tannenberg a manifestation of the devil himself; he was convinced that evil had found a refuge in that man's soul.

"You aren't like your grandfather," the priest said.

"I think I am. My father used to say that I was as hardheaded and stubborn as my grandfather."

"I'm not talking about your personality, I'm talking about your soul."

"But you don't know my grandfather," Clara protested. "You don't know what he's like."

"I've come to know you, though."

"And what do you think you know about me?"

"I know that you're a victim, the victim of a dream, your grandfather's dream. It's governed your life so thoroughly that you've become a prisoner without knowing it."

Clara looked at him hard, then stood up. She wasn't angry with Gian Maria, she couldn't be; everything he had told her was true. Besides, the priest had spoken to her with affection, with no intention to offend her, almost stretching out his hand to her to lead her through the shadows.

"Thank you, Gian Maria."

"Good night, Clara. Sleep well."

Fatima was waiting for her at the door of the house and quietly put her finger over her lips. She led her into her grandfather's room, where Samira, the nurse, was giving Alfred an injection under the close watch of Dr. Najeb.

"He overdid it today," whispered the physician.

Clara could only look on helplessly.

"As soon as he came into the room he fainted. Thank goodness Samira was here waiting to give him medications before he fell asleep; otherwise, I don't know what would have happened," Dr. Najeb explained.

Samira helped Fatima make Tannenberg comfortable in the bed, and as they did, he stretched out his hand toward Clara, who sat down beside him.

"I won't allow you to do this again, Grandfather," she scolded him while she caressed his hand.

"I'm fine, just a little tired."

"Grandfather, you trust me. Shouldn't you tell me what's going on?"

"Clara, you're the only person I trust."

"Then let me in on this other project of yours, tell me what you want done, and I will see that your orders are followed. I can do it."

Alfred Tannenberg closed his eyes as he squeezed his granddaughter's hand. For a second he was tempted to explain Operation Adam to Clara, to turn it over to her; then he'd be able to sleep. But his friends and enemies alike would interpret it as a sign of weakness. Besides, he told himself, Clara wasn't ready to deal with men who so frequently blurred the line between life and death.

"Doctor, I'd like to be alone with my granddaughter."

Fatima opened the door, ready to see that Tannenberg's order was followed. Samira walked out meekly, followed by Dr. Najeb, and then Fatima closed the door after herself.

"Grandfather, you mustn't—"

"The Americans are going to attack on March twentieth. You have only weeks to find the Bible of Clay."

The news stunned Clara; she couldn't find words to speak. It was one thing to think that the war was going to happen but another, very different thing to know exactly what day it would begin.

"Then it's inevitable," she said, the remainder of her once-high spirits depleted.

"Yes, and thanks to the war we're going to make a lot of money."

"Grandfather!"

"Come, Clara, you're an adult. I can't imagine that you haven't learned there is no business so profitable as war. I've always had my hands in conflict and made my fortune thanks to other people's stupidity. I can see in your eyes that you don't want me to tell you the truth. Fine, I won't—but there you have it: The war is going to start on the twentieth. But you mustn't tell anyone that you know this."

"Picot wants to leave."

"Let him go. Let them all go, it doesn't matter. We just have to try to keep them here a few days more. They can leave on the seventeenth or eighteenth. Until then, everyone must keep working."

"What if we don't find the tablets?"

"Then we'll have lost. I'll have lost the only dream I've ever had. I'll speak with Picot tomorrow. I want to propose something to save all this work, and to save you."

"Will we be going to Cairo?"

"I'll let you know. Oh, and be careful with that husband of yours. Don't let him talk you back into your failed marriage."

"Ahmed and I are finished."

"Perhaps. But I am a very wealthy man and I'm dying. Soon you are going to be a very wealthy woman. He may push for a reconciliation; my friends trust him, they know he's a very capable man, so they won't object if he succeeds me as head of the business when I die."

"My God, Grandfather!"

"My child, we have to talk about everything; there's no time for pleasant fictions. Now let me sleep. Tomorrow, offer the men twice their wages to work as hard as they possibly can. They have to keep excavating that blasted temple—until they find the Bible of Clay."

When she left her grandfather's room, Clara found Samira and Fatima waiting for her.

"The doctor said I should sit with him tonight," Samira explained.

"I told her that I could stay," Fatima complained.

"You are not a nurse, Fatima," Clara told her gently.

"But I can take care of him; I've been doing it for forty years!"

"Please, Fatima, go get some rest. This house can't function without you, and if you don't get some sleep we'll all suffer."

She hugged her old servant and motioned Samira into her grandfather's room. Then she retired to her own room.

Ahmed was sitting up in bed, reading. She saw that he hadn't put on pajamas, just a T-shirt and shorts.

"You look exhausted." He set down his book.

"I am."

"I looked for you, but they told me you were talking to the priest."

"We shared a smoke outside."

"You've become friends, then."

"He's a good person. I haven't known many of those in my life."

"Your grandfather is worse, isn't he?"

Clara shot him daggers. "No, and I'm surprised you have that impression."

"Well, there was talk about it in Cairo."

"I imagine Yasir was the talker, but he was wrong. My grandfather is no worse than he was, if you must know."

"Oh, his mind is still clear, of course, but he looks . . . I don't know, more fragile, thinner."

"If you say so. . . . His latest lab results came back fine, Ahmed. He's fine."

"You don't need to be defensive."

"I'm not being defensive; I just know that you're counting the days until he's gone, but he's not going to give you that pleasure."

"Clara!"

"Really, Ahmed, it's been hard for me to see it, but I know how deeply you hate him. I suppose it rubs you the wrong way to be his employee and subordinate to Enrique, Frank, and George."

Ahmed shot to his feet, his fists clenched. Clara looked at him defiantly, knowing that he wouldn't dare lift a finger against her—he would be signing his own death sentence.

"I thought we were going to be able to get through this divorce like two civilized people, without arguments or insults," Ahmed said, crossing the small room to the bottle of mineral water. He poured himself a glass.

"I just want to know the truth."

"Well, then, maybe it's time that we started to talk openly about things. I haven't left because your grandfather hasn't let me. He threatened to have me detained by the Mukhabarat. And he'd have done it too. One phone call from him and I'd have disappeared off the face of the earth. So I accepted his conditions. But not for money, Clara—I did it for my life."

Clara listened stoically as her husband began to spit out the truths that had gone unspoken for so long, truths that he thought would topple the pedestal on which she'd placed her grandfather all these years.

"Do you know what this last operation of his is about? I'll tell you. The archaeological missions he's financed have had one purpose: to steal the most valuable pieces that are found. Nor has he ever had any problem corrupting government officials who earn barely enough to live on between their paltry paychecks. They turn a blind eye to his operations and let thieves carry pieces out of the country's museums. Does that surprise you? It's a lucrative business, moves millions of dollars, and has made your grandfather and his oh-so-respectable friends very, very wealthy. They sell one-of-a-kind pieces to one-of-a-kind clients. Your grandfather runs the business in the Middle East, while Enrique is in charge of Europe and Frank handles South America. George is the spider at the center of the web. He might sell a Roman-period statue stolen from a hermitage in Castille or an altarpiece from a South American cathedral. There are a lot of very wealthy, very greedy people in the world, Clara; they see something and they want it. For them, everything is just a matter of money. A group of art hoarders. There aren't many, but they're very generous. You're pale—do you want some water?"

Ahmed poured her a glassful of water and handed it to her. He was enjoying this. For years he had been suppressing his rising rage at his wife's infantile attitude—she was purposefully blind to what happened around her. She just lived—skirting anything that stood in her way, taking what she wanted—with a willful ignorance through which she steadfastly maintained her innocence about her grandfather's activities.

"Your grandfather needs me for this last operation, so he gave me no choice but to participate. I'll tell you what it consists of. It's a caper, like one of those old American movies, but on a scale not witnessed since the sack of Rome. Alfred's men are going to break into the largest museums all over Iraq, not just in Baghdad. And you want to know who gave them the lists of these one-of-a-kind pieces whose value is literally incalculable? I did. These objects are . . . the patrimony of all humanity. But they'll wind up in the secret museums and dining rooms of a handful of art-greedy millionaires who want to drink out of the same goblet that Hammurabi drank from. But since the teams are risking their necks for those pieces, Alfred's allowing them to carry away a few items for themselves. I've made two lists: one of unique, one-of-a-kind objects, and another of merely important objects."

"That's . . . that's impossible," stammered Clara.

"It's not just possible, it's easy. On March twentieth the war will start, is that not right? Is that not what your grandfather told you? All right, then—that day, his men will break into the museums and get out as fast as they can. Each group has been instructed to reach a border—Kuwait, Turkey, Jordan—where other teams will be waiting to transport the cargo to its final destinations. Enrique has already promised certain pieces to important buyers, as have Frank and George. They'll hang on to the rest and take them out for sale as the market demands. They're in no hurry, even if they are all getting on in years."

"But in the middle of the bombing . . ."

"Oh, that makes it all the easier! When the war starts, nobody's going to be thinking about guarding museums; everybody will be running for their lives. Alfred's men are good, the best thieves in the Middle East."

"Stop it! Don't say another word!"

Clara stood up from her chair, pacing back and forth across the small room. She felt like running, felt like screaming. But she controlled herself. No, she wouldn't do or say anything that Ahmed expected her to do or say. She turned toward him, hating him for having brought her world crashing down around her ears—that lovely, false world in which she'd been living since she was a child, always under the protection of her doting grandfather.

"The war is really going to start on the twentieth?"

"That's right. George called to let us know. You shouldn't be here that day if you want to go on living."

"When will we have to leave Safran?"

"I don't know; your grandfather didn't tell me."

"How will you get out of Iraq?"

"Your grandfather promised to get me out; he's the only one who can."

They stood in silence. Clara felt that she'd aged ten years in the last half hour. She stared at Ahmed. How could she ever have loved this man?

Then it struck her that she didn't care what her grandfather had done. She loved him anyway and would never reproach him for anything, especially in the waning days of his life. She decided that she was going to defend him to her last breath against anyone, including Ahmed or Yasir, who wished to usurp him—who wished to kill him.

Ahmed watched her as she paced the room, and he thought that any moment she was going to collapse, break down completely. He was surprised when she brought herself under control and turned to him with ice-cold eyes. Alfred's eyes.

"I hope you and Yasir are up to doing exactly what my grandfather asks of you. I'll be watching, of course, to make sure you don't decide to change the plan. If you do . . ."

"Are you threatening me?" Ahmed asked, incredulous.

"No, Ahmed. I'm not threatening you. I'm telling you. But I don't imagine that will surprise you, coming as it does from a Tannenberg."

"You want to make a name for yourself in the big business of crime?"

"Spare me the irony. I don't think you know me, Ahmed; you underestimate me, you always have, and you could pay for that mistake dearly."

Ahmed shook his head; he was beginning to think that the woman he'd slept with for the last ten years was a total stranger. But he did believe her—as he'd listened to her talk, he knew that this woman was capable of anything.

"I'm sorry to have upset you, Clara, but it was time that you knew the truth."

"I'm going to sleep in Fatima's room; it stinks in here—it stinks of you. Get out of here, leave Safran as soon as you can, and when the operation is over, try not to bump into me somewhere—I won't be as generous as my grandfather has been."

Clara left the room, gently pulling the door shut behind her. She felt nothing, absolutely nothing for Ahmed; she only regretted the years she'd wasted with him.

Fatima was startled to hear the soft knock at her door. She got out of bed and pulled the door open a crack.

"Clara! What's wrong?"

"Can I sleep here?"

"Yes, of course. Sleep in my bed; I'll make a bed on the floor."

"Just move over, we both fit."

Fatima's presence calmed her. Clara fell into the bed and closed her eyes. She slept deeply until the first ray of sunlight shone brightly through a crack in the blinds.

39

FATIMA ENTERED THE ROOM WITH A TRAY.

"Hurry and eat; Professor Picot wants to see you."

By the time Clara got to the dig, the team had been excavating for hours. Marta came over to her, holding a shard of clay that was clearly distinct from their previous findings.

"Look at this. There was a fire here, in the temple; there's no way to know whether it was an accident or torched on purpose, though when we cleared off the perimeter of another courtyard, this morning, we found a set of stairs and some weapons—swords and spears. They're not terribly well preserved; the ground wasn't dry enough to keep them perfectly. But some of them seem to have been deliberately broken—it looks like the temple was attacked and looted in some battle."

"Temples are usually respected," Clara replied, mystified.

"Yes, but every so often kings overrode the sanctity of the religious establishment out of greed. For example, Nabonidus' plundering caused irreparable changes in the relationship between the throne and the temple. He replaced the temple scribe with a royal administrator, the resh sharri, who was in charge of commercial activities. The priests who oversaw the temple, the qipu and the shatammu, were subordinate to him. Or perhaps there was an invasion, a war between kings, and the temple suffered the same fate as the cities and other sites."

Clara listened attentively to Marta's theorizing. She had developed enormous respect for Marta over the course of their work together, not only for her expertise but also because of her behavior toward everyone on the dig. And Clara envied the deference everyone paid Marta, even Picot, who always treated her as an equal, and the genuine affection in which she was held.

It struck Clara that she'd never earned that kind of respect. In the final analysis, she told herself, there was nothing, absolutely nothing, on her résumé worth noting except her name, Tannenberg, which in the Middle East was respected and feared in equal measure. But even that stemmed from her grandfather's reputation; she just benefited from it as his heir.

"Has Professor Picot seen it?"

"Yves? Yes, of course, and we've decided to allocate more men to this sector. We'll work as late as we can today. We have to make every minute count."

Fabian, dangling by a rope from an improvised crane, its pulleys manned by workers under the close watch of Picot, was being lowered into a hole that seemed to lead into a room buried underground. Everything below was dark.

"Be careful, it looks deep," Picot was saying.

"Don't worry, just let the rope out slowly. We'll see what's down here."

"I am worried—turn on that flashlight. If there's enough space down there, I'll come down too."

The workers slowly lowered Fabian into the hole. They were hoping that this was a lower story of the temple, though it might be just a well. They couldn't be sure until Fabian resurfaced. Picot looked nervous as he peered down into the darkness.

"How is it down there?" he called out to Fabian.

"Lower me a little more—I haven't touched ground yet," Fabian called back, although his voice sounded far away.

They heard a dull thud and then silence. Picot started getting into a harness, as Fabian had done.

"Wait—let Fabian tell us what's down there," Marta told him.

"I don't want to leave him there by himself."

"Me either, but waiting two minutes won't kill anyone. If he doesn't signal us, then we'll go down," she said.

Minutes later, the rope jerked a couple of times. Yves inched closer to the hole, but all he could see was a shaft of light in the blackness.

"Are you all right?" he shouted down, hoping that Fabian could hear him.

They felt another tug on the rope.

"I'm going down. Help me here, and get some more lights so we can see what's down there," Picot grumbled, as he checked his attachment to the crane rope. "Marta, you're in charge."

"I'm going down too."

"No, stay here. If something happens to us, who's going to run the show?"

"I am."

Marta and Picot turned to look at Clara, whose tone left no room for argument.

"I remind you, Professor, that this mission belongs to us both. I'll make sure that nothing happens to you while I'm here."

Yves shrugged and motioned to Marta to follow him.

Some thirty feet down, his feet touched ground. He felt the clamminess of the earth and saw Fabian, on his hands and knees, a few yards away, scraping at a wall with a spatula.

"Nice to have some company," said Fabian without turning around.

"So what are we looking at?" Picot asked.

"I think this is a door—there seems to be another chamber through here. And there's also some sort of fresco—look here, you can see it. It's a winged bull. Beautiful."

"What's this?" Marta said, joining them.

"It appears to be a room. There are some wooden shelves over there—see that wall? The shelves sticking out? It may have been the room where the tablets were held; I don't know, I haven't had much time to look around," Fabian said.

Marta untied two large lanterns from around her waist and placed them on the floor; Picot did the same. The light seemed dim in the large room, but it illuminated what appeared to be a rectangular space that contained, as Fabian had told them, the remains of wooden shelves.

The ground was covered in shards of clay and pieces of ancient wood, as well as vitrified sand.

Picot helped Fabian clean off the section of wall where the traces of the winged bull were painted, while Marta continued to study the floor, where she found pieces of clay tile with bas-reliefs of bulls, lions, falcons, ducks. . . .

"Come look at this!"

"What is it?" Picot asked.

"Bas-reliefs, or what's left of them, but they're gorgeous!"

But the two men remained intent on their work at the doorway.

"What's wrong with you two? Don't you want to see this?" Marta was puzzled.

"There's something here, Marta. Beside the fresco of this bull, the wall sounds hollow—I think there's another room," said Fabian.

"Have it your way, but we ought to let them know up top that we're all right."

"Could you do it?" Picot asked, completely absorbed.

Marta tugged three times at one of the ropes dangling from above to tell the team up at the surface they were all right. Then she went back to her examination of the floor.

An hour later, the three of them reappeared on the surface, smiling in delight.

"What's down there?" Clara asked.

"More rooms in the temple," Picot told her. "So far we've seen the two upper floors, but there are more—exactly how many I can't tell, but there are more for sure. The problem is that we need to shore up from below, because they could collapse and fall in. It won't be easy, and in the time we have left . . ." Picot shook his head dubiously.

"We can get more men," Clara suggested.

"Even so . . . it will be dicey. Normally, it would take months, even years, to do this right," Fabian said.

"And, Clara, I still need to talk to Ahmed and your grandfather," Picot added. "I wasn't able to see them last night, and this morning they were both still asleep when I went over to the house."

"You can see them tonight. For now, tell me what we need to do here."

"We'll do what we can to investigate what's here and to shore it up. But there's no guarantee that we'll find anything at all, and time is against us."

That afternoon, Fatima sent a man to bring Clara back to the house.

When she entered, the eerie silence drew her immediately to her grandfather's room. She took a place quietly just inside the door, watching Dr. Najeb place an oxygen mask over her grandfather's face while Samira changed the intravenous drip bottle. Fatima waited at Alfred's bedside, her eyes brimming with tears.

The doctor whispered to Samira to stay with Tannenberg while he motioned Clara to follow him into the living room.

"I don't think I can go on with this charade of 'medical care,' " the doctor told her without preamble.

"What happened?"

"This morning Mr. Tannenberg lost consciousness—he had a mild coronary. Fortunately, we were able to react quickly. I tried to transfer him to the hospital tent, but he wouldn't hear of it. He insists on hiding his condition, so he's forcing me to treat him in his room. As you saw, I had some equipment brought in, but if we don't take him to a real hospital, he won't last much longer."

"He's dying," Clara said in a tone of voice so calm that it frightened the doctor.

"Yes, he's dying. You've known that for some time—but if he stays here, he's going to die that much sooner."

"We will respect my grandfather's wishes."

There was nothing more Salam Najeb could say, no way to fight the extraordinary irrationality of these two people. They were both so strange to him, following a code of behavior that was beyond his experience or understanding.

"You will be responsible for what happens," the doctor said.

"Of course I will. Now tell me whether my grandfather is able to talk to me."

"He's fully conscious now, but in my opinion he should rest."

"I need to talk to him."

The doctor's expression reflected utter defeat; he shrugged his shoulders, knowing it was useless to argue. All he could do was accompany Clara back to her grandfather's room.

"Samira, Madam Tannenberg wants to talk to her grandfather. Wait at the door, please."

At the same time, Clara motioned to Fatima to leave too. When they were alone, she went over to the bed and took her grandfather's hand. She made an effort to smile.

"Don't try to talk, Grandfather; I want you to rest. I think we've found something—another level to the temple, several more floors. Picot went down with Fabian and Marta, and when they resurfaced they were smiling from ear to ear."

Tannenberg made a motion as though he was about to start talking, but Clara stopped him.

"Please, just listen. You don't need to say a thing. I need you to trust me the way I trust you. I spoke to Ahmed last night and he told me everything."

The old man's eyes filled with rage as he struggled to sit up in bed, tearing the oxygen mask off his face.

"What did he tell you?" he asked furiously, though his voice was barely audible.

"Let me call Samira so she can put this back on you. I . . . I want us to talk, you and I, but you need the oxygen. . . ."

"Stop!" he commanded her. "We'll talk now—then you can call in that idiotic nurse or whoever else you want to. But now tell me what that husband of yours told you."

"He told me about the operation that . . . that's under way, and about George, Frank, and Enrique. About the fortune involved."

Alfred Tannenberg closed his eyes as he gripped Clara's hand to keep her still. When he'd brought his breathing back under control, he opened them again and glared at Clara.

"I told you. Keep your nose out of my business."

"Do you mean you can trust someone else more than me? Please, Grandfather, think about the situation we're in. The war is almost on us. You're . . . you aren't well, and . . . I think you need me. I've heard you say more than once that sometimes, to ensure the success of a business deal, you have to buy loyalties. And if they know you're sick, some of your men are capable of selling you out to the highest bidder."

The old man closed his eyes again. He was surprised by Clara's coolness, the ease with which she'd accepted the fact that they were about to undertake an operation that would leave Iraq stripped of its artistic legacy forever. This young woman, who loved her country, who'd grown up dreaming about discovering its lost cities, who treasured anything from the past, suddenly appeared before him as a woman ready to take over the reins of a business that consisted purely and simply of robbery, theft, looting.

"What do you want, Clara?"

"I want to keep Ahmed and Yasir from taking advantage of our situation. I want you to tell me what I should say to them, what you want me to do."

"We are going to strip Iraq of its past."

"I know that."

"And you don't care?"

Clara hesitated a few moments before answering. She cared, yes, but her loyalty to her grandfather came first—not to mention that she didn't believe that Alfred's men would actually be able to get away with everything. It wasn't easy to empty one museum, let alone ten.

"I won't lie to you. I didn't want to believe Ahmed—I wanted to think he was lying. But I can't change things, or change you either. The sooner this is over, the better. What matters most to me is that you're sick, and they may try to take advantage of you—that I will not allow."

"You can start . . . taking some responsibility. But no mistakes—not from you, or anyone. There are no changes in the operation. I've told Ahmed what I expect of him, Yasir what I expect of him . . ."

The old man's voice trailed off. His eyelids fluttered and his eyes grew dim; Clara could feel his ice-cold hand, almost lifeless. She screamed, and it sounded like a howl.

Dr. Najeb and Samira ran into the room and pushed Clara aside. Fatima followed them and put her arms around Clara.

Two men with drawn pistols burst into the room right on their heels.

"Out—all of you!" the doctor ordered. "You too," he told Clara, somewhat more gently.

Clara gathered herself and motioned to the two men who'd rushed in. Others guards gathered around as they stepped out into the living room.

"Everything's fine—just a little accident. I tripped and almost fell; I think I twisted my ankle. I'm sorry that I alarmed you."

The men clearly didn't believe a word of it.

"I said nothing is wrong!" Clara snapped, drawing herself up. "Go back to your work! And I don't want to hear any talk about this! Any of you who lets your imagination run away can expect to pay the consequences. You two—stay here," she barked at the first two men, as the others withdrew.

"I don't want a word of what you've seen here to get out."

"No, madam, no," one of the guards answered.

"If it does, you'll be whipped. If you keep your mouths closed, I'll show you my gratitude, you can be sure."

"You know we've been with Mr. Tannenberg for years, madam—he trusts us," one of the guards protested.

"I also know that trust has its price, so don't make the mistake of trying to sell information to anybody about what goes on in this house. Now go outside and guard the door. And don't let anybody—anybody—in."

"Yes, madam."

Clara went back to her grandfather's door as quietly as possible. "How is he?" she asked Dr. Najeb.

"His condition is critical. We have to wait to see the EKG, but right now it's his heart that worries me."

"Is he conscious?"

"No. Now let me work. I'll keep you informed. I promise you I'll stay right here beside him."

Ahmed was standing just outside the door when Clara left Alfred's room, irate that Fatima hadn't let him in.

"What's happened? The men are upset; they say you screamed and that something has happened to Alfred."

"I tripped and cried out, that's all. My grandfather is fine—a little tired, but fine."

"I need to talk to him; I've been in Basra today."

"You'll have to talk to me."

Ahmed studied her. "I'm leaving tomorrow, and I want to go over final details with him. As far as I know, your grandfather is in charge; no one's told me that there's been any change. And no one will accept orders from you, including me."

Clara weighed her husband's words and decided not to press the issue. If she did, Ahmed would realize that her grandfather's condition had worsened. So she decided to behave like the Clara she'd always been—though she didn't know how much of that woman was left.

"You'll have to wait until tomorrow. In the meantime, find somewhere else to sleep. I'm sick and tired of pretending."

Ahmed sighed. "Fine. Just tell me where I should go."

"There's a cot in the hospital tent—that should do for now."

"What time can I see Alfred tomorrow morning?"

"I'll let you know."

"Picot wants to talk to me about wrapping things up—will you be there?"

"Yes. He called a meeting to determine when we should close down and what evacuation plans you have in place."

"You know the date, and you know there's not much time left. But we can't tell them."

"That's the problem."

Clara turned away without another word and went back to her grandfather's room.

40

YVES PICOT WAS FORMULATING A PLAN, INSPIRED BY MARTA and Fabian.

The expedition's evacuation was inevitable now, but they needed to return with as many objects as possible—the bas-reliefs, statuettes, tablets, seals, bullae, and calculi they'd found. The harvest had been amazing.

Marta had suggested they mount a big exhibition at a prominent university—her own if possible, the Complutense in Madrid, and then others, with the financial support of some foundation. Fabian agreed: Once the war came, there'd be nothing left of the temple they had discovered. They'd enhance the exhibit with a book of drawings, floor plans, photographs taken by Lion Doyle, and articles contributed by the major members of the team.

But in order to do all that, Picot had to convince Ahmed Husseini to let them take the treasures out of Iraq, which would not be easy. The objects were part of the country's artistic heritage, after all. And under the current circumstances, none of Hussein's government officials would dare permit even a single shard to land safely in one of the countries that was declaring war on them.

Picot thought perhaps Alfred Tannenberg, with his powerful connections, could couch the removal in terms of a rescue operation. Picot was willing to sign whatever papers were necessary, stating that the objects belonged to Iraq and always would, and that they would be returned to the country when it was deemed safe to do so.

Of course, for Alfred Tannenberg, as for his granddaughter, the objective of the expedition had not been achieved—they hadn't found the Bible of Clay—so Tannenberg could very well deny their request in order to pressure them to stay on in Safran and continue the dig. But only a madman would think of remaining in a country that was going to be plunged into war at any moment.

After dinner, when most of the team members had gone their separate ways, Picot asked Lion Doyle and Gian Maria to join him, Marta, and Fabian during their meeting with Ahmed and Clara.

The seasoned archaeologist liked Lion Doyle: He was always in a good mood, ready to give a hand with whatever needed doing. And best of all, he was intelligent.

Clara seemed nervous and distracted; Ahmed, too, seemed tense. Picot had long since picked up on their marital discord and assumed that they were trying to keep up appearances for the sake of the team.

"Ahmed, we need to know what's going on. The reporters said they had it on good authority that the war is virtually upon us."

Ahmed didn't reply immediately. He lit his Egyptian cigarette, exhaled the smoke, and smiled.

"That's what we'd like to know—if you're actually going to attack us, and when."

"That's not funny, Ahmed. Tell me when you think we need to go, and whether you've got a plan to evacuate us," Yves insisted, a bit uncomfortably.

"What we know is that some countries are doing everything they can to avoid a conflict. What I can't tell you, my friends, is whether they'll succeed. As for you and your team . . . I can't make your decisions for you. You may not believe it, but we have no more information than you do, which comes from news reports from the West. I can't be sure that there will be war, nor can I be sure there won't. With regard to when . . . it all depends on when they think they're ready."

Yves and Fabian exchanged a look of disgust. This slippery, cynical bureaucrat was far from the efficient, intelligent archaeologist they'd been accustomed to dealing with, who had persuaded them to come in the first place. It seemed clear that he was being more than evasive—his statement seemed misleading, even untruthful.

"Get off it, Ahmed; what kind of talk is that?" Picot said. "Tell me when you think we should leave."

"If you want to go now, I'll be happy to make all the necessary arrangements for your immediate departure from Iraq."

"What happens if war breaks out tomorrow, tonight? How would you get us out of here?" Fabian insisted.

"I would try to send in helicopters, but I'm not certain they would be made available to me if we were actually under attack."

"So you're recommending that we go now," Marta stated more than asked.

"I think the situation is critical, but I don't have a crystal ball. If you're asking for my advice, I'll give it to you: Go before it gets too hard to leave," Ahmed replied.

"What do you think, Clara?"

That Marta valued her opinion surprised even Clara, not to mention the rest of the participants.

"I don't want you to go; I think we still have a very good chance of finding the Bible of Clay. But we need more time."

"Time is the only thing we don't have," Picot said to her.

"Then you decide—it doesn't make much difference what I think."

"Yves, could I say something?" Lion Doyle asked.

"Yes, of course; I asked you to come because I wanted to know what you think. I want Gian Maria's thoughts too." Picot turned to the priest.

"I think we ought to go. You don't have to be Donald Rumsfeld to know that the United States is going to attack. The information from my colleagues in the press leaves no doubt about that. France, Germany, and Russia have lost the battle in the United Nations, and Bush has been readying his troops and equipment for months. The generals in the Pentagon know that this is the best time of year to wage war in this region; the climate is the determining factor. It's a question of days, maybe weeks—not months.

"Clara may be right: If you kept working you might find the Bible of Clay. But you don't have the time. So I say you should start breaking down the camp and get out of here as soon as possible. If they start bombing, Saddam will leave us to our fate; we can't rely on him to send helicopters to pick us up. It would be crazy even to get into a helicopter in the middle of a war. And trying to cross the border in a convoy would be suicide. As far as I'm concerned, I'm getting ready to go—I don't think there's much more I can do here."

Lion lit a cigarette. It was Gian Maria who finally broke the silence.

"Lion is right. I . . . I think you should leave."

" 'You' should leave? What about you? Are you staying?" Marta asked incredulously.

"I'm staying if Clara stays. I want to help her."

Ahmed looked at Gian Maria in bewilderment. He couldn't fathom why this priest was so determined to help his wife.

"All right, Lion. I think you have it right. Tomorrow we'll start packing up and preparing to move out to Baghdad, and from there home," Picot said. "When do you think you can get us out of here?" He turned to Ahmed.

"As soon as you tell me you're ready."

Picot nodded. "I figure about a week, two at the most, to finish documenting what we have, shoring things up as much as possible, and packing everything properly."

Fabian cleared his throat as he looked over at Marta, seeking her support. He didn't want them to just pack up their equipment and leave Iraq, and Picot seemed even to have forgotten about mounting an exhibit in Europe.

"Yves, I think you should ask Ahmed about the possibility of exhibiting the tablets and bas-reliefs and other objects . . . all the things we've found."

"Yes, Fabian. I was coming to that. You see, Ahmed, Fabian and Marta thought that we should unveil Safran to the scientific community. What we've found here is of incalculable value, as you know. We'd thought about a traveling exhibit, to be presented in several countries. We'll seek funding from universities and private foundations. You, and of course Clara, could help us get things under way."

Ahmed weighed Picot's suggestion. Basically, Yves was asking him to allow everything they'd found in the excavation to be taken out of the country. He felt a wave of anxiety: Many of the objects Picot's team had found had already been sold in advance to private collectors, who would be eager to display their new possessions. Clara, of course, didn't know this, nor did Alfred Tannenberg, but Paul Dukais, the president of Planet Security, had been adamant in his last conversation with Yasir. Some collectors already knew about the existence of the objects through the reports published in *Scientific Archaeology*. They'd contacted intermediaries, who in turn had called Robert Brown, president of the Mundo Antiguo Foundation, which had always been the cover for the illegal antiquities business of George Wagner, Frank dos Santos, and Enrique Gómez Thomson, Alfred's business partners.

"What you're asking is impossible," Ahmed replied curtly.

"I know it's difficult, especially given the current situation, but you're an archaeologist, you know how important the discovery of this temple is. If we leave behind what we've found here . . . Well, all our work, all these months of sacrifice will have been meaningless. If you convince your superiors how significant these findings would be to the archaeological community, your country will most certainly be the first to benefit. And everything, of course, will be returned to Iraq. But first let the world see what we've found, let us organize shows in Paris, Madrid, London, New York, Berlin. We wouldn't be taking these things for ourselves, for our own glory. Your government can appoint you commissioner of the exhibit on Iraq's behalf. We can do it. We've worked hard, Ahmed."

Picot stopped talking, trying to read Ahmed's body language, but it was Clara who spoke.

"Professor Picot, aren't you forgetting me?"

"Not at all, Clara. If we've gotten this far, it's because of you. Nothing we've done here would have been possible without you. We don't want to usurp your contributions—quite the contrary. We're here because you so stubbornly insisted on our coming. That's why I'm asking you to suspend the dig and come with *us*. We need you to help prepare the exhibit, give lectures, participate in seminars, accompany the objects wherever they travel. But we can't do any of that unless your husband persuades his government to let us take what we've found out of Iraq."

"My husband may not be able to do that, but my grandfather can."

Clara's statement didn't surprise them, and Picot was fully prepared to talk to Alfred Tannenberg if Ahmed turned out to be overly reticent. The months he'd spent in Iraq had taught him that there was nothing Tannenberg couldn't do if he wanted to.

"It would be wonderful if Ahmed and your grandfather could convince the government," Picot said.

Ahmed was making his own calculations. This might be his only opportunity to escape from Iraq. Picot was offering him an unexpected cover. It would be best to try to gain time by assuring them that he would do everything in his power to help them—enthusiastically.

"So, will you come with us?" Marta asked Clara.

"No, at least not now, Marta. But I think it's a wonderful idea that the world know what we've uncovered here in Safran. I'll stay on; I know I can find the Bible of Clay."

The camp was silent as Clara, accompanied by Gian Maria, walked back toward her house. Ahmed had discreetly slipped into the hospital tent for the night.

"I like the night—I love the stillness; it's the best time for thinking. Will you go out to the site with me?" she asked the priest.

"If you'd like, I'll go out there with you. Shouldn't we take a jeep?"

"No, let's walk. It's a long way, I know, but it will do us good."

Clara's bodyguards stayed several yards behind them, impassive, as always, at her whims.

When they neared the excavation site, Clara found a place to sit. She patted the sand next to her for Gian Maria.

"Gian Maria, why do you want to stay here? No one can protect you if the Americans start bombing."

"I know, but I'm not afraid. I'm no daredevil, but right now I'm not afraid," he repeated.

"But why don't you leave? You're a priest, and here . . . well, here you haven't been able to do anything very . . . priestly, you know. We're all lost souls, and you've really been very respectful to us—you haven't tried to win us over to the Church at all."

"Clara, I'd like to help you find the Bible of Clay. I'm intrigued by the idea of it. It would be something to know whether Abraham himself revealed the story of Genesis—and if so, whether it is the same Genesis that we know."

"So you're staying out of curiosity."

"I'm staying to help you, Clara. I . . . well, I just wouldn't feel right leaving you alone."

Clara laughed. That Gian Maria believed he could protect her, when she was under the protection of armed men night and day, was amusing. But the priest seemed to really believe that he possessed some special power that could keep anything bad from happening to her.

"What do the other priests in your order say when you talk to them?"

"My superior encourages me to help those who need me; he knows how hard life is in Iraq now."

"But really, you're not saving anybody's soul—you're here with us, working on archaeological matters."

She hadn't really thought much about it up to that point, but it struck her then—as others had pointed out—how odd the priest's tenure with them in Safran had been, working like just any other member of the team.

"They know that, but even so, they think I can be useful here."

"Perhaps, after all, the Church *would* like a chance at the Bible of Clay?" Clara asked with an edge in her voice.

"Please, Clara! The Church has nothing to do with my staying in Safran. It was my choice, and it hurts me that you doubt my motives. I have permission from my superior to be here; he knows what I'm doing and he has no objection. Many priests work; I'm not the only one.

There's nothing strange about it. Of course, at some point I have to go back to Rome, but I've been here months, not years, no matter how long it's seemed to you."

"You know, Gian Maria, sometimes I think that you're the only friend I have here, the only person who'd help me if I needed it."

They sat quietly for a while longer, lost in their own thoughts, untroubled by the occasional noises of the night that were amplified, it seemed, by the prevailing silence.

Soon the night turned cold, and they decided to turn in.

Clara entered the house as quietly as she could, surprised by the total darkness that greeted her. She made her way toward her grandfather's room, where she was sure Samira and Fatima would be sitting with him.

Slipping into the room, she stretched out her hand and followed the wall so that she wouldn't bump into anything. She whispered Samira's name but got no response. There was a metallic, sticky smell in the air. She couldn't see a thing, and neither Fatima nor Samira responded when she called again. She was furious, thinking that the two women had fallen asleep. Then her hand found the light switch.

As the light dimly illuminated the room, she stifled a scream. Nausea rose in her throat.

Samira was lying on the floor, her eyes wide open. A trickle of blood had run out of her mouth and across her pale cheek.

Clara didn't know how long she stood there, frozen, leaning against the wall, but it seemed like an eternity before she marshaled the courage to approach her grandfather's bed. She was certain she'd find him dead.

The oxygen mask was dangling off the side of the bed, and her grandfather lay there unmoving, his face as white as candle wax. Clara touched her fingers to his lips and felt his light breathing, then put her ear to his chest and sensed the quiet, muffled beating of his heart, as though his life was ebbing away. In a panic, she put the oxygen mask back on him and ran out, desperate for help.

Throwing on the living room light, she saw what she had missed in the darkness earlier. The two men guarding her grandfather's door were sprawled on the floor, as dead as Samira. Another wave of panic washed over her. She was alone, terrified that the murderer was still there, in the house.

She ran outside, stopping short with relief when she saw the men who usually stood guard outside the house, the same ones who had greeted her just minutes earlier when they saw her bid good night to Gian Maria. How had someone been able to enter the house without their noticing?

"Madam Tannenberg, what is it?" asked one of them, taken aback by the expression on her face.

"Where's Dr. Najeb?" she asked, her voice barely audible. This man might very well be the murderer of Samira and the other guards.

"He's asleep in his house, madam," said the guard, pointing over to the doctor's small dwelling.

"Call him." Clara's tone betrayed her desperation.

By then, other guards had joined them, and she sent one to find Gian Maria and Picot. She knew she should notify Ahmed, but she didn't want to do that until the Frenchman and the priest had arrived. She didn't trust her husband.

The doctor appeared less than two minutes later. He hadn't had time to comb his hair or even splash water on his face; all the guard had allowed him to do was pull on a pair of pants and a shirt. He was still half asleep.

"What's wrong?" he asked, alarmed by the look on Clara's face.

"What time did you leave my grandfather?" Clara asked, ignoring his question.

"Just after ten. He was resting quietly. Samira was sitting up with him. What's happened?"

Clara returned to the house and her grandfather's room, followed by the doctor. Salam Najeb stood paralyzed at the door, his face reflecting his horror. Then, ignoring the lifeless body of Samira on the floor, he strode decisively over to Tannenberg's bed. He straightened the oxygen mask and took his pulse as he watched the lines on the monitor trace the sick man's vital signs. He examined him thoroughly, until he was sure that he was all right, that he'd not been harmed in any way. Then he prepared a syringe, gave the old man an injection, and changed the bottle of intravenous fluid and medication.

When he had finished, he turned toward Clara, who was standing silently by.

"He seems not to have been harmed." He then went over to Samira's body, knelt, and carefully examined her.

"She's been strangled. She must have tried to defend herself, or defend him," he said, gesturing toward the bed.

Then he gave a start and strode into the far corner of the room. There in the shadows, sprawled in a pool of blood, lay Fatima. Clara couldn't keep back a scream.

"Calm down, she's still alive, she's breathing, although she's taken a terrible blow to the head. We'll take her to the hospital tent; I can't treat her here. I'm going to go get the men outside to help us."

Crying, Clara knelt down next to Fatima. Two guards came in, gathered the old woman up, and carried her out.

When Yves and Gian Maria came in, Clara burst into tears in earnest.

Gian Maria rushed over and put his arms around her. "There, there, now. Are you all right?" the priest murmured.

"Tell us what happened—My God!" Picot said, seeing Samira's body.

"I've asked the guards to take the body to the hospital tent," Dr. Najeb told Clara. "The men outside were shot once in the head, apparently from close range. The killer must have been using a silencer. I've had them taken over to the hospital tent as well."

"What about my grandfather?" cried Clara.

"I've done all I can do for the moment. Someone should watch over him—call me if there's any change at all. But now I need to see to Fatima, and you need to call the authorities and report this. Samira was murdered, and so were the two others."

Salam Najeb turned away. He was crying, for Samira and for himself, for having agreed to come to Safran on this impossible undertaking. He'd done it for the money; Tannenberg had offered him five years' salary to take care of him, in addition to promising that he would buy him an apartment in Cairo. But nothing was worth this.

Ayed Sahadi met the doctor at the door. He looked terrible—pale, fearful, terrified, even, because he knew that Tannenberg would hold him responsible for this and that the Colonel was capable of personally torturing him if the security he was responsible for had failed.

When he entered Tannenberg's room, two of his men were leaving with Samira's body. Clara was still crying and Picot was ordering one of his men to find a woman from the village to sit with the old man.

"Where were you?" Clara screamed at Sahadi when she saw him come in. "You're going to pay dearly for this."

The overseer didn't respond; he didn't even look at her. He began examining the room, the window, the floor, the furniture, everything. The men with him stood by expectantly, not daring to move without his permission.

Several minutes later, the commander of the contingent of soldiers arrived and launched into a heated exchange in Arabic with Sahadi. They were both terrified—they knew that their superiors were even more cruel than they were.

Clara was watching the monitor for her grandfather's vital signs. She thought she saw his eyes twitch and start to open, and he stirred slightly, but then he seemed to subside into a more peaceful slumber.

The village leader arrived, with his wife and two of his daughters. Clara explained what she expected of them. They would be in charge of the house, and the two younger women would not leave her grandfather's bedside.

Ayed Sahadi and the commander of the army detail had agreed to begin investigating immediately; their men would turn both the camp and village upside down for any clue that would lead them to the murderer—and the would-be murderer of Alfred Tannenberg himself, for there was no doubt that he was the actual target. In addition, all the members of the archaeological team, including the workers from the village, would without exception be searched and interrogated. The most difficult decision for them was whether to call the Colonel; they finally decided against it until they could make their own assessment.

Just then Ahmed came in and made his way to Clara's side through the people now crowding the room. "I'm sorry I didn't come sooner; I was with the doctor. He told me what happened, and I've been helping him with Fatima. She's unconscious, and she's lost a lot of blood. She was struck by something heavy. I don't think she'll be able to tell us anything until tomorrow—the doctor has her under sedation."

"Will she live?" Clara asked.

"Yes—or at least Dr. Najeb thinks she will," Ahmed replied.

After making their way past the armed men standing outside the door, Fabian and Marta entered the room. Yves began to fill them in, and Marta immediately took charge.

"I think we all need to move to the living room, given Mr. Tannenberg's state. You," she said, addressing the village leader's wife, "go and make some coffee, please. It's going to be a long night."

Clara gave her a grateful smile. She trusted Marta, and no one was better equipped to bring order to this chaos.

Marta then turned to Ayed Sahadi and the commander, who were still chattering at each other in a corner of the room.

"Have you thoroughly examined everything here?" she asked them.

Both the men bridled. Marta ignored their protests.

"You can continue your discussion outside. You two," she said to the village leader's daughters, "will stay with Mr. Tannenberg as you've been instructed, and in my opinion a couple of armed guards ought to stay in the room too, just in case. But nobody else. Let's go—everybody out," she ordered.

They all filed out. Gian Maria never left Clara's side, and Yves took Fabian aside to speak privately.

Clara settled herself in the living room, only to realize that the man charged by her grandfather with the camp security was looking at her with contained fury.

"Mrs. Husseini, tell us the exact time you went into your grandfather's room, and why," Sahadi demanded. "Did you hear anything strange?"

Clara, in a flat monotone, went through everything that had happened since her walk with Gian Maria.

For almost an hour she answered Sahadi's questions and those of the commander, who urged her to try to recall every possible detail.

"Well, the question that has to be asked of you two," said Picot finally, addressing Sahadi and the commander, "is how it's possible, with the house surrounded by armed men, for someone to get in without being seen and to reach Mr. Tannenberg's room, first killing two guards and the nurse and seriously wounding Fatima."

"Yes," seconded Ahmed. "The Colonel will be arriving tomorrow, and he'll be expecting answers."

The two men looked at each other. Ahmed Husseini had given them the worst possible news—the Colonel was coming personally.

"You called him?" Clara asked her husband.

"Of course. A woman and two men responsible for your grandfather's safety were murdered here tonight. It's not hard to imagine that the real target was him. So it was my duty to inform Baghdad. I assume, Commander, that you'll soon receive a call, but if not, let me tell you: A detail of the Republican Guard is on its way here now to oversee our security properly. It's clear you haven't been able to do that, or prevent this terrible act of betrayal, and the same goes for our friend Sahadi."

"Betrayal? Whose betrayal?" Ayed asked nervously.

"Betrayal by someone here among us, in this camp—I don't know whether he's an Iraqi or a foreigner, but I have no doubt that the killer is one of us," Ahmed stated flatly.

"Including you."

Everyone turned toward Clara. She regretted the words as soon as she uttered them. Accusing her husband of being among the suspects made the rupture between the two of them clear, which she knew was a mistake.

Ahmed glared at her. He didn't respond, although everyone could see the effort he was making to control himself.

"The question is why," said Marta.

"Why?" Fabian repeated.

"Yes, why somebody went into Mr. Tannenberg's room—whether it was really to murder him, as Ahmed thinks, or it was just a thief who was surprised by Samira and the guards and—"

"Marta, it's hard to believe that a mere thief would take on all the security around here," pointed out Picot.

"What do you think, Clara?"

Marta's direct question caught Clara off guard. She didn't know what to say. Her grandfather was a powerful, feared man. He had many enemies, any one of whom might have wanted him dead.

"I don't know. I don't know what to think. I'm . . . I'm . . . I'm exhausted. . . . This is all so awful."

A soldier came in, whispered something in the commander's ear, then left as quickly as he'd come.

"All right," the commander said, "my men have begun questioning the workers and the villagers. So far, no one seems to have seen anything. Professor Picot, we will also be questioning the members of your team, including you."

"Of course. We're happy to cooperate with the investigation in any way we can."

"The sooner we begin, the better. Would you mind going first?" the commander asked him.

"Not at all. Where do you want to talk?"

"What about right here? Mrs. Husseini, would you mind if we worked here?"

"Yes," answered Clara. "Find someplace else. In one of the storerooms, maybe."

Picot and the commander left, followed by Marta, Fabian, and Gian Maria, who would be questioned after Yves. Only Clara, Ahmed, and Ayed remained in the living room.

"Is there anything you haven't told us?" Ahmed asked Clara.

"I've told you everything I remember. You, Ayed, need to tell us how someone was able to get into my grandfather's room."

"I don't know. We've checked every possible point, all the doors and windows. I don't know where they came in, whether it was one man or a team. All of my men swear they saw nothing," Sahadi said. "No one could get in without their noticing."

"But somebody did. And it must have been a person, not a ghost, because ghosts don't shoot people at point-blank range and strangle defenseless women," Ahmed said disgustedly.

"I know, I know. But I just don't understand how it could have happened. Of course, it's possible that it was someone inside the house," Ayed suggested.

"The only people in the house were Fatima, Samira, and the men who were guarding the door to my grandfather's room," Clara pointed out.

"And you—after all, it was you who found the bodies."

Clara looked at Ayed with fire in her eyes, then sprang to her feet and slapped him so hard that the imprint of her fingers remained on his cheek. Ahmed leapt up and grabbed her before Ayed could react.

"Clara! That's enough! Sit down! Have we all gone crazy? And you, Ayed, I don't ever want to hear insinuations like that again. I assure you I won't tolerate any lack of respect toward my wife."

"There were three murders here tonight, and we're all suspects until the guilty party is found," Ayed said.

Ahmed looked like he was about to strike the foreman himself, but instead he just waved him off with a parting shot. "That's right, Ayed. You're a suspect too. Maybe somebody paid you off to kill Tannenberg. Tread very carefully, Ayed."

The foreman turned abruptly and left the living room as Clara slumped back into her chair. Her husband sat down beside her.

"Clara, you have to try to control yourself; you can't let yourself go like that."

"I know, but I'm a wreck. I'm absolutely destroyed, Ahmed."

"Your grandfather is in very bad shape; you should have him moved to Cairo, or at least to Baghdad."

"Is that what Dr. Najeb told you?"

"Nobody has to tell me; all you have to do is look at him to see that he's dying. Admit it; you can't keep up this fiction that he's rallying."

"Leave me alone! You'd love it if he died, but he'll live, you'll see— he'll live, and he'll have you all cut into pieces for the traitors you are!"

"If you won't listen to reason, I'd better go where I can be of some help. If I were you, I'd try to rest."

"I'm going to see Fatima."

"Fine, I'll walk with you."

But they didn't get out of the house, because they met Dr. Najeb at the door. He looked exhausted.

He told them that he still didn't know whether Fatima would recover from the blow to her head. She'd been hit with something heavy, there was no doubt of that, and it had made a deep laceration.

"She's the only person who can tell us what happened—if she had time to see what was going on," Ahmed noted.

Alfred Tannenberg was breathing with difficulty, and his vital signs seemed to have plummeted. Dr. Najeb told the young women in no uncertain terms that they should have called him. Clara cursed herself for not staying at her grandfather's bedside, and she noted Ahmed, not bothering to hide a slight smile of satisfaction as he evaluated the old man's condition.

The doctor prepared a transfusion of plasma and sent them off to sleep for a while if they could, promising that he wouldn't move from Tannenberg's side.

The noise of the helicopter cut through the heavy silence that had fallen over the camp. Picot, Fabian, and Marta had finally agreed to end the adventure. As soon as they received permission from Ayed and the other authorities on-site, they would begin to dismantle the camp and pack up for the trip home. They wouldn't stay a day longer than necessary.

Shortly before dawn, a detachment of the Republican Guard had arrived—Saddam Hussein's feared elite corps of bodyguards and fighters. Nevertheless, Marta thought that they should keep pressing for permission to take the objects they'd unearthed back to Europe.

Picot watched Clara walk with her husband toward the helicopter. The blades hadn't stopped turning when a heavyset man with black hair and a thick black mustache—a veritable carbon copy of Saddam himself—nimbly jumped out. After him came two other soldiers and a woman.

The first man, dressed in military greens, communicated a clear air of authority, and it struck Picot that there was also something sinister about him.

The Colonel shook Ahmed's hand and patted Clara on the shoulder, then walked with them toward Tannenberg's house. He motioned to the woman to follow them.

The woman seemed a bit overwhelmed by the surroundings, and there was also a certain tightness, a tension, around her mouth. Clara waited for her to catch up with them and then greeted her warmly. The Colonel had just told her that the woman was a nurse, eminently trustworthy, from a military hospital. When he heard that Samira had been murdered, he had decided he should bring the nurse to help Dr. Najeb.

The sun was beating down when a soldier came for Picot, with a message that the newcomer would like to speak to him.

Neither Clara nor Ahmed was in the living room of Tannenberg's house, just the man they called the Colonel, who was smoking a cigar and sipping a cup of tea.

He didn't offer his hand or make any effort to greet Picot beyond a brief inclination of his head. Picot decided to sit down, even if the Colonel hadn't asked him to.

The Colonel went straight to the point. "Tell me your opinion of what has happened here."

"I haven't the slightest idea."

"You must have some theory."

"No, really I don't. I've only spoken to Mr. Tannenberg once in my life, so I can't say I know him. Actually, I know almost nothing about him, so I couldn't venture to say why someone would have broken in to his room and killed his nurse and the guards hired to protect him."

"Do you suspect anyone?"

"Me? How could I? I can't imagine that there's a murderer among us."

"But there is, Professor Picot. I hope Fatima will be able to talk. There's a possibility that she saw the person, whoever it was. But at any rate, my men are also going to question the members of your team."

"They already have; they questioned us all last night."

"You must understand that it's necessary. I want you to tell me who is who; I need to know everything about everyone who is here, both Iraqis and foreigners. With the Iraqis there will be no problem; I'll be able to find out everything I need to know about them—more, even, than they know about themselves. But your people . . . Help us, Professor Picot, tell me everything."

"Listen, I've known most of the people here for a long time. They are archaeologists and graduate students. Honest, decent people. You won't find a murderer among them."

"You'd be surprised where one might find people willing to kill someone. Do you know them all? Is there anyone you have known for only a short time?"

Yves Picot remained silent. The Colonel was asking him a question that he didn't want to answer. If he said there were members of the expedition that he'd never seen until his arrival in Iraq, he'd turn them into suspects, and in Iraq, suspects more often than not were "found" to be guilty.

"Think, take your time," the Colonel told him.

"Actually, I know them all. They're people recommended by close friends whom I trust implicitly."

"I, however, have to mistrust everyone implicitly. That's the only way we get results."

"Mister . . ."

"Call me Colonel."

"Colonel, I'm an archaeologist. I'm not in the habit of consorting with killers, and the members of archaeological missions don't tend to go around killing people. Ask all you like; question us as much as you need to, but I doubt very much that you're going to find your killer among our group."

"I have a list here of the members of your group. I'd like to talk to you about each one of them—maybe we can discover something, maybe not. May we begin?"

Yves nodded. He had no choice. This man was not going to take no for an answer. So he'd talk to him, but he'd offer nothing but trivialities.

They had just started when Clara came into the living room. She was smiling, which struck Picot as odd. With three dead bodies and an assassin loose in the camp, there wasn't much to smile about.

"Colonel, my grandfather would like to see you."

"So he's recovered consciousness," the Colonel murmured.

"Yes, and he says he feels better than he has in days."

"I'll be there at once. Professor Picot, we will talk later."

"Whenever you like."

The Colonel left with Clara, while Picot breathed a sigh of relief. He knew he couldn't get out of the interrogation, but at least he had gained some time to gather his thoughts and prepare himself. Meantime, he'd find Fabian and Marta so they could talk this over.

Dr. Najeb gestured to the Colonel and Clara not to come to the bed until the nurse had finished changing the IV.

Salam Najeb was practically asleep on his feet; the signs of exhaustion were patent on his weary face. Clearly, the struggle to keep Alfred Tannenberg and Fatima alive during the last twenty-four hours had taken its toll.

"He seems to have recovered miraculously, but you mustn't tire him," he told Clara and the Colonel, knowing full well that they would do exactly as they pleased.

"You should get some sleep, Doctor," Clara told him.

"Yes, now that Aliya is here, I'll go freshen up and rest for a while. But first I'll stop by and check on Fatima."

"My men are interrogating her," the Colonel said.

"I gave orders that she was not to be disturbed until I made certain she was in a condition to answer questions!" the doctor practically shouted.

"That's enough, Doctor! She is awake and will be very useful to us. Only Mr. Tannenberg and Fatima know what happened in this room, and it is our duty to talk to them both. We have three bodies, Doctor."

The Colonel left no doubt that nothing and no one would stop him from doing his job.

The nurse stepped aside, motioning Clara and the Colonel forward. Clara took her grandfather's hand in hers and squeezed it; she felt better now, seeing him conscious and alert at last.

"You'll bury us all, old friend," the Colonel said in greeting.

Alfred Tannenberg's eyes were sunken, and the pallor of his cheeks showed that death wasn't far off, but the fire in his eyes left no doubt that he would fight to the last.

"What happened?" he asked.

"Only you can tell us that," the Colonel replied.

"I don't remember anything useful. Someone came over to my bed; I thought it was the nurse. They flashed a light in my face, then I heard noises, like slaps or cracks, and I tried to sit up, and then . . . I'm not sure. I think I managed to pull off the oxygen mask. I couldn't see anything . . . It's all confused, I can't remember. . . . But I know someone was here, right next to me. They could have killed me. I want you to punish the guards. They're worthless, worse than worthless—my life isn't safe in their hands."

"Don't worry about that, I've seen to them already. They'll be sorry for the rest of their miserable lives for having allowed this to happen," the Colonel assured him.

"I hope this hasn't affected the work—Clara may still find what we're looking for," Tannenberg said.

"Picot is leaving, Grandfather."

"No. He stays here," the old man declared.

"No, we can't do that. It would . . . it would be a mistake. It's best that he go; I'll stay as long as I can, but you have to leave for a hospital. The Colonel agrees with me."

"I'm staying here with you!" Tannenberg cried.

"You should reconsider, old friend; Dr. Najeb insists that we take you out of here. I personally guarantee Clara's safety. No harm will come to her, I swear that to you, but you must leave."

Alfred Tannenberg didn't reply. He felt so tired, and he was well aware of the thin thread of life to which he clung. If they took him to Cairo, he might live awhile longer, but how much longer? He couldn't leave his granddaughter on the eve of war, because once it started, no one but he could guarantee her safety.

"We'll see; there's time yet," he told the Colonel. "Now I want to meet with Yasir and Ahmed. What happened can't affect our operation."

"Ahmed seems perfectly capable of seeing it through," said the Colonel.

"Ahmed is incapable of doing anything unless he's told exactly what to do. I'm not dead yet, nor is he my heir," Tannenberg replied.

"I'm aware of your differences, but perhaps you should be more flexible just now. You aren't well, is he, Clara?"

Clara didn't respond to the Colonel's question. Her loyalty was to her grandfather and would be to her last breath—and she didn't trust Ahmed either.

"Tell that husband of yours to come, Clara, and I want to see Ayed Sahadi and Yasir too. But first, ready me to meet them. Tell the nurse to help me get dressed."

"You can't get up!" Clara exclaimed in alarm.

"I can and I will. Do as I tell you."

The Colonel's men had not squeezed any useful information from Fatima. She could hardly speak through her sobs but managed to tell them that she had been sitting near Alfred Tannenberg's bed and had dozed off as Samira was preparing bags of intravenous solution. She thought she heard a sound outside the room but kept dozing; she figured the men outside guarding the door had dropped something.

Suddenly there was another sound, this one inside the room, and she woke up and turned toward Samira. She saw someone dressed completely in black from head to toe, with his face covered, and he was strangling the nurse. Fatima had no time to cry out, because the man sprang at her, covered her mouth, and hit her several times with something he had in his hand, until she lost consciousness. That was all she remembered.

She wasn't actually sure it was a man who had attacked her, but it must have been; he was very strong. He was wearing gloves—she knew because she had tried to bite the hand that was keeping her from screaming.

No, she didn't remember any particular odor, and the mysterious figure hadn't spoken a word. All she could recall was the sense of terror, because she was sure he was going to kill her. But Allah was great—her life had been spared, as had that of her master, Alfred Tannenberg.

41

AFTER THE ILLUMINATING DEMONSTRATIONS OF Mauthausen's capabilities, the party from Berlin enjoyed a wonderful dinner. The conversation was lively, but they all skirted the only pertinent topic: Germany was losing the war. They all behaved as though the Wehrmacht were a colossus that was still marching invincibly across the numb landscape of Europe. It was only later, when Alfred Tannenberg was alone with Georg, Heinrich, and Franz, that they voiced their concern in hushed tones, devising plans to escape when Hitler lost the war.

"I'm warning you," Georg said, "you must be prepared. I've already told Franz to ask for a transfer to general headquarters. His father's influence and mine will be enough. What he must not do, under any circumstances, is return to the front."

"Are you certain we will lose?" asked Alfred uneasily.

"Don't believe Goebbels' propaganda; we have lost already. Our soldiers have begun to desert. Hitler doesn't seem to understand what is happening, and his advisers are too frightened to tell him.

"We must be practical, we must face reality: The Allies will overrun Germany, and those of us who have been most loyal to the Führer will pay most dearly. We must prepare to escape before that happens.

"You all know my uncle and his scholarly renown. Before the war, a colleague invited him to work in one of America's secret laboratories, where they have been working on a bomb that could end the war; our scientists are at work on it too, but I fear it will not come in time. But we're lucky—the American has gotten in touch with my uncle again and offered him safe passage out of Germany. There are powerful people in his country who are willing to be generous and pardon any scientists who will work with the United States. My uncle was dubious at first, but I encouraged him to stay in touch with this American, who may be very useful in helping us escape."

"But, Georg, I don't think he can get all four of us out," Heinrich said.

"He's right. We must prepare our own plans," Alfred agreed.

"We will need new identities," Franz mused.

"I have seen to that already. Months ago I had false documents prepared for some very special friends of mine," Georg said with a smile. "One of the benefits of working in the secret service is that you meet some interesting criminal types with unexpected . . . talents. I will provide you all with new identities. But you all must be ready to flee the moment I tell you. I'd suggest that you pack your bags now."

"Neither of us will have a problem," Heinrich assured him, speaking for himself and Alfred.

"I'm currently on leave. No one will be expecting me back at the front right away. Tomorrow when we reach Berlin, I'll request the transfer." Franz nodded.

"*Sehr gut,*" said Georg. "And now, let's think about life after Germany. . . ."

Alfred Tannenberg was nervous.

They had traveled most of the night and arrived in Berlin as the sun was rising. Zieris, the camp commander, had tried to worm out of him why they were leaving in such a rush. Alfred had cut him off short; he and Heinrich were going to Berlin by order of the Reichssicherheitshauptamt, the Reich Security Headquarters.

Heinrich suggested they each stop first to see their parents briefly and to freshen up before presenting themselves at the RSHA, which Alfred thought a splendid idea. He was looking forward to giving his father a great bear hug, even listening to his mother's prattle—he was sure she would tell him how thin he'd gotten.

At eight a.m. sharp, the two officers presented themselves in Georg's office, where they also found Franz. After raising their arms in salute, the four embraced one another warmly.

"It's simply a matter of days now before the whole thing collapses," Georg told them. "The Russians have broken through. Hitler has gone mad, I think, and no one is giving orders. We must go."

"What will Himmler say?" asked Alfred.

"I have convinced Himmler that I should go to Switzerland and meet with a group of our agents there. In light of the course the war was taking, I convinced him of the need to make preparations months ago. We have people in several countries making arrangements for our arrival after the fall of the Reich."

George took three file folders from a box and handed one to each of his friends, who pored over their new identity documents.

"You, Heinrich, will go to Lisbon, and from there to Spain. We have good friends among General Franco's circle. Your name will be Enrique Gómez Thomson. Your father is Spanish, but your mother is English, which is why you don't speak the language; you've lived your entire life outside Spain. There's the number of one of my best men— Eduard Kleen, an old friend of ours from the university—who has been making arrangements for some time to take in a number of us."

Heinrich nodded without taking his eyes off the documents that would make him another man.

"How will I get to Lisbon?"

"By plane, tomorrow afternoon; let's hope the Allies don't shoot you down," Georg said with a wry smile. "Officially, you're leaving for our embassy in Lisbon; you've been made assistant to the military attaché there. But when the end of the war is announced, get out of Lisbon as soon as you can; you'll be in touch with Eduard by then, and he will have your ticket ready for Spain. First, go to Madrid; you'll receive instructions from there. Eduard has done a fine job; there is nothing that friends won't do if you put a large enough stack of bills in their hands."

"And I am going to Brazil . . . ," mused Franz as he looked over the information on his new passport.

"Yes. It was imperative to choose countries where no one will look for us, where we have friends, where the governments turn a blind eye and have no interest in finding out who we are. Brazil is a fine hiding place. Another of my favorite agents is there—a *bon vivant*—and for months he, like Eduard, has been laying the groundwork for your arrival."

"I don't speak Portuguese," Franz complained.

"You'll learn. It's a good destination, Franz; be glad you're going there. We can't all go to the same place. That would be suicide."

"Georg is right," Alfred put in. He was very pleased with the identity he'd been given. He was to be a Swiss businessman from Zurich, but his final destination was Cairo.

"What about you, Georg?" asked Franz.

"I'm leaving tomorrow, first to Switzerland with my uncle, and from there our American friends will transport us to their wonderful country. My parents left today; they'll remain in Switzerland with false identities. As for your parents, talk to them. I need to know within two hours what they want to do. I can give them false documents and send them to Switzerland, but we must do it today; I won't be here tomorrow and I can't trust anyone but myself and you three.

"Go home, talk to your families, but be quiet about it; if any of this reaches the wrong ears, we'll all be shot. I expect you back here in two hours."

"But Himmler isn't going to let you just disappear," said Franz.

"I'm not going to disappear. I'm going to review clandestine routes and safe areas chosen by our agents, logically including our friends in the United States. We have more there than you would imagine."

Alfred Tannenberg was impatiently awaiting his father's decision. The older man had fallen silent, lost in his own thoughts, ignoring the anguished pleas of his wife.

"Papa, please, I want you and Mama to leave," Alfred insisted.

"We will, son, we will, but I do not want to go far from Germany. Even if we lose the war, this is our country."

"Papa, there is no time. . . ."

"So be it—let us pack our bags."

It was not hard for Franz and Heinrich to convince their parents to cross the border into Switzerland, where they would follow the final events of the war cushioned by the safety net of their large Swiss bank accounts.

Georg's superb organizational skills were never more apparent. By the time his friends entered his office two hours later, he had signed visas in hand for every member of their families. They were to leave that very afternoon, that night at the latest.

As he handed over the papers and clapped his friends on the back, he invited them to his house for lunch, where they could talk at length in greater security.

Once they had settled themselves in the privacy of Georg's home, he opened the discussion. "Very well, now begins the second part—what we shall do once we expatriate."

"Get married," Franz said immediately.

"Married?" asked Heinrich.

"Yes, I've talked it over with Alfred; it's the smartest thing to do. Marry a woman native to your new home country, and right away. Alfred can't, of course, since he's already married to Greta, but the rest of us can, and should."

"You two can marry if you like. I've no intention of taking such a step," said Georg. His typical reaction was no surprise to his friends.

"I have a plan."

They all turned to Alfred, as ever respectful of his perverse intelligence, his ability to improvise even in the most difficult circumstances. He had displayed those qualities often.

"I've been thinking of this since we met in Mauthausen. We're going to need money, lots of it—more than we're going to be able to take out of Germany or that we already have in Switzerland. None of us really knows what will happen with the Allies. No matter who our friends are, they may hunt us down. We are, after all, officers of the SS; our names are well known—our parents have seen to that!" He laughed ruefully. "They must stay in Switzerland, for I fear that if the Americans begin to track down those responsible for . . . for what has happened here, some may feel that we, too, bear some of the responsibility. Our families included. We need to insulate ourselves with our own business—a very prosperous business."

They were all listening expectantly.

"We are going to dedicate ourselves to art and antiquities. We go back to our profession—are we not archaeologists?"

"Alfred, get to the point," Franz said impatiently. "Your coyness is becoming irritating."

"I am on my way to Cairo, Georg to the United States, you to Brazil, and Heinrich to Spain—it's perfect!" Alfred was talking more to himself than the others.

"Explain," Georg insisted.

"I still have the tablets we took from those old Jews in Haran, and the other objects we brought back. Do you remember?"

"Yes, of course," said Heinrich. "We all have our share too."

"Well, then, we shall sell antiquities, unique objects. The stuff of collectors' dreams. The Middle East is full of artifacts."

"And where are we going to find these objects?" Franz asked.

"Franz, your university studies were never your strong point," chided Alfred. "The Middle East is littered with artifacts. Ten times what is displayed in museums is still beneath the ground, just begging to be discovered."

"And how are we going to . . . discover these artifacts?"

"The governments of the Middle East are notoriously corrupt; it's all a matter of money—money to excavate, money to keep our finds. Hell, money even to buy objects already sitting in museums. There are people in the world, I assure you, willing to pay whatever we ask for certain objects. All the way from the most knowledgeable scholar to the idiot whose wife thinks a two-thousand-year-old statue might accent their living room nicely. All we have to do is dangle the bait before them.

"I will organize the business in Cairo. From there I can move through Syria, Transjordania, Iran, Palestine. . . . I will supply the goods and you three will sell them. Georg, you will handle the American market, Heinrich, the European, and Franz, the Latin American. Naturally we will need covers, but we can work all that out when the time comes."

Alfred's enthusiasm was infectious. The four men let their imaginations run wild, making plans for the future.

"An import–export business, with offices in our various cities, would be an excellent cover," mused Heinrich.

"Georg, when you get to the United States you must slowly begin to organize a cultural foundation dedicated to promoting art. The Americans have so many foundations—it will fit perfectly. An association that can, in time, finance archaeological expeditions, whose finds, of course, we keep for ourselves. It's so official-sounding, so associated with charity—it's ideal," said Alfred.

"Foundations are not corporations, Alfred," said Franz.

"And neither will ours be. At least that's what people will think. It will belong to us, appear to be one thing but actually be another. Even if we walk out of Germany with all the money in the world, we need respectability. And that's exactly what this will provide," replied Alfred.

"But it isn't easy to just set up a legitimate foundation out of thin air; foundations depend on banks, universities, and I don't know what I'm going to find in the United States," Georg objected.

"You're going to find that the Americans will pay your uncle very well; they will immediately insert him into the highest academic circles and put him to work on central projects. You will meet very important people. The rest will depend on how you comport yourself—you must be able to blend in, become a part of your environment, take advantage of the doors your uncle can open for you. No, we can't create a foundation in one year, or two; first we must integrate ourselves into the societies in which we will be living. When we no longer attract attention, once we're accepted, then we put our plan into operation. Meanwhile, I will start gathering material. As for an import–export business, I think it's a good idea; Europe is going to need everything—we've razed it, and now the reconstruction will begin. Peace will make us rich!" Alfred laughed.

"Shall we sell the Haran tablets?" Georg asked.

"No. Should I find the later tablets written by this scribe Shamas, it would revolutionize the world of archaeology. All the tablets will be priceless. I will arrange further excavations in Haran, where I hope we may at last find those tablets that bear the story of the creation as told by Abraham. What did Abraham know of the creation? Was his version the same as the Bible's? All in good time—we mustn't be in too much of a hurry. But I assure you, I won't stop until I find those tablets, and when I have them we'll decide what to do, together—whatever it is, it will make history. Ever since that day in the desert, even with all we have seen since then, my greatest dream has been to find those tablets. My God, what I would give to find them!"

"You two haven't had to listen to him. Every day, for years, this madman has talked to me about the tablets," Heinrich complained. "The man is obsessed!"

"We may be secure, but what will happen to the Führer?"

"Are you turning sentimental, Franz? What do we care? We can't be associated with a loser. He had a great idea for Germany, but he has lost the war; for us to share in that defeat would be absurd," was Georg's cold answer.

"But where is he?" Franz insisted.

"It seems he has been convinced to retreat into his bunker—I don't know exactly where, but I don't care either. I'm leaving here, just as you three are. He wouldn't protect us if we stayed. Let us save ourselves. He already has his place in history; now it's our turn."

They took their leave of one another, knowing that it would likely be years before they met again, but they each swore loyalty to the others until the end of their days. Their futures were bright. They were going to wrest from the bowels of the Middle East its most precious treasures. They didn't care who the artifacts belonged to, and they knew there would never be a shortage of unscrupulous collectors eager to acquire unique treasures beyond the reach of mere mortals.

They would sell them to the highest bidder.

42

LION DOYLE WAS WANDERING THROUGH THE CAMP, LOOK-
ing for answers. Someone had broken into Alfred
Tannenberg's room, and it wasn't him. Either the clients
who hired him had hedged their bets with a second man, or one of
Tannenberg's enemies had tried to eliminate the bastard.

The Colonel's men had questioned him, of course. They'd been totally ham-handed; Lion could tell that these men were more practiced
with torture as the fastest route to confession.

It had been laughably easy for Lion to breeze through the interrogation as a freelance photographer; he was a pretty good actor, if he did
say so himself. And he was more than accomplished at taking on different personalities, living them out as though it were the most natural
thing on earth.

He'd talked to Picot, who also had more questions than answers.
Fabian and Marta were distressed, but they obviously didn't know anything, nor did Gian Maria, who was visibly shaken by what had
happened.

The only person who seemed unaffected by the violence was the
Croatian, Ante Plaskic. After he'd been interrogated by the Colonel's
men, he'd coolly returned to his computer to finish up some work that
he hadn't been able to get to yesterday.

Lion had always suspected that Ante was not what he claimed to be—he just wasn't the type to be a computer geek, any more than Lion was a photographer. And Ayed Sahadi had revealed himself to be a soldier under the command of the Colonel, although he was still wearing civilian clothes.

So Lion decided to have a little talk with Ante, to probe for a chink in his disguise and get to the bottom of what had happened. He knew it wouldn't be easy to find that opening, though, because Ante looked every bit the professional Lion was. Still, he could give it a try.

When he went into the storeroom where the Croatian was working, Lion found the village leader's son with him. The son was the leader of one of the labor details and often reported in from the excavation site; it wasn't unusual to find him with Ante in the computer house. But what *was* strange was that they seemed to be having a heated argument, which ended the moment Lion came in.

Lion had to admire the Croatian's cool. Ante didn't miss a beat. He sighed and said, "Lion, the workers are upset. They want to know what will happen to the village when we leave. They're afraid that one of them will be blamed for the murders, and our friend here says Professor Picot won't tell them anything. So if you know anything . . ."

"None of us should do anything. I assume we'll have to stay here until this whole thing is cleared up and the murderer or murderers are caught. As for leaving—I think that decision has already been made."

Ante Plaskic turned to the young man and shrugged his shoulders but said nothing. The village leader's son spoke a few words of apology and left.

Lion stared at the computer technician, and Plaskic held his gaze. The two men measured each other for several seconds, and the tacit understanding seemed to be that if it came to a confrontation, the result would be lethal.

"What do you think happened in the house?" Lion Doyle asked, breaking the silence.

"No way to know."

"You must have an opinion."

"No. I never speculate about things unless I have all the facts."

"Ah . . . well, I guess whoever it was, he's got to be here."

"If you say so . . ."

They stared at each other again, and then Lion turned and walked out. The Croatian sat down at the computer, apparently completely absorbed in his work.

Ante was sure that Lion Doyle suspected him, but he also knew that the photographer had nothing on him. He'd been extremely cautious; no one knew about his relationship with Samira. From the day she arrived, the nurse had thrown coy glances his way and gone out of her way to bump into him. They would talk—actually, she would talk, he would listen. She was trying desperately to find a man to get her out of Iraq, and apparently she'd decided that that man was Ante Plaskic. He didn't know why, but it didn't matter—she never stopped throwing herself at him, and she made it clear it could go as far as he wanted it to.

He never touched her, of course. He didn't like Muslim women, even the blond, blue-eyed ones of his home country. So this dark-skinned, black-haired woman with a broad nose through which she seemed to snort rather than breathe left him cold.

But he couldn't afford to reject her: She was far too valuable. Samira was a direct line to everything that went on in Tannenberg's house: the state of his health, who called him, who visited him, even the rift between Clara and her husband.

This inexhaustible source of information allowed Ante to send back detailed reports to Planet Security through his intermediary, the village leader's son. He'd been recruited by Yasir, the Egyptian who'd been Alfred Tannenberg's right-hand man before the two had come to hate each other. It was a perfectly unobstructed flow of information: Yasir would send Ante's reports on by further intermediaries whom he'd also hired, and they, in turn, would convey instructions to him from Planet Security.

Yasir had come into the camp with Ahmed Husseini and had insisted on an accurate report on Tannenberg's health. Neither Yasir nor Ahmed had yet been able to confirm their suspicions that the old man was dying. Dr. Najeb adamantly refused to speak to them about Tannenberg's condition.

So Plaskic had asked Samira to see him, much to her delight. That night, when the camp was asleep, she'd let him into the house.

She had told him that if he could slip through the shadows and get around the guards, they could be together. She detailed the routines of the ten men who surrounded the house, five in front and five in back—not long after midnight they got together for an unauthorized cigarette and coffee break. He need only bide his time until then and slip to the back of the house, where there was a little window that opened into a storeroom; she'd leave it open a crack. Once he got in, he could wait until she came to him.

Ante agreed to the plan, although he had no intention of waiting in the storeroom—he was going straight for the old man.

To a point, it had all gone according to plan. After Picot finished his meeting with the inner circle of the excavation team, Ante waited for the camp to go dark and silence to fall. It was midnight when he got out of his cot and crept to the back of Tannenberg's house, where he waited half an hour in the darkness before one of the guards at the front came to get the others for coffee. They didn't entirely abandon their posts but stayed at the side of the house, maintaining sightlines from which they thought they could catch anyone who tried to approach the back or front of the house.

They were wrong. Plaskic managed to get in with no problem at all. Two men were dozing in chairs at each side of Tannenberg's bedroom door. Both of them had a bullet in the brain before they could open their eyes. The silencer had done its job: The only sound was that of the bodies slumping to the floor and one of the folding chairs tipping over.

Then he pushed the door open. Samira was right. The old servant woman was asleep and never even realized that anybody was in the room.

Samira took one look at the ski mask he was wearing and the pistol in his hand and went crazy. She thought he was going to kill Tannenberg, and she tried to stop him from getting any closer. Plaskic put his hand over her mouth and told her to keep quiet and not to scream, but she wouldn't listen. He throttled her, but it had been her own fault, he told himself, for being so stupid. If she had just shut up, she'd still be alive.

The old servant had also decided to become a problem. She jumped up and started to yell, so he smothered her before smacking her a couple of times with the pistol butt. He thought he'd killed her—God knows she'd bled like a stuck pig. But she'd survived somehow. He'd rather she was dead, but it didn't bother him either way. With the mask and the darkness of the room, there was no way she could identify him.

As instructed, Plaskic had reported in detail on what he'd seen in Tannenberg's room. But this time he didn't write it down; he'd just informed the village leader's son of the old man's condition: hooked up to a monitor with a blood transfusion going in one arm and some kind of clear liquid transfusion in the other.

The village leader's son had asked Ante straight out if he was the one who killed the nurse and the two guards, but Plaskic hadn't answered, sparking a heated argument. The young man told him the Colonel would probably wind up detaining and even killing every Iraqi in the village—but he also knew well what consequences he himself would surely suffer if he betrayed the Croatian. The full implications of the dangerous game he had gotten himself involved in were written all over his face, and he was becoming increasingly agitated. That was when Lion Doyle had walked in on them.

The next day, the Colonel was in a fouler mood than usual. Ahmed Husseini was listening to him patiently, desperately trying not to enrage him further. Yasir sat in silence.

"I'm not leaving here until we find out who did this. He's here, among us, laughing at us. But I'll catch him, and when I do, he'll pray for a quick death."

Aliya, the new nurse, entered the living room. Clara had sent her to report that her grandfather was ready to see them.

They found Alfred sitting in a chair, a blanket covering his knees, no transfusion bag in sight. He was all bones, and his face was ghastly pale.

Beside him sat Clara, smiling slightly. She'd convinced Dr. Najeb to do everything in his power to allow her grandfather to meet with the Colonel in a chair rather than in bed.

Tannenberg knew he had precious little time. He skipped the niceties and got straight to the point.

"My friend," he said, addressing the Colonel, "I must ask you a very special favor. I know it won't be easy and that only a man of your caliber can undertake such a task."

Ahmed Husseini looked at Tannenberg, intrigued, while at the same time taking in the self-assurance that Clara had regained, as though the old man really were going to live forever.

"Ask me anything; you know that you can always count on me," the Colonel assured him.

"Professor Picot and his team wish to leave. I understand that; given the circumstances, we can hardly keep them here. Clara will stay behind for a few more days and then join them later to prepare a grand exhibit of the objects and structures they have found here in Safran. It will be an important exhibition, traveling through several European cities. They will even try to take it to the United States, which I'm sure our friend George will facilitate through the Mundo Antiguo Foundation."

"And what is the favor?" the Colonel asked.

"I want you to secure the permissions Picot will need to remove from Iraq all the things they have found. I know it won't be easy to convince our beloved Saddam, but you can do it. What is urgent is that you requisition helicopters and trucks so that Picot and his people can leave Iraq as soon as possible with their precious cargo."

"And how does that benefit us?" the Colonel asked bluntly.

"It will benefit you, insofar as you will find a half-million dollars in your Swiss account if you do this with the same efficiency you have shown on other occasions."

"Will you speak with the palace?" the Colonel wanted to know.

"I already have. Our leader's sons are informed of the matter and are anxiously awaiting our messenger."

"Then if Baghdad has agreed, I will call my nephew Karim and tell him to set the operation in motion."

"Clara should leave as soon as possible," said Ahmed.

"Clara will leave when she sees fit, just as I will. For the moment she will continue the excavation. I want the work to start again tomorrow; we will not abandon the project because of a dead nurse and a few worthless guards," replied Tannenberg angrily.

"There are pieces that have been found that . . . Well, it's delicate to include them in an exhibition," said Ahmed.

"You've already sold them?" asked Tannenberg, surprising both Ahmed and Yasir. In fact, Yasir could only stare at the floor.

"You always mistrust those around you," Ahmed protested.

"I know those around me. So I think it is quite likely that Robert Brown, the president of the Mundo Antiguo Foundation, has been instructed by George to contact our best clients and announce that there have been important findings in Safran. And that those clients, always eager to add novelties to their collections, have already deposited large sums as an advance against receipt. Am I wrong, Yasir?"

Tannenberg's direct question confounded Yasir, who found that he was suddenly covered in sweat, his white linen shirt sopping wet. He looked over at Ahmed, pleading wordlessly for help, terrified of how Tannenberg would react.

It was the Colonel, concerned about the way the conversation was going, who spoke.

"So there is a conflict of interest with your friends in Washington—"

Tannenberg cut him off. He lied, knowing that the Colonel would not want to be a part of an internecine war of this sort.

"No, there is no conflict of interest. If they've decided in Washington to sell some of the pieces we've found, that's fine with me—that's our business, after all. But one thing has nothing to do with the other. The pieces will leave here first to be shown to the world in the traveling exhibition. They will simply not return to Iraq after being delivered to their buyers. The buyers will have to wait a few months, perhaps as long as a year, before they receive them. That won't be anything new for them; they're accustomed to waiting. They will eventually have what they purchased."

"That's why I enjoy doing business with you, old friend. You have a solution for every problem," the Colonel said, clearly reassured.

"What have you found out about the killings?" Tannenberg inquired.

"Nothing, and that worries me. The killer must be a professional; he must also have a good cover, and a better background. But what is most important is that you are alive, my friend," the Colonel declared.

"I'm alive only because he didn't want to kill me. He never intended to kill me."

The Colonel had no response. The old man was right; if the intruder had wanted to kill him, he'd had a golden opportunity. But, then, what was he looking for in his room?

"We will find the man, Alfred; it's just a matter of time. That is why I'd like to detain Picot here a few more days; it may be one of the people in his group."

"Do it, but see that the clock doesn't run out on us."

"Understood."

"I want Picot out of here by mid-March at the latest," Tannenberg ordered.

"And when will you and Clara be leaving?"

"I'll make the arrangements for that personally, but we will not be here when the war comes, I assure you," the old man declared.

The Colonel bade his friend good-bye and left him with Ahmed and Yasir. Clara also left after giving her grandfather a kiss.

"So you have already betrayed me," Tannenberg said as soon as the door closed behind them.

Yasir and Ahmed squirmed in their seats.

"No one has betrayed you," Ahmed managed to say.

"No? Then how is it that you have already sold pieces from Safran without my knowledge? Shouldn't I have been informed? Do my friends think me so weak that they dare try to deprive me of what's mine?"

"Please, Alfred!" Yasir protested. "No one wants to do that!"

"Yasir, you are a traitor; truly you dream of the day you will see me dead. Your hatred has blinded your intelligence."

Yasir lowered his head and looked out of the corner of his eye at Ahmed, who appeared as nervous as he was.

"We were going to tell you; that is why we came here. George wanted you to know that he had buyers for some of the pieces."

"Oh, really? And why didn't you tell me the other night? When were you planning to give me this surprise?"

"We hardly saw you, and it didn't seem like the right moment . . . ," Ahmed protested.

"You have no guts, Ahmed; you're just an employee, a follower, like Yasir, and you shall remain one for the rest of your days. Men like you don't give orders, you just obey them."

Ahmed Husseini flushed. He fought back an urge, not for the first time, to slap the old man.

"All right," Alfred continued. "I'll take this up with George. No doubt he will explain it all to me."

"That is madness!" Yasir cried. "The spy satellites are monitoring every call, and you know it. If you call George, it'll be like putting it on the front page of the *New York Times!*"

"It's George who's broken the rules, not me. Fortunately, you're both idiots, and you've told me what I need to know about my friends and their plans. Now get out; I have work to do."

The two men left, certain that Alfred Tannenberg would not let the matter rest there, and that the consequences would not be pleasant.

Alfred ordered Aliya to have the guards fetch Ayed Sahadi. Among his other talents, Sahadi was one of the Colonel's best assassins.

Ayed was surprised to find Alfred sitting in a chair, as filled with enmity as ever. And he was even more surprised to hear what Alfred wanted him to do. He weighed the problems of the mission the old man was asking him to carry out. Tannenberg had been paying him very well for such work for years. And the money he'd be paid for this job dispelled all his misgivings.

It was not easy for Clara to convince Picot and Fabian to continue the excavation. But with Marta's help, for which Clara was grateful, she was able to persuade the two men that they had nothing to lose. Gian Maria needed no urging; he was going to stay until the end, as long as Clara remained in Safran.

Picot called the team together to announce they were to continue packing up equipment, so they'd be ready the minute they were told they could leave Safran. But he surprised the group by also informing them that they'd be working right down to the wire. They were going to keep digging, trying to unearth whatever further secrets they could wrest from the saffron-colored earth.

There were murmurs of protest, but Picot silenced them immediately, trying, at the same time, to stir up enough morale for the work ahead and the subsequent exhibit.

Clara returned to her grandfather. Aliya had put him to bed and Dr. Najeb had hooked him up to the monitor again.

Salam Najeb sat down with Clara and spoke as directly as he knew how: He didn't think Alfred Tannenberg could last a week.

Clara almost broke down and wept. She was exhausted and feeling overwhelmed by a growing sense of loneliness and isolation. Even Fatima was no longer there to lean on; she was in a hospital bed, more dead than alive. For her grandfather's sake, she called once again upon reserves of fortitude she'd hardly known she had.

After dinner together, the village leader continued to ply Yasir and Ahmed with sweets in keeping with the laws of hospitality. The two men finally refused any more, but they sat and chatted politely for a while longer, so as not to offend their host by a premature departure. The son offered to walk with them back to the camp, a few hundred yards away.

They walked along together, slowly and in silence, savoring the fine cigars their host had bestowed upon them. They were only about a third of the way to the camp when three men emerged from the shadows by the side of the path, two on one side and one on the other. Before Ahmed could register what was happening, Yasir shrieked and dropped to the ground. The archaeologist had time only to glimpse the knife handle protruding from Yasir's belly before their assailants grabbed up the Egyptian's body and dragged it with them back into the darkness. Ahmed stared at the village leader's son, who made no effort to conceal the blood covering his hands. Then the archaeologist doubled over and vomited. The young villager wiped the blood off his hands with a handkerchief while he waited for Ahmed to compose himself.

"Why?" Ahmed asked when he had recovered.

"Mr. Tannenberg does not forgive betrayal. He wants you to know that."

"When is he going to kill me?" Ahmed asked angrily.

"I do not know," the leader's son replied simply.

Ahmed was aware of the double game the young man had been playing with Yasir, but he was clearly not prepared to resist Alfred's undeniable power at this critical juncture—and at such close range.

"Get away from me." Ahmed stumbled on toward the camp,

intending to leave behind the young man who had killed Yasir without a moment's hesitation or a trace of emotion, but the killer kept pace with him long enough to deliver a parting message:

"I have been instructed to tell you that Mr. Tannenberg will be watching you. If you betray him, even if he is not with us anymore, someone will kill you exactly as I killed Yasir."

Ayed Sahadi approached the caravan. The camels had not yet been loaded with goods, and they were resting. A tall man greeted him with a warm hug.

"May Allah protect you."

"And you," Sahadi responded.

"Come have a cup of tea with us," the man said.

"I can't, I have to get back. But I want you to do me a favor."

"We are friends. You can ask me anything."

"I know, and I thank you. Here," he said, giving him a small package and an envelope. "Make sure this gets to Kuwait as soon as possible. To the address on the envelope, and may Allah be with you."

The man pocketed the sheaf of bills that Ayed gave him. There was no need to count them; he knew that the amount would be, as it had always been, satisfactory. Alfred Tannenberg paid well.

The silence of the dawn was shattered by a scream that awakened the whole camp.

Picot ran out of his house, followed closely by Fabian, and then they froze. Like them, others had jumped out of bed to see what was happening, and they, too, stood speechless.

There, in the middle of the camp, tied to a post, was the body of a man. He had been tortured. His arms and legs and face were bruised and battered, there were deep cuts and bloody wounds on his body, and his hands and feet were missing. Most horribly, his eyes had been pulled out and his ears cut off.

Some of those who'd rushed outdoors couldn't bear to look at the mutilated body and vomited; others just stood there, not knowing what to do, relieved to see the soldiers run up and take charge.

"That's it. We're finished! They're going to kill us all!" Picot shouted furiously as he spun around and stormed back into the house he shared with Fabian.

Marta came into the house, flopped down in a chair, lit a cigarette, and didn't say a word.

"Marta, are you all right?" Fabian asked her.

"Far from it. I've had it. I don't know what's going on here, but this place is turning into a graveyard. I . . . I think we need to get out of here, today if possible."

"Take it easy." Fabian tried to soothe her. "We all have to calm down before we start making decisions. And we need to talk to Clara and Ahmed as soon as we can. They have an obligation to tell us whatever they know."

"That man . . . that man out there is the one who came in with Ahmed," said Marta.

"Yes, the Egyptian, Yasir. Ahmed said he worked for Mr. Tannenberg," Fabian agreed.

"Who could do such a thing?" Marta asked him, her eyes filled with terror.

"I want to see your grandfather."

Ahmed's tone of voice was that of a defeated, frightened man. Clara was shocked by his condition: his clothes and hair rumpled, his eyes bloodshot—*From crying?* Clara wondered—his hands trembling.

"What's wrong?"

"Don't tell me you've missed the spectacle your grandfather mounted. Was it necessary to profane his body? He's a monster . . . that man is a monster—"

"I . . . I don't know what you're talking about," Clara stammered.

"Yasir—he's killed Yasir and mutilated his body and exhibited him out there in the middle of the camp for all to see, so none of us will forget who is in charge, the lord of us all. . . ."

Ahmed was now weeping in earnest, oblivious to the contempt of the guards.

Clara fought back panic. "He won't see you; he's resting."

"I have to see him, I want to know when I'm to die!" Ahmed shouted.

"Not another word! I won't have you spouting this garbage. Get out of here. In fact, I want you back in Baghdad today, where you will follow the instructions my grandfather gave you, to the letter. Now move."

The Colonel's arrival in the midst of their exchange disconcerted Clara, although she refused to wilt under the man's icy glare. "I wish to see Mr. Tannenberg," he told her.

"I don't know whether he's up yet. Wait here."

Clara left him with Ahmed in the living room and went into her grandfather's room. Aliya had just shaved him and Dr. Najeb was about to remove a needle from his arm, leaving him without either plasma or saline solution.

"I told you he shouldn't exert himself," the doctor said to Clara by way of greeting.

"And I told you to keep your mouth shut," said Alfred. "Leave us. I told you I need to be strong today."

"But you're not ready, and I can no longer take responsibility for what you're asking me to do—"

"Leave me alone with my granddaughter," Tannenberg commanded.

Dr. Najeb and Aliya left the room without another word.

"What's wrong, Clara?"

"The Colonel wants to see you. It looks serious. Ahmed came in too. He says that Yasir's body is out in the middle of the camp . . . that you had him killed and mutilated. . . ."

"That's right. Does that surprise you? Betraying me has fatal consequences. That was a reminder to both the men here and my friends in Washington."

"But . . . but what did Yasir do?"

"He conspired against me, spied on me for my friends, did business behind my back."

"How do you know that?"

"How do I know? Really, Clara. Now tell the Colonel to come in and that son of a bitch of a husband of yours to leave—he has his instructions."

"Are you going to kill him?"

"I might; it all depends on what happens in the next few days."

Clara hesitated a moment. "Please, Grandfather, please, don't kill him."

"Clara, not even for you would I fail to do something that I think is necessary to keep my affairs running properly. If I hesitate, if I don't show the others what I can do, then they'll do it to us first. Those are the rules. Not even I am exempt from them. Yasir's death has demonstrated to George, Enrique, and Frankie that I'm alive and well; it's also underscored that to my partners here, including the Colonel. They've all understood the message. Now go and do as I tell you."

"What am I going to say? To Picot, to Marta—they're going to demand answers," asked Clara.

"Don't say anything. They're not in a position to demand anything. Tell them to keep working, keep excavating, trying to find the Bible of Clay before they leave. Or I may have to prevent them from going."

Two hours later, the camp had returned to a strained, false calm. After a heated encounter with Picot, who demanded answers, Clara had gone out to the site to excavate with Gian Maria and a contingent of laborers.

Neither Picot nor anyone else on his team would go with her to the temple, and they couldn't understand how she could just go on with her routine after what had happened. She ignored their reproaches. Otherwise, she'd collapse altogether.

She was preparing to descend to the new chamber they'd found when she heard helicopters taking off in the distance. Ahmed was leaving, and that calmed her. She no longer loved him, but she couldn't have borne it if her grandfather had had him killed; that would have broken down the last of her shaky defenses. She much preferred him gone.

She persuaded Gian Maria to remain above while she went down and explored first. Tied in a sling to the rope that dangled from the pulleys above, she slid down into the blackness until her feet hit the ground. It smelled musty, almost putrid, forcing her to fight off a moment's nausea. She was determined to explore the room the others had discovered, the door Fabian and Picot thought might lead into other spaces in the temple.

She untied the lanterns she'd lashed around her waist, turned them on, and set them out in the most strategic areas. Then she started to feel around the walls and the floor, tapping them for indications of hollow spaces on the other side.

She lost all sense of time, although she periodically tugged at the rope so that the workers up on top would know she was all right. But she didn't give the signal for Gian Maria to join her. She'd made it clear that he was to come down only if she called for him.

She wasn't sure how it happened, but as she tapped at some rock with the handle of a spatula, a whole wall came down, covering her in dust and rubble. When she opened her eyes, she stood frozen, terrified, feeling the loose rubble shifting around her feet. The seconds seemed an eternity; she didn't dare even look down, and she stood so still that she felt nailed to the floor. Suddenly, a light flashed in her face and firm footsteps came toward her.

"Clara, are you all right?"

In the semidarkness she made out the face of Gian Maria; she realized that she'd never in her life been so happy to see another human being. Then the light he was holding shone beyond where she had been working.

"Clara, let's get out of here. It's not stable."

"Gian Maria, look. It's another room! Help me, we've got to look at this. Call some of the workers to help us clear this rubble. We need to get some light down here."

Lion Doyle read the fax from the director of Photomundi, clearly relayed straight from his boss, Tom Martin, president of Global Group:

> We haven't heard from you in quite a while, and our clients are getting impatient. What's happening with the report you promised? If you can't complete it, assignment will end; the media will not continue to pay for random photos. I want news, or else return immediately.

Tom Martin was pressuring Lion because the clients were pressuring him. Those who wanted Alfred Tannenberg dead weren't willing to wait any longer, and Martin was telling Lion that if he didn't kill the old man soon he'd cancel the contract and demand the return of the advance.

Lion made his way to the storeroom that doubled as an office, where he found Fabian giving instructions to Ante Plaskic about making backups and packing up the computer equipment.

"I need to send a fax," Lion told them.

"No problem," Ante said. "Leave it in that tray."

Lion's reply to his "boss" at Photomundi was short and to the point: *You'll have the report this week.*

43

TOM MARTIN READ DOYLE'S BRIEF MESSAGE—BY WAY OF the Photomundi director—and tore up the paper. He'd call Burton right away; the man's patience was wearing thin, as he'd made clear to Tom in no uncertain terms when he'd phoned a couple of days ago. He'd paid a very large advance, he reminded Tom, and he wanted to see results. If the man Tom had sent to Iraq had already located Tannenberg and his granddaughter, if he'd already infiltrated and made contact with them, why weren't they dead?

The president of Global Group had explained that if his man hadn't carried the mission off yet, it must be nearly impossible and he was waiting for his moment. Tom asked Mr. Burton to be patient, but patience was the one quality the gentleman refused to exhibit.

"Do you have news for me, Mr. Martin?" Burton asked as soon as Tom reached him via the British cell number he had provided.

"I've been assured that the contract will be fulfilled this week."

"Do I have your guarantee on that?"

"I'm telling you what my man has told me."

"When will we know that our instructions have been carried out?"

"I said this week I hope to have further news for you—good news."

"I want proof; news is not enough. It's stipulated in our contract."

"I fulfill my contracts, Mr. Burton. I'll be in touch."

"I'll be waiting."

Hans Hausser looked down again at the book he'd been reading before Tom Martin's phone call interrupted him.

It was late, past seven, but he had to call the others. They were impatient to know what was happening in that godforsaken village where the monster seemed to have taken up residence with his granddaughter.

He got up, took his raincoat off the hook in the foyer, and opened the door, trying not to rouse his daughter, Berta, who was feeding her children in the kitchen. But Berta had sharp hearing, and she came out to the hall.

"Papa, where are you going?"

"I need to stretch my legs."

"But it's so late, and it's raining."

"Berta, please! Stop treating me like one of your children! I've been cooped up all day and I feel like taking a walk. I'll be back soon."

He closed the door without giving her time to respond. He knew he was upsetting her, but he couldn't help it; it wouldn't be fair to his friends if he made them wait to hear what he'd learned.

He walked for a long while, until he found a public telephone well away from his home.

Carlo Cipriani was still at the clinic, assisting at the operation of a friend of his whose kidney Antonino was removing. Maria, his secretary, assured Hans that Dr. Cipriani would call him the minute he returned to his office.

The next number he dialed was Bruno Müller's cell phone, which Bruno had been keeping within arm's reach for days.

"Bruno . . . I have news: I've been assured that the job will be done this week."

"Are you sure?"

"That's what they told me, and I hope they keep their word."

"We've waited so many years for this; I guess we can wait another week."

"Yes, although I have to say I'm more impatient than ever. I just hope it'll be over soon."

Bruno Müller sat for a second or two in silence. He was enduring the same heavy weight in his chest that he knew his friend was feeling. They shared the same burning desire to know that Tannenberg was dead at last. That day, as Hans said, that glorious day they would live, they would live differently than they had ever lived before.

"Have you talked to Carlo and Mercedes?"

"Carlo was in the operating room. I'm going to call Mercedes now. I always dread how frantic she is."

"When you talk to Carlo, don't ask him about his son. He still hasn't had any news from him; he's going crazy."

"I think Antonino is with him in the operating room right now."

"No. His other son. The other day when we talked, Carlo told me he hadn't written or called, and that all they could tell him was that he was all right, but they didn't know where he was. Only that he was going through a profound personal crisis. Carlo feels that he's to blame, but he wouldn't say why—he just says he's to blame for it all."

"And your friend at Security Investigations—he can't do anything to help him?"

"I'm afraid the kid said that if his father tried to get in touch with him, he'd never see him again."

"Children can be such a joy."

"What would we be without them, though?"

"I know, my friend, I know. Well, I'm going to call Mercedes, and as soon as I hear anything further I'll let you all know."

After he gave Mercedes the news and reassured her that he'd call as soon as he knew more, Hans hung up the phone and walked in the rain until, soaked through, he decided to hail a taxi and go back home. He was freezing, and he had a cough. Berta would never forgive him—or let him out of the house again—if he'd caught a cold.

The doorbell rang incessantly, and finally, after what seemed an eternity, Robert Brown answered. Paul Dukais was standing there impatiently, and impatience was not something that usually characterized the president of Planet Security.

"Is everyone here?" Dukais asked Brown.

"Ralph's in the study, and I called George to tell him you had news. I told him I'd call back as soon as you tell me what's so urgent."

Dukais went into Brown's luxurious den, where Ralph Barry was sitting with a glass of whiskey. Paul had insisted he be here for this too, since as one of the directors of the Mundo Antiguo Foundation he was part of the operation.

Dukais fixed himself a whiskey and looked at the two men, imagining their reaction to Alfred's latest missive.

"Alfred Tannenberg has had Yasir killed. But that wasn't enough—he had his hands, feet, and ears cut off and his eyes pulled out, and he put it all in a box and sent it to us. I also have a letter from Alfred to George and his associates. And I've talked to one of my men in Cairo, who spoke to Ahmed. This has all pretty much finished *him*—you'll see why. . . ."

As he finished speaking and his two companions watched in horrified silence, Paul Dukais opened a metal box he had brought with him. He took out another box nestled inside and flipped it open. A pair of eyes that were beginning to dry and shrivel stared up at them, perched on top of a bloody mass of flesh and bones.

Brown shot to his feet. His face had lost all color and was distorted by revulsion, his mouth open, his eyes bulging. Barry, too, was in a state of shock, and both men remained speechless. Neither of them seemed able to speak a word. Suddenly, Barry bolted from the room, covering his mouth.

"Close that up!" Brown screamed. "Jesus Christ! He's a fucking lunatic!"

Dukais didn't say anything as he returned the grisly gift to its container, but he was struck by the thought that Brown was no less a monster than Tannenberg; he took part in the same business of stealing and murder, except he did it at a distance, to keep the blood from spattering his nice white shirt. The difference between him and the men he hired to kill people was that hired killers put their lives on the line; Robert Brown sat in a leather-lined den and drank twenty-year-old whiskey from a crystal old-fashioned glass, wielding his telephone as a weapon.

His face pale, Ralph Barry came back, wiping his mouth.

"You son of a bitch!" he said angrily to Dukais.

"You think *I* liked seeing that?" said Dukais, jerking his thumb at the box containing the carnage, which he'd put on a table near the sofa. "I wasn't going to be the only one, you can be damned sure of that. You two get to see *all* the reports." He laughed humorlessly.

Then he got up and poured himself another drink. "Whiskey'll take that bad taste out of your mouth."

"What did Ahmed have to say?" Brown asked.

"Ahmed and my people in Safran seem to agree that Alfred is dying. Last week they were giving him only days, but they were clearly wrong. Alfred's just demonstrated that to us very convincingly. We still have to go through him for everything—that's what this box says. My man in Cairo says the only thing Ahmed wants now is out. Which doesn't mean he won't hold up his end. We've made it clear to him that nobody gets out of this until it's over. So now all we have to do is wait. It won't be long until this damned war starts."

"And what about Clara Tannenberg?" Ralph Barry asked.

"According to her husband, she's turned into a she-devil. I guess she takes after her grandfather."

"Have they found the tablets?"

"No, Ralph, they haven't. But from what Ahmed says, Clara still wants to move a few more tons of dirt. Oh, and he also reported that Picot has talked Clara and Alfred into letting him take everything they've found out of Iraq, for some sort of traveling show they're putting together. They're going to tour seven or eight European cities with it, possibly even here, so sooner or later they'll be calling you. You're a friend of Picot's, right?"

Ralph Barry took a long drink of his whiskey before he answered Dukais.

"We're acquaintances. In academia, everybody at a certain level knows everybody else."

"So the Safran pieces won't be arriving with the rest of the stuff," Robert Brown murmured.

"No, that's one of Clara and Alfred's little surprises. Apparently Alfred isn't opposed to selling some of the pieces, but not until his granddaughter has sashayed all over the world with them."

"He's crazy," Robert Brown said contemptuously.

"Crazy like a fox," Paul Dukais said, grinning wryly. Then the president of Planet Security opened his briefcase and took out three manila folders, which he handed to Robert Brown.

"These are the reports, with a detailed chronology of everything that's happened in the last few days in Safran, including the death of a nurse and two guards."

"What's happened?" asked an increasingly agitated Barry. "Why haven't you told us about this?"

"I'm telling you now. Yasir was our main conduit—I had to set up new lines of communication with my people inside. Everything is in the report. You wanted to know Alfred's condition, but nobody ever sees him, especially since he stays in the equivalent of a bunker in Safran. But my man managed to get into his room. Apparently there was some difficulty and he had to take out the nurse and the guards. He also left Tannenberg's old servant woman badly injured. But he did see Alfred, and he was hooked up to all kinds of machinery and wearing an oxygen mask, so he figures he's in worse shape than anybody has let on. But Alfred seems to have come around, hasn't he?"

The men were exhausted. Clara had hardly let them sleep. Over the last week they had moved tons of earth as they cleared the rubble out of the lower level of the temple.

Yves Picot let her do it her way; his team had helped her as much as they could in the midst of packing up their equipment and anxiously awaiting permission and transportation for their departure.

Fabian and Marta were impressed by the iron will that Clara displayed. She was hardly sleeping and took only five or ten minutes to eat. The only time she ever left the excavation site was to check on her grandfather and Fatima—with Gian Maria in tow—but she never spent more than a few minutes with them before returning to the dig, even though she felt guilty about it. She knew these were the last days of her grandfather's life. Alfred Tannenberg was nothing but skin and bones now, and it was only his enormous strength of will that kept him breathing.

Fatima was beginning to walk again. She'd asked Dr. Najeb to let her stay in Tannenberg's house, so she could be near him.

"Mrs. Husseini."

Clara went on clearing away the dirt from what appeared to be a capital. She paid no attention to anyone who addressed her by her husband's name; she hoped people would start to realize that and stop doing it. But the voice insisted.

"Mrs. Husseini . . ."

She turned, irritated. A boy no more than ten years old was looking at her expectantly.

"Yes?"

"Dr. Najeb sent me for you."

"What's happened?" Clara asked in alarm.

"I don't know, they just told me to come get you."

Clara leapt up and followed the little boy, who ran back toward the camp. Gian Maria followed along behind them. Clara feared the worst.

As they reached the camp, both winded, the boy pointed toward the hospital tent. "They're in there," he told her.

Dr. Najeb and Aliya were trying to revive Alfred Tannenberg. They'd taken him to the hospital tent after he suffered a stroke.

Clara stopped and took in the scene. Neither the doctor nor the nurse came over to her or spoke. Dr. Najeb only looked over at her; the expression on his face said it was hopeless.

Finally the doctor came over and took her arm, leading her outside.

"I don't think he can pull through this."

"How long does he have?"

"I don't know, Clara—maybe several hours, maybe a day, but he can't recover."

At that, Clara burst into tears. The battle against the clock had taken her last reserves. Worse, she'd come to think she couldn't live without her grandfather. She needed to know that he was alive in order to go on.

"Are you sure?" she said, her voice breaking.

"It's a miracle he's lasted even this long. You know that. He's had a cerebral hemorrhage. I don't think he'll regain consciousness, but if he does, he almost certainly won't be able to talk or move. He may not even recognize you. His situation is critical. I'm sorry."

"Can't we get him out of here? To Cairo?" she asked, seeking some ray of hope.

"I suggested that time and time again, but neither of you would hear of it. Now it's too late. If we move him, he'll never survive the trip."

"What can we do?"

"Do? Nothing. We've already done all that can be done. Now we just have to wait and see what happens. Aliya and I will stay with him, and if I were you I'd stay close by. As I say, he could die at any moment."

Ayed Sahadi stood just a few feet from Clara and Dr. Najeb, straining not to miss a word of the conversation. Gian Maria was next to him, ready to help Clara in any way he could.

Clara stood up straight, pulled back her shoulders, and wiped away her tears with the back of her hand, leaving a streak of sand across each cheekbone. She could not show weakness at a time like this. Her grandfather had warned her—men moved only to the sound of the drum and the whip.

"Ayed, double the guard around the hospital. My grandfather has had a setback, but he'll come through it. Dr. Najeb is seeing to that," she said, looking fixedly at Salam Najeb, daring him to contradict her.

"Yes, madam," the foreman murmured.

"And no one stops working, do you hear?"

"I'll stay with you here for a while," said Ayed.

"You'll do as I say. Go to the site to ensure the men keep up their pace."

"Mr. Tannenberg instructed me to stay with you," Ayed said stubbornly. He thought for a moment she was going to hit him—her eyes blazed in anger.

Then, in a very soft voice, she repeated her order: "Ayed, when you're certain that everything is under control and all the men are working, you can come back. Do you understand me?"

"Yes, madam."

"That's better."

Clara whirled around and strode purposefully back toward the hospital tent, followed by Gian Maria, who put his hand on her shoulder.

"Clara, I don't know whether your grandfather was a Christian, but if you like . . . if you like . . . I could administer the last rites to help him in his journey."

"Last rites?"

"Yes, the last sacrament. Help him to die as a Christian, even though his life has not been a Christian one. God is merciful."

"I'm not sure my grandfather would consent to that if . . . if he were conscious."

"I just want to help him, help you. It's my obligation. I'm a priest; I can't see a man who was born a Christian die without offering him the Church's last comfort."

"My grandfather didn't believe in anything. I don't either. God has never been a part of our lives; he just wasn't there, we had no need for him."

"Don't let him die without the last rites," insisted Gian Maria.

"I'm sorry, Gian Maria, I can't let you do that—he never told me to call a priest for him. If I let you perform the last rites over him, it would be . . . a sacrilege."

"What are you saying?" the priest protested.

"I'm saying my grandfather will die as he lived. If your God exists and is merciful, as you say he is, then it won't matter to him whether my grandfather had the last rites or not."

She turned on her heel and went into the tent. She wasn't going to subject her grandfather to any ceremony without his permission. The truth was, she had no idea what the last rites consisted of. She wasn't Catholic, or Christian at all—or Muslim either. God had had no place in either the Yellow House or their home in Cairo. Her grandfather and father had never talked to her about God. For them, religion was a thing for fanatics and the ignorant masses.

Gian Maria just stood there, not knowing what to do. He decided to stay close by; he would pray to God to enlighten Clara and show her the way.

March had come in like the proverbial lion; the days were longer and the stifling heat rose with the added hours of light. The call from Ahmed Husseini, when it came at last, was a godsend.

Picot was smiling broadly after their conversation. The government had granted the team official permission to remove the artifacts from Iraq. But only for an exhibition, Ahmed had added, and one for which Picot and Clara would be co-directors. Furthermore, Picot was to sign a document confirming his responsibility for every piece and, naturally, guaranteeing the return of everything to the Iraqi people.

If they were ready—and Picot had assured him that they would be—the helicopters would pick them up in one week, at dawn on Thursday. They would be taken to Baghdad and from there to the Jordanian border. In ten days at most, they'd be home again.

Clara greeted the news with indifference. Her only concern was her grandfather, and she couldn't have cared less what they'd decided in Baghdad, although sometimes she told herself that she needed silence. She yearned to be alone in the saffron-colored land of their excavation, without Picot and Marta and Fabian and their colleagues. She longed for the solitude that one can find only among one's own people.

Miraculously, Alfred seemed to have survived the cerebral hemorrhage, although Dr. Najeb told her that the improvement was probably deceptive and only temporary.

Her grandfather still could not talk, and he could hardly move. Sometimes he seemed to recognize Clara, but other times his eyes seemed to stare vacantly into space, blind to those around him.

"The master needs to get out of this hospital," Fatima kept saying after her own drawn-out convalescence; she was convinced that Tannenberg would be safer under her care than in the hospital tent, but Dr. Najeb stood his ground.

What pained Clara most was not being able to find her grandfather in those distant lands he seemed to be inhabiting now. Still, she almost never stirred from his side; she didn't dare go out to the excavation site, although Marta informed her of their progress daily.

One afternoon as she sat there holding his hands between her own, the old man began to babble—German, she thought, but she couldn't understand a word of it.

Tannenberg seemed agitated, and he tried to move; anger filled his eyes the few times he found the strength to open them. Dr. Najeb had no explanation for what was happening, and Clara refused to let him administer a sedative; she was convinced that her grandfather was still capable of fully recovering his speech. She was surprised to see him look with interest at his surroundings; he appeared for the first time to actually take it all in. Then she laughed when she saw him smile weakly.

"Grandfather," she whispered. "Can you hear me? Do you know who I am? Grandfather, please, speak to me. Can you hear me?"

Tannenberg's eyes opened wide. He recognized the woman sitting beside him, who seemed to be talking, although he couldn't hear her. Yes, it was Greta, even though he didn't remember her coming to this place with him. He closed his eyes and breathed deep, smelling the air; he felt full of life, even if his wife insisted on babbling on, distracting him from this very pleasant moment.

44

IN MAUTHAUSEN, IT SEEMED THAT SPRING WOULD NEVER arrive. It was cold, and the prisoners, more dead than alive, sensed that something was about to happen. Their guards were on constant, uneasy alert and, with each new day, less concerned with their prisoners' fate—they shot the second someone stumbled.

Alfred Tannenberg was contemplating the camp from the window of Zieris' office. Night had brought a freeze, and the sentinels in the watchtowers were rubbing their hands together to keep warm. Alfred and Heinrich had arrived just over an hour earlier and had gone immediately to the commander's office to submit their new orders. Zieris had listened with curiosity, not daring to question the two well-connected officers too closely. He would try to find out on his own why they were being sent on missions to undisclosed locations outside Austria.

As soon as they left Zieris' office, Heinrich and Alfred went to their warm homes in the village, which stood in such contrast to the hideous conditions of the adjoining camp.

In less than two hours, Heinrich had packed his bags and gathered up all his personal effects. Fräulein Heines, his housekeeper, had shed a tear upon learning that the polite SS officer was leaving, probably never to return, but she was never one for maudlin sentiments, so she quickly pulled herself up and busied herself helping him pack his things into a large trunk. Then, as they said good-bye, he slipped a generous roll of bills into her hand; it would tide her over, he said, until she found another house to which she might lend her excellent services.

A few minutes later, Heinrich was banging on the door of Tannenberg's house. When his friend came to the door, he saw immediately that something was amiss.

"What's wrong?" Heinrich asked, unable to conceal his alarm at Alfred's odd expression. He knew that Greta, Alfred's wife, was expecting a baby, but the due date was still two months away.

"Greta . . . is not well, not well at all. I've sent for the doctor. I hope she doesn't lose the baby; she'd never forgive herself. . . ."

"Come, don't say that! Let me see her."

"Come in, but don't disturb her; the servant is helping her."

"Then I won't stay. But remember, Georg wants us out of here by tomorrow."

"Don't worry—you go on to Berlin and get your plane to Lisbon. I . . . I will see what I can do, but for now I have no choice but to stay here."

"Georg said we must leave immediately!"

"Georg doesn't have a pregnant wife. I'll do what I can—but for the moment, I can't leave. But go, please, go, Heinrich. I won't rest easy until I know you are all safe."

They embraced tightly. They were bound not just by their childhood and university years but also by their shared service at Mauthausen, which had marked them forever. They had made other people's pain their greatest occupation—to such a degree that they had lost count of the number of prisoners they had personally tortured and killed.

The doctor was slow in coming, and when he did arrive, Alfred told him he would pay dearly for the delay. Greta was screaming in agony, and the servant's efforts to allay her pain had proved useless.

For an hour, Alfred waited in the kitchen, drinking cognac, while the doctor struggled to save the lives of his wife and child. He prayed not for God's aid but for the resources to invent a new plan to get out of Austria as soon as possible.

When he saw the doctor at the door and the servant cowering behind him, weeping, he knew that it had not gone well. He got up out of his chair and approached the doctor, waiting for him to speak first.

"I am sorry, Captain Tannenberg; I could not save the child, and your wife . . . Her condition is very delicate. She should be moved to a hospital; she has lost a great deal of blood. If you leave her here, I don't believe she will live."

"Was it a boy . . . or a girl?" Tannenberg stammered, his face red with rage.

"A girl."

Alfred Tannenberg slapped the doctor, who recoiled instantly. He had never had the courage to stand up to an SS officer, much less one like this, whose eyes glared with cruelty and brutality without bounds. So he simply stood there, his cheek red from the slap and the shame, his ear ringing.

"Call for an ambulance—now!" screamed Tannenberg. "And you!" he shouted at the servant. "Go to my wife!"

The woman rushed out of the kitchen, already familiar with her master's abuse. Greta, only half conscious, was moaning, calling out to her lost child.

The ambulance took an hour to arrive, and by then Greta had entered a state of deep unconsciousness. By the time they reached the hospital, she was cold and still and the only thing the doctors could do was certify her death.

Tannenberg was infuriated, not by the loss of his wife and child, but rather at having lost precious hours to escape. Georg had made it clear that time was against them.

Now he had to notify Greta's parents and wait for them to come to the funeral, which would take at least two days. At least, he thought, Heinrich and Franz had gotten away. He would have to stay until Greta was buried; otherwise, he would have to answer to his powerful father-in-law, Fritz Hermann, which was tantamount to answering to Himmler himself. Until Germany collapsed completely, those were the men who pulled the strings of the dying Reich.

He returned to his house and ordered the servant to wrap Greta's body in a shroud. Despite his misgivings about the match planned by his father years ago, she had been a good and loyal wife who had never disappointed him, giving in to all his whims without question or protest. It had taken them several years to conceive—a daughter, the doctor had said—and Greta had been delighted. He had even come to celebrate the idea of having an heir and namesake and was strangely moved that Greta was carrying a child within her. He pictured it blond, with alabaster-white skin and sky-blue eyes, smiling and happy. A perfect child of the Reich.

The commander of Mauthausen was most sympathetic when he learned of Greta's death, and though he questioned whether Alfred's mission outside Austria could wait, Tannenberg simply informed him that his father-in-law, Fritz Hermann, would be arriving at any time and that he should make appropriate arrangements to receive a man in Himmler's inner circle.

Zieris understood the message and did not press, although he did tell Tannenberg a secret.

"A few hours ago I received a telephone call from Berlin. The Red Cross has been calling Herr Himmler very insistently; they want to visit Mauthausen. They have been trying to gain permission to visit the camps for months. I have friends who tell me that the Reichführer is attempting to negotiate with the Allies. I fear that all is lost. The Russians have broken through our lines and occupied part of Germany, and the Allies are about to take Austria. But I imagine you know all this, do you not?"

Tannenberg said nothing; he merely stood at the commander's desk and stared at him.

"It's a shame you're going. A contingent of SS officers is coming to help us evacuate the camp; we must dispose of some of the prisoners. This must look like . . . well . . . a camp for prisoners, not . . . what we've turned it into. Hartheim Castle is going to be made an orphanage. And we are to erase all traces of the gas chambers and crematoria. We have so much work ahead of us—we could have used your help. We don't have much time."

Herr Hermann and his wife wept inconsolably over the death of their daughter and premature granddaughter. Now that the Reich was crumbling, Tannenberg realized that his once-powerful father-in-law was just another man, unaware that shortly after the funeral Alfred would be fleeing the country forever.

When the Hermanns, more stunned than anything else, left to return to Berlin, Tannenberg secured the documents that Georg had given him in a leather traveling wallet. Then, with a small bag in which he had carefully placed the two tablets from Haran and a few articles of clothing, plus two leather satchels—one filled with hard currency and the other with rings, watches, and jewelry pilfered from the prisoners in the camp—he prepared to leave Mauthausen forever.

A car and driver were waiting for him at the door of his house. He left without a word to his servant, nor did he salute the soldier who was to drive him to Switzerland.

When they arrived at the border, Tannenberg smiled with relief. The minute he arrived in Zürich he would find his parents, but he had no intention of staying long. Once he had met the contacts Georg had made for him, he would leave immediately for Cairo. But first he must reach Zürich and adopt the new identity his friend had invented for him.

His parents had moved into a small, quiet hotel near the center of the city, an enviable place where agents from all corners of the world could witness the fall of the Third Reich from a safe distance.

His father, overcome with emotion, embraced him with relief. His mother burst into tears over the death of Greta and their child.

"How long will you be staying?" his father asked. "In Berlin you told me only that we would see each other here and that you had been given a delicate mission."

"I'll be here only one or two days, just long enough to find a seat on an airplane for Lisbon or Casablanca, and from there to Cairo."

"Cairo? Why do you have to go to Egypt?"

"Papa, I shouldn't have to tell you that we've lost the war."

"Don't say that! Germany can still win. Hitler will never surrender."

"Please, Papa, you agreed to come to Switzerland because you were aware of the situation."

"I did it because you convinced me it was better to wait out the war here, but I haven't given it up as lost."

"Well, you might as well—the sooner you recognize that, the better for the family. I know you'll want to go back when it's over, but if I were in your place, I wouldn't. The Allies will hunt down everyone who has played any sort of role in Hitler's campaign, and they will have their revenge. It's best to accept reality; that's why I'm going to Cairo. I will start a new life there; I am leaving everything behind. I can do no more for Germany."

Disbelief and disappointment washed over Herr Tannenberg, who looked incredulously at his son.

"You're leaving us too?" his mother asked him point-blank.

"Mama, we must go our separate ways now. I cannot take you with me; if you heed my advice, you will stay here in Zürich. You have money here, enough to live comfortably for the rest of your lives. If you go back to Germany after the war, you will lose everything."

"Will you be in touch with us?" his mother asked.

"Yes, of course, Mama. But I'm going underground; I'm going to change my name and take on a new identity. So it won't be easy at first, but I'll be in touch when I can, when it is safe to do so—without endangering you and Papa."

His father paced the room, reflecting on his son's words.

"I have spoken to Georg's and Heinrich's parents; Franz's are in Geneva," he said.

"I know, Papa. Georg made meticulous arrangements. If I were you, I would think about starting a business, something that would allow you to settle in Switzerland, keep you busy. And I would do more than that—I would start telling everyone that you are very disappointed in Hitler, who has driven Germany to ruin, that you feel you were deceived."

"That would be despicable!"

"It would be accepting reality. Within a few months, Hitler will be the Antichrist; the Allies will have tried and hanged him. They will hunt down everyone who has collaborated with him. Distance yourself while you still have time."

"I thought that the SS had inculcated a sense of honor in you," his father said reproachfully.

"What the SS taught me was to survive, and that is exactly what I am going to do."

"What will you do in Cairo, my son?" his mother asked softly.

"Get married as soon as possible."

"My God! Your wife died four days ago!"

"I know, Mama, I know. But there is no point in the pretense of mourning for six months. I have to stop being Alfred Tannenberg; I must start a new life. And in order to do that I need someone who can help me grow into my new identity."

"You will no longer call yourself a Tannenberg? You are ashamed of your name?" his father screamed, his face red with anger.

"Of course I am not ashamed of my name. I will always think of myself as Alfred Tannenberg. But I don't want to face the firing squad either. So for the time being, it's best not to call attention to myself—an SS officer can hardly go unnoticed."

"Son," his mother insisted, "tell us what you are going to do in Cairo—what do you need? You can ask us for anything."

"I need money—Swiss francs, American dollars, whatever you can give me, Papa. As for what I'm going to do . . . Heinrich, Georg, Franz, and I have decided that we're going to go into the import–export business, transporting and trading in antiques if possible. But that won't happen until later; the first thing to do is get to Cairo, find the contact Georg has arranged for, and disappear into the background until the war is over. Finding a family who will take me in—that I can marry into—is the best way to cement a new identity."

That night he had dinner with his parents and sisters, along with Heinrich's and Georg's parents. His friends' parents were as worried as his own, although Georg's parents were somewhat relieved to know that their son was with his uncle, on his way to the United States.

They all resisted the idea of becoming exiles, and so they talked about returning to their homes as soon as the war was over. They were convinced that the Allies would not try civilians; if they did, most of the adult population of Germany would be prosecuted.

"You'll see," said Alfred. "The future leaders of Germany will be among the political prisoners who are in the work camps today, unless someone has the foresight to shoot them all."

Two days later, his uniform exchanged for an impeccable civilian suit, Alfred Tannenberg said good-bye to his parents. Deep inside, he knew he would never see them again. He could never return to Germany, so whatever the fate of his parents, their paths were irrevocably diverging.

His heart was heavy as his plane landed in Cairo. This moment marked the beginning of the rest of his life, his new life, and he was filled with uncertainty. He had traveled with his real passport, as Georg had recommended; he would begin using false papers when his instinct told him the time had come—that is, when official word came that Germany had lost the war, which would be in a matter of weeks, perhaps days.

A taxi drove him to an out-of-the-way hotel near the American embassy. He smiled to himself, thinking how close his enemies were—they would never suspect that an SS officer would hole up next door.

The hotel was musty-smelling, and its tenants were mostly Europeans—refugees, spies, low-level diplomats, adventurers. He handed his passport to the clerk at the desk.

"Ah . . . I'm afraid I have only one room left, Herr Tannenberg, a double. If you take it, you'll have to pay for two occupants," said the front-desk clerk, knowing that the tall, steely-eyed German would not refuse.

"That's fine; I'm expecting someone else anyway," he said coolly.

"Yes? And when will this person be arriving?" the reception clerk asked.

"I will let you know," Tannenberg said, never batting an eyelash.

The room boasted a fine view of the Nile from the window. A large bed, a sleeper-sofa, a table, two chairs, and a chest of drawers comprised the room's humble furnishings. A door opened into a small bathroom. Sitting on the bed, Tannenberg resigned himself to his new home until he found Georg's agent, an SS officer who, knowing the situation in Germany, specialized in relocating fellow officers who had been able to get out in time.

The fact was that all four of the old friends had left Berlin with their superiors' permission, even blessings: Georg to supervise agents abroad, Franz to join the SS in Latin America, Heinrich to be part of Germany's diplomatic corps in Portugal, and Alfred to work with agents dispatched to Cairo.

Alfred decided to be prudent. After he committed a map of Cairo to memory, he went out to scout the nearby neighborhoods. He walked for upward of an hour, and what he saw was a city filled with foreigners, almost all Europeans. He was struck by the chaotic traffic; taxis sped through intersections without looking in either direction, drivers seemed to use their horns more than their brakes, and the pedestrians, though they seemed remarkably cool, sometimes had to leap out of the way of oncoming vehicles.

He was pleased to see an inviting sign over a door: *Restaurant Kababgy.*

He pushed open the door and went in. A perfectly uniformed waiter greeted him in English, much to Alfred's confusion, which the waiter picked up on.

"*Parlez-vous Français, sprechen sie Deutsch, parla Italiano, habla Español . . . ?*"

"*Deutsch . . . ja, ja, Deutsch,*" stammered Tannenberg.

"Ah! *Willkommen!* Do you have a reservation?"

"No, I didn't have time, I just arrived, and . . . well, a friend told me this was one of the best restaurants in the city."

"Thank you, sir. Can you tell me who your friend is?"

"You may not know him. He is . . . German, like me."

"There are many Europeans who dine with us. But come this way, we will find you a table."

The restaurant was very full, and the only free table was a small one in a far corner.

Alfred ate hungrily while studying the clientele, which was extremely varied. When he returned to the hotel, he told himself that the next day he would track down his contact. Georg had given him an address near Khan el-Khalili, the market where the artisans of Cairo made and sold their crafts.

He woke up shortly before dawn, feeling full of life. He would have liked to go on exploring the city, visit the pyramids, even go to Alexandria, but he told himself that those excursions would have to wait.

Khan el-Khalili turned out to be a city within the city. Its twisting, narrow streets all looked alike to him, and the dense fragrance of spices tickled his nose and stomach. He walked for a long time and, upon realizing his map wasn't quite as updated as he'd thought, at last decided to ask for directions from a man sitting in front of a small shop, smoking a long, aromatic cigarette. The stranger was quite friendly and was soon explaining how to find the shop Alfred was looking for. As Alfred walked away, the man called out to tell him there was no way to get lost—everyone in Cairo knew Yasir Mubak's store.

The three-story building looked better cared for than most structures in the area. A sign announced the offices of an import–export business and a shop that promised true antiques.

When Alfred pushed open the door, he was surprised to see the shop filled to the ceiling with furniture, lamps, rugs—everything. There was not a spare inch of surface, although a quick glance revealed that these "true antiques" were in fact cheap imitations and reproductions. A very neat, well-groomed young man approached him.

"How may I help you?"

"I'm looking for Yasir Mubak."

"Is he expecting you?"

"No, I don't believe he knew that I was coming today, but tell him I am a friend of Herr Wolter."

The young man looked him up and down and hesitated. Motioning toward a chair, he invited Alfred to take a seat while he sent for Mr. Mubak, then disappeared up a flight of stairs at the back of the store.

Tannenberg waited for more than a quarter hour, conscious of being watched, before Yasir Mubak came down the stairs and walked over, smiling.

"Please, come in, come in. Friends of Herr Wolter are always welcome. Shall we talk in my office?"

Alfred followed Mubak upstairs into a large room decorated in traditional Egyptian fashion, then through another door into a private office. Alfred couldn't locate their source through the clutter of the store, but he could hear voices and the clicking of typewriters nearby.

"Well, Herr . . . ? I don't believe you've told me your name."

"No, I haven't. I'm Alfred Tannenberg, and it's urgent that I get in touch with Herr Wolter."

"Of course, of course. I will be happy to relay that to Herr Wolter, and he will contact you. Would you like to send him a note yourself or have me say anything in particular?"

Tannenberg took out a sealed envelope and handed it to Mubak.

"Give this to Herr Wolter for me, please, and tell him that I am at the Hotel National."

"Indeed, indeed. And how else may I be of service?"

Alfred was about to reply when the door to the office opened and a dark-skinned woman vaguely resembling Mubak entered. The woman, like Mubak, was dressed in Western clothing—a dark gray suit and white blouse, black high-heeled shoes, hair in a fashionable chignon.

"Sorry! I thought you were alone," she said apologetically.

"No bother. Come in, come in. . . . Alia, this is Herr Tannenberg. Alia is my sister, and a fine asset to my business."

Alfred stood up and clicked his heels together, slightly bowing his head. He did not dare offer his hand, because although the woman looked Westernized, she might still be offended if a man touched her.

"Miss . . ."

"Freut mich, sie kennen zu lernen," she said in passable German.

"You speak my language."

"Yes, I lived for several years in Hamburg with my younger sister, who's married to a German businessman."

"My brother-in-law is a clothing manufacturer," Yasir explained, "who bought cotton from us. He met my sister and . . . well, they fell in love, got married, and lived in Hamburg until two or three years ago, when they moved here. The war . . ." Mubak had to say no more.

"I lived for months at a time in Hamburg, helping my sister with her four rambunctious children," Alia continued comfortably. Clearly she had none of the reservations Alfred had expected from a Middle Eastern woman.

Yasir invited Tannenberg to share a cup of tea, which he was happy to accept. As they sat and conversed, he watched Alia. She was neither beautiful nor ugly, short nor tall, but there was something about her— Tannenberg felt there was a certain magnetism at work. For the hour he was in Mubak's office, he never took his eyes off her. He figured that she must be about thirty, and she seemed quite acceptable. And that was when he made the decision. He would marry Alia Mubak—if, that is, his SS contact could confirm that this was a family that could be trusted wholeheartedly and was well positioned to advance his interests. Certainly the fact that Mubak's office was the rendezvous for SS agents retreating from Germany spoke volumes.

That same night Alfred received a visit from SS Commander Helmut Wolter.

The two men were more or less the same age; with Wolter's blond hair and steel-blue eyes, they looked almost like twins, though Wolter's white skin had been noticeably tanned by the sun. He was tall, with an athletic build—the model SS officer.

Commander Wolter brought Tannenberg up to date on the situation in Egypt. Like the other countries in the region, Egyptians were sympathetic to the Nazi cause, and their hatred of Jews was second only to the Germans'. SS officers were safe there, they had nothing to fear, and during the war Wolter and other agents had established a strong network of friends and allies. Now that Germany's cause seemed lost, they were going to put that network to good use. The SS, he told Tannenberg, would never surrender.

Aside from the obligatory patriotic discourse, Alfred liked the agent, who for the past five long years had been based in Cairo while traveling all over the Middle East, studying the lay of the land and doling out money to buy loyalty.

"Can Yasir Mubak be trusted?" Alfred asked.

"Yes, of course. He is the brother-in-law of a German factory owner, a Nazi like us, who has provided many services to the Reich. His entire family sympathizes with our cause and has helped us unconditionally. We can trust Yasir as we would trust one another," the commander assured him.

"Is he working for us?"

"He's working with us; he provides us with a great deal of very valuable information. He has his own network of agents all over the Middle East. He is a businessman and believes, quite rightly, that businessmen must keep themselves well informed. His help to us is free; he has never accepted money."

"I don't trust men who don't charge for their work," said Tannenberg.

"He does not work for us, as I said, he works with us. There is a differnce, Captain."

"What about his family?"

"Yasir is married and has five or six children, several brothers and sisters, and heaven knows how many aunts, uncles, cousins, and so on. His parents are quite aged. If he likes you, someday he will invite you into his home; it's quite an experience."

"I met his sister Alia."

"Ah, yes, Alia! She is a peculiar woman but very capable. She helps Yasir with the business, since she speaks English, French, and German. She learned in Hamburg; she was the caregiver to her sister's four children. The old maid of the family, so to speak."

"Old maid?"

"She is thirty, after all, and in Egypt if a woman reaches that age without marrying, she will most likely never find a husband—unless, that is, her family bestows a very large dowry. But she doesn't seem to mind. People here do find her a bit odd; she doesn't want to dress like other women, and she's judged for that, although no one dares reprimand her publicly. Yasir is well connected to the spheres of power in the government."

Alfred Tannenberg took in this information and quickly processed it. The two men then talked about the immediate future and the role that Alfred might play in the SS underground in Egypt.

In the days that followed, Alfred pieced together his plan of action. The news that arrived from Germany was unambiguous: The Allies were drawing ever closer to winning the war outright. And the international community filling the Cairo hotels to capacity had no doubt that with the defeat of the Reich, a new era in German governance would begin. One that would not favor the old Aryan masters.

One evening when Tannenberg was visiting Mubak in his office in Khan el-Khalili, he boldly made him two proposals.

"Yasir, my friend, forgive me if what I am about to say offends you, but I would like to ask your permission to see more of Alia, to court her, in a word. My intentions are clear: If she wishes, and you and your family give your blessing, it would be an honor for me to make her my wife."

Yasir could do nothing but stare at Alfred. He could not understand how this wealthy, handsome German had fixed upon his beloved sister. Alia was not attractive, he knew, nor distinguished in any way except for her knowledge of English, French, and German. Ah, yes, she also knew how to type. But he doubted that those skills qualified her to be a good wife, and his family had resigned itself to the fact that Alia would remain unmarried. Now suddenly this upstanding German was asking his permission to marry her. *Why?* he wondered.

"I will do nothing without your consent," Tannenberg assured him as he saw the doubt cover his new friend's face.

"I will speak with our father; it is he who must grant permission. If my father wishes to consider your proposal, he will send for you."

But there was yet another surprise in store for Yasir.

"Very well, my friend, now I would like us to talk trade. I want to start a business—an antiques business—and I also want to finance archaeological expeditions. You know I'm an archaeologist—or at least I was, before the war."

During the time he'd been in Cairo, Tannenberg had taken the measure of Yasir Mubak and reached the conclusion that only profit mattered to him—the more the better. Alfred had the distinct impression that in Mubak he had found the perfect partner, the perfect means by which to achieve the objective that he, Georg, Franz, and Heinrich had set themselves—looting the archaeological treasures of the Middle East and selling them on the black market.

After five hours—Yasir had given instructions to his staff that they not be interrupted—the two men reached an agreement: They would form an antiques trading company. Yasir would continue with his own business, but he would also become Tannenberg's partner. The contacts of the one combined with the ingenuity of the other could make them both very, very wealthy. And they discovered they had one other very important thing in common: a complete lack of scruples.

The answer from Alia and Yasir's father came a week later, in a note sent by the old man. He invited Tannenberg to lunch with the family the following Friday.

At that, Alfred Tannenberg smiled in self-satisfaction. Things could not be going better: He had just formed a business, well ahead of schedule, and he was going to be married. A strategic union with Alia came with its advantages, among them becoming part of the Mubak clan, which meant he would be under the protection of one of the principal families of Egypt. He was going to need protection now that the war in Europe was in its final days. Additionally, his partnership with Yasir would open doors all across the Middle East that might otherwise have been closed to a foreigner.

Given the pressures of living in wartime, Tannenberg was able to convince Alia's father not to delay the wedding overlong—even so, he still had to agree to wait several months for traditional preparations.

The day Commander Wolter telephoned to inform him of Hitler's suicide, Tannenberg was surprised at how little he cared; in fact, his only concern was the legal obstacles that SS officers "deployed" in the Middle East might have to face. But Commander Wolter assured him that they were well prepared for this eventuality: They would all go underground immediately. They had the money and false documents to do so without a trace. And the sooner they disappeared, the better. In the closing days of the war, the Allies had discovered that hell existed on earth—in concentration camps located all over Germany, Austria, Poland . . . every country over which Hilter's boot had trod. And the Allies vowed to hunt down every German who had had anything to do with what they insisted on calling an outrage, a genocide, even a holocaust.

Alfred Tannenberg consulted with both Wolter and Yasir as to whether he should now adopt his new identity. Wolter insisted upon it, while Yasir claimed no one would come to Egypt looking for SS officers and that his father wouldn't approve of his daughter marrying a man with a false name. That argument decided the case: Alfred Tannenberg would continue to be Alfred Tannenberg. He knew there was risk involved, but he agreed with Yasir that in Egypt, and especially with his new connections, he could survive under his own identity if he exercised discretion.

A year after the war had ended, Alfred Tannenberg had married Alia Mubak and, better yet, business was booming. He had managed to contact Georg, who, with his uncle's protection, was starting a new life in the United States. Heinrich was in Madrid under the protective mantle of Franco, and Franz was living the high life in Brazil, where the SS network had shown itself to be extraordinarily efficient in protecting its own. Of course, more time still had to pass before they could comfortably embark on the actual theft of antiquities, but Tannenberg was doing everything possible to prepare for that stage of the business, identifying and seeking out the objects they would put on the market when the time came.

Yasir had introduced him to all the relevant contacts—grave robbers who knew the Valley of the Kings like the palm of their hand, gray-market excavators of archaeological sites, corrupt museum officials. . . . But it was Tannenberg himself who, applying his knowledge of ancient history, conceived detailed plans for financing expeditions in Syria, Jordan, Iraq . . . with special emphasis on his desire to personally lead a team to dig in Haran.

His great dream, still unfulfilled, was to find the tablets of the patriarch Abraham, the stories transcribed by Shamas.

Tannenberg's enthusiasm soon infected Alia, and he even convinced Yasir of the importance of the search.

The tablets were his obsession, the driving force of his life; he was certain that the day he had them, his stature as a renowned archaeologist would secure his place in history and no one would care what he once had been.

In Egypt, and later in Syria and Iraq, he found a secure refuge, as did many of his former comrades. He learned, in snatches here and there, of the Nuremberg Trials as he was excavating once again in Haran. There, Alia conceived and bore their son, Helmut, while Alfred's hands were digging in the sands of the desert of the Middle East.

45

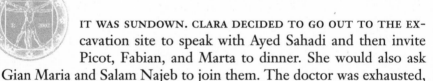 IT WAS SUNDOWN. CLARA DECIDED TO GO OUT TO THE EX-
cavation site to speak with Ayed Sahadi and then invite
Picot, Fabian, and Marta to dinner. She would also ask
Gian Maria and Salam Najeb to join them. The doctor was exhausted,
and it would do him good to relax for a while.

After changing his IV bottle, Aliya took Clara's place beside
Tannenberg. She would remain there until Clara returned to her vigil
after dinner.

Salam Najeb looked in on his patient before dinner. He found
Tannenberg agitated, shouting orders in a strange tongue. When he
went over to the bedside to administer a sedative, the old man's eyes
filled with terror and he tried to fend the doctor off with the arm he
could still move, but Aliya and one of the guards managed to hold him
still for the injection, while he hurled obvious insults at them all. But
once the sedative took effect, he fell into a fitful sleep.

"Don't move from his side, Aliya, and if you observe any change,
call me immediately," Dr. Najeb ordered.

"Yes, Doctor."

The nurse sat down again beside the sick man's bed and opened a
book to entertain herself as the camp began to stir for dinner. She

sighed resignedly, and as Tannenberg tossed and stirred in his bed, she turned out all the lights save for one small lamp whose beam fell squarely on the pages of her book.

She neither heard nor saw the figure that suddenly appeared, holding her tight with one hand and putting the other over her mouth. The last thing she felt was the cold steel at her throat. It sliced through so neatly that she had no time to scream or even move. She died without knowing that she'd been killed.

Lion Doyle told himself he was sorry he'd had to kill Aliya, but he'd had no choice. He couldn't leave any witnesses.

He stood over the bed in which Tannenberg was sleeping—the man's eyes, darting back and forth under his eyelids, and a quiver in his legs and hands indicated that his dreams were not restful.

Lion didn't lose a second; he cut Alfred Tannenberg's throat just as neatly as he had the nurse's, and then he made sure the old man would not survive by stabbing him just under the breastbone and slicing him from sternum to navel.

Tannenberg never awoke, never stirred. Lion crept out of the hospital tent in silence, as quickly as he'd slipped in. No one could have missed him. Picot, Fabian, and Marta were with Clara, and the rest of the team was packing, since the next day the helicopters were coming to transport them to Baghdad.

He'd be leaving with them. The truth was, he'd been stupid not to eliminate Tannenberg earlier. He'd been kidding himself that there were too many obstacles. The fact was, he'd enjoyed being there, working like just another member of Picot's team. He was sorry he wasn't who he said he was, except, of course, for the fact that he missed his farm. And Marian—but he knew that if she'd been there, she'd have been happy too.

He took advantage of the darkness and the shadows of the tents to dispose of his weapon and his bloody clothes. He'd just have a smoke until he heard the alarm.

Dinner had been pleasant, since everyone had apparently come to the same decision—it was best not to talk about any of the bad things that had happened over the last couple of weeks. Fabian had entertained them with anecdote after anecdote about his many years in the classroom.

As the rest of the group started back to camp, Clara and Dr. Najeb headed for the hospital tent. The guards nodded a greeting as they went in. Clara was first, followed by the doctor, and her scream of horror echoed throughout the camp. It was a shriek—a high-pitched, drawn-out wail that seemed to go on forever.

Aliya was lying on the ground in a pool of blood. Tannenberg was as white as candle wax, his hands lying limp on the bloodstained sheets.

Dr. Najeb tried to pull Clara back out of the tent as she clawed at his face, and when she saw the guards rush in she threw herself at them, hitting them with her fists and kicking them, cursing them, her lips covered with spittle.

"Pigs! Imbeciles! I'll kill you all!"

Clara's cries echoed like those of a wounded beast, bringing shivers to the rest of the team. Picot, Fabian, Marta, and Ayed Sahadi ran to the hospital, followed closely by Gian Maria and other members of the expedition, among them Lion Doyle and Ante Plaskic.

Gian Maria put his arms around Clara and led her out of the hospital, but only after Dr. Najeb had managed to inject her with a powerful tranquilizer.

It was a long night, filled with shouts and cries, reproaches and confusion. No one had seen anything, none of the guards who'd withstood Clara's rampage could tell them what had happened—none of them had heard or seen a thing. Neither Ayed's brutal interrogation techniques nor the no-less-brutal techniques of the commander of the guard managed to elicit any information—no one knew anything.

"We have a murderer among us," Picot declared for the second time in as many weeks.

"Yes, whoever killed Tannenberg and Aliya almost certainly killed Samira and the two guards," replied Marta glumly as she lit a cigarette with a shaking hand.

Lion Doyle listened to the speculation with the same doleful expression on his face as the rest of the members of the team, although he could feel Ante Plaskic's gaze burning coldly into his back.

"I'm ready to get the hell out of here," said Fabian.

"Me too, Fabian, me too," responded Yves Picot. "And thank God that will happen tomorrow. I wouldn't stay another minute for all the tea in China."

Clara wasn't able to see them off. Dr. Najeb had mercifully administered another tranquilizer: She was in bed, hardly aware of her surroundings. Fatima, despite her own condition, had taken charge of the situation.

Now, except for Gian Maria, all the members of Picot's archaeological team had left. They had wasted no time getting themselves on the helicopters, terrified that their exit would be blocked again, given the previous night's horror.

Lion Doyle, flying toward Baghdad with the rest of the group, knew that he still had to kill Clara, but trying to do that under the circumstances in the camp seemed logistically impossible. Ayed Sahadi had put six men at Clara's door and posted men all around the house. Lion could have kicked himself for not doing the job sooner, but it was a tough job, after all—and sometimes he felt as though killing the heavily guarded Tannenberg had made his mission a success in itself, which meant his employer ought not only to pay him full price but also congratulate him. Of course, Tom Martin wasn't one to give pats on the back; he just expected his employees to do the job they'd been hired to do.

Ahmed Husseini had arranged for the archaeological team to spend two days in Baghdad before being helicoptered to the Jordanian border. From there they would be transported to Amman, and from Amman each member of the team would fly out to his or her own country: Picot to Paris, Marta and Fabian to Madrid, others to Berlin, London, Rome.

Lion Doyle sent a short but very clear fax to Photomundi: *Returning tomorrow. Bringing a lot of material, but not all of it. It's been hard to work the last few days. But the most important part is done.*

They were all experiencing what felt like a kind of claustrophobia, as though the very air was pressing in on them, and they were desperate to leave Iraq as soon as possible, but Ahmed had asked them to be patient—finding helicopters to move them just then was not easy, nor was it advisable to risk their lives by driving to the Jordanian border.

In the lobby of the Hotel Palestina, they ran into some of the reporters who'd visited them in Safran. All the international news desks at all the wire services were telling their correspondents that the war was going to start in a matter of days. Some were hurrying to return home before the invasion began, but most of them were making arrangements for when the fireworks started—arrangements not just for transportation, but also for interpreters and bodyguards, and food and bottled water, just in case.

That night, Picot and the rest of the team had dinner with Miranda and some other reporters.

"Why don't you come with us?" Picot asked Miranda.

"Because that's not what I do. I haven't sat around here this long just to bail out at the last minute."

"You could spend a few days with me in Paris—in fact, you could stay as long as you like."

Miranda looked at Picot with a conspiratorial smile. She liked this archaeologist as much as he seemed smitten with her, but they both knew they lived parallel lives that could never cross, and that if they did, they would wind up doing each other no good.

"It wouldn't work out, Yves."

"Why? You said there was nobody in your life right now."

"There's not."

"Then . . ."

"Then nothing. You're terrific, really, so terrific that I don't want to think of you as a one-night stand."

"I'm not talking about a one-night stand," Picot protested.

Miranda couldn't help holding out some hope for them. "When this damned war is over, I'll go visit you in Paris, or wherever you are, I promise, and then we'll laugh about this and have a drink and each either go our own way or . . . or the other."

Picot seemed satisfied. He knew that Miranda was going to stay on in Baghdad and could only hope she'd be safe, so she could make good on her promise.

Ahmed Husseini, who had come to dinner with them, was drinking one whiskey after another despite Fabian's attempts to slow him down. The secure, elegant director of the Bureau of Archaeological Excavations they had first met was now unkempt, unshaven, and clearly sleepless. He had dark rings around his eyes, and there was pain, anxiety, grief, anguish—Fabian didn't know what to call it—his restless eyes, which darted nervously from one place to another, as though he feared for his life.

"Are you going back to Safran?" Marta asked him.

"I'm not sure. Clara won't speak to me, but certainly I'll go if there's anything I can do to help her."

"She's your wife!" exclaimed Marta. "How can you not go to her at a time like this?"

"I don't know, Marta, I don't know. . . . I . . . Everything that's happened . . . It's so terrible, and now the war . . . I don't know what's going to happen. . . . Clara should come back to Baghdad, though she's chosen not to; I don't think she can stay there much longer alone."

Fabian made a sign to Marta not to pursue the subject, and he turned the conversation to the exhibit they were planning.

"We're grateful that you were able to convince the authorities to let us mount this exhibition."

"Yes, Professor Picot has already signed all the papers." Ahmed nodded.

"What about you? When will you be joining us?" Fabian asked.

"Me? I'm not sure. It all depends on Clara; I'd like to leave now, to-morrow, if I could, but it's not easy to leave Iraq, and now that Tannenberg is dead they may not let me."

Ahmed's cell phone interrupted him. He didn't get up to go talk more discreetly somewhere else, though—he listened in silence to the voice on the other end, which seemed to be giving him orders.

He nodded over and over, his face pale and his expression tense.

"Who was that?" Marta asked, not caring in the slightest if she was being nosy.

"It . . . it was the Colonel. He's very important."

"He seemed terrible," Marta murmured.

"I'll be heading back to Safran first thing tomorrow to attend Alfred's funeral. The presidential palace wants him buried with full honors. I've been ordered to go, to be with Clara, and to convince her to return to Baghdad."

"That's the most sensible thing," Lion Doyle declared.

"What about us, though?" asked Picot with a note of worry.

"You will be leaving Baghdad the day after tomorrow at first light. Karim, my assistant, is the Colonel's nephew, and he'll make sure you run into no problems; he'll accompany you to the air base if I don't get back in time. But I should be back tomorrow evening—with Clara, if possible."

Ahmed then excused himself. He had drunk too much—his head was spinning, he felt like throwing up, and his eyes burned. He knew that the best thing he could do was try to get some sleep.

Picot suggested that the group retire to the bar for a nightcap, and almost everyone came along. Only Ante Plaskic refused. He said good night and went up to his room.

"What a strange guy," Miranda said as she watched him cross the lobby toward the elevators.

"He is," agreed Picot. "I think my intuition about him may have been right all along. All these months he hasn't made one attempt to be pleasant or sociable with the rest of us. He's been totally distant."

"He was good at his job, though," said Marta, in his defense. "Without him, none of the data would have been catalogued. And he's always been polite; he's done everything we asked him to do. I don't think it's fair to criticize him for not being friendly, especially when no one seemed to like him from the start. It's not as though any of us went out of our way to make him feel welcome," she insisted.

"Whatever," Picot said. "I still think he's strange."

They sat up until late, drinking and talking about the war.

Three helicopters hovered over the yellow sand, just a few yards from what remained of the archaeological camp.

Clara, standing beside the Colonel, waited with a distracted look for the delegation to land. She'd been informed that the government had sent its most distinguished representatives to attend her grandfather's funeral: several generals, two ministers, and several members of Saddam's own family.

As they filed toward her from the helicopters, they all grasped her hand and expressed their condolences. Iraq, they said, had lost one of its best friends and most distinguished citizens. But Clara hardly heard their words of comfort; in fact, it was hard for her to understand what they were saying at all. She was so overcome with grief, her heart so dulled, that she found it almost impossible to concentrate on what was happening around her.

She could not erase the image of her grandfather's slit throat and horribly wounded body from her mind. Whoever had done it had made certain not just to kill him but to hurt him to exact revenge for who knew what offense.

Until now she had never in her life felt alone, not even when her parents died. She couldn't bear the pain of this ceremonial confirmation that her grandfather would no longer be with her, and she could find no consolation in any of the words she heard—not even in the heartfelt attentions of Fatima, who held her in her arms like a little girl trying to give her some sense of comfort.

Ahmed came up and kissed her softly on the cheek, then took her arm and led her back to the house. Clara offered no resistance. She didn't care one way or another whether Ahmed was there, although Fatima had urged her to let her husband try to help her, at least for appearances' sake.

Once they reached the house, Fatima served tea and sweet pastries to the men as they waited to form the funeral cortege that would bear Tannenberg's casket to his grave.

At first Clara had considered asking the Colonel to helicopter her and the casket to Cairo, so that her grandfather might be buried there. Then she realized that her grandfather wouldn't have cared where he was buried; one place was as good as another. She knew him well, knew that he had never had any special feeling for any place in particular. But she did believe in the value of symbols, so she decided that it was right that he be buried near the ruins of the temple where they were still so eagerly searching for the tablets that had been his obsession.

Clara didn't stay in the small living room with the men but went instead into the room where Fatima had washed and prepared the body of the man to whom she had been loyal for over forty years. The servant had done it with the same respect and reverence she'd shown when he was alive.

Clara took her grandfather's lifeless hand in hers, and she broke down.

"Grandfather, Grandfather," she moaned as the tears flowed. "Why did they do this to you?"

A soft knock came on the door, and Fatima quietly entered the room to tell her that the time had come to take the body.

Clara's weeping became more uncontrollable and she embraced the lifeless body of her grandfather as she wailed in despair.

With the help of Ahmed, Fatima pulled Clara away while the Colonel closed the casket and, with the aid of five other men, carried it to the open jeep that would drive it a few hundred yards to the grave that had been dug in the saffron-colored earth.

Dr. Najeb approached Clara and offered her a pill, which she refused. She wanted to come out of the haze she'd been in for two days, no matter how much pain she had to bear. The doctor didn't insist.

There was no religious ceremony at all, Catholic or Muslim. Nor did anyone speak a word of farewell to Alfred Tannenberg. It had been Clara's express desire that her grandfather be buried without any ceremony but the silence of the desert and the grief of those who had loved him, and she knew that of all those gathered around the grave, only she and Fatima truly had.

The men lowered the casket into the dry sand. Ahmed held Clara tightly, but as they started throwing dirt into the grave, he couldn't prevent her from trying to throw herself on top of the casket. It was finally the Colonel's firm hand that stopped her and led her away.

The return to the house took place in silence.

The Colonel seated Clara in the room that had been Alfred Tannenberg's office. Ahmed sat down next to her.

"Are you strong enough for us to have a talk?" the officer asked solicitously.

"Yes, yes . . ." she replied, wiping away the tears that she couldn't seem to stop.

"Then listen to me, and listen to me as the father you no longer have, for your grandfather was everything to you. Ahmed has told me that you know about your grandfather's business dealings; if that's true, then you will understand that we cannot stop the operation that is under way. Your husband will take over and manage it, and you will go. In my opinion, the sooner you leave Iraq, the better. I think you should go to Cairo, to your house there, where you will be safe until all this is over. You can also work on the exhibit that Professor Picot is planning. I can't say what Iraq will be like within a month; I do not even know whether we will still be alive, but I am trusting Picot to keep his word and make you the co-director of the exhibit."

"I don't want to leave," Clara murmured.

"Clara, look at me. It would be madness for you to stay here unless you want to die. I must advise you to leave; your grandfather would have done the same."

"I want to stay for a few more days."

"A few more days, then, but you must leave Iraq before March twentieth. And I also warn you—I cannot leave many soldiers here. Soon every available man, including those in this village, will be called up to serve in the armed forces. The twentieth, Clara. If you wait any longer, I will not be able to get you out of Iraq," said the Colonel gravely.

Once the helicopters had gone, Clara felt better. The delegation from Iraq had been in Safran for barely five hours, but she felt a desperate need to be alone, to not talk or listen to anyone, so that she could try to pull herself together and begin to face life without her grandfather.

Gian Maria had remained at a respectful distance during the burial, in fact during the entire time Saddam's representatives had been there. He had been able to speak to Ahmed for a few minutes, and he'd assured him that he would take care of Clara and try to persuade her to go back to Baghdad as soon as possible.

Ahmed had asked him to call when they needed transportation back to the capital or, if necessary, straight to the Jordanian border.

The leader of the village sent a boy to ask to meet with Clara. He wanted to know whether his men were to keep working the excavation or return to their normal lives; some of them had already received orders to report for military mobilization.

Clara met with him; with her were Fatima, Ayed Sahadi, and Salam Najeb, whom the Colonel had charged with watching over her.

To the distress of Fatima and Dr. Najeb, Clara assured the village leader that the archaeological work would go on for a few days more and that she needed all the men available; she was willing to double their wages if they worked night and day.

When the leader left, Ayed asked her if it wouldn't be best to end the dig now.

"We will stay for a few more days, and for that length of time we'll work as hard as humanly possible. We may yet find what we're looking for."

No one dared contradict her. Ayed assured her that they would work hard, but he cautioned her that it would be with fewer laborers than they'd had, since many of them had been mobilized. But that didn't seem to faze Clara—she would dig alone if she had to.

Lion Doyle tossed in his sleep. He couldn't decide whether to stay in Baghdad.

After returning from Safran, Ahmed had told the group that Clara had insisted on staying for a few more days, despite his and the Colonel's advice. She'd agreed to leave Safran soon, though, and Lion asked himself whether it was worth trying to kill her in the confines of Baghdad or better to wait for her to meet Picot in some European city, where it would be much easier to eliminate her. Getting into Iraq had been easy; what would be tough would be leaving if the damned war broke out. So either he left with the archaeologists or he figured out a way for himself later, which he had no idea how to do.

To stay, he'd need an excuse. But that, he told himself, wouldn't be hard—he'd just tell everyone that he was going to keep working. He decided to call London to consult with the director of Photomundi. They'd already have his fax and have passed it on to Tom Martin, but still, he'd feel better if he could speak to them directly, so there'd be no doubt that Tannenberg was dead. His excuse would be that he was calling for instructions—he'd leave it to Tom Martin whether he stayed or went.

Ante Plaskic's decision to stay in Baghdad had been simple. He'd overheard the cross-table conversations during dinner, so he knew that Clara would be back in the city soon. He only needed to learn whether she was coming back with those damned tablets they'd all been after. If she was, he had to get his hands on them and leave Iraq immediately. He was determined to finish the job that he was going to be paid so generously for.

He wondered who Tannenberg's killer was, and he kept coming back to the photographer, Lion Doyle, although he also suspected the foreman, Ayed Sahadi. He thought it was more likely that it had been

Sahadi, who could have been paid by almost anybody to take revenge on the monstrous man that Alfred Tannenberg had been.

It wasn't likely that Clara would find the tablets, but he couldn't run that risk so he was going to stay. He'd tell Picot that he'd run into some friends and would be going back a day or two later. He didn't really care whether the archaeologist believed him or not.

46

IT WAS LATE, AND TOM MARTIN HAD JUST GOTTEN BACK from a meeting in Paris, but he stopped by his office the minute he left the airport—his secretary had called him to say a fax from Iraq had come in. Even though the fax's message was clear enough, he wanted to hear the news direct, so he picked up the phone and called the director of Photomundi.

The man was sleeping when the telephone jolted him awake.

"Hello?" he answered groggily.

"Hey, it's me."

"What time is it?"

"Two."

"You're working at this hour?" asked the grumpy director.

"I work twenty-four hours a day. Listen, have you gotten anything else from your man in Baghdad?"

"No."

"Not even a phone call?"

"Nothing."

"Get yourself to the office. He'll be getting in touch with you."

"At this hour?" the man protested.

"Do what I tell you—get going. I'm expecting news, and I know we're going to get it tonight."

The director of Photomundi grumbled, but he rolled out of bed. He couldn't tell Tom Martin where to shove it because he was a good customer, one of the best. If Martin told him to get up and go to the office at two in the morning, he got up and went to the office. He jumped into the shower, hoping that would revive him.

He was putting on his jacket when his cell phone rang. He recognized Lion Doyle's voice immediately, and he hit the record button so he could make sure Tom Martin heard the whole conversation.

"So, how're things at home? Get my fax?"

"Yes, thanks a lot. How are you?"

"Surprised you haven't called. Ready to get back home—especially because of what's gone down these last few days. You don't know how terrible things have been. You know Clara Tannenberg, the archaeologist who was co-financing the expedition with Picto? Well, her grandfather was murdered. Somebody just sneaked in and slit his throat—did the same thing to a nurse taking care of him. He was sick, dying of cancer, so nobody can figure out why anybody would kill him instead of just letting him die. But they did. There were guards all over the place, but they turned out to be useless. You can imagine what it's been like—although now, fortunately, we're back in Baghdad, getting ready to fly to Jordan later this morning. Unless you want me to stay and do some kind of special report or something. There's always something to shoot. By the way, I took some shots of what happened in Safran—you probably won't be able to sell them, but you never know. . . ."

The director of Photomundi made encouraging noises at everything Lion said, then told him he'd call around to some news agencies and newspapers and see whether they were interested enough in his shots for him to stay. He'd call back—Lion needed to stay off the phone for a while so he could get through.

By three, Tom Martin was listening to the recording of the conversation.

He grinned when he heard Lion's story. *What an actor,* he thought.

Lion had done at least half the job—the hardest part, killing Alfred Tannenberg—so, Tom thought, his clients were going to be very pleased. Of course, he'd have to contact them right away to find out whether they wanted to forget about killing Clara Tannenberg or whether she had to die too. He didn't care one way or another, but he had to say that killing a man like Tannenberg was quite a feat in a country like Iraq, where the target was one of Saddam's favorites.

Hans Hausser was sleeping the light sleep of a man whose youth was behind him. He awoke immediately when one of his several cell phones rang—it had to be news of Alfred. He turned on his bedside light and answered before the third ring.

"Hello?"

"Mr. Burton?"

"Yes." Hans felt a twinge of indigestion. He looked at the clock: four-fifteen.

"This is Tom Martin."

"Yes."

"The job has been done—well, half the job, the most important part, shall we say. The principal objective has been eliminated."

"Are you certain?"

"Absolutely certain."

"Do you have proof?"

"Of course; it's on the way."

"And what happened to . . . to . . . the other part?"

"Just getting this far has been a miracle. Do you know what the conditions are in the place where this happened?"

"I don't care. When will the rest of the job be done?"

"That's why I'm calling you; maybe it can be done here in Europe. Over there, it's much harder, given the circumstances; there are risks. But if you wish, we can try. I'm calling you for instructions—we can either wait awhile for the second part to be completed in Europe or we can try again abroad. But I want you to know that the possibilities abroad are not good."

The professor breathed deep to gain some time; he didn't know what to say. He couldn't make this decision by himself; he needed to consult the others.

"Give me a few minutes. I'll call you back."

"I'll be waiting, but I need an answer before six, my time."

"You'll have it long before that."

Carlo Cipriani had been at a dinner with some old friends of his, doctors, and when he got back home he'd sat down to read for two or three hours and enjoy the evening's silence. When he heard the phone ring hours later he jumped up and answered it immediately.

"Carlo . . ."

"Hans?"

"Yes, old friend, it's me. It's done. He's dead."

"You mean . . ."

"He's dead, he's dead. I just got the call. And there's proof."

"Are you certain?"

"I'm certain. It's done."

They fell silent, not knowing what to say, both men searching deep within themselves for some special emotion. But they couldn't find it, despite having waited almost their whole lives for this moment.

"The monster is dead," Carlo finally murmured, almost to himself.

"He's dead, Carlo. And we did it," Hausser said, his voice emotionless. "But you know, I feel empty inside."

"And yet . . ."

"And yet we had to do it—we couldn't have died in peace otherwise."

"Have you called Bruno and Mercedes?"

"No, I called you first. We have to make a decision about his granddaughter."

"She's still alive?" Carlo asked.

"Yes. There were difficulties enough, apparently, with the first half of the job. They're asking me whether they should pursue her over there or whether to do it here, in Europe. Apparently she'll be staying here for some time."

"Staying where?"

"I don't know, but she's leaving where she is now." They had already said too much—Hans didn't want to be more specific on the phone.

"So what do you think we should do?"

"I don't know; we could leave things as they stand, or . . ."

"Mercedes won't hear of that," Carlo declared, his heart heavy.

"What about us, Carlo? Will we hear of it?"

"Do you think our conscience can bear it?"

"Mine can, I assure you," Hausser told him; he had not one iota of doubt that he could sleep easily for the rest of his life no matter how many more Tannenbergs were killed.

"You're right. I guess I'm still just trying to . . . to get used to the news."

"I am too, but we have to make a decision," Hausser said firmly.

"Maybe we should let them make the decision. They know about these things. They can decide where it would be best to do it," Carlo finally said, knowing that Mercedes would never consent to stopping halfway.

"That suits me fine."

"At any rate, tell them that we will hold them to the second part."

"Yes, we have to; we've waited our whole lives for this, and today God has finally answered our prayers."

"It has nothing to do with God, Hans, and never has—God wasn't there, he's never been with us. Mercedes is right: If God ever existed, he abandoned us long ago."

They fell silent again, each lost in his own thoughts, wandering through a past that never receded far in their memories.

"I'll call Bruno and then Mercedes, and if there's anything new I'll let you know."

"All rights, Hans. This is going to be a very long night."

"I personally am going to sleep very well."

Deborah jerked awake when the telephone rang, then she bolted upright in bed. She clutched her chest and waited—a premonition of sorrow swept over her.

"Deborah, for heaven's sake, it's all right—it's just the telephone," her husband told her.

"It's almost dawn, Bruno—who would be calling?"

Bruno Müller got up and went into the hall to answer the phone. Deborah followed him, shivering with cold and uncertainty.

"Hello?" Bruno answered, his voice firm and steady.

"Bruno . . . it's Hans."

"Hans! What's wrong?" Bruno asked, now alarmed.

"The monster is dead."

"My God!" Bruno exclaimed, breathless at the news, staring at his disheveled wife leaning against the doorway.

Bruno felt a wave of warmth pass through his body, and then an icy cold settled in the pit of his stomach. Myriad emotions washed over his face, and he felt faint.

"Bruno! Bruno! What is it?!" Deborah asked, her voice edging toward hysteria.

"I'm all right, Deborah. Go back to bed."

"But, Bruno . . ."

"Go back to bed!" barked the usually quiet Bruno.

Hans, listening, knew firsthand what a chaos of emotions Bruno was feeling.

"Are you sure, Hans?" Bruno asked, back on the line.

"I'm sure. We've killed him at last."

"We did it, we finally did it. Oh, my God, we've won!" Bruno knew now that he could finally die in peace.

Hans nodded in silence at his friend's words.

Mercedes had taken a sleeping pill—over the last few months she'd been lucky to get four hours' sleep a night, and she'd finally given in to medication.

The phone rang and rang and rang before it finally penetrated her dream state.

"Hello?"

"Mercedes?"

It sounded to Hans as though she were speaking from beyond the grave. The slurring of her words and the grogginess of her voice worried him. "Are you all right?"

"Who is it?" Mercedes asked vaguely, trying to wake up, focus her eyes, think.

"It's Hans."

"Hans? Hans . . . What's happened?"

"Good news—that's why I didn't wait to call. I'm sorry I woke you."

"It's all right—what is it?"

"He's dead. The monster is dead."

Mercedes cried out, a sound almost like keening. Then she managed to sit up on the side of the bed and put her feet on the floor.

"Mercedes, are you all right?" Hans asked again.

"I was . . . I was so asleep. I couldn't sleep, so I took a pill and . . . Hans, is it true?"

"Yes, absolutely true. He's dead, and there's proof."

"What was it like? When did it happen?" Mercedes was all questions.

"He's already been buried."

"Did he suffer?"

"I don't know—I don't have the details yet."

"I hope he did—I hope he knew he was dying. What about the girl? The granddaughter?"

"She's alive."

"Why? I won't forgive *any* member of his family," Mercedes declared, her voice rising.

"There is no forgiveness, that's right, but things have to be done carefully. Apparently there were some problems, and now they want to know whether to finish it there or whether it can be done in Europe, where she'll be staying for a few months."

"And how are we supposed to know which way is best?" Mercedes shot back.

"Well, we could defer to them. They're experts, after all."

"Then we tell them to do what we hired them to do—the whole job, and the sooner the better. . . . Hans, are you sure? Sure? That monster is dead, truly dead?"

"He's dead, Mercedes, I'm sure."

Mercedes began to weep then, and her sobs moved her old friend so deeply that he, too, at last was able to shed tears of joy and relief. The world was finally free of Alfred Tannenberg.

"Mercedes, please, don't cry. . . ."

Bruno's words seemed powerless to console her.

Carlo brought her a glass of water, and Hans took an immaculate white handkerchief from his jacket pocket and thrust it upon her.

At that hour of the evening in Barcelona, the noises of the street filtered through the windows of Mercedes' house.

Hans had suggested that they meet to mark the fulfillment of the vow they had taken so long ago. Within hours the three friends had landed in Barcelona; they were all deeply concerned about Mercedes, who had been in an emotional crisis since she'd learned of the death of Alfred Tannenberg.

"I'm sorry, I'm sorry," Mercedes sniffled. "I can't help it; I haven't stopped crying since you called me. . . . You know, I think it's a miracle we were able to kill that monster. I always thought that someday we'd do it, but sometimes I would get so desperate, I would think we might never . . ." She began to break down again.

"I still remember the day the Americans arrived," Carlo said gently to her. "You were in the so-called orphanage, hiding with us. You looked like a little boy. That wonderful Polish doctor saved your life and convinced the others to let you stay with us."

"If they'd ever discovered you . . . ," Hans said.

"I don't know what they'd have done to us, but they'd certainly have made the doctor pay," Bruno reflected.

"You were tougher then than you're acting now—you certainly didn't cry as much," said Carlo, attempting to lighten the mood.

Mercedes wiped away her tears with Hans' handkerchief and took a sip of water. She even tried to laugh with Carlo.

"I'm sorry . . . I'm . . . I'm going to wash my face. I'll be back."

When she left, the three friends looked at one another, their faces still troubled.

"I don't know how that monster was able to live all these years in the Middle East without being recognized and reported. His name alone should have exposed him." Bruno shook his head.

"A lot of Nazis took refuge in Syria, Egypt, Iraq, just as they did in Brazil, Paraguay, and other Latin American countries. Tannenberg's case is not the only one; there are still Nazis living very respectable lives, old men nobody pays any mind to," said Hans.

"Don't forget that the grand mufti of Jerusalem was one of Hitler's staunch allies and that the Arabs were supporters of the Nazi regime. We shouldn't be surprised by Tannenberg," Carlo said.

"But why weren't we able to find him for so many years?" Bruno asked.

"Because even if a person changes his name, it's easier to find him in a democratic country than in an autocracy," replied Carlo.

Mercedes came back looking more composed, although her eyes were still red.

"I still haven't thanked you all for coming," she said, smiling uncertainly.

"We all needed to see one another again," replied Hans.

"God, what a long road it's been!" Mercedes exclaimed.

"Yes, but it's all been worth it. All these years of suffering, of nightmares, and we've finally been repaid. Vengeance," Bruno said, "is ours."

"Vengeance, yes, vengeance," said Mercedes, her eyes filled with tears but her voice strong and hard. "Not for a single minute in all these years have I doubted that we would keep our vow. What we went through . . . It was . . . it was hell, and that's why I don't care if God exists; his punishment could never be worse than Mauthausen."

"Did you talk to Tom Martin again?" Carlo asked Hans, trying to distract Mercedes.

"Yes, and I told him that they were to finish the job, the sooner the better. He assured me that his man would do what he'd been hired to do, but he underscored the tremendous difficulties he's already had to face with Alfred. He keeps saying that we can't fathom the obstacles he had to overcome to kill a man under the protection of Saddam in Iraq," Hans replied.

"It's certainly taken long enough," remarked Bruno.

"And that's why it's cost us a fortune. But in the final analysis, our man did it—we have to be grateful for that. Global Group isn't staffed by thugs and hoodlums; if they were, they would never have been able to kill Tannenberg. Anyway, I told him that the second half of the job had to be done, and quicker than the first," Hans said.

"Getting rid of Clara Tannenberg may be even more complicated than getting rid of the old man; when the war starts, it won't be easy for Martin's man to finish what he started. And the Americans have made their decision. There's a great deal at stake, including saving face," Carlo said with a hint of concern.

"You know, it's always surprised me that you could be a Communist," Hans said to him.

Carlo laughed, although his laughter was bitter.

"My mother was in Mauthausen for being a Communist, or rather, because my father was a Communist. He died before he got to the camp, and my mother . . . my mother worshipped him, so she became a Communist for him—though her parents had also been Reds. What could I do? What can I do? I still believe there's value in Communism, despite the horrors that Stalin perpetrated, all that went on behind the Iron Curtain, in the gulags and all that."

"I'm torn about this war, although I'll never be anti-American—we owe them our lives," Bruno said.

"How many innocent people died to free us?" Hans replied. "If the United States hadn't sacrificed thousands of its own men, we'd have died in Mauthausen."

They fell silent, adrift in their thoughts. Their view of the world had been irrevocably colored by the horror of the camp.

Carlo got up out of the chair he was sitting in, clapped his hands once, and in a tone of voice that strove for cheerfulness, suggested that they all go out to dinner to celebrate.

"You're our hostess, Mercedes. Surprise us. But it better be memorable—we've been waiting for this moment for sixty years."

All four of them knew that they needed to make an effort to get past the emotions of the last hours. Mercedes promised that she'd take them to the best dinner they could ever dream of. None of them had ever gotten over their experience of starvation. It had been many years since they'd left Mauthausen physically, but pain and hunger were with them always.

47

"SHAMAS! WAKE UP! WAKE UP!"

Lia's voice was filled with fear. Shamas opened his eyes and sat up in his bed. Through the window came the first light of day.

"What is it?"

"Ili has sent for you. You must go to the temple."

"So early? Did he say why?"

"No, the servant who came said only that Ili wished to see you."

Shamas dressed quickly and left for the temple, filled with worry by his old master's call.

When he reached the rectangular room in which Ili and a number of other scribes awaited him, his misgivings were confirmed. Something grave had clearly happened.

"Shamas, the lord of Safran has demanded our lands," Ili told him. "He is envious of the temple's prosperity."

"What does he want of us?"

"All that we have: wheat, the fruits of our trees, the date palms, our water. He wants our livestock and our houses. He says that there is little fruit in his lands, and that the waters of his streams have dried up. He demands that we increase our tributes to him, for he says that in comparison with what we have, we pay little."

"We have enough grain in the storehouses so that there will be no want of it."

"That is not the problem, Shamas. The truth is that the lord of the palace lacks nothing but wants everything. He sees that we have much, and he would have it. He is the grandson of my predecessor, the last grand master, and he thinks that it is his birthright to govern not just the palace but the temple as well. He shall seek to place an administrator over us, to oversee our labors and decide what portion of our harvests shall be sent to the royal treasury and what portion shall remain here.

"I withheld this from you yesterday, so as not to mar your ceremony. But I received the lord's orders several days ago, and today, before dawn, one of his soldiers came to demand my answer. I believed that we could continue to talk about the matter, that I might persuade him of the injustice of his demands, but I was mistaken."

"And is there no way to oppose him? Can we not rise up against him?"

"He would destroy us—he would salt our land, sack our storehouses. . . . We have no choice. We are men of peace; we know not how to make war," said Ili.

The scribes, distraught, were silent, pondering what tribulations their lord's demand might bring upon them. Some looked toward Shamas, hoping that his restless mind might find a solution.

"We can seek aid from the king of Ur," said Shamas. "He is more powerful than our lord, who would not dare match arms against him."

They agreed to send an emissary to Ur to seek the king's aid and implore his protection. Ili appointed a young scribe and bade him set out immediately. But the question they all asked themselves was whether the king of Ur would hear their pleas. Kings were capricious beings, and their logic was not the logic of men. Thus, it was possible that the king of Ur might ask in exchange for his aid a price larger than that demanded by the lord of Safran. They were left to await their fate.

The sun was shining in all its splendor, bathing the yellow land of Safran with light, when the cry of a man rose above the noise of the market.

Ili and Shamas looked at each other, knowing that that cry was the augury of death and destruction.

All the scribes ran to the doors of the temple, where soldiers from the lord of Safran were already making ready to enter. The crackling of flames and the weeping of women rose toward the sky, and citizens shouted as the soldiers attacked men's houses and their defenseless inhabitants.

Shamas realized that there was nothing they could do but bend like the rushes along the banks of the Euphrates, waiting for the storm to pass. But his instinct was more powerful than his reason, and he confronted the soldiers, though Ili begged him to stand aside.

He knew that his effort would be futile, but he would not surrender to the injustice that was being done against them.

How much time had passed? Perhaps a second, perhaps hours—he felt profoundly weary, and confusion reigned within his mind.

No man is eternal, even a king. Someday someone in this temple will live once again in peace, looking after the fields and pastures, caring for the livestock and the houses of men who trust in the good work of scribes who, as we have, labor from dawn to dusk to bring order and justice to the community, thought Shamas as he was dragged away by a soldier.

He saw Ili, his master, lying on the ground, with a wound to his face from which a stream of blood was flowing. Other scribes lay motionless around him, and among the bodies were also servants of the temple who had run to defend the place where until today peace and tranquillity had reigned.

His head hurt, his limbs were heavy, he could hardly move one of his arms, and his eyesight was clouded.

Am I dying, like the others? Am I already dead?

Then he realized that the pain he was feeling was too intense for the dead. He knew that there still remained in him some breath of life, but how much? And Lia—was Lia still alive? The soldier kicked him in the face and left him to die—Shamas was hardly breathing, and the soldier feared little that he would stand again.

Why has God willed that this should be my end? Shamas thought. Then he smiled to himself—Ili would have reproached him for asking such a question at a moment like this, a question to God. But would the others not ask the same of Marduk?

If Abraham were here, Shamas would ask him why God allowed His creatures to die violent deaths. Was such an end truly necessary?

He was not certain whether his eyes were closed, but he could not see; his life was ebbing away, all because of one man's greed. How absurd that seemed to him! Where was God? Would he see Him in the end? He heard a voice, the voice of Abraham, begging him to trust in God. Then a white light illuminated the corner in which he lay, and he felt a firm hand help him stand. He felt no more pain and melted into eternity.

48

GIAN MARIA WAS CAREFULLY CLEANING A TABLET ON WHICH the marks of cuneiform were barely visible when a laborer practically ran over him.

"Come, come!" he shouted. "There is another room! A wall has fallen!"

"What wall? What's happened?"

He received no answer from the man, who took off running back toward the excavation site. Gian Maria followed with curiosity. Ayed Sahadi, looking very excited, was shouting orders to a group of laborers.

"What's happened?" Gian Maria asked the foreman.

"That man there hit the wall with his pick—it just collapsed. We've found another room full of tablets. I've sent for Clara."

Clara herself ran up at that precise moment, with Fatima, her head still wrapped in bandages, not far behind.

"What have they found?" Clara asked breathlessly.

"Another room and more tablets," Gian Maria told her.

Clara gave instructions to the laborers to shore up what was left of the wall and erect supports to hold up the ceiling—but first, wherever possible, to gather up the tablets. Gian Maria sat down on the floor to have a look at the new finds. His eyes were burning from trying to read so much cuneiform blurred by time, but he knew that sooner or later, Clara would want him to examine all these new tablets.

He found none that were particularly interesting, but with Ante's help he carefully began lining them up so the laborers could transport them to the camp, where over the last few days they had been putting together some of the pieces that Picot had left behind when he and his team left Safran.

It occurred to Gian Maria how fortunate they were that Ante Plaskic had come back. Ahmed had called Clara to tell her that at the last minute Ante had decided, against Picot's advice, to stay in Iraq and return to Safran. He'd then convinced Ahmed to arrange transportation for him, despite the fact that Clara would be staying no more than a week longer. But the effort had paid off—since Ante had returned to the camp, he'd done nothing but work; he was with them at the dig every moment.

"Is there anything there?" Clara asked, walking over to where Gian Maria was concentrating on categorizing the tablets under Ante's watchful eye.

"I'm not sure; there are shards of commercial transactions, and some prayers, but I haven't had time to review them closely. We'll gather them all up—I imagine you'll want to take them with you to Baghdad."

"Yes, but I wish you'd try to . . . well, examine them more closely before then, just in case," Clara prodded.

"I'll try, Clara, but we have to be realistic about what we can still hope to accomplish. There are hardly any laborers left. Ayed is doing all he can, but the army is calling up most of the men. And others . . . Well, you know what's happening; they want to be at home with their families."

"We have two days, Gian Maria—in two days Ahmed is going to take us out. The ministry is terminating the expedition."

Ante Plaskic listened in silence to their conversation. Clara had been keyed up and driven since her grandfather's murder; she seemed to have inherited her grandfather's all-consuming obsession with the tablets. It hadn't mattered to her that Ante had come back to the camp—she hadn't even questioned his motives. She'd greeted him absentmindedly and put him to work with the others.

It had been only a few days since Picot and his team had left, but to Clara it seemed an eternity. Where the camp had once stood, with all its frenetic activity, there was now nothing but the empty mud houses and the permanent calm of the desert. Time had stopped once more in the remote enclave.

Gian Maria was right: There were hardly any workers left. And those who remained looked at Clara differently now. The absence of her grandfather had stripped her of her authority, even her ability to command respect.

Only the presence of Ayed Sahadi fostered a certain degree of order and ensured that the workers kept at it.

As for Clara herself, her mind was a mass of contradictions—she knew that the war was going to start on March 20 and that she had to be out of Iraq by March 19, yet she felt that something was holding her in that dusty land. She also knew full well of course, that if she stayed she could easily die. Fighter planes make no distinction between friends and enemies, those who betrayed the country and those who were loyal to it. And then there were the tablets . . .

It was five a.m. when her cell phone woke her.

"Clara . . ." Ahmed's unsteady voice scared her.

"Ahmed! What's wrong?"

"Clara, you need to get out now."

"Has there been . . . has there been some change?"

"I'm worried."

"You're panicking."

"Call it what you want, but you can't wait until the last minute. All hell is about to break loose. And listen, I spoke to Picot last night—you need to be there, keeping an eye on the exhibition planning."

"Where is he?"

"In Paris."

"Paris?" sighed Clara.

"He says things have already started coming together and he wants to know whether you're going with them."

"Going where?"

"I don't know, wherever they're putting it together. I didn't ask."

"What about you, Ahmed? Are you going?"

"I'd like to go with you," he answered carefully. He knew that the Ministry of the Interior recorded every conversation, and after the murder of Alfred Tannenberg an exhaustive investigation had been launched. Saddam and his circle had always been obsessed with betrayal, so of course they believed that Tannenberg's murderer must have been a close friend, family member, or ally.

"It's five o'clock in the morning; if you don't have anything else to tell me—"

"I'm telling you that you need to come out now. Today is the eighteenth of March—"

"I know what day it is. I'm staying until the nineteenth; we found another room yesterday and several dozen new tablets. We're close, Ahmed. I can feel it."

"Clara, you should be in Baghdad, in your own house. The army is mobilizing every man; you won't have any workers."

"One more day, Ahmed."

"No, Clara, no—I'll send the helicopter later today."

"I'm not leaving today, Ahmed."

"Tomorrow, then, at sunrise."

Gian Maria hadn't slept all night. He'd stayed up to classify the last tablets they'd found, before the workers packed them up and sealed them in the container destined for Baghdad.

His eyes were killing him, but he still had quite a few tablets to decipher. He picked one up at random, and as he looked at it, he gave a start and almost dropped it—across the top was incised the name *Shamas*. He could feel his heart beat faster and his breathing become shallower as he passed his finger over the lines of cuneiform.

> *As dictated to me by our patriarch Abraham:*
>
> *In the beginning God created the heavens and the earth. And the earth was without form, and void; and the darkness was upon the face of the deep. And the spirit of God moved upon the face of the waters.*
>
> *And God said, Let there be light: and there was light. And God saw the light, that it was good: and God divided the light from the darkness. And God called the light Day, and the darkness He called Night. And the evening and the morning were the first day.*

Tears flowed from the priest's eyes. He was profoundly moved, and he felt an irresistible need to fall on his knees and give thanks to God.

Here in his hands he held the story of the Creation, its words pressed into wet clay over three thousand years ago by the scribe Shamas himself so that men might learn the truth. This clay tablet bore the very words of Abraham the patriarch, inspired by God, the words which many centuries later would be gathered into the book called the Bible.

Gian Maria could hardly go on reading, so great was the emotion he was feeling.

> *And God said, Let there be a firmament in the midst of the waters, and let it divide the waters from the waters. And God made the firmament and divided the waters which were under the firmament from the waters which were above the firmament: and it was so. And God called the firmament Heaven. And the evening and the morning were the second day.*

He went on reading, not realizing that he was doing so out loud. He felt closer to God than he had ever felt before. And then he realized that in the stack of tablets he had not yet examined, there were yet others bearing the distinctive mark of Shamas.

He began to search feverishly through the tablets, scanning the top of each one, where the scribes wrote their names. First he found one piece of tablet, then others, and in a while he had managed to find eight—eight pieces, some shards and some whole, inscribed by Shamas.

Gian Maria prayed, laughed, cried, such was the chaos of emotions that swept over him as he found clay tablet after clay tablet containing the words of Abraham.

He knew he should tell Clara, but he felt the need to be alone with them in this moment so charged with a spirituality that probably only he felt. It was a miracle, and he gave thanks to God for having allowed him to be the one to discover this clay fired with the mark of the deity.

The Bible made no mention of Shamas, so as Gian Maria tried to decipher the signs carefully incised by Shamas' stylus, he wondered who this scribe might have been, how he knew Abraham, and how Abraham had come to tell him the story of the Creation. He also wondered about the strange wanderings of this man who first announced that Abraham was going to tell him the story of Genesis on two tablets that had been secreted in Haran. And yet Shamas had left traces of himself here in Safran too, in the temple near Ur, where the team had found shards of legal statements, official reports and communications, lists of plants, poems. . . .

The room where these new tablets had been found was not distinguished from the others in any way. It was rather small, actually, undecorated, defined only by the slots in the walls where there had once been shelves upon which the scribes would line up their tablets. Clara had mentioned that it may not have been a ceremonial room in the temple but rather, a man's private room—the study, perhaps, of an um-mi-a, a master scribe.

Gian Maria mused on the turn his life had taken over the last few months. He had left the security of the Vatican's walls, left the comfortable routine he shared with other priests, the tranquillity of spirit. He no longer remembered the last time he had slept comfortably through the whole night, since hearing that terrifying confession months ago.

Once again, his eyes filled with tears as he read the words that transported him back to the moment when God created man:

> *And God said, Let us make a man in our image, after our likeness: and let him have dominion over the fish of the sea, and over the fowl of the air, and over the cattle, and over all the earth, and over every creeping thing that creepeth upon the earth.*

> *So God created man in His own image, in the image of God created He him; male and female created He them.*

> *And God blessed them, and God said unto them, Be fruitful, and multiply, and replenish the earth, and subdue it: and have dominion over the fish of the sea, and over the fowl of the air, and over every living thing that moveth upon the earth.*

> *And God said, Behold, I have given you every herb bearing seed, which is upon the face of all the earth, and every tree, in which is the fruit of a tree yielding seed: to you it shall be for meat.*

Light was beginning to come through the window when Gian Maria realized that Ante Plaskic was watching him. He'd been so engrossed in reading the tablets that he hadn't been aware of the Croatian's arrival.

"Ante, you can't imagine what I've found!"

"What?" he asked casually.

"Clara's grandfather was right—he always thought that Abraham had been aware of the story of Genesis. Here it is. The tablets he spent his life looking for. They exist! Look . . ."

Ante came over to Gian Maria and picked up one of the tablets. It was hard to believe that people could kill over something as simple as a piece of dried clay, but they did, and he wouldn't hesitate to do so as well if anyone tried to stop him from taking them now.

"How many are there?" he asked the priest.

"Eight, I've found eight. Thank God for allowing me to do this work!" Gian Maria answered joyously.

"We should wrap them carefully to keep them intact. Let me help."

"No, no, we have to tell Clara first. Nothing can compensate for the loss of her grandfather, but at least she's finally made his dream come true. This is a miracle!"

Just then, Ayed Sahadi entered the room and eyed the men.

"What's happened?" he asked in a tone of voice that matched his suspicious look.

"Ayed, we've found the tablets!" Gian Maria exclaimed, excited as a child, all traces of his characteristic shyness absent.

"The tablets? What tablets?" Ayed asked.

"The Bible of Clay! Mr. Tannenberg was right. Clara was right. Abraham told the story of creation to a scribe. It's a revolutionary discovery, one of the greatest in history," Gian Maria explained, emerging from the shock of the discovery and his spiritual reflections and growing more excited by the second.

The foreman came over to the workbench where the eight tablets were laid out side by side, three of them reconstructed from broken pieces—pieces that fit together perfectly after Gian Maria had solved their jigsaw puzzle. The tablets couldn't be restored in Safran, though; that had to be done by experts, and Gian Maria prayed that Clara would let him take them to Rome, where they could be examined and authenticated by Vatican authorities, even reconstructed with the advanced techniques developed in Europe.

Ayed assessed the situation instantly and asked Gian Maria to go to Clara's house to give her the news—he didn't want to leave Ante alone with the tablets. Gian Maria agreed, nodding eagerly, his eyes bright as he rushed out to tell Clara. When he got to the house, he found her already dressed, sipping a cup of tea with Fatima.

"I see you're up early," she greeted him.

"Clara, the Bible of Clay is real—it exists!" he blurted out.

"Of course it exists, Gian Maria. I'm sure of it—I have two tablets that prove it."

"No, I mean we've found it—we found the Bible of Clay!"

Clara just stared at him, as though she couldn't understand what he was saying.

"They were stored in the room we discovered yesterday; there are eight of them, eight tablets, Clara, each twenty centimeters long. I've read them and it's no mistake. It's . . . it's the Bible of Clay!"

As Clara shot to her feet, Gian Maria seized her hand and pulled her out the door. They ran to the workroom, Gian Maria chattering and telling her what had happened during the night.

Ayed and Ante were visibly tense when Clara and Gian Maria burst into the room, breaking off what looked to be a heated discussion, but Clara paid them no mind. She ran to the workbench where the eight tablets were laid out.

She picked up one of them and was elated to see the cuneiform signs that denoted *Shamas* at the top. Then she began to silently read the wedge-shaped markings that had been pressed into wet clay more than three thousand years earlier.

Tears came to her eyes, and Gian Maria was swept up in emotion all over again. They were laughing and crying, going over the tablets, touching them, as though to reassure themselves that they were real.

Afterward, they wrapped them carefully, and Clara insisted on keeping them near her.

"I'll put them in the same case as the first two. I don't want to lose sight of them for a second."

"We need to put a guard on them," Ayed told her.

"Ayed, you haven't let me out of your sight, twenty-four hours a day, so if the tablets are with me they're safe."

Ayed shrugged his shoulders; he had no intention of fighting again with this impossible woman. He couldn't have cared less about her fate or the fate of those damned tablets. If the Colonel hadn't ordered him to protect her—with his own life—he'd have left when the old man died.

"I want the workers to clear out a little more of the area where we found the tablets. There may be more . . . ," Clara continued.

"No. I just called the Colonel, and he's sending a helicopter for us this afternoon. We're going back to Baghdad."

"We can't go now! We have to look for more!" Clara cried desperately.

"You know you can't stay any longer. Don't tempt fate, Clara, and don't risk everyone else's life in the bargain," Ayed Sahadi replied harshly, to Clara's surprise. "You've got what you came for. I have my orders, and I'm following them. Get everything ready you want to take—we're leaving before nightfall."

49

THE BUZZ OF THE INTERCOM WOKE GEORGE WAGNER FROM a brief nap. He opened his eyes in irritation. The buzzer sounded again, and his secretary's apologetic voice broke the silence.

"Mr. Wagner, it's Robert Brown. He says it's urgent and can't wait."

Brown was practically screaming when Wagner picked up the phone. "You'll never guess what's happened, George! They've found it! It fucking exists!"

"What are you talking about? Stop babbling—get ahold of yourself. Tell me what happened."

Robert Brown swallowed hard, trying to calm himself.

"The Bible of Clay—it exists. They've found it. Eight tablets, Genesis, signed by Shamas, as dictated by Abraham," Brown finally said, as coherently as he could.

George Wagner could hardly believe what he was hearing. He gripped the arm of the chair, trying to keep control of his emotions.

"How . . ." he said.

"I just got word that yesterday, at their dig in Safran, another room was discovered in the ziggurat. Apparently it was a study where a scribe might have lived. They found several dozen tablets but didn't realize until a few hours ago that the Bible of Clay was among them. It's comprised of eight full tablets, three of them in pretty bad shape—they'll need to be reconstructed. But there's no doubt that they're Alfred's Bible of Clay," Brown said, slowing down.

Wagner felt like someone had kicked him in the chest. A few days earlier, Alfred had been murdered, and now the Bible of Clay turned up. Destiny had played its last dirty trick on his old friend, denying him what he'd wanted most in all the world.

"Where are the tablets now?" he asked.

"Still in Safran. They're going to fly Clara to Baghdad with the tablets. Our man is with her, and he'll grab them as soon as he can. It's going to be tricky, though. She's well guarded, to say the least."

"I want him to secure those tablets now, and the minute he has them we'll get him out. Call Paul Dukais, tell him it's top priority—getting the tablets comes before anything else, even the rest of the operation."

"I haven't been able to talk to our man directly yet; it's our friends who relayed the message," Robert Brown told him.

"Oh," Wagner said, now more skeptical. "And are they sure, then? They've found it?"

"Absolutely, I assure you."

"What about Ahmed Husseini?"

"He has the same instructions as our man—get the tablets. Don't worry, we will," Brown replied.

"I *am* worried. We get them, or I'll have their heads. Literally."

Robert Brown didn't answer for a few seconds. He knew Wagner didn't make idle threats.

"I'll call Paul right now," he said.

"Do."

"But what if she . . . what if Clara resists?"

"Clara is but a speck of sand in our lives," Wagner answered.

The Colonel could still feel the presence of Alfred Tannenberg in his office in the Yellow House, where Clara and he were now meeting.

An obviously nervous Ahmed Husseini was there too.

"My dear girl, the best thing is to entrust the tablets to me," the Colonel told Clara. "I will get them out of Iraq and see that they are deposited in a safe place."

"But you just told me that I have to be out of Iraq tomorrow myself. Why can't I just take them with me?"

The Colonel was too preoccupied with the military situation and the urgency of this new crisis to call on his powers of diplomacy.

"Clara, your grandfather had some partners, and you know what is going to happen here the minute the war starts. So don't be stubborn—let's make this as easy as possible."

"These tablets have nothing to do with my grandfather's business dealings. They're mine and nobody else's."

"Your grandfather's partners do not share that view. Give the tablets to me and you will receive your share when the time comes."

"They're not for sale, and they never will be," Clara replied defiantly.

"Please, Clara, don't make all this harder than it already is!" Ahmed pleaded.

"I'm not making things harder, I'm just refusing to let you rob me. My grandfather detailed the business operation under way right now, and he assured me that these tablets are not part of the deal. They're mine."

The Colonel stood up and approached Clara. She could see in his eyes that he was willing to do anything to get his hands on the tablets. She felt a shiver of fear run down her spine. She looked over at Ahmed, but his expression projected only anguish and resignation. The man she'd fallen in love with had vanished long ago. She realized that she had to gain some time—otherwise, she could lose everything, even her life.

"If I give them to you, will you promise me that you won't sell them until I can speak directly to my grandfather's partners?" she asked, her tone now more conciliatory.

"Of course, of course . . . They are reasonable men and have no desire to cheat you. Or harm you, for God's sake. You should absolutely discuss this with them. Right now we must cease wasting time."

"All right," she replied wearily. "Wait here."

She left the office and ran up the stairs two at a time. Fatima was still unpacking the luggage.

"Go to your room and bring me up some of your clothes!" she ordered her servant.

"What? What's happening?" Fatima asked in alarm.

"They want to take the Bible of Clay from me. We have to get out of here now. If they catch me they'll kill us both, so you must decide for yourself whether to come with me or not. Now hurry, bring me a burka."

"What about Gian Maria and that other man, Ante Plaskic? I took them to the guest rooms. They can help you. I'll tell them—"

"No! Don't tell them. Do as I say—go!"

Clara pulled out a small bag and crammed a few pieces of clothing into it. Then she slipped the tablets inside. She hoped they wouldn't wind up in a million pieces, but she'd have to run that risk—anything to keep them out of the Colonel's hands. Otherwise, she'd never see them again.

Fatima came rushing back in with an armful of her clothes. Within thirty seconds, Clara had pulled on a black robe and covered her head with a black veil that fell almost to her feet.

"Are you coming?" she asked Fatima.

"I won't leave you," answered the terrified woman.

Ayed Sahadi was on the landing, waiting for the two women to appear. The Colonel had ordered him to stand watch on the stairway, and he had posted himself there on the landing, where he could see the door to Clara's room.

Fatima stifled a cry of fear when she saw the Colonel's man leaning against the wall, smoking one of his unmistakable Egyptian cigarettes.

Clara glared at Sahadi. "What are you doing here?" she asked him angrily.

"The Colonel sent me," he answered, shrugging.

"The Colonel doesn't trust me?" Clara said.

"I can't think why that would be," Sahadi replied sarcastically, looking sidewise at her black robes and veil.

"He wants the Bible of Clay," Clara answered.

"Your grandfather's partners want it. It's nothing personal—it's just business," Ayed replied.

"No it isn't. You know better than anyone how hard we've worked to find it—those tablets are much more than an archaeological treasure; they're my grandfather's dream made tangible."

"Don't go looking for trouble, Clara—if you don't hand them over, they'll take them by force. Be smart."

"How much do you want for helping me?"

Clara's offer surprised him. He'd never have expected her to bribe him—they both knew that double-crossing the Colonel would be signing his own death warrant.

"My life isn't for sale," he replied very seriously.

"Everybody has a price, even you. Tell me how much you want for helping me get out of here."

"Out of this house?"

"Out of Iraq."

"You have an Egyptian passport, you can leave whenever you like—and you have got the Colonel's permission."

"What good is his permission if I don't give him the tablets? Is two hundred fifty thousand enough? Dollars?"

Greed flickered in Sahadi's eyes. He could feel the temptation pulsing through his veins, knowing full well that accepting would almost certainly be fatal.

"I'm going to make a lot of money either way—I've been working for the Colonel for a long time; I know the rules."

"Then you also know the laws of supply and demand. I need to get out of Iraq and you can help me. How much? Name the amount—I'll pay it."

"You can pay me half a million dollars?"

"I can pay you that in Egypt or in Switzerland, anyplace but Iraq. I don't have that kind of money here."

"And how do I know you'll pay me?"

"Because if I don't you can kill me, or turn me over to the Colonel, which would amount to the same thing."

"I could turn you over to him now."

"Then do it or take my offer. We're out of time."

The sound of a door opening distracted them both. Gian Maria had just come out of one of the guest rooms and had stopped cold seeing them.

"What's going on?" he asked, puzzled at why Clara was in Shiite dress.

"The Colonel wants the Bible of Clay and I don't want to give it to him. I'm asking Ayed to help me escape."

Gian Maria was still puzzled—the implications of what Clara was saying hadn't sunk in.

Ayed grimaced and waved them all into Gian Maria's room. When they were inside, he paced the floor, his greed for the money and his fear of the Colonel clearly at war inside him. He reached the conclusion that it was a pure toss of a coin—all or nothing.

"If he finds us, he'll kill us," he whispered.

"Yes," Clara answered.

"You know this house better than I do—you know there are soldiers standing guard outside."

"I can leave as Fatima; no one will give it a second thought."

"Do it, then—go to the kitchen, get a basket, and leave through the back door, as though you were going to the market. Fatima will have to stay in her room, and you, Gian Maria, in yours."

"But where will Clara go?" Gian Maria asked.

"I think the only place she can be safe, at least for a few hours, is in the Hotel Palestina," Ayed said.

"You're crazy! The hotel is full of reporters, and a lot of them know Clara from Safran," Gian Maria said, increasingly anxious.

"That's why she needs to find somebody she can trust, maybe that reporter who hit it off with Picot. Ask her to hide you until I can retrieve you. But don't leave her room. Not for one minute."

"You think I can trust her?" Clara asked.

"I think she likes Picot, and I don't think he'd want to find out that something happened to you because she didn't help you—he might think less of her, so to speak," Sahadi said. "So even though she's not crazy about you, she'll help you."

"You're quite a psychologist," Clara said acidly.

"Let's not waste time—go. Hide your face. Fatima will help you with the veil so you'll look like a Shiite. And leave that bag—you'll have to hide the tablets somewhere else. Find something smaller."

"They don't fit . . . ," Clara protested.

"We have a shopping cart," Fatima offered. "They may fit there."

"Good idea!" exclaimed Clara.

"I'm going with you," Gian Maria declared, regaining his equilibrium.

"No!" Ayed shot back. "Do you want them to kill us all? Go, Clara." Then, turning to Fatima and Gian Maria, he continued to lay out the scenario: "In a few minutes, this house is going to be a living hell. The Colonel will interrogate you both, and you'll get the worst of it, Fatima."

"Then she's coming with me," said Clara.

"She can't. This is our only chance; don't blow it. Everything depends on Fatima now. The Colonel will figure she knows where you've gone, so he'll have her tortured. If she talks, we're all dead . . . unless . . ."

"Unless what?" Gian Maria asked.

"Unless we make them think either that Clara left without saying anything or that somebody kidnapped her and took the tablets too," said Ayed, thinking out loud.

"But the soldiers will say they saw a Shiite woman—Fatima—leave, so the kidnapping story won't wash," said Clara.

"Then we'll just have to stake everything on one shot. . . . All right, both of you try to leave—and hope the soldiers don't stop you. Go to the Hotel Palestina; I'll come for you. I don't know how soon, but I will. And you, Gian Maria, lock yourself in here and pretend to be asleep. Where's the Croatian?" Ayed suddenly asked.

"In a room on the first floor, near the door into the garage," Fatima told him.

"Good. Let's hope he doesn't realize what's going on. If he doesn't know anything, he can't say anything."

The two women slipped stealthily down to the kitchen, desperately trying not to make a sound. They barely dared breathe. Gian Maria, sweating profusely, closed the door to his room, fell to his knees, and started praying: *Please, God, help them.*

Clara emptied the contents of the bag into the shopping cart, arranging everything as best she could to cushion the tablets. Then she embraced Fatima.

They opened the kitchen door into the back lawn and walked out, standing tall, toward the wrought-iron gate at the rear of the property. No one seemed to pay them any mind. Once they reached the street, Clara whispered to Fatima not to hurry, not to draw attention, just to walk as slowly and casually as always. Soon the Yellow House was blocks behind them.

Ayed Sahadi was lighting another cigarette when Ahmed appeared at the foot of the stairs, meekly asking for Clara.

"I haven't moved. She must be up in her room," Sahadi answered, taking a puff of his cigarette.

Ahmed went to the bedroom where he had once slept, and knocked. There was no answer.

"Clara, it's me!"

He turned toward Sahadi and asked again if he had seen Clara.

"I told you I haven't moved since the Colonel sent me up here. I didn't see her leave, so she has to be in there."

Ahmed opened the door and went into the bedroom. The fragrance of flowers Fatima had brought in mixed with Clara's perfume and filled the room, bringing Ahmed a sharp pang of nostalgia.

"Clara . . ." he called softly, expecting his wife to appear out of the shadows that were beginning to creep into the room—but clearly she wasn't there.

He came out of the room, and with a look bordering on contrition, asked Ayed again where his wife was.

"She's not in her room?" Ayed tried to make his voice sound worried.

"No—she must have left. You must have seen her leave!"

"No, Ahmed, I'm telling you, nobody's been in or out of that room since the Colonel sent me up here. She has to be there—"

"She's not there!" Ahmed screamed.

Ayed went up to the room and opened the door. He went in as though he really thought he was going to find Clara.

"We have to tell the Colonel," said Ahmed.

"Wait—she may be somewhere else in the house," Ayed replied.

Each of them searched part of the house but could locate neither Clara nor Fatima. Two of the servants said they thought they'd seen Fatima leave the house with somebody, probably one of her cousins, since she was dressed in the same black robes and veil as Fatima.

When Ahmed and Ayed went into Tannenberg's office, the Colonel was talking on his cell phone, and from his tone of voice it wasn't hard to conclude that he was arguing with someone.

When he saw the two men come in alone, the Colonel immediately knew the worst—Clara had gotten away.

"Where is she?" he asked icily.

"She isn't in her room," Ahmed said.

"Where is she?" the Colonel asked Ayed directly, and this time it was obvious that he was not ready to believe a word the man said.

"I don't know. I went up and stood on the landing directly outside her room, stood there until Ahmed came up. So she must have escaped before you sent me up there. I never moved off that landing."

"We've searched the entire house for her," said Ahmed, almost trembling in anticipation of the Colonel's reaction.

"How could you have been so stupid!" the Colonel shouted. "She's as slippery as her grandfather, and now we've lost her."

He ran out of the front door, shouting orders to the soldiers guarding the house. A minute later the two servant women were being interrogated. One of the Colonel's men dragged Gian Maria out of his room and shoved him down to the living room, where Ante Plaskic was already answering the Colonel's questions.

"You helped her get away!" the Colonel was yelling in his face.

"I assure you I did not," the Croatian answered, showing no fear.

"You did, and you shall confess! And you will too!" he shouted at Gian Maria.

"What's happening?" Gian Maria asked, praying for God to forgive his lie.

"Where is Clara Tannenberg? You know, Gian Maria! She never took a step without you! Tell me where she is!"

"But . . . but . . . I . . . I don't . . . Clara . . . Clara . . . ," Gian Maria babbled. He was honestly overwhelmed by the Colonel's livid face, the shouting, the rage in his eyes.

One of the soldiers came in and whispered something in the Colonel's ear. Neither of the two servant women knew anything. They had seen Fatima leaving the house with another woman, a Shiite, and the shopping cart. They had thought the woman was one of her relatives.

"So she's dressed like a Shiite. Send men to look for her in Fatima's relatives' houses. Do whatever you have to do—I want answers," ordered the Colonel.

One of the Colonel's men began to punch Gian Maria in the face and body. The priest didn't think he could withstand the pain, and once more he prayed for strength; he couldn't betray Clara. Nor did he, although he lost two teeth and blood was seeping out of his ear by the time the soldier finished with him.

Ante Plaskic was not in good shape either, after his interrogator got all he could out of him, which was nothing. But Ante realized that he was lucky—ordinarily, the interrogator would have killed him; this time, he was satisfied after a few harsh blows to the head.

"They don't know anything," Ayed told the Colonel.

"How do you know that?" the Colonel asked him.

"Because if she left the way it appears she did, she wouldn't have told anybody. She knows us, she knows we can get a confession out of a rock, so she wouldn't have run the risk of trusting anybody."

The Colonel thought about that for a moment and realized that Ayed was probably right. Clara knew that he would interrogate everyone in the house, maybe even kill them, so she wouldn't have confided her plans to anyone.

"You're right, Ayed, you're right. All right, let these two go. They're worthless. But I want men watching the house day and night," he ordered. "We'll go to headquarters and start the search for them. Little Miss Tannenberg is going to pay dearly for this stunt."

"Colonel, we don't have much time—shouldn't we forget about Clara for now?" said Ahmed, making an effort to appear calm.

"Are you trying to protect her? Forget it—nobody screws with me and gets away with it, not even Clara Tannenberg!"

"In two days, the Americans and British are going to start bombing; we have work to do. Mike Fernandez called me this morning. He's worried—really worried. He's afraid that Tannenberg's death is going to complicate the operation," Ahmed insisted.

"That Green Beret is always worried. We're doing our part; tell him to do his. Our friends in Washington want the Bible of Clay; it's the most important part of the haul, and they're going to get it. I want to see you in my office in half an hour—call my nephew and tell him to come too," the Colonel replied.

When the Colonel left, Ahmed helped Gian Maria up off the floor and into a chair. Then he asked one of the servants to go to the medicine cabinet and find some antiseptic and bandages.

Ante Plaskic was still lying on the floor, unmoving, and Ahmed tried to help him to stand up too, but the Croatian was in worse shape than Gian Maria; he was barely breathing. Ahmed thought it best to let him lie for the moment.

The two soldiers who'd just interrogated the two men had stayed behind in the living room, looking on indifferently; they couldn't have cared less whether the men lived or died—they were just doing their job, which was to follow the Colonel's orders.

Ayed took charge of the situation and ordered the soldiers to search the house again and be sure men were posted on the outside as well, as the Colonel had ordered.

"Gian Maria, where's Clara?" Ahmed asked him.

"I don't know . . . ," the priest answered in a raspy whisper.

"She trusts you," Ahmed insisted.

"Yes, but I don't know where she is—I haven't seen her since I got to the house. I . . . I'd like to find her too. I'm worried about what might happen to her. The Colonel . . . is a monster."

Ahmed shrugged his shoulders wearily. He had a feeling of terrible dread, almost nausea, in the pit of his stomach.

"I don't want anything to happen to Clara; tell me where she is so I can help her. She's my wife, Gian Maria."

"I don't know where she is, Ahmed—but I fear for her life," the priest replied, looking over at Ayed Sahadi, who had just gotten Ante up and dropped him on the couch.

"I have to go—the Colonel is expecting me," Ahmed said resignedly. "You too, Ayed. We can't stay. The servants will help you two, though. Get out, get out of Iraq as soon as you can; today, if possible. I'll call my office and leave instructions so you can pass through the checkpoints if you leave by car. But if I were you, I'd start moving as soon as possible."

Gian Maria nodded. He could hardly move, but he knew he had to do as Ahmed said.

"I'll go to the Hotel Palestina," he whispered.

"The Palestina? What for?" Ahmed asked.

"Because most of the foreigners are there, and they can tell me the best way to get out of here. Maybe I can go with somebody, if they help me. . . ."

"I can try to get a car to take you to the Jordanian border, but I can't promise anything," Ahmed told them.

"If there's no other way, I'll ask for your help, but I'd rather go it on my own," Gian Maria replied.

"Go to the Palestina, then—you'll both be better off there," Ayed told the two men. With a look to Gian Maria that was not lost on Ante

Plaskic, he warned, "And listen to what Ahmed is telling you: Get out of Iraq as soon as you can."

Before he left, Sahadi went over to the priest and told him softly, "Don't tell that man where Clara is. I don't trust him."

Gian Maria didn't even respond. Later, when Ahmed and Ayed had left, silence fell over the room. The only sounds were from outside on the lawn, words exchanged by the soldiers guarding the house.

It was more than half an hour before either man could bring himself to move. Meanwhile, the two servants treated their bruises and contusions, the cuts on their faces and torsos, and made them more comfortable—although the women were so nervous that their hands shook.

Ante asked them to bring him aspirin for the pain as he finished swabbing the rest of the blood off his face. But it was still a while before the two men could move around, much less talk.

50

CLARA AND FATIMA HURRIED INTO THE HOTEL PALESTINA before the doorman had a chance to ask what business they had there. At the front desk, Clara managed to persuade the clerk to call Miranda in her room and then to let her speak to the reporter herself.

"Hello, Miranda? I'm a friend of Professor Picot's. You and I met in Safran. Could I come up and speak to you?"

Miranda recognized Clara's voice. She thought it was odd that Clara used the artifice of mentioning Picot but gave her the room number and told her she was welcome to come up.

Two minutes later, when Miranda opened the door to her room, she was met with the spectacle of two Shiite women covered in black from head to toe. She invited them in, then closed the door, turned, and stood there, obviously waiting for some explanation.

"Thank you. I can't tell you how badly we need your help," Clara said as she removed her veil, then gestured toward Fatima to sit down in the room's only chair.

"I knew it was you—I recognized your voice. What's going on?"

"I have to get out of Iraq. Miranda, I found it—I found the Bible of Clay! But now they're trying to take it away from me," Clara explained, the words tumbling out.

"The Bible of Clay? You mean it actually exists? My God, Yves won't believe it!"

The fact that Miranda had referred to Picot by his first name wasn't lost on Clara. Apparently there *was* something more than friendship between the professor and the reporter, and Clara could exploit that.

"Will you help me?"

"Help you what?"

"I told you—I have to get out of Iraq."

"Wait. Tell me what's happened first. Who wants to take the Bible of Clay away from you? Do you have it with you? Can I see it?"

Clara reached down into the shopping cart and carefully removed a package wrapped in several layers of cloth. She laid it on Miranda's bed and started unwrapping; soon, eight clay tablets were laid out over the sheets. In a smaller package were the two tablets her grandfather had found in Haran decades ago.

Miranda was unimpressed. The tablets, inscribed with unintelligible signs, were almost identical to scores of others she had seen at the dig. Her well-honed reporter's instincts demanded more.

"Are you sure this is the creation story?" she asked, her eyes drilling into Clara's.

Slowly, Clara traced the words written in the clay, translating for Miranda. As she read, the battle-hardened reporter was surprised to find herself first moved, then electrified. And thoroughly convinced.

"How did you find them?" she asked.

"It was Gian Maria, actually. . . . We found another room in the temple, with dozens more tablets, many of them in shards. Gian Maria was classifying them when he discovered these."

"And who wants to take them away from you?" the reporter wanted to know.

"Everyone—my husband, Saddam's people, the Colonel . . . They think they belong to Iraq," Clara told her, finding the easiest excuse.

"They do," Miranda replied seriously.

"Do you really think that Iraq is in any position to guarantee their safety—their existence? Do you think Saddam cares about them? You know as well as I do that right now, archaeology is the last thing the authorities will protect."

Miranda didn't seem convinced by Clara's argument; it was clear there was much more to the story.

"You should call Picot," Miranda suggested.

"All outgoing calls are being monitored. If I call him and tell him what I've found, they'll track me down and take the tablets."

"So what is it you want?"

"I want to get them out of Iraq and present them to the world," Clara lied. "I want them to be part of the exhibition that Picot is organizing in Europe. You know my husband obtained permission for Picot to take some of the Safran pieces with him. Well, these were found in Safran. We can get them out as part of that. Miranda, this is the greatest archaeological discovery in the last fifty years, maybe more. The Bible of Clay is going to make people rethink their ideas about history and archaeology. And it's going to cause a huge commotion among Judeo–Christian scholarship, because it *proves* the existence of Abraham, and it *proves* that Genesis as it appears in the Bible came down from him."

The two women looked at each other for a few seconds in silence. Neither trusted the other, maybe because there was an unconscious rivalry between them, a rivalry that centered on Yves Picot, albeit for very different reasons. Clara knew, too, that Miranda thought of her as a pet in Saddam's court who couldn't be trusted.

"You're asking me to help get these tablets out of Iraq?"

"Yes . . . and me too."

"What about Gian Maria?"

"He's at the Yellow House; he stayed behind with Ante Plaskic."

"Why? Why aren't they with you?"

"Because I had to escape—I had to run. Ayed Sahadi covered for me, for a price. But if anyone finds out they'll kill him—and us too. Gian Maria will meet up with me here if he can."

"What about Ante Plaskic?"

"He doesn't know anything; I didn't talk to him."

"Why not?"

"I don't know. . . . I . . . I don't trust anyone but Gian Maria."

"What about Ayed?"

"He's helping me for money, Miranda. Although he's capable of turning me in if he gets a better offer."

"And your husband?"

"My husband doesn't know I'm here. I don't think he would denounce me, but I don't want to take that chance. I don't want to expose him either." Clara sighed. "We're getting a divorce; we haven't been living together for months."

Now Miranda knew she was beginning to hear the truth. "But why come to me? I have no connections here. I can't do anything," she protested.

"You can let Fatima and me stay here. Nobody will look for us in your room. We won't be a bother; we'll sleep on the floor. Ayed promised to come for us when the time was right, and if he doesn't . . . I don't know, something will turn up."

"The Colonel will look for you here too. They'll search every room. And he'll find you."

"No, it would never occur to them that I would stay in Baghdad. They'll think I'm trying to cross one of the borders, and since Fatima has family in Tehran, they'll look for us along the Iranian border."

Miranda lit a cigarette and went to the window. She needed to think. Clearly the two women were scared, but she knew Clara wasn't telling her the whole story. There were pieces that didn't fit, and she knew she could get into big trouble if she helped them. Besides, she really believed that a discovery of this magnitude rightfully belonged to Iraq, the Iraqi people, and the tablets should leave the country only with permission. Yes, Iraq was on the verge of war, but there was still hope—Russia, France, and Germany were still vehemently arguing in the UN Security Council against U.S. intervention.

Clara could sense Miranda's doubts.

"At least let us stay here until Sahadi comes," she pleaded. "Then we'll leave. That way, you won't be compromised. With the curfew in effect, if we're out on the street at night, we'll be arrested. We can't run that risk."

"I'd like to know what you've done to make your friend Saddam want to arrest you," Miranda said.

"I haven't done anything. But right now even the privileged aren't safe. If I can manage to get out of Iraq, you'll see that I haven't lied to you in any way—Picot and I will show this discovery to the entire world."

"All right. You can stay tonight. There's not much space, but I guess we can figure something out. We'll talk more tomorrow, but I've got to go now—people are waiting for me downstairs."

When Miranda closed the hotel room door behind her, Clara breathed a very deep sigh of relief. She'd managed to overcome the reporter's reluctance, although she knew Miranda hadn't decided how far she was willing to go to help her. What Clara was sure of was that the reporter wouldn't expose her, and that in itself was all she needed for the moment. It would give Ayed Sahadi enough time to contact her.

In the Colonel's office at the headquarters of the Secret Police, activity was more intense than usual. The Colonel was on the phone, shouting at some poor soul on the other end of the line. Soldiers moved in and out, delivering documents, packing others into black courier bags marked *Classified.*

Ahmed Husseini was drinking a whiskey, and Ayed Sahadi was chain-smoking his Egyptian cigarettes, waiting for the Colonel to finish his phone call.

He finally slammed down the phone and turned to them.

"They won't allow me to leave—the palace needs me to stay here in Baghdad. I told the president's aide that I am a soldier and I want to be with my unit in Basra, to personally appraise the situation on the Kuwait border," he told them, not bothering to hide his disappointment.

"You need to be at the border the day after tomorrow; Mike Fernandez is waiting so he can get you out of Iraq and into Egypt. He's going to provide the documents and money you need to make a new life for yourself," Ahmed said wearily.

"You think I don't know my own job? You think you have to explain that to me? If we don't get out of here by the twentieth, we may never be able to get out," the Colonel said.

"I have to stay," Ahmed said bitterly.

"Yes, you do. It's your duty," the Colonel said firmly, then switched to a tone of reassurance. "You have to coordinate the operation, Ahmed. The Yankees won't do anything to you; Tannenberg's friends have made sure of that."

"Who knows what will happen," Ahmed insisted.

"Nothing will happen! Nothing! They will get you out of here. Ayed too. He'll stay with you, and you'll make sure the operation goes smoothly. Listen, my friend, Tannenberg's men are in position, and you must appear in control. If you do not, if you waver, the whole operation will collapse. Tannenberg is no longer with us—the men need someone else to follow, someone with authority whom they can trust. You are his granddaughter's husband, the head of the family now, so act like it!" The Colonel had no patience for Ahmed's weakening resolve.

"Where in the hell is Clara?" Ahmed mused aloud.

"We're looking for her. I've put out a special alert to all the border checkpoints. But we have to be careful not to alert the palace," Ayed reminded them.

"Your wife is very clever," the Colonel said to Ahmed, "but not clever enough to keep us from finding her."

"I think we ought to go over the operation one more time with the men, Colonel," Ayed suggested.

"Then let's go to it," the Colonel replied, slapping the arm of his chair and standing up, ready for action.

Miranda was distracted throughout dinner. She couldn't erase Clara from her mind. She was tempted to call Picot in Paris, or that other archaeologist, Marta Gómez, to ask for advice. But if the telephones were being monitored, she'd only get Clara arrested—and herself too, for having sheltered a fugitive.

"Are you not feeling well?"

"No, I'm okay, Daniel. Just tired."

The cameraman shrugged. It was obvious that she hadn't paid any attention to the conversation over dinner, and her furrowed brow was a clear sign that something was worrying her.

"Well, as Lauren Bacall said to Humphrey Bogart, if you need me, just whistle. . . . You know how to whistle, don't you, Miranda? You just put your lips together and blow."

Miranda couldn't help but laugh. "Thanks, Daniel, but I'm really okay. It's that this whole business is so exhausting. Too much hurry up and wait."

"Well, you might as well get over it, because it's either wait or leave," Daniel replied.

"I don't want to leave, but I almost wish they'd give the word and start, you know? I hate the idea of war, but this is killing me."

"Politically incorrect, as always," said an English reporter Miranda had run into in other battle zones.

"I know, Margaret, I know, but you're all as sick of this waiting as I am, and I'll bet deep down you're wishing the same thing."

When she returned to the hotel after dinner, Miranda turned down a nightcap and went straight up to her room, anxious to learn whether Clara was still there.

She opened the door cautiously and found the two women sound asleep, huddled on the floor next to the wall, with the bedspread over them.

Miranda undressed quietly and slipped into bed, trying to decide whether to invite her guests to share the bed with her. But the bed was small, and there was no way all three of them would fit. She rolled over and drifted off to sleep.

The Croatian eyed the priest suspiciously. "Where's Clara?"

Gian Maria had been waiting for Ante Plaskic to ask and was prepared to lie. "I don't know—I wish I did—I'm afraid for her."

"She wouldn't have left without saying good-bye to you," Ante postulated.

"Do you think that if I knew where she was I wouldn't tell you? I'd have told those men who beat us. I . . . I'm not used to violence."

"No, you wouldn't have said a word. You'd have protected her," Ante Plaskic shot back, unconvinced.

"I'm a priest, Ante."

"And I know what priests are capable of. In the war, the priest in my village helped people. One day a paramilitary patrol came in looking for a man, the leader of our militia. The priest had hidden him in the church, and he refused to confess. He was tortured in front of the whole village—they pulled the flesh off his bones, but he never talked. Not that his sacrifice made any difference; they found the man and killed him, after wiping out the entire village."

Gian Maria knew that Ante was sending a message, but he chose to ignore it. Instead, he forced himself to be personable and laid his hand sympathetically on the Croatian's shoulder.

"What you've been through must have been terrible."

"I'm not looking for compassion," Ante told him flatly.

"We all need understanding and compassion," Gian Maria replied.

"Not me."

As the hours passed, the two men had pulled themselves together and felt recovered enough to leave the Yellow House. The two servant women helped them pack the few belongings they'd brought. One of them said she had a cousin who lived nearby and that if they paid him, he could drive them to the Hotel Palestina. They agreed, then sat back and waited.

The servant returned with her cousin, who helped them into the car, and within fifteen minutes they were at the Hotel Palestina. Although it was almost midnight, there were still people hanging around the lobby and bar. The desk clerk swore he had not a single free room; only after continued insistence and the stealthy exchange of considerable money did he agree to show them two rooms, which he told them had been dismantled for a remodeling that had recently been put on hold.

The desk clerk wasn't lying—the rooms didn't just need a coat of paint. The carpet in both was stained and musty-smelling, and the bathrooms looked as though they hadn't been cleaned in months. But they would do, at least for one night. Ante took the first room they were shown, while the clerk took Gian Maria to the second, on a higher floor.

As the desk clerk turned to return downstairs, Gian Maria had another question. "Are the reporters from Safran still in the hotel?"

The clerk told him they were.

"Thank God. Maybe tomorrow some of them will take us in," Gian Maria said, thinking of course of Miranda. A ray of hope had just appeared on his horizon.

Miranda was dreaming of a strange war between unknown opponents when insistent knocking on her door dragged her out of sleep. She jumped up, but as she struggled groggily toward the door she tripped over Clara, who remained sound asleep.

"Who is it?" Miranda asked softly, and the answer surprised her.

"It's Gian Maria—open the door, hurry!"

The priest entered the room, looking over his shoulder, concerned that someone might be following him. He had gone back downstairs where he ran into Daniel, who gave him Miranda's room number. Although he had waited, and made every effort to be discreet, he knew he might have attracted unwanted attention.

"Are they here? Oh, thank God!" he said upon seeing the two women asleep on the floor.

"I hope you'll be able to tell me what's happened," Miranda told him. "These two haven't been much help."

"If the Colonel finds her, he'll kill her," Gian Maria answered, pointing toward Clara, who seemed to be stirring and waking up.

"But why?" Miranda insisted.

"Because she found the Bible of Clay, and they want to take it from her," Gian Maria answered.

"Those tablets don't belong to her; they belong to the Iraqi people," Miranda shot back.

"So you're not going to help us?" Clara, now more fully awake, asked, sitting up.

"It's stealing, Clara, no matter how you slice it. I can't be a party to that, even if we're on the verge of war."

"It's mine, Miranda!" Clara said, her voice pleading, filled with anguish.

"Either way, I don't think you're telling me the whole story."

Clara began to explain, but Miranda cut her off.

"And another thing—I don't understand why they're after *you.* Unless, that is, you want to keep something that's not yours, which makes you a thief—here or anywhere. So I'd appreciate it if you'd find somewhere else to hide. I want nothing to do with this black-market secret, and I doubt Professor Picot would approve of what you're doing."

Miranda's words hit Clara like a pitcher of ice water. Fatima, who had woken up and sat watching the scene, covered her face with her hands.

"And you, Gian Maria," Miranda went on, "I find your part in all this very odd. You're a priest, but you don't care if she breaks the Ten Commandments. Honestly, I don't understand you."

Her words shook the priest, who had never questioned the fact that the tablets were Clara's. But after a few seconds, he found a way to reply to Miranda's accusation.

"You're right, or at least partly right. But . . . well, I don't think things are quite what they seem, quite the way you're describing them. Look at my face—turn on the light."

Miranda flicked on the lamp switch on the nightstand and gasped when she saw Gian Maria's battered and bruised face.

"What happened to you?" she asked in alarm.

"The Colonel wanted to know where Clara was," he answered. "And I refused to tell him."

"I remember him from Safran."

"Well, he's a very influential officer in Saddam's inner circle. He wants the tablets, but not for Iraq—for some sort of business deal. I imagine Clara could it explain it to us, but what I heard at the Yellow House was something about some friends in Washington and that the war is going to start tomorrow, things like that."

"The war is starting tomorrow? How could the Colonel know that?" Miranda said.

"It's very complicated," said Clara. "I don't know if I can explain it all. But he wants the Bible of Clay so he can sell it. So does my husband. That's why they're after me, to take it from me. I'm not stealing it, Miranda, I'm saving it. After the exhibition in Europe, I'll put it in a safe place until the war is over, then it can come back to Iraq," she said. She'd invented this story on the spur of the moment to try to assuage Miranda's doubts.

"Your husband is corrupt too? Come on, Clara!"

"Think whatever you want. If you aren't going to help me, Fatima and I will go, but at least let us stay till daylight. If we're seen out in the street now, we'll be arrested. Ayed promised to come and get us out of here—it was his idea for us to come here in the first place. But don't worry; as soon as the sun is up, we'll leave, I promise."

Miranda stood looking at Clara, not knowing quite what to do. She didn't trust her—in fact, she didn't like her, and sensed that behind all the high-minded promises and desperation, there was some sort of imposture.

"At first light, you're out of here," she finally said.

"Fine. But please, at least help Gian Maria," Clara asked.

"No, I don't need anything, don't worry," Gian Maria said.

"Yes you do. You have to get out of Iraq tomorrow morning, before the invasion. If you stay here, they'll kill you. Or did the Colonel let you come here?" Clara asked.

"No. He left Ante Plaskic and me lying on the floor bleeding after we were interrogated. Ayed persuaded him that you're more than familiar with the Colonel's methods, so you'd never have told us where you were going. That seemed to satisfy him, so he left us. Your husband seemed desperate; he's with the Colonel, but I think he wants to try to help you."

"He doesn't want to help me—he wants the Bible of Clay."

"Ahmed is not a bad man, Clara," Gian Maria told her.

"How touching!" Miranda interrupted. "You people are—" She stopped, searching for words, then gave up and dropped her hands to her side in frustration. "As for the war starting tomorrow, are you sure?"

"My understanding is that it's going to start on the twentieth," Clara said quietly, "which means that Gian Maria still has time to get out of Iraq if he leaves first thing tomorrow."

"And how can you be so sure the war will start on the twentieth?" Miranda insisted.

"The Colonel said it would."

"But the Colonel is an officer in Saddam's army, not the Americans'—I doubt he knows the exact date the war is going to start . . . unless . . ."

"What planet are you living on, Miranda?" asked Clara bitterly.

"Me? What about you?"

"I'm living on the one where business decides who lives and who dies—good, profitable business. A lot of people are going to make a lot of money on this war," Clara answered angrily.

"You know, it's spoiled brats like you who make ordinary people miserable," replied Miranda contemptuously.

"Please! Please!" Gian Maria tried to calm things. "This is absurd. Look, we're all on edge."

"On edge? Did you just hear what she said? This woman doesn't care about anything but satisfying her own needs and saving her own life. So far as I'm concerned, she's as bad as her grandfather."

Miranda's declaration stunned them all into silence. It was two or three hours before dawn, and the tension in the room was beginning to be unbearable for them all.

Clara ignored Miranda and turned to Gian Maria.

"Will you go? Please?"

"But what about you? I want to help you."

"Gian Maria, all our chances are slim at best. Together we have none. Do you think I can get out of Iraq with a priest? Do you think you're invisible? It won't be long until the Colonel tracks us down. I have one chance, and I can't afford to risk it because of you. Nor can you jeopardize your own safety."

"I don't want anything to happen to you because of me; I just want to help you," Gian Maria insisted.

A knock at the door shocked them into silence. Miranda waved all three into the bathroom, then opened the door.

Ayed Sahadi looked nervous as he pushed his way into the room without saying a word. When the door was closed, he asked, "Where are they?"

"Who?"

"I don't have time to play games! Where's Clara?"

He strode over to the bathroom door, opened it, and smiled in spite of the fraught circumstances. Gian Maria, Clara, and Fatima were huddled together in the shower. Fatima was clearly terrified, Gian Maria worried, and Clara, as always, defiant.

"Come on, we're leaving," he ordered Clara and Fatima.

"I want to go with you," Gian Maria insisted.

"You'll be the death of us all," Clara said, exasperated.

"Can you help him get out of here?" Ayed asked Miranda.

"How? Just tell me how I can do that. According to Clara, the war is going to start within a day. Trying to get to the border would be suicide."

Ayed looked at Clara reproachfully, astounded that she had chosen to tell a reporter that the war was about to start. "He can stay here—the Americans know that the press has hunkered down here. The hotel is safe—they won't bomb it."

"Clara, I want to go with you," Gian Maria said forcefully.

"Gian Maria, you aren't coming. It's my life at stake, and the safety of the Bible. The answer is no. No." Clara's words left no room for argument, but Ayed continued to mull over whether there might be some way Gian Maria could be useful to them.

"Where are you going to take them?" Gian Maria asked him.

"You know I can't tell you that—if the Colonel decides to interrogate you again, he won't be as nice as the last time," Ayed told him.

"But if they torture him, he could tell them that Clara went with you," Miranda pointed out.

"He doesn't know where, so it doesn't matter. And let's hope that doesn't happen, and that we'll all be well beyond his reach. Put on your veils and follow my instructions. There are Secret Police everywhere," Ayed told the women.

"Then how are we going to get out?" Clara asked.

"In a carpet—actually, in two. There's a truck at the service entrance downstairs waiting to load up. You'll meet up with me later. Come on, into the service elevator."

After checking to make sure no one was in the hall, they slipped out of the room, leaving Miranda and Gian Maria behind. The reporter looked relieved, while the priest seemed desolate.

"Want a drink?" Miranda asked him.

"I don't drink," he answered, his voice little more than a whisper.

"Me either, but I've got some bottles I use to persuade people to talk to me. And I think I'm going to have one."

She went into the bathroom for a glass, then opened the door in the bottom of the nightstand and pulled out a bottle of bourbon. She twisted off the top, poured herself a shot, and took a long swallow.

"What exactly is Clara to you, Gian Maria?" she asked the priest abruptly.

The priest hesitated. He couldn't tell her the truth, so at last he resorted to vagueness.

"Nothing—it's not what you think. I have a moral obligation toward her, that's all."

"A moral obligation? What on earth for?"

"Because I'm a priest, Miranda, that's what for. Sometimes God puts us in situations that we'd never have expected, and that's all I can say. I won't break confidence. I'm sorry."

Miranda accepted his answer. She knew he wasn't lying, just not telling the whole truth. Besides, she could practically see the spiritual conflict tearing him in half.

"Is it true the war is starting tomorrow?" she asked him.

"That's what the Colonel and Ahmed said."

"Today is the nineteenth. . . ."

"And tomorrow is the twentieth, and on the twentieth the war is going to start."

"And where's Ante Plaskic?"

"In his room. The Colonel was tougher on him than he was on me. We could hardly stand up by the time his men were finished with us."

"Then how'd you get here?"

"Some relative of Clara's maid brought us."

"And now what are you going to do?"

"Me? I have no idea. I feel like . . . I feel like I'm about to fail completely in my purpose. I can't leave Iraq without knowing that Clara is all right."

"There's no way she's going to contact you. You heard her—you have to look to yourself."

Rapid knocking at the door startled them both, and as they froze in apprehension they recognized Ayed's voice outside.

They were back. Clara was pale, Fatima was shaking, and Ayed looked furious.

"There's no way out of here! The hotel is surrounded. The Colonel's probably posted soldiers next to the truck. The only reason they haven't caught us is because the driver didn't know anything. They'll have to stay here."

"Oh, no—I've had enough. I assure you, whatever happens, they aren't going to stay here. Find somewhere else, some other room," Miranda told him.

"Then go out there and tell the soldiers to come detain them," Ayed challenged her. "They either stay here or in jail."

"They can't stay in my room!" the reporter hissed. "Not with the police here!"

"They can stay in mine," Gian Maria said quietly.

"You have a room? Where?" Ayed asked.

"The fourth floor. It's terrible—dirty, just one bed, and the shower doesn't work very well—but we can make do."

"What about Ante Plaskic?" Clara asked.

"He's on the second floor."

"He may want to talk to you—he might come up to your room," said Ayed.

"Maybe, but if he does I'll put Clara and Fatima in the bathroom."

"All right," said Ayed. "They'll go to Gian Maria's room. We have to hope the Colonel won't have the whole hotel searched." He turned to Gian Maria. "Let's go."

The four of them left. Miranda poured herself another drink, knocked it back in one gulp, and lay down on the bed. She was beat—she needed some sleep, though she knew it wouldn't come easy. She couldn't stop thinking about her recent guests' claim that the war was going to start in twenty-four hours or less. Just how did Clara, Ayed, the Colonel, and Ahmed—all these Iraqis—know *that*?

It was the telephone's ringing that woke her. Some of the other re-porters were waiting for her at breakfast downstairs; they were all plan-ning to go out to get shots of the streets of Baghdad, stories on the run-up to the war. Fifteen minutes later, her hair wet from the shower, she was downstairs in the lobby.

The rest of the day she was nervous, unsure of what to do—should she tell the other reporters what she knew or keep quiet?

She called her chief in London, and he confirmed there were con-stant rumors that the war would be under way within mere hours, but when she asked him about the twentieth specifically, he laughed.

"If I only knew—now that would be a scoop! Day before yesterday Bush gave Saddam an ultimatum; that was the seventeenth. All the em-bassies are being evacuated and all foreigners are being urged to leave the country, so it could start any minute, I suppose. Call me—I figure you'll know before anyone else!"

Miranda made no effort to check on Clara or Gian Maria. She knew they were in the hotel, on the floor below hers. She was worried about what might happen to them, but at the same time she told herself that she didn't want any part in their scheme.

That night she sat up late talking to the other reporters, half-waiting for the bombs to start dropping. When the sky suddenly began to light up with tracer shells after a series of deafening blasts, for the first time she was truly frightened. It was March 20, and the war was under way.

Hours later, reporters were hearing from their main offices in cap-itals around the world that the coalition forces had entered Iraq. The die was cast.

51

MIKE FERNANDEZ LOOKED AT HIS WATCH. THE AMERICAN and British land war in Iraq had begun, and so had the operation that Tannenberg had so meticulously planned over the last year.

The former Green Beret told himself that it was going to go off without a hitch—not even the old man's death could stop the machine already in progress. There was a shitload of money at stake, and the men knew they'd be paid only if they made off with the whole list and successfully delivered the material to the drop-off point. In a matter of hours, they'd all be out of Iraq for good.

In Baghdad, at that same moment, a group of men in military uniforms was awaiting the signal to leave the warehouse where they'd holed up a few hours earlier.

All of them had worked under Alfred Tannenberg for years. His murder shook them, but Ahmed had assured them that the operation would remain unchanged. He was now the head of the Tannenberg family, he had told them, and he expected the same level of efficiency and loyalty they had always shown to Tannenberg himself.

The money the men would earn from the operation would assure them a comfortable future, to put it mildly, so they had all agreed to go ahead with everything as planned. What they did afterward was up to them. The only pledge they had made was to cross the border into Kuwait and turn over the haul to the former American army officer, a good commander who knew how to inspire trust.

The team leader's cell phone rang; the time had come. He listened as the order came.

"Let's move," he told them.

They all stood up and rechecked their weapons one last time. Then they pulled ski masks over their faces and suddenly, in their black camouflage suits, became invisible in the darkness as they climbed up into the military transport truck waiting outside for them.

Bombs and antiaircraft shells lit up the nighttime skyline of Baghdad. Sirens terrified the civilians of the city, who were huddled together in their homes.

The team passed other military vehicles but attracted no attention. At last they reached the back door of the National Museum. Within seconds, they were inside.

Most of the guards had left hours ago, but some of them had insisted on staying that night. The noise of the bombs and the flickering of the lights as electricity came and went didn't seem to faze them—they'd disconnected the alarm system and the museum was as open to marauders as a jar of candy on a table.

The men in ski masks—carrying nylon, plastic, and felt bags—went from floor to floor, carefully selecting the artifacts from Ahmed's list. No one spoke. Following explicit instructions from the Colonel, the man in charge made sure that none of the artifacts was damaged—and especially that none of his men gave in to temptation and pocketed some small item.

In less than fifteen minutes the team had bagged dozens upon dozens of artifacts: finely carved marble panels, ancient weapons, tools, terra-cotta urns and vases, tablets, statuettes, and bas-reliefs in basalt, sandstone, diorite, and alabaster, objects fashioned of gold and silver and wood, cylinder seals . . . There was so much loot they could hardly carry it.

Then, as quickly as they'd entered, they left. No one within a thousand miles of Iraq would suppose that the country's entire artistic and historical patrimony was being stolen.

Ahmed was waiting impatiently in his darkened office. When his cell phone rang, he felt his heart race.

"Team One: We've got it—we're moving out," the leader of the commando team reported.

"Did everything go as planned?"

"Like clockwork."

Two minutes later another call came in—the second team had just left the museum in Mosul. As in Baghdad, there'd been no problem getting in and out within scant minutes. Other calls—from Kairah, Tikrit, and Basra—came in. Throughout the country, Alfred Tannenberg's commando teams had successfully completed their missions, and their bags now contained the soul of Iraq, its history—indeed, a good part of the history of humanity.

Ahmed lit a cigar. Beside him, the Colonel's nephew was talking on his cell phone, informing his uncle of the operation's success. Ahmed, however, would postpone celebration until each team reached its destination—Kuwait, Syria, Jordan . . .

The two men were alone in the ministry building; the Colonel had ordered them not to leave. They had lowered the blinds and closed the windows to minimize, as much as possible, their exposure to the bombs falling all over the city.

How were they to get out of Iraq? The Colonel had assured Ahmed that Ayed Sahadi would get him out when the time came, but there had been no word from Ayed. By now he might well be fighting with his unit, or he might have even gone with the Colonel to Basra, at which point he would try to make his way on to Kuwait. With Tannenberg dead, Ahmed didn't trust the Colonel—he didn't trust anybody, in fact, because he knew that he had no authority over any of Tannenberg's associates in this operation. If they felt they had to sacrifice him, they would do so without a second thought.

Paul Dukais lit up a cigar in his office in New York. He'd just gotten a call from Mike Fernandez confirming the success of the operation.

"We've done the impossible—now it's up to you guys to do what's merely difficult," the former Green Beret had joked.

"I hope we can make you proud," Dukais replied, his mood elated. "You guys did good."

"Yes, sir, we did."

"Any casualties?"

"Some of the teams had to defend themselves, but nothing serious."

"Good—as soon as you're out and back home, your mission is over."

The president of Planet Security was delighted with the night's work. Based on the two percent commission he was taking from the sale of every artifact, this cargo was going to make him a fortune.

Robert Brown and Ralph Barry were putting together the annual report on the Mundo Antiguo Foundation when Dukais called them with the good news. The two men celebrated with a scotch—if George Wagner didn't smile at this, Ralph Barry thought, then he'd never smile at anything.

"So, Paul, now what?" Robert Brown asked.

"Now the merchandise gets crated up very carefully, and within a few days it'll land. Some of it will go directly to Spain, some to Brazil, and some here.

"Ayed Sahadi's got a detailed list explaining which lots are going where. If there are no problems—and there's no reason there would be—we'll have pulled this thing off."

"What do you know about Ahmed?" Robert Brown asked.

"He'll be taken out of Iraq as soon as our boys go in—a matter of days."

"Are you sure they'll be able to get him out? He was one of Saddam's select few."

"Ahmed was one of the select few that *Tannenberg* drew into Saddam's inner circle—let's not forget that," Dukais answered cynically.

"Of course, of course. And we have to appreciate his expertise—it was a tremendous help." Brown nodded. "And what about Clara?"

"Don't worry, we'll find her. Nobody carrying such an archaeological treasure can disappear forever. The Colonel is looking for her, and I've got another, very special man on the search too. He's been close to her over the last few months. If anybody can find her, he can."

"And he's in Baghdad?"

"My man? Oh, yeah—he stayed with Clara. Don't worry, he'll find her."

"What worries me is the Bible of Clay."

"If we find Clara, we find the Bible—and we'll make her an offer for it that she can't refuse," Paul Dukais laughed.

Clara was becoming stir crazy in the tiny hotel room—she hadn't been out in two days. She was afraid that at any moment the door would open and the Colonel would walk in and shoot her point-blank. She hadn't seen Miranda after their argument, although Gian Maria intimated that the reporter had been worried about her. At least she hadn't told anybody Clara was right there in the hotel.

Gian Maria, in turn, was dodging Ante Plaskic's questions regarding Clara's whereabouts. The Croatian didn't trust him, and the priest had finally realized that Ante's insistent questions were decidedly suspicious. Fortunately, the confusion surrounding the war had given Gian Maria a little break—everyone had enough to do just staying alive.

"Ayed hasn't been back," Clara complained.

"Don't worry—we'll get out of here somehow," the priest consoled her.

"How? Don't you realize that we're in the middle of a war? If the Americans win, they'll detain me, and if Saddam wins . . ." Her voice trailed off worriedly.

"You must put your faith in God, Clara. Thanks to him we've survived so far."

Clara didn't want to hurt the priest's feelings by telling him that she didn't trust God in the slightest, she trusted only her own abilities, so she just nodded and said nothing.

She worried about Fatima. The older woman was hardly eating, and she was growing thinner by the day. She didn't complain, but her silence showed how much she was suffering. Clara begged that she confide in her, but Fatima wouldn't talk. She just passed her hand lightly over Clara's face as the tears rolled down her cheeks.

Clara glued herself to a portable radio Gian Maria had borrowed from Miranda in order to pick up the BBC, but it was Gian Maria who provided her with the best information, which the war correspondents in Baghdad were getting directly from their home offices.

After several intense days of waiting, Gian Maria announced that the Americans had reached the outskirts of Baghdad; the next day he reported that they'd taken over the airport, south of the city.

"Where is Ayed Sahadi? Why hasn't he come for us?" Clara kept asking.

Gian Maria had no answer for that. He'd called Ayed's telephone numbers—all of them—several times, and at first a man with a snippy voice had told him Ayed was unavailable, but in recent days the telephone rang and rang and no one answered.

"Do you think he's betrayed me?"

"If he had, we'd have been arrested by now," Gian Maria argued.

"Then why hasn't he come or at least sent me a message?"

"Because he hasn't been able to—the Colonel may have him under surveillance."

One afternoon when Gian Maria came in, Miranda was with him.

"Your Croatian friend is asking a lot of questions about you," she told Clara.

"I know, but Ayed warned me about him—said he couldn't be trusted."

"He thinks you're here, but I suppose that was one secret you couldn't keep forever," Miranda told her.

"And who told him that?" Clara shot her an accusatory glance.

"The hotel is full of Iraqis," Miranda said. "My colleagues hire them as interpreters; others have befriended them. And, of course, the hotel employees are harboring their entire families here because they know the Americans won't bomb this hotel. That's why nobody in housekeeping cares that you're here—they figure you're just taking shelter, like everybody else. Gian Maria didn't have to be so generous with his tips—they'd have looked the other way anyway.

"So sooner or later your friend Ante Plaskic was going to find out. Honestly, not ten minutes ago he stopped me in the lobby to ask about you again. When I told him I didn't know anything, he told me he knew you were here, in Gian Maria's room. I lied—I told him Gian Maria had taken in some other people, refugees, but I doubt he believed me. I wouldn't have. I just wanted to tell you, so you'd know."

"What can we do?" Gian Maria asked Miranda.

"I don't know. I don't understand why you don't trust him—but anyway, he's determined to find you, so he'll be up here any minute to find out whether I was lying."

"Then I've got to get out," Clara said determinedly.

"But you can't! They'll catch you!" Gian Maria cried in alarm.

"I'm tired of this!" Clara shouted.

"Calm down!" Miranda barked. "Getting hysterical isn't going to help."

"Let her hide in your room," Gian Maria implored Miranda. "It'll be for just a few hours."

"No—I'm sorry, I told you I want no part of what you're doing."

"Look," Clara said, "you know as well as I that there's word from the reporters that the National Museum has been looted. If I give these tablets up, they'll end up in the hands of the highest bidder."

Miranda didn't say anything as she weighed Clara's argument.

"All right, then, go to my room, but just until this Croatian is convinced you're not staying here. Here's the key—I'm leaving; they're waiting for me downstairs. I'm not sure if you've heard yet, but there are American units raiding some of the suburbs. They'll be entering the city any minute."

"Be careful," Gian Maria told her. "And thank you."

Miranda looked at him and left without a good-bye.

When she came back several hours later, she found Clara and Fatima sitting on the bed in her room.

"They've started razing statues of your friend Saddam," were the first words out of her mouth.

"Who?" Clara asked.

"The Iraqis."

"The Americans must have paid them," Clara mused aloud, as Fatima began to weep softly again.

"It's being filmed by television crews from all over the world," Miranda said. "The Americans have taken control of almost the whole city, without nearly the resistance anyone anticipated. A day that'll go down in history," Miranda told them, her voice caustic.

"I don't know what to do . . . ," Clara said softly.

"What can you do?"

"Where is Saddam?" Fatima asked all of a sudden, surprising the two women.

"Nobody knows—in hiding somewhere, in all probability," Miranda told her. "Officially, the war has been won by the coalition troops, but there are guerrillas all over the city still shooting, and some army units haven't surrendered yet."

"Then who is leading the country?" asked Fatima.

"Right now, nobody. Baghdad is a city at war: The winners haven't taken control yet and the losers still haven't completely given up, although a lot of Iraqis have taken to the streets to welcome the Americans. In situations like this, it's hard to tell what's happening—confusion is the only constant," Miranda explained.

"Are the borders open?" asked Clara.

"I don't know, but I'd guess not. I'll bet there are lots of Iraqis trying to flee to neighboring countries."

"And you—how long will you be staying in Iraq?" Clara asked Miranda.

"Until my boss pulls me out. When this stops being news, I'll be out of here—but whether it's a week or a month, I couldn't say."

The long conversation consisted of one lie after another. Gian Maria knew he hadn't convinced Ante that he knew nothing of Clara's whereabouts. He told Plaskic he could have a look at the room, mistakenly thinking that would satisfy him.

"Don't you think the time has come for us to get out of here?" Ante had asked.

"Easier said than done," the priest had answered. "First they'll have to reestablish transportation—the roads have been bombed and no traffic is allowed to cross the borders—and then, finding a car to take us out . . . I don't know, I think it's too soon. It's still dangerous to be out on the streets, much less the highways."

"Let's ask Miranda," Ante had insisted. "I heard some of the reporters saying that as soon as the Americans declare victory, they'll be out of here."

"I guess we could get a lift with them, although I may stay behind to give a hand with the reconstruction—people are going to need all the help they can get. The wreckage everywhere, the families that have been destroyed, the children who have lost their parents, innocent men and women wounded . . . I'm a priest, Ante, and I'm needed here," Gian Maria had replied, trying to justify his reluctance to leave.

On May 1, the coalition forces declared an end to the war and a coalition victory. Baghdad was in chaos, and the Iraqis were bemoaning the widespread and devastating destruction the foreigners had unleashed. The National Museum had been looted, as had almost every museum in Iraq, and many Iraqis felt that their national pride had been violated.

Ahmed Husseini was overcome with guilt. Ayed Sahadi had told him that the stolen pieces were already outside Iraq, in safe locations, and that soon both of them would be immensely wealthy. All they had to do was wait for their contact. Paul Dukais had it all planned out— one of his men would come for them, carrying the necessary permits allowing for their timely exit, and nobody would ask any embarrassing questions.

But before he left Iraq, Ayed Sahadi was going to do everything in his power to earn the money Clara had promised him. He hadn't gone back to the hotel for her, knowing she'd be safer there than with him, especially considering that the Colonel had eyes and ears everywhere. He had run an unnecessary risk the night he'd gone to the hotel, so he had decided to leave her there until the situation cooled. He knew that the Colonel was safely out of the country by now, across the border into Kuwait. With a new passport he'd begun his life under a new identity, as an ordinary citizen living in a luxury hotel near Cairo. Now might be the time. . . .

When Ayed entered the lobby of the Hotel Palestina, he saw Miranda with a group of other reporters, arguing heatedly with three American officers. He waited for her to step away from the group before he approached her.

"Miranda . . ."

"Ayed! God, I thought you'd disappeared forever. Your friends have missed you."

"I imagine, but if I'd come to see them any earlier, I'd have put their lives in danger. And I knew they were in good hands with you and Gian Maria."

"Great. So you're one of those people who leave others to do the dirty work?" Miranda shot back resentfully, causing Ayed to burst out laughing.

"Well, thank you, Miranda. Now, where are they?"

"Holed up in my room again. That Croatian is searching madly for Clara, certain that she's in the hotel."

"Don't worry—I'm here to take them off your hands."

"And where are they going, if I may ask?"

"First to Jordan, then to Egypt. Clara has a lovely house in Cairo, and her grandfather's fortune is waiting for her there—didn't she tell you?"

"And how are you getting to Jordan?"

"Some friends are taking us."

"What about Gian Maria?"

Ayed shrugged his shoulders and raised his eyebrows to signal his absolute indifference to the fate of the young priest. He had no intention of dragging him along. That wasn't part of the deal he'd made with Clara. As far as he was concerned, the priest was on his own.

Miranda took Ayed straight up to her room—she wanted to get rid of Clara as soon as possible.

Clara listened to Ayed's explanations in silence.

"I'll see that nothing happens to you," he assured her.

"If it does, you won't collect a penny," she warned him.

"I know."

"I want to go with you," Gian Maria interrupted.

Clara looked at Ayed and preempted any response. "He's coming with us. He's part of the deal."

"I'll have to charge more—and I can't guarantee that my men will be willing to take on another passenger."

"He comes with me," Clara said flatly.

"And what about your friend Ante Plaskic?" Miranda asked.

"Say good-bye for us," Ayed told her.

"Very funny," Miranda snapped.

No one seemed to notice Ayed Sahadi and the two Shiite women veiled in black leaving the hotel. But neither Ayed nor the two women spotted Ante Plaskic watching them from a corner of the lobby.

The Croatian saw at once that Clara was clutching a bag tightly to her side—inside which, he was certain, was the Bible of Clay. All he had to do was follow her and take the tablets—the easy way or the hard way. He figured that would mean killing Ayed, but that was a detail he could live with. And then there came the priest, tagging along behind. Another collateral casualty, but war was war. . . .

And then his plans turned to shit. The two men and two women got into a car that screeched away and disappeared into the chaos of the city. He'd lost Clara again, and now he'd have to hunt her down outside Iraq. But he knew where to go. Sooner or later she'd meet with Yves Picot. It was just a matter of beating her to him.

Lion Doyle had reached the same conclusion long before. Lion, too, intended to finish his mission and eliminate Clara Tannenberg. Professor Picot would lead him to her.

52

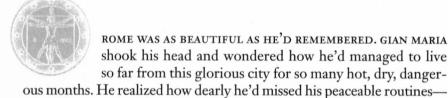 ROME WAS AS BEAUTIFUL AS HE'D REMEMBERED. GIAN MARIA shook his head and wondered how he'd managed to live so far from this glorious city for so many hot, dry, dangerous months. He realized how dearly he'd missed his peaceable routines—the prayers at dawn, the quiet reading in the evening.

He entered the clinic and walked down the hall to his father's office. Maria, Dr. Carlo Cipriani's secretary, greeted him warmly.

"Gian Maria! How wonderful to see you!"

"*Grazie*, Maria."

"Go right in, please. Your father is alone—he didn't tell me you were coming."

"He doesn't know—it's a surprise." He put his finger to his lips and smiled.

He knocked softly at the door of his father's inner office, then turned the doorknob and entered.

Carlo Cipriani froze when he saw his son. He stood up, but found himself unable to speak. Gian Maria just looked at him, unblinking, standing in the middle of the office. His father saw that he was thinner, his skin tanned by the wind and sun. He no longer looked the frail, studious boy he'd always been; he was a man now, a different man, who was clearly taking the measure of his father.

"*Figlio mìo!*" the old man exclaimed almost shyly, going to his son and taking him in his arms.

To Carlo's relief, the priest responded to his embrace.

"Sit down, sit down, I'll call your brother and sister. Antonino and Lara have been very worried about you. Your superior has given us very little news, my son. Only that you were well, but he refused to tell us where you were. Why did you go away, *figlio mìo?*"

"To keep you from committing murder, Papa."

At those words, Carlo Cipriani felt the weight of his entire life upon his shoulders—his legs almost failed him, as though he had aged twenty years in that instant, and he lowered himself with difficulty into the chair.

"You know who I am, you know who I was. I have never hidden that from any of my children. How can you judge me? I went to ask your forgiveness and understanding, and God's forgiveness as well."

"Alfred Tannenberg is dead, Papa—murdered. But I suppose you already know that."

"I know, I know, and don't ask me to . . ."

"To ask forgiveness? Didn't you go to confession to ask forgiveness for that sin, that crime? You cannot imagine what I've been through to try to ease that burden on my conscience, but I have failed. I assure you that I would have given my life in order to prevent you from committing this mortal sin."

"I'm sorry. I'm sorry for the pain and trouble I caused you, my son, but I do not think that God will condemn me for having . . . for having facilitated the death of that monster."

"Even the life of a monster belongs to God, Papa, and only he can take it."

"I see you have not forgiven me."

"Do you truly repent for what you've done, Papa?"

"No." Carlo Cipriani's voice was once again strong and full of conviction, without a hint of doubt, as he looked straight into his son's eyes.

"And what have you gained by this, Papa?"

"I have gained justice, the justice that was denied us when we were helpless children, when that monster ordered us to beat our own mothers, as though they were mules, beasts of burden! I watched my mother die, then my sister, as unable to stop it as you were unable to prevent Alfred's death. Because of him you will never know your grandmother or your aunt. You are not one to judge me."

"I am just a priest and a son, and I love you, Papa."

Gian Maria bent over his father and took him in his arms again, as tears came to both men's eyes.

"Where have you been, my son?"

"In Iraq, in a little village called Safran, fearing for the life of Alfred's granddaughter, Clara. Is she also to pay for the death of your mother and sister?" Gian Maria asked solemnly, stepping away from his father.

The old doctor didn't answer. He got up out of the chair and turned his back, beginning to pace the office, not looking at his son.

"She is innocent; she's done nothing to any of you," the younger man pleaded.

"Gian Maria, you don't understand. You're a priest; I'm just a man, perhaps the worst of men in your eyes, but don't judge me, *figlio mìo*, just forgive me."

"Whom are you asking to forgive you, the priest or the son?"

"Both, my son, both."

"Where is Clara?" Enrique asked.

It irritated George Wagner that even over the secure phone connection, static broke up Enrique's voice. But everything irritated him now—his complications were mounting.

"In Paris, with Professor Picot," Wagner answered. "But don't worry, I've just talked to Paul Dukais, and he's got a man in. He assures me we'll have the tablets soon."

"He should have gotten them sooner," Enrique complained from the quiet shadows of his house in Seville.

"Yes, he should have, and I told Dukais not to pay him if he doesn't deliver. But apparently the contractor has just come back from Iraq and has rekindled his relationship with Picot, so he knows exactly where the tablets are."

"We should put together a group," Enrique suggested.

"That's what Frankie said. We will, in due time. From what we can tell, Picot wants to mount a public exhibition with all the artifacts they found in Safran, including the Bible of Clay. But they've locked it away in a safety-deposit box in a bank, where it will remain until the exhibition is ready. We just have to wait. Until then, Dukais' man can still be useful to us, since he's part of the group that worked with Picot in Iraq—he can tell us what Clara and Picot are up to."

"What about the husband?"

"Ahmed? We told him not to lose sight of Clara, but they've separated and filed for divorce. Clara doesn't want anything to do with him—she knows he's working for us. So I don't know whether he can help. Or if he ever *was* of any help."

"Christ, George, Ahmed has been incredibly useful to us. If it hadn't been for him, the operation to sack the museums could never have succeeded."

"Alfred planned it," George replied softly.

"True. But Ahmed took it the rest of the way, with the help of the Colonel, so let's give recognition where recognition's due, eh?"

"Don't worry. He'll receive his share. But now, my friend, the first priority is getting our hands on the Bible of Clay. I have a very special buyer, a man who's willing to pay millions for it."

"Let's be prudent, George; it would be crazy to put it on the market so soon."

"We'll wait long enough, but the person who wants the Bible of Clay has no intention, I assure you, of exhibiting it."

"Have your people at the foundation inventoried the merchandise?" Enrique asked.

"They're doing that right now. Ahmed's helping them."

"I need you to help me with the merchandise on this end too."

"I know—so does Frankie. Don't worry, I've let Robert Brown and Ralph Barry know; they'll take care of it. But if you want to get started, Ahmed can come to Seville."

"What do we do with Clara?"

"She's not making any waves for the moment, aside from not cooperating with us. If she stays out of our way and keeps quiet, I don't give a damn about her. If she starts to make trouble, she goes the way of her grandfather."

"Agreed, my friend."

Yves Picot was listening in silence to the voice on the other end of the line, a voice that seemed to be in no hurry to finish what it was saying. It had been over ten minutes since Picot had uttered a word. When he finally hung up, he gave a sigh of relief. Clara had been pressuring him to mount the exhibition as soon as possible, ignoring the mountains of paperwork and the myriad difficulties involved in putting together an exhibition of this magnitude. Clara Tannenberg, in fact, had insisted that they weren't working fast enough. The artifacts were packed and crated, Lion Doyle's photographs were ready, all the archaeologists who'd taken part in the excavation had written articles on the aspects of the work that they had overseen and the objects they'd found. And as though that weren't enough, there was the Bible of Clay itself. Clara wanted to show the world those tablets, which seemed to be burning a hole in their packaging, since their chances of "misplacement" increased with every passing day, even from the safety-deposit box in the Swiss bank.

So Clara would hear nothing of a break from their months-long labor, and ever since she'd shown up in Paris she'd been hounding them. Every day another phone call.

Thank goodness, Picot thought, that Marta Gómez was as efficient in the art gallery as she was on the dig. And a pleasure to work with besides. Although she shared Clara's burning desire to mount the exhibition, she wasn't blind to the realities of the enterprise. Within mere weeks, Marta had mobilized foundations and universities in search of support funds. Picot, too, had done his part, calling influential friends in academia and finance to tempt them with the news that the exhibition was going to make public a truly revolutionary discovery.

From what Fabian had just told him, Marta had finalized arrangements for the exhibit's first venue, the National Archaeological Museum in Madrid. Picot himself would have preferred it to be in Paris, in the Louvre, but scheduling conflicts had made that impossible for several months, so Madrid it would have to be.

Fabian also told him that a Spanish banking house and two large corporations had agreed to finance the exhibit's first stop. And that didn't even take into account the upper echelons of the Universidad Complutense in Madrid; the Spanish Ministry of Education and Culture had been very enthusiastic about the show as well. It was a great opportunity for Madrid—the first European city to host the exhibit. Then it would move on to Paris, Berlin, Amsterdam, London, and, last, New York.

He was going to call Clara with the good news, although he was almost certain Marta had already done so. The two women seemed to have grown closer through their dedication to seeing this exhibit up and running.

The four old friends had met in Berlin. After his recent travels, Hans Hausser had asked to meet near his home; in the last few days he hadn't been feeling too well. When Mercedes saw him, she was worried—he'd grown so thin, and his face had a sickly pallor.

"I went to London, as we discussed, to see Tom Martin. I told him that we were not going to pay the last installment until the job was finished. I'd already told him that on the phone, but in person there can be no misunderstanding."

"And what did he say?" Mercedes asked.

"He said the price had gone up because it had taken his man longer than expected to do the job—the difficulties had been greater than they'd imagined. But I made it perfectly clear that not only were we not going to pay more—not a euro more, I told him—if he didn't keep his end of the contract, but that we'd pay only a portion of it if his man doesn't complete the job. We went back and forth, but we finally reached an agreement. If his man solves the problem within the next few days, he'll get the full fee plus a bonus; if it takes longer, they'll get the original price."

"Where is Clara Tannenberg?" Bruno wanted to know.

"Until a few days ago she was in Paris," Hans told them, "but now she's in Madrid, organizing an exhibit to showcase the artifacts she uncovered in a temple in Iraq. Apparently, she'd been excavating there for several months with a team of archaeologists from all over Europe. I honestly don't know how they did it, given the situation there."

Carlo Cipriani looked sad and withdrawn; he barely said a word, and seemed to stare into space, without really seeing his friends.

"What's on your mind, Carlo?" Hans asked him.

"Nothing . . . I've wanted to tell you all that Gian Maria is back. . . . I just can't believe it. . . . I've been thinking that we ought to let Clara go. Her death would not rest easy on my conscience. Alfred Tannenberg is dead; we've kept our vow."

"I'm happy to hear about Gian Maria, but no," said Mercedes. "We are going to see this out. We swore that we would kill him and all his descendants. Clara Tannenberg is his only living relative, the last Tannenberg, and she must die."

Bruno Müller and Hans Hausser lowered their heads, knowing that no one would ever convince Mercedes to settle for anything but total revenge, as she saw it.

"We'll do it—we'll go through with it, but I understand what Carlo is saying. The girl is innocent—" Hans finally murmured.

"Innocent?" Mercedes repeated the word incredulously. "Innocent? My mother was innocent, and yours, and our brothers and sisters. Every one of us in that camp was innocent. No, she's not innocent, she's that monster's legacy. If you people are going to back out now . . . tell me . . . because I'm going ahead with this, even if I have to do it alone."

"Please, Mercedes, let's not argue! We'll do what we vowed to do, but Carlo's concern seems to me worth taking into account," Bruno said, trying to forestall her spiraling fury.

"Clara Tannenberg will die, whether you people like it or not, I assure you," Mercedes said flatly. "I will not discuss it further."

Under the watchful eye of one of the security guards in the Archaeological Museum, Ante Plaskic was lifting the newly published books out of boxes and placing them carefully on the empty shelves.

It struck him that Yves Picot was a sentimental guy: The Frenchman had argued with Clara that it wouldn't be fair to exclude Ante or any of the others who'd been part of the team in Safran. Marta Gómez had agreed.

So for two weeks Ante had been in Madrid doing a little of everything. Picot had put him under Marta's supervision, and Marta had been as trusting as Picot. They both believed his story: He just wanted to be a part of this historic exhibit.

Fabian and Marta had managed to piece together a catalogue in record time—a two-hundred-page book detailing the temple in Safran. Picot was optimistic that sales would be considerable.

Ante watched Lion Doyle out of the corner of his eye. It hadn't surprised him to find Lion working here too. However, unlike Ante, Lion was beloved by everyone on the team, who saw him as a personable, cheery, devil-may-care photographer. But Ante assured himself again that Lion wasn't what he seemed, just as Ayed Sahadi had been more than a mere foreman at an archaeological dig.

From snatches of overheard conversations, Ante learned that Sahadi had managed to get Clara out of Iraq safe and sound with the Bible of Clay and that Ahmed had been with them. They'd gone first to Cairo, where Clara had apparently decided to live until the situation in Iraq became clearer. It was also, apparently, where she decided to break off the marriage, because Ahmed was nowhere to be seen in Madrid, although Ante had heard that he'd make an appearance at the opening.

As he shelved the books, he told himself that he couldn't afford to fail again. This time, he had to do it.

The man at Planet Security who'd hired him had decided to take out an insurance policy: Ante was being provided with a team of operatives waiting for his signal to move in on the Bible of Clay. All Ante had to do was say the word.

During the last two weeks, he'd barely left the museum. He'd familiarized himself with it completely and, more importantly, the guards who worked the museum had become accustomed to his comings and goings. He'd made a special effort to chat up the guards who monitored the alarm system.

He'd told the men in the commando team to scout the building too, without calling attention to themselves. Almost all of them had come in as tourists, walking through the galleries and poking into hallways and offices as though they'd gotten lost. They wouldn't have much time to snatch the tablets, Ante knew, and getting out of the building was going to be tough. Ante planned to make the grab before the museum opened the gallery where the Bible was going to be displayed; getting them afterward would be impossible. Plus, Picot had commissioned exact replicas of the tablets to be made, which might mean they would leave the reproductions in the museum after the exhibit opened and put the originals back in the safety-deposit box. Ante couldn't run that risk.

It concerned him that he hadn't managed to find out when they were planning to bring the tablets to the museum. Marta told him that even the very existence of the Bible of Clay was a closely guarded secret. Not until opening day would they announce their priceless find to the world press.

Clara hadn't allowed the experts in the Vatican to examine the tablets. Gian Maria had insisted the path to authenticity would be through the Holy See, but Clara had told him that the Vatican wouldn't have any choice but to bow to the clear evidence—when she deigned to make that evidence available.

It was two days until the opening, and the museum administrators had prepared a gallery with every security measure known to man in order to ensure the tablets' safety.

Clara, Picot, Fabian, and Marta had personally designed the exhibit and its display within the gallery—from the lighting to the wall panels to the display cases themselves. And the tablets wouldn't be brought in until an hour before the museum's doors opened for the show.

"Nervous?" Picot asked Clara.

"Yes, a little. It's been a long road. . . . I miss my grandfather, you know? He didn't deserve to miss this moment. He lived his whole life for this."

"You still don't have any leads on his murder?"

Clara shook her head as she tried to hold back tears.

"Well, then! Let's talk about something else," Picot said, putting his hand on her shoulder and leaning over her protectively.

"Am I interrupting something?"

Yves jumped and pulled back as he turned and saw Miranda standing there; he seemed flustered to see her. Miranda had talked her way into the museum before the opening.

Clara went over to Miranda and gave her a kiss on the cheek, telling her she was glad to see her. Then she left the gallery, leaving Miranda and Picot alone.

"You don't seem so glad to see me," the reporter remarked to the still-flustered-looking professor.

"I've tried and tried to get in touch with you—don't tell me your agency didn't tell you," he said by way of protest.

"I know, but I had to stay in Iraq longer than I'd expected—you know what a mess it is over there."

"But how do you know about this?" Picot asked her, gesturing to the gallery.

"Good heavens, Yves, I'm a reporter; I read the newspapers. In London they say there's going to be a revelation. . . ."

"Yes, the Bible of Clay."

"I know—Clara and I have a serious difference of opinion about those tablets."

"What do you mean?"

"The way I see it, they're stolen—they belong to Iraq and they shouldn't have been removed without permission."

"And just who could have given that permission? Remember, a war had just started."

"Her own husband—his name is Ahmed Husseini if I'm not mistaken. Even if getting permission from Saddam Hussein himself failed, Ahmed was the head of the Bureau of Archaeological Excavations. Who better to legitimize all this?"

"Miranda, what's done is done. Anyway, we're not going to keep the tablets. When the situation in Iraq clears up, they'll be repatriated. Meanwhile, they'll go to the Louvre, which in addition to having the most important collection of Mesopotamian art and artifacts is incredibly secure."

Fabian interrupted them; he looked nervous.

"Yves, they called from the bank; the armored truck has just left—it's on its way."

"Let's go to the loading dock—come along, Miranda."

When the tablets were laid out in their display case, Clara turned the key in the lock and squeezed Gian Maria's arm emotionally. Then she turned to Picot, Fabian, and Marta, who were standing close by, and smiled.

The museum's chief of security explained once again the extraordinary measures the museum had taken to safeguard the treasures, and Clara seemed happy with what she heard.

"You look awfully nice," Fabian complimented her.

She gave him a peck on the cheek and thanked him. Her two-piece fire-red suit illuminated her tanned face and set off her steel-blue eyes to great effect.

Ten minutes later, the doors of the museum opened to officials of the Spanish government, the vice president and two ministers, and academics from all over the world who'd come to witness what promised to be a truly extraordinary exhibition.

European and American archaeologists alike praised the objects found in Iraq, which were displayed in cases throughout three galleries in the museum. Meanwhile, Marta and Fabian were guiding a group of Spanish authorities, pointing out details of the artifacts and explaining their historical and cultural significance.

Waiters carrying trays of drinks and hors d'oeuvres passed among the guests, who seemed to enjoy the food and drink almost as much as the treasures on display.

Picot and Clara had decided that they wouldn't open the "special" gallery until an hour after the exhibit had opened. At that time, they would solemnly invite the guests and world press into the sanctuary where the greatest treasure of the entire exhibit—the eight clay tablets of the Bible of Clay—was set out in a brilliantly lighted display case.

As they milled about, the guests speculated on what great surprise lay in store for them.

Ante Plaskic spotted his team from Planet Security spread out among the guests, some camouflaged as waiters, some as security guards, some even as invited guests. Nor did he fail to notice that Lion Doyle, despite the constant smile on his face, appeared slightly tense.

The way the theft had been planned, there was no choice but to steal the tablets before the doors to the gallery were opened. They'd be running a huge risk, but it was their only chance. Ante went over the long list of security measures the museum had instituted for the gallery, and then he made his way to the alarm control room. He had ten minutes to grab the tablets and get out.

"Ladies and gentlemen, if I could have your attention, please . . . ," Yves Picot said loudly, standing in the middle of the crowded gallery. "I would ask that you complete your visit to these galleries soon, because in fifteen minutes I am going to ask you to accompany me into a very special gallery, where you will be presented with an archaeological treasure of incalculable value. This groundbreaking find will have worldwide repercussions, not only in academia but also in archaeology itself, in society, and in the Church. Fifteen minutes . . ."

Picot then turned to a group near him, in which Marta and Fabian were talking to the vice president of Spain. Behind them was Clara, in conversation with a government minister and the chancellor of the University of Madrid. Miranda circled toward them through the crowd.

They all started moving slowly toward the closed gallery doors, chatting animatedly. An elegantly dressed older woman in a Chanel suit, her face beautiful and her expression serene, crossed the gallery toward Clara. The woman smiled at Clara, who returned her pleasant greeting; Clara didn't know her, but thought how striking she was. Suddenly the woman stumbled and fell hard against Clara; someone must have accidentally run into her. As the woman regained her balance and walked away, apologizing, Clara winced in pain. She failed to see the slight smile on the elegant, serene face.

Clara went on chatting with the chancellor, telling him that they were about to see cuneiform tablets with a remarkable text inscribed on them, when she abruptly clutched her chest and fell to the floor, to the astonishment of everyone around them.

Yves and Fabian hurried over and knelt down beside her, trying to elicit some reaction—all Clara did was open and close her eyes and gasp, as though trying to wake up from an underwater nightmare.

Fabian called out for a doctor and ambulance, while Ante Plaskic gave a sign to the men of Planet Security's team, who went immediately into action.

One of the guests was a doctor, and he bent down to examine Clara. He discovered a small prick on her left breast, near her sternum—near her heart.

"Quick, call an ambulance!" he repeated. "She's bleeding!"

Two security guards, followed by a tuxedo-clad man, slipped from the room and hurried toward the gallery containing the Bible of Clay.

Ante, too, was rushing, but toward the security-system control room, where monitors displayed every inch of the museum interior. He walked in and put two bullets in the head of the security guard keeping watch on the monitors. Then he pulled the man's body into a corner and locked the door—he couldn't be disturbed now. He skillfully disconnected all the museum's alarms, even as he watched his team enter the gallery and neutralize the two security guards inside. In less than two minutes they'd slipped the tablets into a bag and made their getaway.

The Croatian smiled to himself. The mission was almost complete. Without him as a mole, there was no way anyone could have pulled this off. He was proud.

His eyes then turned to another monitor, where he saw Yves Picot kneeling beside Clara, holding her in his arms, then picking her up and, with Fabian and security guards opening a way through the crowd, carrying her out.

He didn't know why—maybe because she looked so indifferent to all the chaos in the room—but his attention was drawn to a stately, striking older woman who appeared on one of the other monitors. She was the only person who showed no concern for Clara, no worry about her collapse, not even curiosity—she just walked very elegantly toward the exit.

He asked himself what it was the woman had in her hand, because she seemed to be carrying something, but he couldn't make it out through the monitor.

Mercedes Barreda left the museum and took a deep, grateful breath of the warm spring air. She'd always loved the tranquillity and calm of this part of Madrid, a neighborhood called Salamanca. She started walking, a bit aimlessly, immensely happy. She didn't notice two elegantly dressed men toting a large bag hurry out of the museum and jump into a waiting car. The only thing she was thinking about was how to get rid of the awl that she'd just plunged into Clara's heart. She wouldn't leave any fingerprints, because she'd worn a pair of lovely kidskin gloves, so she could toss it into any drain, but not here, not in this neighborhood where the police would certainly look for it. No, she'd find another spot, far away.

She walked for over an hour, strolling through the tree-shaded streets, then hailed a taxi. "Hotel Ritz," she told the driver.

She thought about going back to Barcelona but decided not to—there was no reason for her to run: Nobody was looking for her, nobody would associate her with the death of Clara Tannenberg. Still, she changed clothes and left the hotel, walking toward the Atocha train station. She found a storm drain near the Prado Museum and threw the long, thin instrument away. Then, walking back toward the hotel, she congratulated herself on how easy it had been to end Clara's life. Why had it been so difficult for those hired guns when she'd done it in just one night?

She'd never wavered in her determination to kill Alfred's granddaughter. When she was just a teenager, living in Barcelona, her grandmother had told her the story of the assassination of Elisabeth of Austria. A man had come up to the empress and plunged a stiletto into her; the empress had died shortly afterward, with only a few drops of blood staining her dress.

When she began dreaming of killing Clara, she'd visualized the moment when she'd plunge the stiletto into her heart. It hadn't been easy to find the weapon she finally used—nobody sold stilettos anymore. She'd looked in all the secondhand stores, even a few souvenir shops, to see if she could find a reproduction. She'd eventually wound up looking through the scrap metal left by the workers of her construction company. Finally she found an awl—almost an ice pick, she thought, but longer and triangular—which she cleaned and sharpened and polished as though it were a work of art.

Back in her hotel room, she opened the refrigerator, took out a bottle of champagne, and drank a toast to her triumph. For the first time in her entire long life, she felt fully, completely, truly happy.

Lion Doyle was furious. Clara Tannenberg was dead, but he hadn't killed her, and that meant he wouldn't get paid the rest of his fee. From what he could see, the killer had been a professional—who else would have had the courage and sangfroid to kill Clara in front of hundreds of people? The killer had stabbed her with something long and thin and sharp that had gone straight into Clara's heart and hardly left a trace. But who had it been?

He'd planned to kill her that night. She was staying at Marta Gómez's house, and he knew no one would think anything of it if he turned up there. They'd invite him in, and he'd eliminate the only remaining Tannenberg. He'd figured he would also have to kill Marta, but that was just collateral damage. The problem now, though, was that he couldn't tell Tom Martin he'd finished the job. And it bugged him to see Gian Maria crying like some damned schoolkid as he left the museum with Miranda to go to the hospital where Clara's body had been taken—the authorities had immediately called for an autopsy.

Lion walked into a phone booth and reluctantly called Tom Martin.

"Clara Tannenberg's been killed," he told him.

"And . . . ?"

"I don't know who did it," Lion reported shamefacedly.

"What! . . . Okay, get back here. We have to talk."

"I'll be there tomorrow."

George Wagner had just finished a meeting when his secretary put through an urgent call from Paul Dukais.

"It's done," Paul said jubilantly. "Mission accomplished."

"Everything?"

"Everything! We've got the merchandise. And, by the way, somebody killed your friend's granddaughter."

George gave only the slightest pause. "The package, Paul—when will it be arriving?"

"It's on its way; it'll be there tomorrow."

Wagner had nothing to say about Clara. And there was no objection to Clara's murder from Enrique Gómez or Frankie dos Santos either. She hadn't mattered to them. Her murder, in fact, had nothing to do with them. Their only concern was placing the artifacts on the market as soon as possible. George had suggested that just this once, they all get together to drink to the success of their greatest operation—not just the looting of the Iraqi museums but also the theft of the Bible of Clay. He was itching to get his hands on it, to touch it, even if it would soon be on its way to its buyer.

In the waiting room at the hospital, Yves was pacing back and forth, unable to talk. Miranda, Fabian, and Marta were in the same shape, and all Gian Maria could do was cry.

Two police inspectors were waiting, like the others, for the results of the autopsy. Inspector García, a man in his late forties, had asked the archaeologists to go with him to the police station to try to establish what had happened.

At last, the coroner came out. "Are any of you relatives of Clara Tannenberg?" he asked.

Picot and Fabian looked at each other, not knowing what to say. Marta, as usual, took charge.

"We're friends—she has no one else in Madrid. We've tried to contact her husband, but so far we've been unsuccessful."

"Very well. Señora Tannenberg was killed with a sharp object—a stiletto, an ice pick, very long and extremely thin; we aren't sure exactly what it was, but it pierced her heart. I'm sorry."

The coroner gave the police a few more details, then handed his report to Inspector García.

"I'll be here awhile longer, Inspector, if you should need anything."

The inspector nodded. The case, he thought, was more complicated than it might seem, and he needed to get results fast. The press was calling the ministry for information. And the whole thing couldn't have been more sensational: an Iraqi archaeologist murdered in Madrid's National Archaeological Museum at the opening of an exhibit attended by politicians, government officials, and academics, at which a treasure was to be revealed. And the treasure, in turn, had been stolen from under the noses of the museum guards and security agents practically within sight of two hundred invited guests, including the vice president of the Spanish government himself.

He could just imagine the headlines the next day, and not only in Spain—the international press would pick this up from the wire services. He'd already gotten two calls from his superiors, wanting to know what he'd been able to find—especially the motive for the crime, which everyone figured was related to the mysterious treasure. The vice president had been clear—he wanted results now.

And that was precisely what the inspector hoped to get when he interviewed the dead archaeologist's friends.

It was hot at the police station, so he opened the window to let in a little cool air, at the same time motioning Picot and the others to sit down. The young priest was a wreck, clinging to Marta.

It was going to be a long night, since he was going to have to interview each of them, one by one, to try to answer two questions: Who had wanted Clara Tannenberg dead, and why?

The inspector's assistant turned on the TV set in the office, just in time for the nine o'clock news. They all fell silent, watching the images from that afternoon they'd never forget.

The news anchor was saying that in addition to the murder of the Iraqi archaeologist and a security guard whose body had been found later, a brazen robbery had taken place in the Archaeological Museum—someone had just walked out of the heavily fortified building with eight cuneiform clay tablets, priceless Mesopotamian treasures that some archaeologists had called the "Bible of Clay." That was the much-publicized "secret treasure" to be unveiled.

Yves Picot slammed his fist down on the desk; Fabian cursed incredulously. They'd killed Clara in order to steal the Bible of Clay, Picot said, and the rest agreed with him completely—undoubtedly that explained the murder.

Gian Maria's cry of anguish shocked them all. The priest was watching the screen, and a look of horror had come to his face as the museum's surveillance tape was aired and he saw Clara walking across the gallery with the chancellor, the two of them surrounded by attendees. Suddenly Clara seemed to stumble and then kept walking, until two or three seconds later she fell senseless to the floor.

But Gian Maria saw something else, something the others were incapable of seeing. In the midst of the crowd, for just one split second, he had glimpsed the profile of a woman he knew very, very well.

It was Mercedes Barreda, the little girl from Mauthausen, the little girl who, with his father and his other lifelong friends, had suffered the mind-numbing cruelty of Hitler's concentration camps and watched her mother die.

Instantly, Gian Maria realized that Mercedes was Clara's killer, and he felt a terrible sharp pain in his chest—his very soul was on fire. He couldn't tell anyone, could never denounce her, because that would be tantamount to denouncing his father. Yet not reporting her would make him an accomplice to Clara's murder and a sinner in the eyes of the Lord.

Inspector García was asking him questions: What had he seen on the screen? What did he see there? But Gian Maria, his voice strained and thready, said it was nothing, just the shock of once again watching Clara die.

Yves Picot, Marta Gómez, and Fabian Tudela believed him, but Gian Maria's behavior had planted the seed of doubt in Inspector García's mind—and in Miranda's too. She told herself that she had to get her hands on that news report so she could go over it with a fine-tooth comb, until she found some clue that would explain the priest's behavior.

Yves explained to Inspector García in great detail what the tablets looked like and alerted him to not just the archaeological value of the Bible of Clay but also its religious value. The inspector was fascinated by the story Professor Picot told him of their last few months in Iraq. Out of Gian Maria he got little more than stammered monosyllables.

Time after time, the inspector asked Picot and the others to tell him everything about the last hours before the murder—who was invited to the opening, whom they'd seen, who knew about the existence of the tablets, whom they suspected. He wanted a list of everyone who'd had any contact whatever with the tablets. The five of them left the police station exhausted, convinced that the clues to the murder–theft led somewhere so dark they couldn't see it.

What's to become of me after this? Gian Maria asked himself in desolation when, late that night, he returned to the hotel with Miranda and Picot.

Carlo Cipriani got into the taxi. He was tired, bone-weary, actually, despite the fact that the flight from Barcelona had taken only two hours.

It had been hard for him to say good-bye to Mercedes, Hans, and Bruno. They had tried so hard to convince him that the bonds that joined them were stronger than life or death. They were right—except for his children, he loved no one as much as he loved his three friends. He would sacrifice anything for them, but he thought the time had come to finally find some peace in his life, and he could do that only by distancing himself from them.

He had no reproach for Mercedes, nor had Bruno and Hans. She hadn't told them what she'd done—there was no reason to; they'd known the minute they saw her. She looked wonderful, transformed, radiant, and she told them that for the first time in her life she'd been sleeping like a baby. Hans couldn't bear to tell her how he felt about what she'd done, and Bruno simply wept.

Now, back in Rome, Carlo told himself that he had to make a new start on what remained of his life. He told the taxi to take him to St. Peter's Square, in the Vatican.

When he entered the basilica, the shadowy quietness of the space brought him calm.

Inspector García was entering St. Peter's Square at the same time, on his way to the basilica to find Gian Maria. He'd convinced his superiors to let him follow a hunch and go to Rome, to talk to the young priest one more time.

Once inside the cathedral, the inspector hesitated, scanning the immense space. He paid no attention to the old man making his way to one of the confessionals.

As Carlo Cipriani closed the curtain behind him and knelt, he could see how the young priest had aged—his once-serene face was clouded with bitterness, and his eyes had changed.

"Mi benedica, Padre, perché ho peccato."

"What is your sin, my son?"

"I am responsible for the murder of two people. May God forgive me, and may my son forgive me also!"

"Do you repent of these sins?"

"Yes, Father."

"Then may God forgive you, and may God forgive me for not forgiving you."

Inspector García saw the old man emerge from the confessional, his eyes filled with tears. It looked like he was having trouble breathing, and he seemed about to faint.

"Are you all right?"

"I'm fine—thank you," said Cipriani, walking away and not looking back.

Gian Maria came out of the confessional. He looked unsurprised to see the inspector and moved forward to shake his hand.

"I'm sorry to have come all this way to bother you, Father, but I'd like to talk to you again. You don't have to if you don't want to . . . ," the inspector said to him.

Gian Maria looked at Inspector García without answering. Then, as he began to walk alongside him, he saw his father fall to his knees before Michelangelo's "Pietà" and hide his face in his hands. He felt a wave of pity for the old man, and for himself.

The skies were gray in Rome that day, and rain was falling over all the living and the dead.

JULIA NAVARRO is a Madrid-based journalist and political analyst for Agencia OTR/Europa Press, and a correspondent for other prominent Spanish radio and television networks and print media; she also writes a weekly column for *Tiempo* magazine and is the author of several non-fiction books on contemporary political affairs. Bantam Dell published the English translation of her first novel, the international bestseller *The Brotherhood of the Holy Shroud*, in 2006. Her latest historical thriller, *The Blood of the Innocents*, is currently topping bestseller lists in Europe.

ANDREW HURLEY is best known for his translation of Jorge Luis Borges's *Collected Fictions* and Reinaldo Arenas's "Pentagony" novels, among many other translated works of literature, criticism, history, and memoir. He lives and works in San Juan, Puerto Rico.